P9-DFK-033

A CENTURY OF BRITISH MYSTERY AND SUSPENSE

A Century of British Mystery and Suspense

Edited and with an Introduction by
ANNE PERRY

and a Foreword by
JON L. BREEN

Garden City, New York

P.O. Box 8296
Greenbay, WI 54308

For all permissions information, see pages 564–66

ISBN: 0-7394-0777-5

Manufactured in the United States of America

CONTENTS

INTRODUCTION

'Age cannot wither her, nor custom stale their infinite variety'. With apologies! But mystery stories cover such a range and colour, such shadings and flavours, and yet all carry the essence of drama, the dangerous, the unknown, the nature of human passions, that there is an ever evolving form wherein surely there is something for every taste and occasion.

Do you care for something light and entertaining to fill a little while pleasantly, perhaps before you go to sleep? How about P. G. Wodehouse's 'Jeeves and the Stolen Venus'? It has familiar characters that offer a unique satisfaction, a confection of crime and amusement to leave you smiling.

Or if you would like a nicely rounded, quirky, individual tale of natural justice to leave you with a warm satisfaction, try Dick Francis's 'Twenty-One Good Men and True'. As you would expect, this is an adventure to do with horse racing, but with a delicate twist at the end and a highly individual flavour. 'The Wasp', by Peter Lovesey, is set in Australia, and again gives you memorable characters, a wrench of pity, and at the end a sigh of total satisfaction. It is perfectly rounded off. Gillian Linscott's 'Poison Peach' had me agonising all the way through. Would justice be served, or the law? My compassion was engaged, and my anger as I raced through it. But I should have trusted!

Similarly with Frederick Forsyth's 'There Are No Snakes in Ireland', vivid and involving, or Catherine Aird's 'Home Is the Hunter'. I am not quite sure why, but 'The African Tree Beavers' by Michael Gilbert pleases me out of all proportion. There is a flavour in it both familiar and satisfying, a rounding off that left me saying 'yes, . . . yes!'

Do you like to dip into the 'Golden Age' for its elegance, its classic plots, its sheer reliability for story-telling skill? Do you admire the unfailing intricacy of Agatha Christie who never cheats or sells you short? How about Miss Marple in 'The Four Suspects'? Or the forthright decency of Roderick Alleyn from Dame Ngaio March, another writer who never fails your trust, then read 'Death on the Air'. Still golden, Albert Campion in Margery Allingham's 'One Morning They'll Hang Him'.

And there are other classic detection stories, a little less well-known one can relax with, certain they will not disappoint, such as 'A Study in White' by Nicholas Blake, (anyone who has travelled on an English train will shiver with this in remembered familiarity). I both shivered and laughed aloud at 'Lesson in Anatomy' by Michael Innes, and remembered how many of his books I had enjoyed.

Perhaps you are now ready for something darker and more modern, a touch of psychological suspense, a vivid journey into alienation, loneliness and the reality of outwardly ordinary people, so well told you see the harsh distortions through their eyes? Try Frances Fyfield's 'Nothing to Lose', or Patricia Highsmith's 'Woodrow Wilson's Necktie'. A story with a sweet and sour taste, atmosphere perfectly caught, questions answered and unanswered, is Julian Symons' 'Flowers that Bloom in the Spring'.

A thoroughly modern tale, a vignette of tragedy told through the eyes of a protagonist whose abiding sense of loss we understand only too easily, is Simon Brett's 'An Unmentionable Death'. This is not comfortable, entertaining fiction, but a reminder of reality too sharp to ignore.

A nicely turned domestic story with an ending that startles and lingers in the memory is Antonia Fraser's 'Have a Nice Death'.

Ready for another change of mood? Still essentially British in character and style, but perhaps a thoroughly exotic setting? How about warm seas with blue skies, languid, rippling water and hidden horror, regret, and a touch of espionage? Ian Fleming and 'Octopussy' is your answer.

And after James Bond, how about Simon Templer? Another tropical beach, something more traditional in Leslie Charteris' 'The Arrow of God'? Or something subtler and harder, more of a short story than a mystery, but a perfectly polished gem, and as British as four o'clock tea and hot crumpets—Reginald Hill's 'The Worst Crime Known to Man'.

Can anyone have a more supreme gift for depicting the humanity of seemingly repellent people, and making you feel their pain in a way you can neither dismiss nor forget, than W. Somerset Maugham? 'The Traitor' is profoundly of its time and patterns of thought, and yet is always passionately and intensely true.

While we are with the sadness that twists at our stomach, the pity wrung from you in spite of yourself, how about another dip in warm, deadly waters, this time in Crete, the stirring of one evil ancient and unknowable, another modern and all too familiar? Try 'Don't Look Now' by Daphne du Maurier.

Do you fancy a complete change, a different beat, something to lift your spirits and make you feel that in spite of occasional blips, life is on the whole good, full of passion and laughter and essentially decent people, and justice triumphs in the end?

Who could be more British than G. K. Chesterton? Meet Father Brown in 'The Man in the Passage', with all Chesterton's beloved paradox, colour, outsize characters and love of life. If it is a trifle over the top, does it matter? One is invigorated for having participated in it and everything is a little brighter, a little sharper and sweeter in flavour.

More happy resolutions? How about the greatest consulting detective in fiction? Go with Sherlock Holmes and Dr. Watson to solve the mystery of 'The Copper Beeches', that darkly sinister house where danger finally explodes in fearful violence. Follow the relentlessly logical deductions of reasoning, uncover the horror at the conclusion, and see it all become right. Here are all the idiosyncrasies we love, copy, and parody, sometimes forgetting how sharp the originals were. It is not by chance that they have survived.

'The Haunted Policeman' is one of Dorothy L. Sayers' lightest, most charming short stories, and yet the mystery is intensely satisfying. One can see in it echoes of her fellowship with G. K. Chesterton. Peter Wimsey is clever, amusing, full of character, and one feels happier for having spent time in his company, and wishes for more.

I had had no idea A. A. Milne wrote mystery short stories. I associated him with 'Pooh, Piglet', and 'Where the Woogle Wasn't', and wonderful verses about good and bad bears. 'A Perfectly Ordinary Case of Blackmail' deals with good and bad also, but is a well-turned crime story. I should dearly like to meet the extraordinary Mr. Scroope again, and see him unravel and re-ravel other cases with such finesse.

Ready to be let down gently? How about a delicate character study with a sweet-sad twist, a short story that happens to include crime, in a profoundly English setting with a delicious touch of history? Try Peter Robinson's 'The Two Ladies of Rose Cottage'.

Now for something a trifle sharper, justice and irony, a darkness to balance the light—'Justice in My Own Hands', by Elizabeth Ferrars, 'Breakfast Television', by Robert Barnard, 'The Honest Blackmailer' by Patricia Moyes. All are perfectly crafted, with the sting in the tail the ideal conclusion, leaving you complete.

Sharper still? Darker? Lord Dunsany's 'The Two Bottles of Relish' exemplifies a total horror with the classic elements of mystery and detection.

No one crafts these ingredients better than Ruth Rendell, as in 'Means of Evil'. And yet what stayed with me were sudden, vivid illuminations of character in Wexford's observation of Burden, a moment of loneliness lit so brilliantly it remains in the memory long after the page is closed.

Another modern master is Jonathan Gash and 'Eyes for Offa Rex' is a dark story with the intimate knowledge of antiques and objects of beauty which has given us delight throughout his books. Here the plot unfolds with bitter horror, but leaves us with the feeling of justice served, satisfying and highly individual.

Eric Ambler is better known for tales of espionage, but 'The Case of the Emerald Sky' is a straight detective story introducing the highly individual Dr. Jan Czissar, another one of those harmless, even slightly comical-seeming sleuths who succeed in turning all the evidence on its head and proving that nothing is as it looks. That always pleases some element in us, and we relish seeing it again.

This is a collection of British stories, and I ask you to excuse us for including that master of Britishness John Dickson Carr who created H.M., and Gideon Fell. We do know he was American. But he was so GOOD at utterly English eccentricity! 'The Clue of the Red Wig' has all the elements, twists, surprises, grisly horror and some violence, but no lies to the reader, no disappointment and no cheap evasions. The atmosphere is sharp, the characters entertaining and the mystery thoroughly well plotted.

Wry humour has always sat well in detective stories, especially within a particular flavour of modern ones. 'Looking for Thelma', by Gillian Slovo, borrows, tongue in cheek, from Raymond Chandler, who so expertly crossed the Atlantic in the opposite direction. This tale has neat turns, pathos, the abiding flavour the title suggests.

Michael Z. Lewin's 'Family Business' is a short story with the characterisation of a novel, full of people I feel must be a beginning, a foretaste of more, and yet the plot is complete in itself.

'Lucky Dip' by Liza Cody is another exploration of a unique viewpoint, superbly told so that for a brief time we live another life, sense its flavour and care fiercely for the protagonist. We are left smiling and satisfied. There is darkness, but there is also justice, and sometimes there are the little grace notes that lift the spirits, like a shaft of sunlight on a grey landscape.

Lastly there is 'Heroes', my own contribution, set in the trenches of the First World War. It is a short story which happens to have a mystery in it, and a reluctant detective, whose concern is not retribution but as much justice as can serve both the living and the dead.

'The Best' must always be an arbitrary choice. This is our attempt to represent as many facets as possible of the brilliant gem that is mystery short story, with something for almost every mood, every taste, for the connoisseur to enjoy.

Bon Appetit!

Anne Perry

FOREWORD

The year is 1900. Depending on how you choose to count, it is either the first year of the 20th century or the last of the 19th. Technology is running rampant. The telegraph and telephone, with their revolution in instantaneous communication, have been joined by automobiles and moving pictures, with more wonders on the horizon. Life seems to move ever faster, grow more complex, produce new sources of stress. Spare time is rare and precious.

In your leisure reading, you have developed an appetite for detective stories, a well-established genre of popular literature. Tales of detection are thrilling and suspenseful, but, you tell yourself, more than mere light entertainment. Indeed, they are improving; they test the intellect, hone the reader's reasoning skills, educate about social problems. While giving pleasure, they also equip you to deal with the increasing pressures of modern times. But can there ever be enough good detective fiction to satisfy your craving? You anxiously scan the pages of magazines and the shelves of bookshops. As each new practitioner appears, you eagerly pounce. As a turn-of-the-century mystery buff, what are your options?

To begin, the American Edgar Allan Poe's founding fatherhood notwithstanding, the British stand at the top of the mystery food chain. Sherlock Holmes, the most famous detective in fiction, is officially dead, his impatient and ungrateful creator Sir Arthur Conan Doyle, having killed him off in the final story of *The Memoirs of Sherlock Holmes* (1893). (The Baker Street sleuth won't be revived provisionally until *The Hound of the Baskervilles* [1902] or permanently until *The Return of Sherlock Holmes* [1905].) Still, his influence continues to be pervasive. Most of the other well-known detectives follow his lead: preternaturally gifted, supplied with a full panoply or a pointed lack of eccentricities, able to pursue their investigations unencumbered by police procedures and red tape, concentrating their activities in the short-story form to take advantage of the lucrative magazine market. Arthur Morrison's Martin Hewitt, perhaps the best-known of them, finished his magazine career in the waning years of the century. (The final collection of his cases, *The Red Triangle,* will appear in 1903.)

Burglar A. J. Raffles, the anti-Holmes figure created by Doyle's brother-in-law E.W. Hornung, is at his peak, having been collected last year in *The Amateur Cracksman,* with a second group coming next year in *The Black Mask* (American title, *Raffles: Further Adventures of the Amateur Cracksman*). Old Dick Donovan is still at it: his 1900 collection is *The Adventures of Tyler Tatlock, Private Detective.*

Various professions are represented by fictional detectives, and not only the physicians and lawyers whose connections to criminal investigation seem obvious. The cases of reporter/sleuth Beverley Gretton have been gathered this year in Herbert Cadett's *The Adventures of a Journalist.* All manner of crime solvers are plying their trade, even (would you believe it?) *female* ones: the cases of George R. Sims' *Dorcas Dene, Detective* were collected three years ago, in 1897, and this year the adventures of M. McDonnell Bodkin's *Dora Myrl, the Lady Detective* have appeared in book form. Female *writers* of detective stories are not quite as unusual: L. T. Meade (Elizabeth Thomasina Meade Smith) has been writing in the field for nearly a decade. This year her collection is *The Sanctuary Club,* written in collaboration with Robert Eustace.

With the short fiction market so bullish, detective novels have taken a back seat, but there have been a few milestones since Wilkie Collins' classic *The Moonstone* (1868). In 1892, Israel Zangwill produced the first great locked-room novel, *The Big Bow Mystery,* which also pioneered a classic whodunit surprise gimmick, one that was turned up a notch by Marie and Robert Leighton in last year's *Michael Dred, Detective.* Fergus Hume, who made such a splash with *The Mystery of a Hansom Cab* (1886), will have a half-dozen new novels in the shops this year. Surely no future detective novelist will ever be so prolific.

Yes, there's plenty of interesting stuff around for the mystery reader of 1900. But what new wonders does the century to come hold in store?

The Short Story Tradition Continues

Between 1900 and the beginning of World War I, most of the best British writers of detective fiction continued to specialize in the short form. The first great sleuth to be introduced in the 20th century was Baroness Orczy's Old Man in the Corner, the armchair detective whose cases were first collected in *The Case of Miss Elliott* (1905). He lives only in short stories, as does Orczy's memorable female sleuth, *Lady Molly of Scotland Yard* (1910). Contemporaries like Robert Barr in *The Triumphs of Eugene Valmont* (1906), with its satirical contrast of British and French police methods, also kept it short. Although one of the most famous sleuths of the era, R. Austin Freeman's scientific detective Dr. John Thorndyke, first appeared in the novel *The Red Thumb Mark* (1907) and would have many other book-length cases, his short-story appearances, first collected in *John Thorndyke's Cases* (1909), have generally been more highly valued. Similarly, though Ernest Bramah's pioneering blind detective Max Carrados would appear in a single novel, *The Bravo of London* (1934), his most notable work is in short stories, first collected in *Max Carrados* (1914).

As Hugh Greene pointed out in introducing his 1970 anthology *The Rivals of Sherlock Holmes,* much of this pre-war British detective fiction had been grittier and in some ways more realistic than the work that would follow: "The setting of most of these stories is much closer to Raymond Chandler's 'mean streets' down which Philip Marlowe walked than to the unreal country house, ye old English village, world of the English detective story in the years between the wars. . . ."

The greatest British sleuth to be introduced between 1900 and World War I did not belong to this tradition of urban realism, however. G. K. Chesterton's Father Brown solved bizarre, sometimes impossible, crimes while coining paradoxes and making subtle theological points. More than any other writer, he foreshadowed the games-playing and puzzle-spinning of post-war detective fiction. The brilliant though unobtrusive amateur sleuth, first in a long line of Roman Catholic religious detectives, never appeared at greater than short-story length in a career that spanned a quarter of a century.

There were a few key novels in the period before the Great War. *Trent's Last Case* (1913), by Chesterton's friend E. C. Bentley, was credited with augmenting the realism of detective fiction by stressing the humanity of the sleuth. Ironically, journalist Philip Trent's purported last case was actually his first, and, despite his failure (a reversal of the normal infallibility of fictional detectives), became popular enough to be revived in a series of short stories. A.E.W. Mason's *At the Villa Rose* (1910) introduced, at a time when most fictional sleuths were amateurs or private enquiry agents, the French police detective Hanaud, who would have another notable case in *The House of the Arrow* (1924) and whose career would extend into the '40s, concluding with *The House in Lordship Lane* (1946). Mrs. Belloc Lowndes' *The Lodger* (1912) fictionalized the Jack the Ripper murders, a frequent ploy of crime fiction writers ever since, and in its psychological approach foreshadowed the modern crime novel.

The trauma of World War I brought British detective fiction to a virtual halt. In the new wave of fiction after the war, emphasis would shift to the novel, though short stories remained popular. The early stories about Agatha Christie's Hercule Poirot, narrated by Captain Hastings, are solidly Holmesian in structure and atmosphere, and most of the other great sleuths of the period appeared at least occasionally in short stories. (The same is true of the leading series sleuths, as well as non-series writers, today.)

The Golden Age of the '20s

Post-war Britain, a generation of its male population decimated (through death or disability) by the conflict, returned to relative peacetime stability, though in a society markedly changed in attitudes, standards of moral behavior and worldly experience. The populace was ready for some light relief, some of which was provided by the amusing, artificial, but intellectually rigorous detective fiction of what would be called the Golden Age of Detection. To some readers, the detective story became a game more than a literary form, a brain teaser as surely as the crossword puzzles that gained popularity around the same time. But the Golden Age detective story's remoteness from real life and real humanity has been exaggerated: the work of its best writers was always rooted in character and, while its plots and situations may have been unlikely, they were usually no more so than those of the allegedly more realistic crime fiction of later decades.

The year 1920 is considered a milestone in British (and thus all) detective fiction, largely but not entirely because of the debut of Agatha Christie. *The Mysterious Affair at Styles* introduced her great detective Hercule Poirot with an early example of the audacious reader bamboozlement that would reach its peak in the controversial *The Murder of Roger Ackroyd* (1926). Christie was a pioneer in establishing the concept of fair play to the reader, offering all the clues a clever reader needed to beat the great detective to the solution. Fair clues had *sometimes* been presented in detective stories extending all the way back to Poe, but they were far from the rule. It had been more common for Sherlock Holmes and his imitators to conceal the clues until explaining them in the denouement. The greater space for expanding the plot and hiding the clues in plain sight afforded by the novel length may have helped to account for the rise of fair play, but the best of the post-1920 practitioners practiced it in short stories as rigorously as in novels.

Decades after her death, Christie is still among the most famous and most widely reprinted writers of detective fiction. She has been so successful, so influential, so maddeningly persistent in her dominance of the paperback shelves that an inevitable backlash has occurred. Nothing better demonstrates Christie's dominance than the way later writers fall over themselves asserting how unlike her they are, dutifully saluting her plot spinning while exaggerating the flatness of her characters and underestimating the subtle charm of her style.

Freeman Wills Crofts, master of the time-table puzzle, also appeared for the first time in 1920 with *The Cask,* while H. C. Bailey, harking back to the short story emphasis of an earlier era, published his first collection of stories, *Call Mr. Fortune.*

Three years later, the second great female British writer of the period, Dorothy L. Sayers, introduced Lord Peter Wimsey in *Whose Body?* (1923). Christie and Sayers have been the most written about Golden Age writers, the former for her mastery of puzzlemaking and reader misdirection, the latter for her fusion of the detective novel with the mainstream novel. Ironically, the early Sayers was as committed to the detective story's game elements as anyone, even incorporating a crossword puzzle into one of her short stories. But by the time Sayers left detective fiction for other literary pursuits in the late '30s, she had shown how a detective character can grow and deepen over a series of novels and how romance (scorned by the rules-makers of the '20s) could be integrated into the detective story. With the romance came a feminist icon, detective novelist Harriet Vane, who, over the course of several books, is saved from the gallows, pursued and finally married by Lord Peter Wimsey.

A figure whose historical importance equals that of Christie and

Sayers has been relatively neglected. Journalist and humorist A. B. Cox had two distinctive authorial identities: as Anthony Berkeley, he created an intentionally offensive detective in Roger Sheringham and produced the classic traditional detective novel *The Poisoned Chocolates Case* (1929); as Francis Iles, he pioneered the modern crime novel that stresses psychology over detection in two classics, *Malice Aforethought* (1931) and *Before the Fact* (1932).

Though he is not usually regarded as a writer of detective fiction, humorist P. G. Wodehouse merits at least a mention. The perfect butler Jeeves often acted very much like a detective in bailing employer Bertie Wooster out of trouble, and the relationship of the pair influenced Sayers in her creation of Wimsey and his ever-reliable manservant Bunter. The upper-class, amusedly observed milieu of Wodehouse's stories helped set the tone for other mystery writers of the era, and in his prolific provision of jacket quotes over the years, he constantly revealed his enthusiasm for the form.

Like Elizabethan drama and any other literary school, British detective fiction is defined in terms of its giants. But many writers of the period kept to a high standard. Others who debuted in the '20s included John Rhode, the creator of the irascible Dr. Priestley, whose career extended from 1926 to 1961; Philip MacDonald, whose great contributions may have been overshadowed by a couple of American writers with the same surname; and Margery Allingham, whose Albert Campion changed and developed as interestingly as Lord Peter Wimsey. Gladys Mitchell, whose Beatrice Lestrange Bradley first appeared in 1929's *Speedy Death,* gave her sleuth a 55-year run matched only by Hercule Poirot. Even some of the lesser writers of the period—names like Anthony Wynne, J. J. Connington and R.A.J. Walling—produced work that is still enjoyable for present-day readers, if they can find it.

The Golden Age Tradition Continues

The mystery reader of 1930 was well-adapted to the idea of detective fiction as a game. The narratives were often accompanied by character lists, maps and floor plans, and the clues had better be there. A number of writers, notably the American S. S. Van Dine and the Briton Ronald A. Knox, had drawn up sometimes facetious but essentially serious lists of rules. Aside from fair play, they added seemingly arbitrary strictures. In his "Detective Story Decalogue," Knox insisted the story contain no Chinaman (a term that is now deemed racist but may not have been intentionally offensive at the time), no "more than one secret room or passage," no poison unknown to science, no accident or sixth sense that helps the detective. In his "Twenty Rules for Writing Detective Fiction," Van Dine insisted there could be no love interest, no extended descriptions or literary flourishes; there must be one murderer and he or she can't be a servant. Members of the Detection Club, of which Chesterton, Sayers and Berkeley were prominent members, had to swear they would shun solutions by "Divine Revelation, Feminine Intuition, Mumbo-Jumbo, Jiggery-Pokery, Coincidence, or the Act of God." New writers in the field flouted the rules at their peril—but often to the great advantage of their work.

In the '30s, more writers in the tradition of the '20s appeared, most notably Ngaio Marsh, Michael Innes and Nicholas Blake. They held to the tradition of fair play to the reader while helping effect a steady rise in the general literary quality of the field. Marsh and Innes used police detectives, Roderic Alleyn and John Appleby, respectively, but very unusual ones—well-educated, intellectual, even aristocratic—that had more resemblance to the gentleman sleuths of the Wimsey school than to the police procedural heroes of later years. Innes matched or surpassed Sayers in loading his dialogue with literary allusions and quotations.

The beginning of World War II is generally taken to mark the end of the Golden Age of Detection. Unlike the previous global war, it did not have the effect of shutting down production of detective stories in Great Britain, though paper shortages limited the number of books that could be published. In his essay "The Whodunit in World War II and After," Howard Haycraft noted, "At the height of the Nazi blitz of London in 1940 special 'raid libraries' were set up at the reeking entrances of the underground shelters to supply, by popular demand, detective stories and nothing else." The category had become a staple of the population's leisure reading, a literary comfort food in a time of increasing stress. The war inspired some writers of classical detection to introduce elements of espionage and thriller fiction into their plots—see, for example, Michael Innes' *The Secret Vanguard* (1940) and Margery Allingham's *Traitor's Purse* (1941).

After the war, fashions in crime fiction changed, and new subgenres rose to prominence. But at no time since has there been a lack of British writers in the classical tradition, including, in rough chronological order Christianna Brand, Elizabeth (known in the U.S. as E.X.) Ferrars, Edmund Crispin, Patricia Moyes, Catherine Aird, Robert Barnard, Colin Dexter and other traditionalists. The two most celebrated contemporary icons of British detection, P. D. James and Ruth Rendell, for all their ambition and success in increasing the depth and literary interest of their works, began with classical detection and still observe its standards and conventions in at least some of their novels.

Confusions of Nationality

Mutual attraction, whether geographically or stylistically, has sometimes blurred the distinction between American and British writers of crime fiction. Though John Dickson Carr, master of the locked-room puzzle, was not of British nationality, he lived in England for much of his life, usually employed a British setting and British detectives (Dr. Gideon Fell and, under his pseudonym Carter Dickson, Sir Henry Merrivale), stayed put in his adopted homeland in the dangerous days of World War II and earned a place in British mystery fiction by being more British than the British. In later years, American novelists Patricia Highsmith and Michael Z. Lewin achieved similar honorary British status. Some writers moved in the other direction, born British but gravitating to America: Leslie Charteris, creator of the Saint who occasionally functioned as a detective but usually as a Robin Hood-ish criminal, and the Q. Patrick/Patrick Quentin collaborators, Richard Webb and Hugh Wheeler, who were born British but lived and set most of their work in the United States.

Apart from the Anglo-Americans, there is some ambiguity about Down Under crime writers. Ngaio Marsh, a New Zealander, set most of her novels in Great Britain and is generally claimed by the British, while Arthur W. Upfield, whose series about Inspector Napoleon Bonaparte is probably the most notable series of Australian detective novels, was born an Englishman.

The Broadening of the Crime Story

Early histories of mystery fiction, notably H. Douglas Thomson's *Masters of Mystery* (1931) and Howard Haycraft's *Murder for Pleasure* (1941), focused on detection, and to many readers the solidly clued whodunit remains crime fiction's Main Street (or in British terms, High Street). Still there are many other subgenres under the broad crime-mystery umbrella, and British writers have been prominent in most of them.

The Crime Novel: As noted earlier, Anthony Berkeley writing as Francis Iles was a pioneer of the transition from detective to crime novel traced by Julian Symons in his history *Bloody Murder* (1972; third revised edition 1992). Some of the ways the crime novel differs from the detective story as summed up by Symons: "Based on psychology of characters . . . or an intolerable situation that must end in violence. No deceptions of the locked-room or faked-print kind, no obscure poisons . . . Often no detective . . . Quite often no clues in the detective story sense . . . The lives of characters are shown continuing after the crime . . . [O]ften radical in the sense of questioning some aspect of law, justice or the way society is run." The modern crime story began in the '30s as a trend paralleling the continuation of classical detection. Some of Iles' fellow crime writers of the '30s were satirist C. E. Vulliamy (a.k.a. Anthony Rolls) and F. Tennyson Jesse. Later came the transplanted American Highsmith, Symons himself, and such present-day writers as Minette Walters and Frances Fyfield.

The Thriller: Though sometimes used in Britain as a term for the whole field of crime fiction, it properly describes stories where the stress is on action, adventure and intrigue more than detection. In its lowbrow form (and don't take that necessarily as pejorative), examples include writers like William Le Queux, a spy and future-war specialist who debuted in the 1890s; E. Phillips Oppenheim, author of the classic *The Great Impersonation* (1920); the extremely prolific Edgar Wallace; "Sapper" (H. C. McNeile), creator of the celebrated and reviled Bulldog Drummond; Sax Rohmer, whose creation of the sinister villain Fu Manchu may have been a factor in Father Knox's ban on "Chinamen"; and, of course, Ian Fleming, whose super-agent James Bond spawned nearly as many imitators as Sherlock Holmes. The higher-browed thriller encompasses the work of Somerset Maugham (in *Ashenden*), Graham Greene, Eric Ambler, John le Carré, Len Deighton and Frederick Forsyth. Operating somewhere between the brows, and overlapping traditional detection, is the jockey-turned-novelist Dick Francis.

The Police Procedural: Though many fictional detectives have always been police, their cases were not usually police procedurals, a relatively recent form in which much of the interest lies in the everyday workings of a law enforcement agency. John Creasey, whose output surpassed that of Fergus Hume and Edgar Wallace by a considerable margin, made his greatest contribution to crime fiction with the police procedural novels he wrote under the name J. J. Marric, beginning with *Gideon's Day* (1955). Among other important British practitioners were two who drew on their own experiences as police, Maurice Procter and John Wainwright. Many of the major contemporary British sleuths are official police, including P. D. James' Adam Dalgliesh, Ruth Rendell's Wexford, H.R.F. Keating's Inspector Ghote, Peter Lovesey's Peter Diamond, and Reginald Hill's Dalziel and Pascoe. Some of their more prominent colleagues are defined by their musical interests, including John Harvey's Charlie Resnick (jazz), Colin Dexter's Inspector Morse (choral music and classics), Peter Robinson's Alan Banks (opera) and Ian Rankin's John Rebus (rock).

Romantic Suspense: Since the romantic suspense novel (or modern gothic) can be traced to Charlotte Brontë's *Jane Eyre* (1847), as well as the original gothic novels of writers like Ann Radcliffe and Matthew G. (Monk) Lewis, it should be no surprise British influence has continued strong. Daphne du Maurier's *Rebecca* (1938) is a 20th-century classic of the form. Among the successful later practitioners have been Victoria Holt, Mary Stewart and the less-well-known but outstanding Anna Gilbert.

The Historical Mystery: Though the detective story was once contemporary almost by definition, in recent years historical crime stories have become more and more popular. Agatha Christie was again a pioneer, with the ancient Egyptian whodunit *Death Comes as the End* (1944). After a false start in 1934, *Devil Kinsmere* (as by Roger Fairbairn), John Dickson Carr produced much historical detection through the '50s, including *The Bride of Newgate* (1950) and the time-travel fantasy *Fire, Burn!* (1957). But historical mysteries didn't catch on in a big way until the '70s when various British writers were mining the past for story material, notably Peter Lovesey in his series about Victorian-era police detectives Sergeant Cribb and Constable Thackeray, beginning with *Wobble to Death* (1970), and Francis Selwyn (pseudonym of Donald Thomas), whose slightly earlier Victorian Sergeant Verity first appeared in *Cracksman on Velvet* (1974). Ellis Peters' introduction of Brother Cadfael in *A Morbid Taste for Bones* (1977) started a vogue for medieval sleuths, while Anne Perry achieved great success with backgrounds of Victorian England, introducing Charlotte and Thomas Pitt in *The Cater Street Hangman* (1979), and beginning a second series about amnesiac private detective Thomas Monk and Crimean War nurse Hester Latterly in *The Face of a Stranger* (1990). Also of note are Gillian Linscott, whose novels trace feminist movement of the early twentieth century through the adventures of suffragette Nell Bray, beginning with *Sister Beneath the Sheet* (1991), and the incredibly prolific (if not *quite* to a John Creasey level) P. C. Doherty, who writes novels of various historical periods under various names.

Sherlock Holmes pastiches have been appearing at a dizzying rate since the 1970s. While much of the impetus has come, surprisingly, from Americans, much of the best work has been done by British writers such as Michael Hardwick (*Prisoner of the Devil* [1980] and *Revenge of the Hound* [1987]), June Thomson (several short-story collections beginning with *The Secret Files of Sherlock Holmes* [1990]) and Donald Thomas (*The Secret Cases of Sherlock Holmes* [1997]).

Courtroom Novels: There have been relatively few British legal thrillers in the tradition of John Grisham, but there are an abundance of courtroom crime novels, including such classics as Edgar Lustgarten's *A Case to Answer* (1947; American title *One More Unfortunate*), Cyril Hare's *Tragedy at Law* (1942), Gerald Bullett's *The Jury* (1935), Raymond Postgate's *Verdict of Twelve* (1940), and Anthony Berkeley's *Trial and Error* (1937). Sara Woods' Antony Maitland laid claim to the title of British Perry Mason in a long series of novels beginning with *Bloody Instructions* (1962). Henry Cecil mined a Wodehouse-like vein of legal humor in novels beginning with *The Painswick Line* (1951). Many of solicitor Michael Gilbert's novels, notably *Death Has Deep Roots* (1951) and *Blood and Judgement* (1959), display his legal expertise in outstanding courtroom scenes. (Gilbert has written almost every type of crime fiction, which made it hard to decide where to insert his name in this survey.) The most famous British lawyer and sometime detective is probably John Mortimer's Rumpole of the Bailey, created for television but in book form since 1978.

The Hard-boiled: The one area at which the British have not traditionally excelled is the hard-boiled novel popularized by American writers like Dashiell Hammett, Raymond Chandler and James M. Cain—not that they haven't tried. The British who have practiced it have usually used American backgrounds and characters. Hartley Howard and Basil Copper wrote about American private eyes in a way convincing to British readers, if not to Americans. James Hadley Chase, who rarely visited the United States, had a major success with the gangster epic *No Orchids for Miss Blandish* (1939) and followed it up with many more American-based thrillers. Peter Cheyney sometimes used American settings and characters, introducing G-man Lemmy Caution in *This Man Is Dangerous* (1936), but also created a British equivalent of the American private eye in Slim Callaghan, who first appeared in *The Urgent Hangman* (1938). The recent rise of the

Brit Noir school shows them still trying and with greater success. Writers like John Harvey, whose Charlie Resnick novels beginning with *Lonely Hearts* (1989) were inspired by Elmore Leonard, Ross Thomas, and TV's *Hill Street Blues,* and Liza Cody, who introduced British female private eye Anna Lee in *Dupe* (1980), show a strong influence of the American tough school. A whole new generation of down-and-dirty British writers has been represented in the *Fresh Blood* anthology series edited by Maxim Jakubowski and Mike Ripley. Prominent names apart from the editors themselves include Derek Raymond, Mark Timlin, Denise Danks, Russell James, Ken Bruen and Phil Lovesey.

Why the British?

How have the British compiled such a remarkable record in the field of crime fiction? One measure of the high British standard of quality in the field is seen in how many of its practitioners, both one-shots and specialists, also distinguished themselves in other areas of writing. Victorian novelists Charles Dickens and Wilkie Collins set the pattern. Conan Doyle created a vast body of work, both historical fiction and non-fiction, that had nothing to do with crime and detection. Chesterton, of course, was a celebrated essayist, journalist and critic. Father Ronald Knox produced a huge body of theological writings. G.D.H. Cole, a Golden Age staple writing with wife Margaret Cole, was a noted economist. Eden Phillpotts, a respected mainstream writer, entered the field in 1921 with *The Grey Room.* A. A. Milne, whose one-shot *The Red House Mystery* (1922) was hailed an instant classic, was most famous as a writer of children's books like *Winnie-the-Pooh.* Peter Dickinson, quite possibly the finest crime fiction writer on the contemporary scene, also is noted for his children's books. Sayers would become a distinguished translator of Dante and a religious playwright after abandoning detective fiction, while Nicholas Blake (C. Day-Lewis) became poet laureate. Both John Harvey and Peter Robinson have produced volumes of poetry. C. P. Snow, who started and ended his novelistic career with detective fiction, became a respected mainstream literary figure with his *Strangers and Brothers* series of novels. Lady Antonia Fraser was a distinguished popular biographer of British royalty before she began recounting the adventures of Jemima Shore. Julian Symons was a formidable critic, poet and historian outside his crime fiction specialty. Detective fiction may have been seen as a recreational activity, but serious writers have taken its creation seriously.

Another reason for British leadership in this particular mode may lie in the national character. The detective story from its beginnings has been a very moral form, one that has assumed (or at least sought after) a norm of stability. If crime upsets the order, the order must be restored, not by the force of dictatorship, but by the rationality and common sense of democracy. What nation is more historically stable, traditional and orderly than Great Britain? What nation with such a low murder rate can boast such a long history of colorful and memorable crimes? What country has more faithfully preserved its traditions, its great buildings, its landmarks?

What Is to Come?

The year is now 2000. Depending on how you count, the first year of the 21st century and third millennium or the last year of the 20th and second. Technology is sweeping us ahead in a way the citizen of a hundred years ago could not have imagined. There is no problem whatsoever finding enough good mysteries to read. Every crime writer could shut down production tomorrow, and you would never run out of reading matter, even if you were a speed reader and medical science found a way to grant you a second century of life. A concerted effort to read even all the *good* mysteries of the past would prove an insurmountable folly. A less ambitious program of reading all the good *new* mystery fiction being published, even confining yourself to the good new *British* mysteries, would leave you little time for anything else.

The crime story shows no signs of flagging, in the English-speaking world or elsewhere. There may be changes in delivery modes (downloaded a good e-book lately?), but it is still safe to say that all the variants of the crime-mystery-detective story will continue into the foreseeable future. And while no one country or even one language can lay claim to the whole field, continued British leadership is at least arguable.

Jon L. Breen

The Copper Beeches

SIR ARTHUR CONAN DOYLE

Sherlock Holmes is without doubt the greatest literary creation of all time. Holmes personified the man of science, valued by the Industrial Revolution, who brought the scientific method to crime detection. Dr. Watson, Moriarty, and 221B Baker Street are almost as well known as the great sleuth himself, and are known to five generations of readers. Films, television shows, and radio dramas have all been produced to star Holmes—he is one of the very few literary creations to be brought to life by every form of mass communication, and he continues to fascinate readers in many cultures.

Sir Arthur Conan Doyle (1859–1930), a British physician as well as a novelist and detective-story writer, based Holmes on a doctor he knew. No man ever received a greater tribute.

"To the man who loves art for its own sake," remarked Sherlock Holmes, tossing aside the advertisement sheet of the *Daily Telegraph*, "it is frequently in its least important and lowliest manifestations that the keenest pleasure is to be derived. It is pleasant to me to observe, Watson, that you have so far grasped this truth that in these little records of our cases which you have been good enough to draw up, and, I am bound to say, occasionally to embellish, you have given prominence not so much to the many *causes célèbres* and sensational trials in which I have figured, but rather to those incidents which may have been trivial in themselves, but which have given room for those faculties of deduction and of logical synthesis which I have made my special province."

"And yet," said I, smiling, "I cannot quite hold myself absolved from the charge of sensationalism which has been urged against my records."

"You have erred, perhaps," he observed, taking up a glowing cinder with the tongs, and lighting with it the long cherrywood pipe which was wont to replace his clay when he was in a disputatious rather than a meditative mood—"you have erred, perhaps, in attempting to put colour and life into each of your statements, instead of confining yourself to the task of placing upon record that severe reasoning from cause to effect which is really the only notable feature about the thing."

"It seems to me that I have done you full justice in the matter," I remarked with some coldness, for I was repelled by the egotism which I had more than once observed to be a strong factor in my friend's singular character.

"No, it is not selfishness or conceit," said he, answering, as was his wont, my thoughts rather than my words. "If I claim full justice for my art, it is because it is an impersonal thing—a thing beyond myself. Crime is common. Logic is rare. Therefore it is upon the logic rather than upon the crime that you should dwell. You have degraded what should have been a course of lectures into a series of tales."

It was a cold morning of the early spring, and we sat after breakfast on either side of a cheery fire in the old room in Baker Street. A thick fog rolled down between the lines of dun-coloured houses, and the opposing windows loomed like dark, shapeless blurs, through the heavy yellow wreaths. Our gas was lit, and shone on the white cloth, and glimmer of china and metal, for the table had not been cleared yet. Sherlock Holmes had been silent all the morning, dipping continuously into the advertisement columns of a succession of papers, until at last, having apparently given up his search, he had emerged in no very sweet temper to lecture me upon my literary shortcomings.

"At the same time," he remarked, after a pause, during which he had sat puffing at his long pipe and gazing down into the fire, "you can hardly be open to a charge of sensationalism, for out of these cases which you have been so kind as to interest yourself in, a fair proportion do not treat of crime, in its legal sense, at all. The small matter in which I endeavoured to help the King of Bohemia, the singular experience of Miss Mary Sutherland, the problem connected with the man with the twisted lip, and the incident of the noble bachelor, were all matters which are outside the pale of the law. But in avoiding the sensational, I fear that you may have bordered on the trivial."

"The end may have been so," I answered, "but the methods I hold to have been novel and of interest."

"Pshaw, my dear fellow, what do the public, the great unobservant public, who could hardly tell a weaver by his tooth or a compositor by his left thumb, care about the finer shades of analysis and deduction! But, indeed, if you are trivial, I cannot blame you, for the days of the great cases are past. Man, or at least criminal man, has lost all enterprise and originality. As to my own little practice, it seems to be degenerating into an agency for recovering lost lead pencils and giving advice to young ladies from boarding-schools. I think that I have touched bottom at last, however. This note I had this morning marks my zero point, I fancy. Read it!" He tossed a crumpled letter across to me.

It was dated from Montague Place upon the proceding evening, and ran thus:

Dear Mr Holmes—I am very anxious to consult you as to whether I should or should not accept a situation which has been offered to me as governess. I shall call at half-past ten tomorrow, if I do not inconvenience you—Yours faithfully,

Violet Hunter.

"Do you know the young lady?" I asked.
"Not I."
"It is half-past ten now."
"Yes, and I have no doubt that is her ring."
"It may turn out to be of more interest than you think. You remember that the affair of the blue carbuncle, which appeared to be a mere whim at first, developed into a serious investigation. It may be so in this case also."
"Well, let us hope so! But our doubts will very soon be solved, for here, unless I am much mistaken, is the person in question."
As he spoke the door opened, and a young lady entered the room. She was plainly but neatly dressed, with a bright, quick face, freckled like a plover's egg, and with the brisk manner of a woman who has had her own way to make in the world.
"You will excuse my troubling you, I am sure," said she, as my companion rose to greet her; "but I have had a very strange experience, and as I have no parents or relations of any sort from whom I could ask advice, I thought that perhaps you would be kind enough to tell me what I should do."
"Pray take a seat, Miss Hunter. I shall be happy to do anything that I can to serve you."
I could see that Holmes was favourably impressed by the manner and speech of his new client. He looked her over in his searching fashion, and then composed himself with his lids drooping and his fingertips together to listen to her story.
"I have been a governess for five years," said she, "in the family of Colonel Spence Munro, but two months ago the Colonel received an appointment at Halifax, in Nova Scotia, and took his children over to America with him, so that I found myself without a situation. I advertised, and I answered advertisements, but without success. At last the little money which I had saved began to run short, and I was at my wit's end as to what I should do.

"There is a well-known agency for governesses in the West End called Westaway's, and there I used to call about once a week in order to see whether anything had turned up which might suit me. Westaway was the name of the founder of the business, but it is really managed by Miss Stoper. She sits in her own little office, and the ladies who are seeking employment wait in an anteroom, and are then shown in one by one, when she consults her ledgers and sees whether she has anything which would suit them.

"Well, when I called last week I was shown into the little office as usual, but I found that Miss Stoper was not alone. A prodigiously stout man with a very smiling face and a great heavy chin which rolled down in fold upon fold over his throat sat at her elbow with a pair of glasses on his nose, looking very earnestly at the ladies who entered. As I came in he gave quite a jump in his chair and turned quickly to Miss Stoper.

" 'That will do,' said he; 'I could not ask for anything better. Capital! capital!' He seemed quite enthusiastic and rubbed his hands together in the most genial fashion. He was such a comfortable-looking man that it was quite a pleasure to look at him.

" 'You are looking for a situation, miss?' he asked.

" 'Yes, sir.'

" 'As governess?'

" 'Yes, sir.'

" 'And what salary do you ask?'

" 'I had £4 a month in my last place with Colonel Spence Munro.'

" 'Oh, tut, tut! sweating—rank sweating!' he cried, throwing his fat hands out into the air like a man who is in a boiling passion. 'How could anyone offer so pitiful a sum to a lady with such attractions and accomplishments?'

" 'My accomplishments, sir, may be less than you imagine,' said I. 'A little French, a little German, music, and drawing—'

" 'Tut, tut!' he cried. 'This is all quite beside the question. The point is, have you or have you not the bearing and deportment of a lady? There it is in a nutshell. If you have not, you are not fitted for the rearing of a child who may some day play a considerable part in the history of the country. But if you have, why, then, how could any gentleman ask you to condescend to accept anything under the three figures? Your salary with me, madam, would commence at £100 a year.'

"You may imagine, Mr. Holmes, that to me, destitute as I was, such an offer seemed almost too good to be true. The gentleman, however, seeing perhaps the look of incredulity upon my face, opened a pocketbook and took out a note.

" 'It is also my custom,' said he smiling in the most pleasant fashion until his eyes were just two little shining slits amid the white creases of his face, 'to advance to my young ladies half their salary beforehand, so that they may meet any little expenses of their journey and their wardrobe.'

"It seemed to me that I had never met so fascinating and so thoughtful a man. As I was already in debt to my tradesmen, the advance was a great convenience, and yet there was something unnatural about the whole transaction which made me wish to know a little more before I quite committed myself.

" 'May I ask where you live, sir?' said I.

" 'Hampshire. Charming rural place. The Copper Beeches, five miles on the far side of Winchester. It is the most lovely country, my dear young lady, and the dearest old country-house.'

" 'And my duties, sir? I should be glad to know what they would be.'

" 'One child—one dear little romper just six years old. Oh, if you could see him killing cockroaches with a slipper! Smack! smack! smack! Three gone before you could wink!' He leaned back in his chair and laughed his eyes into his head again.

"I was a little startled at the nature of the child's amusement, but the father's laughter made me think that perhaps he was joking.

" 'My sole duties, then,' I asked, 'are to take charge of a single child?'

" 'No, no, not the sole, not the sole, my dear young lady,' he cried. 'Your duty would be, as I am sure your good sense would suggest, to obey any little commands my wife might give, provided always that they were such commands as a lady might with propriety obey. You see no difficulty, heh?'

" 'I should be happy to make myself useful.'

" 'Quite so. In dress now, for example, We are faddy people, you know—faddy, but kind-hearted. If you were asked to wear any dress which we might give you, you would not object to our little whim. Heh?'

" 'No,' said I, considerably astonished at his words.

" 'Or to sit here, or sit there, that would not be offensive to you?'

" 'Oh, no.'

" 'Or, to cut your hair quite short before you come to us?'

"I could hardly believe my ears. As you may observe, Mr Holmes, my hair is somewhat luxuriant, and of a rather peculiar tint of chestnut. It has been considered artistic. I could not dream of sacrificing it in this offhand fashion.

" 'I am afraid that that is quite impossible,' said I. He had been watching me eagerly out of his small eyes, and I could see a shadow pass over his face as I spoke.

" 'I am afraid that it is quite essential,' said he. 'It is a little fancy of my wife's, and ladies' fancies, you know, madam, ladies' fancies must be consulted. And so you won't cut your hair?'

" 'No, sir, I really could not,' I answered firmly.

" 'Ah, very well; then that quite settles the matter. It is a pity, because in other respects you would really have done very nicely. In that case, Miss Stoper, I had best inspect a few more of your young ladies.'

"The manageress had sat all this while busy with her papers without a word to either of us, but she glanced at me now with so much annoyance upon her face that I could not help suspecting that she had lost a handsome commission through my refusal.

" 'Do you desire your name to be kept upon the books?' she asked.

" 'If you please, Miss Stoper.'

" 'Well, really, it seems rather useless, since you refuse the most excellent offers in this fashion,' said she sharply. 'You can hardly expect us to exert ourselves to find another such opening for you. Good day to you, Miss Hunter.' She struck a gong upon the table, and I was shown out by the page.

"Well, Mr. Holmes, when I got back to my lodgings and found little enough in the cupboard, and two or three bills upon the table, I began to ask myself whether I had not done a very foolish thing. After all, if these people had strange fads, and expected obedience on the most extraordinary matters, they were at least ready to pay for their eccentricity. Very few governesses in England are getting a hundred a year. Besides, what use was my hair to me? Many people are improved by wearing it short, and perhaps I should be among the number. Next day I was inclined to think that I had made a mistake, and by the day after I was sure of it. I had almost overcome my pride, so far as to go back to the agency and inquire whether the place was still open, when I received this letter from the gentleman himself. I have it here, and I will read it to you:

The Copper Beeches, near Winchester.

Dear Miss Hunter—Miss Stoper has very kindly given me your address, and I write from here to ask you whether you have reconsidered your decision. My wife is very anxious that you should come, for she has been much attracted by my description of you. We are willing to give thirty pounds a quarter, or £120 a year, so as to recompense you for any little inconvenience which our fads may cause you. They are not very exacting after all. My wife is fond of a particular shade of electric blue, and would like you to wear such a dress indoors in the morning. You need not, however, go to the expense of purchasing one, as we have one belonging to my dear daughter Alice (now in Philadelphia) which would, I should think, fit you very well. Then, as to sitting here or there, or amusing yourself in any manner indicated, that need cause you no inconvenience. As regards your hair, it is no doubt a pity, especially as I could not help remarking its beauty during our short interview, but I am afraid that I must remain firm upon this point, and I only hope that the increased salary may recompense you for the loss. Your duties, as far as the child is concerned, are very light. Now do try to come, and I shall meet you with the dog-cart at Winchester. Let me know your train—Yours faithfully,

Jephro Rucastle.

"That is the letter which I have just received, Mr Holmes, and my mind is made up that I will accept it. I thought, however, that before taking the final step, I should like to submit the whole matter to your consideration."

"Well, Miss Hunter, if your mind is made up, that settles the question," said Holmes, smiling.

"But you would not advise me to refuse?"

"I confess that it is not the situation which I should like to see a sister of mine apply for."

"What is the meaning of it all, Mr Holmes?"

"Ah, I have no data. I cannot tell. Perhaps you have yourself formed some opinion?"

"Well, there seems to me to be only one possible solution. Mr Rucastle seemed to be a very kind, good-natured man. Is it not possible that his wife is a lunatic, that he desires to keep the matter quiet for fear she should be taken to any asylum, and that he humours her fancies in every way in order to prevent an outbreak."

"That is a possible solution—in fact, as matters stand, it is the most probable one. But in any case it does not seem to be a nice household for a young lady."

"But the money, Mr Holmes, the money!"

"Well, yes, of course, the pay is good—too good. That is what makes me uneasy. Why should they give you £120 a year, when they could have the pick for £40? There must be some strong reason behind."

"I thought that if I told you the circumstances you would understand afterwards if I wanted your help. I should feel so much stronger if I felt that you were at the back of me."

"Oh, you may carry that feeling away with you. I assure you that your little problem promises to be the most interesting which has come my way for some months. There is something distinctly novel about some of the features. If you should find yourself in doubt or in danger—"

"Danger! What danger do you foresee?"

Holmes shook his head gravely. "It would cease to be a danger if we could define it," said he. "But at any time, day or night, a telegram would bring me down to your help."

"That is enough." She rose briskly from her chair with the anxiety all swept from her face. "I shall go down to Hampshire quite easy in my mind now. I shall write to Mr Rucastle at once, sacrifice my poor hair tonight, and start for Winchester tomorrow." With a few grateful words to Holmes she bade us both good-night, and bustled off upon her way.

"At least," said I, as we heard her quick, firm step descending the stairs, "she seems to be a young lady who is very well able to take care of herself."

"And she would need to be," said Holmes gravely; "I am much mistaken if we do not hear from her before many days are past."

It was not very long before my friend's prediction was fulfilled. A fortnight went by, during which I frequently found my thoughts turning in her direction, and wondering what strange side alley of human experience this lonely woman had strayed into. The unusual salary, the curious conditions, the light duties, all pointed to something abnormal, though whether a fad or a plot, or whether the man were a philanthropist or a villain, it was quite beyond my powers to determine. As to Holmes, I observed that he sat frequently for half an hour on end, with knitted brows and an abstracted air, but he swept the matter away with a wave of his hand when I mentioned it. "Data! data! data!" he cried impatiently. "I can't make bricks without clay."

And yet he would always wind up by muttering that no sister of his should ever have accepted such a situation.

The telegram which we eventually received came late one night, just as I was thinking of turning in, and Holmes was settling down to one of those all-night researches which he frequently indulged in, when I would leave him stooping over a retort and a test-tube at night, and find him in the same position when I came down to breakfast in the morning. He opened the yellow envelope, and then, glancing at the message, threw it across to me.

"Just look up the trains in Bradshaw," said he, and turned back to his chemical studies.

The summons was a brief and urgent one.

Please be at the Black Swan Hotel at Winchester at midday tomorrow (it said). Do come! I am at my wits' end.

Hunter.

"Will you come with me?" asked Holmes, glancing up.

"I should wish to."

"Just look it up, then."

"There is a train at half-past nine," said I, glancing over my Bradshaw. "It is due at Winchester at 11:30."

"That will do very nicely. Then perhaps I had better postpone my analysis of the acetones, as we may need to be at our best in the morning."

By eleven o'clock the next day we were well upon our way to the old English capital. Holmes had been buried in the morning papers all the way down, but after we had passed the Hampshire border he threw them down, and began to admire the scenery. It was an ideal spring day, a light blue sky, flecked with little fleecy white clouds drifting across from west to east. The sun was shining very brightly, and yet there was an exhilarating nip in the air, which set an edge to a man's energy. All over the countryside, away to the rolling hills around Aldershot, the little red and grey roofs of the farm-steadings peeped out from amidst the light green of the new foliage.

"Are they not fresh and beautiful?" I cried, with all the enthusiasm of a man fresh from the fogs of Baker Street.

But Holmes shook his head gravely.

"Do you know, Watson," said he, "that it is one of the curses of a mind with a turn like mine that I must look at everything with reference to my own special subject. You look at these scattered houses, and you are impressed by their beauty. I look at them, and the only thought which comes to me is a feeling of their isolation, and of the impunity with which crime may be committed there."

"Good heavens!" I cried. "Who would associate crime with these dear old homesteads?"

"They always fill me with a certain horror. It is my belief, Watson, founded upon my experience, that the lowest and vilest alleys in London do not present a more dreadful record of sin than does the smiling and beautiful countryside."

"You horrify me!"

"But the reason is very obvious. The pressure of public opinion can do in the town what the law cannot accomplish. There is no lane so vile that the scream of a tortured child, or the thud of a drunkard's blow, does not beget sympathy and indignation among the neighbours, and then the whole machinery of justice is ever so close that a word of complaint can set it going, and there is but a step between the crime and the dock. But look at these lonely houses, each in its own fields, filled for the most part with poor ignorant folk who know little of the law. Think of the deeds of hellish cruelty, the hidden wickedness which may go on, year in, year out, in such places, and none the wiser. Had this lady who appeals to us for help gone to live in Winchester, I should never have had a fear for her. It is the five miles of country which makes the danger. Still, it is clear that she is not personally threatened."

"No. If she can come to Winchester to meet us she can get away."

"Quite so. She has her freedom."

"What *can* be the matter, then? Can you suggest no explanation?"

"I have devised seven separate explanations, each of which would cover the facts as far as we know them. But which of these is correct can only be determined by the fresh information which we shall no doubt find waiting for us. Well, there is the tower of the Cathedral, and we shall soon learn all that Miss Hunter has to tell."

The "Black Swan" is an inn of repute in the High Street, at no distance from the station, and there we found the young lady waiting for us. She had engaged a sitting-room, and our lunch awaited us upon the table.

"I am so delighted that you have come," she said earnestly, "it is so kind of you both; but indeed I do not know what I should do. Your advice will be altogether invaluable to me."

"Pray tell us what has happened to you."

"I will do so, and I must be quick, for I have promised Mr Rucastle to be back before three. I got his leave to come into town this morning, though he little knew for what purpose."

"Let us have everything in its due order." Holmes thrust his long thin legs out towards the fire, and composed himself to listen.

"In the first place, I may say that I have met, on the whole, with no actual ill-treatment from Mr and Mrs Rucastle. It is only fair to them to say that. But I cannot understand them, and I am not easy in my mind about them."

"What can you not understand?"

"Their reasons for their conduct. But you shall have it all just as it occurred. When I came down Mr Rucastle met me here, and drove me in his dog-cart to Copper Beeches. It is, as he said, beautifully situated, but it is not beautiful in itself, for it is a large square block of a house, whitewashed; but all stained and streaked with damp and bad weather. There are grounds round it, woods on three sides, and on the fourth a field which slopes down to the Southampton high-road, which curves past about a hundred yards from the front door. This ground in front belongs to the house, but the woods all round are part of Lord Southerton's preserves. A clump of copper beeches immediately in front of the hall door has given its name to the place.

"I was driven over by my employer, who was as amiable as ever, and was introduced by him that evening to his wife and the child. There was no truth, Mr Holmes, in the conjecture which seemed to us to be probable in your rooms at Baker Street. Mrs Rucastle is not mad. I found her to be a silent, pale-faced woman, much younger than her husband, not more than thirty, I should think, while he can hardly be less than forty-five. From their conversation I have gathered that they have been married about seven years, that he was a widower, and that his only child by the first wife was the daughter who has gone to Philadelphia. Mr Rucastle told me in private that the reason why she had left them was that she had an unreasoning aversion to her stepmother. As the daughter could not have been less than twenty, I can quite imagine that her position must have been uncomfortable with her father's young wife.

"Mrs Rucastle seemed to me to be colourless in mind as well as in feature. She impressed me neither favourably nor the reverse. She was a nonentity. It was easy to see that she was passionately devoted both to her husband and to her little son. Her light grey eyes wandered continually from one to the other, noting every little want and forestalling it if possible. He was kind to her also in his bluff, boisterous fashion, and on the whole they seemed to be a happy couple. And yet she had some secret sorrow, this woman. She would often be lost in deep thought, with the saddest look upon her face. More than once I have surprised her in tears. I have thought sometimes that it was the disposition of her child which weighted upon her mind, for I have never met so utterly spoilt and so ill-natured a little creature. He is small for his age, with a head which is quite disproportionately large. His whole life appears to be spent in an alternation between savage fits of passion and gloomy intervals of sulking. Giving pain to any creature weaker than himself seems to be his one idea of amusement, and he shows quite remarkable talent in planning the capture of mice, little birds, and insects. But I would rather not talk about the creature, Mr Holmes, and, indeed, he has little to do with my story."

"I am glad of all details," remarked my friend, "whether they seem to you to be relevant or not."

"I shall try not to miss anything of importance. The one unpleasant thing about the house, which struck me at once, was the appearance and conduct of the servants. There are only two, a man and his wife. Toller, for that's his name, is a rough, uncouth man, with grizzled hair and whiskers, and a perpetual smell of drink. Twice since I have been with them he has been quite drunk, and yet Mr Rucastle seemed to take no notice of it. His wife is a very tall and strong woman with a sour face, as silent as Mrs Rucastle, and much less amiable. They are a most unpleasant couple, but fortunately I spend most of my time in the nursery and my own room, which are next to each other in one corner of the building.

"For two days after my arrival at the Copper Beeches my life was very quiet; on the third, Mrs Rucastle came down just after breakfast and whispered something to her husband.

" 'Oh yes,' said he, turning to me, 'we are very much obliged to you, Miss Hunter, for falling in with our whims so far as to cut your hair. I assure you that it has not detracted in the tiniest iota from your appearance. We shall now see how the electric blue dress will become you. You will find it laid out upon the bed in your room, and if you would be so good as to put it on we should both be extremely obliged.'

"The dress which I found waiting for me was of a peculiar shade of blue. It was of excellent material, a sort of beige, but it bore unmistakable signs of having been worn before. It could not have been a better fit if I had been measured for it. Both Mr and Mrs Rucastle expressed a delight at the look of it which seemed quite exaggerated in its vehemence. They were waiting for me in the drawing-room, which is a very large room, stretching along the entire front of the house, with three long windows reaching down to the floor. A chair had been placed close to the central window, with its back turned towards it. In this I was asked to sit, and then Mr Rucastle, walking up and down on the other side of the room, began to tell me a series of the funniest stories that I have ever listened to. You cannot imagine how comical he was, and I laughed until I was quite weary. Mrs Rucastle, however, who has evidently no sense of humour, never so much as smiled, but sat with her hands in her lap, and a sad, anxious look upon her face. After an hour or so, Mr Rucastle suddenly remarked that it was time to commence the duties of the day, and that I might change my dress, and go to little Edward in the nursery.

"Two days later this same performance was gone through under exactly similar circumstances. Again I changed my dress, again I sat in the window, and again I laughed very heartily at the funny stories of which my employer had an immense repertoire, and which he told inimitably. Then he handed me a yellow-backed novel, and, moving my chair a little sideways, that my own shadow might not fall upon the page, he begged me to read aloud to him. I read for about ten minutes, beginning in the heart of a chapter, and then suddenly, in the middle of a sentence, he ordered me to cease and change my dress.

"You can easily imagine, Mr Holmes, how curious I became as to what the meaning of this extraordinary performance could possibly be. They were always very careful, I observed, to turn my face away from the window, so that I became consumed with the desire to see what was going on behind my back. At first it seemed to be impossible, but I soon devised a means. My hand mirror had been broken, so a happy thought seized me, and I concealed a little of the glass in my handkerchief. On the next occasion, in the midst of my laughter, I put my handkerchief up to my eyes, and was able with a little management to see all that there was behind me. I confess that I was disappointed. There was nothing.

"At least, that was my first impression. At the second glance, however, I perceived that there was a man standing in the Southampton road, a small bearded man in a grey suit, who seemed to be looking in my direction. The road is an important highway, and there are usually people there. This man, however, was leaning against the railings which bordered our field, and was looking earnestly. I lowered my handkerchief, and glanced at Mrs Rucastle to find her eyes fixed upon me with a most searching gaze. She said nothing, but I am convinced that she had divined that I had a mirror in my hand, and had seen what was behind me. She rose at once.

" 'Jephro,' said she, 'there is an impertinent fellow upon the road there who stares up at Miss Hunter.'

" 'No friend of yours, Miss Hunter?' he asked.

" 'No; I know no one in these parts.'

" 'Dear me! How very impertinent! Kindly turn round, and motion him to go away.'

" 'Surely it would be better to take no notice?'

" 'No, no, we should have him loitering here always. Kindly turn round, and wave him away like that.'

"I did as I was told, and at the same instant Mrs Rucastle drew down the blind. That was a week ago, and from that time I have not sat again in the window, nor have I worn the blue dress, nor seen the man in the road."

"Pray continue," said Holmes. "Your narrative promises to be a most interesting one."

"You will find it rather disconnected, I fear, and there may prove to be little relation between the different incidents of which I speak. On the very first day that I was at Copper Beeches, Mr Rucastle took me to a small outhouse which stands near the kitchen door. As we approached it I heard the sharp rattling of a chain, and the sound as of a large animal moving about.

" 'Look in here!' said Mr Rucastle, showing me a slit between two planks. 'Is he not a beauty?'

"I looked through, and was conscious of two glowing eyes, and of a vague figure huddled up in the darkness.

" 'Don't be frightened,' said my employer, laughing at the start which I had given. 'It's only Carlo, my mastiff. I call him mine, but really old Toller, my groom, is the only man who can do anything with him. We feed him once a day, and not too much then, so that he is always as keen as mustard. Toller lets him loose every night, and God help the trespasser whom he lays his fangs upon. For goodness' sake don't you ever on any pretext set your foot over the threshold at night, for it is as much as your life is worth.'

"The warning was no idle one, for two nights later I happened to look out of my bedroom window about two o'clock in the morning. It was a beautiful moonlight night, and the lawn in front of the house was silvered over and almost as bright as day. I was standing wrapped in the peaceful beauty of the scene, when I was aware that something was moving under the shadow of the copper beeches. As it emerged into the moonshine I saw what it was. It was a giant dog, as large as a calf, tawny-tinted, with hanging jowl, black muzzle, and huge projecting bones. It walked slowly across the lawn and vanished into the shadow upon the other side. That dreadful silent sentinel sent a chill to my heart, which I do not think that any burglar could have done.

"And now I have a very strange experience to tell you. I had, as you know, cut off my hair in London, and I had placed it in a great coil at the bottom of my trunk. One evening, after the child was in bed, I began to amuse myself by examining the furniture of my room, and by rearranging my own little things. There was an old chest of drawers in the room, the two upper ones empty and open, the lower one locked. I had filled the two first with my linen, and as I had still much to pack away, I was naturally annoyed at not having the use of the third drawer. It struck me that it might have been fastened by a mere oversight, so I took out my bunch of keys and tried to open it. The very first key fitted to perfection, and I drew the drawer open. There was only one thing in it, but I am sure that you would never guess what it was. It was my coil of hair.

"I took it up and examined it. It was of the same peculiar tint, and the same thickness. But then the impossibility of the thing obtruded itself upon me. How *could* my hair have been locked in the drawer? With trembling hands I undid my trunk, turned out the contents, and drew from the bottom my own hair. I laid the two tresses together, and I assure you they were identical. Was it not extraordinary? Puzzle as I would I could make nothing at all of what it meant. I returned the strange hair to the drawer, and I said nothing of the matter to the Rucastles, as I felt that I had put myself in the wrong by opening a drawer which they had locked.

"I am naturally observant as you may have remarked, Mr Holmes, and I soon had a pretty good plan of the whole house in my head. There was one wing, however, which appeared not to be inhabited at all. A door which faced that which led into the quarters of the Tollers opened into this suite, but it was invariably locked. One day, however, as I ascended the stair, I met Mr Rucastle coming out through this door, his keys in his hand, and a look on his face which made him a very different person to the round jovial man to whom I was accustomed. His cheeks were red, his brow was all crinkled with anger, and the veins stood out at his temples with passion. He locked the door, and hurried past me without a word or a look.

"This aroused my curiosity; so when I went out for a walk in the grounds with my charge, I strolled round to the side from which I could see the windows of this part of the house. There were four of them in a row, three of which were simply dirty, while the fourth was shuttered up. They were evidently all deserted. As I strolled up and down, glancing at them occasionally, Mr Rucastle came out to me, looking as merry and jovial as ever.

" 'Ah!' said he, 'you must not think me rude if I passed you without a word, my dear young lady. I was preoccupied with business matters.'

"I assured him that I was not offended. 'By the way,' said I, 'you seem to have quite a suite of spare rooms up there, and one of them has the shutters up.'

" 'Photography is one of my hobbies,' said he. 'I have made my darkroom up there. But, dear me! what an observant young lady we have come upon. Who would have believed it? Who would have ever believed it?' He spoke in a jesting tone, but there was no jest in his eyes as he looked at me. I read suspicion there, and annoyance, but no jest.

"Well, Mr Holmes, from the moment that I understood that there was something about that suite of rooms which I was not to know, I was all on fire to go over them. It was not mere curiosity, though I have my share of that. It was more a feeling of duty—a feeling that some good might come from my penetrating to this place. They talk of woman's instinct; perhaps it was woman's instinct which gave me that feeling. At any rate, it was there; and I was keenly on the look-out for any chance to pass the forbidden door.

"It was only yesterday that the chance came. I may tell you that, besides Mr Rucastle, both Toller and his wife find something to do in these deserted rooms, and I once saw him carrying a large black linen bag with him through the door. Recently he has been drinking hard, and yesterday evening he was very drunk; and, when I came upstairs, there was the key in the door. I have no doubt at all that he had left it there. Mr and Mrs Rucastle were both downstairs, and the child was with them, so that I had an admirable opportunity. I turned the key gently in the lock, opened the door, and slipped through.

"There was a little passage in front of me, unpapered and uncarpeted, which turned at a right angle at the farther end. Round this corner were three doors in a line, the first and third of which were open. They each led into an empty room, dusty and cheerless, with two windows in the one, and one in the other, so thick with dirt that the evening light glimmered dimly through them. The center door was closed, and across the outside of it had been fastened one of the broad bars of an iron bed, padlocked at one end to a ring in the wall, and fastened at the other with stout cord. The door itself was locked as well, and the key was not there. This barricaded door corresponded clearly with the shuttered window outside, and yet I could see by the glimmer from beneath it that the room was not in darkness. Evidently there was a skylight which let in light from above. As I stood in the passage gazing at this sinister door, and wondering what secret it might veil, I suddenly heard the sound of steps within the room, and saw a shadow pass backwards and forwards against the little slit of dim light which shone out from under the door. A mad, unreasoning terror rose up in me at the sight, Mr Holmes. My overstrung nerves failed me suddenly, and I turned and ran—ran as though some dreadful hand were behind me, clutching at the skirt of my dress. I rushed down the passage, through the door, and straight into the arms of Mr Rucastle, who was waiting outside.

" 'So,' said he, smiling, 'it was you, then. I thought it must be when I saw the door open.'

" 'Oh, I am so frightened!' I panted.

" 'My dear young lady! my dear young lady!'—you cannot think how caressing and soothing his manner was—'and what has frightened you, my dear young lady?'

"But his voice was just a little too coaxing. He overdid it. I was keenly on my guard against him.

" 'I was foolish enough to go into the empty wing,' I answered. 'But it is so lonely and eerie in this dim light that I was frightened and ran out again. Oh, it is so dreadful still in there!'

" 'Only that?' said he, looking at me keenly.

" 'Why, what do you think?' I asked.

" 'Why do you think that I lock this door?'

" 'I am sure that I do not know.'

" 'It is to keep people out who have no business there. Do you see?' He was still smiling in the most amiable manner.

" 'I am sure if I had known—'

" 'Well, then, you know now. And if you ever put your foot over that threshold again—' here in an instant the smile hardened into a grin of rage, and he glared down at me with the face of a demon, 'I'll throw you to the mastiff.'

"I was so terrified that I do not know what I did. I suppose that I must have rushed past him into my room. I remember nothing until I found myself lying on my bed trembling all over. Then I thought of you, Mr Holmes. I could not live there longer without some advice. I was frightened of the house, of the man, of the woman, of the servants, even of the child. They were all horrible to me. If I could only bring you down all would be well. Of course I might have fled from the house, but my curiosity was almost as strong as my fears. My mind was soon made up. I would send you a wire. I put on my hat and cloak, went down to the office, which is about half a mile from the house, and then returned, feeling very much easier. A horrible doubt came into my mind as I approached the door lest the dog might be loose, but I remembered that Toller had drunk himself into a state of insensibility that evening, and I knew that he was the only one in the household who had any influence with the savage creature, or who would venture to set him free. I slipped in in safety, and lay awake half the night in my joy at the thought of seeing you. I had no difficulty in getting leave to come into Winchester this morning, but I must be back before three o'clock, for Mr and Mrs Rucastle are going on a visit, and will be away all the evening, so that I must look after the child. Now I have told you all my adventures, Mr Holmes, and I should be very glad if you could tell me what it all means, and, above all, what I should do."

Holmes and I had listened spellbound to this extraordinary story. My friend rose now, and paced up and down the room, his hands in his pockets, and an expression of the most profound gravity upon his face.

"Is Toller still drunk?" he asked.

"Yes. I heard his wife tell Mrs Rucastle that she could do nothing with him."

"That is well. And the Rucastles go out tonight?"

"Yes."

"Is there a cellar with a good strong lock?"

"Yes, the wine cellar."

"You seem to me to have acted all through this matter like a brave and sensible girl, Miss Hunter. Do you think that you could perform one more feat? I should not ask it of you if I did not think you a quite exceptional woman."

"I will try. What is it?"

"We shall be at the Copper Beeches by seven o'clock, my friend and I. The Rucastles will be gone by that time, and Toller will, we hope, be incapable. There only remains Mrs Toller, who might give the alarm. If you could send her into the cellar, on some errand, and then turn the key upon her, you would facilitate matters immensely."

"I will do it."

"Excellent! We shall then look thoroughly into the affair. Of course there is only one feasible explanation. You have been brought there to personate someone, and the real person is imprisoned in this chamber. That is obvious. As to who this prisoner is, I have no doubt that it is the daughter, Miss Alice Rucastle, if I remember right, who was said to have gone to America. You were chosen, doubtless, as resembling her in height, figure, and the colour of your hair. Hers had been cut off, very possibly in some illness through which she has passed, and so, of course, yours had to be sacrificed also. By a curious chance you came upon her tresses. The man in the road was, undoubtedly, some friend of hers—possibly her fiancé and no doubt as you wore the girl's dress, and were so like her, he was convinced from your laughter, whenever he saw you, and afterwards from your gesture, that Miss Rucastle was perfectly happy, and that she no longer desired his attentions. The dog is let loose at night to prevent him from endeavouring to communicate with her. So much is fairly clear. The most serious point in the case is the disposition of the child."

"What on earth has that to do with it?" I ejaculated.

"My dear Watson, you as a medical man are continually gaining light as to the tendencies of a child by the study of the parents. Don't you see that the converse is equally valid? I have frequently gained my first real insight into the character of parents by studying their children. This child's disposition is abnormally cruel, merely for cruelty's sake, and whether he derives this from his smiling father, as I should suspect, or from his mother, it bodes evil for the poor girl who is in their power."

"I am sure that you are right, Mr Holmes," cried our client. "A thousand things come back to me which make me certain that you have hit it. Oh, let us lose not an instant in bringing help to this poor creature."

"We must be circumspect, for we are dealing with a very cunning man. We can do nothing until seven o'clock. At that hour we shall be with you, and it will not be long before we solve the mystery."

We were as good as our word, for it was just seven when we reached the Copper Beeches, having put up our trap at the wayside public-house. The group of trees, with their dark leaves shining like burnished metal in the light of the setting sun, were sufficient to mark the house even had Miss Hunter not been standing smiling on the doorstep.

"Have you managed it?" asked Holmes.

A loud thudding noise came from somewhere downstairs. "That is

Mrs Toller in the cellar," said she. "Her husband lies snoring on the kitchen rug. Here are his keys which are the duplicates of Mr Rucastle's."

"You have done well indeed!" cried Holmes, with enthusiasm. "Now lead the way, and we shall soon see the end of this black business."

We passed up the stair, unlocked the door, followed on down a passage, and found ourselves in front of the barricade which Miss Hunter had described. Holmes cut the cord and removed the transverse bar. Then he tried the various keys in the lock, but without success. No sound came from within, and at the silence Holmes' face clouded over.

"I trust that we are not too late," said he. "I think, Miss Hunter, that we had better go in without you. Now, Watson, put your shoulder to it, and we shall see whether we cannot make our way in."

It was an old rickety door and gave at once before our united strength. Together we rushed into the room. It was empty. There was no furniture save a little pallet bed, a small table, and a basketful of linen. The skylight above was open, and the prisoner gone.

"There has been some villainy here," said Holmes; "this beauty has guessed Miss Hunter's intentions, and has carried his victim off."

"But how?"

"Through the skylight. We shall soon see how he managed it." He swung himself up on to the roof. "Ah, yes," he cried, "here's the end of a long light ladder against the eaves. That is how he did it."

"But it is impossible," said Miss Hunter, "the ladder was not there when the Rucastles went away."

"He has come back and done it. I tell you that he is a clever and dangerous man. I should not be very much surprised if this were he whose step I hear now upon the stair. I think, Watson, that it would be as well for you to have your pistol ready."

The words were hardly out of his mouth before a man appeared at the door of the room, a very fat and burly man, with a heavy stick in his hand. Miss Hunter screamed and shrunk against the wall at the sight of him, but Sherlock Holmes sprang forward and confronted him.

"You villain," said he, "where's your daughter?"

The fat man cast his eyes round, and then up at the open skylight.

"It is for me to ask you that," he shrieked, "you thieves! Spies and thieves! I have caught you, have I! You are in my power. I'll serve you!" He turned and clattered down the stairs as hard as he could go.

"He's gone for the dog!" cried Miss Hunter.

"I have my revolver," said I.

"Better close the front door," cried Holmes, and we all rushed down the stairs together. We had hardly reached the hall when we heard the baying of a hound, and then a scream of agony, with a horrible worrying sound which it was dreadful to listen to. An elderly man with a red face and shaking limbs came staggering out at a side-door.

"My God!" he cried. "Someone has loosed the dog. It's not been fed for two days. Quick, quick, or it'll be too late!"

Holmes and I rushed out, and round the angle of the house, with Toller hurrying behind us. There was the huge famished brute, its black muzzle buried in Rucastle's throat, while he writhed and screamed upon the ground. Running up, I blew its brains out, and it fell over with its keen white teeth still meeting in the great creases of his neck. With much labour we separated them, and carried him, living but horribly mangled, into the house. We laid him upon the drawing-room sofa, and having despatched the sobered Toller to bear the news to his wife, I did what I could to relieve his pain. We were all assembled round him when the door opened, and a tall, gaunt woman entered the room.

"Mrs Toller!" cried Miss Hunter.

"Yes, miss. Mr Rucastle let me out when he came back before he went up to you. Ah, miss, it is a pity you didn't let me know what you were planning, for I would have told you that your pains were wasted."

"Ha!" said Holmes, looking keenly at her. "It is clear that Mrs Toller knows more about this matter than anyone else."

"Yes, sir, I do, and I am ready enough to tell what I know."

"Then pray sit down, and let us hear it, for there are several points on which I must confess that I am still in the dark."

"I will soon make it clear to you," said she; "and I'd have done so before now if I could ha' got out from the cellar. If there's police-court business over this, you'll remember that I was the one that stood your friend, and that I was Miss Alice's friend too.

"She was never happy at home, Miss Alice wasn't, from the time that her father married again. She was slighted like, and had no say in anything; but it never really became bad for her until after she met Mr Fowler at a friend's house. As well as I could learn, Miss Alice had rights of her own by will, but she was so quiet and patient, she was, that she never said a word about them, but just left everything in Mr

Rucastle's hands. He knew he was safe with her; but when there was a chance of a husband coming forward, who would ask for all that the law could give him, then her father thought it time to put a stop on it. He wanted her to sign a paper so that whether she married or not, he could use her money. When she wouldn't do it, he kept on worrying her until she got brain fever, and for six weeks was at death's door. Then she got better at last, all worn to a shadow, and with her beautiful hair cut off; but that didn't make no change in her young man, and he stuck to her as true as man could be."

"Ah," said Holmes, "I think that what you have been good enough to tell us makes the matter fairly clear, and that I can deduce all that remains. Mr Rucastle, then, I presume, took to this system of imprisonment?"

"Yes, sir."

"And brought Miss Hunter down from London in order to get rid of the disagreeable persistence of Mr Fowler."

"That was it, sir."

"But Mr Fowler, being a preserving man, as a good seaman should be, blockaded the house, and, having met you, succeeded by certain arguments, metallic or otherwise, in convincing you that your interests were the same as his."

"Mr Fowler was a very kind-spoken, free-handed gentleman," said Mrs Toller serenely.

"And in this way he managed that your good man should have no want of drink, and that a ladder should be ready at the moment when your master had gone."

"You have it, sir, just as it happened."

"I am sure we owe you an apology, Mrs. Toller," said Holmes, "for you have certainly cleared up everything which puzzled us. And here comes the country surgeon and Mrs Rucastle, so I think, Watson, that we had best escort Miss Hunter back to Winchester, as it seems to me that our *locus standi* now is rather a questionable one."

And thus was solved the mystery of the sinister house with the copper beeches in front of the door. Mr Rucastle survived, but was always a broken man, kept alive solely through the care of his devoted wife. They still live with their old servants, who probably know so much of Rucastle's past life that he finds it difficult to part from them. Mr Fowler and Miss Rucastle were married, by special license, in Southampton the day after their flight, and he is now the holder of a Government appointment in the Island of Mauritius. As to Miss Violet Hunter, my friend Holmes, rather to my disappointment, manifested no further interest in her when once she had ceased to be the centre of one of his problems, and she is now the head of a private school at Walsall, where I believe that she has met with considerable success.

The Man in the Passage

GILBERT K. CHESTERTON

Gilbert Keith Chesterton, essayist, man-of-letters and creator of Father Brown, was born on May 29, 1874, in London. He did not distinguish himself at St. Paul's or at Slade, the art school of University College, London, though he became a light comic draftsman of some merit and later illustrated a number of books by himself and with E. C. Bentley and Hilaire Belloc. As a widely read and heard journalist, debater and after-dinner speaker, even his opponents granted him credit for his wit, his humanity and personal kindness, his love of liberty and gift of paradox.

Two men appeared simultaneously at the two ends of a sort of passage running along the side of the Apollo Theater in the Adelphi. The evening daylight in the streets was large and luminous, opalescent and empty. The passage was comparatively long and dark, so each man could see the other as a mere black silhouette at the other end. Nevertheless, each man knew the other, even in that inky outline, for they were both men of striking appearance, and they hated each other.

The covered passage opened at one end on one of the steep streets of the Adelphi, and at the other on a terrace overlooking the sunset-colored river. One side of the passage was a blank wall, for the building it supported was an old unsuccessful theater restaurant, now shut up. The other side of the passage contained two doors, one at each end. Neither was what was commonly called the stage door; they were a sort of special and private stage doors, used by very special performers, and in this case by the star actor and actress in the Shakespearean performance of the day. Persons of that eminence often like to have such private exits and entrances, for meeting friends or avoiding them.

The two men in question were certainly two such friends, men who evidently knew the doors and counted on their opening, for each approached the door at the upper end with equal coolness and confidence. Not, however, with equal speed; but the man who walked fast was the man from the other end of the tunnel, so they both arrived before the secret stage door almost at the same instant. They saluted each other with civility, and waited a moment before one of them, the sharper walker, who seemed to have the shorter patience, knocked at the door.

In this and everything else each man was opposite and neither could be called inferior. As private persons, both were handsome, capable, and popular. As public persons, both were in the first public rank. But everything about them, from their glory to their good looks, was of a diverse and incomparable kind. Sir Wilson Seymour was the kind of man whose importance is known to everybody who knows. The more you mixed with the innermost ring in every polity or profession, the more often you met Sir Wilson Seymour. He was the one intelligent man on twenty unintelligent committees—on every sort of subject, from the reform of the Royal Academy to the project of bimetallism for Greater Britain. In the arts especially he was omnipotent. He was so unique that nobody could quite decide whether he was a great aristocrat who had taken up art, or a great artist whom the aristocrats had taken up. But you could not meet him for five minutes without realizing that you had really been ruled by him all your life.

His appearance was "distinguished" in exactly the same sense; it was at once conventional and unique. Fashion could have found no fault with his high silk hat; yet it was unlike anyone else's hat—a little higher, perhaps, and adding something to his natural height. His tall, slender figure had a slight stoop, yet it looked the reverse of feeble. His hair was silver-gray, but he did not look old; it was worn longer than the common, yet he did not look effeminate; it was curly, but it did not look curled. His carefully pointed beard made him look more manly and militant rather than otherwise, as it does in those old admirals of Velasquez with whose dark portraits his house was hung. His gray gloves were a shade bluer, his silver-knobbed cane a shade longer than scores of such gloves and canes flapped and flourished about the theaters and the restaurants.

The other man was not so tall, yet would have struck nobody as short, but merely as strong and handsome. His hair also was curly, but fair and cropped close to a strong, massive head—the sort of head you break a door with, as Chaucer said of the Miller's. His military mustache and the carriage of his shoulders showed him a soldier, but he had a pair of those peculiar, frank, and piercing blue eyes which are more common in sailors. His face was somewhat square, his jaw was square; his shoulders were square, even his jacket was square. Indeed, in the wild school of caricature then current, Mr. Max Beerbohm had represented him as a proposition in the fourth book of Euclid.

For he also was a public man, though with quite another sort of success. You did not have to be in the best society to have heard of Captain Cutler, of the siege of Hong-Kong and the great march across China. You could not get away from hearing of him wherever you were; his portrait was on every other post card; his maps and battles in every other illustrated paper; songs in his honor in every other music-hall turn or on every other barrel organ. His fame, though probably more temporary, was ten times more wide, popular, and spontaneous than the other man's. In thousands of English homes he appeared enormous above England, like Nelson. Yet he had infinitely less power in England than Sir Wilson Seymour.

The door was opened to them by an aged servant or "dresser," whose broken-down face and figure and black, shabby coat and trousers contrasted queerly with the glittering interior of the great actress's dressing room. It was fitted and filled with looking glasses at every angle of refraction, so that they looked like the hundred facets of one huge diamond—if one could get inside a diamond. The other features of luxury—a few flowers, a few colored cushions, a few scraps of stage costume—were multiplied by all the mirrors into the madness of the Arabian Nights, and danced and changed places perpetually as the shuffling attendant shifted a mirror outwards or shot one back against the wall.

They both spoke to the dingy dresser by name, calling him Parkinson, and asking for the lady as Miss Aurora Rome. Parkinson said she was in the other room, but he would go and tell her. A shade crossed the brow of both visitors; for the other room was the private room of the great actor with whom Miss Aurora was performing, and she was of the kind that does not inflame admiration without inflaming jealousy. In about half a minute, however, the inner door opened, and she entered as she always did, even in private life, so that the very silence seemed to be a roar of applause, and one well deserved. She was clad in a somewhat strange garb of peacock green and peacock blue satins, that gleamed like blue and green metals, such as delight children and esthetes, and her heavy, hot brown hair framed one of those magic faces which are dangerous to all men, but especially to boys and to men growing gray. In company with her male colleague, the great American actor, Isidore Bruno, she was producing a particularly poetical and fantastic interpretation of *Midsummer Night's Dream*, in which the artistic prominence was given to Oberon and Titania, or in other words to Bruno and herself.

Set in dreamy and exquisite scenery, moving in mystical dances, the green costume, like burnished beetle wings, expressed all the elusive individuality of an elfin queen. But when personally confronted in what was still broad daylight, a man looked only at her face.

She greeted both men with the beaming and baffling smile which kept so many males at the same just dangerous distance from her. She accepted some flowers from Cutler, which were as tropical and expensive as his victories; and another sort of present from Sir Wilson Seymour, offered later on and more nonchalantly by that gentleman. For it was against his breeding to show eagerness, and against his conventional unconventionality to give anything so obvious as flowers. He had picked up a trifle, he said, which was rather a curiosity; it was an ancient Greek dagger of the Mycenean Epoch, and might have been well worn in the time of Theseus and Hippolyta. It was made of brass like all the Heroic weapons, but, oddly enough, sharp enough to prick anyone still. He had really been attracted to it by the leaflike shape; it was as perfect as a Greek vase. If it was of any interest to Miss Rome or could come in anywhere in the play, he hoped she would—

The inner door burst open and a big figure appeared, who was more of a contrast to the explanatory Seymour than even Captain Cutler. Nearly six-foot-six, and of more than theatrical thews and muscles, Isidore Bruno, in the gorgeous leopard skin and golden-brown garments of Oberon, looked like a barbaric god. He leaned on a sort of hunting spear, which across a theater looked a slight, silvery wand, but which in the small and comparatively crowded room looked as plain as a pikestaff—and as menacing. His vivid, black eyes rolled volcanically, his bronze face, handsome as it was, showed at that moment a combination of high cheekbones with set white teeth, which recalled certain American conjectures about his origin in the Southern plantations.

"Aurora," he began, in that deep voice like a drum of passion that had moved so many audiences, "will you—"

He stopped indecisively because a sixth figure had suddenly presented itself just inside the doorway—a figure so incongruous in the scene as to be almost comic. It was a very short man in the black uniform of the Roman secular clergy, and looking (especially in such a presence as Bruno's and Aurora's) rather like the wooden Noah out of an ark. He did not, however, seem conscious of any contrast, but said with dull civility, "I believe Miss Rome sent for me."

A shrewd observer might have remarked that the emotional temperature rather rose at so unemotional an interruption. The detachment of a professional celebate seemed to reveal to the others that they stood round the woman as a ring of amorous rivals; just as a stranger coming in with frost on his coat will reveal that a room is like a furnace. The presence of the one man who did not care about her increased Miss Rome's sense that everybody else was in love with her, and each in a somewhat dangerous way: the actor with all the appetite of a savage and a spoiled child; the soldier with all the simple selfishness of a man of will rather than mind; Sir Wilson with that daily hardening concentration with which old Hedonists take to a hobby; nay, even the abject Parkinson, who had known her before her triumphs, and who followed her about the room with eyes or feet, with the dumb fascination of a dog.

A shrewd person might also have noted a yet odder thing. The man like a black wooden Noah (who was not wholly without shrewdness) noted it with a considerable but contained amusement. It was evident that the great Aurora, though by no means indifferent to the admiration of the other sex, wanted at this moment to get rid of all the men who admired her and be left alone with the man who did not—did not admire her in that sense, at least; for the little priest did admire and even enjoy the firm feminine diplomacy with which she went about her task. There was, perhaps, only one thing that Aurora Rome was clever about, and that was one half of humanity—the other half. The little priest watched, like a Napoleonic campaign, the swift precision of her policy for expelling all while banishing none. Bruno, the big actor, was so babyish that it was easy to send him off in brute sulks, banging the door. Cutler, the British officer, was pachydermatous to ideas, but punctilious about behavior. He would ignore all hints, but he would die rather than ignore a definite commission from a lady. As to old Seymour he had to be treated differently; he had to be left to the last. The only way to move him was to appeal to him in confidence as an old friend, to let him into the secret of the clearance. The priest did really admire Miss Rome as she achieved all these three objects in one selected action.

She went across to Captain Cutler and said in her sweetest manner, "I shall value all these flowers because they must be your favorite flowers. But they won't be complete, you know, without *my* favorite flower. *Do* go over to that shop around the corner and get me some lilies-of-the-valley and then it will be *quite lovely*."

The first object of her diplomacy, the exit of the enraged Bruno, was at once achieved. He had already handed his spear in a lordly style like a scepter to the piteous Parkinson, and was about to assume one of the cushioned seats like a throne. But at this open appeal to his rival there glowed in his opal eyeballs all the sensitive insolence of the slave; he knotted his enormous brown fists for an instant, and then, dashing open the door, disappeared into his own apartments beyond. But meanwhile Miss Rome's experiment in mobilizing the British

Army had not succeeded so simply as seemed probable. Cutler had indeed risen stiffly and suddenly, and walked towards the door, hatless, as if at a word of command. But perhaps there was something ostentatiously elegant about the languid figure of Seymour leaning against one of the looking glasses, that brought him up short at the entrance, turning his head this way and that like a bewildered bulldog.

"I must show this stupid man where to go," said Aurora in a whisper to Seymour, and ran out to the threshold to speed the parting guest.

Seymour seemed to be listening, elegant and unconscious as was his posture, and he seemed relieved when he heard the lady call out some last instructions to the Captain, and then turn sharply and run laughing down the passage towards the other end, the end on the terrace above the Thames. Yet a second or two after, Seymour's brow darkened again. A man in his position has so many rivals, and he remembered that at the other end of the passage was the corresponding entrance to Bruno's private room. He did not lose his dignity; he said some civil words to Father Brown about the revival of Byzantine architecture in the Westminster Cathedral, and then, quite naturally, strolled out himself into the upper end of the passage. Father Brown and Parkinson were left alone, and they were neither of them men with a taste for superfluous conversation. The dresser went round the room, pulling out looking glasses and pushing them in again, his dingy dark coat and trousers looking all the more dismal since he was still holding the festive fairy spear of King Oberon. Every time he pulled out the frame of a new glass, a new black figure of Father Brown appeared; the absurd glass chamber was full of Father Browns, upside down in the air like angels, turning somersaults like acrobats, turning their backs to everybody like very rude persons.

Father Brown seemed quite unconscious of this cloud of witnesses, but followed Parkinson with an idly attentive eye till he took himself and his absurd spear into the farther room of Bruno. Then he abandoned himself to such abstract meditations as always amused him—calculating the angles of the mirrors, the angles of each refraction, the angle at which each must fit into the wall . . . when he heard a strong but strangled cry.

He sprang to his feet and stood rigidly listening. After the same instant Sir Wilson Seymour burst back into the room, white as ivory. "Who's that man in the passage?" he cried. "Where's that dagger of mine?"

Before Father Brown could turn in his heavy boots, Seymour was plunging about the room looking for the weapon. And before he could possibly find that weapon or any other, a brisk running of feet broke upon the pavement outside, and the square face of Cutler was thrust into the same doorway. He was still grotesquely grasping a bunch of lilies-of-the-valley. "What's this?" he cried. "What's that creature down the passage? Is this some of your tricks?"

"My tricks!" exclaimed his pale rival, and made a stride towards him.

In the instant of time in which all this happened, Father Brown stepped out into the top of the passage, looked down it, and at once walked briskly towards what he saw.

At this the other two men dropped their quarrel and darted after him, Cutler calling out, "What are you doing? Who are you?"

"My name is Brown," said the priest sadly, as he bent over something and straightened himself again. "Miss Rome sent for me, and I came as quickly as I could. I have come too late."

The three men looked down, and in one of them at least the life died in that late light of afternoon. It ran along the passage like a path of gold, and in the midst of it Aurora Rome lay lustrous in her robes of green and gold, with her dead face turned upwards. Her dress was torn away as in a struggle, leaving the right shoulder bare, but the wound from which the blood was welling was on the other side. The brass dagger lay flat and gleaming a yard or so away.

There was a blank stillness for a measurable time; so that they could hear far off a flower girl's laugh outside Charing Cross, and someone whistling furiously for a taxicab in one of the streets off the Strand. Then the Captain, with a movement so sudden that it might have been passion or playacting, took Sir Wilson Seymour by the throat.

Seymour looked at him steadily without either fight or fear, "You need not kill me," he said, in a voice quite cold. "I shall do that on my own account."

The Captain's hand hesitated and dropped; and the other added with the same icy candor, "If I find I haven't the nerve to do it with that dagger, I can do it in a month with drink."

"Drink isn't good enough for me," replied Cutler, "but I'll have blood for this before I die. Not yours—but I think I know whose."

And before the others could appreciate his intention he snatched up the dagger, sprang at the other door at the lower end of the passage, burst it open, bolt and all, confronted Bruno in his dressing room. As he did so, old Parkinson tottered in his wavering way out of the door and caught sight of the corpse lying in the passage. He moved shakily towards it; looked at it weakly with a working face; then moved shakily back into the dressing room again, and sat down suddenly on one of the richly cushioned chairs. Father Brown instantly ran across to him, taking no notice of Cutler and the colossal actor, though the room already rang with their blows and they began to struggle for the dagger. Seymour, who retained some practical sense, was whistling for the police at the end of the passage.

When the police arrived it was to tear the two men from an almost apelike grapple; and, after a few formal inquiries, to arrest Isidore Bruno upon a charge of murder, brought against him by his furious opponent. The idea that the great national hero of the hour had arrested a wrongdoer with his own hand doubtless had its weight with the police, who are not without elements of the journalist. They treated Cutler with a certain solemn attention, and pointed out that he had got a slight slash on the hand. Even as Cutler bore him back across tilted chair and table, Bruno had twisted the dagger out of his grasp and disabled him just below the wrist. The injury was really slight, but till he was removed from the room the half savage prisoner stared at the running blood with a steady smile.

"Looks a cannibal sort of chap, don't he?" said the constable confidentially to Cutler.

Cutler made no answer, but said sharply a moment after, "We must attend to the . . . death . . ." and his voice escaped from articulation.

"The two deaths," came in the voice of the priest from the farther side of the room. "This poor fellow was gone when I got across to him." And he stood looking down at old Parkinson, who sat in a black huddle on the gorgeous chair. He also had paid his tribute, not without eloquence, to the woman who had died.

The silence was first broken by Cutler, who seemed not untouched by a rough tenderness. "I wish I was him," he said huskily. "I remember he used to watch her wherever she walked more than—anybody. She was his air, and he's dried up. He's just dead."

"We are all dead," said Seymour, in a strange voice, looking down the road.

They took leave of Father Brown at the corner of the road, with some random apologies for any rudeness they might have shown. Both their faces were tragic, but also cryptic.

The mind of the little priest was always a rabbit warren of wild thoughts that jumped too quickly for him to catch them. Like the white tail of a rabbit, he had the vanishing thought that he was certain of their grief, but not so certain of their innocence.

"We had better all be going," said Seymour heavily. "We have done all we can to help."

"Will you understand my motives," asked Father Brown quietly, "if I say you have done all you can to hurt?"

They both started as if guiltily, and Cutler said sharply, "To hurt?"

"To hurt yourselves," answered the priest. "I would not add to your troubles if it weren't common justice to warn you. You've done nearly everything you could do to hang yourselves, if this actor should be acquitted. They'll be sure to subpoena me; I shall be bound to say that after the cry was heard each of you rushed into the room in a wild state and began quarreling about a dagger. As far as my words on oath can go, either of you might have done it. You hurt yourselves with that; and then Captain Cutler must hurt himself with the dagger."

"Hurt myself!" exclaimed the Captain, with contempt. "A silly little scratch."

"Which drew blood," replied the priest, nodding. "We know there's blood on the brass now. And so we shall never know whether there was blood on it before."

There was a silence; and then Seymour said, with an emphasis quite alien to his daily accent, "But I saw a man in the passage."

"I know you did," answered the cleric Brown, with a face of wood; "so did Captain Cutler. That's what seems so improbable."

Before either could make sufficient sense of it even to answer, Father Brown had politely excused himself and gone stumping up the road with his stumpy old umbrella.

As modern newspapers are conducted, the most honest and most important news is the police news. If it be true that in the twentieth century more space was given to murder than to politics, it was for the excellent reason that murder is a more serious subject. But even this would hardly explain the enormous omnipresence and widely distributed detail of "The Bruno Case," or "The Passage Mystery," in the Press of London and the excitement that for some weeks the Press really told the truth; and the reports of examination and cross-examination, if interminable, even if intolerable, are at least reliable coincidence of persons. The victim was a popular actor; and the accused had been caught red-handed, as it were, by the most popular soldier of the patriotic season. In those extraordinary circumstances the Press was paralyzed into probity and accuracy; and the rest of this somewhat singular business can practically be recorded from the reports of Bruno's trial.

The trial was presided over by Mr. Justice Monkhouse, one of those who are jeered at as humorous judges, but who are generally much more serious than the serious judges, for their levity comes from a living impatience of professional solemnity; while the serious judge is really filled with frivolity, because he is filled with vanity. All the chief actors being of a worldly importance, the barristers were well balanced; the prosecutor for the Crown was Sir Walter Cowdray, a heavy but weighty advocate of the sort that knows how to seem English and trustworthy, and how to be rhetorical with reluctance. The prisoner was defended by Mr. Patrick Butler, K. C., who was mistaken for a mere *flâneur* by those who misunderstand the Irish character—and those who had not been examined by him. The medical evidence involved no contradictions, the doctor whom Seymour had summoned on the spot, agreeing with the eminent surgeon who had later examined the body. Aurora Rome had been stabbed with some sharp instrument such as knife or dagger; some instrument, at least, of which the blade was short. The wound was just over the heart, and she had died instantly. When the first doctor saw her she could hardly have been dead for twenty minutes. Therefore, when Father Brown found her, she could hardly have been dead for three.

Some official detective evidence followed, chiefly concerned with the presence or absence of any proof of a struggle: the only suggestion of this was the tearing of the dress at the shoulder, and this did not seem to fit in particularly well with the direction and finality of the blow. When these details had been supplied, though not explained, the first of the important witnesses was called.

Sir Wilson Seymour gave evidence as he did everything else that he did at all—not only well, but perfectly. Though himself much more of a public man than the judge, he conveyed exactly the fine shade of self-effacement before the King's Justice; and though everyone looked at him as they would at the Prime Minister or the Archbishop of Canterbury, they could have said nothing of his part in it but that it was that of a private gentleman, with an accent on the noun. He was also refreshingly lucid, as he was on the committees. He had been calling on Miss Rome at the theater; he had met Captain Cutler there; they had been joined for a short time by the accused, who had then returned to his own dressing room; they had then been joined by a Roman Catholic priest, who asked for the deceased lady and said his name was Brown. Miss Rome had then gone just outside the theater to the entrance of the passage, in order to point out to Captain Cutler a flower shop at which he was to buy her some more flowers; and the witness had remained in the room, exchanging a few words with the priest. He had then distinctly heard the deceased, having sent the Captain on his errand, turn round laughing and run down the passage towards its other end, where was the prisoner's dressing room. In idle curiosity as to the rapid movements of his friends, he had strolled out to the head of the passage himself and looked down it towards the prisoner's door. Did he see anything in the passage? Yes, he saw something in the passage.

Sir Walter Cowdray allowed an impressive interval, during which the witness looked down, and for all his usual composure seemed to have more than his usual pallor. Then the barrister said in a lower voice, which seemed at once sympathetic and creepy, "Did you see it distinctly?"

Sir Wilson Seymour, however moved, had his excellent brains in full working order. "Very distinctly as regards its outline, but quite indistinctly—indeed not at all—as regards the details inside the outline. The passage is of such length that anyone in the middle of it appears quite black against the light at the other end." The witness lowered his steady eyes once more and added, "I had noticed the fact before, when Captain Cutler first entered it." There was another silence, and the judge leaned forward and made a note.

"Well," said Sir Walter patiently, "what was the outline like? Was it, for instance, like the figure of the murdered woman?"

"Not in the least," answered Seymour quietly.

"What did it look to you like?"

"It looked to me," replied the witness, "like a tall man."

Everyone in court kept his eyes riveted on his pen or his umbrella handle or his book or his boots or whatever he happened to be looking at. They seemed to be holding their eyes away from the prisoner by main force; but they felt his figure in the dock, and they felt it as gigantic. Tall as Bruno was to the eye, he seemed to swell taller and taller when all eyes had been torn away from him.

Cowdray was resuming his seat with his solemn face, smoothing his black silk robes and white silk whiskers. Sir Wilson was leaving the witness box, after a few final particular to witnesses, when the counsel for the defense sprang up and stopped him.

"I shall only detain you a moment," said Mr. Butler, who was a rustic-looking person with red eyebrows and an expression of partial slumber. "Will you tell his lordship how you knew it was a man?"

A faint, refined smile seemed to pass over Seymour's features. "I'm afraid it is the vulgar test of trousers," he said. "When I saw daylight between the long legs I was sure it was a man, after all."

Butler's sleepy eyes opened as suddenly as some silent explosion. "After all!" he repeated slowly. "So you did think first it was a woman?" The red brows quivered.

Seymour looked troubled for the first time. "It is hardly a point of fact," he said, "but if his lordship would like me to answer for my impression, of course I shall do so. There was something about the thing that was not exactly a woman and yet was not quite a man; somehow the curves were different. And it had something that looked like long hair."

"Thank you," said Mr. Butler, K. C., and sat down suddenly, as if he had got what he wanted.

Captain Cutler was a far less plausible and composed witness than Sir Wilson, but his account of the opening incidents was solidly the same. He described the return of Bruno to his dressing room, the dispatching of himself to buy a bunch of lilies-of-the-valley, his return to the upper end of the passage, the thing he saw in the passage, his suspicion of Seymour, and his struggle with Bruno. But he could give little artistic assistance about the black figure that he and Seymour had seen. Asked about its outline, he said he was no art critic—with a somewhat too obvious sneer at Seymour. Asked if it was a man or a woman, he said it looked more like a beast—with a too obvious snarl at the prisoner. But the man was plainly shaken with sorrow and sincere anger, and Cowdray quickly excused him from confirming facts that were already fairly clear.

The defending counsel also was again brief in his cross-examination; although (as was his custom) even in being brief, he seemed to take a long time about it. "You used a rather remarkable expression," he said, looking at Cutler sleepily. "What do you mean by saying that it looked more like a beast than a man or a woman?"

Cutler seemed seriously agitated. "Perhaps I oughtn't to have said that," he said, "but when the brute has huge humped shoulders like a chimpanzee, and bristles sticking out of its head like a pig—"

Mr. Butler cut short his curious impatience in the middle. "Never mind whether its hair was like a pig's," he said. "Was it like a woman's?"

"A woman's!" cried the soldier. "Great Scott, no!"

"The last witness said it was," commented the counsel, with unscrupulous swiftness. "And did the figure have any of those serpentine and semi-feminine curves to which eloquent allusion has been made? No? No feminine curves? The figure, if I understand you, was rather heavy and square than otherwise?"

"He may have been bending forward," said Cutler, in a hoarse and rather faint voice.

"Or again, he may not," said Mr. Butler, and sat down suddenly for the second time.

The third witness called by Sir Walter Cowdray was the little Catholic clergyman, so little compared with the others, that his head seemed hardly to come above the box, so that it was like cross-examining a child. But unfortunately Sir Walter had somehow got it into his head (mostly by some ramifications of his family's religion) that Father Brown was on the side of the prisoner, because the prisoner was wicked and foreign and even partly black. Therefore, he took Father Brown up sharply whenever that proud pontiff tried to explain anything; and told him to answer yes or no, and merely tell the plain facts. When Father Brown began, in his simplicity, to say who he thought the man in the passage was, the barrister told him that he did not want his theories.

"A black shape was seen in the passage. And you say you saw the black shape. Well, what shape was it?"

Father Brown blinked as under rebuke; but he had long known the literal nature of obedience. "The shape," he said, "was short and thick, but had two sharp, black projections curved upwards on each side of the head or top, rather like horns, and—"

"Oh, the devil with horns, no doubt," ejaculated Cowdray, sitting down in triumphant jocularity.

"No," said the priest dispassionately. "I know who it was."

Those in court had been wrought up to an irrational but real sense of some monstrosity. They had forgotten the figure in the dock and thought only of the figure in the passage. And the figure in the passage, described by three capable and respectable men who had all seen it, was a shifting nightmare: one called it a woman, and the other a beast, and the other a devil . . .

The judge was looking at Father Brown with level and piercing eyes. "You are a most extraordinary witness," he said, "but there is something about you that makes me think you are trying to tell the truth. Well, who was the man you saw in the passage?"

"He was myself," said Father Brown.

Butler, K. C., sprang to his feet in an extraordinary stillness, and said quite calmly, "Your lordship will allow me to cross-examine?"

And then, without stopping, he shot at Brown the apparently disconnected question, "You have heard about this dagger; you know the experts say the crime was committed with a short blade?"

"A short blade," assented Brown, nodding solemnly like an owl, "but a very long hilt."

Before the audience could quite dismiss the idea that the priest had really seen himself doing murder with a short dagger with a long hilt (which seemed somehow to make it more horrible), he had himself hurried on to explain.

"I mean daggers aren't the only thing with short blades. Spears have short blades. And spears catch at the end of the steel just like daggers, if they're that sort of fancy spear they have in theaters; like the spear poor old Parkinson killed his wife with, just when she'd sent for me to settle their family troubles—and I came just too late, God forgive me! But he died penitent—he just died of being penitent. He couldn't bear what he'd done."

The general impression in court was that the little priest, who was gabbling away, had literally gone mad in the box. But the judge still looked at him with bright and steady eyes of interest; and the counsel for the defense went on with his questions, unperturbed.

"If Parkinson did it with that pantomime spear," asked Butler, "he must have thrust from four yards away. How do you account for signs of struggle, like the dress dragged off the shoulder?" He had slipped into treating this mere witness as an expert; but no one noticed it now.

"The poor lady's dress was torn," said the witness, "because it was caught in a panel that slid to just behind her. She struggled to free herself, and as she did so Parkinson came out of the prisoner's room and lunged with the spear."

"A panel?" repeated the barrister in a curious voice.

"It was a looking glass on the other side," explained Father Brown. "When I was in the dressing room I noticed that some of them could probably be slid out into the passage."

There was another vast and unnatural silence, and this time it was the judge who spoke. "So you really mean that, when you looked down that passage, the man you saw was yourself—in a mirror?"

"Yes, my lord; that was what I was trying to say," said Brown, "but they asked me for the shape; and our hats have corners just like horns, and so I—"

The judge leaned forward, his old eyes yet more brilliant, and said in specially distinct tones, "Do you really mean to say that when Sir

Wilson Seymour saw that wild what-you-call-him with curves and a woman's hair and a man's trousers, what he saw was Sir Wilson Seymour?"

"Yes, my lord," said Father Brown.

"And you mean to say that when Captain Cutler saw that chimpanzee with humped shoulders and hog's bristles, he simply saw himself?"

"Yes, my lord."

The judge leaned back in his chair with a luxuriance in which it was hard to separate the cynicism and the admiration. "And can you tell us why," he asked, "you should know your own figure in a looking glass, when two such distinguished men don't?"

Father Brown blinked even more painfully than before; then he stammered, "Really, my lord, I don't know . . . unless it's because I don't look at it so often."

There Are No Snakes in Ireland

FREDERICK FORSYTH

Frederick Forsyth was born in Ashford, Kent, England in 1938. After service in the Royal Air Force he was a reporter for Reuters and the BBC for several years, before publishing his acclaimed first novel *The Day of the Jackal* in 1971. That book was a best-seller and a successful motion picture, and won the MWA Edgar Award as the best novel of the year.

It was followed by *The Odessa File* (1972), also a best-seller and a motion picture. Forsyth has published only eight suspense thrillers to date, but each has been highly successful and several have been filmed. All reflect his journalistic training and sense of a well-told story.

His short stories carry the same feeling of reality as his novels. They have been collected as *No Comebacks* (1982). The classic "There Are No Snakes in Ireland" won the MWA Edgar Award as best short story of the year. It first appeared in *No Comebacks* and has been reprinted in *The Year's Best Mystery and Suspense Stories—1983, Ellery Queen's Mystery Magazine* and *The New Edgar Winners.*

McQueen looked across his desk at the new applicant for a job with some scepticism. He had never employed such a one before. But he was not an unkind man, and if the job-seeker needed the money and was prepared to work, McQueen was not averse to giving him a chance.

"You know it's damn hard work?" he said in his broad Belfast accent.

"Yes, sir," said the applicant.

"It's a quick in-and-out job, ye know. No questions, no pack drill. You'll be working on the lump. Do you know what that means?"

"No, Mr. McQueen."

"Well, it means you'll be paid well but you'll be paid in cash. No red tape. Geddit?"

What he meant was there would be no income tax paid, no National Health contributions deducted at source. He might also have added that there would be no National Insurance cover and that the Health and Safety standards would be completely ignored. Quick profits for all were the order of the day, with a fat slice off the top for himself as the contractor. The job-seeker nodded his head to indicate he had "goddit" though in fact he had not. McQueen looked at him speculatively.

"You say you're a medical student, in your last year at the Royal Victoria?" Another nod "On the summer vacation?"

Another nod. The applicant was evidently one of those students who needed money over and above his grant to put himself through medical school. McQueen, sitting in his dingy Bangor office running a hole-and-corner business as a demolition contractor with assets consisting of a battered truck and a ton of second-hand sledgehammers, considered himself a self-made man and heartily approved of the Ulster Protestant work ethic. He was not one to put down another such thinker, whatever he looked like.

"All right," he said, "you'd better take lodgings here in Bangor. You'll never get from Belfast and back in time each day. We work from seven in the morning until sundown. It's work by the hour, hard but well paid. Mention one word to the authorities and you'll lose the job like shit off a shovel. OK?"

"Yes, sir. Please, when do I start and where?"

"The truck picks the gang up at the main station yard every morning at six-thirty. Be there Monday morning. The gang foreman is Big Billie Cameron. I'll tell him you'll be there."

"Yes, Mr. McQueen." The applicant turned to go.

"One last thing," said McQueen, pencil poised. "What's your name?"

"Harkishan Ram Lal," said the student. McQueen looked at his pencil, the list of names in front of him and the student.

"We'll call you Ram," he said, and that was the name he wrote down on the list.

The student walked out into the bright July sunshine of Bangor, on the north coast of County Down, Northern Ireland.

By that Saturday evening he had found himself cheap lodgings in a dingy boarding house halfway up Railway View Street, the heart of Bangor's bed-and-breakfast land. At least it was convenient to the main station from which the works truck would depart every morning just after sun-up. From the grimy window of his room he could look straight at the side of the shored embankment that carried the trains from Belfast into the station.

It had taken him several tries to get a room. Most of those houses with a B-and-B notice in the window seemed to be fully booked when he presented himself on the doorstep. But then it was true that a lot of casual labor drifted into the town in the height of summer. True also that Mrs. McGurk was a Catholic and she still had rooms left.

He spent Sunday morning bringing his belongings over from Belfast, most of them medical textbooks. In the afternoon he lay on his bed and thought of the bright hard light on the brown hills of his native Punjab. In one more year he would be a qualified physician, and after another year of intern work he would return home to cope with the sicknesses of his own people. Such was his dream. He calculated he could make enough money this summer to tide himself through to his finals and after that he would have a salary of his own.

On the Monday morning he rose at a quarter to six at the bidding of his alarm clock, washed in cold water and was in the station yard just after six. There was time to spare. He found an early-opening café and took two cups of black tea. It was his only sustenance. The battered truck, driven by one of the demolition gang, was there at a quarter past six and a dozen men assembled near it. Harkishan Ram Lal did not know whether to approach them and introduce himself, or wait at a distance. He waited.

At twenty-five past the hour the foreman arrived in his own car, parked it down a side road and strode up to the truck. He had McQueen's list in his hand. He glanced at the dozen men, recognized them all and nodded. The Indian approached. The foreman glared at him.

"Is youse the darkie McQueen has put on the job?" he demanded.

Ram Lal stopped in his tracks. "Harkishan Ram Lal," he said. "Yes."

There was no need to ask how Big Billie Cameron had earned his name. He stood 6 feet and 3 inches in his stockings but was wearing enormous nail-studded steel-toed boots. Arms like tree trunks hung from huge shoulders and his head was surmounted by a shock of ginger hair. Two small, pale-lashed eyes stared down balefully at the sight and wiry Indian. It was plain he was not best pleased. He spat on the ground.

"Well, get in the fecking truck," he said.

On the journey out to the work site Cameron sat up in the cab which had no partition dividing it from the back of the lorry, where the dozen laborers sat on two wooden benches down the sides. Ram Lal was near the tailboard next to a small, nut-hard man with bright blue eyes, whose name turned out to be Tommy Burns. He seemed friendly.

"Where are youse from?" he asked with genuine curiosity.

"India," said Ram Lal. "The Punjab."

"Well which?" said Tommy Burns.

Ram Lal smiled. "The Punjab is a part of India," he said.

Burns thought about this for a while. "You Protestant or Catholic?" he asked at length.

"Neither," said Ram Lal patiently. "I am a Hindu."

"You mean you're not a Christian?" asked Burns in amazement.

"No. Mine is the Hindu religion."

"Hey," said Burns to the others, "your man's not a Christian at all." He was not outraged, just curious, like a small child who has come across a new and intriguing toy.

Cameron turned from the cab up front. "Aye," he snarled, "a heathen."

The smile dropped off Ram Lal's face. He stared at the opposite canvas wall of the truck. By now they were well south of Bangor, clattering down the motorway towards Newtownards. After a while Burns began to introduce him to the others. There was a Craig, a Munroe, a Patterson, a Boyd and two Browns. Ram Lal had been long enough in Belfast to recognize the names as being originally Scottish, the sign of the hard Presbyterians who make up the backbone of the Protestant majority of the Six Counties. The men seemed amiable and nodded back at him.

"Have you not got a lunch box, laddie?" asked the elderly man called Patterson.

"No," said Ram Lal, "it was too early to ask my landlady to make one up."

"You'll need lunch," said Burns, "aye, and breakfast. We'll be making tay ourselves on a fire."

"I will make sure to buy a box and bring some food tomorrow," said Ram Lal.

Burns looked at the Indian's rubber-soled soft boots. "Have you not done this kind of work before?" he asked.

Ram Lal shook his head.

"You'll need a pair of heavy boots. To save your feet, you see."

Ram Lal promised he would also buy a pair of heavy ammunition boots from a store if he could find one open late at night. They were through Newtownards and still heading south on the A21 towards the small town of Comber. Craig looked across at him.

"What's your real job?" he asked.

"I'm a medical student at the Royal Victoria in Belfast," said Ram Lal. "I hope to quality next year."

Tommy Burns was delighted. "That's near to being a real doctor," he said. "Hey, Big Billie, if one of us gets a knock young Ram could take care of it."

Big Billie grunted. "He's not putting a finger on me," he said.

That killed further conversation until they arrived at the work site. The driver had pulled northwest out of Comber and two miles up the Dundonald road he bumped down a track to the right until they came to a stop where the trees ended and saw the building to be demolished.

It was a huge old whiskey distillery, a sheer-sided, long derelict. It had been one of two in these parts that had once turned out good Irish whiskey but had gone out of business years before. It stood beside the River Comber, which had once powdered its great waterwheel as it flowed down from Dundonald to Comber and on to empty itself in Strangford Lough. The malt had arrived by horse-drawn cart down the track and the barrels of whiskey had left the same way. The sweet water that had powdered the machines had also been used in the vats. But the distillery had stood alone, abandoned and empty for years.

Of course the local children had broken in and found it an ideal place to play. Until one had slipped and broken a leg. Then the county council had surveyed it, declared it a hazard and the owner found himself with a compulsory demolition order.

He, scion of an old family of squires who had known better days, wanted the job done as cheaply as possible. That was where McQueen came in. It could be done faster but more expensively with heavy machinery; Big Billie and his team would do it with sledges and crowbars. McQueen had even lined up a deal to sell the best timbers and the hundreds of tons of mature bricks to a jobbing builder. After all, the wealthy nowadays wanted their new houses to have "style" and that meant looking old. So there was a premium on antique sun-bleached old bricks and genuine ancient timber beams to adorn the new-look-old "manor" houses of the top executives. McQueen would do all right.

"Right lads," said Big Billie as the truck rumbled away back to Bangor. "There it is. We'll start with the roof tiles. You know what to do."

The group of men stood beside their pile of equipment. There were great sledgehammers with 7-pound heads; crowbars 6 feet long and over an inch thick; nailbars a yard long with curved split tips for extracting nails; short-handled, heavy-headed lump hammers and a variety of timber saws. The only concessions to human safety were a number of webbing belts with dogclips and hundreds of feet of rope. Ram Lal looked up at the building and swallowed. It was four storeys high and he hated heights. But scaffolding is expensive.

One of the men unbidden went to the building, prised off a plank door, tore it up like a playing card and started a fire. Soon a billycan of water from the river was boiling away and tea was made. They all had their enamel mugs except Ram Lal. He made a mental note to buy that also. It was going to be thirsty, dusty work. Tommy Burns finished his own mug and offered it, refilled, to Ram Lal.

"Do they have tea in India?" he asked.

Ram Lal took the proffered mug. The tea was ready-mixed, sweet and off-white. He hated it.

They worked through the first morning perched high on the roof. The tiles were not to be salvaged, so they tore them off manually and hurled them to the ground away from the river. There was an instruction not to block the river with falling rubble. So it all had to land on the other side of the building, in the long grass, weeds, broom and gorse which covered the area round the distillery. The men were roped together so that if one lost his grip and began to slither down the roof, the next man would take the strain. As the tiles disappeared, great yawning holes appeared between the rafters. Down below them was the floor of the top storey, the malt store.

At ten they came down the rickety internal stairs for breakfast on the grass, with another billycan of tea. Ram Lal ate no breakfast. At two they broke for lunch. The gang tucked into their piles of thick sandwiches. Ram Lal looked at his hands. They were nicked in several places and bleeding. His muscles ached and he was very hungry. He made another mental note about buying some heavy work gloves.

Tommy Burns held up a sandwich from his own box. "Are you not hungry, Ram?" he asked. "Sure, I have enough here."

"What do you think you're doing?" asked Big Billie from where he sat across the circle round the fire.

Burns looked defensive. "Just offering the lad a sandwich," he said.

"Let the darkie bring his own fecking sandwiches," said Cameron. "You look after yourself."

The men looked down at their lunch boxes and ate in silence. It was obvious no one argued the toss with Big Billie.

"Thank you, I am not hungry," said Ram Lal to Burns. He walked away and sat by the river where he bathed his burning hands.

By sundown when the truck came to collect them half the tiles on the great roof were gone. One more day and they would start on the rafters, work for saw and nailbar.

Throughout the week the work went on, and the once proud building was stripped of its rafters, planks and beams until it stood hollow and open, its gaping windows like open eyes staring at the prospect of its imminent death. Ram Lal was unaccustomed to the arduousness of this kind of labor. His muscles ached endlessly, his hands were blistered, but he toiled on for the money he needed so badly.

He had acquired a tin lunch box, enamel mug, hard boots and a pair of heavy gloves, which no one else wore. Their hands were hard enough from years of manual work. Throughout the week Big Billie Cameron needled him without let-up, giving him the hardest work and positioning him on the highest points once he had learned Ram Lal hated heights. The Punjabi bit on his anger because he needed the money. The crunch came on the Saturday.

The timbers were gone and they were working on the masonry. The simplest way to bring the edifice down away from the river would have been to plant explosive charges in the corners of the side wall facing the open clearing. But dynamite was out of the question. It would have required special licences in Northern Ireland of all places, and that would have alerted the tax man. McQueen and all his gang would have been required to pay substantial sums in income tax, and McQueen in National Insurance contributions. So they were chipping the walls down in square-yard chunks, standing hazardously on sagging floors as the supporting walls splintered and cracked under the hammers.

During lunch Cameron walked round the building a couple of times and came back to the circle round the fire. He began to describe how they were going to bring down a sizable chunk of one outer wall at third-floor level. He turned to Ram Lal.

"I want you up on the top there," he said. "When it starts to go, kick it outwards."

Ram Lal looked up at the section of wall in question. A great crack ran along the bottom of it.

"That brickwork is going to fall at any moment," he said evenly. "Anyone sitting on top there is going to come down with it."

Cameron stared at him, his face suffusing, his eyes pink with rage where they should have been white. "Don't you tell me my job; you do as you're told, you stupid fecking nigger." He turned and stalked away.

Ram Lal rose to his feet. When his voice came, it was in a hard-edged shout. "*Mister Cameron . . .*"

Cameron turned in amazement. The men sat openmouthed. Ram Lal walked slowly up to the big ganger.

"Let us get one thing plain," said Ram Lal, and his voice carried clearly to everyone else in the clearing. "I am from the Punjab in northern India. I am also a Kshatria, member of the warrior caste. I may not have enough money to pay for my medical studies, but my ancestors were soldiers and princes, rulers and scholars, two thousand years ago when yours were crawling on all fours dressed in skins. Please do not insult me any further."

Big Billie Cameron stared down at the Indian student. The whites of his eyes had turned a bright red. The other laborers sat in stunned amazement.

"Is that so?" said Cameron quietly. "Is that so, now? Well, things are a bit different now, you black bastard. So what are you going to do about that?"

On the last word he swung his arm, open-palmed, and his hand crashed into the side of Ram Lal's face. The youth was thrown bodily to the ground several feet away. His head sang. He heard Tommy Burns call out, "Stay down, laddie. Big Billie will kill you if you get up."

Ram Lal looked up into the sunlight. The giant stood over him, fists bunched. He realized he had not a chance in combat against the big Ulsterman. Feelings of shame and humiliation flooded over him. His ancestors had ridden, sword and lance in hand, across plains a hundred times bigger than these six counties, conquering all before them.

Ram Lal closed his eyes and lay still. After several seconds he heard the big man move away. A low conversation started among the others. He squeezed his eyes tighter shut to hold back the tears of shame. In the blackness he saw the baking plains of the Punjab and men riding over them; proud, fierce men, hook-nosed, bearded, turbaned, black-eyed, the warriors from the land of Five Rivers.

Once, long ago in the world's morning, Iskander of Macedon had ridden over these plains with his hot and hungry eyes; Alexander, the young god, whom they called The Great, who at twenty-five had wept because there were no more worlds to conquer. These riders were the descendants of his captains, and the ancestors of Harkishan Ram Lal.

He was lying in the dust as they rode by, and they looked down at him in passing. As they rode each of them mouthed one single word to him. Vengeance.

Ram Lal picked himself up in silence. It was done, and what still had to be done had to be done. That was the way of his people. He spent the rest of the day working in complete silence. He spoke to no one and no one spoke to him.

That evening in his room he began his preparations as night was about to fall. He cleared away the brush and comb from the battered dressing table and removed also the soiled doily and the mirror from its stand. He took his book of the Hindu religion and from it cut a page-sized portrait of the great goddess Shakti, she of power and justice. This he pinned to the wall above the dressing table to convert it into a shrine.

He had bought a bunch of flowers from a seller in front of the main station, and these had been woven into a garland. To one side of the portrait of the goddess he placed a shallow bowl half-filled with sand, and in the sand stuck a candle which he lit. From his suitcase he took a cloth roll and extracted half a dozen joss sticks. Taking a cheap, narrow-necked vase from the bookshelf, he placed them in it and lit the ends. The sweet, heady odor of the incense began to fill the room. Outside, big thunderheads rolled up from the sea.

When his shrine was ready he stood before it, head bowed, the garland in his fingers, and began to pray for guidance. The first rumble of thunder rolled over Bangor. He used not the modern Punjabi but the ancient Sanskrit, language of prayer. "*Devi Shakti* . . . *Maa* . . . Goddess Shakti . . . great mother . . ."

The thunder crashed again and the first raindrops fell. He plucked the first flower and placed it in front of the portrait of Shakti.

"I have been previously wronged. I ask vengeance upon the wrongdoer . . ." He plucked the second flower and put it beside the first.

He prayed for an hour while the rain came down. It drummed on the tiles above his head, streamed past the window behind him. He finished praying as the storm subsided. He needed to know what form the retribution should take. He needed the goddess to send him a sign.

When he had finished, the joss sticks had burned themselves out and the room was thick with their scent. The candle guttered low. The flowers all lay on the lacquered surface of the dressing table in front of the portrait. Shakti stared back at him unmoved.

He turned and walked to the window to look out. The rain had stopped but everything beyond the panes dripped water. As he watched, a dribble of rain sprang from the guttering above the window and a trickle ran down the dusty glass, cutting a path through the grime. Because of the dirt it did not run straight but meandered sideways, drawing his eye farther and farther to the corner of the window as he followed its path. When it stopped he was staring at the corner of his room, where his dressing gown hung on a nail.

He noticed that during the storm the dressing-gown cord had

slipped and fallen to the floor. It lay coiled upon itself, one knotted end hidden from view, the other lying visible on the carpet. Of the dozen tassels only two were exposed, like a forked tongue. The coiled dressing-gown cord resembled nothing so much as a snake in the corner. Ram Lal understood. The next day he took a train to Belfast to see the Sikh.

Ranjit Singh was also a medical student, but he was more fortunate. His parents were rich and sent him a handsome allowance. He received Ram Lal in his well-furnished room at the hostel.

"I have received word from home," said Ram Lal. "My father is dying."

"I am sorry," said Ranjit Singh, "you have my sympathies."

"He asks to see me. I am his first born. I should return."

"Of course," said Singh. "The first-born son should always be by his father when he dies."

"It is a matter of the air fare," said Ram Lal. "I am working and making good money. But I do not have enough. If you will lend me the balance I will continue working when I return and repay you."

Sikhs are no strangers to moneylending if the interest is right and repayment secure. Ranjit Singh promised to withdraw the money from the bank on Monday morning.

That Sunday evening Ram Lal visited Mr. McQueen at his home at Groomsport. The contractor was in front of his television set with a can of beer at his elbow. It was his favorite way to spend a Sunday evening. But he turned the sound down as Ram Lal was shown in by his wife.

"It is about my father," said Ram Lal. "He is dying."

"Oh, I'm sorry to hear that, laddie," said McQueen.

"I should go to him. The first-born son should be with his father at this time. It is the custom of our people."

McQueen had a son in Canada whom he had not seen for seven years.

"Aye," he said, "that seems right and proper."

"I have borrowed the money for the air fare," said Ram Lal. "If I went tomorrow I could be back by the end of the week. The point is, Mr. McQueen, I need the job more than ever now; to repay the loan and for my studies next term. If I am back by the weekend, will you keep the job open for me?"

"All right," said the contractor. "I can't pay you for the time you're away. Nor keep the job open for a further week. But if you're back by the weekend, you can go back to work. Same terms, mind."

"Thank you," said Ram, "you are very kind."

He retained his room in Railway View Street but spent the night at his hostel in Belfast. On the Monday morning he accompanied Ranjit Singh to the bank where the Sikh withdrew the necessary money and gave it to the Hindu. Ram took a taxi to Aldergrove airport and the shuttle to London where he bought an economy-class ticket on the next flight to India. Twenty-four hours later he touched down in the blistering heat of Bombay.

On the Wednesday he found what he sought in the teeming bazaar at Grant Road Bridge. Mr. Chatterjee's Tropical Fish and Reptile Emporium was almost deserted when the young student, with his textbook on reptiles under his arm, wandered in. He found the old proprietor sitting near the back of his shop in half-darkness, surrounded by his tanks of fish and glass-fronted cases in which his snakes and lizards dozed through the hot day.

Mr. Chatterjee was no stranger to the academic world. He supplied several medical centers with samples for study and dissection, and occasionally filled a lucrative order from abroad. He nodded his white-bearded head knowledgeably as the student explained what he sought.

"Ah yes," said the old Gujerati merchant, "I know the snake. You are in luck. I have one, but a few days arrived from Rajputana."

He led Ram Lal into his private sanctum and the two men stared silently through the glass of the snake's new home.

Echis carinatus, said the textbook, but of course the book had been written by an Englishman, who had used the Latin nomenclature. In English, the saw-scaled viper, smallest and deadliest of all his lethal breed.

Wide distribution, said the textbook, being found from West Africa eastwards and northwards to Iran, and on to India and Pakistan. Very adaptable, able to acclimatize to almost any environment, from the moist bush of western Africa to the cold hills of Iran in winter to the baking hills of India.

Something stirred beneath the leaves in the box.

In size, said the textbook, between 9 and 13 inches long and very slim. Olive brown in color with a few paler spots, sometimes hardly distinguishable, and a faint undulating darker line down the side of the body. Nocturnal in dry, hot weather, seeking cover during the heat of the day.

The leaves in the box rustled again and a tiny head appeared.

Exceptionally dangerous to handle, said the textbook, causing more deaths than even the more famous cobra, largely because of its size which makes it so easy to touch unwittingly with hand or foot. The author of the book had added a footnote to the effect that the small but lethal snake mentioned by Kipling in his marvelous story "Rikki-Tikki-Tavy" was almost certainly not the krait, which is about 2 feet long, but more probably the saw-scaled viper. The author was obviously pleased to have caught out the great Kipling in a matter of accuracy.

In the box, a little black forked tongue flickered towards the two Indians beyond the glass.

Very alert and irritable, the long-gone English naturalist had concluded his chapter on *Echis carinatus*. Strikes quickly without warning. The fangs are so small they make a virtually unnoticeable puncture, like two tiny thorns. There is no pain, but death is almost inevitable, usually taking between two and four hours, depending on the bodyweight of the victim and the level of his physical exertions at the time and afterwards. Cause of death is invariably a brain hemorrhage.

"How much do you want for him?" whispered Ram Lal.

The old Gujerati spread his hands helplessly. "Such a prime specimen," he said regretfully, "and so hard to come by. Five hundred rupees."

Ram Lal clinched the deal at 350 rupees and took the snake away in a jar.

For his journey back to London Ram Lal purchased a box of cigars, which he emptied of their contents and in whose lid he punctured twenty small holes for air. The tiny viper, he knew, would need no food for a week and no water for two or three days. It could breathe on an infinitesimal supply of air, so he wrapped the cigar box, resealed and with the viper inside it among his leaves, in several towels whose thick sponginess would contain enough air even inside a suitcase.

He had arrived with a handgrip, but he bought a cheap fiber suitcase and packed it with clothes from market stalls, the cigar box going in the center. It was only minutes before he left his hotel for Bombay airport that he closed and locked the case. For the flight back to London he checked the suitcase into the hold of the Boeing airliner. His hand baggage was searched, but it contained nothing of interest.

The Air India jet landed at London Heathrow on Friday morning and Ram Lal joined the long queue of Indians trying to get into Britain. He was able to prove he was a medical student and not an immigrant, and was allowed through quite quickly. He even reached the luggage carousel as the first suitcases were tumbling onto it, and saw his own in the first two dozen. He took it to the toilet, where he extracted the cigar box and put it in his handgrip.

In the Nothing-to-Declare channel he was stopped all the same, but it was his suitcase that was ransacked. The customs officer glanced in his shoulder bag and let him pass. Ram Lal crossed Heathrow by courtesy bus to Number One Building and caught the midday shuttle to Belfast. He was in Bangor by teatime and able at last to examine his import.

He took a sheet of glass from the bedside table and slipped it carefully between the lid of the cigar box and its deadly contents before opening wide. Through the glass he saw the viper going round and round inside. It paused and stared with angry black eyes back at him. He pulled the lid shut, withdrawing the pane of glass quickly as the box top came down.

"Sleep, little friend," he said, "if your breed ever sleep. In the morning you will do Shakti's bidding for her."

Before dark he bought a small screw-top jar of coffee and poured the contents into a china pot in his room. In the morning, using his heavy gloves, he transferred the viper from the box to the jar. The enraged snake bit his glove once, but he did not mind. It would have recovered its venom by midday. For a moment he studied the snake, coiled and cramped inside the glass coffee jar, before giving the top a last, hard twist and placing it in his lunch box. Then he went to catch the works truck.

Big Billie Cameron had a habit of taking off his jacket the moment he arrived at the work site, and hanging it on a convenient nail or twig. During the lunch break, as Ram Lal had observed, the giant foreman never failed to go to his jacket after eating, and from the right-hand pocket extract his pipe and tobacco pouch. The routine did not vary. After a satisfying pipe, he would knock out the dottle, rise and say, "Right, lads, back to work," as he dropped his pipe back into the pocket of his jacket. By the time he turned round everyone had to be on their feet.

Ram Lal's plan was simple but foolproof. During the morning he would slip the snake into the right-hand pocket of the hanging jacket. After his sandwiches the bullying Cameron would rise from the fire, go to his jacket and plunge his hand into the pocket. The snake would do what great Shakti had ordered that he be brought halfway across the world to do. It would be he, the viper, not Ram Lal, who would be the Ulsterman's executioner.

Cameron would withdraw his hand with an oath from the pocket, the viper hanging from his finger, its fangs deep in the flesh. Ram Lal would leap up, tear the snake away, throw it to the ground and stamp upon its head. It would by then be harmless, its venom expended. Finally, with a gesture of disgust he, Ram Lal, would hurl the dead viper far into the River Comber, which would carry all evidence away to the sea. There might be suspicion, but that was all there would ever be.

Shortly after eleven o'clock, on the excuse of fetching a fresh sledgehammer, Harkishan Ram Lal opened his lunch box, took out the coffee jar, unscrewed the lid and shook the contents into the right-hand pocket of the hanging jacket. Within sixty seconds he was back at his work, his act unnoticed.

During lunch he found it hard to eat. The men sat as usual in a circle round the fire; the dry old timber baulks crackled and spat, the billycan bubbled above them. The men joshed and joked as ever, while Big Billie munched his way through the pile of doorstep sandwiches his wife had prepared for him. Ram Lal had made a point of choosing a place in the circle near to the jacket. He forced himself to eat. In his chest his heart was pounding and the tension in him rose steadily.

Finally Big Billie crumpled the paper of his eaten sandwiches, threw it in the fire and belched. He rose with a grunt and walked towards his jacket. Ram Lal turned his head to watch. The other men took no notice. Billie Cameron reached his jacket and plunged his hand into the right-hand pocket. Ram Lal held his breath. Cameron's hand rummaged for several seconds and then withdrew his pipe and pouch. He began to fill the bowl with fresh tobacco. As he did so he caught Ram Lal staring at him.

"What are youse looking at?" he demanded belligerently.

"Nothing," said Ram Lal, and turned to face the fire. But he could not stay still. He rose and stretched, contriving to half turn as he did so. From the corner of his eye he saw Cameron replace the pouch in the pocket and again withdraw his hand with a box of matches in it. The foreman lit his pipe and pulled contentedly. He strolled back to the fire.

Ram Lal resumed his seat and stared at the flames in disbelief. Why, he asked himself, why had great Shakti done this to him? The snake had been her tool, her instrument brought at her command. But she had held it back, refused to use her own implement of retribution.

He turned and sneaked another glance at the jacket. Deep down in the lining at the very hem, on the extreme left-hand side, something stirred and was still. Ram Lal closed his eyes in shock. A hole, a tiny hole in the lining, had undone all his planning. He worked the rest of the afternoon in a daze of indecision and worry.

On the truck ride back to Bangor, Big Billie Cameron sat up front as usual, but in view of the heat folded his jacket and put it on his knees. In front of the station Ram Lal saw him throw the still-folded jacket onto the back seat of his car and drive away. Ram Lal caught up with Tommy Burns as the little man waited for his bus.

"Tell me," he asked, "does Mr. Cameron have a family?"

"Sure," said the little laborer innocently, "a wife and two children."

"Does he live far from here?" said Ram Lal. "I mean, he drives a car."

"Not far," said Burns, "up on the Kilcooley estate. Ganaway Gardens, I think. Going visiting are you?"

"No, no," said Ram Lal, "see you Monday."

Back in his room Ram Lal stared at the impassive image of the goddess of justice.

"I did not mean to bring death to his wife and children," he told her. "They have done nothing to me."

The goddess from far away stared back and gave no reply.

Harkishan Ram Lal spent the rest of the weekend in an agony of anxiety. That evening he walked to the Kilcooley housing estate on the ring road and found Ganaway Gardens. It lay just off Owenroe Gardens and opposite Woburn Walk. At the corner of Woburn Walk there was a telephone kiosk, and here he waited for an hour, pretending to make a call, while he watched the short street across the road. He thought he spotted Big Billie Cameron at one of the windows and noted the house.

He saw a teenage girl come out of it and walk away to join some friends. For a moment he was tempted to accost her and tell her what demon slept inside her father's jacket, but he dared not.

Shortly before dusk a woman came out of the house carrying a shopping basket. He followed her down to the Clandeboye shopping center, which was open late for those who took their wage packets on a Saturday. The woman he thought to be Mrs. Cameron entered Stewarts supermarket and the Indian student trailed round the shelves behind her, trying to pick up the courage to approach her and reveal the danger in her house. Again his nerve failed him. He might, after all, have the wrong woman, even be mistaken about the house. In that case they would take him away as a madman.

He slept ill that night, his mind racked by visions of the saw-scaled viper coming out of its hiding place in the jacket lining to slither, silent and deadly, through the sleeping council house.

On the Sunday he again haunted the Kilcooley estate, and firmly identified the house of the Cameron family. He saw Big Billie clearly in the back garden. By mid-afternoon he was attracting attention locally and knew he must either walk boldly up to the front door and admit what he had done, or depart and leave all in the hands of the goddess. The thought of facing the terrible Cameron with the news of what deadly danger had been brought so close to his children was too much. He walked back to Railway View Street.

On Monday morning the Cameron family rose at a quarter to six, a bright and sunny August morning. By six the four of them were at breakfast in the tiny kitchen at the back of the house, the son, daughter and wife in their dressing gowns, Big Billie dressed for work. His jacket was where it had spent the weekend, in a closet in the hallway.

Just after six his daughter Jenny rose, stuffing a piece of marmaladed toast into her mouth.

"I'm away to wash," she said.

"Before ye go, girl, get my jacket from the press," said her father, working his way through a plate of cereal. The girl reappeared a few seconds later with the jacket, held by the collar. She proffered it to her father. He hardly looked up.

"Hang it behind the door," he said. The girl did as she was bid, but the jacket had no hanging tab and the hook was no rusty nail but a smooth chrome affair. The jacket hung for a moment, then fell to the kitchen floor. Her father looked up as she left the room.

"Jenny," he shouted, "pick the damn thing up."

No one in the Cameron household argued with the head of the family. Jenny came back, picked up the jacket and hung it more firmly. As she did, something thin and dark slipped from its folds and slithered into the corner with a dry rustle across the linoleum. She stared at it in horror.

"Dad, what's that in your jacket?"

Big Billie Cameron paused, a spoonful of cereal halfway to his mouth. Mrs. Cameron turned from the cooker. Fourteen-year-old Bobby ceased buttering a piece of toast and stared. The small creature lay curled in the corner by the row of cabinets, tight-bunched, defensive, glaring back at the world, tiny tongue flickering fast.

"Lord save us, it's a snake," said Mrs. Cameron.

"Don't be a bloody fool, woman. Don't you know there are no snakes in Ireland? Everyone knows that," said her husband. He put down the spoon. "What is it, Bobby?"

Though a tyrant inside and outside his house, Big Billie had a grudging respect for the knowledge of his young son, who was good at school and was being taught many strange things. The boy stared at the snake through his owlish glasses.

"It must be a slowworm, Dad," he said. "They had some at school last term for the biology class. Brought them in for dissection. From across the water."

"It doesn't look like a worm to me," said his father.

"It isn't really a worm," said Bobby. "It's a lizard with no legs."

"Then why do they call it a worm?" asked his truculent father.

"I don't know," said Bobby.

"Then what the hell are you going to school for?"

"Will it bite?" asked Mrs. Cameron fearfully.

"Not at all," said Bobby. "It's harmless."

"Kill it," said Cameron senior, and "throw it in the dustbin."

His son rose from the table and removed one of his slippers, which he held like a flyswat in one hand. He was advancing, bare-ankled towards the corner, when his father changed his mind. Big Billie looked up from his plate with a gleeful smile.

"Hold on a minute, just hold on there, Bobby," he said, "I have an idea. Woman, get me a jar."

"What kind of a jar?" asked Mrs. Cameron.

"How should I know what kind of jar? A jar with a lid on it."

Mrs. Cameron sighed, skirted the snake and opened a cupboard. She examined her store of jars.

"There's a jamjar, with dried peas in it," she said.

"Put the peas somewhere else and give me the jar," commanded Cameron. She passed him the jar.

"What are you going to do, Dad?" asked Bobby.

"There's a darkie we have at work. A heathen man. He comes from a land with a lot of snakes in it. I have in mind to have some fun with him. A wee joke, like. Pass me that oven glove, Jenny."

"You'll not need a glove," said Bobby. "He can't bite you."

"I'm not touching the dirty thing," said Cameron.

"He's not dirty," said Bobby. "They're very clean creatures."

"You're a fool, boy, for all your school learning. Does the Good Book not say: 'On thy belly shalt thou go, and dust shalt thou eat . . .'? Aye, and more than dust, no doubt. I'll not touch him with me hand."

Jenny passed her father the oven glove. Open jamjar in his left hand, right hand protected by the glove, Big Billie Cameron stood over the viper. Slowly his right hand descended. When it dropped, it was fast; but the small snake was faster. Its tiny fangs went harmlessly into the padding of the glove at the center of the palm. Cameron did not notice, for the act was masked from his view by his own hands. In a trice the snake was inside the jamjar and the lid was on. Through the glass they watched it wriggle furiously.

"I hate them, harmless or not," said Mrs. Cameron. "I'll thank you to get it out of the house."

"I'll be doing that right now," said her husband, "for I'm late as it is."

He slipped the jamjar into his shoulder bag, already containing his lunch box, stuffed his pipe and pouch into the right-hand pocket of his jacket and took both out to the car. He arrived at the station yard five minutes late and was surprised to find the Indian student staring at him fixedly.

"I suppose he wouldn't have the second sight," thought Big Billie as they trundled south to Newtownards and Comber.

By mid-morning all the gang had been let into Big Billie's secret joke on pain of a thumping if they let on to "the darkie." There was no chance of that; assured that the slowworm was perfectly harmless, they too thought it a good leg-pull. Only Ram Lal worked on in ignorance, consumed by his private thoughts and worries.

At the lunch break he should have suspected something. The tension was palpable. The men sat in a circle around the fire as usual, but the conversation was stilted and had he not been so preoccupied he would have noticed the half-concealed grins and the looks darted in his direction. He did not notice. He placed his own lunch box between his knees and opened it. Coiled between the sandwiches and the apple, head back to strike, was the viper.

The Indian's scream echoed across the clearing, just ahead of the roar of laughter from the laborers. Simultaneously with the scream, the lunch box flew high in the air as he threw it away from himself with all his strength. All the contents of the box flew in a score of directions, landing in the long grass, the broom and gorse all around them.

Ram Lal was on his feet, shouting. The gangers rolled helplessly in their mirth, Big Billie most of all. He had not had such a laugh in months.

"It's a snake," screamed Ram Lal, "a poisonous snake. Get out of here, all of you. It's deadly."

The laughter redoubled; the men could not contain themselves. The reaction of the joke's victim surpassed all their expectations.

"Please, believe me. It's a snake, a deadly snake."

Big Billie's face was suffused. He wiped tears from his eyes, seated across the clearing from Ram Lal, who was standing looking wildly round.

"You ignorant darkie," he gasped, "don't you know? There are no snakes in Ireland. Understand? There aren't any."

His sides ached with laughing and he leaned back in the grass, his hands behind him to support him. He failed to notice the two pricks, like tiny thorns, that went into the vein on the inside of the right wrist.

The joke was over and the hungry men tucked into their lunches. Harkishan Ram Lal reluctantly took his seat, constantly glancing round him, a mug of steaming tea held ready, eating only with his left hand, staying clear of the long grass. After lunch they returned to work. The old distillery was almost down, the mountains of rubble and savable timbers lying dusty under the August sun.

At half past three Big Billie Cameron stood up from his work, rested on his pick and passed a hand across his forehead. He licked at a slight swelling on the inside of his wrist, then started work again. Five minutes later he straightened up again.

"I'm not feeling so good," he told Patterson, who was next to him. "I'm going to take a spell in the shade."

He sat under a tree for a while and then held his head in his hands. At a quarter past four, still clutching his splitting head, he gave one convulsion and toppled sideways. It was several minutes before Tommy Burns noticed him. He walked across and called to Patterson.

"Big Billie's sick," he called. "He won't answer me."

The gang broke and came over to the tree in whose shade the foreman lay. His sightless eyes were staring at the grass a few inches from his face. Patterson bent over him. He had been long enough in the laboring business to have seen a few dead ones.

"Ram," he said, "you have medical training. What do you think?"

Ram Lal did not need to make an examination, but he did. When he straightened up he said nothing, but Patterson understood.

"Stay here all of you," he said, taking command. "I'm going to phone an ambulance and call McQueen." He set off down the track to the main road.

The ambulance got there first, half an hour later. It reversed down the track and two men heaved Cameron onto a stretcher. They took him away to Newtownards General Hospital, which has the nearest casualty unit, and there the foreman was logged in as DOA—dead on arrival. An extremely worried McQueen arrived thirty minutes after that.

Because of the unknown circumstance of the death an autopsy had to be performed and it was, by the North Down area pathologist, in the Newtownards municipal mortuary to which the body had been transferred. That was on the Tuesday. By that evening the pathologist's report was on its way to the office of the coroner for North Down, in Belfast.

The report said nothing extraordinary. The deceased had been a man of forty-one years, big-built and immensely strong. There were upon the body various minor cuts and abrasions, mainly on the hands and wrists, quite consistent with the job of navvy, and none of these were in any way associated with the cause of death. The latter, beyond a doubt, had been a massive brain hemorrhage, itself probably caused by extreme exertion in conditions of great heat.

Possessed of this report, the coroner would normally not hold an inquest, being able to issue a certificate of death by natural causes to the registrar at Bangor. But there was something Harkishan Ram Lal did not know.

Big Billie Cameron had been a leading member of the Bangor council of the outlawed Ulster Volunteer Force, the hard-line Protestant paramilitary organization. The computer at Lurgan, into which all deaths in the province of Ulster, however innocent, are programmed, threw this out and someone in Lurgan picked up the phone to call the Royal Ulster Constabulary at Castlereagh.

Someone there called the coroner's office in Belfast, and a formal inquest was ordered. In Ulster death must not only be accidental; it must be seen to be accidental. For certain people, at least. The inquest was in the Town Hall at Bangor on the Wednesday. It meant a lot of trouble for McQueen, for the Inland Revenue attended. So did two quiet men of extreme Loyalist persuasion from the UVF council. They sat at the back. Most of the dead man's workmates sat near the front, a few feet from Mrs. Cameron.

Only Patterson was called to give evidence. He related the events of the Monday, prompted by the coroner, and as there was no dispute none of the other laborers was called, not even Ram Lal. The coroner read the pathologist's report aloud and it was clear enough. When he had finished, he summed up before giving his verdict.

"The pathologist's report is quite unequivocal. We have heard from Mr. Patterson of the events of that lunch break, of the perhaps rather foolish prank played by the deceased upon the Indian student. It would seem that Mr. Cameron was so amused that he laughed himself almost to the verge of apoplexy. The subsequent heavy labor with pick and shovel in the blazing sun did the rest, provoking the rupture of a large blood vessel in the brain or, as the pathologist puts it in more medical language, a cerebral hemorrhage. This court extends its sympathy to the widow and her children, and finds that Mr. William Cameron died of accidental causes."

Outside on the lawns that spread before Bangor Town Hall McQueen talked to his navvies.

"I'll stand fair by you, lads," he said. "The job's still on, but I can't afford not to deduct tax and all the rest, not with the Revenue breathing down my neck. The funeral's tomorrow, you can take the day off. Those who want to go on can report on Friday."

Harkishan Ram Lal did not attend the funeral. While it was in progress at the Bangor cemetery he took a taxi back to Comber and asked the driver to wait on the road while he walked down the track. The driver was a Bangor man and had heard about the death of Cameron.

"Going to pay your respects on the spot, are you?" he asked.

"In a way," said Ram Lal.

"That the manner of your people?" asked the driver.

"You could say so," said Ram Lal.

"Aye, well, I'll not say it's any better or worse than our way, by the graveside," said the driver, and prepared to read his paper while he waited.

Harkishan Ram Lal walked down the track to the clearing and stood where the camp fire had been. He looked around at the long grass, the broom and the gorse in its sandy soil.

"Visha serp," he called out to the hidden viper. "O venomous snake, can you hear me? You have done what I brought you so far from the hills of Rajputana to achieve. But you were supposed to die. I should have killed you myself, had it all gone as I planned, and thrown your foul carcass in the river.

"Are you listening, deadly one? Then hear this. You may live a little longer but then you will die, as all things die. And you will die alone, without a female with which to mate, because there are no snakes in Ireland."

The saw-scaled viper did not hear him, or if it did, gave no hint of understanding. Deep in its hole in the warm sand beneath him, it was busy, totally absorbed in doing what nature commanded it must do.

At the base of a snake's tail are two overlapping plate-scales which obscure the cloaca. The viper's tail was erect, the body throbbed in ancient rhythm. The plates were parted, and from the cloaca, one by one, each an inch long in its transparent sac, each as deadly at birth as its parent, she was bringing her dozen babies into the world.

Death on the Air

DAME NGAIO MARSH

Dame Ngaio (pronounced "Ny'o") Marsh (1899–1982) is the most famous writer from New Zealand. An actress and theatrical producer from 1920–1952, Dame Ngaio brought to her fiction a background in the theater. She created one of the great series detectives of the twentieth century, Inspector (later Superintendent) Roderick Alleyn, who is featured in every one of her thirty-two published novels. A good measure of the success of Dame Ngaio rests on the way she allowed Alleyn to grow emotionally, to marry his beloved Agatha Troy, and to advance in his profession. Her impact on the mystery field can be seen in her selection as a Grand Master by the Mystery Writers of America.

"Death on the Air" finds Roderick Alleyn facing one of his most interesting and puzzling cases, set on Christmas Day.

On the 25th of December at 7:30 a.m. Mr. Septimus Tonks was found dead beside his wireless set.

It was Emily Parks, an under-housemaid, who discovered him. She butted open the door and entered, carrying mop, duster, and carpet-sweeper. At that precise moment she was greatly startled by a voice that spoke out of the darkness.

"Good morning, everybody," said the voice in superbly inflected syllables, "and a Merry Christmas!"

Emily yelped, but not loudly, as she immediately realized what had happened. Mr. Tonks had omitted to turn off his wireless before going to bed. She drew back the curtains, revealing a kind of pale murk which was a London Christmas dawn, switched on the light, and saw Septimus.

He was seated in front of the radio. It was a small but expensive set, specially built for him. Septimus sat in an armchair, his back to Emily, his body tilted towards the radio.

His hands, the fingers curiously bunched, were on the ledge of the cabinet under the tuning and volume knobs. His chest rested against the shelf below and his head leaned on the front panel.

He looked rather as though he was listening intently to the interior secrets of the wireless. His head was bent so that Emily could see his bald top with its trail of oiled hairs. He did not move.

"Beg pardon, sir," gasped Emily. She was again greatly startled. Mr. Tonks' enthusiasm for radio had never before induced him to tune in at seven-thirty in the morning.

"Special Christmas service," the cultured voice was saying. Mr. Tonks sat very still. Emily, in common with the other servants, was terrified of her master. She did not know whether to go or to stay. She gazed wildly at Septimus and realized that he wore a dinner-jacket. The room was now filled with the clamor of pealing bells.

Emily opened her mouth as wide as it would go and screamed and screamed and screamed . . .

Chase, the butler, was the first to arrive. He was a pale, flabby man but authoritative. He said: "What's the meaning of this outrage?" and then saw Septimus. He went to the arm-chair, bent down, and looked into his master's face.

He did not lose his head, but said in a loud voice: "My Gawd!" And then to Emily: "Shut your face." By this vulgarism he betrayed his agitation. He seized Emily by the shoulders and thrust her towards the door, where they were met by Mr. Hislop, the secretary, in his dressing-gown. Mr. Hislop said: "Good heavens, Chase, what is the meaning—" and then his voice too was drowned in the clamor of bells and renewed screams.

Chase put his fat white hand over Emily's mouth.

"In the study if you please, sir. An accident. Go to your room, will you, and stop that noise or I'll give you something to make you." This to Emily, who bolted down the hall, where she was received by the rest of the staff who had congregated there.

Chase returned to the study with Mr. Hislop and locked the door. They both looked down at the body of Septimus Tonks. The secretary was the first to speak.

"But—but—he's dead," said little Mr. Hislop.

"I suppose there can't be any doubt," whispered Chase.

"Look at the face. Any doubt! My God!"

Mr. Hislop put out a delicate hand towards the bent head and then drew it back. Chase, less fastidious, touched one of the hard wrists, gripped, and then lifted it. The body at once tipped backwards as if it was made of wood. One of the hands knocked against the butler's face. He sprang back with an oath.

There lay Septimus, his knees and his hands in the air, his terrible face turned up to the light. Chase pointed to the right hand. Two fingers and the thumb were slightly blackened.

Ding, dong, dang, ding.

"For God's sake stop those bells," cried Mr. Hislop. Chase turned off the wall switch. Into the sudden silence came the sound of the door-handle being rattled and Guy Tonks' voice on the other side.

"Hislop! Mr. Hislop! Chase! What's the matter?"

"Just a moment, Mr. Guy." Chase looked at the secretary. "You go, sir."

So it was left to Mr. Hislop to break the news to the family. They listened to his stammering revelation in stupefied silence. It was not until Guy, the eldest of the three children, stood in the study that any practical suggestion was made.

"What has killed him?" asked Guy.

"It's extraordinary," burbled Hislop. "Extraordinary. He looks as if he'd been—"

"Galvanized," said Guy.

"We ought to send for a doctor," suggested Hislop timidly.

"Of course. Will you, Mr. Hislop? Dr. Meadows."

Hislop went to the telephone and Guy returned to his family. Dr. Meadows lived on the other side of the square and arrived in five minutes. He examined the body without moving it. He questioned Chase and Hislop. Chase was very voluble about the burns on the hand. He uttered the word "electrocution" over and over again.

"I had a cousin, sir, that was struck by lighting. As soon as I saw the hand—"

"Yes, yes," said Dr. Meadows. "So you said. I can see the burns for myself."

"Electrocution," repeated Chase. "There'll have to be an inquest."

Dr. Meadows snapped at him, summoned Emily, and then saw the rest of the family—Guy, Arthur, Phillipa, and their mother. They were clustered round a cold grate in the drawing-room. Phillipa was on her knees, trying to light the fire.

"What was it?" asked Arthur as soon as the doctor came in.

"Looks like electric shock. Guy, I'll have a word with you if you please. Phillipa, look after your mother, there's a good child. Coffee with a dash of brandy. Where are those damn maids? Come on, Guy."

Alone with Guy, he said they'd have to send for the police.

"The police!" Guy's dark face turned very pale. "Why? What's it got to do with them?"

"Nothing, as like as not, but they'll have to be notified. I can't give a certificate as things are. If it's electrocution, how did it happen?"

"But the police!" said Guy. "That's simply ghastly. Dr. Meadows, for God's sake couldn't you—?"

"No," said Dr. Meadows, "I couldn't. Sorry, Guy, but there it is."

"But can't we wait a moment? Look at him again. You haven't examined him properly."

"I don't want to move him, that's why. Pull yourself together, boy. Look here. I've got a pal in the C.I.D.—Alleyn. He's a gentleman and all that. He'll curse me like a fury, but he'll come if he's in London, and he'll make things easier for you. Go back to your mother. I'll ring Alleyn up."

That was how it came about that Chief Detective-Inspector Roderick Alleyn spent his Christmas Day in harness. As a matter of fact he was on duty, and as he pointed out to Dr. Meadows, would have had to turn out and visit his miserable Tonkses in any case. When he did arrive it was with his usual air of remote courtesy. He was accompanied by a tall, thick-set officer—Inspector Fox—and by the divisional police-surgeon. Dr. Meadows took them into the study. Alleyn, in his turn, looked at the horror that had been Septimus.

"Was he like this when he was found?"

"No. I understand he was leaning forward with his hands on the ledge of the cabinet. He must have slumped forward and been propped up by the chair arms and the cabinet."

"Who moved him?"

"Chase, the butler. He said he only meant to raise the arm. *Rigor* is well established."

Alleyn put his hand behind the rigid neck and pushed. The body fell forward into its original position.

"There you are, Curtis," said Alleyn to the divisional surgeon. He turned to Fox. "Get the camera man, will you, Fox?"

The photographer took four shots and departed. Alleyn marked the position of the hands and feet with chalk, made a careful plan of the room and turned to the doctors.

"Is it electrocution, do you think?"

"Looks like it," said Curtis. "Have to be a p.m. of course."

"Of course. Still, look at the hands. Burns. Thumb and two fingers bunched together and exactly the distance between the two knobs apart. He'd been tuning his hurdy-gurdy."

"By gum," said Inspector Fox, speaking for the first time.

"D'you mean he got a lethal shock from his radio?" asked Dr. Meadows.

"I don't know. I merely conclude he had his hands on the knobs when he died."

"It was still going when the house-maid found him. Chase turned it off and got no shock."

"Yours, partner," said Alleyn, turning to Fox. Fox stooped down to the wall switch.

"Careful," said Alleyn.

"I've got rubber soles," said Fox, and switched it on. The radio hummed, gathered volume, and found itself.

"No-oel, No-o-el," it roared. Fox cut it off and pulled out the wall plug.

"I'd like to have a look inside this set," he said.

"So you shall, old boy, so you shall," rejoined Alleyn. "Before you begin, I think we'd better move the body. Will you see to that, Meadows? Fox, get Bailey, will you? He's out in the car."

Curtis, Hislop, and Meadows carried Septimus Tonks into a spare downstairs room. It was a difficult and horrible business with that contorted body. Dr. Meadows came back alone, mopping his brow, to find Detective-Sergeant Bailey, a fingerprint expert, at work on the wireless cabinet.

"What's all this?" asked Dr. Meadows. "Do you want to find out if he'd been fooling round with the innards?"

"He," said Alleyn, "or—somebody else."

"Umph!" Dr. Meadows looked at the Inspector. "You agree with me, it seems. Do you suspect—?"

"Suspect? I'm the least suspicious man alive. I'm merely being tidy. Well, Bailey?"

"I've got a good one off the chair arm. That'll be the deceased's, won't it, sir?"

"No doubt. We'll check up later. What about the wireless?"

Fox, wearing a glove, pulled off the knob of the volume control.

"Seems to be O.K." said Bailey. "It's a sweet bit of work. Not too bad at all, sir." He turned his torch into the back of the radio, undid a couple of screws underneath the set, lifted out the works.

"What's the little hole for?" asked Alleyn.

"What's that, sir?" said Fox.

"There's a hole bored through the panel above the knob. About an eighth of an inch in diameter. The rim of the knob hides it. One might easily miss it. Move your torch, Bailey. Yes. There, do you see?"

Fox bent down and uttered a bass growl. A fine needle of light came through the front of the radio.

"That's peculiar, sir," said Bailey from the other side. "I don't get the idea at all."

Alleyn pulled out the tuning knob.

"There's another one there," he murmured. "Yes. Nice clean little holes. Newly bored. Unusual, I take it?"

"Unusual's the word, sir," said Fox.

"Run away, Meadows," said Alleyn.

"Why the devil?" asked Dr. Meadows indignantly. "What are you driving at? Why shouldn't I be here?"

"You ought to be with the sorrowing relatives. Where's your corpse-side manner?"

"I've settled them. What are you up to?"

"Who's being suspicious now?" asked Alleyn mildly. "You may stay for a moment. Tell me about the Tonkses. Who are they? What are they? What sort of a man was Septimus?"

"If you must know, he was a damned unpleasant sort of a man."

"Tell me about him."

Dr. Meadows sat down and lit a cigarette.

"He was a self-made bloke," he said, "as hard as nails and—well, coarse rather than vulgar."

"Like Dr. Johnson perhaps?"

"Not in the least. Don't interrupt. I've known him for twenty-five years. His wife was a neighbor of ours in Dorset. Isabel Foreston. I brought the children into this vale of tears and, by jove, in many ways it's been one for them. It's an extraordinary household. For the last ten years Isabel's condition has been the sort that sends these psycho-jokers dizzy with rapture. I'm only an out-of-date G.P., and I'd just say she is in an advanced stage of hysterical neurosis. Frightened into fits of her husband."

"I can't understand these holes," grumbled Fox to Bailey.

"Go on, Meadows," said Alleyn.

"I tackled Sep about her eighteen months ago. Told him the trouble was in her mind. He eyed me with a sort of grin on his face and said: 'I'm surprised to learn that my wife has enough mentality to—' But look here, Alleyn, I can't talk about my patients like this. What the devil am I thinking about."

"You know perfectly well it'll go no further unless—"

"Unless what?"

"Unless it has to. Do go on."

But Dr. Meadows hurriedly withdrew behind his professional rectitude. All he would say was that Mr. Tonks had suffered from high blood pressure and a weak heart, that Guy was in his father's city office, that Arthur had wanted to study art and had been told to read for law, and that Phillipa wanted to go on the stage and had been told to do nothing of the sort.

"Bullied his children," commented Alleyn.

"Find out for yourself. I'm off." Dr. Meadows got as far as the door and came back.

"Look here," he said, "I'll tell you one thing. There was a row here last night. I'd asked Hislop, who's a sensible little beggar, to let me know if anything happened to upset Mrs. Sep. Upset her badly, you know. To be indiscreet again, I said he'd better let me know if Sep cut up rough because Isabel and the young had had about as much of that as they could stand. He was drinking pretty heavily. Hislop rang me up at ten-twenty last night to say there'd been a hell of a row; Sep bullying Phips—Phillipa, you know; always call her Phips—in her room. He said Isabel—Mrs. Sep—had gone to bed. I'd had a big day and I didn't want to turn out. I told him to ring again in half an hour if things hadn't quieted down. I told him to keep out of Sep's way and stay in his own room, which is next to Phips' and see if she was all right when Sep cleared out. Hislop was involved. I won't tell you how. The servants were all out. I said that if I didn't hear from him in half an hour I'd ring again and if there was no answer I'd know they were all in bed and quiet. I did ring, got no answer, and went to bed myself. That's all. I'm off. Curtis knows where to find me. You'll want me for the inquest, I suppose. Goodbye."

When he had gone Alleyn embarked on a systematic prowl round the room. Fox and Bailey were still deeply engrossed with the wireless.

"I don't see how the gentleman could have got a bump-off from the instrument," grumbled Fox. "These control knobs are quite in order. Everything's as it should be. Look here, sir."

He turned on the wall switch and tuned in. There was a prolonged humming.

". . . concludes the program of Christmas carols," said the radio.

"A very nice tone," said Fox approvingly.

"Here's something, sir," announced Bailey suddenly.

"Found the sawdust, have you?" said Alleyn.

"Got it in one," said the startled Bailey.

Alleyn peered into the instrument, using the torch. He scooped up two tiny traces of sawdust from under the holes.

" 'Vantage number one," said Alleyn. He bent down to the wall plug. "Hullo! A two-way adapter. Serves the radio and the radiator. Thought they were illegal. This is a rum business. Let's have another look at those knobs."

He had his look. They were the usual wireless fitments, bakelite knobs fitting snugly to the steel shafts that projected from the front panel.

"As you say," he murmured, "quite in order. Wait a bit." He

produced a pocket lens and squinted at one of the shafts. "Ye-es. Do they ever wrap blotting-paper round these objects, Fox?"

"Blotting-paper!" ejaculated Fox. "They do not."

Alleyn scraped at both the shafts with his penknife, holding an envelope underneath. He rose, groaning, and crossed to the desk. "A corner torn off the bottom bit of blotch," he said presently. "No prints on the wireless, I think you said, Bailey?"

"That's right," agreed Bailey morosely.

"There'll be none, or too many, on the blotter, but try, Bailey, try," said Alleyn. He wandered about the room, his eyes on the floor; got as far as the window and stopped.

"Fox!" he said. "A clue. A very palpable clue."

"What is it?" asked Fox.

"The odd wisp of blotting-paper, no less." Alleyn's gaze traveled up the side of the window curtain. "Can I believe my eyes?"

He got a chair, stood on the seat, and with his gloved hand pulled the buttons from the ends of the curtain rod.

"Look at this." He turned to the radio, detached the control knobs, and laid them beside the ones he had removed from the curtain rod.

Ten minutes later Inspector Fox knocked on the drawing-room door and was admitted by Guy Tonks. Phillipa had got the fire going and the family was gathered round it. They looked as though they had not moved or spoken to one another for a long time.

It was Phillipa who spoke first to Fox. "Do you want one of us?"

"If you please, miss," said Fox. "Inspector Alleyn would like to see Mr. Guy Tonks for a moment, if convenient."

"I'll come," said Guy, and led the way to the study. At the door he paused. "Is he—my father—still—?"

"No, no, sir," said Fox comfortably. "It's all ship-shape in there again."

With a lift of his chin Guy opened the door and went in, followed by Fox. Alleyn was alone, seated at the desk. He rose to his feet.

"You want to speak to me?" asked Guy.

"Yes, if I may. This has all been a great shock to you, of course. Won't you sit down?"

Guy sat in the chair farthest away from the radio.

"What killed my father? Was it a stroke?"

"The doctors are not quite certain. There will have to be a *post-mortem*."

"Good God! And an inquest?"

"I'm afraid so."

"Horrible!" said Guy violently. "What do you think was the matter? Why the devil do these quacks have to be so mysterious? What killed him?"

"They think an electric shock."

"How did it happen?"

"We don't know. It looks as if he got it from the wireless."

"Surely that's impossible. I thought they were fool-proof."

"I believe they are, if left to themselves."

For a second undoubtedly Guy was startled. Then a look of relief came into his eyes. He seemed to relax all over.

"Of course," he said, "he was always monkeying about with it. What had he done?"

"Nothing."

"But you said—if it killed him he must have done something to it."

"If anyone interfered with the set it was put right afterwards."

Guy's lips parted but he did not speak. He had gone very white.

"So you see," said Alleyn, "your father could not have done anything."

"Then it was not the radio that killed him."

"That we hope will be determined by the *post-mortem*."

"I don't know anything about wireless," said Guy suddenly. "I don't understand. This doesn't seem to make sense. Nobody ever touched the thing except my father. He was most particular about it. Nobody went near the wireless."

"I see. He was an enthusiast?"

"Yes, it was his only enthusiasm except—except his business."

"One of my men is a bit of an expert," Alleyn said. "He says this is a remarkably good set. You are not an expert you say. Is there anyone in the house who is?"

"My young brother was interested at one time. He's given it up. My father wouldn't allow another radio in the house."

"Perhaps he may be able to suggest something."

"But if the thing's all right now—"

"We've got to explore every possibility."

"You speak as if—as—if—"

"I speak as I am bound to speak before there has been an inquest," said Alleyn. "Had anyone a grudge against your father, Mr. Tonks?"

Up went Guy's chin again. He looked Alleyn squarely in the eyes.

"Almost everyone who knew him," said Guy.

"Is that an exaggeration?"

"No. You think he was murdered, don't you?"

Alleyn suddenly pointed to the desk beside him.

"Have you ever seen those before?" he asked abruptly. Guy stared at two black knobs that lay side by side on an ashtray.

"Those?" he said. "No. What are they?"

"I believe they are the agents of your father's death."

The study door opened and Arthur Tonks came in.

"Guy," he said, "what's happening? We can't stay cooped up together all day. I can't stand it. For God's sake what happened to him?"

"They think those things killed him," said Guy.

"Those?" For a split second Arthur's glance slewed to the curtainrods. Then, with a characteristic flicker of his eyelids, he looked away again.

"What do you mean?" he asked Alleyn.

"Will you try one of those knobs on the shaft of the volume control?"

"But," said Arthur, "they're metal."

"It's disconnected," said Alleyn.

Arthur picked one of the knobs from the tray, turned to the radio, and fitted the knob over one of the exposed shafts.

"It's too loose," he said quickly, "it would fall off."

"Not if it was packed—with blotting-paper, for instance."

"Where did you find these things?" demanded Arthur.

"I think you recognized them, didn't you? I saw you glance at the curtain-rod."

"Of course I recognized them. I did a portrait of Phillipa against those curtains when—he—was away last year. I've painted the damn things."

"Look here," interrupted Guy, "exactly what are you driving at, Mr. Alleyn? If you mean to suggest that my brother—"

"I!" cried Arthur. "What's it got to do with me? Why should you suppose—"

"I found traces of blotting-paper on the shafts and inside the metal knobs," said Alleyn. "It suggested a substitution of the metal knobs for the bakelite ones. It is remarkable, don't you think, that they should so closely resemble one another? If you examine them, of course, you find they are not identical. Still, the difference is scarcely perceptible."

Arthur did not answer this. He was still looking at the wireless.

"I've always wanted to have a look at this set," he said surprisingly.

"You are free to do so now," said Alleyn politely. "We have finished with it for the time being."

"Look here," said Arthur suddenly, "suppose metal knobs were substituted for bakelite ones, it couldn't kill him. He wouldn't get a shock at all. Both the controls are grounded."

"Have you noticed those very small holes drilled through the panel?" asked Alleyn. "Should they be there, do you think?"

Arthur peered at the little steel shafts. "By God, he's right, Guy," he said. "That's how it was done."

"Inspector Fox," said Alleyn, "tells me those holes could be used for conducting wires and that a lead could be taken from the—transformer, is it?—to one of the knobs."

"And the other connected to earth," said Fox. "It's a job for an expert. He could get three hundred volts or so that way."

"That's not good enough," said Arthur quickly; "there wouldn't be enough current to do any damage—only a few hundredths of an amp."

"I'm not an expert," said Alleyn, "but I'm sure you're right. Why were the holes drilled then? Do you imagine someone wanted to play a practical joke on your father?"

"A practical joke? On *him?*" Arthur gave an unpleasant screech of laughter. "Do you hear that, Guy?"

"Shut up," said Guy. "After all, he is dead."

"It seems almost too good to be true, doesn't it?"

"Don't be a bloody fool, Arthur. Pull yourself together. Can't you see what this means? They think he's been murdered."

"Murdered! They're wrong. None of us had the nerve for that, Mr. Inspector. Look at me. My hands are so shaky they told me I'd never be able to paint. That dates from when I was a kid and he shut me up in the cellars for a night. Look at me. Look at Guy. He's not so vulnerable, but he caved in like the rest of us. We were conditioned to surrender. Do you know—"

"Wait a moment," said Alleyn quietly. "Your brother is quite right, you know. You'd better think before you speak. This may be a case of homicide."

"Thank you, sir," said Guy quickly. "That's extraordinarily decent of you. Arthur's a bit above himself. It's a shock."

"The relief, you mean," said Arthur. "Don't be such an ass. I didn't kill him and they'll find it out soon enough. Nobody killed him. There must be some explanation."

"I suggest that you listen to me," said Alleyn. "I'm going to put several questions to both of you. You need not answer them, but it will be more sensible to do so. I understand no one but your father touched this radio. Did any of you ever come into this room while it was in use?"

"Not unless he wanted to vary the program with a little bullying." said Arthur.

Alleyn turned to Guy, who was glaring at his brother.

"I want to know exactly what happened in this house last night. As far as the doctors can tell us, your father died not less than three and not more than eight hours before he was found. We must try to fix the time as accurately as possible."

"I saw him at about a quarter to nine," began Guy slowly. "I was going out to a supper-party at the Savoy and had come downstairs. He was crossing the hall from the drawing-room to his room."

"Did you see him after a quarter to nine, Mr. Arthur?"

"No. I heard him, though. He was working in here with Hislop. Hislop had asked to go away for Christmas. Quite enough. My father discovered some urgent correspondence. Really, Guy, you know, he was pathological. I'm sure Dr. Meadows thinks so."

"When did you hear him?" asked Alleyn.

"Some time after Guy had gone. I was working on a drawing in my room upstairs. It's above his. I heard him bawling at little Hislop. It must have been before ten o'clock, because I went out to a studio party at ten. I heard him bawling as I crossed the hall."

"And when," said Alleyn, "did you both return?"

"I came home at about twenty past twelve," said Guy immediately. "I can fix the time because we had gone on to Chez Carlo, and they had a midnight stunt there. We left immediately afterwards. I came home in a taxi. The radio was on full blast."

"You heard no voices?"

"None. Just the wireless."

"And you, Mr. Arthur?"

"Lord knows when I got in. After one. The house was in darkness. Not a sound."

"You had your own key?"

"Yes," said Guy. "Each of us has one. They're always left on a hook in the lobby. When I came in I noticed Arthur's was gone."

"What about the others? How did you know it was his?"

"Mother hasn't got one and Phips lost hers weeks ago. Anyway, I knew they were staying in and that it must be Arthur who was out."

"Thank you," said Arthur ironically.

"You didn't look in the study when you came in," Alleyn asked him.

"Good Lord, no," said Arthur as if the suggestion was fantastic. "I say," he said suddenly, "I suppose he was sitting here—dead. That's a queer thought." He laughed nervously. "Just sitting here, behind the door in the dark."

"How do you know it was in the dark?"

"What d'you mean? Of course it was. There was no light under the door."

"I see. Now do you two mind joining your mother again? Perhaps your sister will be kind enough to come in here for a moment. Fox, ask her, will you?"

Fox returned to the drawing-room with Guy and Arthur and remained there, blandly unconscious of any embarrassment his presence might cause the Tonkses. Bailey was already there, ostensibly examining the electric points.

Phillipa went to the study at once. Her first remark was characteristic. "Can I be of any help?" asked Phillipa.

"It's extremely nice of you to put it like that," said Alleyn. "I don't want to worry you for long. I'm sure this discovery has been a shock to you."

"Probably," said Phillipa. Alleyn glanced quickly at her. "I mean," she explained, "that I suppose I must be shocked but I can't feel anything much. I just want to get it all over as soon as possible. And then think. Please tell me what has happened."

Alleyn told her they believed her father had been electrocuted and that the circumstances were unusual and puzzling. He said nothing to suggest that the police suspected murder.

"I don't think I'll be much help," said Phillipa, "but go ahead."

"I want to try to discover who was the last person to see your father or speak to him."

"I should think very likely I was," said Phillipa composedly. "I had a row with him before I went to bed."

"What about?"

"I don't see that it matters."

Alleyn considered this. When he spoke again it was with deliberation.

"Look here," he said, "I think there is very little doubt that your father was killed by an electric shock from his wireless set. As far as I know the circumstances are unique. Radios are normally incapable of giving a lethal shock to anyone. We have examined the cabinet and are inclined to think that its internal arrangements were disturbed last night. Very radically disturbed. Your father may have experimented with it. If anything happened to interrupt or upset him, it is possible that in the excitement of the moment he made some dangerous readjustment."

"You don't believe that, do you?" asked Phillipa calmly.

"Since you ask me," said Alleyn, "no."

"I see," said Phillipa; "you think he was murdered, but you're not sure." She had gone very white, but she spoke crisply. "Naturally you want to find out about my row."

"About everything that happened last evening," amended Alleyn.

"What happened was this," said Phillipa; "I came into the hall some time after ten. I'd heard Arthur go out and had looked at the clock at five past. I ran into my father's secretary, Richard Hislop. He turned aside, but not before I saw . . . not quickly enough. I blurted out: 'You're crying.' We looked at each other. I asked him why he stood it. None of the other secretaries could. He said he had to. He's a widower with two children. There have been doctor's bills and things. I needn't tell you about his . . . about his damnable servitude to my father nor about the refinements of cruelty he'd had to put up with. I think my father was mad, really mad, I mean. Richard gabbled it all out to me higgledy-piggledy in a sort of horrified whisper. He's been here two years, but I'd never realized until that moment that we . . . that . . ." A faint flush came into her cheeks. "He's such a funny little man. Not at all the sort I've always thought . . . not good-looking or exciting or anything."

She stopped, looking bewildered.

"Yes?" said Alleyn.

"Well, you see—I suddenly realized I was in love with him. He realized it too. He said: 'Of course, it's quite hopeless, you know. Us, I mean. Laughable, almost.' Then I put my arms around his neck and kissed him. It was very odd, but it seemed quite natural. The point is my father came out of his room into the hall and saw us."

"That was bad luck," said Alleyn.

"Yes, it was. My father really seemed delighted. He almost licked his lips. Richard's efficiency had irritated my father for a long time. It was difficult to find excuses for being beastly to him. Now, of course . . . He ordered Richard to the study and me to my room. He followed me upstairs. Richard tried to come too, but I asked him not to. My father . . . I needn't tell you what he said. He put the worst possible construction on what he'd seen. He was absolutely foul, screaming at me like a madman. He was insane. Perhaps it was D. Ts. He drank terribly, you know. I dare say it's silly of me to tell you all this."

"No," said Alleyn.

"I can't feel anything at all. Not even relief. The boys are frankly relieved. I can't feel afraid either." She stared meditatively at Alleyn. "Innocent people needn't feel afraid, need they?"

"It's an axiom of police investigation," said Alleyn and wondered if indeed she was innocent.

"It just *can't* be murder," said Phillipa. "We were all too much afraid to kill him. I believe he'd win even if you murdered him. He'd hit back somehow." She put her hands to her eyes. "I'm all muddled."

"I think you are more upset than you realized. I'll be as quick as I can. Your father made this scene in your room. You say he screamed. Did anyone hear him?"

"Yes. Mummy did. She came in."

"What happened?"

"I said: 'Go away, darling, it's all right.' I didn't want her to be involved. He nearly killed her with the things he did. Sometimes he'd . . . we never knew what happened between them. It was all secret, like a door shutting quietly as you walk along a passage."

"Did she go away?"

"Not at once. He told her he'd found out that Richard and I were lovers. He said . . . it doesn't matter. I don't want to tell you. She was terrified. He was stabbing at her in some way I couldn't understand. Then, quite suddenly, he told her to go to her own room. She went at once and he followed her. He locked me in. That's the last I saw of him, but I heard him go downstairs later."

"Were you locked in all night?"

"No. Richard Hislop's room is next to mine. He came up and spoke through the wall to me. He wanted to unlock the door, but I said better not in case—he—came back. Then, much later, Guy came home. As he passed my door I tapped on it. The key was in the lock and he turned it."

"Did you tell him what had happened?"

"Just that there'd been a row. He only stayed a moment."

"Can you hear the radio from your room?"

She seemed surprised.

"The wireless? Why, yes. Faintly."

"Did you hear it after your father returned to the study?"

"I don't remember."

"Think. While you lay awake all that long time until your brother came home?"

"I'll try. When he came out and found Richard and me, it was not going. They had been working, you see. No, I can't remember hearing it at all unless—wait a moment. Yes. After he had gone back to the study from mother's room I remember there was a loud crash of static. Very loud. Then I think it was quiet for some time. I fancy I heard it again later. Oh, I've remembered something else. After the static my bedside radiator went out. I suppose there was something wrong with the electric supply. That would account for both, wouldn't it? The heater went on again about ten minutes later."

"And did the radio begin again then, do you think?"

"I don't know. I'm very vague about that. It started again sometime before I went to sleep."

"Thank you very much indeed. I won't bother you any longer now."

"All right," said Phillipa calmly, and went away.

Alleyn sent for Chase and questioned him about the rest of the staff and about the discovery of the body. Emily was summoned and dealt with. When she departed, awestruck but complacent, Alleyn turned to the butler.

"Chase," he said, "had your master any peculiar habits?"

"Yes, sir."

"In regard to the wireless?"

"I beg pardon, sir. I thought you meant generally speaking."

"Well, then, generally speaking."

"If I may say so, sir, he was a mass of them."

"How long have you been with him?"

"Two months, sir, and due to leave at the end of this week."

"Oh. Why are you leaving?"

Chase produced the classic remark of his kind.

"There are some things," he said, "that flesh and blood will not stand, sir. One of them's being spoke to like Mr. Tonks spoke to his staff."

"Ah. His peculiar habits, in fact?"

"It's my opinion, sir, he was mad. Stark, staring."

"With regard to the radio. Did he tinker with it?"

"I can't say I've ever noticed, sir. I believe he knew quite a lot about wireless."

"When he turned the thing, had he any particular method? Any characteristic attitude or gesture?"

"I don't think so, sir. I never noticed, and yet I've often come into the room when he was at it. I can seem to see him now, sir."

"Yes, yes," said Alleyn swiftly. "That's what we want. A clear mental picture. How was it now? Like this?"

In a moment he was across the room and seated in Septimus's chair. He swung round to the cabinet and raised his right hand to the tuning control.

"Like this?"

"No, sir," said Chase promptly, "that's not him at all. Both hands it should be."

"Ah." Up went Alleyn's left hand to the volume control. "More like this?"

"Yes, sir," said Chase slowly. "But there's something else and I can't recollect what it was. Something he was always doing. It's in the back of my head. You know, sir. Just on the edge of my memory, as you might say."

"I know."

"It's a kind—something—to do with irritation," said Chase slowly.

"Irritation? His?"

"No. It's no good, sir. I can't get it."

"Perhaps later. Now look here, Chase, what happened to all of you last night? All the servants, I mean."

"We were all out, sir. It being Christmas Eve. The mistress sent for me yesterday morning. She said we could take the evening off as soon as I had taken in Mr. Tonks's grog-tray at nine o'clock. So we went," ended Chase simply.

"When?"

"The rest of the staff got away about nine. I left at ten past, sir, and returned about eleven-twenty. The others were back then, and all in bed. I went straight to bed myself, sir."

"You came in by a back door, I suppose?"

"Yes, sir. We've been talking it over. None of us noticed anything unusual."

"Can you hear the wireless in your part of the house?"

"No, sir."

"Well," said Alleyn, looking up from his notes, "that'll do, thank you."

Before Chase reached the door Fox came in.

"Beg pardon, sir," said Fox. "I just want to take a look at the *Radio Times* on the desk."

He bent over the paper, wetted a gigantic thumb, and turned a page.

"That's it, sir," shouted Chase suddenly. "That's what I tried to think of. That's what he was always doing."

"But what?"

"Licking his fingers, sir. It was a habit," said Chase. "That's what he always did when he sat down to the radio. I heard Mr. Hislop tell the doctor it nearly drove him demented, the way the master couldn't touch a thing without first licking his fingers."

"Quite so," said Alleyn. "In about ten minutes, ask Mr. Hislop if he will be good enough to come in for a moment. That will be all, thank you, Chase."

"Well, sir," remarked Fox when Chase had gone, "if that's the case and what I think's right, it'd certainly make matters worse."

"Good heavens, Fox, what an elaborate remark. What does it mean?"

"If metal knobs were substituted for bakelite ones and fine wires brought through those holes to make contact, then he'd get a bigger bump if he tuned in with *damp* fingers."

"Yes. And he always used both hands. Fox!"

"Sir."

"Approach the Tonkses again. You haven't left them alone, of course?"

"Bailey's in there making out he's interested in the light switches. He's found the main switchboard under the stairs. There's signs of a blown fuse having been fixed recently. In a cupboard underneath there are odd lengths of flex and so on. Same brand as this on the wireless and the heater."

"Ah, yes. Could the cord from the adapter to the radiator be brought into play?"

"By gum," said Fox, "you're right! That's how it was done, Chief. The heavier flex was cut away the radiator and shoved through. There was a fire, so he wouldn't want the radiator and wouldn't notice."

"It might have been done that way, certainly, but there's little to prove it. Return to the bereaved Tonkses, my Fox, and ask prettily if any of them remember Septimus's peculiarities when tuning his wireless."

Fox met little Mr. Hislop at the door and left him alone with Alleyn. Phillipa had been right, reflected the Inspector, when she said Richard Hislop was not a noticeable man. He was nondescript. Grey eyes, drab hair; rather pale, rather short, rather insignificant; and yet last night there had flashed up between those two the realization of love. Romantic but rum, thought Alleyn.

"Do sit down," he said. "I want you, if you will, to tell me what happened between you and Mr. Tonks last evening."

"What happened?"

"Yes. You all dined at eight, I understand. Then you and Mr. Tonks came in here?"

"Yes."

"What did you do?"

"He dictated several letters."

"Anything unusual take place?"

"Oh, no."

"Why did you quarrel?"

"Quarrel!" The quiet voice jumped a tone. "We did not quarrel, Mr. Alleyn."

"Perhaps that was the wrong word. What upset you?"

"Phillipa has told you?"

"Yes. She was wise to do so. What was the matter, Mr. Hislop?"

"Apart from the . . . what she told you . . . Mr. Tonks was a difficult man to please. I often irritated him. I did so last night."

"In what way?"

"In almost every way. He shouted at me. I was startled and nervous, clumsy with papers, and making mistakes. I wasn't well. I blundered and then . . . I . . . I broke down. I have always irritated him. My very mannerisms—"

"Had he no irritating mannerisms, himself?"

"He! My God!"

"What were they?"

"I can't think of anything in particular. It doesn't matter does it?"

"Anything to do with the wireless, for instance?"

There was a short silence.

"No," said Hislop.

"Was the radio on in here last night, after dinner?"

"For a little while. Not after—after the incident in the hall. At least, I don't think so. I don't remember."

"What did you do after Miss Phillipa and her father had gone upstairs?"

"I followed and listened outside the door for a moment." He had gone very white and had backed away from the desk.

"And then?"

"I heard someone coming. I remembered Dr. Meadows had told me to ring him up if there was one of the scenes. I returned here and rang him up. He told me to go to my room and listen. If things got any worse I was to telephone again. Otherwise I was to stay in my room. It is next to hers."

"And you did this?" He nodded. "Could you hear what Mr. Tonks said to her?"

"A—a good deal of it."

"What did you hear?"

"He insulted her. Mrs. Tonks was there. I was just thinking of ringing Dr. Meadows up again when she and Mr. Tonks came out and went along the passage. I stayed in my room."

"You did not try to speak to Miss Phillipa?"

"We spoke through the wall. She asked me not to ring Dr. Meadows, but to stay in my room. In a little while, perhaps it was as much as twenty minutes—I really don't know—I heard him come back and go downstairs. I again spoke to Phillipa. She implored me not to do anything and said that she herself would speak to Dr. Meadows in the morning. So I waited a little longer and then went to bed."

"And to sleep?"

"My God, no!"

"Did you hear the wireless again?"

"Yes. At least I heard static."

"Are you an expert on wireless?"

"No. I know the ordinary things. Nothing much."

"How did you come to take this job, Mr. Hislop?"

"I answered an advertisement."

"You are sure you don't remember any particular mannerism of Mr. Tonks's in connection with the radio?"

"No."

"And you can tell me no more about your interview in the study that led to the scene in the hall?"

"No."

"Will you please ask Mrs. Tonks if she will be kind enough to speak to me for a moment?"

"Certainly," said Hislop, and went away.

Septimus's wife came in looking like death. Alleyn got her to sit down and asked her about her movements on the preceding evening. She said she was feeling unwell and dined in her room. She went to bed immediately afterwards. She heard Septimus yelling at Phillipa and went to Phillipa's room. Septimus accused Mr. Hislop and her daughter of "terrible things." She got as far as this and then broke down quietly. Alleyn was very gentle with her. After a little while he learned that Septimus had gone to her room with her and had continued to speak of "terrible things."

"What sort of things?" asked Alleyn.

"He was not responsible," said Isabel. "He did not know what he was saying. I think he had been drinking."

She thought he had remained with her for perhaps a quarter of an hour. Possibly longer. He left her abruptly and she heard him go along the passage, past Phillipa's door, and presumably downstairs. She had stayed awake for a long time. The wireless could not be heard from her room. Alleyn showed her the curtain knobs, but she seemed quite unable to take in their significance. He let her go, summoned Fox, and went over the whole case.

"What's your idea on the show?" he asked when he had finished.

"Well, sir," said Fox, in his stolid way, "on the face of it the young gentlemen have got alibis. We'll have to check them up, of course, and I don't see we can go much further until we have done so."

"For the moment," said Alleyn, "let us suppose Masters Guy and Arthur to be safely established behind cast-iron alibis. What then?"

"Then we've got the young lady, the old lady, the secretary, and the servants."

"Let us parade them. But first let us go over the wireless game. You'll have to watch me here. I gather that the only way in which the radio could be fixed to give Mr. Tonks his quietus is like this: Control knobs removed. Holes bored in front panel with fine drill. Metal knobs substituted and packed with blotting paper to insulate them from metal shafts and make them stay put. Heavier flex from adapter to radiator cut and the ends of the wires pushed through the drilled holes to make contact with the new knobs. Thus we have a positive and negative pole. Mr. Tonks bridges the gap, gets a mighty wallop as the current passes through him to the earth. The switchboard fuse is blown almost immediately. All this is rigged by murderer while Sep was upstairs bullying wife and daughter. Sep revisited study some time after ten-twenty. Whole thing was made ready between ten, when Arthur went out, and the time Sep returned—say, about ten-forty-five.

The murderer reappeared, connected radiator with flex, removed wires, changed back knobs, and left the thing tuned in. Now I take it that the burst of static described by Phillipa and Hislop would be caused by the short-circuit that killed our Septimus?"

"That's right."

"It also affected all the heaters in the house. *Vide* Miss Tonks's radiator."

"Yes. He put all that right again. It would be a simple enough matter for anyone who knew how. He'd just have to fix the fuse on the main switchboard. How long do you say it would take to—what's the horrible word?—to recondition the whole show?"

"M'm," said Fox deeply. "At a guess, sir, fifteen minutes. He'd have to be nippy."

"Yes," agreed Alleyn. "He or she."

"I don't see a female making a success of it," grunted Fox. "Look here, Chief, you know what I'm thinking. Why did Mr. Hislop lie about deceased's habit of licking his thumbs? You say Hislop told you he remembered nothing and Chase says he overheard him saying the trick nearly drove him dippy."

"Exactly," said Alleyn. He was silent for so long that Fox felt moved to utter a discreet cough.

"Eh?" said Alleyn. "Yes, Fox, yes. It'll have to be done." He consulted the telephone directory and dialed a number.

"May I speak to Dr. Meadows? Oh, it's you, is it? Do you remember Mr. Hislop telling you that Septimus Tonks's trick of wetting his fingers nearly drove Hislop demented. Are you there? You don't? Sure? All right. All right. Hislop rang you up at ten-twenty, you said? And you telephoned him? At eleven. Sure of the times? I see. I'd be glad if you'd come round. Can you? Well, do if you can."

He hung up the receiver.

"Get Chase again, will you, Fox?"

Chase, recalled, was most insistent that Mr. Hislop had spoken about it to Dr. Meadows.

"It was when Mr. Hislop had flu, sir. I went up with the doctor. Mr. Hislop had a high temperature and was talking very excited. He kept on and on, saying the master had guessed his ways had driven him crazy and that the master kept on purposely to aggravate. He said if it went on much longer he'd . . . he didn't know what he was talking about, sir, really."

"What did he say he'd do?"

"Well, sir, he said he'd—he'd do something desperate to the master. But it was only his rambling, sir. I daresay he wouldn't remember anything about it."

"No," said Alleyn, "I daresay he wouldn't." When Chase had gone he said to Fox: "Go and find out about those boys and their alibis. See if they can put you on to a quick means of checking up. Get Master Guy to corroborate Miss Phillipa's statement that she was locked in her room."

Fox had been gone for some time and Alleyn was still busy with his notes when the study door burst open and in came Dr. Meadows.

"Look here, my giddy sleuth-hound," he shouted, "what's all this about Hislop? Who says he disliked Sep's abominable habits?"

"Chase does. And don't bawl at me like that. I'm worried."

"So am I, blast you. What are you driving at? You can't imagine that . . . that poor little broken-down hack is capable of electrocuting anybody, let alone Sep?"

"I have no imagination," said Alleyn wearily.

"I wish to God I hadn't called you in. If the wireless killed Sep, it was because he'd monkeyed with it."

"And put it right after it had killed him?"

Dr. Meadows stared at Alleyn in silence.

"Now," said Alleyn, "you've got to give me a straight answer, Meadows. Did Hislop, while he was semi-delirious, say that this habit of Tonks's made him feel like murdering him?"

"I'd forgotten Chase was there," said Dr. Meadows.

"Yes, you'd forgotten that."

"But even if he did talk wildly, Alleyn, what of it? Damn it, you can't arrest a man on the strength of a remark made in delirium."

"I don't propose to do so. Another motive has come to light."

"You mean—Phips—last night?"

"Did he tell you about that?"

"She whispered something to me this morning. I'm very fond of Phips. My God, are you sure of your grounds?"

"Yes," said Alleyn. "I'm sorry. I think you'd better go, Meadows."

"Are you going to arrest him?"

"I have to do my job."

There was a long silence.

"Yes," said Dr. Meadows at last. "You have to do your job. Good-bye, Alleyn."

Fox returned to say that Guy and Arthur had never left their parties. He had got hold of two of their friends. Guy and Mrs. Tonks confirmed the story of the locked door.

"It's a process of elimination," said Fox. "It must be the secretary. He fixed the radio while deceased was upstairs. He must have dodged back to whisper through the door to Miss Tonks. I suppose he waited somewhere down here until he heard deceased blow himself to blazes and then put everything straight again, leaving the radio turned on."

Alleyn was silent.

"What do we do now, sir?" asked Fox.

"I want to see the hook inside the front-door where they hang their keys."

Fox, looking dazed, followed his superior to the little entrance hall.

"Yes, there they are," said Alleyn. He pointed to a hook with two latch-keys hanging from it. "You could scarcely miss them. Come on, Fox."

Back in the study they found Hislop with Bailey in attendance.

Hislop looked from one Yard man to another.

"I want to know if it's murder."

"We think so," said Alleyn.

"I want you to realize that Phillipa—Miss Tonks—was locked in her room all last night."

"Until her brother came home and unlocked the door," said Alleyn.

"That was too late. He was dead by then."

"How do you know when he died?"

"It must have been when there was that crash of static."

"Mr. Hislop," said Alleyn, "why would you not tell me how much that trick of licking his fingers exasperated you?"

"But—how do you know! I never told anyone."

"You told Dr. Meadows when you were ill."

"I don't remember." He stopped short. His lips trembled. Then, suddenly he began to speak.

"Very well. It's true. For two years he's tortured me. You see, he knew something about me. Two years ago when my wife was dying, I took money from the cash-box in that desk. I paid it back and thought he hadn't noticed. He knew all the time. From then on he had me where he wanted me. He used to sit there like a spider. I'd hand him a paper. He'd wet his thumbs with a clicking noise and a sort of complacent grimace. Click, click. Then he'd thumb the papers. He knew it drove me crazy. He'd look at me and then . . . click, click. And then he'd say something about the cash. He'd never quite accused me, just hinted. And I was impotent. You think I'm insane. I'm not. I could have murdered him. Often and often I've thought how I'd do it. Now you think I've done it. I haven't. There's the joke of it. I hadn't the pluck. And last night when Phillipa showed me she cared, it was like Heaven—unbelievable. For the first time since I've been here I *didn't* feel like killing him. And last night someone else *did!*"

He stood there trembling and vehement. Fox and Bailey, who had watched him with bewildered concern, turned to Alleyn. He was about to speak when Chase came in. "A note for you, sir," he said to Alleyn. "It came by hand."

Alleyn opened it and glanced at the first few words. He looked up.

"You may go, Mr. Hislop. Now I've got what I expected—what I fished for."

When Hislop had gone they read the letter.

Dear Alleyn,

Don't arrest Hislop. I did it. Let him go at once if you've arrested him and don't tell Phips you ever suspected him. I was in love with Isabel before she met Sep. I've tried to get her to divorce him, but she wouldn't because of the kids. Damned nonsense, but there's no time to discuss it now. I've got to be quick. He suspected us. He reduced her to a nervous wreck. I was afraid she'd go under altogether. I thought it all out. Some weeks ago I took Phips's key from the hook inside the front door. I had the tools and the flex and wire all ready. I knew where the main switchboard was and the cupboard. I meant to wait until they all went away at the New Year, but last night when Hislop rang me I made up my mind to act at once. He said the boys and servants were out and Phips locked in her room. I told him to stay in his room and to ring me up in half an hour if things hadn't quieted down. He didn't ring up. I did. No answer, so I knew Sep wasn't in his study.

I came round, let myself in, and listened. All quiet upstairs, but the lamp still on in the study, so I knew he would come down again. He'd said he wanted to get the midnight broadcast from somewhere.

I locked myself in and got to work. When Sep was away last year, Arthur did one of his modern monstrosities of paintings in the study. He talked about the knobs making good pattern. I noticed then that they were very like the ones on the radio and later on I tried one and saw that it would fit if I packed it up a bit. Well, I did the job just as you worked it out, and it only took twelve minutes. Then I went into the drawing-room and waited.

He came down from Isabel's room and evidently went straight to the radio. I hadn't thought it would make such a row, and half expected someone would come down. No one came. I went back, switched off the wireless, mended the fuse in the main switchboard, using my torch. Then I put everything right in the study.

There was no particular hurry. No one would come in while he was there and I got the radio going as soon as possible to suggest he was at it. I knew I'd be called in when they found him. My idea was to tell them he had died of a stroke. I'd been warning Isabel it might happen at any time. As soon as I saw the burned hand I knew that cat wouldn't jump. I'd have tried to get away with it if Chase hadn't gone round bleating about electrocution and burned fingers. Hislop saw the hand. I daren't do anything but report the case to the police, but I thought you'd never twig the knobs. One up to you.

I might have bluffed through if you hadn't suspected Hislop. Can't let you hang the blighter. I'm enclosing a note to Isabel, who won't forgive me, and an official one for you to use. You'll find me in my bedroom upstairs. I'm using cyanide. It's quick.

I'm sorry, Alleyn. I think you knew, didn't you? I've bungled the whole game, but if you will be a supersleuth . . . Goodbye.

Henry Meadows

Breakfast Television

ROBERT BARNARD

Born in Burnham-on-Crouch, Essex, England, Robert Barnard graduated from Balliol College, Oxford, and received his Ph.D. from the University of Bergen, Norway. After lecturing at universities in Australia and Norway, he published his first novel *Death of an Old Goat,* in 1974. With the novel *Sheer Torture,* published in 1981, he created his series character, Scotland Yard Detective Perry Trethowan, who has appeared in several novels since. His short fiction consists of marvelously dark humored slice of life British mysteries that often make the best of year collections, and have been nominated several times for the Edgar and the Agatha award, winning the latter in 1988 for his short short "More Final Than Divorce." He lives with his wife in Leeds, England.

The coming of Breakfast Television has been a great boon to the British.

Caroline Worsley thought so anyway, as she sat in bed eating toast and sipping tea, the flesh of her arm companionably warm against the flesh of Michael's arm. Soon they would make love again, perhaps while the consumer lady had her spot about dangerous toys, or during the review of the papers, or the resident doctor's phone-in on acne. They would do it when and how the fancy took them—or as Michael's fancy took him, for he was very imperative at times—and this implied no dislike or disrespect for the breakfast-time performer concerned. For Caroline liked them all, and could lie there quite happily watching any one of them: David the doctor, Jason the pop-chart commentator, Selma the fashion expert, Jemima the problems expert, Reg the sports round-up man, and Maria the link-up lady. And of course Ben, the link-up man.

Ben, her husband.

It had all worked out very nicely indeed. Ben was called for by the studio at four-thirty. Michael always waited for half an hour after that, in case Ben had forgotten something and made a sudden dash back to the flat for it. Michael was a serious, slightly gauche young man, who would hate to be caught out in a situation both compromising and ridiculous. Michael was that rare thing, a studious student—though very well-built too, Caroline told herself appreciatively. His interests were work, athletics, and sex. It was Caroline who had initiated him into the pleasures of regular sex. At five o'clock his alarm clock went off, though as he told Caroline, it was rarely necessary. His parents were away in Africa, dispensing aid, know-how and Oxfam beatitudes in some godforsaken part of Africa, so he was alone in their flat. He put his tracksuit on, so that in the unlikely event of his being seen in the corridor he could pretend to be going running. But he never had been. By five past he was in Caroline's flat, and in the bedroom she shared with Ben. They had almost an hour and a half of sleeping and love-making before breakfast television began.

Not that Michael watched it with the enthusiasm of Caroline. Sometimes he took a book along and read it while Caroline was drawing in her breath in horror at combustible toys, or tut-tutting at some defaulting businessman who had left his customers in the lurch. He would lie there immersed in *The Mechanics of the Money Supply* or *Some Problems of Exchange-Rate Theory*—something reasonably straight-forward, anyway, because he had to read against the voice from the set, and from time to time he was conscious of Ben looking directly at him. He never quite got used to that.

It didn't bother Caroline at all.

'Oh look, his tie's gone askew,' she would say, or: 'You know, Ben's much balder than he was twelve months ago—I've never noticed it in the flesh.' Michael seldom managed to assent to such propositions with any easy grace. He was much too conscious of balding, genial, avuncular Ben, grinning out from the television screen, as he tried to wring from some graceless pop-star three words strung together consecutively that actually made sense. 'I think he's getting fatter in the face,' said Caroline, licking marmalade off her fingers.

'I am not getting fatter in the face,' shouted Ben. 'Balder, yes, fatter in the face definitely not.' He added in a voice soaked in vitriol: 'Bitch!'

He was watching a video of yesterday's love-making on a set in his dressing-room, after the morning's television session had ended. His friend Frank, from the technical staff, had rigged up the camera in the cupboard of his study, next door to the bedroom. The small hole that was necessary in the wall had been expertly disguised. Luckily Caroline was a deplorable housewife. Eventually she might have discovered the sound apparatus under the double bed, but even then she would probably have assumed it was some junk of Ben's that he had shoved there out of harm's way. Anyway, long before then . . .

Long before then—what?

'Hypocritical swine!' yelled Ben, as he heard Caroline laughing with Michael that the Shadow Foreign Secretary had really wiped the floor with him in that interview. 'She told me when I got home yesterday how well I'd handled it.'

As the shadowy figures on the screen turned to each other again, their bare flesh glistening dully in the dim light, Ben hissed: 'Whore!'

The make-up girl concentrated on removing the traces of powder from his neck and shirt-collar, and studiously avoided comment.

'I suppose you think this is sick, don't you?' demanded Ben.

'It's none of my business,' the girl said, but added: 'If she is carrying on, it's not surprising, is it? Not with the hours we work.'

'Not surprising? I tell you, I was bloody surprised! Just think how you would feel if your husband, or bloke, was two-timing you while you were at the studio.'

'He is,' said the girl. But Ben hadn't heard. He frequently didn't hear other people when he was off camera. His comfortable, sympathetic-daddy image was something that seldom spilled over into his private life. Indeed, at his worst, he could slip up even on camera: he could be leant forwards, listening to his interviewees with appearance of the warmest interest, then reveal by his next question that he hadn't heard a word they were saying. But that happened very infrequently, and only when he was extremely preoccupied. Ben was very good at his job.

'Now they'll have tea,' he said. 'Everyone needs a tea-break in their working morning.'

Tea . . .

Shortly after this there was a break in Caroline's delicious early-morning routine: her son Malcolm came home for a long weekend from school. Michael became no more than the neighbor's son, at whom she smiled in the corridor. She and Malcolm had breakfast round the kitchen table. It was on Tuesday morning, when Malcolm was due to depart later in the day, that Ben made one of his little slips.

He was interviewing Cassy Le Beau from the long-running pop group The Crunch, and as he leaned forward to introduce a clip from the video of their latest musical crime, he said:

'Now, this is going to interest Caroline and Michael, watching at home—'

'Why did he say Michael?' asked Caroline aloud, before she could stop herself.

'He meant Malcolm,' said their son. 'Anyway, it's bloody insulting, him thinking I'd be interested in The Crunch.'

Because Malcolm was currently rehearsing Elgar's Second with the London Youth Orchestra. Ben was about two years out of date with his interests.

* * *

'Did you see that yesterday morning?' Caroline asked Michael, the next day.

'What?'

'Ben's slip on *Wake Up, Britain yesterday.'*

'I don't watch breakfast telly when I'm not with you.'

'Well, he did one of those "little messages home" that he does—you probably don't remember, but there was all this publicity about the families when *Wake Up, Britain* started, and Ben got into the habit of putting little messages to Malcolm and me into the programme. Ever so cosy and ever so bogus. Anyway, he did one yesterday, as Malcolm was home, only he said "Caroline and Michael". Not Malcolm, but Michael.'

Michael shrugged.

'Just a slip of the tongue.'

'But his own *son*, for Christ's sake! And for the slip to come out as *Michael!'*

'These things happen,' said Michael, putting his arm around her and pushing her head back on to the pillow. 'Was there a Michael on the show yesterday?'

'There was Michael Heseltine on, as usual.'

'There you are, you see.'

'But Heseltine's an ex-cabinet minister. He would *never* call him Michael.'

'But the name was in his head. These things happen. Remember, Ben's getting old.'

'True,' said Caroline, who was two years younger than her husband.

'Old!' shouted Ben, dabbing at his artificially-darkened eyebrows, one eye on the screen. 'You think I'm old? I'll show you I've still got some bolts left in my locker.'

He had dispensed with the services of the make-up girl. He had been the only regular on *Wake Up, Britain* to demand one anyway, and the studio was surprised but pleased when Ben decided she was no longer required. Now he could watch the previous evening's cavortings without the damper of her adolescent disapproval from behind his shoulder.

And now he could plan.

One of the factors that just had to be turned to his advantage was Caroline's deplorable housekeeping. All the table-tops of the kitchen were littered with bits of this and that—herbs, spices, sauces, old margarine tubs, bits of jam on dishes. The fridge was like the basement of the Victoria and Albert Museum, and the freezer was a record of their married life. And on the window-ledge in the kitchen were the things he used to do his little bit of gardening . . .

Ben and Caroline inhabited one of twenty modern service flats in a block. Most of the gardening was done by employees of the landlords, yet some little patches were allotted to tenants who expressed an interest. Ben had always kept up his patch, though (as was the way of such things) it was more productive of self-satisfaction than of fruit or veg. 'From our own garden', he would say, as he served his guests horrid little bowls of red currants.

Already on the window-ledge in the kitchen there was a little bottle of paraquat.

That afternoon he pottered around in his mouldy little patch. By the time he had finished and washed his hands under the kitchen tap the paraquat had found its way next to the box of tea-bags standing by the kettle. The top of the paraquat was loose, having been screwed only about half way round.

'Does you good to get out on your own patch of earth,' Ben observed to Caroline, as he went through to his study.

The next question that presented itself was: when? There were all sorts of possibilities—including that the police would immediately arrest him for murder, he was reconciled to that—but he thought that on the whole it would be best to do it on the morning when he was latest home. Paraquat could be a long time in taking effect, he knew, but there was always a chance that they would not decide to call medical help until it was too late. If he was to come home to a poisoned wife and lover in the flat, he wanted them to be well and truly dead. Wednesday was the day when all the Breakfast TV team met in committee to hear what was planned for the next week: which ageing star would be plugging her memoirs, which singer plugging his forthcoming British tour. Wednesdays Ben often didn't get home till early afternoon. Wednesday it was.

Tentatively in his mental engagements book he pencilled in Wednesday, May 15.

Whether the paraquat would be in the teapot of the Teasmade, or in the tea-bag, or how it would be administered, was a minor matter that he could settle long before the crucial Tuesday night when the tea-things for the morning had to be got ready. The main thing was that everything was decided.

May 15—undoubtedly a turning-point in her life—began badly for Caroline. First of all Ben kissed her goodbye before he set off for the studio, something he had not done since the early days of his engagement on Breakfast Television. Michael had come in at five o'clock as usual, but his love-making was forced, lacking in tenderness. Caroline lay there for an hour in his arms afterwards, wondering if anything was worrying him. He didn't say anything for some time—not till the television was switched on. Probably he relied on the bromides and the plugs to distract Caroline's attention from what he was going to say.

He had taken up his textbook, and the kettle of the Teasmade was beginning to hum, when he said, in his gruff, teenage way:

'Won't be much more of this.'

Caroline was watching clips from a Frank Bruno fight, and not giving him her full attention. When it was over, she turned to him:

'Sorry—what did you say?'

'I said there won't be much more of this.'

A dagger went to her heart, which seemed to stop beating for minutes. When she could speak, the words came out terribly middle-class-matron.

'I don't quite understand. Much more of what?'

'This. You and me together in the mornings.'

'You don't mean your parents are coming home early?'

'No. I've . . . got a flat. Nearer college. So there's not so much travelling in the morning and evenings.'

'You're just *moving out?'*

'Pretty much so. Can't live with my parents for ever.'

Caroline's voice grew louder and higher.

'You're not living with your parents. It's six months before they come home. You're moving out *on me*. Do you have the impression that I'm the sort of person you can just move in with when it suits you, and then flit away from when it doesn't suit you any longer?'

'Well . . . yes, actually. I'm a free agent.'

'You *bas*tard! You *bas*tard!'

She would have liked to take him by the shoulder and shake him till the teeth rattled in his head. Instead she sat there on the bed, coldly furious. It was 7.15. The kettle whistled and poured boiling water on to the tea-bags in the teapot.

'Have some tea or coffee,' said Ben on the screen to his politician guest, with a smile that came out as a death's head grin. 'It's about early morning tea-time.'

'It's someone else, isn't it?' finally said Caroline, her voice kept steady with difficulty. 'A new girlfriend.'

'All right, it's a new girlfriend,' agreed Michael.

'Someone younger.'

'Of course someone younger,' said Michael, taking up his book again, and sinking into monetarist theory.

Silently Caroline screamed: *Of course someone younger*: What the hell's that supposed to mean? They don't come any older than you? Of course I was just passing the time with a crone like you until someone my own age came along?

'You're moving in with a girl,' she said, the desolation throbbing in her voice.

'Yeah,' said Michael, from within his Hayek.

'Tea all right?' Ben asked his guest.

Caroline sat there, watching the flickering images on the screen, while the tea in the pot turned from hot to warm. The future spread before her like a desert—a future as wife and mother. What kind of life was that, for God's sake? For some odd reason a future as *lover* had seemed, when she had thought about it at all, fulfilling, traditional and dignified. Now any picture she might have of the years to come was turned into a hideous, mocking, negative image, just as the body beside her in the bed had turned from a glamorous sex object into a boorish, ungrateful teenager.

They were having trouble in the *Wake Up, Britain* studio, where the two anchor people had got mixed up as to who was introducing what. Caroline focused on the screen: she always enjoyed it when Ben muffed something.

'Sorry,' said Ben, smiling his kindly-uncle smile. 'I thought it was Maria, but in fact it's me. Let's see . . . I know it's David, our resident medico, but actually I don't know what your subject is today, David.'

'Poison,' said David.

But the camera had not switched to him, and the instant he dropped the word into the ambient atmosphere Caroline (and one million other viewers) saw Ben's jaw drop, and an expression of panic flash like lightning through his eyes.

'I've had a lot of letters from parents of small children,' said David, in his calm, everything-will-be-all-right voice, 'about what to do if the kids get hold of poison. Old medicines, household detergents, gardening stuff—they can all be dangerous, and some can be deadly.' Caroline saw Ben, the camera still agonizingly on him, swallow hard and put his hand up to his throat. Then, mercifully, the producer changed the shot at last to the doctor, leaning forward and doing his thing. 'So here are a few basic rules about what to do in that sort of emergency . . .'

Caroline's was not a quick mind, but suddenly a succession of images came together: Ben's kiss that morning, his smile as he offered his guest early morning tea, a bottle of paraquat standing next to the box of tea-bags in the kitchen, Ben's dropping jaw at the sudden mention of poison.

'Michael,' she said.

'What?' he asked, hardly bothering to take his head out of his book.

She looked at the self-absorbed, casually cruel body, and her blood boiled.

'Oh, nothing,' she said. 'Let's have tea. It'll be practically cold by now.'

She poured two cups, and handed him his. He put aside his book, which he had hardly been reading, congratulating himself in his mind on having got out of this so lightly. He took the cup, and sat on the bed watching the screen, where the sports man was now introducing highlights of last night's athletics meeting from Oslo.

'Boy!' said Michael appreciatively, stirring his tea. 'That was a great run!'

He took a great gulp of the tea, then hurriedly put the cup down, turned to look at Caroline, and then choked.

Caroline had not taken up her tea, but sat there looking at the graceless youth. Round her lips there played a smile of triumphal revenge—a smile that the camera whirring away in the secrecy of the study cupboard perfectly caught for Ben, and for the criminal court that tried them, ironically, together.

An Unmentionable Death

SIMON BRETT

Simon Brett is adept at both the traditional mystery as well as the historical, his recent novels include *Mrs. Pargeter's Plot* and *Sicken and So Die.* His main series features Charles Paris, an actor as well as amateur detective, stumbling into the middle of crimes usually set against the backdrop of the London theater scene. His other series concerns the mysterious Mrs. Pargeter, a detective who skirts the edge of the law in her unusual investigations. He's also quite accomplished in the short form as well, with stories appearing in the *Malice Domestic* series, as well as the anthologies *Once Upon a Crime* and *Funny Bones.* A winner of the Writer's Guild of Great Britain award for his radio plays, he has also written non-fiction books and edited several books in the Faber series, including *The Faber Book of Useful Verse* and *The Faber Book of Parodies.* He lives in Burpham, England.

Harriet Chailey rang the doorbell of Number 73, Drefford Road. It was a large Edwardian house in that part of the city where property prices had rocketed in the last decade. Through the open doors of the garage she could see the discreet chromium gleam of a vintage Bentley.

Two undergraduates, propped on their bicycles in the street behind her, indulged in the common delusion of their age that the whole world wanted to hear what they had to say. They talked loudly of a party that evening, anatomising its probable guest list. The banter was comfortingly familiar. It seemed such a short time ago that she had been in the town to visit Dickie, Dickie before he took his degree, before he started his research. Dickie had talked just like that in those days, in the days before he became obsessed by his subject, in the days when there had been room in his life for something other than work.

But that had been more than five years ago. And now, as she had to remind herself so many times in the last three days, Dickie was dead.

She felt again the surge of guilt. She should have kept more closely in touch with her younger brother after their parents died. But it had become decreasingly easy to do so. Of latter years it had been almost impossible to get Dickie talking about anything outside his subject. That subject—some detail of Old French syntax—was so obscure that people incautious enough to enquire about it condemned themselves to a half-hour lecture.

Mind you, Dickie had been good at it. A world expert. Invited to conferences all over the globe—Tokyo, San Francisco, even Paris—to give lectures about the subject. Apparently highly respected in academic circles. But, for the average member of the public—that is, for anyone with interests outside that particular crux of Old French syntax—there were no two ways about it, Dickie's obsession had turned him into a bore.

Though maybe, Harriet thought wryly, he wasn't alone in that. A family failing . . . ? She knew she was equally single-minded about her own work at the British Embassy in Rome. Get her on to her special subject and perhaps the effect wasn't so very different . . .

If only they had both relaxed sometimes. Let up for a while. Thought about other things. Taken time to bridge their eight-year age difference, time to get to know each other.

It was too late now for such hopes.

The door of 73 Drefford Road opened to reveal a man in his fifties. He was tweed-suited and round-faced, with white hair worn almost rakishly long. He looked at her quizzically, unsurprised by a visit from a stranger but with no idea as to who she might be.

'Good afternoon. I'm Harriet Chailey,' she announced in her startlingly deep, almost masculine voice.

His face instantly composed itself into an expression of compassion.

'I'm so dreadfully sorry about what happened. Do come in.' He ushered her across a tall hallway, heavy with dark wood, into a sitting room of subsided leather chairs and piles of overspilling files, rather like the staff room of a prep school. Naive paintings of South American origin hung on the walls, between framed photographs of vintage Bentley rallies.

'My name's Michael Brewer. I was Richard's . . . well, landlord I suppose I have to say, but I hope his friend, too. Do sit down.'

'Thank you.'

'Could I get you a cup of tea? Or coffee if you'd rather . . . ?'

'No, thank you. I've only just finished lunch.'

'Ah.' He perched diffidently on the arm of a sofa. 'I don't know if Richard ever mentioned me to you in his letters or . . . ?'

'No. No, we didn't correspond that much, I'm afraid. Rather lost touch over the last few years.'

'Yes. Well, of course. Otherwise I'd have known you were his next-of-kin and wouldn't have dreamed of making the arrangements so quickly or . . .'

He petered out, embarrassed, and then, although Harriet had made no accusation, returned to his own defence.

'I feel dreadful. It's just that he'd never mentioned having any family while he was living here. No one in college seemed to know much about his background. He kept himself to himself.'

'Yes.'

'And since very few people came to visit him here—and those who did were . . . well, didn't seem to be close friends . . . To put it bluntly, it seemed as though I was the nearest to a friend he had, so when it came to funeral arrangements, I thought the quicker everything was sorted out, the better.'

Harriet nodded firmly. 'I am very grateful to you.'

'Take my word for it, please, Miss Chailey, that, had I had any idea that Richard had a sister, I wouldn't have—'

'Of course not. Don't worry. It's just unfortunate. One of those things.'

'Yes.'

But Michael Brewer didn't look fully comforted. His expression remained anxious, and Harriet felt she should try to put him at his ease. After all, the man had done more than many would have done in the circumstances.

'I really *am* very grateful to you, Mr Brewer. At least somebody saw to it that my brother had a proper funeral.'

'Yes.' He shrugged. 'Well, it was the least I could do.'

'Hm. Was it in the college chapel?'

'The funeral?'

'Yes.'

Michael Brewer looked embarrassed. 'No. No.'

'Oh.' Some instinct restrained Harriet from pursuing this. 'I would like to see Dickie's—Richard's—grave, Mr Brewer. You know, I mean, pay my last respects, as it were . . .'

His embarrassment grew. 'I'm sorry. Your brother's funeral was at a crematorium and . . .'

'Ah.' Somehow this was the greatest shock. When the news had come through to the Embassy three days before, she had been knocked sideways, but she had clung on to the image of Dickie's body, the thought that, even though he was dead, there was something of him left. But now she knew even that perverse comfort to be illusory.

Firmly, remembering her diplomatic training, she shifted the conversation away from this emotive area. 'Are you connected with the university yourself, Mr Brewer?'

'I used to teach a certain amount,' he acknowledged. 'But, as you have probably read in the press, there have been a lot of cutbacks in education recently. I'm afraid three years ago I was found to be "surplus to requirements".'

'Oh, I'm sorry,' she said formally. 'What was your subject?'

'Spanish.'

Harriet gestured to the walls. 'Hence the paintings?'

'Yes. I still go to South America most summers.'

'Really? I was posted to Bogota for a while some years back.'

'Ah?'

'I'm in the Foreign Office,' she explained.

He nodded. 'I don't know Bogota well. Only ever spent a few days there.'

'Oh.'

The small talk was slowly to a standstill. There was no point in further evasion. 'Mr Brewer,' asked Harriet with characteristic directness, 'how did my brother die?'

'Erm . . .'

'I mean, what did he die of?'

The man's embarrassment was now painful to witness. 'I think,' he said eventually, 'it said "Pneumonia" on the death certificate. But you'd have to ask his doctor if you want the full details.'

Dr Hart, like his surgery, was a bit run-down and seedy. He and his sports jacket looked tired, as if they had both seen enough of sickbeds and symptoms. He had a full waiting room of coughers and complainers and students with psychosomatic essay crises. The way he kept glancing at his watch left Harriet in no doubt that she had been squeezed in on sufferance.

'Your brother first came to see me about three months ago, I suppose. Complaining of gastric trouble. Diarrhoea, occasional vomiting, he said. I prescribed for him, but he didn't seem to get better. Came in a couple more times, still no improvement. Towards the end I went and saw him at the house. But by then the pneumonia had set in and . . .'

The doctor shrugged. Another case ended as all cases will eventually end. The only difference was with this one the end had come a little earlier than might have been expected.

'But surely he should have gone into hospital?' Harriet protested.

Dr Hart nodded wearily. 'I tried to persuade him to go in when he came to the surgery. I wanted some tests done. But he didn't want to know about it. Said he hadn't got the time . . .'

'Had to get on with his work . . .'

'Yes. That was it. And by the last time I saw him, I'm afraid he was beyond tests.' The doctor sighed. 'I'm sorry, Miss Chailey, but if a patient's determined *not* to look after himself, there's not a lot we doctors can do about it.'

'No. And there wasn't a post-mortem?'

'There was no need. I had seen your brother just before he died. It wasn't a case of a sudden, unexplained illness.'

'No.' Harriet was silent for a moment. 'Dr Hart, what do you think made him ill?'

The reply was brusque almost to the point of rudeness. 'Self-neglect. As I said, he didn't look after himself. God knows what he ate or when he ate it. I think Mr Brewer tried to make him eat the occasional proper meal, but most of the time . . . He just let himself go, I'm afraid. And under those circumstances, he would be prey to any infection that came along. He had so weakened himself by the end that the slightest chill could have turned to pneumonia. Your brother led a rather eccentric life, Miss Chailey.' Another, undisguised, look at the watch. 'And now, if you'll excuse me . . .'

Harriet rose from her chair. At the door she stopped.

'You are telling me everything you know, Dr Hart, aren't you?'

'Yes,' he replied gruffly, turning his attention to the pile of notes on his desk. 'Of course I am.'

'It just seems so sad,' Harriet said, pausing in her removal of books from shelves and looking across the chaos of paper covering her late brother's room, 'that Dickie never got married. I'm sure if he'd had someone else to think about, he wouldn't have got so immersed in his work. I mean, no wife would have let him get *that* immersed, would she?'

'No,' Michael Brewer concurred gently.

'You didn't see any evidence of girl friends? I mean, no one came around on a regular basis . . . ?'

'Very few people on any sort of basis.'

'No. It seems as if my brother was completely sexless.'

Michael Brewer grunted agreement.

Harriet sighed. 'I know there are people like that. But as a child he was always lively . . . sociable. He must have been dreadfully lonely.'

'I honestly don't think he was,' said Michael Brewer, offering what comfort he could. 'I think his work so absorbed him that he didn't really notice whether he was with people or on his own.'

'Hm. It's strange. Somehow, now, the work itself just seems irrelevant.' She picked another book off the shelf. 'I mean, I can't even understand the titles of these—God knows what I'd make of the contents. No doubt they're worth quite a lot, but certainly not to the average man in the street.'

'No.'

'Do you think there'd be any chance of getting rid of them through the university? I mean, one of the libraries . . . someone working in the same field . . . ?'

'I'm sure that'd be possible. Would you like me to handle it, Miss Chailey?'

'Well, if you wouldn't mind, I'd be extremely grateful.'

'No problem. Would you be hoping to make some money from the sale?'

'Oh, goodness, no. Just so long as they go somewhere where they're appreciated.'

'Of course.'

She looked round the room with a kind of hopelessness. 'He didn't really have much, did he? I mean, all these files and books and journals, yes, but not much personal stuff.'

'No. Obviously there are his clothes and . . . Do you want to check through all those?'

'No, no. I'll give them to Oxfam or . . .'

'Would you like me to organise that, too?'

'Well, it does seem rather an imposition . . .'

'Not at all. I'm on the spot. It's quite easy for me. And you said you had to get back to Rome . . .'

'Yes, I told them it would only be a few days. Compassionate leave.'

The thought of all the work piling up in her office came to her with sudden urgency. And the Ambassador was giving that party on Saturday. There's no way they'd get it all organised properly without her. Hm, there was a good flight the following afternoon. . . .

'Look, you leave it all with me,' Michael Brewer said soothingly. 'If you're sure there's nothing you want . . . ?'

'Well, I'd better keep looking. There might be some odd family photographs or . . .'

'Stay as long as you like. It's no problem.'

'Thanks.'

Harriet yawned, and sneaked a look at her watch. Nearly eight o'clock. Been a long couple of days. Still, she should really keep checking through. There might be something, some memory to keep open the book of her brother's life.

But the thought of the next afternoon's flight had lodged in her mind. Just another half-hour here, she thought with a hint of guilt, and then back to the hotel. Quick dinner, early night and train to London in the morning. There was nothing for her here.

'Mr Brewer,' she asked diffidently, 'about Dickie's illness . . .'

The man stiffened. 'Yes . . . ?'

'How long was he actually bedridden at the end?'

'I suppose about three weeks.'

'And was he eating properly then?'

'Well, I tried to make him, but he wasn't interested. And when he did eat something, he had difficulty keeping it down.'

'It was very good of you to look after him.'

Michael Brewer shrugged. 'Only sorry I wasn't more effective.'

'And he kept on working?'

'Yes. Right to the end. I tried to persuade him to stop, to go into hospital, but . . . he was very strong-willed.'

'Yes.'

The doorbell rang. With a muttered 'Excuse me', Michael Brewer went downstairs. He left the door open, and Harriet could hear the conversation from the hall.

First, Michael Brewer's urbane 'Good evening'.

Then an unexpected voice. Young, rough, slightly furtive.

'Oh, hello. I was given this address by a friend.'

'Really?'

'Friend called Rod.'

'Oh?' Apparently the name meant nothing to Michael Brewer.

'He said this was the place to come to. . . . Said there was someone here who—'

'I'm sorry. You've been misinformed. I think you have the wrong address. There's no one here who can help you.'

Intrigued by the conversation, Harriet had been drawn to the doorway of Dickie's room. Through the banisters she could see the visitor at the front door. A boy in his late teens, spiked black punk hair, torn denim jeans and jacket. A haunted face, an air of twitchiness, but, as well, a kind of insolence.

As she looked, Michael Brewer closed the front door. Harriet went back hastily into the room and, to look busy, knelt down by a pile of files at the foot of a bookcase. She tugged to dislodge them, and released a pile of glossy magazines from under the files.

She opened one.

In spite of her occasionally spinsterish manner, Harriet Chailey's experience of life had been broader than might be supposed. She recognised pornography when she saw it.

But she had never seen pornography like this before. There were no female bodies in the pictures. They were all men.

She reached further under the bookcase and pulled out a thin cigar box. Lifting the lid revealed a couple of plastic syringes, some blood-stained bandages and a small polythene bag with dregs of white powder at the bottom.

'Ah.'

She turned to see Michael Brewer framed in the doorway. His face was a mask of pity.

'I'm sorry,' he said. 'I thought I'd got rid of all that stuff. I was hoping you wouldn't have to find out about it.'

'What?' asked Harriet, bewildered. 'Do you mean that Dickie died from a drug overdose?'

'No,' Michael Brewer replied sadly. 'No. That wasn't it.'

'I still find it hard to believe,' said Harriet. 'I mean, from what I remember of Dickie . . .'

'You said you hadn't seen him for a long time . . .' Michael Brewer's voice was gentle and compassionate.

'True.'

'And you said it seemed odd that there was no sexual dimension to his life . . .'

'Yes . . .'

'No, I'm sorry. From the time he moved in, there was no question about it.'

'Oh.'

'Boys used to call here. Ask any of the neighbours. Young men calling late at night. For your brother.'

'I see.' A thought struck her. 'You mean . . . was that young man this evening . . . ?'

Michael Brewer nodded. 'I'm sorry. I really didn't want you to find out about it.'

'Better I should know.'

'Why? Why do you say that? I'd have thought you'd got enough to come to terms with—just having heard your brother's died—without *this*.'

'No. I want to find out as much as I can about him. I regret I didn't get to know him better while he was alive. Now I just want to find out everything about Dickie.'

'Ah.'

'Maybe it's my way of coping with the bereavement.'

'Maybe . . .' Michael Brewer shook his head sorrowfully. 'I think you may just be making more pain for yourself.'

'Perhaps I need the pain. As a kind of expiation. Punishment for not having got to know him while he was alive.'

Michael Brewer nodded, accepting this interpretation.

'Why didn't Dr Hart tell me?'

'We discussed it, Miss Chailey. We both felt the less people who knew, the better.'

'That was not very professional of him, as a doctor.'

'Perhaps not. But as a human being . . . well, it was at least compassionate.'

'Yes.' Harriet looked at her watch. 'He wouldn't still be at the surgery, would he?'

'No.'

'Do you have his home phone number?'

'Yes,' said Michael Brewer, with a rueful nod.

'Are you saying you didn't make the diagnosis straight away?'

'All right, I am, yes.' Dr Hart's voice was testy. He was annoyed enough at being rung at home; and now to have his professional expertise questioned was even more annoying. 'Look, Miss Chailey, have you any idea how many patients I see in a day? I get them all through—pensioners with arthritis, menopausal women, students with God knows what problems. Sex, depression, drugs—have you any idea of the scale of the drugs problem in this university? And it just gets worse and worse, because the pushers never seem to get caught—or as soon as one is caught, another two appear to take his place.

'Well, as a result of all this, there's not a lot of time, you know. So, on the whole, as a doctor, you go for the obvious. Someone comes in complaining of diarrhoea, you tend to prescribe something for diarrhoea. Look, for God's sake, until just before he died, I didn't even know your brother was homosexual.'

'Nor did I.'

'No. Well, there you are. You grew up with him and didn't know. I met him for what . . . three . . . four ten-minute consultations? So how am I expected to know every detail of his life?'

'I see your point. I mean the drugs thing . . . that's the biggest shock to me. He used to be so anti-drugs. Really priggish about it. Still, I suppose I'm talking about a long time ago.'

'People change.'

'Yes. Did you know about his drug habit?'

'Again, not till the end, no. If I had known, I might have been able to do something about it.'

'Did Michael Brewer tell you?'

'No. God, he tried to keep it from me. He did everything to try and stop me from finding out.'

'Why?'

'Because he was a good friend to your brother.'

'He wasn't more than that, was he?'

'What do you mean?'

Michael Brewer had left Harriet discreetly alone in his study to make the phone call, so she felt she could risk this line of questioning. 'Well,' she continued, 'we've established that Dickie was gay . . .'

'No. Absolutely not. I'm certain Michael isn't. No, he's just that rarity in this day and age—a good man. He found himself in the situation of having a sick man on his hands, and he just did his best to look after that sick man.'

'But if Michael didn't tell you, how did you find out about the drugs?'

'I . . . came across some stuff in your brother's room. Syringes, what have you . . .' Just as I did, thought Harriet, as the doctor went on, 'Michael Brewer wasn't even there at the time.'

'Did you talk to Dickie about it?'

'No. He was too far gone with the pneumonia by then. Virtually unconscious.'

'But surely that was the time to get him into hospital?'

'Look, Miss Chailey, your brother was going to die. There was nothing I could do about it, nothing anyone could do about it at that stage. I agreed with Michael Brewer that it would be more compassionate to let him die in his own surroundings than in the exposed anonymity of a hospital ward.'

'And was another consideration the fact that you didn't want your failure to be known to the hospital doctors?'

'Failure? What do you mean, Miss Chailey?'

'I mean your failure to diagnose earlier what was really wrong with Dickie.'

There was a silence from the other end of the line. Then, grudgingly, Dr Hart conceded, 'All right. Yes. I should have been alert to it, and I wasn't. As I say, so many people come through the surgery. With some types you're immediately suspicious. You spot them as high-risk the minute they walk in. But with someone like your brother . . . who seemed so . . . well, eccentric, yes, but otherwise quite ordinary . . . I mean, the last person you would associate with either homosexuality or drugs.'

'True,' Harriet agreed. 'And it was because you didn't want your mistake shown up that you signed the death certificate with "Pneumonia" and—?'

'Pneumonia was what he died of,' Dr Hart objected.

'All right, that was what he died of, but it wasn't what killed him.'

'You're splitting hairs.'

'No, I'm not.' Harriet pressed on relentlessly. 'And for the same reason you were happy to see the funeral arrangements made as quickly as possible? Happy that he should be cremated? To destroy the evidence of your blunder?'

'All right. If that's how you choose to put it, yes.'

There was a silence after this admission. Then the doctor came again to his own defence. 'Listen, Miss Chailey, I don't feel particularly proud of how I've behaved over this. But AIDS is a new disease, it's currently an incurable disease, about which your average GP—and I've never claimed to be more than your average GP—knows very little. Now, if a known drug addict—or one of the local rent boys—comes into my surgery complaining of diarrhoea or weight loss . . . all right, I'm on my guard. With someone like your brother . . .' he repeated, 'when he comes in with something that could be caused by food poisoning or one of any number of viruses, well . . .'

'Yes.' Harriet sighed. Through her anger and frustration, she couldn't help seeing the doctor's point of view. 'And how do you suppose my brother contracted it?' she asked dully.

'Take your pick. Given his promiscuous active homosexuality . . . given the fact that he'd been to a conference in San Francisco within the last year . . . given the drug habit . . . given all the facts I didn't know about him until just before he died . . . he was a prime target.'

'Yes.' Harriet felt empty and listless. 'Well, thank you, Doctor, for telling me the truth.'

'I'm sorry I didn't tell you first time round, but . . . Quite honestly, I really didn't think it was necessary for you to know something that could only cause you pain.'

'Thanks for the thought.'

The doctor cleared his throat at the other end of the line. 'If it's any comfort to you, Miss Chailey,' he said, 'you've made me feel an incompetent old fool.'

Harriet wasn't hungry when she got back to her hotel that night. The quick dinner she had been promising herself had lost its appeal. So had the early night. The revelations of the evening had made sleep a very distant possibility.

Even the next day's flight to Rome had become remote and unimportant. The Ambassador's party on Saturday had lost its urgency. It would still happen somehow, whether she was there or not.

The fact that her brother had died of AIDS made everything else seem trivial.

She had found almost nothing of personal relevance in his room. Just his keys. Still, she noticed with a pang as she put them in her handbag, that they were attached to the brass Italian key ring she had given him for a birthday in the days when they still remembered each other's birthdays.

Ironically, the only other items she had brought from 73 Drefford Road were the gay magazines and the box of drug equipment. In a perverse way, as if it made any difference at this stage of her brother's life (or rather death), she felt she should remove this incriminating evidence from his room.

She glanced through the magazines, not disgusted or intrigued by their contents, just bewildered. And bewildered at the sidelights they offered on her brother's life. How little she had known him.

The magazines, she noticed, went in sequence. Published every month. Dickie's collection covered the last six months. Maybe there had once been other back-numbers. Michael Brewer had implied that he had checked through the room to remove all the evidence of homosexuality he could find. He had presumably only missed this lot because they were jammed under the files.

Abstractedly, trying to control and organise her thoughts, Harriet placed the magazines in order. She put down the oldest first. Six months ago, five months, four months, three months, two months. Then the latest.

She looked at the cover of the most recent magazine and felt a sudden dryness in her mouth. Oh my God, she thought.

The taxi driver seemed confused by her request.

'It's not that I don't know where to take you,' he said. 'It's just you don't seem the sort to want to go there.'

'I know where I want to go,' said Harriet, firmness as ever further deepening her husky voice.

This seemed to explain things for the taxi driver. 'Oh,' he said to her considerable amusement, 'I get it. You're one of them transsexuals, aren't you?'

It was a small pub behind the bus station. 'Small and run-down. Outside motor bikes clustered like insects round a rotten fruit.

Harriet's determination was so strong that she didn't stop to think how incongruous her smart Italian coat must look amidst the studded leather and frayed denim of the interior. As she ordered a red wine, she was unaware of the quizzical eyebrows of thc car-ringed and heavily moustached barman, or of the open amazement and muttered comments of the other drinkers.

She looked eagerly round the bar. There were a few other women, though their livid, streak-dyed hair and black vampire make-up gave them the look of another species from her own. But most of the occupants of the bar were male. Young men with blonded hair and haggard eyes, shrieking jokey insults at each other. Thickset men in heavy leathers. Older men in furtive raincoats.

She tried to imagine Dickie in this environment. She tried to picture the young man she remembered from her childhood leaning twitchily against the bar like these other men, but her mind could not encompass the image.

And then she saw it.

A familiar, haunted face. Pained and putty-coloured under black spiked hair. The boy sat alone, uninterested in the half of beer in his hand. His eyes darted anxiously around the bar.

Harriet Chailey moved across to sit beside him. He gave no sign of having noticed her.

She touched his arm. He recoiled as if she'd burnt him, and the sunken, paranoid eyes found hers.

'What do you want?' he hissed.

'I want to talk to you.'

'I haven't done nothing wrong. I haven't got nothing on me.'

Their dialogue was attracting attention from the drinkers around them, who seemed to bristle and move almost imperceptibly closer. The atmosphere was not friendly.

'I just want to talk,' Harriet persisted, again placing a gentle hand on the boy's denim sleeve.

This time he sprang to his feet, and a flicker of menace went through the watching crowd.

'I'll pay you,' said Harriet.

The hollow eyes turned back to her.

'Money?'

She nodded.

'How much?'

'Twenty pounds.'

The boy nodded, and sat back down again. As he did so, he flicked a message with his head to the protective crowd around him. They relaxed and returned to their drinks.

'What do you want to know?' he asked truculently.

'I want to know about Seventy-three Drefford Road,' said Harriet.

Michael Brewer came back from the shops the next morning and let himself in through the front door of 73 Drefford Road. As he closed it, he was shocked to hear a deep female voice from the top of the stairs.

'Good morning.'

He spun round to face her. 'Miss Chailey.'

'I apologise for letting myself in. I had Dickie's keys.'

'Of course. I must confess to being somewhat surprised to see you. I understood that you were catching a plane back to Rome this afternoon.'

'That was my intention, yes.'

'And can I ask what made you change your mind?'

'If you come up to Dickie's room, I'll tell you.'

'Very well.' Michael Brewer nodded slowly. 'Will you just allow me to put my shopping in the kitchen?'

'Of course.'

'Can I offer you a cup of coffee or anything of the sort?'

'No, thank you.'

Harriet was sitting in an armchair in front of the bathroom door when Michael Brewer entered his late tenant's room. 'Now,' he asked amiably, apparently unperturbed by her trespass, 'what is this? Is there something else of Richard's you want to look for? Or something you've found and want to show me . . . ?'

'This is the only thing I want to show you.' She indicated the latest edition of the gay magazine on the table beside her.

'Oh?'

'But time enough for that. Do sit down.'

'Thank you,' said Michael Brewer, acting on the invitation.

'I'm sorry. It's ridiculous my offering you a chair in your own house.'

He shrugged to indicate that he was unworried by this social solecism. 'Well, now . . . ?' He raised a quizzical eyebrow.

'I just wanted to say how much care you put into looking after Dickie, and . . .'

He made a gesture of self-depreciation. 'The least I could do.'

'Yes. How soon did you realise what was actually wrong with him?'

'I didn't have any suspicions until near the end. I should have thought of it earlier. You know, knowing the life he led. I mean, when he started getting recurrent diarrhoea . . .'

'Losing weight . . .'

'Yes. And also getting this sort of skin infection. . . . I should have put two and two together. . . . But I'm afraid I didn't. Until it was too late.'

'Do you think Dickie himself knew what was wrong with him?'

'No, I'm sure he had no idea. Right up to the end. I certainly didn't say anything about it to him. I wanted to spare him as much pain as I could.'

'That was very thoughtful.'

'Well . . . Anyway, Richard didn't really think about his health. For him being ill was just an inconvenience . . .'

'Something that kept him from the dissection of Old French syntax?'

'Precisely.'

'It was unfortunate, Mr Brewer, that Dr Hart didn't spot what was really wrong with Dickie.'

'Yes. Perhaps it was.'

'Didn't you feel that you should share your suspicions with him the minute you realised what it was?'

'I did think about that, yes. But, quite honestly—and this may have been very wrong of me—by the time I realised what was happening, which was very near the end, I thought it better to keep quiet. I mean, the point is, with AIDS, there is no cure. Richard was under a death sentence from the moment he contracted the dreadful thing. And, given a choice between having a load of tests, being labelled as a plague victim, being hospitalised—and the alternative, which was dying with a degree of dignity . . .'

'And in ignorance . . .'

'Yes. Well, I'm afraid I chose the second course.'

'Hm.' Harriet looked pensive. 'It's a strange disease, AIDS. Nobody yet knows much about it.'

'No. That's what makes it so terrifying.'

'Yes. There have even been cases of pathologists refusing to do post-mortems on AIDS victims.'

'So I've heard.'

'And I dare say ordinary doctors aren't immune from that kind of fear. They're only human, after all. I dare say some of them would rather not investigate an AIDS patient too closely.'

'Maybe not.'

'And be quite happy if the victim's body is disposed of as soon as possible without too many questions asked.'

'I suppose that could happen, yes.'

'The other strange thing is that a lot of the symptoms—at least the early symptoms—could be mistaken for all kinds of other ailments.'

'So I believe.'

'Did you know, for instance,' said Harriet suddenly, 'that systematic poisoning could produce a lot of the same symptoms as AIDS?'

There was a half-beat pause before Michael Brewer replied, 'No. No, I didn't.'

'Arsenic, for instance.'

'Really?'

'Oh yes. Diarrhoea . . . vomiting . . . weight-loss certainly, because the victim can't keep anything down . . . discoloration of the skin . . . dermatitis—all classic symptoms of arsenic poisoning. So long as the case wasn't investigated too closely, it would be quite easy to confuse the symptoms.'

'Oh.' Michael Brewer smiled urbanely. 'What a mine of information you are, Miss Chailey. I'm sure you're very good at Trivial Pursuits.'

'Thank you. Yes, I'm not bad at it.'

'But, of course, I believe that nowadays it is extremely difficult to obtain arsenic in this country, so I can't imagine that the confusion you describe would be very likely ever to occur in real life.'

'No. No. Mind you, in other countries arsenic is still relatively easy to obtain.'

'Really? Another Trivial Pursuit answer?'

'No. All I'm saying is that smuggling arsenic into this country would be quite as easy as—perhaps even easier than—smuggling in other illegal substances.'

Michael Brewer was icily silent. When he finally spoke, there was a new cold detachment in his voice. 'May I ask precisely what you're saying, Miss Chailey?'

"What I'm saying is that there is a lot of drug abuse in this city. In the university and with the local youngsters . . .'

'So I've heard.'

'And the young people must get their supplies from somewhere . . .'

'Presumably.'

'One of their sources is this address. Seventy-three Drefford Road.'

'What?' His face was suddenly pale. 'Where did you hear that from?'

'A young addict.'

'You can't believe what they say!'

'I believed this one. He was the boy who came round here last night.'

'He wasn't looking for drugs. He was—'

Harriet overruled him. 'The boy was looking for drugs. He told me. Oh, you played it very cleverly, yes. You made it seem as if he was a rent boy coming round looking for Dickie. But he wasn't. He was after drugs. Just like all the other late-night visitors to this house.'

'But your brother—'

'My brother wasn't homosexual.'

'Look, I know it's hard for you to believe that a member of your family—'

'You can stop all that, Mr Brewer. There's no point in trying to maintain that pretence any longer. I know what's been going on here.'

'Oh?' The voice was icier than ever.

'You've been smuggling in drugs from South America for some years. I don't know how long, but certainly since you lost your job.'

'What do you mean?'

'Come on, Mr Brewer. Vintage Bentleys are an expensive hobby. You need a fairly healthy income from somewhere to keep that going.'

'But I—'

'Good little system you had worked out. All ticking over fine. Until Dickie found out what you were up to. He'd always hated drugs, hated what they did to people, and I think he must have threatened to expose what you were doing.'

'You don't know what you're talking about.'

'Yes I do,' said Harriet implacably. 'You fobbed Dickie off for a while . . . maybe said you'd stop dealing, maybe said you'd confess voluntarily . . . somehow you bought time. But my brother remained a threat . . . until you saw a way of getting rid of him—a way which would never be investigated too closely. You started systematically to poison him, and at the same time worked out how to make it appear that he was in a high-risk category for catching AIDS.'

Michael Brewer was calmer now. Once again he had control of himself. He rubbed his chin reflectively. 'Say that what you're suggesting was true . . . what was it that started you thinking that way?'

'Two things,' Harriet replied firmly. 'First,'—she pointed at it—'this magazine.'

'What about it?'

'Good idea, getting the magazines. I think you built up the collection privately, then slipped them into this room towards the end, when Dickie was too ill to notice what was going on. You hid them, but you didn't hide them too well. Hid them just badly enough, in fact, so that Dr Hart couldn't fail to find them. Just as I couldn't fail to find them yesterday.'

'You have no proof of that.'

'But I think I do. Circumstantial evidence, at least.'

'Oh?'

'You see, this one . . .'—again she indicated the magazine on the table—'was only published a fortnight ago . . .'

'But—'

'And by then Dickie was far too ill to get out of bed—let alone go out and buy magazines.'

'Ah.' Michael Brewer nodded ruefully, acknowledging his carelessness. 'You mentioned two things . . . ?' He was now almost diffident in his casualness.

'The other thing was the drugs.'

'Oh?'

'That made me suspicious. It seemed like overkill. All right, we all know by now—no one could help knowing from all the publicity campaigns—that AIDS can be contracted by promiscuous homosexual activity or by drug addicts sharing needles. One or other would have been good enough to start people wondering about the nature of Dickie's illness. To build him up as both a promiscuous gay *and* an intravenous drug abuser seemed excessive. It also started me thinking that perhaps you had access to drugs yourself.'

'Ah!' Michael Brewer bowed his head contritely. 'Yes, I agree that was maybe a bit over the top.'

'You realise,' said Harriet, 'that what you've just said is tantamount to an admission that you did kill my brother?'

'Yes.' He smiled grimly. 'Yes, I realise that.' Slowly, he started to loosen his tie. 'And you must realise why I am not afraid to make that admission to you.'

'The admission that you killed Dickie?'

'Yes. I killed him. And I can tell you that in complete confidence, because, I'm afraid, Miss Chailey, there is no chance that you are going to leave this house alive.'

He tugged savagely at one end of his tie, which came loose and flicked out across the room like a whip.

'You're going to kill me too?'

'You've left me no alternative. Just as your brother left me no alternative. I had to kill him, I'm afraid. Self-protection. It's dog-eat-dog out there, you know.'

'I know,' said Harriet. 'I do work for the British Foreign Office, after all.'

Michael Brewer smiled condescendingly as he started to wind the ends of the tie around his hands. 'Always worth trying a little joke, isn't it? Playing for time. Won't work, but worth trying.'

'Strangling,' observed Harriet, 'won't be nearly such a good murder as the other one. Not nearly so ingenious. And all that dreadful business of getting rid of the body to cope with.'

'Needs must when the devil drives, my dear.' Michael Brewer moved slowly towards her. 'And, though I appreciate your concern, don't worry, I'll think of something.'

'What's more,' Harriet went on gamely, 'I don't think even Dr Hart will sign a death certificate describing a strangling as "natural causes".'

'NO, HE BLOODY WELL WON'T!'

The new voice took them both by surprise, as the bathroom door was flung open and Dr Hart crashed into the room.

Michael Brewer gazed at the apparition with his mouth open. It closed with a snap as Dr Hart's fist caught him on the point of the jaw. The murderer crumpled backwards in a heap, and offered no resistance as the doctor plunged a syringe into his wrist.

'That'll keep him quiet till the police come.'

'Good heavens,' said Harriet.

Dr Hart looked slightly sheepish. 'I'm sorry. I'm not normally a violent man, but I'm afraid, with drugs, I just see red. When I hit him I was hitting all the pushers in the world. When I think of the wreckage of young lives which I've seen pass through my surgery . . .'

'Yes. Are you sure it was all recorded?'

'Certain.' He went back into the bathroom and emerged with a cassette recorder. He spooled it back some way and pressed the 'Play' button. Michael Brewer's confession was reassuringly repeated.

Harriet looked wistfully around the room. 'I'll never forgive myself,' she said, 'for not getting to know Dickie better, but at least now I'll know that what I remember of him was what he was really like.'

'Yes.' Dr Hart looked at her. 'Thank you for asking me to help.'

'There was no one else I could ask.'

'No. Still, at least I feel I've done something. I told you how you made me feel last night. . . .'

'Yes.'

'Well, at least this morning I feel less of an incompetent old fool.' He gave her a weary grin. 'Marginally less, anyway.'

The African Tree-Beavers

MICHAEL GILBERT

A long career filled with fine novels and stories earned Michael Gilbert (1912–) the coveted Grand Master Award of the Mystery Writers of America in 1987. A solicitor and partner in a major London legal firm, Mr. Gilbert frequently includes events surrounding the law, solicitors, and courts in his fiction, which now totals more than two dozen novels, numerous radio and television scripts, and hundreds of short stories. Michael Gilbert is especially adept at the espionage story, and his collection *Game Without Rules* (1967) contains some of the best writing ever done in that genre. Among his series characters is the estimable Patrick Petrella, Detective Chief Inspector of the Metropolitan Police, who appears in some masterful police procedurals.

"The African Tree-Beavers" is not a procedural, but it is one of the most fascinating and challenging mysteries you will ever read.

Like many practical and unimaginative men, Mr Calder believed in certain private superstitions. He would never take a train which left at one minute to the hour, distrusted the number twenty-nine, and refused to open any parcel or letter on which the stamp had been fixed upside down. This, incidentally, saved his life when he refused to open an innocent-looking parcel bearing the imprint of a bookseller from whom he had made many purchases in the past, but which proved, on this occasion, to contain three ounces of tri-toluene and a contact fuse. Mr Behrens sneered at the superstition, but agreed that his friend was lucky.

Mr Calder also believed in coincidences. To be more precise, he believed in a specific law of coincidence. If you heard a new name, or a hitherto unknown fact, twice within twelve hours, you would hear it again before a further twelve hours was up. Not all the schoolmasterly logic of Mr Behrens could shake him in this belief. If challenged to produce an example he will cite the case of the Reverend Francis Osbaldestone.

The first time Mr Calder heard this name was at eleven o'clock at night, at the Old Comrades' Reunion of the infantry regiment with which he had fought for a memorable eight months in the Western Desert in 1942. He attended these reunions once every three years. His real interest was not in reminiscences of the war, but in observation of what had taken place since. It delighted him to see that a Motor Transport Corporal, whom he remembered slouching round in a pair of oily denims, should have become a prosperous garage proprietor, and that the Orderly Room Clerk, who had sold places on the leave roster, had developed his talents, first as a bookmakers' runner, and now as a bookmaker; and that the God-like Company Sergeant-

Major should have risen no higher than commissionaire in a block of flats at Putney, and would be forced, if he met him in ordinary life, to call his former clerk, 'Sir'.

Several very old friends were there. Freddie Faulkner, who had stayed on in the army and had risen to command the battalion, surged through the crowd and pressed a large whisky into his hand. Mr Calder accepted it gratefully. One of the penalties of growing old, he had found, was a weak bladder for beer.

Colonel Faulkner shouted above the roar of conversation, "When are you going to keep your promise?"

"What promise?" said Mr Calder. "How many whiskies *is* this? Three or four?"

"I thought I'd get you a fairly large one. It's difficult to get near the bar. Have you forgotten? You promised to come and look me up."

"I hadn't forgotten. It's difficult to get away."

"Nonsense. You're a bachelor. You can up-sticks whenever you like."

"It's difficult to leave Rasselas behind."

"That dog of yours? For God's sake! Where do you think I live? In Hampstead Garden Suburb? Bring him with you! He'll have the time of his life. He can chase anything that moves, except my pheasants."

"He's a very well-behaved dog," said Mr Calder, "and does exactly what I tell him. If you really want me—"

"Certainly I do. Moreover, I can introduce Rasselas to another animal lover. Our rector. Francis Osbaldestone. A remarkable chap. Now get your diary out, and fix a date. . . ."

It was ten o'clock on the following morning when the name cropped up next. Mr Calder was stretched in one chair in front of the fire, his eyes shut, nursing the lingering remains of a not disagreeable hangover. Mr Behrens was in the other chair, reading the Sunday newspapers. Rasselas occupied most of the space between them.

Mr Behrens said, "Have you read this? It's very interesting. There's a clergyman who performs miracles."

"The biggest miracle any clergyman can perform nowadays," said Mr Calder sleepily, "is to get people to come to church."

"Oh, they come to *his* church all right. Full house, every Sunday. Standing-room only."

"How does he do it?"

"Personal attraction. He's equally successful with animals. However savage or shy they are, he can make them come to him, and behave themselves."

"He ought to try it on a bull."

"He has. Listen to this: *On one occasion, a bull got loose and threatened some children who were picnicking in a field. The rector, who happened to be passing, quelled the bull with a few well-chosen words. The children were soon taking rides on the bull's back.*"

"Animal magnetism."

"I suppose, if you'd met St Francis of Assisi, you'd have sniffed and said, 'Animal magnetism.' "

"He was a saint."

"How do you know this man isn't?"

"He may be. But it would need more than a few tricks with animals to convince me."

"Then what about miracles? *On another occasion, the rector was woken on a night of storm by an alarm of fire. The verger ran down to the rectory to tell the rector that a barn had been struck by lightning. The telephone line to the nearest town with a fire brigade was down. The rector said, 'Not a moment to lose. The bells must be rung.' As he spoke, the bells started to ring themselves.*"

Mr Calder snorted.

"It's gospel truth," Mr Behrens said. "Mr Penny, the verger, vouches for it. He says that by the time he got back to his cottage, where the only key of the bell-chamber is kept, and got across with it to the church, the bells had *stopped* ringing. He went up into the belfry. There was no one there. The ropes were on their hooks. Everything was in perfect order. At that moment, the brigade arrived. They had heard the bells, and were in time to save the barn."

Mr Calder said, "It sounds like a tall story to me. What do you think, Rasselas?" The dog showed his long white teeth in a smile. "He agrees. What is the name of this paragon?"

"He is the Reverend Francis Osbaldestone."

"Rector of Hedgeborn, in the heart of rural Norfolk."

"Do you know him?"

"I heard his name for the first time at about eleven o'clock last night."

"In that case," said Mr Behrens, "according to the fantastic rules propounded and believed in by you, you will hear it again before ten o'clock this evening."

It was at this precise moment that the telephone rang.

Since Mr Calder's telephone number was not only ex-directory, but was changed every six months, his incoming calls were likely to be matters of business. He was not surprised, therefore, to recognise the voice of Mr Fortescue, who was the Manager of the Westminster Branch of the London and Home Counties Bank, and other things besides.

Mr Fortescue said, "I'd like to see you and Behrens, as soon as possible. Shall we say tomorrow afternoon?"

"Certainly," said Mr Calder. "Can you give me any idea what it's about?"

"You'll find it all in your *Observer*. An article about a clergyman who performs miracles. Francis Osbaldestone."

"Ah!" said Mr Calder

"You sound pleased about something," said Mr Fortescue.

Mr Calder said, "You've just proved a theory."

"I understand," said Mr Fortescue, "that you know Colonel Faulkner quite well, in the army."

"He was my company commander," said Mr Calder.

"Would you say he was an imaginative man?"

"I should think he's got about as much imagination as a No. 11 bus."

"Or a man who would be easily deluded?"

"I'd hate to try."

Mr Fortescue pursed his lips primly, and said, "That was my impression, too. Do you know Hedgeborn?"

"Not the village. But I know that part of Norfolk. It's fairly primitive. The army had a battle school near there during the war. They were a bit slow about handing it back, too."

"I seem to remember," said Mr Behrens, "that there was a row about it. Questions in Parliament. Did they give it back in the end?"

"Most of it. They kept Snelsham Manor, with its park. After all the trouble at Porton Experimental Station, they moved the gas section down to Cornwall, and transferred the Bacterial Warfare Establishment to Snelsham, which is less than two miles from Hedgeborn."

"I can understand," said Mr Calder, "that Security would keep a careful eye on an establishment like Snelsham. But why should they be alarmed by a saintly parson two miles down the valley?"

"You are not aware of what happened last week?"

"Ought we to be?"

"It has been kept out of the press. It's bound to leak out sooner or later. Your saintly parson led what I can only describe as a village task force. It was composed of the members of the Parochial Church Council, and a couple of dozen of the villagers and farmers. They broke into Snelsham Manor."

"But, good God," said Calder, "the security arrangements must have been pretty ropy."

"The security was adequate: a double wire fence, patrolling guards and dogs. The village blacksmith cut the fence in two places. A farm tractor dragged it clear. They had no trouble with the guards, who were armed with truncheons. The farmers had shot-guns."

"And the dogs?"

"They made such a fuss of the rector that he was, I understand, in some danger of being licked to death."

"What did they do when they got in?" said Behrens.

"They broke into the experimental wing and liberated twenty rabbits, a dozen guinea-pigs and nearly fifty rats."

Mr Behrens started to laugh, and managed to turn it into a cough when he observed Mr Fortescue's eyes on him.

"I hope you don't think it was funny, Behrens. A number of the rats had been infected with Asiatic plague. They *hope* that they recaptured or destroyed the whole of that batch."

"Has no action been taken against the rector?"

"Naturally. The police were informed. An inspector and a sergeant drove over from Thetford to see the rector. They were refused access."

"Refused?"

"They were told," said Mr Fortescue gently, "that if they attempted to lay hands on the rector they would be resisted—by force."

"But surely—" said Mr Behrens. And stopped.

"Yes," said Mr Fortescue. "Do think before you say anything. Try to visualize the unparalleled propaganda value to our friends in the various CND and Peace Groups if an armed force had to be despatched to seize a village clergyman."

Mr Behrens said, "I'm visualizing it. Do you think one of the more enterprising bodies—the International Brotherhood Group occurs to me as a possibility—might have planted someone in Hedgeborn? Someone who is using the rector's exceptional influence—"

"It's a possibility. You must remember that the Bacterial Warfare Wing has only been there for two years. If anyone *has* been planted, it has been done comparatively recently."

"How long has the rector been there?" said Mr Calder.

"Eighteen months."

"I see."

"The situation is full of possibilities, I agree. I suggest you tackle it from both ends. I should suppose, Behrens, that there are few people who know more about the IBG and its ramifications than you do. Can you find out whether they have been active in this area recently?"

"I'll do my best."

"We can none of us do more than our best," agreed Mr Fortescue. "And you, Calder, must go down to Hedgeborn immediately. I imagine that Colonel Faulkner would invite you?"

"I have a standing invitation," said Mr Calder. "For the shooting."

Hedgeborn has changed in the last four hundred years, but not very much. The church was built in the reign of Charles the Martyr, and the Manor in the reign of Anne the Good. There is a village smithy, where a farmer can still get his horses shod. He can also buy diesel oil for his tractor. The cottages have thatched roofs, and television aerials.

Mr Calder leaned out of his bedroom window at the Manor and surveyed the village, asleep under a full moon. He could see the church, at the far end of the village street, perched on a slight rise, its bell-tower outlined against the sky. There was a huddle of cottages round it. The one with a light in it would belong to Mr Penny, the verger, who had come running down the street to tell the rector that Farmer Alsop's farm was on fire. If he leaned out of the window, Mr Calder could just see the roof of the rectory, at the far end of the street, masked by trees.

Could there be any truth in the story of the bells? It had seemed fantastic in London. It seemed less so now.

A soft knock at the door heralded the arrival of Stokes, once the Colonel's batman, now his factotum.

"Would you care for a nightcap before you turn in, sir?"

"Certainly not," said Mr Calder. "Not after that lovely dinner. Did you cook it yourself?"

Stokes looked gratified. "It wasn't what you might call hote kweezeen."

"It was excellent. Tell me, don't you find things a bit quiet down here?"

"I'm used to it, sir. I was born here."

"I didn't realize that," said Mr Calder.

"I saw you looking at the smithy this afternoon. Enoch Clavering's my first cousin. Come to that, we're mostly first or second cousins. Alsops, and Stokes, and Vowles, and Claverings."

"It would have been Enoch who cut down the fence at Snelsham Manor?"

"That's right, sir." Stokes' voice was respectful, but there was a hint of wariness in it. "How did you know about that, if you don't mind me asking? It hasn't been in the papers."

"The colonel told me."

"Oh, of course. All the same, I do wonder how *he* knew about Enoch cutting down the fence. He wasn't with us."

"With *you?*" said Mr Calder. "Do I gather, Stokes, that you took part in this—this enterprise?"

"Well, naturally, sir. Seeing I'm a member of the Parochial Church Council. Would there be anything more?"

"Nothing more," said Mr Calder. "Goodnight."

He lay awake for a long time, listening to the owls talking to each other in the elms. . . .

"It's true," said Colonel Faulkner next morning. "We are a bit in-bred. All Norfolk men are odd. It makes us just a bit odder, that's all."

"Tell me about your rector."

"He was some sort of missionary, I believe. In darkest Africa. Got malaria very badly, and was invalided out."

"From darkest Africa to darkest Norfolk. What do you make of him?"

The colonel was lighting his after-breakfast pipe, and took time to think about that. He said, "I just don't know, Calder. Might be a saint. Might be a scoundrel. He's got a touch with animals. No denying that."

"What about the miracles?"

"No doubt they've been exaggerated in the telling. But—well—that business of the bells . . . I can give chapter and verse for that. There only *is* one key to the bell-chamber. I remember what a fuss there was when it was mislaid last year. And no-one could have got it from Penny's cottage, opened the tower up, rung the bells, *and* put the key back without someone seeing him. Stark impossibility."

"How many bells rang?"

"The tenor and the treble. That's the way we always ring them for an alarm. One of the farmers across the valley heard them, got out of bed, spotted the fire, and phoned for the brigade."

"Two bells," said Mr Calder thoughtfully. "So one man *could* have rung them."

"If he could have got in."

"Quite so." Mr Calder was looking at a list. "There are three people I should like to meet. A man called Smedley . . ."

"The rector's warden. I'm people's warden. He's my opposite number. Don't like him much."

"Miss Martin, your organist. I believe she has a cottage near the church. And Mr Smallpiece, your village postmaster."

"Why those three?"

"Because," said Calder, "apart from the rector himself, they are the only people who have come to live in this village during the past two years—so Stokes tells me."

"He ought to know," said Colonel. "He's related to half the village."

Mr Smedley lived in a small, dark cottage. It was tucked away behind the Viscount Townshend public house, which had a signboard outside it with a picture of the Second Viscount looking remarkably like the turnip which had become associated with his name.

Mr Smedley was old and thin, and inclined to be cautious. He thawed very slightly when he discovered that his visitor was the son of Canon Calder of Salisbury.

"A world authority on monumental brasses," he said. "You must be proud of him."

"I'd no idea."

"Yes, indeed. I have a copy somewhere of a paper he wrote on the brasses at Verden, in Hanover. A most scholarly work. We have some fine brasses in the church here, too. Not as old or as notable as Stoke d'Abernon, but very fine."

"It's an interesting village altogether. You've been getting into the papers."

"I'd no idea that our brasses were *that* famous."

"Not your brasses. Your rector. He's been written up as a miracle-worker."

"I'm not surprised."

"Oh, why?"

Mr Smedley blinked maliciously, and said, "I'm not surprised at the ability of the press to cheapen anything it touches."

"But *are* they miracles?"

"You'll have to define your terms. If you accept the Shavian definition of a miracle as an event which creates faith, then certainly, yes. They are miracles."

It occurred to Mr Calder that Mr Smedley was enjoying this conversation more than he was. He said, "You know quite well what I mean. Is there a rational explanation for them?"

"Again, it depends what you mean by rational."

"I mean," said Mr Calder bluntly, "are they miracles or conjuring tricks?"

Mr Smedley considered the matter, his head on one side. Then he said, "Isn't that a question which you should put to the rector? After all, if they are conjuring tricks, he must be the conjurer."

"I was planning to do just that," said Mr Calder, and prepared to take his leave.

When he was at the door, his host checked him by laying a claw-like hand on his arm. He said, "Might I offer a word of advice? This is not an ordinary village. I suppose the word which would come most readily to mind is—primitive. I don't mean anything sinister. But, being so isolated, it has grown up rather more slowly than the outside world. And another thing . . ." Mr Smedley paused, and Mr Calder was reminded of an old black crow, cautiously approaching a tempting morsel, wondering whether he dared to seize it. "I ought to warn you that the people here are very fond of their rector. If what they regarded as divine manifestations were described by you as conjuring tricks, well—you see what I mean."

"I see what you mean," said Mr Calder. He went out into the village street, took a couple of deep breaths, and made his way to the post office.

The post office was dark, dusty and empty. He could hear the postmaster, in the back room, wrestling with a manual telephone exchange. He realised, as he listened, that Mr Smallpiece was no Norfolkman. His voice suggested that he had been brought up within sound of Bow Bells. When he emerged, Mr Calder confirmed the diagnosis. If Mr Smedley was a country crow, Mr Smallpiece was a cockney sparrow.

Mr Smallpiece said, "Nice to see a new face around. You'll be staying with the colonel. "I 'ope his aunt gets over it."

"Gets over what?"

"Called away ten minutes ago. The old lady 'ad a fit. Not the first one neither. If you ask me, she 'as one whenever she feels lonely."

"Old people are like that," agreed Mr Calder. "Your job must keep you very busy."

"*'Oh, I am the cook and the captain bold, and the mate of the Nancy brig',*" agreed Mr Smallpiece. "I work the exchange—eighteen lines—deliver the mail, sell stamps, send telegrams, and run errands. 'Owever, there's no overtime in this job, and what you don't get paid for you don't get thanked for." He looked at the clock above the counter, which showed five minutes to twelve, pushed the hand on five minutes, turned a card in the door from 'Open' to 'Closed', and said, "Since the colonel won't be back much before two, what price a pint at the Viscount?"

"You take the words out of my mouth," said Mr Calder. "What happens if anyone wants to ring up someone whilst you're out?"

"Well, they can't, can they?" said Mr Smallpiece.

When the colonel returned—his aunt, Mr Calder was glad to learn, was much better—he reported the negative results of his inquiries to date.

"If you want to see Miss Martin, you can probably kill two birds with one stone. She goes along to the rectory most Wednesdays, to practice the harmonium. You'll find the rectory at the far end of the street. The original one was alongside the church, but it was burned down about a hundred years ago. I'm afraid it isn't an architectural gem. Built in the worst style of Victorian ecclesiastical red brick."

Mr Calder, as he lifted the heavy wrought-iron knocker, was inclined to agree. The house was not beautiful. But it had a certain old-fashioned dignity and solidity.

The rector answered the door himself. Mr Calder had hardly known what to expect. A warrior-ecclesiastic in the Norman mould? A fanatical priest, prepared to face stake and faggots for his faith? A subtle Jesuit living by the Rule of Ignatius Loyola in solitude and prayer? What he had not been prepared for was a slight, nondescript man with an apologetic smile who said, "Come in, come in. Don't stand on ceremony. We never lock our doors here. I know you, don't I? Wait! You're Mr Calder, and you're staying at the Manor. *What* a lovely dog! A genuine Persian deerhound of the royal breed. What's his name?"

"He's called Rasselas."

"Rasselas," said the rector. He wasn't looking at the dog, but was staring over his shoulder, as though he could see something of interest behind him in the garden. "Rasselas." The dog gave a rumbling growl. The rector said, "Rasselas," again, very softly. The rumble changed to a snarl. The rector stood perfectly still, and said nothing. The snarl changed back into a rumble.

"Well, that's much better," said the rector. "Did you see? He was fighting me. I wonder why."

"He's usually very well behaved with strangers."

"I'm sure he is. Intelligent, too. Why should he have *assumed* that I was an enemy? You heard him assuming it, didn't you?"

"I heard him changing his mind, too."

"I was able to reassure him. The interesting point is, why should he have started with hostile thoughts? I trust he didn't derive them from you? But I'm being fanciful. Why should you have thoughts about us at all? Come along in and meet our organist, Miss Martin. Such a helpful person, and a spirited performer on almost any instrument."

The opening of an inner door had released a powerful blast of Purcell's overture to *Dido and Aeneas*, played on the harmonium with all stops out.

"Miss Martin. *Miss Martin!*"

"I'm so sorry, Rector. I didn't hear you."

"This is Mr Calder. He's a wartime friend of Colonel Faulkner. Curious that such an evil thing as war should have produced the fine friendships it did."

"Good sometimes comes out of evil, don't you think?"

"No," said the rector. "I'm afraid I don't believe that at all. Good sometimes comes in spite of evil. A very different proposition."

"A beautiful rose," said Miss Martin, "can grow on a dunghill."

"Am I the rose, and Colonel Faulkner the dunghill, or vice-versa?"

Miss Martin tittered. The rector said, "Let that be a warning to you not to take an analogy too far."

"I have to dash along now, but please stay. Miss Martin will do the honours. Have a cup of tea. You will? Splendid."

Over the teacups, as Mr. Calder was wondering how to bring the conversation round to the point he required, Miss Martin did it for him. She said, "This is a terrible village for gossip, Mr Calder. Although you've hardly been down here two days, people are already beginning to wonder what you're up to. Particularly as you've been getting round, talking to people."

"I am naturally gregarious," said Mr Calder.

"Now, now. You won't pull the wool over *my* eyes. I know better. You've been sent."

Mr Calder said, trying to keep the surprise out of his voice, "Sent by whom?"

"I'll mention no names. We all know that there are sects and factions in the Church who would find our rector's teachings abhorrent to their own narrow dogma. And who would be envious of his growing reputation."

"Oh, I see," said Mr Calder.

"I'm not asking you to tell me if my guess is correct. What I do want to impress on you is that there is nothing exaggerated in these stories. I'll give you one instance which I can vouch for myself. It was a tea-party we were giving for the Brownies. I'd made a terrible miscalculation. The most appalling disaster faced us. *There wasn't enough to eat*. Can you imagine it?"

"Easily," said Mr Calder, with a shudder.

"I called the rector aside, and told him. He just smiled, and said, 'Look in that cupboard, Miss Martin.' I simply stared at him. It was a cupboard I use myself for music and anthems. I have the only key. I walked over and unlocked it. And what do you think I found? A large plate of freshly cut bread and butter, and two plates of biscuits."

"Enough to feed the five thousand."

"It's odd you should say that. It was the precise analogy that occurred to me."

"Did you tell people about this?"

"I don't gossip. But one of my helpers was there. She must have spread the story. Ah, here is the rector. Don't say a word about it to him. He denies it all, of course."

"I'm glad to see that Miss Martin has been looking after you," said the rector. "A thought has occurred to me. Do you sing?"

"Only under duress."

"Recite, perhaps? We are getting up a village concert. Miss Martin is a tower of strength in such matters . . ."

"It would appear from his reports," said Mr Fortescue, "that your colleague is entering fully into the life of the village. Last Saturday, according to the *East Anglian Gazette*, he took part in a village concert in aid of the RSPCA. He obliged with a moving rendering of *The Wreck of the Hesperus*."

"Good gracious!" said Mr Behrens. "How very versatile!"

"He would not, however, appear to have advanced very far in the matter I sent him down to investigate. He thinks that the rector is a perfectly sincere enthusiast. He has his eye on three people, any one of whom *might* have been planted in the village to work on him. Have you been able to discover anything?"

"I'm not sure," said Mr Behrens. "I've made the round of our usual contacts. I felt that the International Brotherhood Group was the most likely. It's a line they've tried with some success in the past. Stirring up local prejudice, and working it up into a national campaign. You remember the schoolchildren who trespassed on that missile base in Scotland and were roughly handled?"

"Were alleged to have been roughly handled."

"Yes. It was a put-up job. But they made a lot of capital out of it. I have a line on their chief organizer. My contact thinks they *are* up to something. Which means they've got an agent planted in Hedgeborn."

"Or that the rector is their agent."

"Yes. The difficulty will be to prove it. Their security is rather good."

Mr Fortescue considered the matter, running his thumb down the angle of his promiment chin. He said, "Might you be able to contrive, through your contact, to transmit a particular item of information to their agent in Hedgeborn?"

"I might. But I hardly see—"

"In medicine," said Mr Fortescue, "I am told that, when it proves impossible to clear up a condition by direct treatment, it is sometimes possible to precipitate an artificial crisis which *can* be dealt with."

"Always bearing in mind that, if we do precipitate a crisis, poor old Calder will be in the middle of it."

"Exactly," said Mr Fortescue.

It was on the Friday of the second week of his stay that Mr Calder noticed the change. There was no open hostility. No one attacked him. No one was even rude to him. It was simply that he had ceased to be acceptable to the village. People who had been prepared to chat with him in the bar of the Viscount Townshend now had business of their own to discuss when he appeared. Mr Smedley did not answer his knock, although he could see him through the front window, reading a book. Mr Smallpiece avoided him in the street.

It was like the moment, in a theatre, when the iron safety-curtain descends, cutting off the actors and all on the stage from the audience. Suddenly, he was on one side. The village was on the other.

By the Saturday, the atmosphere had become so oppressive that Mr Calder decided to do something about it. Stokes had driven the Colonel into Thetford on business. He was alone in the house. He decided, on the spur of the moment, to have a word with the rector.

Although it was a fine afternoon, the village street was completely empty. As he walked, he noted the occasional stirring of a curtain, and knew that he was not unobserved, but the silence of the early autumn afternoon lay heavily over everything. On this occasion he had left a strangely subdued Rasselas behind.

His knock at the rectory door was unanswered. Remembering the rector saying, "We never lock our doors here," he turned the handle and went in. The house was silent. He took a few steps along the hall, and stopped. The door on his left was ajar. He looked in. The rector was there. He was kneeling at a carved prie-dieu, as motionless as if he had himself been part of the carving. If he had heard Mr Calder's approach, he took absolutely no notice of it. Feeling extremely foolish, Mr Calder withdrew by the way he had come.

Walking back down the street, he was visited by a recollection of his days with the Military Mission in wartime Albania. The mission had visited a remote village, and had been received with the same silent disregard. They had usually been well received, and it had puzzled them. When he returned to the village some months later, Mr Calder had learned the truth. The village had caught an informer, and were waiting for the mission to go before they dealt with him. He had heard what they had done to the informer, and, although he was not naturally queasy, it had turned his stomach. . . .

That evening, Stokes waited on them in unusual silence. When he had gone, the colonel said, "Whatever it is, it's tomorrow."

"How do you know?"

"I'm told that the rector has been fasting since Thursday. Also that morning service tomorrow has been cancelled, and Evensong brought forward to four o'clock. That's when it'll break."

"It will be a relief," said Mr Calder.

"Stokes thinks you ought to leave tonight. He thinks I shall be all right. You might not be."

"That was thoughtful of Stokes. But I'd as soon stay. That is, unless you want to get rid of me."

"Glad to have you," said the colonel. "Besides, if they see you've gone, they may put it off. Then we shall have to start all over again."

"Did you contact the number I asked you to?"

"Yes. From a public call-box in Thetford."

"And what was the answer?"

"It was so odd," said the colonel, "that I was afraid I might get it wrong, and I wrote it down."

He handed Mr Calder a piece of paper. Mr Calder read it carefully, folded it up, and put it in his pocket.

"Is it good news or bad?"

"I'm not sure," said Mr Calder. "But I can promise you one thing. You'll hear a sermon tomorrow which you won't forget."

When the rector stepped into the pulpit, his face was pale and composed, but it was no longer gentle. Mr Calder wondered how he could ever have considered him nondescript. There was a blazing conviction about the man, a fire and a warmth which lit up the whole church. This was no longer the gentle St Francis. This was Peter the Hermit, "Whose eyes were a flame and whose tongue was a sword."

He stood for a moment, upright and motionless. Then he turned his head slowly, looking from face to face in the crowded congregation, as if searching for support and guidance from his flock. When he started to speak, it was in a quiet, almost conversational voice.

"The anti-Christ has raised his head once more. The Devil is at his work again. We deceived ourselves into thinking that we had dealt him a shrewd blow. We were mistaken. Our former warning has not been heeded. I fear that it will have to be repeated, and this time more strongly."

The colonel looked anxiously at Mr Calder, who mouthed the word, "Wait."

"Far from abandoning the foul work at Snelsham Manor, I have learned that it is not only continuing, but intensifying. More of God's creatures are being imprisoned and tortured by methods which would have shamed the Gestapo. In the name of science, mice, small rabbits, guinea-pigs and hamsters are being put to obscene and painful deaths. Yesterday, a cargo of African tree-beavers, harmless and friendly little animals, arrived at this . . . at this scientific slaughter-house. They are to be inoculated with a virus which will first paralyse their limbs, then cause them to go mad with pain, and, finally, die. The object of the experiment is to hold off the moment of death as long as possible . . ."

Mr Calder, who was listening with strained attention, had found it difficult to hear the closing sentence, and realized that the rector was now speaking against a ground-swell of noise.

The noise burst out suddenly into a roar. The rector's voice rode over the tumult like a trumpet.

"Are we going to allow this?"

A second roar crashed out with startling violence.

"We will pull down this foul place, stone by stone. We will purge what remains with fire. All who will help, follow me!"

"What do we do?" said the Colonel.

"Sit still," said Mr Calder.

In a moment they were alone in their pew, with a hundred angry faces round them. The rector, still standing in the pulpit, quelled the storm with an upraised hand. He said, "We will have no bloodshed. We cannot fight evil with evil. Those who are not with us are against us. Enoch, take one of them. Two of you the other. Into the vestry with them!"

Mr Calder said, "Go with it. Don't fight."

As they were swirled down the aisle, the colonel saw one anxious face in the crowd. He shouted, "Are you in this, too, Stokes?" The next moment they were in the vestry. The door had clanged shut, and they heard the key turn in the lock. The thick walls and nine inches of stout oak cut down the sound, but they could hear the organ playing. It sounded like Miss Martin's idea of the *Battle Hymn of the Republic*.

"Well," said the colonel. "What do we do now?"

"We give them five minutes to get to the rectory. There'll be some sort of conference there, I imagine."

"And then?"

Mr Calder had seated himself on a pile of hassocks, and sat there, swinging his short legs. He said, "As we have five minutes to kill, maybe I'd better put you in the picture. Why don't you sit down?"

The colonel grunted, and subsided.

Mr Calder said, "Hasn't it struck you that the miracles we've been hearing about were of two quite different types?"

"I don't follow you."

"One sort was simple animal magnetism. No doubt about that. I saw the rector operating on Rasselas. Nearly hypnotized the poor dog. The other sort—well, there's been a lot of talk about them, but I've only heard any real evidence of two. The bells that rang themselves and the food that materialized in a locked cupboard. Isolate them from the general hysteria, and what do they amount to? You told me yourself that the key of the vestry had been mislaid."

"You think someone stole it? Had it copied?"

"Of course."

"Who?"

"Oh," said Mr Calder impatiently, "the person who organized the other miracles, of course. I think it's time we got out of here, don't you?"

"How?"

"Get someone to unlock the door. I notice they left the key in it. There must be some sane folk about."

The colonel said, "Seeing that the nearest farm likely to be helpful to us is a good quarter of a mile away, I'd be interested to know how you intend to shout for help."

"Follow me up that ladder," said Mr Calder. "I'll show you."

In the crowded room at the rectory the rector said, "Is that clear? They'll be expecting us on the southern side, where we attacked before, so we'll come through the woods, on the north. Stokes, can you get the colonel's Land Rover up that side?"

"Easily enough, Rector."

"Have the grappling irons laid out at the back. Tom's tractor follows you. Enoch, how long to cut the wire?"

"Ten seconds."

This produced a rumbling laugh.

"Good. We don't want any unnecessary delay. We drive the tractors straight through the gap and ride in on the back of them. The fire-raising material will be in the trailers behind the rear tractor. The Scouts can see to that under you, Mr Smedley."

"Certainly, Rector. Scouts are experts at lighting fires."

"Excellent. Now, the diversion at the front gate. That will be under you, Miss Martin. You'll have the Guides and Brownies. You demand to be let in. When they refuse, you all start screaming. If you can get hold of the sentry, I suggest you scratch him."

"I'll let Matilda Briggs do *that*," said Miss Martin.

Enoch Clavering touched the rector on the arm and said, "Listen." Then he went over to the window and opened it.

"What is it, Enoch?"

"I thought I heard the bells some minutes ago, but I didn't like to interrupt. They've stopped now. It's like it was the last time. The bells rang themselves. What does it signify?"

"It means," said the rector cheerfully, "that I've been a duffer. I ought to have seen that the trap-door to the belfry was padlocked. Our prisoners must have climbed up and started clapping the tenor and the treble. Since they've stopped, I imagine someone heard them and let them out."

Miss Martin said, "What are we going to do?"

"What we're not going to do is lose our heads. Stokes, you've immobilized the colonel's car?"

Stokes nodded.

"And you've put the telephone line out of communication, Mr Smallpiece?"

"Same as last time."

"Then I don't see how they can summon help in under half an hour. We should have ample time to do all we have to."

"I advise you against it," said Mr Calder.

He was standing in the doorway, one hand in his pocket. He looked placid, but determined. Behind him they could see the great dog, Rasselas, his head almost level with Mr Calder's shoulder, his amber eyes glowing.

For a moment there was complete silence. Then a low growl of anger broke out from the crowded room. The rector said, "Ah, Calder. Tell me who let you out?"

"Jack Collins. And he's gone in his own car to Thetford. The police will be here in half an hour."

"Then they will be too late."

"That's just what I was afraid of," said Mr Calder. "It's why I came down as fast as I could, to stop you."

There was another growl, louder and more menacing. Enoch Clavering stepped forward. He said, "Bundle him down into the cellar, Rector, and let's get on with it."

"I shouldn't try it," said Mr Calder. His voice was still peaceful. "First, because if you put a hand on me this dog will have that hand off. Secondly, because the colonel is outside in the garden. He's got a shotgun, and he'll use it, if he has to."

The rector said gently, "You mustn't think you can frighten us. The colonel won't shoot. He's not a murderer. And Rasselas won't attack me. Will you, Rasselas?"

"You've got this all wrong," said Mr Calder. "My object is to prevent *you* attacking *us*. Just long enough for me to tell you two things. First, the guards at Snelsham have been doubled. They are armed. And they have orders to shoot. What you're leading your flock to isn't a jamboree, like last time. It's a massacre."

"I think he's lying," said Mr Smedley.

"There's one way of finding out," said Mr Calder. "But it's not the real point. The question which really matters—what our American friends would refer to as the sixty-four thousand dollar question—is, have any of you ever seen a tree-beaver?"

The question fell into a sudden pool of silence.

"Come, come," said Mr Calder. "There must be some naturalists here. Rector, I see the *Universal Encyclopaedia of Wild Life* on your shelf. Would you care to turn its pages and give us a few facts about the habits of this curious creature?"

The reactor said, with a half-smile of comprehension on his face, "What are you getting at, Mr Calder?"

"I can save you some unnecessary research. The animal does not exist. Indeed, it could not exist. Beavers live in rivers, not in trees. The animal was invented by an old friend of mine, a Mr Behrens. And, having invented this remarkable animal, he thought it would be a pity to keep it all to himself. He had news of its arrival at Snelsham passed to a friend of his, who passed it on to a subversive organization known as the International Brotherhood Group. Who, in turn, passed it to you, Rector, through their local agent."

The rector was smiling now. He said, "So I have been led up the garden path. *Sancta simplicitas!* Who is this agent?"

"That's easy. Who told you about the tree-beavers?"

There was a flurry of movement. A shout, a crash, and the sound of a shot. . . .

"It is far from clear," said Mr Calder, "whether Miss Martin intended to shoot the rector or me. In fact Rasselas knocked her over, and she shot herself. As soon as they realized they had been fooled, the village closed its ranks. They concocted a story that Miss Martin, who was nervous of burglars, was known to possess a revolver, a relic of the last war. She must have been carrying it in her handbag, and the supposition was that, in pulling it out to show to someone, it had gone off and killed her. It was the thinnest story you ever heard, and the Coroner was suspicious as a cat. But he couldn't shake them. And, after all, it was difficult to cast doubt on the evidence of the entire Parochial Church Council, supported by their rector. The verdict was accidental death."

"Excellent," said Mr Fortescue. "It would have been hard to prove anything. In spite of your beavers. How did the rector take it?"

"Very well indeed. I had to stay for the inquest, and made a point of attending Evensong on the following Sunday. The church was so full that it was difficult to find a seat. The rector preached an excellent sermon, on the text, "Render unto Caesar the things that are Caesar's'."

"A dangerous opponent," said Mr Fortescue. "On the whole, I cannot feel sorry that the authorities should have decided to close Snelsham Manor."

Have a Nice Death

ANTONIA FRASER

One of the most enjoyable female sleuths to emerge in the last decade is television reporter Jemima Shore, the creation of Lady Antonia Fraser (1932–) one of the very few titled (before achieving fame as a writer) women to produce mystery fiction. Her writing career debuted in 1977 with *Quiet as a Nun,* and she has since produced some half-dozen additional books, all of which feature the resourceful Ms. Shore. Earlier, Lady Antonia was known for her nonfiction books, including *A History of Toys,* and *King Charles II,* and she remains a noted historian of the British monarchy.

"Have a Nice Death" is a wonderful puzzle story that has no sleuth, although the reader can have great fun playing the part.

Everyone was being extraordinarily courteous to Sammy Luke in New York.

Take Sammy's arrival at Kennedy Airport, for example: Sammy had been quite struck by the warmth of the welcome. Sammy thought: how relieved Zara would be! Zara (his wife) was inclined to worry about Sammy—he had to admit, with some cause; in the past, that is. In the past Sammy had been nervous, delicate, highly strung, whatever you liked to call it—Sammy suspected that some of Zara's women friends had a harsher name for it; the fact was that things tended to go wrong where Sammy was concerned, unless Zara was there to iron them out. But that was in England. Sammy was quite sure he was not going to be nervous in America; perhaps, cured by the New World, he would never be nervous again.

Take the immigration officials—hadn't Sammy been warned about them?

"They're nothing but gorillas"—Zara's friend, wealthy Tess, who traveled frequently to the States, had pronounced the word in a dark voice. For an instant Sammy, still in his nervous English state, visualized immigration checkpoints manned by terrorists armed with machine guns. But the official seated in a booth, who summoned Sammy in, was slightly built, perhaps even slighter than Sammy himself, though the protection of the booth made it difficult to tell. And he was smiling as he cried:

"C'mon, c'mon, bring the family!" A notice outside the booth stated that only one person—or one family—was permitted inside at a time.

"I'm afraid my wife's not traveling with me," stated Sammy apologetically.

"I sure wish my wife wasn't with me either," answered the official, with ever-increasing bonhomie.

Sammy wondered confusedly—it had been a long flight after all—whether he should explain his own very different feelings about his wife, his passionate regret that Zara had not been able to accompany him. But his new friend was already examining his passport, flipping through a large black directory, talking again:

"A writer . . . Would I know any of your books?"

This was an opportunity for Sammy to explain intelligently the purpose of his visit. Sammy Luke was the author of six novels. Five of them had sold well, if not astoundingly well, in England and not at all in the United States. The sixth, *Women Weeping*, due perhaps to its macabrely fashionable subject matter, had hit some kind of publishing jackpot in both countries. Only a few weeks after publication in the States its sales were phenomenal and rising; an option on the film rights (maybe Jane Fonda and Meryl Streep as the masochists?) had already been bought. As a result of all this, Sammy's new American publishers believed hotly that only one further thing was necessary to ensure the vast, the *total* success of *Women Weeping* in the States, and that was to make of its author a television celebrity. Earnestly defending his own position on the subject of violence and female masochism on a series of television interviews and talk shows, Sammy Luke was expected to shoot *Women Weeping* high, high into the best-seller lists and keep it there. All this was the firm conviction of Sammy's editor at Porlock Publishers, Clodagh Jansen.

"You'll be great on the talk shows, Sammy," Clodagh had cawed down the line from the States. "So little and cute and then—" Clodagh made a loud noise with her lips as if someone was gobbling someone else up. Presumably it was not Sammy who was to be gobbled. Clodagh was a committed feminist, as she had carefully explained to Sammy on her visit to England, when she had bought *Women Weeping*, against much competition, for a huge sum. But she believed in the social role of best-sellers like *Women Weeping* to finance radical feminist works. Sammy had tried to explain that his book was in no way anti-feminist, no way at all, witness the fact that Zara herself, his Egeria, had not complained . . .

"Save it for the talk shows, Sammy," was all that Clodagh had replied.

While Sammy was still wondering how to put all this concisely, but to his best advantage, at Kennedy Airport, the man in the booth asked: "And the purpose of your visit, Mr. Luke?"

Sammy was suddenly aware that he had drunk a great deal on the long flight—courtesy of Porlock's first class ticket—and slept too heavily as well. His head began to sing. But whatever answer he gave, it was apparently satisfactory. The man stamped the white sheet inside his passport and handed it back. Then:

"Enjoy your visit to the United States of America, Mr. Luke. Have a nice day now."

"Oh I will, I know I will," promised Sammy. "It seems a lovely day here already."

Sammy's experiences at the famous Barraclough Hotel (accommodation arranged by Clodagh) were if anything even more heartwarming. Everyone, but everyone at the Barraclough wanted Sammy to enjoy himself during his visit.

"Have a nice day now, Mr. Luke": most conversations ended like that, whether they were with the hotel telephonists, the agreeable men who operated the lifts or the gentlemanly *concierge*. Even the New York taxi drivers, from whose guarded expressions Sammy would not otherwise have suspected such warm hearts, wanted Sammy to have a nice day.

"Oh I will, I will," Sammy began by answering. After a bit he added: "I just adore New York," said with a grin and the very suspicion of an American twang.

"This is the friendliest city in the world," he told Zara down the long-distance telephone, shouting, so that his words were accompanied by little vibratory echoes.

"Tess says they don't really mean it." Zara's voice in contrast was thin, diminished into a tiny wail by the line. "They're not sincere, you know."

"Tess was wrong about the gorillas at Immigration. She could be wrong about that too. Tess doesn't *own* the whole country, you know. She just inherited a small slice of it."

"Darling, you do sound funny," countered Zara; her familiar anxiety on the subject of Sammy made her sound stronger. "Are you all right? I mean, are you all right over there all by yourself—?"

"I'm mainly on television during the day," Sammy cut in with a laugh. "Alone except for the chat show host and forty million people." Sammy was deciding whether to add, truthfully, that actually not all the shows were networked; some of his audiences being as low as a million, or, say, a million and a half, when he realized that Zara was saying in a voice of distinct reproach:

"And you haven't asked after Mummy yet." It was the sudden

illness of Zara's mother, another person emotionally dependent upon her, which had prevented Zara's trip to New York with Sammy, at the last moment.

It was only after Sammy had rung off—having asked tenderly after Zara's mother and apologized for his crude crack about Tess before doing so—that he realized Zara was quite right. He *had* sounded rather funny: even to himself. That is, he would never have dared to make such a remark about Tess in London. Dared? Sammy pulled himself up.

To Zara, his strong and lovely Zara, he could of course say anything. She was his wife. As a couple, they were exceptionally close as all their circle agreed; being childless (a decision begun through poverty in the early days and somehow never rescinded) only increased their intimacy. Because their marriage had not been founded on a flash-in-the-pan sexual attraction but something deeper, more companionate—sex had never played a great part in it, even at the beginning—the bond had only grown stronger with the years. Sammy doubted whether there was a more genuinely united pair in London.

All this was true; and comforting to recollect. It was just that in recent years Tess had become an omnipresent force in their lives: Tess on clothes, Tess on interior decoration, especially Tess on curtains, that was the real pits—a new expression which Sammy had picked up from Clodagh; and somehow Tess's famous money always seemed to reinforce her opinions in a way which was rather curious, considering Zara's own radical contempt for unearned wealth.

"Well, I've got money now. Lots and lots of it. Earned money," thought Sammy, squaring his thin shoulders in the new pale blue jacket which Zara, yes Zara, had made him buy. He looked in one of the huge gilded mirrors which decorated his suite at the Barraclough, pushing aside the large floral arrangement, a gift from the hotel manager (or was it Clodagh?) to do so. Sammy Luke, the conqueror of New York, or at least American television; then he had to laugh at his own absurdity.

He went on to the little balcony which led off the suite's sitting room and looked down at the ribbon of streets which stretched below; the roofs of lesser buildings; the blur of green where Central Park nestled, at his disposal, in the center of it all. The plain truth was that he was just very, very happy. The reason was not purely the success of his book, nor even his instant highly commercial fame, as predicted by Clodagh, on television, nor yet the attentions of the press, parts of which had after all been quite violently critical of his book, again as predicted by Clodagh. The reason was that Sammy Luke felt loved in New York in a vast, wonderful, impersonal way: Nothing was demanded of him by this love; it was like an electric fire which simulated red-hot coals even when it was switched off. New York glowed but it could not scorch. In his heart Sammy knew that he had never been so happy before.

It was at this point that the telephone rang again. Sammy left the balcony. Sammy was expecting one of three calls. The first, and most likely, was Clodagh's daily checking call: "Hi, Sammy, it's Clodagh Pegoda . . . listen, that show was great, the one they taped. Our publicity girl actually told me it didn't go too well at the time, she was frightened they were mauling you . . . but the way it came out . . . Zouch!" More interesting sounds from Clodagh's mobile and rather sensual lips. "That's my Sam. You really had them licked. I guess the little girl was just protective. Sue-May, was it? Joanie. Yes, Joanie. She's crazy about you. I'll have to talk to her; what's a nice girl like that doing being crazy about a man, and a married man at that. . . ."

Clodagh's physical preference for her own sex was a robust joke between them; it was odd how being in New York made that, too, innocuous. In England Sammy had been secretly rather shocked by the frankness of Clodagh's allusions: more alarmingly she had once goosed him, apparently fooling, but with the accompanying words "You're a bit like a girl yourself, Sammy," which were not totally reassuring. Even that was preferable to the embarrassing occasion when Clodagh had playfully declared a physical attraction to Zara, wondered—outside the money that was now coming in—how Zara put up with Sammy. In New York, however, Sammy entered enthusiastically into the fun.

He was also pleased to hear, however lightly meant, that Joanie, the publicity girl in charge of his day-to-day arrangements, was crazy about him; for Joanie, unlike handsome, piratical, frightening Clodagh, was small and tender.

The second possibility for the call was Joanie herself. In which case she would be down in the lobby of the Barraclough, ready to escort him to an afternoon taping at a television studio across town. Later Joanie would drop Sammy back at the Barraclough, paying carefully and slightly earnestly for the taxi as though Sammy's nerves might be ruffled if the ceremony was not carried out correctly. One of these days, Sammy thought with a smile, he might even ask Joanie up to his suite at the Barraclough . . . after all what were suites for? (Sammy had never had a suite in a hotel before, his English publisher having an old-fashioned taste for providing his authors with plain bedrooms while on promotional tours.)

The third possibility was that Zara was calling him back: their conversations, for all Sammy's apologies, had not really ended on a satisfactory note; alone in London, Zara was doubtless feeling anxious about Sammy as a result. He detected a little complacency in himself about Zara: after all, there was for once nothing for her to feel anxious about (except perhaps Joanie, he added to himself with a smile).

Sammy's complacency was shattered by the voice on the telephone:

"I saw you on television last night," began the voice—female, whispering. "You bastard, Sammy Luke, I'm coming up to your room and I'm going to cut off your little—" A detailed anatomical description followed of what the voice was going to do to Sammy Luke. The low, violent obscenities, so horrible, so surprising, coming out of the innocent white hotel telephone, continued for a while unstopped, assaulting his ears like the rustle of some appalling cowrie shell; until Sammy thought to clutch the instrument to his chest, and thus stifle the voice in the surface of his new blue jacket.

After a moment, thinking he might have put an end to the terrible whispering, Sammy raised the instrument again. He was in time to hear the voice say:

"Have a nice death, Mr. Luke."

Then there was silence.

Sammy felt quite sick. A moment later he was running across the ornate sitting room of the splendid Barraclough suite, retching; the bathroom seemed miles away at the far end of the spacious bedroom;he only just reached it in time.

Sammy was lying, panting, on the nearest twin bed to the door—the one which had been meant for Zara—when the telephone rang again. He picked it up and held it at a distance, then recognized the merry, interested voice of the hotel telephonist.

"Oh, Mr. Luke," she was saying. "While your line was busy just now, Joanie Lazlo called from Porlock Publishers, and she'll call right back. But she says to tell you that the taping for this afternoon has been canceled, Max Syegrand is still tied up on the Coast and can't make it. Too bad about that, Mr. Luke. It's a good show. Anyway, she'll come by this evening with some more books to sign . . . Have a nice day now, Mr. Luke." And the merry telephonist rang off. But this time Sammy shuddered when he heard the familiar cheerful farewell.

It seemed a long time before Joanie rang to say that she was downstairs in the hotel lobby, and should she bring the copies of *Women Weeping* up to the suite? When she arrived at the sitting room door, carrying a Mexican tote bag weighed down by books, Joanie's pretty little pink face was glowing and she gave Sammy her usual softly enthusiastic welcome. All the same Sammy could hardly believe that he had contemplated seducing her—or indeed anyone—in his gilded suite amid the floral arrangements. That all seemed a very long while ago.

For in the hours before Joanie's arrival, Sammy received two more calls. The whispering voice grew bolder still in its descriptions of Sammy's fate; but it did not grow stronger. For some reason, Sammy listened through the first call to the end. At last the phrase came: although he was half expecting it, his heart still thumped when he heard the words:

"Have a nice death now, Mr. Luke."

With the second call, he slammed down the telephone immediately and then called back the operator:

"No more," he said loudly and rather breathlessly. "No more, I don't want any more."

"Pardon me, Mr. Luke?"

"I meant, I don't want any more calls, not like that, not now."

"Alrighty." The operator—it was another voice, not the merry woman who habitually watched television, but just as friendly. "I'll hold your calls for now, Mr. Luke. I'll be happy to do it. Goodbye now. Have a nice evening."

Should Sammy perhaps have questioned this new operator about his recent caller? No doubt she would declare herself happy to discuss the matter. But he dreaded a further cheerful, impersonal New York encounter in his shaken state. Besides, the very first call had been put through by the merry television-watcher. Zara. He needed to talk to Zara. She would know what to do; or rather she would know what *he* should do.

"What's going on?" she exclaimed. "I tried to ring you three times and that bloody woman on the hotel switchboard wouldn't put me through. Are you all right? I rang you back because you sounded so peculiar. Sort of high, you were laughing at things, things which weren't really funny; it's not like you, is it; in New York people are supposed to get this energy, but I never thought . . ."

"I'm not all right, not all right at all," Sammy interrupted her; he was aware of a high, rather tremulous note in his voice. "I was all right then, more than all right, but now I'm not, not at all." Zara couldn't at first grasp what Sammy was telling her, and in the end he had to abandon all explanations of his previous state of exhilaration. For one thing, Zara couldn't seem to grasp what he was saying, and for another Sammy was guiltily aware that absence from Zara's side had played more than a little part in this temporary madness. So Sammy settled for agreeing that he had been acting rather oddly since he had arrived in New York, and then appealed to Zara to advise him how next to proceed.

Once Sammy had made this admission, Zara sounded more like her normal brisk but caring self. She told Sammy to ring up Clodagh at Porlock.

"Frankly, Sammy, I can't think why you didn't ring her straightaway." Zara pointed out that if Sammy could not, Clodagh certainly could and would deal with the hotel switchboard, so that calls were filtered, the lawful distinguished from the unlawful.

"Clodagh might even know the woman," observed Sammy weakly at one point. "She has some very odd friends."

Zara laughed. "Not *that* odd, I hope." Altogether she was in a better temper. Sammy remembered to ask after Zara's mother before he rang off; and on hearing that Tess had flown to America on business, he went so far as to say that he would love to have a drink with her.

When Joanie arrived in the suite, Sammy told her about the threatening calls and was vaguely gratified by her distress.

"I think that's just dreadful, Sammy," she murmured, her light hazel eyes swimming with some tender emotion. "Clodagh's not in the office right now, but let me talk with the hotel manager right away. . . ." Yet it was odd how Joanie no longer seemed in the slightest bit attractive to Sammy. There was even something cloying about her friendliness; perhaps there was a shallowness there, a surface brightness concealing nothing; perhaps Tess was right and New Yorkers were after all insincere. All in all, Sammy was pleased to see Joanie depart with the signed books.

He did not offer her a second drink, although she had brought him an advance copy of the *New York Times* Book Section for Sunday, showing that *Women Weeping* had jumped four places in the best-seller list.

"Have a nice evening, Sammy," said Joanie softly as she closed the door of the suite. "I've left a message with Clodagh's answering service and I'll call you tomorrow."

But Sammy did not have a very nice evening. Foolishly he decided to have dinner in his suite; the reason was that he had some idiotic lurking fear that the woman with the whispering voice would be lying in wait for him outside the Barraclough.

"Have a nice day," said the waiter, automatically, who delivered the meal on a heated trolley covered in a white damask cloth, after Sammy had signed the chit. Sammy hated him.

"The day is over. It is evening." Sammy spoke in a voice which was pointed, almost vicious; he had just deposited a tip on the white chit. By this time the waiter, stowing the dollars rapidly and expertly in his pocket, was already on his way to the door; he turned and flashed a quick smile.

"Yeah. Sure. Thank you, Mr. Luke. Have a nice day." The waiter's hand was on the door handle.

"It is evening here!" exclaimed Sammy. He found he was shaking. "Do you understand? Do you agree that it is *evening?*" The man, mildly startled, but not at all discomposed, said again: "Yeah. Sure. Evening. Goodbye now." And he went.

Sammy poured himself a whiskey from the suite's mini-bar. He no longer felt hungry. The vast white expanse of his dinner trolley depressed him, because it reminded him of his encounter with the waiter; at the same time he lacked the courage to push the trolley boldly out of the suite into the corridor. Having avoided leaving the Barraclough he now found that even more foolishly he did not care to open the door of his own suite.

Clodagh being out of the office, it was doubtless Joanie's fault that the hotel operators still ignored their instructions. Another whispering call was let through, about ten o'clock at night, as Sammy was watching a movie starring the young Elizabeth Taylor, much cut up by commercials, on television. (If he stayed awake till midnight, he could see himself on one of the talk shows he had recorded.) The operator was now supposed to announce the name of each caller, for Sammy's inspection; but this call came straight through.

There was a nasty new urgency in what the voice was promising: "Have a nice death now. I'll be coming by quite soon, Sammy Luke."

In spite of the whiskey—he drained yet another of the tiny bottles—Sammy was still shaking when he called down to the operator and protested: "I'm still getting these calls. You've got to do something. You're supposed to be keeping them away from me."

The operator, not a voice he recognized, sounded rather puzzled, but full of goodwill; spurious goodwill, Sammy now felt. Even if she was sincere, she was certainly stupid. She did not seem to recall having put through anyone to Sammy within the last ten minutes. Sammy did not dare instruct her to hold all calls in case Zara rang up again (or Clodagh, for that matter; where was Clodagh, now that he needed protection from this kind of feminist nut?) He felt too desperate to cut himself off altogether from contact with the outside world. What would Zara advise?

The answer was really quite simple, once it had occurred to him. Sammy rang down to the front desk and complained to the house manager who was on night duty. The house manager, like the operator, was rather puzzled, but extremely polite.

"Threats, Mr. Luke? I assure you you'll be very secure at the Barraclough. We have guards naturally, and we are accustomed . . . but if you'd like me to come up to discuss the matter, why I'd be happy to. . . ."

When the house manager arrived, he was quite charming. He referred not only to Sammy's appearance on television but to his actual book. He told Sammy he'd loved the book; what was more he'd given another copy to his eighty-three-year-old mother (who'd seen Sammy on the *Today* show) and she'd loved it too. Sammy was too weary to wonder more than passingly what an eighty-three-year-old mother would make of *Women Weeping*. He was further depressed by the house manager's elaborate courtesy; it wasn't absolutely clear whether he believed Sammy's story, or merely thought he was suffering from the delightful strain of being a celebrity. Maybe the guests at the Barraclough behaved like that all the time, describing imaginary death threats? That possibility also Sammy was too exhausted to explore.

At midnight he turned the television on again and watched himself, on the chat show in the blue jacket, laughing and wriggling with his own humour, denying for the tenth time that he had any curious sadistic tastes himself, that *Women Weeping* was founded on any incident in his private life.

When the telephone rang sharply into the silence of the suite shortly after the end of the show, Sammy knew that it would be his persecutor; nevertheless the sight of his erstwhile New York self, so debonair, so confident, had given him back some strength. Sammy was no longer shaking as he picked up the receiver.

It was Clodagh on the other end of the line, who had just returned to New York from somewhere out of town and picked up Joanie's message from her answering service. Clodagh listened carefully to what Sammy had to say and answered him with something less than her usual loud-hailing zest.

"I'm not too happy about this one!" she said after what—for Clodagh—was quite a lengthy silence. "Ever since Andy Warhol, we can never be quite sure what these jokers will do. Maybe a press release tomorrow? Sort of protect you with publicity *and* sell a few more copies. Maybe not. I'll think about that one, I'll call Joanie in the morning." To Sammy's relief, Clodagh was in charge.

There was another pause. When Clodagh spoke again, her tone was kindly, almost maternal; she reminded him, surprisingly, of Zara.

"Listen, little Sammy, stay right there and I'll be over. We don't want to lose an author, do we?"

Sammy went on to the little balcony which led off the sitting room and gazed down at the streetlights far far below; he did not gaze too long, partly because Sammy suffered from vertigo (although that had become much better in New York) and partly because he wondered whether an enemy was waiting for him down below. Sammy no longer thought all the lights were twinkling with goodwill. Looking downwards he imagined Clodagh, a strong Zara-substitute, striding towards him, to save him.

When Clodagh did arrive, rather suddenly at the door of the suite—maybe she did not want to alarm him by telephoning up from the lobby of the hotel?—she did look very strong, as well as handsome, in her black designer jeans and black silk shirt; through her shirt he could see the shape of her flat, muscular chest, with the nipples clearly defined, like the chest of a young Greek athlete.

"Little Sammy," said Clodagh quite tenderly. "Who would want to frighten you?"

The balcony windows were still open. Clodagh made Sammy pour himself yet another whiskey and one for her too (there was a trace of the old Clodagh in the acerbity with which she gave these orders). Masterfully she also imposed two mysterious bomb-like pills upon Sammy which she promised, together with the whiskey, would give him sweet dreams "and no nasty calls to frighten you."

Because Clodagh was showing a tendency to stand very close to him, one of her long arms affectionately and irremovably round his shoulders, Sammy was not all that unhappy when Clodagh ordered him to take both their drinks on to the balcony, away from the slightly worrying intimacy of the suite.

Sammy stood at the edge of the parapet, holding both glasses, and looked downwards. He felt better. Some of his previous benevolence towards New York came flooding back as the whiskey and pills began to take effect. Sammy no longer imagined that his enemy was down there in the street outside the Barraclough, waiting for him.

In a way of course, Sammy was quite right. For Sammy's enemy was not down there in the street below, but standing silently right there behind him, on the balcony, black gloves on her big, capable, strong hands where they extended from the cuffs of her chic black silk shirt.

"Have a nice death now, Sammy Luke." Even the familiar phrase hardly had time to strike a chill into his heart as Sammy found himself falling, falling into the deep trough of the New York street twenty-three stories below. The two whiskey glasses flew from his hands and little icy glass fragments scattered far and wide, far far from Sammy's tiny slumped body where it hit the pavement; the whiskey vanished altogether, for no one recorded drops of whiskey falling on their face in Madison Avenue.

Softhearted Joanie cried when the police showed her Sammy's typewritten suicide note with that signature so familiar from the signing of the books; the text itself, the last product of the battered, portable typewriter Sammy had brought with him to New York. But Joanie had to confirm Sammy's distressed state at her last visit to the suite; an impression more than confirmed by the amount of whiskey Sammy had consumed before his death—a glass in each hand as he fell, said the police—to say nothing of the pills.

The waiter contributed to the picture too.

"I guess the guy seemed quite upset when I brought him his dinner." He added as an afterthought: "He was pretty lonesome too. Wanted to talk. You know the sort. Tried to stop me going away. Wanted to have a conversation. I shoulda stopped, but I was busy." The waiter was genuinely regretful.

The hotel manager was regretful too, which considering the fact that Sammy's death had been duly reported in the press as occurring from a Barraclough balcony, was decent of him.

One of the operators—Sammy's merry friend—went further and was dreadfully distressed: "Jesus, I don't believe it. For Christ's sake, I just saw him on television!" The other operator made a calmer statement simply saying that Sammy had seemed very indecisive about whether he wished to receive calls or not in the course of the evening.

Zara Luke, in England, told the story of Sammy's last day and his pathetic tales of persecution, not otherwise substantiated. She also revealed—not totally to the surprise of her friends—that Sammy had a secret history of mental breakdowns and was particularly scared of traveling by himself.

"I shall always blame myself for letting him go," ended Zara, brokenly.

Clodagh Jansen of Porlock Publishers made a dignified statement about the tragedy.

It was Clodagh, too, who met the author's widow at the airport when Zara flew out a week later to make all the dreadful arrangements consequent upon poor Sammy's death.

At the airport Clodagh and Zara embraced discreetly, tearfully. It was only in private later at Clodagh's apartment—for Zara to stay at the Barraclough would certainly have been totally inappropriate—that more intimate caresses of a richer quality began. Began, but did not end: neither had any reason to hurry things.

"After all, we've all the time in the world," murmured Sammy's widow to Sammy's publisher.

"And all the money too," Clodagh whispered back; she must remember to tell Zara that *Women Weeping* would reach the Number One spot in the best-seller list on Sunday.

The Honest Blackmailer

PATRICIA MOYES

Patricia Moyes (1923–), a resident of the British Virgin Islands, has been called the last of the Golden Age writers because her mysteries are in the tradition of Agatha Christie, Dorothy L. Sayers, and the other greats who published between WWI and WWII. She emphasizes well-plotted, clever stories with fully realized characters. All of her more than sixteen novels feature the husband-and-wife team of Henry and Emmy Tibbett; in Moyes' later books, Henry is a Detective Chief Superintendent of Scotland Yard, while Emmy assists him and sometimes leads him through his cases. Among her flawlessly plotted books are *Death on the Agenda* (1962), *Season of Snows and Sins* (1971), and *A Six-Letter Word for Death* (1983).

Patricia Moyes' short stories are also excellent, and the present selection, which concerns a blackmailer with principles, was one of the best mystery stories published in 1982.

Any young man starting out in life to be a serious blackmailer should realize that he is entering a very delicate and possibly dangerous profession, requiring great judgment, finesse, and knowledge of human nature. Above all, he must learn not to be greedy. If Harry Bessemer had not been greedy, he might still be pursuing his lucrative career in London.

Harry came to his chosen profession in a conventional, almost classic way. His parents were blunt, North country, lower middle-class people, and they were proud, in a way, when Harry—after an adequate but not brilliant school career—informed them that he intended to go to London. Shows the lad has spunk, independence. They were even more pleased when he wrote to tell them that he had been accepted by the Metropolitan Police as a trainee. A right good start for the boy—shows you what he's made of. End up Chief Inspector, I wouldn't wonder.

In fact, Harry did not enjoy his years on the Force—for his taste, the work was too hard, the hours too long and the pay inadequate. However, it provided him with precious experience and training, so that when he resigned from the police he had no difficulty in getting a job as an investigator for a highly reputable firm of private detectives.

At the beginning there was a lot of tedious legwork on divorce cases—British law in those days still demanded the kind of sordid evidence that only a hired detective could produce. However, he worked doggedly and well, and in time was promoted to more sensitive and interesting cases, involving important and wealthy clients who for one reason or another did not care to call in the law. What he discovered on those cases—the vulnerability of human beings, however exalted—finally decided him to become a blackmailer.

It was, of course, vital that he should lay hands on and keep the tangible evidence that he was sent out to locate—letters, photographs, and even tapes, although he never found them very satisfactory. He would report back to his firm that he had had no success in finding the required evidence. The client might go away happily, convinced that the incriminating document no longer existed; on the other hand, the client might decide to call in another firm of private detectives, and it was imperative that they, too, should find nothing.

There remained the question of where to store these valuable documents until he was ready to use them. Harry moved from the small suburban house which he was renting to another, similar one on the other side of London, which he rented under an assumed name. Here, in the cellar, he installed an efficient safe, a photocopier, and basic darkroom equipment for developing and printing photographs. When he had a sizable collection of potentially damaging evidence in his hands, he resigned from his job as investigator and set up privately as a professional blackmailer.

It is a moot point whether a career blackmailer should marry or remain single. A wife may provide a useful cloak of respectability—on the other hand, it admits another person into that very private world. Harry made a nice compromise. With his savings, together with the small legacy left by his parents, he bought a small dry-cleaning establishment in yet another London suburb, which included living accommodations over the shop. He then married a nice, pretty but not very bright girl named Susan. She ran the shop and did a fair amount of perfectly legitimate business.

Susan had no knowledge of the rented house in the distant suburb, and she genuinely believed that Harry's fairly frequent absences from home were connected with some vague real-estate business up North. This, in her simple mind, accounted for the comparative affluence in which she and her husband lived, which could hardly have been produced by the small dry-cleaning establishment.

Harry knew very well that one of the big difficulties a blackmailer has to overcome is the actual transfer of money from the blackmailee, without any obvious contact between himself and his victim, and, of course, without any written or bank records. His terms, which were reasonable, were strictly cash; and for this, the dry-cleaning shop provided an ingenious front. He bought a van with the name—Clean-U-Quik—painted on the side of it. He himself drove the van to make special pickups and deliveries, exclusively to the homes of his various victims.

Posing as a mere driver, in the employment of Clean-U-Quik, he identified himself by a different and assumed name to each of his prospects. The system was simple. He made a weekly or fortnightly call, the victim's clothes were actually cleaned and returned, and there was always an envelope—ostensibly with a check for the cleaning bill—left for Harry to pick up. It contained the required sum in cash. Thus, if his clients were rich enough (and most of them were) to employ a domestic staff, the latter had no suspicion of what was going on. Harry felt justifiably proud of his scheme.

For some years all went well. Then Harry became aware of a growing worry about the permissiveness of modern London society. He soon realized that actors and actresses, rich though they might be, were useless prospects. They would merely laugh in his face, having probably already sold the scandalous story to a newspaper for a large amount of money. Even the aristocracy had become, by Harry's strict standards, notoriously lax, and were only of any practical use if they were closely connected in some way with the royal family. Income-tax dodgers were still a possibility, but unfortunately the Inland Revenue Service was becoming altogether too efficient at catching its own offenders. Homosexuality was no longer a crime, and eminent people were jostling each other to get out of the closet. About the only promising prospects left were politicians and diplomats. What with all this, and inflation too, the life of an honest blackmailer was becoming more difficult by the day.

One of Harry's good, solid clients who never let him down was the Right Honourable Mr.—better call him X. Mr. X was a Member of Parliament, Under-Secretary of State for something or other, eminently respectable, married to a rich and aristocratic wife, and known for his implacable stand against the Provisional I.R.A. in Northern Ireland. Harry had acquired beautiful evidence—both photographs and letters—to show that Mr. X in fact enjoyed a homosexual relationship with a young Irishman, whom he kept in a discreet apartment on the fringes of Islington, in East London, well away from his stylish West London house in Kensington. What was more, the young Irishman was strongly suspected of having illegal connections with Ulster terrorists. It was, from Harry's point of view, an ideal setup.

What was even more, a sense of confidence—you could almost call it friendship—sprang up between Harry and Mr. X. Harry's fortnightly demand was a perfectly reasonable sum to pay for his discretion, and he did not abuse it. Moreover, he made a special point of seeing that Mr. and Mrs. X's clothes were impeccably cleaned and pressed. The arrangement would have gone along very satisfactorily for a long time if Harry had not become greedy.

The unfortunate fact was that, in a single week, Harry lost two steady clients. One was a bestselling writer of tough, macho novels who suddenly burst into print with details of his love affair with a private in the Royal Marines. This doubled his sales, and rendered Harry's compromising photograph worthless. The other was a Member of Parliament—a tax-evasion case which the authorities had not spotted, but Harry had—who was blown up when he opened one of the letterbombs which Irish terrorists had taken to sending to politicians known to oppose their views.

This double blow to Harry's finances made him take a drastic step. He wrote a letter to the Rt. Hon. Mr. X., addressed to the House of Commons and purporting to come from one of Mr. X's constituents. It requested an urgent interview with the Member concerning rates and taxes in the constituency. Every British voter has the right to speak to his M.P. on such questions, and private rooms in the House are set aside for such meetings. It was in this way that Harry had made his original contact with Mr. X, and of course he signed the letter with the name by which Mr. X knew him. By return of post Harry received a letter from Mr. X's secretary, granting him an interview the following week.

The Right Honourable Mr. X was not a fool. He had a shrewd suspicion of what was coming, and he was right. In the privacy of the interview room Harry told him bluntly that the fortnightly bills for dry-cleaning were to be trebled, starting from the next pickup day, at the end of the week.

Mr. X smiled, as he always did. He agreed with Harry that these were inflationary times, and that an increase was only to be expected. Harry was momentarily taken aback, feeling that he had trodden on a stair which was not there. He had expected at least a show of opposition.

"There's just one snag, though," Mr. X went on. "The banks are closed for today, and I'm off to Belgium for that NATO conference tomorrow morning. Would you take a check?"

"You know my terms," said Harry, smelling a rat. "Cash only."

"Well . . ." Mr. X sighed. "I don't see how it can be done. If you'd wait until next month—"

"I said this week and I mean this week," said Harry, who had financial troubles of his own.

A sudden light broke upon Mr. X. "I know," he said. "There are banks at London Airport which will be open tomorrow before I have to board my plane. I'll draw the money there and send it to you."

"Send it?"

"By post. If you'll just give me your address—"

"Oh, no," said Harry. "I don't want cash like that arriving at the shop."

"Then perhaps you have another address—a private one?"

"You don't catch me like that," said Harry. "I pick the money up at your house—in cash."

"Oh, Harry," said Mr. X, full of regret, "don't you see I'm trying to help you? After all, we trust each other, don't we?"

"Up to a point," said Harry cautiously.

"Ah, well now, how's this for an idea? I'll mail the money from London Airport in an envelope addressed to myself, at my home. I'll have to disguise my handwriting, of course, but that won't be too difficult. I'll mark the envelope Private and Confidential, and I'll underline the word Private three times. That way, you'll be able to recognize it at once."

"How do you mean?"

"Well, while I'm away, my mail will be waiting for me on the marble table in the hall. You know the one. When the butler goes off to collect the clothes for cleaning, you can just pick up the envelope and slip it in your pocket. How's that?"

"Not bad," said Harry, nodding slowly. "Not bad." He smiled. "It's a real pleasure to do business with you, sir. You're a real gentleman."

That evening Mr. X said to his young Irish boy friend, "You know, Paddy, I think it might not be a bad idea if I got one of those letterbombs."

"But—"

"Oh, don't worry. I'll be able to identify it, and take it straight to the police. But there are rumors going round that perhaps I'm not so unsympathetic to the provisionals as I appear to be—"

"Okay," said Paddy, who was a practical young man. "What do you want?"

"It must be posted tomorrow morning at London Airport," said Mr. X.

"Hey, that doesn't give me much time—"

"You can arrange it," said Mr. X.

"Well—yes, okay. I suppose I can."

"I'll address the envelope myself. Get me one—not too small."

"Yes, *sir*," said Paddy, with an impish grin and a mock salute. He brought a large envelope.

Mr. X began writing, in apparently uneducated capital letters, his own name and address. He added Private and Confidential in the top left-hand corner and underlined the word Private three times. Then he handed the envelope to Paddy. "Make sure the device is well-padded with newspaper or something," he said. "It should look as though the envelope was pretty full. Got it? All clear?"

"Yes, *sir*," said Paddy again. He took the envelope. "I'll be getting around to the boys to get this done right away."

"You're a good lad," said Mr. X.

Three days later Harry turned up in his dry-cleaning van at the Kensington house, as usual. As usual, the butler asked him to wait in the hall while he went to get the dirty clothes. It was a great trial to the butler, who had been trained in a grand house, that the mews cottage at the back had been sold for an enormous sum, so that tradesmen had to be admitted through the front door.

As soon as the butler had gone, Harry went to the hall table. Sure enough, there was the envelope, well-stuffed, written in a hand which, from long experience, he could recognize was that of the Right Honourable Mr. X., thinly disguised. He picked up the envelope and put it in his pocket, just as the butler returned with his laundry bag.

"I'll have these back by Tuesday," said Harry cheerfully, as he went out the front door. He could hardly have been more wrong. As soon as he got into the van, he could not resist opening the envelope. He, the van, the clothes, and part of Mr. X's front steps were blown to smithereens.

Harry had made another grave error, as great as his sin of greed. He had not bothered to check that there was no conference in Belgium that week. The Right Honourable, who had simply gone to stay for a few days with his sister in the country, came back to London at once when he heard the news, expressing profound shock and surprise.

The police were efficient—they were becoming accustomed to dealing with such incidents. They found a few fragments of the envelope, and the butler affirmed that he had noticed, after the explosion, that an envelope marked Private and Confidential, which had been on the table awaiting Mr. X's return, had disappeared. He could only conclude that the dry-cleaning man had taken it—either to steal it, but more likely in mistake for an exactly similar one which was still there, marked Clean-U-Quik, and containing Mr. X's check for three pounds and thirty pence for cleaning, as per invoice.

Since poor Harry was dead, the police decided to give him the benefit of the doubt, and concluded that it had been an error on his part to take the wrong envelope. They congratulated Mr. X on his fortunate escape.

The terrorists, however, took a different point of view. Paddy stood a lot higher in the organization than Mr. X had ever realized, and he began to be worried. If the rumors that Mr. X was playing a double game were so prevalent that Mr. X had actually suggested an apparent letterbomb attack on himself, then Mr. X ceased to be an asset and became a positive danger. The Right Honourable Mr. X, having disposed of Harry, was in a light-hearted mood—even possibly in a state of grace—when he opened an innocuous-looking letter in his mail at the House of Commons a couple of weeks later, and had his head blown off. So a rough sort of justice may be said to have been done.

The Worst Crime Known to Man

REGINALD HILL

Reginald Hill has written more than forty novels, included the well-known Dalziel and Pascoe series. He has won the Crime Writers' Association Gold Dagger for best crime novel of the year, has been shortlisted for the MWA Edgar, and in 1995 was awarded the CWA Cartier Diamond Dagger for his outstanding contribution to the genre, He lives quietly in Cumbria, England with his wife, Pat; his cats, Pip and Marty; and his conscience.

"A middle-aged man was removed from the Centre Court crowd yesterday for causing a disturbance during a line-call dispute."

On summer evenings when I was young, I used to sit with Mamma on the verandah of our bungalow and watch the flamingoes gliding over the tennis court to roost on the distant lake.

This was my favorite time of day and the verandah was my favorite place. It was simply furnished with a low table, a scatter of cane chairs, and an old English farmhouse rocker with its broad seat molded and polished by long use.

This was Father's special chair. At the end of the day he would fold his great length into it, lean back with a sigh of contentment, and more often than not say, "This was your grandfather's chair, Colley, did I ever tell you that?"

"Yes, Father."

"Did I? Then probably I told you what it was my father used to tell me while sitting in this chair."

"Life is a game and you play to the rules, and cheating's the worst crime known to man," I would chant.

"Good boy," he would exclaim, laughing and glancing at Mamma, who would smile sweetly, making me smile too. I always smiled when Mamma smiled. She seemed to me then a raving beauty, and she was certainly the most attractive of the only three white women within five hundred square miles. I suppose she seemed so to many others too. "Boff" Gorton, a young District Officer from a better school than Father, used to tell her so after his third gin and tonic, and she would smile and my father would laugh. Boff came round quite a lot, ostensibly to check that all was well (there had already been the first stirrings of the Troubles) and to have a couple of sets on our lush green tennis court. I was too young to wonder how serious Boff's admiration of Mamma really was. During one of his visits, when Father had been held up in the bush, I got up in the night for a drink of water and heard a noise of violent rocking on the verandah. When I went to investigate I discovered Mamma relaxing in the rocking chair and

Boff, flushed and rather breathless, sitting on the floor. Curiously, Boff's situation struck me as less remarkable than Mamma's. This was the first time in my life I had ever known her to occupy the rocker.

Father's attitude to Boff was that of an older and rather patronizingly helpful brother. Only on the tennis court did anything like passion show, and that may have been due to natural competitiveness rather than jealousy. At any rate, their games were gargantuan struggles, with Boff's youth and Father's skill in such balance that the outcome was always in doubt.

The court itself was beautiful, a rectangle of English green it had taken ten years to perfect. It was completely enclosed in a cage of wire mesh, erected more to keep wildlife out than balls in. Human entry was effected through a small, tight-fitting gate, shut at night with a heavy chain and large padlock.

Father and Boff played their last match there one spring afternoon that had all the warmth and richness of the best of English summer evenings. Mamma was away superintending the *accouchement* of our nearest female neighbor, who had foolishly delayed her transfer down-country overlong. Curiously, Mamma's absence seemed to stir things up between the two men more than her presence ever did, and Father's invitation to Boff to play tennis came out like a challenge to a duel.

Boff tried to lighten matters by saying to me, "Colley, old chum, why don't you come along and be ball boy?"

"Yes, Colley," said Father. "You come along. You can be umpire too, and see fair play."

"I say," said Boff, flushing. "Do we need an umpire? I mean, neither of us is likely to cheat, are we?"

"Life is a game and you play to the rules and cheating's the worst crime known to man," I piped up.

"How right you are, Colley," said Father, observing Boff grimly. "You umpire!"

There was no more discussion, but even in the pre-match knock-up I recognized a ferocity that both excited and disturbed me. And when the match proper began it was such a hard-fought struggle that for a long time none of us noticed the arrival of the spectators. Usually only the duty houseboy watched from a respectful distance, waiting to be summoned forward with refreshing drinks, though occasionally some nomadic tribesmen would gaze from the fringes of the bush with courteous puzzlement. But this was different. Suddenly I realized that the court was entirely surrounded. There must have been two hundred of them, all standing quietly enough, but all marked with the symbols of their intent and bearing its instruments—machetes and spears.

"Father!" I choked out.

The two men glanced toward me, then saw what I had seen. For a second no one moved; then, with a fearsome roar, the natives rushed forward. Boff hurled himself towards the gate in the fence, and for a moment I thought he was making a suicidal attempt at flight. But District Officers are trained in other schools than that, and the next minute I saw he had seized the retaining chain, pulled it round the gate post and snapped shut the padlock.

The enemy was locked out. At the same time, of course, we were locked in.

If they had been carrying guns, in, out, it would have made no difference. Fortunately they were not, and the mesh was too close for the broad heads of their throwing spears. Even so, they could soon have hacked a way through the wire had not Boff for the second time revealed the quality of his training. Father in his eagerness for the fray had come from the house unarmed, but Boff had brought his revolver, and as soon as a group of our invaders began to hack at the fence he took careful aim and shot the most enthusiastic of them between the eyes.

They fell back in panic, but only for a moment. When they realized that Boff wasn't following up his attack, they returned to the fence, but no one offered to lead another demolition attempt.

"I've got just five bullets left," murmured Boff. "The only thing holding these chaps back is that they know the first to make a move will certainly die. But eventually not even that will matter."

"Why don't we make a dash for the house?" asked Father. "It's only fifty yards. And once we get to the rifles . . ."

"For God's sake!" said Boff. "Don't you understand? Outside this fence we're finished! And please don't talk about rifles. Once one of this lot gets that idea . . ."

Suddenly there came a great cry from the direction of the bungalow and I thought someone *had* got the idea. But a puff of smoke and a sudden tongue of flame revealed the truth, at the same time better and worse. Worse, because my home was going up in flames; better, because this act of arson would destroy their only source of weaponry and might even attract attention to our plight.

Father, perhaps feeling annoyed at the lead Boff had taken in dealing with the situation, suddenly picked up his racket.

"We might as well do something till help comes," he said. "My service, I believe."

It may have started as a gesture, but very rapidly that match developed into the hard, bitter struggle it had promised to be before the attack. I stood at the net holding the revolver, at first keeping an eye on the enemy outside. But soon my judgment of line calls and lets was being required so frequently that I had to give my full attention to the game.

But the most curious thing of all was the reaction of the rebels. At first there'd been some jabbering about ways of winkling us out. Then they fell silent except for one man, some renegade houseboy, I presume, who rather self-importantly began to offer a mixture of explanation of, and commentary on, the game, till his voice too died away; and at four-all in the first set I realized they had become as absorbed in the match as the players themselves. It was quite amazing, like watching a highly sunburned Wimbledon crowd. The heads moved from side to side following the flight of the ball, and at particularly strong or clever shots they beat their spear shafts against the earth and made approving booming noises deep in their throats.

Father took the first set seven-five, and looked as if he might run away with the second. But at one-four Boff's youth began to tell, and suddenly Father was on the defensive. At four-four he seemed to fold up completely, but I guessed that he was merely admitting the inevitable and taking a rest with a view to the climax.

The policy seemed to pay off. Boff won that set six-four, but now he too seemed to have shot his bolt and neither man could gain an ascendancy in the final set. Six-six it went, seven-seven, eight-eight, nine-nine, then into double figures. The light was fading fast.

"Look," said Boff coming up to the net and speaking in a low voice. "Shall we try to keep it going as long as possible? I don't know what these fellows may do when we finish. All right?"

Father didn't answer, but returned to the base line to serve. They came hard and straight, four aces. The crowd boomed. I forgot my official neutrality and joined in the applause. Father stood back to receive service.

I don't know. Perhaps he *was* trying to keep the match going. Perhaps he just intended to give away points by lashing out wildly at Boff's far from puny service. But the result was devastating. Three times in a row the ball streaked from his racket quite unplayably, putting up baseline chalk. Love-forty. Three match points. Father settled down, Boff served. Again the flashing return, but this time Boff, driven by resentment or fear, flung himself after it and sent it floating back. Father smashed, Boff retrieved. Father smashed. Boff retrieved again.

"For God's sake!" he pleaded.

Father, at the net, drove the ball deep into the corner and Boff managed to reach this only by flinging himself full length across the grass. But what a shot he produced! A perfect lob, drifting over Father's head and making for the extreme backhand corner.

Father turned with a speed I had not believed him capable of and went in pursuit. There was topspin on the ball. Once it bounced, it would be away beyond mortal reach. The situation looked hopeless.

But Father had no intention of letting it bounce. I drew in my breath as I saw he was going to attempt that most difficult of shots, a reverse backhand volley on the run. I swear the spectating natives drew in their breath too.

Father stretched—but it wasn't enough. He leapt. He connected. It was superb. The ball floated towards Boff, who still lay prostrate on the base line, and bounced gently a couple of feet from his face.

"Out!" he called desperately.

Father's roar of triumph turned to a howl of incredulity.

"Out?" he demanded. *"Out?"*

He turned to me and flung his arms wide in appeal. Boff called to me.

"Please, Colley. It *was* out, wasn't it? It *was!"*

He spoke with all the authority of a District Officer. But I was the umpire and I knew that in this matter my powers exceeded his. I shook my head.

"In!" I called. "Game, set and match to . . ."

With a cry of triumph, Father jumped over the net. And at the same moment a big black fellow with a face painted like a Halloween lantern twisted his spear butt in the chain till it snapped, and the howling mob poured in.

They were only inside the fence for about ten seconds before the first Land Rover full of troops arrived. But in that time they managed to carve the recumbent Boff into several pieces. Father on his feet and wielding his racket like a cavalry sabre managed to get away with a few unpleasant wounds, while I—perhaps because I still held the revolver, though I was too petrified to use it—escaped without threat, let alone violence.

On her return Mamma was naturally upset. I would have thought the survival of her husband and only son would have compensated for the loss of the house, but the more this was urged, the greater waxed her grief. Later, when I told the story of the match, describing with the detail befitting a noble death how Boff had so heroically attempted to keep the final game going, she had a relapse. When she recovered, things changed. I don't think I ever saw her smile again at Father's jokes.

Not that there were many more to smile at. One of Father's wounds turned septic and he had to have his right arm amputated just above the elbow. He tried to learn to play left-handed thereafter, but it never amounted to more than pat ball, and within a twelvemonth only the metal supports rising from the luxuriant undergrowth showed where the tennis court had been.

Soon after that I was sent back to the old country for schooling, and midway through my first term the Head sent for me to tell me there'd been a tragic accident. Father had been cleaning a gun and it had gone off. Or perhaps my mother had been cleaning the gun. Or perhaps, as they both died, they'd both been cleaning guns. I never discovered any details. Out there in the old days they still knew how to draw a decent veil over such things.

I was deeply grieved, of course, but school's a good place for forgetting and I never went back. Sending me to England had been their last known wish for my future. I did not feel able to go against it, not even when I was old enough to have some freedom of choice. And I have been happy enough here with my English job, English marriage, English health. I dig my little patch of garden, read political biographies, play a bit of golf.

But no tennis. I never got interested at school somehow, and I don't suppose I would ever have bothered with tennis again if my managing director hadn't offered me a spare Centre Court ticket. Well, I had to be in town anyway, and it seemed silly to miss the chance of visiting Wimbledon.

I was enjoying it thoroughly too, enjoying the crowd and the place and the game, here, now, with never a thought for the old days, till the Australian played that deep cross-court lob which sent the short-tempered American sprawling.

Then suddenly I saw it all again.

The white ball drifting through the richly scented, darkling air.

The outstretched figure on the baseline.

The pleading, despairing look on Boff's face as he watches the ball bounce out of his reach.

And with it his youth and his hopes and his life.

I saw the same anguish on the American's face today, heard the same accusing disbelief in his voice.

Of course, it wasn't his life and hopes and youth that were at stake. But as Father used to say, life is a game, and you play to the rules, and cheating's the worst crime known to man.

And the American and Boff did have one thing in common.

Both balls were a good six inches out.

Jeeves and the Stolen Venus

P. G. WODEHOUSE

Pelham Grenville Wodehouse, one of this century's most popular writers of light fiction, was born at Guildford, England, on October 15, 1881. He was educated at Dulwich College, then served two years as a bank clerk before leaving to conduct a column, "By the Way," in the London *Globe.* Over the years he wrote close to 100 novels, 500 stories and essays, 16 plays, and some lyrics. He and his wife made their home in France until they were arrested by the Nazis in 1941 and brought to Berlin. He became an American citizen in 1956. He was knighted in 1975 and died that same year at 93.

The telephone rang, and I heard Jeeves out in the hall dealing with it. Presently he trickled in.

"Mrs. Travers, sir."

"Aunt Dahlia? What does she want?"

"She did not confide in me, sir."

A bit oddish, it seems to me, looking back on it now, that as I went to the instrument I should have had no premonition, if that's the word I want, of an impending doom. Not psychic, that's my trouble.

"Hullo, old blood relation."

"Hullo, Bertie, you revolting young blot," she responded in her hearty way. "Are you sober?"

"As a judge."

"Then listen attentively. I'm speaking from an undersized hamlet in Hampshire called Marsham-in-the-Vale. I'm staying at Marsham Manor with Cornelia Fothergill, the novelist. Ever heard of her?"

"She is not on my library list."

"She would be, if you were a woman. I'm trying to persuade her to let me have her new novel as a serial for the *Boudoir*."

I got the gist. This aunt is the proprietor or proprietress of a weekly paper for the half-witted woman called *Milady's Boudoir*.

"How's it coming?" I asked.

"She's weakening. I have the feeling that one more shove will do the trick. That's why you're coming here for the week-end."

"Who, me? Why me?"

"To help me sway her. You will exercise all your charm—"

"I haven't much."

"Well, exercise what you've got."

I'm not keen on these blind dates. And if life has taught me one thing, it is that the prudent man keeps away from female novelists.

"Will anyone else be there? Is there any bright young society. I mean?"

"I wouldn't call the society young, but it's very bright. There's Cornelia's husband. Edward Fothergill, the artist, and his father, Edward Fothergill. He's an artist, too, of a sort. You won't have a dull moment. So tell Jeeves to pack your effects."

It surprises many people, I believe, that Bertram Wooster, as a general rule a man of iron, is as wax in the hands of his Aunt Dahlia. They do not know that this woman possesses a secret weapon by which she can always bend me to her will—viz., the threat that if I give her any of my lip she will bar me from her dinner table and deprive me of the roasts and boilers of her French chef, Anatole, God's gift to the gastric juices.

And so it came about that towards the quiet evenfall of Friday the 22nd inst. I was at the wheel of the old sports model, tooling through Hants with Jeeves at my side, the brow furrowed and the spirits low.

Arrival at Marsham Manor did little to smooth the former and raise the latter. Shown into the hall, I found myself in as cozy an interior as one could wish to find—large log fire, comfortable chairs, and a tea-table that gave out an invigorating aroma of buttered toast and muffins. But a single glance at the personnel was enough to tell me that I had struck one of those joints where every prospect pleases and only man is vile.

Three human souls were present, each as outstanding a piece of cheese as Hampshire could provide. One was a small, thin citizen with a beard of the type that causes so much distress—my host, I presumed—and seated near him another bloke of much the same construction but an earlier model, whom I took to be the father. He, too, was bearded. The third was a large, spreading woman wearing the horn-rimmed spectacles which are always an occupational risk for pen-pushers of the gentler sex.

After a brief pause for identification, she introduced me to the gang, and presently Aunt Dahlia blew in, and we chatted of this and that. The Fothergill contingent pushed off, and I was heading in the same direction when Aunt Dahlia arrested my progress.

"Just a second, Bertie," she said. "I would like to show you something."

"And I," I riposted, "would like to know what this job is you say you want me to do for you."

"I'll be coming to that shortly. This thing I'm going to show you is tied in with it. But first a word from our sponsor. Did you notice how jumpy Everard Fothergill is?"

"No. I didn't spot that. Is he jumpy?"

"He's a nervous wreck. Ask me why."

"Why?"

"Because of this picture I'm going to show you. Step this way."

She led me into the dining-room and switched on the light.

"Look," she said.

What she was drawing to my attention was a large oil painting. A classical picture, I suppose you would have called it: stout female in the minimum of clothing in conference with what appeared to be a dove.

"Venus?" I said. It's usually a safe bet.

"Yes. Old Fothergill painted it. He's just the sort of man who would paint a picture of Ladies' Night in a Turkish Bath and call it Venus. He gave it to Everard as a wedding present."

"I like the patine," I said. Another safe bet.

"No, you don't. The thing's a mess. The old boy's just an incompetent amateur. I got the whole strength of it from Cornelia one night. As I say, he gave this eyesore to Everard as a wedding present, and naturally, being devoted to his father and not wanting to hurt his feelings, Everard can't have it taken down and put in the cellar. So he has to sit looking at it every time he has a meal, and he suffers profusely. You see, Everard's a real artist. His stuff's good. Look at this," she said, indicating the picture next to old Fothergill's. "That's one of his things."

I took a steady look at Everard's effort. It, too, was a classical picture, and it seemed to me very like the other one.

"Venus?"

"Don't be an ass. Jocund Spring."

"Oh, sorry. Though, mark you, Sherlock Holmes would have made the same mistake. On the evidence, I mean."

"So now you understand."

"Far from it."

"I'll put it in words of one syllable. If a man can paint anything as good as that, it cuts him to the quick to have to glue his eyes on a daub like the Venus every time he puts on the nosebag."

"Oh, I see that, and the heart bleeds, of course. But I don't see there's anything to be done."

"I do. Ask me what."

"What?"

"You're going to steal that Venus."

"Steal it?"

"Tonight."

"When you say, 'steal it,' do you mean '*steal* it'?"

"That's right. That's the job I alluded to. Good heavens," she said, "you're always stealing policemen's helmets, aren't you?"

I had to correct this.

"Not always. Only as an occasional treat, as it might be on Boat Race night. And stealing pictures is a very different thing from lifting the headgear of the Force."

"There's nothing complex about it. You just cut it out of the frame with a sharp knife. You know, Bertie," she said, all enthusiasm, "it's extraordinary how things fit in. These last weeks there's been a gang of picture thieves working around this neighborhood. They pinched a Romney at a house near here and a Gainsborough from another house. When his Venus disappears, there won't be a chance of old Fothergill suspecting anything. These marauders are connoisseurs, he'll say to himself, only the best is good enough for them. Cornelia agreed with me."

"You told her?"

"Well, naturally. I was naming the Price of the Papers. I said that if she gave me her solemn word that she would let the *Boudoir* have this slush she's writing, shaving her usual price a bit, you would liquidate the Venus."

"You did, did you? And what did she say?"

"She thanked me brokenly, so go to it, boy, and heaven speed your efforts. All you have to do is open one of the windows, to make it look like an outside job, collect the picture, take it back to your room, and burn it. I'll see you have a good fire."

"Oh, thanks."

It was with bowed head and the feeling that the curse had come upon me that I proceeded to my room. Jeeves was there, studding the shirt, and I lost no time in putting him *au courant*, if that's the expression.

"Jeeves," I said, "here's a nice state of things. Do you know what Aunt Dahlia has just been springing on me?"

"Yes, sir. I chanced to be passing the door of the dining-room, and could not but overhear her observations. Mrs. Travers has a carrying voice."

"I suppose I'll have to do it, Jeeves."

"I fear so, sir. Taking into consideration the probability that, should you demur, Mrs. Travers will place sanctions on you in the matter of Anatole's cooking, you would appear to have no option but to fall in with her wishes. Are you in pain, sir?"

"No, just chafing. This has shocked me, Jeeves. Forcing a Wooster to become a picture-pincher! I wouldn't have thought such an idea would ever have occurred to her, would you?"

"The female of the species is more deadly than the male, sir. May I ask if you have formulated a plan of action?"

"Well, you heard the set-up as she envisages it. I open window—"

"Pardon me for interrupting, sir, but there I think Mrs. Travers is in error. A broken window would lend greater verisimilitude."

"It would also bring the whole ruddy household starting from their slumbers and coming to see what was going on."

"No, sir, it can be done quite noiselessly by smearing treacle on a sheet of brown paper, attaching the paper to the pane, and striking it with the fist."

"But where's the brown paper? Where's the treacle?"

"I can procure them, sir, and I shall be happy to perform the operation for you, if you wish."

"You will? That's very decent of you, Jeeves."

"Not at all, sir. It is my aim to give satisfaction. Excuse me, I think I hear someone knocking."

He went to the door and opened it, and I caught a glimpse of what looked like a butler.

"Your knife, sir," he said, coming back with it on a salver.

"Thank you, Jeeves, curse it." I regarded the object with a shudder. "I wish I could slide out of this binge."

"I can readily imagine it, sir."

After some deliberation we scheduled the kick-off for one o'clock in the morning, when the household might be expected to be getting their eight hours, and at one on the dot Jeeves shimmered in.

"Everything is in readiness, sir."

"The treacle?"

"Yes, sir."

"The brown paper?"

"Yes, sir."

"Then just bust the window, would you mind?"

"I have already done so, sir."

"You have? Well, you were right about it being noiseless. I didn't hear a sound. Then, Ho for the dining-room, I suppose. No sense in putting it off."

"No, sir. If it were done when 'tis done, then 'twere well it were done quickly," he said.

It would be idle to pretend that, as I made my way down the stairs, I was my usual calm, debonair self. The feet were cold, and if there had been any sudden noises I would have started at them. My meditations on Aunt Dahlia, who had let me in for this, were rather markedly lacking in a nephew's love.

However, in one respect you had to hand it to her. She had said the thing would be as easy as falling off a log, and so it proved. She had in no way overestimated the sharpness of the knife with which she provided me. Four quick cuts, and the canvas fell out of the frame. I rolled it up and streaked back to my room with it.

Jeeves in my absence had been stoking the fire. I was about to feed Edward Fothergill's regrettable product to the flames and push it home with the poker, but he stopped me.

"It would be injudicious to burn so large an object in one piece, sir. There is the risk of setting the chimney on fire."

"Ah, yes. I see what you mean. Snip it up, you think?"

"I fear it is unavoidable, sir. Might I suggest that it would relieve the monotony of the task if I were to provide you with whisky and a syphon?"

"You know where they keep it?"

"Yes, sir."

"Then lead it to me, Jeeves."

"Very good, sir."

I was making good progress when the door opened without my hearing it and Aunt Dahlia stole in. She spoke before I knew she was there, causing me to shoot up to the ceiling with a stifled cry.

"Everything all right, Bertie?"

"I wish you'd blow your horn," I said, coming back to earth and speaking with not a little bitterness. "You made me bite my tongue. Yes, everything has gone according to plan. But Jeeves insists on burning the *corpus delicti* bit by bit."

"Well, of course. You don't want to set the chimney on fire."

"That's what he said."

"And he was right, as always. I've brought my scissors. Where is Jeeves, by the way? Why not at your side, giving selfless service?"

"Because he's giving selfless service elsewhere. He will be returning shortly with the whisky decanter and all the trimmings."

"What a man! There is none like him, none. Bless my soul," said the relative, some minutes later, "how this brings back memories of the dear old school and our girlish cocoa parties. We used to sneak down to the headmistress's study and toast wholewheat bread on the end of pens, with the kettle simmering on the hob. Happy days, happy days. Ah, Jeeves, come right in and put it down well within my reach. We're getting on, you see. What is that you have on your arm?"

"The garden shears, madam. I am anxious to lend all the assistance that is within my power."

"Then start lending. Edward Fothergill's masterpiece awaits you."

With the three of us working away, we soon completed the job. I had scarcely got through my first whisky and *s.* and begun on another when all that was left of the Venus, not counting the ashes, was the little bit at the southwest end which Jeeves was holding. He was regarding it with what seemed to me a rather thoughtful eye.

"Excuse me, madam," he said, "did I understand you to say that Mr. Fothergill senior's name was Edward?"

"That's right. Think of him as Eddie, if you wish. Why?"

"It is merely that the picture we have with us tonight is signed 'Everard Fothergill,' madam."

To say that aunt and nephew did not take this big would be paltering with the truth. We skipped like the high hills.

"Give me that fragment, Jeeves. It looks like Edward to me," I pronounced, having scrutinized it.

"You're crazy," said Aunt Dahlia, wrenching it from my grasp. "It's Everard, isn't it, Jeeves?"

"That was certainly the impression I formed, madam."

"Bertie," said Aunt Dahlia speaking in a voice of the kind which I believe is usually called strangled, and directing at me the sort of look which in the old hunting days she would have given a hound engaged in chasing a rabbit, "if you've burned the wrong picture—"

"Of course I haven't," I replied stoutly. "But if it will ease your mind, I'll go and see."

I had spoken, as I say, stoutly, and hearing me you would have said to yourself, "All is well with Bertram. He is unperturbed." But I wasn't. I feared the worst, and already I was wincing at the thought of the impassioned speech, touching on my mental and moral defects, which Aunt Dahlia would be delivering when we foregathered once more.

I was in no vein for another shock, but I got this when I reached journey's end, for as I entered the dining-room somebody inside it came bounding out and rammed me between wind and water. We staggered into the hall together, and as I had switched on the lights there, to avoid bumping into pieces of furniture, I was enabled to see him steadily and see him whole, as Jeeves says.

It was old Fothergill, in bedroom slippers and a dressing-gown. In his right hand he had a knife, and at his feet there was a bundle of some sort which he had dropped at the moment of impact, and when I picked it up for him in my courteous way and it came unrolled, what I saw brought a startled "Golly!" to my lips. It dead-heated with a yip of anguish from his. He had paled beneath his beard.

"Mr. Wooster!" he—quavered is, I think, the word. "Thank God you are not Everard!"

Well, I was pretty pleased about that, too, of course.

"No doubt," he proceeded, still quavering, "you are surprised to find me removing my picture by stealth in this way. But I can explain everything."

"Well, that's fine, isn't it?"

"You are not an artist—"

"No, more a literary man. I once wrote an article on What the Well-Dressed Man Is Wearing for *Milady's Boudoir*."

"Nevertheless, I think I can make you understand what this picture means to me. I was two years painting it. It was my child. I watched it grow. I loved it. And then Everard married, and in a mad moment I gave it to him as a wedding present. You cannot imagine what agonies I suffered. I saw how he valued the picture. His eyes at meal times were always riveted on it. I could not bring myself to ask him for it back. And yet I was lost without it."

"So you decided to pinch it?"

"Exactly. I told myself that Everard would never suspect. There have been picture robberies in the neighborhood recently, and he would assume that this was the work of the same gang. And I yielded to temptation. Mr. Wooster, you would not betray me?"

"I wouldn't what?"

"You will not tell Everard?"

"Oh, I see what you mean. No, of course not, if you don't want me to. Sealed lips, you suggest?"

"Precisely."

"Right ho."

"Thank you, thank you. I knew you would not fail me. Well, one might as well be turning in, I suppose, so I will say good night," he said, and having done so, shot up the stairs like a homing rabbit. And scarcely had he disappeared when I found Aunt Dahlia and Jeeves at my side.

"Oh, there you are," I said.

"Yes, here we are. What's kept you all this time?"

"I would have made it snappier, but I was somewhat impeded in my movements by bearded artists."

"By what?"

"I've been chatting with Edward Fothergill."

"Bertie, you're blotto."

"Not blotto, but much shaken. Aunt Dahlia, I have an amazing story to relate."

I related my amazing story.

"And so," I concluded, "we learn once again the lesson never, however dark the outlook, to despair. The storm clouds lowered, the skies were black, but now what do we see? The sun shining and the bluebird working at the old stand. La Fothergill wanted the Venus expunged, and it has been expunged. Voila!" I said, becoming a bit Parisian.

"And when she finds that Everard's Jocund Spring has also been expunged?"

I h'med. I saw what she had in mind.

"Yes, there's that," I agreed.

"There isn't a chance now that she'll give me that serial."

"No, you have a point there. I had overlooked that."

She inflated her lungs, and it could have been perceived by the dullest eye that she was about to begin.

"Bertie—"

Jeeves coughed that soft cough of his, the one that sounds like a sheep clearing its throat on a distant mountainside.

"I wonder if I might make a suggestion, madam?"

"Yes, Jeeves? Remind me," she said, turning to me, "to go on with what I was saying later."

"It is merely that it occurs to me as a passing thought, madam, that there *is* a solution to the difficulty that confronts us. If Mr. Wooster were to be found here lying stunned, the window broken and *both* pictures removed, Mrs. Fothergill could scarcely but assume that he had been overcome, while endeavoring to protect her property, by miscreants making a burglarious entry."

Aunt Dahlia came up like a rocket from the depths of gloom.

"I see what you mean. She would be so all over him for his plucky conduct that she couldn't decently fail to let me have that serial at my own price."

"Precisely, madam."

"Thank you, Jeeves."

"Not at all, madam."

"A colossal scheme, don't you think, Bertie?"

"Supercolossal," I assented, "but with one rather serious flaw. I allude to the fact that I am not lying stunned."

"We can arrange that. I could give you a tiny little tap on the head . . . with what, Jeeves?"

"The gong stick suggests itself, madam."

"That's right, with the gong stick. You would hardly feel it."

"I'm not going to feel it."

"You mean you won't play ball? Think well, Bertram Wooster. Reflect what the harvest will be. Not a smell of Anatole's cooking will you get for months and months and months. He will dish up his Sylphides à la crême d'Ecrivisses and his Timbales de ris de veau Toulousiane and whatnot, but you will not be there to dig in and get yours. This is official."

I drew myself to my full height.

"There is no terror, Aunt Dahlia, in your threats, for . . . how does it go, Jeeves?"

"For you are armed so strong in honesty, sir, that they pass by you like the idle wind, which you respect not."

"Exactly. I have been giving considerable thought, Aunt Dahlia, to this matter of Anatole's cooking, and I have reached the conclusion that the thing is one that cuts both ways. Heaven, of course, to chew his smoked offerings, but what of the waistline? The last time I enjoyed your hospitality I put on a full inch around the middle. I am better without Anatole's cooking. I don't want to get to the stage of looking like Uncle George."

I was alluding to the present Lord Yaxley, a prominent clubman who gets more prominent yearly, especially seen sideways.

"So," I continued, "agony though it may be, I am prepared to kiss those Timbales of which you speak goodbye, and I, therefore, meet your suggestion that you should give me tiny little taps on the head with a resolute nolle prosequi."

"That is your last word, is it?"

"It is," I said, turning on my heel, and it was, for even as I spoke something struck me a violent blow on the back hair, and I fell like some monarch of the forest beneath the axe of the woodman.

The next thing I remember with any clarity is finding myself in bed with a sort of booming noise going on close by. This, the mists having lifted, I was able to diagnose as Aunt Dahlia talking.

"Bertie," she was saying, "I wish you would listen and not let your attention wander. I've got news that will send you singing about the house."

"It will be some little time," I responded coldly, "before I go singing about any ruddy houses. My head—"

"A little the worse for wear, no doubt. But don't let's go off into side issues. I want to tell you the final score. The dirty work is attributed on all sides to the gang, probably international, which got away with the Gainsborough and the Romney. The Fothergill is all over you, as Jeeves foresaw she would be, and she's given me the serial on easy terms. You were right about the bluebird. It's singing."

"So is my head."

"I know. And, as you would say, the heart bleeds. But you can't make an omelette without breaking eggs."

"Your own?"

"No, Jeeves's. He said it in a hushed voice as we stood viewing the remains."

"He did, did he? Well, I trust that in future . . . Oh, Jeeves," I said, as he entered carrying what looked like a cooling drink.

"Sir?"

"This matter of eggs and omelettes?"

"Yes, sir?"

"From now on, if you could see your way to cutting out the eggs and laying off the omelettes, I should be greatly obliged."

"Very good, sir. I will bear it in mind."

The Haunted Policeman

DOROTHY L. SAYERS

Dorothy Leigh Sayers was born on June 13, 1893, the only child of the headmaster of the Christchurch Choir School, Oxford. She grew up in the East Anglian fen country familiar to readers of *The Nine Tailors* and was one of the first women to obtain a degree from Oxford. She was editor of *Oxford Poetry* and wrote advertising copy before writing her first mystery, featuring Lord Peter Wimsey—*Whose Body?* (1923). She secretly gave birth to a son in 1924 and later married journalist Oswold Atherton Fleming. She wrote 11 novels and 44 stories and is highly regarded as an anthologist. She died on December 17, 1957.

"Good God!" said his lordship. "Did I do that?"

"All the evidence points that way," replied his wife.

"Then I can only say that I never knew so convincing a body of evidence produce such an inadequate result."

The nurse appeared to take this reflection personally. She said in a tone of rebuke: "He's a *beautiful* boy."

"H'm," said Peter. He adjusted his eyeglass carefully. "Well, you're the expert witness. Hand him over."

The nurse did so, with a dubious air. She was relieved to see that this disconcerting parent handled the child competently; as, in a man who was an experienced uncle, was not, after all, so very surprising. Lord Peter sat down gingerly on the bed.

"Do you feel it's up to standard?" he inquired with some anxiety. "Of course, *your* workmanship's always sound—but you never know with these collaborate efforts."

"I think it'll do," said Harriet.

"Good." He turned abruptly to the nurse. "All right; we'll keep it. Take it and put it away, and tell 'em to invoice it to me. It's a very interesting addition to you, Harriet; but it would have been a hell of a rotten substitute." His voice wavered a little, for in the last twenty-four hours he had had the fright of his life.

The doctor, who had been doing something in the other room, entered in time to catch the last words.

"There was never any likelihood of that, you goop," he said, cheerfully. "Now, you've seen all there is to be seen, and you'd better run away and play." He led his charge firmly to the door. "Go to bed," he advised him in kindly accents; "you look all in."

"I'm all right," said Peter. "I haven't been doing anything. And look here—" He stabbed a belligerent finger in the direction of the adjoining room. "Tell those nurses of yours, if I want to pick my son up, I'll pick him up. If his mother wants to kiss him, she can kiss him. I'll have none of your infernal hygiene in *my* house."

"Very well," said the doctor, "just as you like. Anything for a quiet life. I rather believe in a few healthy germs myself. Builds up resistance. No, thanks, I won't have a drink. I've got to go to another one, and an alcoholic breath impairs confidence."

"Another one?" said Peter, aghast.

"One of my hospital mothers. You're not the only fish in the sea by a long chalk. One born every minute."

"God! what a world." They passed down the great curved stair. In the hall a sleepy footman clung, yawning, to his post of duty.

"All right, William," said Peter. "Buzz off now; I'll lock up." He let the doctor out. "Good night—and thanks very much, old man. I'm sorry I swore at you."

"They mostly do," replied the doctor philosophically. "Well, bung-ho, Flim. I'll look in again later, just to carn my fee, but I shan't be wanted. You've married into a good tough family, and I congratulate you."

The car, spluttering and protesting a little after its long wait in the cold, drove off, leaving Peter alone on the door-step. Now that it was all over and he could go to bed, he felt extraordinarily wakeful. He would have liked to go to a party. He leaned back against the wrought-iron railings and lit a cigarette, staring vaguely into the lamp-lit dusk of the square. It was thus that he saw the policeman.

The blue-uniformed figure came up from the direction of South Audley Street. He too was smoking, and he walked, not with the firm tramp of a constable on his beat, but with the hesitating step of a man who has lost his bearings. When he came in sight he had pushed back his helmet and was rubbing his head in a puzzled manner. Official habit made him look sharply at the bare-headed gentleman in evening dress, abandoned on a doorstep at three in the morning, but since the gentleman appeared to be sober and bore no signs of being about to commit a felony, he averted his gaze and prepared to pass on.

" 'Morning officer," said the gentleman, as he came abreast with him.

" 'Morning sir," said the policeman.

"You're off duty early," pursued Peter, who wanted somebody to talk to. "Come in and have a drink."

This offer reawakened all the official suspicion.

"Not just now, sir, thank you," replied the policeman guardedly.

"Yes, now. That's the point." Peter tossed away his cigarette. It described a fiery arc in the air and shot out a little train of sparks as it struck the pavement. "I've got a son."

"Oh, ah!" said the policeman, relieved by this innocent confidence. "Your first, eh?"

"And last, if I know anything about it."

"That's what my brother says, every time," said the policeman. "Never no more, he says. He's got eleven. Well, sir, good luck to it. I see how you're situtated, and thank you kindly, but after what the sergeant said I dunno as I better. Though if I was to die this moment, not a drop 'as passed me lips since me supper beer."

Peter put his head on one side and considered this.

"The sergeant said you were drunk?"

"He did, sir."

"And you were not?"

"No, sir. I saw everything just the same as I told him, though what's become of it now is more than I can say. But drunk I was not, sir."

"Then," said Peter, "as Mr. Joseph Surface remarked to Lady Teazle, what is troubling you is the consciousness of your own innocence. He insinuated that you had looked on the wine when it was red—you'd better come in and make it so. You'll feel better."

The policeman hesitated.

"Well, sir, I dunno. Fact is, I've had a bit of a shock."

"So've I," said Peter. "Come in for God's sake and keep me company."

"Well, sir—" said the policeman again. He mounted the steps.

The logs in the hall-chimney were glowing a deep red through their ashes. Peter raked them apart, so that the young flame shot up between them. "Sit down," he said; "I'll be back in a moment."

The policeman sat down, removed his helmet, and stared about him, trying to remember who occupied the big house at the corner of the Square. The engraved coat-of-arms upon the great silver bowl on the chimney-piece told him nothing, even though it was repeated in color upon the backs of two tapestried chairs: three white mice skipping upon a black ground. Peter, returning from the shadows beneath the stair, caught him as he traced the outlines with a thick finger.

"A student of heraldry?" he said. "Seventeenth-century work and not very graceful. You're new to this beat, aren't you? My name's Wimsey."

He put down a tray on the table.

"If you'd rather have beer or whisky, say so. These bottles are only a concession to my mood."

The policeman eyed the long necks and bulging silver-wrapped corks with curiosity. "Champagne?" he said. "Never tasted it, sir. But I'd like to try the stuff."

"You'll find it thin," said Peter, "but if you drink enough of it, you'll tell me the story of your life." The cork popped, and the wine frothed out into the wide glasses, glinting as it caught the firelight.

"Well!" said the policeman. "Here's to your good lady, sir, and the new young gentleman. Long life and all the best. A bit in the nature of cider, ain't it, sir?"

"Just a trifle. Give me your opinion after the third glass, if you can put up with it so long. And thanks for your good wishes. You a married man?"

"Not yet, sir. Hoping to be when I get promotion. If only the sergeant—but that's neither here nor there. You been married long, sir, if I may ask?"

"Just over a year."

"Ah! and do you find it comfortable, sir?"

Peter laughed.

"I've spent the past twenty-four hours wondering why, when I'd had the blazing luck to get onto a perfectly good thing, I should be fool enough to risk the whole show on a silly experiment."

The policeman nodded sympathetically.

"I see what you mean, sir. Seems to me, life's like that. If you don't take risks, you get nowhere. If you do, they may go wrong, and then where are you? And 'alf the time, when things happen, they happen first, before you can even think about 'em."

"Quite right," said Peter, and filled the glasses again. He found the policeman soothing. True to his class and training, he turned naturally in moments of emotion to the company of the common man. Indeed, when the recent domestic crisis had threatened to destroy his nerve, he had headed for the butler's pantry with the swift instinct of the homing pigeon. There, they had treated him with great humanity, and allowed him to clean the silver.

With a mind oddly clarified by champagne and lack of sleep, he watched the constable's reaction to Pol Roger 1926. The first glass had produced a philosophy of life; the second produced a name—Alfred Burt—and further hints of some mysterious grievance against the station sergeant; the third glass, as prophesied, produced the story.

"You were right, sir" (said the policeman) "when you spotted I was new to the beat. I only come on it at the beginning of the week, and that accounts for me not being acquainted with you, sir, nor with most of the residents about here. Jessop, now, he knows everybody, and so did Pinker—but he's been took off to another division. You'd remember Pinker—big chap, make two o' me, with a sandy mustache. Yes, I thought you would.

"Well, sir, as I was saying, me knowing the district in a general way, but not, so to speak, like the palm o' me 'and, might account for me making a bit of a fool of myself, but it don't account for me seeing what I did see. See it I did, and not drunk nor nothing like it. And as for making a mistake in the number, well, that might happen to anybody. All the same, sir, thirteen was the number I see, plain as the nose on your face."

"You can't put it stronger than that," said Peter, whose nose was of a kind difficult to overlook.

"You know Merriman's End, sir?"

"I think I do. Isn't it a long cul-de-sac running somewhere at the back of South Audley Street, with a row of houses on one side and a high wall on the other?"

"That's right, sir. Tall, narrow houses they are, all alike, with deep porches and pillars to them."

"Yes. Like an escape from the worst square in Pimlico. Horrible. Fortunately, I believe the street was never finished, or we should have had another row of the monstrosities on the opposite side. This house is pure eighteenth century. How does it strike you?"

P. G. Burt contemplated the wide hall—the Adam fireplace and paneling with their graceful shallow moldings, the pedimented doorways, the high roundheaded window lighting hall and gallery, the noble proportions of the stair. He sought for a phrase.

"It's a gentleman's house," he pronounced at length. "Room to breathe, if you see what I mean. Seems like you couldn't act vulgar in it." He shook his head. "Mind you, I wouldn't call it cosy. It ain't the place I'd choose to sit down to a kipper in me shirtsleeves. But it's got class. I never thought about it before, but now you mention it I see what's wrong with them other houses in Merriman's End. They're sort of squeezed-like. I been into more'n one o' them tonight, and that's what they are; they're squeezed. But I was going to tell you about that.

"Just upon midnight it was" (pursued the policeman) "when I turns into Merriman's End in the ordinary course of my dooties. I'd got pretty near down towards the far end, when I see a fellow lurking about in a suspicious way under the wall. There's back gates there, you know, sir, leading into some gardens, and this chap was hanging about inside one of the gateways. A rough-looking fellow, in a baggy old coat—might a-been a tramp off the Embankment. I turned my light on him—that street's not very well lit, and it's a dark night—but I couldn't see much of his face, because he had on a ragged old hat and a big scarf round his neck. I thought he was up to no good, and I was about to ask him what he was doing there, when I hear a most awful yell come out o' one o' them houses opposite. Ghastly it was, sir. 'Help!' it said. 'Murder! help!' fit to freeze your marrow."

"Man's voice or woman's?"

"Man's, sir, I think. More of a roaring kind of yell, if you take my meaning. I says, 'Hullo! What's up there? Which house is it?' The chap says nothing, but he points, and him and me runs across together. Just as we gets to the house, there's a noise like as if someone was being strangled just inside, and a thump, as it might be something falling against the door."

"Good God!" said Peter.

"I gives a shout and rings the bell. 'Hoy!' I says. 'What's up here?' and then I knocks on the door. There's no answer, so I rings and knocks again. Then the chap who was with me, he pushes open the letter-flap and squints through it."

"Was there a light in the house?"

"It was all dark, sir, except the fanlight over the door. That was lit up bright, and when I looks up, I see the number of the house—Number Thirteen, painted plain as you like on the transom. Well, this chap peers in, and all of a sudden he gives a kind of gurgle and falls back. 'Here!' I says, 'what's amiss? Let me have a look.' So I puts me eye to the flap and I looks in."

P. C. Burt paused and drew a long breath. Peter cut the wire of the second bottle.

"Now, sir," said the policeman. "believe me or believe me not, I was as sober at that moment as I am now. I can tell you everything I see in that house, same as if it was wrote up there on that wall. Not as it was a great lot, because the flap wasn't all that wide, but by squinnying a bit, I could make shift to see right across the hall and a piece on both sides and part way up the stairs. And here's what I see, and you take notice of every word, on account of what came after."

He took another gulp of the Pol Roger to loosen his tongue and continued:

"There was the floor of the hall. I could see that very plain. All black and white squares it was, like marble, and it stretched back a good long way. About halfway along, on the left, was the staircase, with a red carpet, and the statue of a white naked woman at the foot, carrying a big pot full of blue and yellow flowers. In the wall next the stairs there was an open door, and a room all lit up. I could just see the end of a table, with a lot of glass and silver on it. Between that door and the front door there was a big black cabinet, shiny with gold figures painted on it, like them things they had at the Exhibition. Right at the back of the hall there was a place like a conservatory, but I couldn't see what was in it, only it looked very gay. There was a door on the right, and that was open, too. A very pretty drawing-room, by what I could see of it, with pale-blue paper and pictures on the walls. There were pictures in the hall, too, and a table on the right with copper bowl, like as it might be for visitors' cards to be put in. Now, I see all that, sir, and I put it to you, if it hadn't a' been there, how could I describe it so plain?"

"I have known people describe what wasn't there," said Peter thoughtfully, "but it was seldom anything of that kind. Rats, cats, and snakes I have heard of and occasionally naked female figures; but delirious lacquer cabinets and hall-tables are new to me."

"As you say, sir," agreed the policeman, "and I see you believe me so far. But here's something else, what you mayn't find quite so easy. There was a man laying in that hall, sir, as sure as I sit here, and he was dead. He was a big man and clean-shaven, and he wore evening dress. Somebody had stuck a knife into his throat. I could see the handle of it—it looked like a carving-knife, and the blood had run out, all shiny, over the marble squares."

The policeman looked at Peter, passed his handkerchief over his forehead, and finished the fourth glass of champagne.

"His head was up against the end of the hall table," he went on, "and his feet must have been up against the door, but I couldn't see anything quite close to me, because of the letter-box. You understand, sir, I was looking through the wire cage of the box, and there was something inside—letters, I suppose—that cut off my view downwards. But I see all the rest—in front and a bit of both sides; and it must have been regularly burnt in upon me brain, as they say, for I don't suppose I was looking more than a quarter of a minute or so. Then all the lights went out at once, same as if somebody had turned off the main switch. So I looks round, and I don't mind telling you I felt a bit queer. And *when* I looks round, lo and behold! my bloke in the muffler had hopped it."

"The devil he had," said Peter.

"Hopped it," repeated the policeman, "and there I was. And just there, sir, is where I made my big mistake, for I thought he couldn't a-got far, and I started off up the street after him. But I couldn't see him, and I couldn't see nobody. All the houses was dark, and it come over me what a sight of funny things may go on and nobody take a mite o' notice. The way I'd shouted and banged on the door, you'd a-thought it'd a-brought out every soul in the street, not to mention that awful yelling. But there—you may have noticed it yourself, sir. A man may leave his ground-floor windows open, or have his chimney afire, and you may make noise enough to wake the dead, trying to draw his attention, and nobody give no heed. He's fast asleep, and the neighbors say, 'Blast that row, but it's no business of mine,' and stick their 'eads under the bedclothes."

"Yes," said Peter. "London's like that."

"That's right, sir. A village is different. You can't pick up a pin there without somebody coming up to ask where you got it from—but London keeps itself to itself. . . . Well, something'll have to be done, I thinks to myself, and I blows me whistle. They heard that all right. Windows started to go up all the street. That's London, too."

Peter nodded. "London will sleep through the last trump. Puddley-in-the-Rut and Doddering-in-the-Dumps will look down their noses and put on virtuous airs. But God, Who is never surprised, will say to His angel, 'Whistle 'em up, Michael, whistle 'em up; East and West will rise from the dead at the sound of the policeman's whistle.' "

"Quite so, sir," said P. C. Burt; and wondered for the first time whether there might not be something in this champagne stuff after all. He waited for a moment and then resumed:

"Well, it so happened that just when I sounded my whistle, Withers—that's the man on the other beat—was in Audley Square, coming to meet me. You know, sir, we has times for meeting one another, arranged different-like every night; and twelve o'clock in the square was our rendyvoos tonight. So up he comes in, you might say, no time at all, and finds me there, with everyone a-hollering at me from the windows to know what was up. Well, naturally I didn't want the whole bunch of 'em running out into the street and our man getting away in the crowd, so I just tells 'em there's nothing, only a bit of an accident farther along. And then I see Withers and glad enough I was. We stands there at the top o' the street, and I tells him there's a dead man laying in the hall at Number Thirteen, and it looks to me like murder. 'Number Thirteen' he says, 'you can't mean Number Thirteen. There ain't no Number Thirteen in Merriman's End, you fathead; it's all even numbers.' And so it is, sir, for the houses on the other side were never built, so there's no odd numbers at all.

"Well, that give me a bit of a jolt. I wasn't so much put out at not having remembered about the numbers, for as I tell you, I never was on the beat before this week. No; but I knew I'd seen that there number writ up plain as pie on the fanlight, and I didn't see how I could have been mistaken. But when Withers heard the rest of the story, he thought maybe I'd misread it for Number Twelve. It couldn't be Eighteen, for there's only the eight houses in the road; nor it couldn't be Sixteen neither, for I knew it wasn't the end house. But we thought it might be Twelve or Ten; so away we goes to look.

"We didn't have no difficulty about getting in at Number Twelve. There was a very pleasant old gentleman came down in his dressing-gown, asking what the disturbance was, and could he be of use. I apologized for disturbing him, and said I was afraid there'd been an accident in one of the houses, and had he heard anything. Of course, the minute he opened the door I could see it wasn't Number Twelve we wanted; there was only a little hall with polished boards, and the walls plain paneled—all very bare and neat and no black cabinet nor naked woman nor nothing. The old gentleman said, yes, his son had heard somebody shouting and knocking a few minutes earlier. He'd got up and put his head out of the window, but couldn't see nothing, but they thought from the sound it was Number Fourteen forgotten his latch-key again. So we thanked him very much and went on to Number Fourteen.

"We had a bit of a job to get Number Fourteen downstairs. A fiery sort of gentleman he was, something in the military way, I thought, but he turned out to be a retired Indian Civil Servant. A dark gentleman, with a big voice, and his servant was dark, too. The gentleman wanted to know what the blazes all this row was about, and why a decent citizen wasn't allowed to get his proper sleep. He supposed that young fool at Number Twelve was drunk again. Withers had to speak a bit sharp to him; but at last the servant came down and let us in. Well, we had to apologize once more. The hall was not a bit like—the staircase was on the wrong side, for one thing and though there was a statue at the foot of it, it was some kind of a heathen idol with a lot of heads and arms, and the walls were covered with all sorts of brass stuff and native goods—you know the kind of thing. There was a black-and-white linoleum on the floor and that was about all there was to it. The servant had a soft sort of way with him I didn't half like. He said he slept at the back and had heard nothing till his master rang for him. Then the gentleman came to the top of the stairs and shouted out it was no use disturbing him; the noise came from Number Twelve as usual, and if that young man didn't stop his blanky Bohemian goings-on, he'd have the law on his father. I asked if he'd seen anything, and he said, no, he hadn't. Of course, sir, me and that other chap was inside the porch, and you can't see anything what goes on inside those porches from the other houses, because they're filled in at the sides with colored glass—all the lot of them."

Lord Peter Wimsey looked at the policeman and then looked at the bottle, as though estimating the alcoholic content of each. With deliberation, he filled both glasses again.

"Well, sir," said P. C. Burt, after refreshing himself, "by this time Withers was looking at me in rather an old-fashioned manner. However, he said nothing, and we went back to Number Ten, where there was two maiden ladies and a hall full of stuffed birds and wallpaper like a florist's catalogue. The one who slept in the front was deaf as a post, and the one who slept at the back hadn't heard nothing. But we got hold of their maids, and the cook said she'd heard the voice calling 'Help!' and thought it was in Number Twelve, and she'd hid her head in the pillow and said her prayers. The housemaid was a sensible girl. She'd looked out when she'd heard me knocking. She couldn't see anything at first, owing to us being in the porch, but she thought something must be going on, so, not wishing to catch cold, she went back to put on her bedroom slippers. When she got back to the window, she was just in time to see a man running up the road. He went very quick and very silent, as if he had galoshes on, and she could see the ends of his muffler flying out behind him. She saw him run out of the street and turn to the right, and then she heard me coming along after him. Unfortunately, her eye being on the man, she didn't notice which porch I came out of. Well, that showed I wasn't inventing the whole story at any rate, because there was my bloke in the muffler. The girl didn't recognize him at all, but that wasn't surprising, because she'd only just entered the old ladies' service. Besides, it wasn't likely the man had anything to do with it, because he was outside with me when the yelling started. My belief is, he was the sort as doesn't care to have his pockets examined too close, and the minute my back was turned he thought he'd be better and more comfortable elsewhere.

"Now there ain't no need" (continued the policeman), "for me to trouble you, sir, with all them houses what we went into. We made inquiries at the whole lot, from Number Two to Number Sixteen, and there wasn't one of them had a hall in any ways conformable to what that chap and I saw through the letter-box. Nor there wasn't a soul in 'em could give us any help more than what we'd had already. You see, sir, though it took me a bit o' time telling, it all went very quick. There was the yells; they didn't last beyond a few seconds or so, and before they was finished, we was across the road and inside the porch. Then there was me shouting and knocking; but I hadn't been long at that afore the chap with me looks through the box. Then I has my look inside, for fifteen seconds it might be, and while I'm doing that, my chap's away up the street. Then I runs after him, and then I blows me whistle. The whole thing might take a minute or a minute and a half. Not more.

"Well, sir, by the time we'd been into every house in Merriman's End, I was feeling a bit queer again, I can tell you, and Withers, he was looking queerer. He says to me. 'Burt,' he says, 'is this your idea of a joke? Because if so, the 'Olborn Empire's where you ought to be, not the police force.' So I tells him over again, most solemn, what I seen—'and,' I says, 'if only we could lay hands on that chap in the muffler, he could tell you he seen it, too. And what's more,' I says, 'do you think I'd risk me job, playing a silly trick like that?' He says, 'Well, it beats me,' he says. 'If I didn't know you was a sober kind of chap, I'd say you was seein' things.'

" 'Things?' I says to him. 'I see that there corpse a-layin' there with the knife in his neck, and that was enough for me. 'Orrible, he looked, and the blood all over the floor.' 'Well,' he says, 'maybe he wasn't dead after all, and they've cleared him out of the way.' 'And cleared the house away too, I suppose,' I said to him. So Withers says, in an odd sort o' voice, 'You're sure about the house? You wasn't letting your imagination run away with you over naked females and such?' That was a nice thing to say. I said, 'No, I wasn't. There's been some monkey business going on in this street and I'm going to get to the bottom of it, if we has to comb out London for that chap in the muffler.' 'Yes,' says Withers, nasty like, 'it's a pity he cleared off so sudden.' 'Well,' I says, 'you can't say I imagined *him,* anyhow, because that there girl saw him, and a mercy she did,' I said, 'or you'd be saying next I ought to be in Colney Hatch.' 'Well,' he says, 'I dunno what you think you're going to do about it. You better ring up the station and ask for instructions.'

"Which I did. And Sergeant Jones, he come down himself, and he listens attentive-like to what we both has to say, and then he walks along the street, slow-like, from end to end. And then he comes back and says to me, 'Now, Burt,' he says, 'just you describe that hall to me again, careful.' Which I does, same as I described it to you, sir. And he says, 'You're sure there was the room on the left of the stairs with the glass and silver on the table; and the room on the right with the pictures in it?' And I says, 'Yes, Sergeant, I'm quite sure of that.' And Withers says, 'Ah!' in a kind of got-you-now-voice, if you take my meaning. And the sergeant says, 'Now, Burt,' he says, 'pull yourself together and take a look at these here houses. Don't you see they're all single-fronted? There ain't one of 'em has rooms both sides o' the front hall. Look at the windows, you fool,' he says."

Lord Peter squinted at the bottle and poured out the last of the champagne.

"I don't mind telling you, sir" (went on the policeman) "that I was fair knocked silly. To think of me never noticing that! Withers had noticed it all right, and that's what made him think I was drunk or barmy. But I stuck to what I'd seen. I said, there must be two of them houses knocked into one, somewhere; but that didn't work, because we'd been into all of them, and there wasn't no such thing—not without there was one o'them concealed doors like you read about in crook stories. 'Well, anyhow,' I says to the sergeant, 'the yells was real all right, because other people heard 'em. Just you ask, and they'll tell you.' So the sergeant says, 'Well, Burt, I'll give you every chance.'

"So he knocks up Number Twelve again—not wishing to annoy Number Fourteen any more than he was already—and this time the son come down. An agreeable gentleman he was, too; not a bit put out. He says, Oh, yes, he'd heard the yells and his father'd heard them too. 'Number Fourteen,' he says, 'that's where the trouble is. A very old bloke, is Number Fourteen, and I shouldn't be surprised if he beats that unfortunate servant of his. The Englishman abroad, you know! The outposts of Empire and all that kind of thing. They're rough and ready—and then the curry in them parts is bad for the liver.' So I was for inquiring at Number Fourteen again; but the sergeant, he loses patience, and says, 'You know quite well,' he says, 'it ain't Number Fourteen, and, in my opinion, Burt, you're either dotty or drunk. You best go home straight away,' he says, 'and sober up, and I'll see you again when you can give a better account of yourself.' So I argues a bit, but it ain't no use, and away he goes, and Withers goes back to his beat. And I walks up and down a bit till Jessop comes to take over, and then I comes away, and that's when I sees you, sir.

"But I ain't drunk, sir—at least, I wasn't then, though there do seem to be a kind of swimming in me head at this moment. Maybe that stuff's stronger than it tastes. But I wasn't drunk then, and I'm pretty sure I'm not dotty. I'm haunted, sir, that's what it is—haunted. It might be there was someone killed in one of them houses a many years ago, and that's what I see tonight. Perhaps they changed the numbering of the street on account of it—I've heard tell of such things—and when the same night come round, the house goes back to what it was before. But there I am, with a black mark against me, and it ain't a fair trick for no ghost to go getting a plain man into trouble. And I'm sure, sir, you'll agree with me."

The policeman's narrative had lasted some time, and the hands of the grandfather clock stood at a quarter to five. Peter Wimsey gazed benevolently at his companion, for whom he was beginning to feel a positive affection. He was, if anything, slightly more drunk than the policeman, for he had missed tea and had no appetite for his dinner; but the wine had not clouded his wits; it had only increased excitability and postponed sleep. He said:

"When you looked through the letter-box, could you see any part of the ceiling, or the lights?"

"No, sir; on account, you see, of the flap. I could see right and left and straight forward; but not upwards, and none of the near part of the floor."

"When you looked at the house from outside, there was no light except through the fanlight. But when you looked through the flap, all the rooms were lit, right and left and at the back?"

"That's so, sir."

"Are there back doors to the houses?"

"Yes, sir. Coming out of Merriman's End, you turn to the right, and there's an opening a little way along which takes you to the back doors."

"You seem to have a very distinct visual memory. I wonder if your other kinds of memory are as good. Can you tell me, say, whether any of the houses you went into had any particular smell? Especially Ten, Twelve, and Fourteen?"

"Smell, sir?" The policeman closed his eyes to stimulate recollection. "Why, yes, sir. Number Ten, where the two ladies live, that had a sort of an old-fashioned smell. I can't put me tongue to it. Not lavender—but something as ladies keeps in bowls and such—rose-leaves and what not. Potpourri, that's the stuff. Potpourri. And Number Twelve—well, no, there was nothing particular there, except I remember thinking they must keep pretty good servants, though we didn't see anybody except the family. All that floor and paneling was polished beautiful—you could see your face in it. Beeswax and turpentine, I says to meself. And elbow-grease. What you'd call a clean house with a good, clean smell. But Number Fourteen—that was different. I didn't like the smell of that. Stuffy, like as if the servant had been burning some o' that there incense to his idols, maybe."

"Ah!" said Peter. "What you say is very suggestive." He placed his fingertips together and shot his last question over them:

"Ever been inside the National Gallery?"

"No, sir," said the policeman, astonished. "I can't say as I ever was."

"That's London again," said Peter. "We're the last people in the world to know anything of our great metropolitan institutions. Now, what is the best way to tackle this bunch of toughs, I wonder? It's a little early for a call. Still, there's nothing like doing one's good deed before breakfast, and the sooner you're set right with the sergeant, the better. Let me see. Yes—I think that may do it. Costume pieces are not as a rule in my line, but my routine has been so much upset already, one way and another, that an irregularity more or less will hardly matter. Wait here for me while I have a bath and change. I may be a little time; but it would hardly be decent to get there before six."

The bath had been an attractive thought, but was perhaps ill-advised, for a curious languor stole over him with the touch of the hot water. The champagne was losing its effervescence. It was with an effort that he dragged himself out and reawakened himself with a cold shower.

The matter of dress required a little thought. A pair of gray flannel trousers was easily found, and though they were rather too well creased for the part he meant to play, he thought that with luck they would probably pass unnoticed. The shirt was a difficulty. His collection of shirts was a notable one, but they were mostly of an inconspicuous and gentlemanly sort. He hesitated for some time over a white shirt with an open sports collar, but decided at length upon a blue one, bought as an experiment and held to be not quite successful. A red tie, if he had possessed such a thing, would have been convincing. After some consideration, he remembered that he had seen his wife in a rather wide Liberty tie, whose prevailing color was orange. That, he felt, would do if he could find it. On her it had looked rather well; on him, it would be completely abominable.

He went through into the next room; it was queer to find it empty. A peculiar sensation came over him. Here *he* was, rifling his wife's drawers, and there *she* was, spirited out of reach at the top of the house with a couple of nurses and an entirely new baby, which might turn into goodness knew what. He sat down before the glass and stared at himself. He felt as though he ought to have changed somehow in the night; but he only looked unshaven and, he thought, a trifle intoxicated. Both were quite good things to look at the moment, though hardly suitable for the father of a family. He pulled out all the drawers in the dressing-table; they emitted vaguely familiar smells of face-powder and handkerchief sachet. He tried the big built-in wardrobe: frocks, costumes, and trays full of underwear, which made him feel sentimental. At last he struck a promising vein of gloves and stockings. The next tray held ties, the orange of the desired Liberty creation gleaming in a friendly way among them. He put it on, and observed with pleasure that the effect was Bohemian beyond description.

He wandered out again, leaving all the drawers open behind him as though a burglar had passed through the room. An ancient tweed jacket of his own, of a very countrified pattern, suitable only for fishing in Scotland, was next unearthed, together with a pair of brown canvas shoes. He secured his trousers by a belt, searched for and found an old soft-brimmed felt hat of no recognizable color, and, after removing a few trout-flies from the hat-band and tucking his shirt-sleeves well up inside the coat-sleeve, decided that he would do. As an afterthought, he returned to his wife's room and selected a wide woolen scarf in a shade of greenish blue. Thus equipped, he came downstairs again, to find P. C. Burt fast asleep, with his mouth open and snoring.

Peter was hurt. Here he was, sacrificing himself in the interests of this policeman, and the man hadn't the common decency to appreciate it. However, there was no point in waking him yet. He yawned horribly and sat down. . . .

It was the footman who wakened the sleepers at half-past six. If he was surprised to see his master, very strangely attired, slumbering in the hall in company with a large policeman, he was too well trained to admit the fact even to himself. He merely removed the tray. The faint clink of glass roused Peter, who slept like a cat at all times.

"Hullo, William," he said. "Have I overslept myself? What's the time?"

"Five and twenty to seven, my lord."

"Just about right." He remembered that the footman slept on the top floor. "All quiet on the Western Front, William?"

"Not altogether quiet, my lord." William permitted himself a slight smile. "The young master was lively about five. But all satisfactory, I gather from Nurse Jenkyn."

"Nurse Jenkyn? Is that the young one? Don't let yourself be run away with, William. I say, just give P. C. Burt a light prod in the ribs, would you? He and I have business together."

In Merriman's End, the activities of the morning were beginning. The milkman came jingling out of the cul-de-sac; lights were twinkling in upper rooms; hands were withdrawing curtains; in front of Number Ten, the housemaid was already scrubbing the steps. Peter posted his policeman at the top of the street.

"I don't want to make my first appearance with official accompaniment," he said. "Come along when I beckon. What, by the way, is the name of the agreeable gentleman in Number Twelve? I think he may be of some assistance to us."

"Mr. O'Halloran, sir."

The policeman looked at Peter expectantly. He seemed to have abandoned all initiative and to place implicit confidence in this hospitable and eccentric gentleman. Peter slouched down the street with his hands in his trousers pockets and his shabby hat pulled rakishly over his eyes. At Number Twelve he paused and examined the windows. Those on the ground floor were open; the house was awake. He marched up the steps, took a brief glance through the flap of the letter-box, and rang the bell. A maid in a neat blue dress and white cap and apron opened the door.

"Good morning," said Peter, slightly raising the shabby hat; "is Mr. O'Halloran in?" He gave the *r* a soft continental roll. "Not the old gentleman. I mean young Mr. O'Halloran?"

"He's in," said the maid, doubtfully, "but he isn't up yet."

"Oh!" said Peter. "Well, it is a little early for a visit. But I desire to see him urgently. I am—there is a a little trouble where I live. Could you entreat him—would you be so kind? I have walked all the way," he added, pathetically, and with perfect truth.

"Have you, sir?" said the maid. She added kindly, "You do look tired, sir, and that's a fact."

"It is nothing," said Peter. "It is only that I forgot to have any dinner. But if I can see Mr. O'Halloran it will be all right."

"You'd better come in, sir," said the maid. "I'll see if I can wake him." She conducted the exhausted stranger in and offered him a chair. "What name shall I say, sir?"

"Petrovinsky," said his lordship, hardily. As he had rather expected, neither the unusual name nor the unusual clothes of this unusually early visitor seemed to cause very much surprise. The maid left him in the tidy little paneled hall and went upstairs without so much as a glance at the umbrella stand.

Left to himself, Peter sat still, noticing that the hall was remarkably bare of furniture, and was lit by a single electric pendant almost immediately inside the front door. The letter-box was the usual wire-cage, the bottom of which had been carefully lined with brown paper. From the back of the house came a smell of frying bacon.

Presently there was the sound of somebody running downstairs. A young man appeared in a dressing-gown. He called out as he came: "Is that you, Stefan? Your name came up as Mr. Whiskey. Has Marfa run away again, or—What the hell? Who the devil are you, sir?"

"Wimsey," said Peter, mildly, "not Whiskey; Wimsey the policeman's friend. I just looked in to congratulate you on a mastery of the art of false perspective which I thought had perished with the ingenious Van Hoogstraaten, or at least with Grace and Lambelet."

"Oh!" said the young man. He had a pleasant countenance, with humorous eyes and ears pointed like a faun's. He laughed a little ruefully. "I suppose my beautiful murder is out. It was too good to last. Those bobbies! I hope to God they gave Number Fourteen a bad night. May I ask you how you come to be involved in the matter?"

"I," said Peter, "am the kind of person in whom distressed constables confide—I cannot imagine why. And when I had the picture of that sturdy blue-clad figure, led so persuasively by a Bohemian stranger and invited to peer through a hole. I was irresistibly transported in mind to the National Gallery. Many a time have I squinted sideways through those holes into the little black box, and admired that Dutch interior of many vistas painted so convincingly on the four flat sides of the box. How right you were to preserve your eloquent silence! Your Irish brogue would have given you away. The servants, I gather, were purposely kept out of sight."

"Tell me," said Mr. O'Halloran, seating himself sideways upon the hall table, "do you know by heart the occupation of every resident in this quarter of London? I do not paint under my own name."

"No," said Peter. "Like the good Dr. Watson, the constable could observe, though he could not reason from his observation; it was the smell of turpentine that betrayed you. I gather that at the time of his first call the apparatus was not far off."

"It was folded together and lying under the stairs," replied the painter. "It has since been removed to the studio. My father had only just had time to get it out of the way and hitch down the 'Number

Thirteen' from the fanlight before the police reinforcements arrived. He had not even time to put back this table I am sitting on; a brief search would have discovered it in the dining-room. My father is a remarkable sportsman; I cannot too highly recommend the presence of mind he displayed while I was haring round the houses and leaving him to hold the fort. It would have been so simple and so unenterprising to explain; but my father, being an Irishman, enjoys treading on the coattails of authority."

"I should like to meet your father. The only thing I do not thoroughly understand is the reason of this elaborate plot. Were you by any chance executing a burglary round the corner, and keeping the police in play while you did it?"

"I never thought of that," said the young man, with regret in his voice. "No. The bobby was not the predestined victim. He happened to be present at a full-dress rehearsal, and the joke was too good to be lost. The fact is, my uncle is Sir Lucius Preston, the R.A."

"Ah!" said Peter. "The light begins to break."

"My own style of draftsmanship," pursued Mr. O'Halloran, "is modern. My uncle has on several occasions informed me that I draw like that only because I do not know how to draw. The idea was that he should be invited to dinner tomorrow and regaled with a story of the mysterious 'Number Thirteen,' said to appear from time to time in this street and to be haunted by strange noises. Having thus detained him till close upon midnight, I should have set out to see him to the top of the street. As we went along, the cries would have broken out. I should have led him back—"

"Nothing," said Peter, "could be clearer. After the preliminary shock he would have been forced to confess that your draftsmanship was a triumph of academic accuracy."

"I hope," said Mr. O'Halloran, "the performance may still go forward as originally intended." He looked at Peter, who replied:

"I hope so, indeed. I also hope that your uncle's heart is a strong one. But may I, in the meantime, signal to my unfortunate policeman and relieve his mind? He is in danger of losing his promotion, through a suspicion that he was drunk on duty."

"Good God!" said Mr. O'Halloran. "No—I don't want that to happen. Fetch him in."

The difficulty was to make P. C. Burt recognize in the daylight what he had seen by night through the letter-flap. Of the framework of painted canvas, with its forms and figures oddly foreshortened and distorted, he could make little. Only when the thing was set up and lighted in the curtained studio was he at length reluctantly convinced.

"It's wonderful," he said. "It's like Maskelyne and Devant. I wish the sergeant could a-seen it."

"Lure him down here tomorrow night," said Mr. O'Halloran. "Let him come as my uncle's bodyguard. You—" he turned to Peter—"you seem to have a way with policemen. Can't you inveigle the fellow along? Your impersonation of starving and disconsolate Bloomsbury is fully as convincing as mine. How about it?"

"I don't know," said Peter. "The costume gives me pain. Besides, is it kind to a poor policeman? I give you the R.A., but when it comes to the guardian of the law—Blast it all! I'm a family man, and I must have *some* sense of responsibility."

A Perfectly Ordinary Case of Blackmail

A. A. MILNE

A. A. Milne was born on January 18, 1882, in London. At Trinity College he edited the *Granta*. After graduation in 1903 he returned to London to become a journalist, with little success until 1906, when he was offered the assistant editorship of *Punch*. He married Dorothy de Sélincourt and in 1915 joined the Royal Warwickshire Regiment. By the time he was demobilized he was sufficiently recognized as a writer so that he could turn to writing full-time. Although best known for his Winnie-the-Pooh stories, his detective fiction is noteworthy. Alexander Woollcott called *The Red House Mystery* one of the three best mystery stories of all time.

A stout, old-young man of forty, Mr. Cedric Watherston of Watherston & Reeves, Solicitors, sat at his office table, knitting. He was not a good knitter, but he was proud of the fact that he could knit at all. He had learned when a prisoner of war in 1917, having walked straight into a German trench on his first journey up the line; and with the passage of years the circumstance of his capture had also become, in some odd way, a matter for pride. He liked sentences which began, "I remember when I was a prisoner in Holzminden." When a client was announced, he put the ball of wool, the needles, and the unfinished sock in the top left-hand drawer, smoothed his hair with both hands, and waited for the visitor to be shown in.

"Sir Vernon Filmer."

Mr. Watherston rose to shake hands with one of his most distinguished clients. "Glad to see you, Sir Vernon. You don't often give us the pleasure. On no unpleasant business, I trust?"

Sir Vernon did not look as if he were glad to see Mr. Watherston. He was a tall, fair, cold man, with pale-blue eyes, a prominent nose, and a small prim mouth. He was one of those natural politicians who are always conveniently there when ministerial posts are being given out. If there were to be ten knighthoods on New Year's Day for what could only be described as "public services," and nine had been decided upon, his name would come irresistibly to the mind for the tenth place.

"Cigarette?"

Sir Vernon waved it away. Mr. Watherston lighted one for himself, leaned back in his chair, remembered to put his fingertips together.

"I am being blackmailed," Sir Vernon said.

"Dear, dear, we must do something about that," said Mr. Watherston with an exaggerated calm which hid most of his emotions. Surprise was the least of these, for he had a dislike of politicians.

"That is naturally what I am expecting."

Mr. Watherston tried over a few sentences in his mind until he got the right opening. "Blackmail," he said delicately, "implies the previous commission, or alleged commission, of some offense. Offenses can be classified as offenses against the law, offenses against morality, and offenses against the social code. Perhaps, in this case, one should add political offenses. Which class or classes of offense, Sir Vernon, does the threatened exposure allege?"

"Legal," said Sir Vernon, adding primly, "I have nothing whatever on my conscience."

Yes, yes, thought Mr. Watherston, but your conscience must be in pretty good training by now.

"To put it frankly, then, Sir Vernon, the blackmailer is threatening to reveal some action of yours which is punishable by law?"

"Yes. To put it with greater accuracy, if the truth had come out at the time, I might have been prosecuted, but need not necessarily have been convicted. I should think that today there was no possibility of conviction."

"When did this happen?"

"Nearly thirty years ago—1909, to be exact."

"Ah! So it is the social and political consequences which really matter today?"

"Obviously. As they did, to an overwhelming extent, at the time. Do you not think it would be illuminating if I told you about it?"

Mr. Watherston held up a hasty hand. He had had no experience of blackmail, and he disliked the idea of being accessory after the fact to an apparently undiscovered crime. His mind wandered vaguely back to 1909, trying to think of the sort of contemporary illegalities in which Sir Vernon, then a young man of twenty-two, might have been mixed up. Having himself been a boy of twelve at the time, he came to no conclusion.

"Sir Vernon," he said. "It will be distressing for you to confide this story to anyone. Let us consider the matter on general lines for the moment. There are three ways of dealing with a blackmailer. The first is to submit to his demands."

Sir Vernon indicated what he thought of that.

"The second is to prosecute him. As you know, this can be done anonymously, under the disarming name of Mr. X."

Sir Vernon gave a short, unpleasant laugh.

"The only remaining method is to settle with the blackmailer out of court. I could pay his demands for you; I could instruct the prosecution for you. But frankly, Sir Vernon, I am not competent to get the better of a scoundrel whether by negotiation, threat, or personal violence." He let this sink in for a moment and then added, "Fortunately I know the man who is."

"Private detective or shady solicitor?"

"Solicitor. A shady solicitor in the sense that he usually acts for the submerged classes, but entirely loyal to his clients, whether prostitutes or Prime Ministers. And a very able man."

"You know him personally?"

"Oh, yes. The fortunes of war threw us together at Holzminden, where we happened to be prisoners."

"H'm," said Sir Vernon doubtfully.

"I understand your dislike of confiding in a stranger. Perhaps I should have added that he has very strong feelings about the detestable crime of blackmail. It is the one charge which he has always refused to defend in court—which is more than can be said for the whole of the bar. To get the better of a blackmailer he would go to the extreme length of his purse, his time, and—the law."

"Very well," said Sir Vernon. "I agree to accept your advice. I had better see this fellow in my own house at, say nine o'clock this evening. Will you arrange that?"

Mr. Watherston made a note, saying, "His name is Scroope." He got up and held out his hand. "Perhaps you will let me know how the matter goes on. And if there is anything else I can do, Sir Vernon—"

They shook hands and went to the door together.

"Cold fish," thought Mr. Watherston, as he returned to his table. "One can't help disliking him. I wonder what he did."

He picked up the telephone. Afterward, there being nothing else to do, he went back to his knitting.

Being asked by an interviewer to what he attributed his success in life Mr. Scroope replied, "My eyebrows." These had a natural quirk which seemed to express a good-tempered amusement with the world, and to admit his companion of the moment to an equal share in that amusement. "You and I," they seemed to say, "*we* know." It is doubtful if anybody had ever had a private joke with Sir Vernon, nor was he the man to wish to be on confidential terms with anyone less important than himself, least of all a shady solicitor; but even he recognized the eyebrows as evidence of a knowledge of the world. Mr. Scroope obviously knew his way about.

"A cigar, thanks," said Mr. Scroope. "Nothing to drink. Now then, Sir Vernon, Watherston tells me that you are being blackmailed. Who told *you*?"

"I don't understand," said Sir Vernon coldly.

"Dammit, one doesn't wake up in the morning and say, 'I've a sort of feeling that there are blackmailers about.' Something must have given you the idea."

"Naturally I had a letter," Sir Vernon said.

"Why 'naturally'? You might have had a telephone message. Is that the letter?"

Sir Vernon released it. "It came this morning through the post."

"H'm. Typed. Signed, 'Well-Wisher.' Humorous. D'you know who wrote it?"

"Not with any certainty."

"Five hundred in pound notes on Saturday as a guarantee of good faith, followed by five hundred every six weeks. Sounds as if he wanted to get married. Well, that gives us six weeks before the second payment. Six weeks in which to think of something."

"You suggest I should pay the five hundred?"

"Oh, certainly. At least, *you* won't, I will. We'll keep you out of it."

"Read the rest of the letter."

"I have. You are given till Saturday to get the money; you are to communicate with nobody; you are to have your car waiting outside your door on Saturday morning, ready to drive yourself to a rendezvous which will be given you by letter before you start."

"Perhaps you are not aware that I am lunching at Chequers on Saturday?"

"Nobody tells me anything," said Mr. Scroope sadly. "But then, why shouldn't you? The food's quite good, I hear. And who could give you a better alibi than the Prime Minister?"

"You propose to keep the rendezvous yourself?"

"As Sir Vernon Filmer? Do I look like it? But I daresay I can find somebody who will pass for you at a distance. All you'll be asked to do, I fancy, is to leave the money in a certain spot, where the blackmailer will pick it up afterward. He's giving nothing away. Now then, he says, 'I have a letter written on board the *Ladybird* on September 15, 1909. Don't tell me you've forgotten it.' " He looked up. "Have you forgotten it?"

"No."

"Right. Then you'd better tell me."

"There were three of us on the *Ladybird* that summer afternoon:

Robert Hayforth, the owner, myself, and a local hand called Towers. We had been fishing close inshore. Hayforth, a powerful and devoted swimmer, had suggested a swim. The wind was freshening, the sea uninviting, and I stayed on board. Hayforth, whose idea of a swim was half a mile out and half a mile back, had been gone about ten minutes, when suddenly Towers came sidling up to me, his right hand behind his back. I'd never liked him, nobody in the place did, but he was a useful man in a boat, and Hayforth often took him on. He had a bottle in his hand, and he was holding it like a club. He—he accused me of"—Sir Vernon's face could still show disgust at the idea—" 'messing about with his wife.' "

"Were you?"

Sir Vernon looked at Scroope contemptuously, and went on: "I asked him what the devil he was talking about. I thought he was drunk. He said that when he had finished with me I'd have the sort of face that nobody's girl would want to mess about with. It was horrible. Such a foul weapon, and he was much more powerful than I. Hayforth was out of sight and hailing distance. I was at the man's mercy. It was his life or mine. I saw red."

He poured himself out a brandy and swallowed it quickly. In another moment, thought Scroope, all his past life will flash before his eyes. Why must politicians always talk in clichés?

"And you killed him," Scroope said. "How?"

"I don't know to this day how I did it. I seemed to be endowed with superhuman strength. Fear, I suppose, and furious indignation at that loathsome weapon."

"You killed him, and you went on killing him. Is that right?"

"Yes."

"And when you had finished, it didn't look like self-defense, it looked like deliberate, premeditated, brutal murder. Is that right?"

"Yes, but it wasn't."

"It's what things look like which matter to the law. Well, and then Hayforth yelled, 'Ship ahoy!' and you helped him on board, and he saw the body and said. 'Lawks a mussy, what's all this?' And you told him. And he agreed to help you. Is that right?"

"Agreed on conditions."

"Ah, yes, now I'm seeing it. That letter was to him. Exonerating him and admitting sole responsibility. Why a letter? Couldn't he trust you?"

"If anything had happened to me, if the body had been washed up—"

"It would have been awkward for him. Because—stop me if I'm wrong—*he* was the man who had been messing about."

"Yes. I had no idea of it, but I suppose there were other people who had guessed."

"So, when he had got the letter safely in his pocket, you put out to sea—the wind was freshening, you said—and it sounded sufficiently plausible to say that Towers had been washed overboard. No attempts to save him?"

"It blew up into a gale, and we didn't pick up our moorings until three o'clock next morning; we put the accident at just after midnight. In the dark, in that weather, with only two of us to work the boat, what could we have done? We nearly followed him as it was. I never expected to see land again."

"Convincing. And no suspicions by anybody?"

"None that I heard of. Towers was a thoroughgoing rascal. Nobody missed him."

"Not even his wife?"

"She least of all." Sir Vernon cleared his throat and added, "I should explain that my whole career was in the balance at this time, and that I had no other course open to me. I had just left Oxford with unusually brilliant prospects—"

Scroope picked up the letter. "D'you think this is Hayforth, Sir Vernon?" he asked.

"It might be, of course. Equally, I suppose, he might be dead, and somebody might have found my letter among his papers. I lost sight of him in the war, and haven't heard of him since."

"That sort of man?"

"Obviously not in those days," said Sir Vernon somewhat stiffly, "or he wouldn't have been my friend. But he was always a reckless fellow, and might have been knocked about by the war, have fallen on hard times, and slowly sunk to—this. The war," said Sir Vernon, who had fortunately missed it, "did not improve people's characters."

"Is there anything in this letter which indicates knowledge not contained in your letter to Hayforth?"

"I don't think so."

"For instance, why should it be taken for granted that you can drive your own car? Lots of people can't."

For the first time that evening Sir Vernon looked at Scroope with respect. "That's true," he said thoughtfully.

"Were you driving a car at that time?"

"My wife gave me a Rolls as a wedding present a few months later."

"I congratulate you. Driven Hayforth in it?"

"Probably. I saw something of him up until the war began."

Scroope got up and threw the end of his cigar into the fire. "Obviously we must find the man first. I shall sleep here on Friday night, so as to be with you when your instructions come." He took a notebook and pencil from his pocket. "Turn your head to one side, I want the profile." He began to draw. "About five feet eleven inches, aren't you? I think I've got just the man. Muffled and goggled, of course, which is what anyone would be who was keeping a date with a blackmailer. My man—Dean is his name—will come in the back way at eight o'clock on Saturday morning. With a false mustache. This is going to be fun. There, that's not bad." He had the drawing up and admired it. "Thank God, it's money he wants."

"What else are blackmailers ever after?" asked Sir Vernon contemptuously.

"Seats in the Cabinet," said Mr. Scroope. "The way I'm going to work, that would have made it more difficult."

On Saturday morning at 8:30, Sir Vernon stepped nervously from his front door and walked across to his garage. It was a chilly February morning, and even for that short distance he thought it well to wear a thick fawn traveling coat and a checked cap. He brought his car round to the front door and left it there. Mr. Scroope and breakfast were waiting for him in the morning room.

"Now then, Sir Vernon," Mr. Scroope said, his mouth full of omelette, "let's get down to it. You are to be at the fifth milestone between Wellborough and Chiselton at twelve-thirty. You say you know the road. How?"

"It was near Chiselton that Hayforth kept his boat."

"Good. How long would it take you to get there?"

"Three hours."

"Then Dean must take three hours. He's just arrived; we'll have him in directly, and you can show him the place on the map. What's the country like?"

"Quite flat. No houses, no trees, no possibility of concealment, as I remember. A long, almost straight road."

"Dean will hide the money behind the milestone—nothing elaborate, just enough not to catch the eye of a passer-by. Then he'll drive on, turning off at Chiselton and coming back to London another way. Obviously, the blackmailer will be a little way behind him up to the milestone. He may be outside the house now—he was in London last night to post the letter—in which case he'll follow your car down. Dean, in your coat and cap, will be good enough for him."

Sir Vernon had picked up the letter again, and was studying it. "You talk of 'him' all the time," he said. "Does it not occur to you that it is more likely to be the work of a gang?"

"With a mastermind at the center of the spider's web?" said Mr. Scroope hopefully.

"I gather," said Sir Vernon coldly, "that you think otherwise."

Scroope pushed the toast away, and spoke seriously. "I'll tell you what I think," he said, "and then I'll tell you my plans. You're paying for this treat, and you're entitled to know. I think that if two young men go out in a boat for a summer afternoon's offshore fishing and bathing, they will not be wearing oilskins. I think that if one of them has just had a desperate fight for his life, any letter which he writes immediately after, with a shaking hand and under the stress of great emotion, will be uncharacteristic and only just legible. I think that if a small boat, manned by two people in flannels, is fighting a gale for eight hours, the occupants will not merely be wet, but soaked literally to the skin. And I think that after it's all over, and now that the unexpected storm has removed all possibility of suspicion, Mr. Robert Hayforth will find a piece of sodden paper in his pocket with not a single decipherable word on it, will wonder what the devil it is, and then throw it away with a laugh at the ridiculous caution which inspired it. What that piece of paper would have looked like thirty years later baffles the imagination. In short, you may be certain that the blackmailer is Hayforth himself, and that it is only his word against yours."

Sir Vernon permitted himself a little enthusiasm. "But that is most satisfactory, Mr. Scroope. You relieve my mind considerably."

"Yes, but even so, he can be extremely mischievous. So, since blackmailers are better out of action, I propose, with your financial assistance, to put him out of action."

"Now that we know who he is—"

"We don't. We only know who he was: a face and a name of thirty years ago. That doesn't help. But this letter shows that he is sticking to familiar ground. It is probable that he is living in the district, and almost certain that he has a car. Ever studied history?"

"I got a first in history in my finals at Oxford," said Sir Vernon.

"Pooh, I don't mean that sort of dead-alive history. Real history. Criminal history. Ever studied the Lindbergh case?"

There was no need to wait for an answer; Sir Vernon's delicate shrug had given it.

"What it came to in the end was that they knew all about the man except who he was. However, he had the ransom notes—numbers taken, of course—and one day he would use them. That was their only hope of getting him. But how? Every gasoline station in the neighborhod was given a list of the notes, and told to write down secretly on the back of any ten-dollar bill paid in exchange for gas the number of the car which was filled. Then the list of ransom notes could be consulted at leisure in the evening."

"Most ingenious. And now you have taken the numbers of the notes?"

"Of course. And I shall go down to Wellborough this afternoon, and make arrangements. Not being official, it will cost money. But by the time we've made the second payment to Hayforth, I shall know what he's calling himself and where he lives. I'll tell you something else. He says that he will give you the second rendezvous on March twenty-fifth, and that it will be in an entirely different part of the country. It won't. If his plan works successfully today, as I mean it to do, he will repeat it exactly. It leaves you just as uncertain until the last moment, and saves him the trouble of looking for an equally convenient place."

"And when you've found him?"

"Then," said Mr. Scroope with happy smile, "the real fun begins."

When a man calling himself Mr. Richard Hastings was arrested for possessing and passing forged notes, he did what all intelligent prisoners do. He sent for Mr. Scroope.

"Well," said Mr. Scroope, twinkling at him, "what's the story, Mr. Hastings?" He looked at the man with interest, summed him up as a gentleman gone to the bad, and offered him a cigarette.

"Thanks. I've been arrested, the Lord only knows why, for—"

"Yes, I know the police story, now I want to know yours."

"I swear to you that I am—"

"—absolutely innocent. Naturally. But we still need a story to explain why a quantity of forged notes was found in your safe, and why several others which had been passed in the neighborhood were traced to you. What is that story?"

"They were planted on me."

"By whom?"

"Some enemy, I suppose."

"I see. What about the notes in circulation which have been through your hands?"

"They must have gone through many hands. Why pick on me?"

"Obviously because you had such a large store of them in your safe. We want a better story than you're giving me, Mr. Hastings."

"I can't tell you anything better."

"Then," said Mr. Scroope politely, "I will wish you good morning." He got up. "Just one word of advice, if I may. The story which you will be telling to some other solicitor need not be true; but it must sound sufficiently like the truth to allow him a temporary hallucination that it was possible." He held out his hand with a smile.

Richard Hastings waved the hand away. "Wait," he said. "You'd better have it. I found the damned things."

"That's better. Where?"

"Oh, hidden under a stone."

"You know, I don't think that that will quite carry conviction—using the word 'conviction' in its less technical sense, of course. It must have been rather a moment in your life when you found such a large packet of notes. You would be expected to remember the historic spot."

"Oh, well, if you want the exact place, it was behind the fifth milestone on the Wellborough-Chiselton road."

"You counted—and remembered?"

Richard Hastings looked up angrily. "What the devil do you mean? It said. 'Wellborough, five miles,' didn't it?"

"You were looking behind milestones for something?"

"I happened to sit down there. Convenient to lean against for a few minutes. I noticed that the ground was disturbed, and investigated."

"And said 'Hallo, what's this?' "

"Exactly."

"And what was it?"

"A parcel of one-pound notes. Damned odd, I thought."

"And so you decided to steal them?"

"What's that?"

"You wish to plead guilty to an alternative charge of stealing by finding. Is that right?"

"Right!" Hastings said suddenly. "I stole them. That's not very serious, is it? Well, now you've got the truth."

"It's odd," Mr. Scroope said, "that a man, driving along the Wellborough-Chiselton road on a cold and frosty morning, should stop at precisely the fifth milestone, lean against it rather than against the cushions of his car."

Richard Hastings jumped to his feet, and said angrily, "What's all this? You trying to trap me?"

"I'm trying to do," said Scroope mildly, "what counsel for the prosecution will do much more thoroughly."

"Sorry. I see the point; but naturally"—he gave an awkward little laugh—"I'm a bit upset about the whole thing. But I do absolutely swear, and it's gospel truth, that I didn't know that the notes were forged, and that I found them precisely where I said I did."

"Oh, come, we must tell them a little more. When you happened to find them."

"I can't remember the exact date."

"Which date can't you remember?"

Mr. Richard Hastings wiped his forehead with the back of his hand and said, "I haven't the vaguest idea what you're talking about."

"I want the date which you can't exactly remember, when you got out of your car, leaned against the fifth milestone, and accidentally found a packet of notes. Just venture a rough guess."

"The first week in February."

"About seven weeks ago. The first forged note which came to hand was paid to the Lion Garage at Chiselton on February eighteenth. So that fits nicely. Now what about the second date? When you again got out of your car, leaned against the fifth milestone, and accidentally found a second packet of notes."

Mr. Richard Hastings licked his lips. "What makes you think I did that?"

"Two parcels were found in your safe. One, opened, contained about four hundred fifty forged notes. The other, unopened—or, possibly, opened, examined and tied up again—contained five hundred."

"I can explain that. It's all coming back to me. The parcel which I found—"

"In the first week in February?"

"Yes. It was really two parcels, done up together. I counted the top one and it was five hundred. I was forgetting for the moment about the other parcel, which I didn't open. Obviously there was another five hundred in that. Making the thousand, as you were saying. Silly of me."

"Not at all. Very natural. Then all that we have left to explain," said Mr. Scroope cheerfully, "is why the inner wrapper of the second parcel was a sheet of *The Western Morning News* dated March twenty-fourth—six weeks later."

Robert Hayforth banged the table with his hand, and cried, "Blast him, he's framed me! The sniveling devil!"

"Sniveling—? Who is he?"

"The Right Honorable Sir Vernon Filmer." He dragged the words out sneeringly. "All right, you've got it. It was hush money. He killed a man, murdered him; that's your smug, hypocritical Right Honorable. You want me to tell the truth in court. Right, I'll tell it—and we'll go down together."

Mr. Scroope got up. "I've chosen never to defend blackmail cases. Everything which you have told me is, of course, in the strictest confidence, and I now fade out of the case. I warn you, the penalty for blackmail is, next to that for murder, the severest known to the law. Any written evidence which you may have had against Sir Vernon Filmer will be in possession of the police, and you will not be permitted to use it. An unsupported accusation made in your defense would only make your case worse and your punishment more severe. If you take my unprofessional advice, you will plead 'Not Guilty' to the present charge, give no evidence, and leave it to your counsel to suggest that in some way you are the innocent victim of a conspiracy."

He picked up his hat and went to the door. "Oh, by the way," he added, "if it gets about, though I don't see why it should, that I declined this case, it will not prejudice the court against you." The eyebrows went up in that humorous quirk of his. "It may even do you good. There is an absurd legend in legal circles that I defend only the guilty."

Mr. Cedric Watherston picked up the telephone and said, "Watherston here."

"Busy?"

"Just turning the heel."

"Anyone listening in?" the voice said.

"My dear fellow!"

"Right. Then I thought you would like to know that your honorable friend is relieved of all anxiety for five years."

"Fancy! I do congratulate you. I was reading an interesting case this morning, forging and passing and all that sort of thing, and oddly enough—but, of course, it's only a coincidence."

"I expect so. A respectable family lawyer really shouldn't read criminal cases."

"It just caught the eye. Ah, what do you think will happen at the end of the five years?"

"I think that you will lose a distinguished client, and the country a distinguished servant. Quite suddenly."

"Ah! I was fearing the same thing myself." Mr. Watherston chuckled. "You know, you're a very naughty man. Here was a perfectly ordinary case of blackmail and there is hardly a crime in the calendar which you have not committed in order to bring the blackmailer to justice. If," he added, "you know what I mean by justice."

"Well, you see," the voice said apologetically, "I don't *like* blackmailers."

"Neither do I."

"Comes to that, I don't like Sir Vernon Filmer."

"How right you are," said Mr. Watherston cheerfully.

Lucky Dip

LIZA CODY

Liza Cody is the winner of a Creasey Award for her very popular Anna Lee series of mysteries and has also been nominated for the Edgar. Her rich novels featuring private eye Anna include *Under Contract, Bad Company, Dupe, Head Case,* and *Stalker,* while *Rift* is a stunning novel of suspense set in East Africa. She makes her home in England.

He was sitting against a bit of broken wall, looking almost normal. I could see him because of the full moon. It was a lovely moon with wispy clouds like old lady's hair across its face.

I watched the man for a couple of minutes, but he didn't move. Well, he wouldn't, would he? I could see he didn't belong—he was far too well dressed—and I wondered how he got there. This is not a part of the city men dressed like him go.

He had not been dead long. You could tell that at a glance because he still had his shoes on. If you die here you won't keep your shoes for ten minutes. You won't keep your wallet for ten seconds, dead or alive.

With this in mind I had a quick look, right and left, for anyone lurking in the shadows. If I'd seen anyone bigger than me, I'd have stayed where I was. Moon shadows are blacker than hearses, and I knew I wasn't the only one out that night. But in the Trenches only the big are bold, and someone big would have been rummaging in the remains already. So I hopped out from behind my pile of rubble and made a run for it.

I reached him in no time at all and grabbed his left lapel. Seven out of ten men are right-handed, and the chances are seven to three anything valuable will be in a left-hand inside pocket. I took a swift dip and came up with the winnings.

By now I could hear stirrings—a snap of rotten wood, a slide of brick dust. I flicked his watch off his wrist and almost in the same motion made a dive into his jacket pocket. Then I got on my toes and legged it.

I legged it out of the Trenches completely, because, although there are plenty of places to hide, the people I wanted to hide from know them as well as I do. The Trenches are useful as long as it's only the law you want to avoid. Robbing a corpse isn't nice, and I didn't want to take all that trouble only to be robbed myself.

It was just a quick jog to the High Street. On the way I stopped under a street lamp to look at what I had in my hand. The wallet was fat snakeskin, the watch was heavy gold, and the loose change was all pound coins and fifty-pence pieces. For once in my short life I'd struck oil.

All the same you don't break old habits for the sake of one lucky dip, and when I saw all those plump taxpayers doing their late Christmas shopping on the High Street, I stuck out my hand as usual.

"Got any spare change, please?" I said, as always. "For a cup of tea. For a bed for the night. For a hot meal."

And as always they coughed up like princes or told me to get myself a job. It was nice that night. I perform best when there's no pressure, and by the time I'd worked my way down to the station, I'd made a nice little pile. But it doesn't do to loll around and count your takings in public, so I jumped a tube to Paddington.

My sister has this room in Paddington. She lives in Camberwell with her boyfriend, so this room's just for business. I don't trust my sister's boyfriend, but I do trust my sister, up to a point, which was why I went to her business address. You may meet all sorts of funny blokes there, but you won't meet her boyfriend, and that suits me. It suits him, too, if you want to know the truth: he doesn't like me any more than I like him.

When we first came down to the city, Dawn and me, we relied on each other; we didn't have anyone else to turn to. But after she took up with him and he set her up in business, she didn't need me like she used to, and we drifted apart.

The trouble with Dawn is she always needs a man. She says she doesn't feel real without one. Feeling real is important to Dawn so I suppose I shouldn't criticize. But her men have been nothing but a disappointment. You could say I'm lucky to have an older sister like Dawn: she's an example to me. I'd rather die than turn out like her.

Still, she is my sister, and we've been through a lot together. Especially in this last year when we came down to the city together. And before that, when our mum kicked us out, or rather, kicked Dawn out because of the baby. And after that when Dawn's boyfriend kicked Dawn out because of the baby.

I have never been hungrier than I was last year trying to look after Dawn. She lost the baby in the end, which was a bit of a relief to me. I don't know how we would have managed if she'd had it. I don't think she would have coped very well either. It's much harder to get a man when you've got a little baby to look after.

Anyway, that's all in the past, and now Dawn has business premises in Paddington.

I waited outside until I was sure she was alone, and then I went up and knocked on the door.

"Crystal!" she said when she opened the door. "What you doing here? You got to be more careful—I might've had company."

"Well, you haven't," I said. And she let me in, wrinkling her nose and pulling her kimono tight. I don't like that kimono—it's all hot and slippery. Since she got her hair streaked, Dawn has taken to wearing colors that would look all right on a tree in autumn but turn her hard and brassy.

"Gawd," she said, "you don't half look clatty. Can't you get your hair cut? That coat looks like it's got rats living in it."

I took the coat off, but she didn't like the one underneath either.

"What a pong," she said.

"I had a wash last week," I told her. "But I would like to use your bathroom." I wanted somewhere private to look at what I'd got off the dead man.

"You can't stop around here," she said, worried. "I got someone coming in half an hour." She looked at her watch.

I sat in her bathroom and looked at the dead man's watch. It had *Cartier* written on the face, and it really was proper gold. Quality, I thought, and felt a bit sad. By rights a man with a watch like that shouldn't end up in the Trenches without a stitch on. Because that's how he'd be by now, pale and naked in the moonlight. Nobody would recognize him without his coat and suit and shoes. He'd just look like anyone. We're into recycling in the Trenches.

To cheer myself up I looked at his wallet, and when I counted up I found I had 743 pounds and 89 pence. And I couldn't use half of it.

Imagine me trying to change a fifty-pound note! There's a chance in a million a cat with cream on his whiskers milked a cow, but that's good odds compared to the chance I'd come by a fifty-quid note honestly. I couldn't even pop the watch. One look at a watch like that and any honest pawnbroker would turn me in. A dishonest one would rip me off quick as a wink. Either way the watch was no good for me.

I borrowed my sister's toothbrush and had a fast swipe with her deodorant before I joined her again. You never know when you're going to find clean water next so it pays to make use of what there is.

"Do me a favor, Crystal," she said, when she saw me. "Bugger off before you frighten the horses."

"Brought you a Christmas present," I said and handed her the watch.

"You're barmy, Crystal." She stared at the watch like it was a spider in her bed. "Who'd you nick this off?"

"I never," I told her. "I found it." And it was true because the feller was dead. It wasn't as if it was his property because there wasn't a him anymore for it to belong to. When you're dead you're gone. And that's final. Dead men don't own watches.

Even with a Christmas present, Dawn wouldn't let me stop for the night. It's a funny thing, if I hadn't had 743 pounds, 89 pence in my pocket, I wouldn't have wanted to. If it had just been the 89 pence, I'd been quite happy sleeping out.

But having things is dangerous. Having things makes you a mark. It's like being pretty. If you don't believe me, look at Dawn. She's pretty and she's been a mark from the time she was eleven. Being pretty brought her nothing but trouble. She's always had to have someone to protect her. I'm glad I'm not pretty.

There's a hospital down the Harrow Road so I went there. I couldn't decide what to do, so I sat in Casualty till they chucked me out. It's a pity there aren't more places you can go and sit in at night to have a quiet think. It's hard to think on the hoof, and if you are cold or hungry, thinking is not on your mind at all.

It seemed to me, after a while, that the best place to go was where I slept last night. Some might say it was a daft idea to go back to a place that was rousted, but I thought if the police had been there last night, it would be deserted tonight.

Twenty-seven Alma-Tadema Road is a condemned house. They say it's unsafe. There are holes in the roof and holes in the floors, but it is perfectly safe if you are sober, tread carefully, and don't light fires. That was what went wrong last night: we had a couple of winos in, and one of them got cold just before daybreak.

When I got there, I saw that they had nailed more boards across the front door and downstairs windows. I could get in, but it would take time. There were still people up and about so, to be on the safe side, I would have to come back later if I wanted more than a few minutes' kip.

I walked on past and went down to the Embankment. It is quite a long walk, and by the time I got there I was hungry. Actually, I'm hungry all the time. Dawn says she thinks I must have worms and I probably do, but mostly I think it's just my age. Someone like Bloody Mary does almost as much walking as I do, but she doesn't seem to need half the fuel. She stopped growing years ago.

There are a lot of women like Bloody Mary, but I mention her because she was the one I picked up on the Embankment that night, huffing and puffing along with her basket on wheels.

"Oh, me poor veins," she said, and we walked on together. I slowed down a bit so she could keep up.

"There's a stall open by the Arches," she said. "Couldn't half murder a cuppa."

She used to sing in the streets—walk up and down Oxford Street bellowing "Paper Moon" with her hand held out—but after a bad dose of bronchitis last year her voice went.

At the Arches I got us both a cup of tea and a sausage sandwich.

"Come into money, Crys?" Johnny Pavlova asked. It is his stall and he has a right to ask, because now and then when there's no one around to see, he gives me a cup free. As he always says, he's not a charitable institution, but catch him in the right mood and he'll slip you one like the best of them.

All the same it reminded me to be careful.

"Christmas," I said. "They were feeling generous down the High Street."

"Down the High Street?" he said. "You ain't been on that demolition site, have you? I heard they found this stiff bollock-naked there this evening."

"Did they?" I said as if I couldn't care less. "I didn't hear nothing. I was just working the High Street."

I went over and sat with Bloody Mary under the Arches. Johnny Pavlova doesn't like us hanging too close round his stall. He says we put the respectable people off their hot dogs.

"Will you look at that moon," Bloody Mary said, and she pulled her coats tight.

It was higher in the sky now and smaller, but there was still a good light to see by.

"Where you kipping tonight, Crystal?" she asked. I knew what she meant. A moon like that is a freezing moon this time of year.

Just then, Brainy Brian came slithering in beside us so I didn't have to answer. He was coughing his lungs out as usual, and he didn't say anything for a while. I think he's dying. You can't cough like that and live long. He used to go to college in Edinburgh, but then he started taking drugs and he failed all his exams. He did all right down here in the city because to begin with he was very pretty. But druggies don't keep their looks any longer than they keep their promises. Now he's got a face like a violin and ulcers all over his arms and legs.

When he recovered his breath he said, "Share your tea, Crystal?"

We'd already finished ours so we didn't say anything for a while. But Brian was so sorry-looking, in the end I went to get another two, one for him and one for Bloody Mary. While they were sucking it up I slipped away.

"Watch yourself, Crys," Johnny Pavlova said as I went by. He gave me a funny look.

The first thing you do when you break into a house is find another way out. A good house has to have more than one way out because you don't want to go running like the clappers to get out the same door the Law is coming in.

The house on Alma-Tadema Road has a kitchen door through to the garden. I loosened the boards on that before lying down to sleep. I also made sure I had the snakeskin wallet safe.

I had made the right decision: there was no one but me there. A heap of damp ashes marked the spot where the winos had lit their fire, and they blew in little eddies from draught. Otherwise nothing stirred.

I went over the house collecting all the paper and rags I could find to build myself a nest, then I curled up in it and shut my eyes.

Nighttime is not the best time for me. It's when I can't keep busy and in control of my thoughts that bad memories and dreams burst out of my brain. It's hard to keep cheerful alone in the dark, so I need to be very, very tired before I'll lie down and close my eyes. Sometimes I say things over and over in my head until I get to sleep—things like the words of a song or a poem I learned at school—over and over so there's no spare room in my brain for the bad stuff.

That night I must have been very tired because I only got part of the way through "What's Love Got to Do with It," when I dropped off. Dawn used to play that song all the time when we were still living at home. She played it so often it used to drive me up the wall. But it is songs like that, songs I didn't even know I'd learned the words to, that help me through the night nowadays.

The next thing I knew someone was coughing. I opened my eyes but it was still dark, and there was this cough, cough, cough coming my way. Brainy Brain, I thought, and relaxed a bit. It's something you have to watch out for—people coming up on you when you're alone in the dark.

"It's cold," he said when he found me. "It's hard, hard cold out there." He crawled into my nest. I was quite warm and I didn't want to leave but I knew his coughing would keep me awake.

"Give us a cuddle, Crystal," he said. "I got to get warm."

"Shove off," I said. His hands remind me of a fork. Some people do it to keep warm. Not me. I've seen too much and I want to die innocent.

He started coughing again. Then he said, "You got any dosh, Crystal?"

"Enough for a tea in the morning," I said. I really did not want to go. It was one of my better nests and it didn't seem fair to give it up to Brian.

"They're looking for you," he said. "Someone saw you in the Trenches."

"Not me," I said. "Who saw me?"

"You know that little kid?" he said. "Marvin, I think he's called. Well, they hurt him bad. He said he saw you."

"Who wants to know?" I sat up.

"Lay down," he said, "I got to get warm." He grabbed me and pulled me down, but he didn't start anything so I kept still.

After a while he said, "Johnny Pavlova says you got dosh. They asked him too."

I waited till he finished coughing. Then I said, "Who's asking? The Law?"

"Not them," he said. He knew something, I thought. And then I thought, he talked to Johnny Pavlova, he's talked to Marvin, and Marvin saw me in the Trenches. Maybe Brain talked to whoever is looking for me.

I said, "Did they send you, Brian? Did they send you to find me?"

He doubled over, coughing. Later he said, "You don't understand, Crystal. I got to get some money. I lost my fixings, and I haven't scored for days."

So that was that. I left him and went out the kitchen way. Brain was right—it was hard cold outside. And I was right, too—having things makes you a mark. I dumped the snakeskin wallet in the garden before I climbed over the fence. And then I climbed right back and picked it up again. Dumping the wallet wouldn't stop anyone looking for me. Not having it would be no protection. Marvin didn't have it and he got hurt. I wondered why they picked on Marvin to clobber. Perhaps he got the dead man's shoes, or his coat. Perhaps they saw a little kid in a big thick coat and they recognized the coat.

No one ever looked for me before. There was no one interested. I thought maybe I should run away—somewhere up north, or maybe to the West Country. But when I ran away the first time, it was me and Dawn together. And it was difficult because we didn't know the city. It took us ages to get sorted.

I thought about it walking down the road. The moon had gone and the sky had that dirty look it gets just before day. My nose was runny from the cold and I was hungry, so I went to the Kashmir takeaway. The Kashmir is a good one because it has a bin not twenty paces away. What happens is that when the pubs close a lot of folks want an Indian takeaway, but because they've been drinking they order too much and chuck what's left over in this bin. I've had breakfast there many times. The great thing about a Kashmir breakfast is that although the food is cold by the time you get it, the spices are still hot, and it warms you up no end. From this point of view Indian food is the best in the city.

I felt much more cheerful after breakfast, and I found a lighted shopwindow with a doorway to sit in. It was there I had a proper look at the wallet. Before, at Dawn's business premises, I only counted the money and redistributed it in the pockets of my coats. Now I studied the credit cards, library cards, and business stuff.

These are not things I am normally interested in. I can't use them. But this time, it seemed to me, the only way out of trouble was to give them back. The dead man in the Trenches might be dead but he was still dangerous.

His name was Philip Walker-Jones. He belonged to a diners club, a bridge club, and a chess club. He had two business cards—Data Services Ltd. and Safe Systems Plc. He was managing director twice over, which seemed quite clever because both companies had the same address in Southwark Road. Southwark Road is not far from where I found him. Maybe he walked out of his office and died on the way to the station. But that didn't explain what he was doing in the Trenches. Nobody like him goes in the Trenches.

I thought about Philip Walker-Jones sitting in the moonlight against the broken brickwork. He had looked as if he'd just sat down for a bit of a breather. But he wasn't resting. He was dead. There wasn't a mark on him that I could see. It didn't look as if anyone had bumped him—he was just sitting there in all his finery. Quite dignified, really.

Little Marvin would have been there watching like I was, and probably a few others too—waiting to see if it was safe to take a dip. We were wrong, weren't we?

I didn't want to go back too close to the Trenches, but if I was going to give the wallet back I had to. It was too early yet for public transport so I started walking. A good breakfast does wonders for the brain, so while I was walking I went on thinking.

I didn't know anything about data and systems except that they sounded like something to do with computers, but I do know that dining, bridge, and chess are all things you do sitting down. Philip Walker-Jones didn't have any cards saying he belonged to a squash club or a swimming club, and if he spent all that time sitting down, maybe he wasn't very fit. If he wasn't very fit, and he started to run suddenly, he could have had a heart attack.

It was a satisfying bit of thinking that took me down to the river without really noticing. Crossing over, it occurred to me that computers, bridge, and chess were things that really brainy people did, and in my experience brainy people all wear glasses and don't run around much. A really brainy man would not go running into the Trenches after dark, unless he was being chased. A scared, unfit man running in the Trenches would have no bother getting a heart attack. Easy.

The wind off the river was sharp and cold, but it wasn't the only thing making me shiver. Because if Philip Walker-Jones had a reason to be scared to death, so did I.

Give the rotten wallet back, I thought, *and do it double quick. Say, "Here's your money, now leave me be." And then do a runner.* I'm good at that.

I stopped for a pint of milk to fuel up. And I went through my pockets to find some of the fifty-pound notes, which I stuffed back in the wallet to make it look better.

I felt quite good. I had made my plan and it was almost as if I didn't have the wallet anymore. It was as good as gone, and by the time I reached Southwark Road I wasn't bothering much about keeping out of sight. It was daylight now and there were other people in the streets, and cars on the roads, and as usual no one seemed to notice me.

All the same, I gave the Trenches a miss. I walked down Southwark Road bold as brass looking at numbers and signs. And when I found one that read *Safe Systems Plc*, I walked right up to the door.

It was a new door in an old building, and it was locked. Perhaps it was too early. Not having a watch myself, I don't keep track of office hours. I stood there wondering if I should hike on to the station where there's a clock and a cup of tea, and just then the door opened from the inside. It gave me such a fright I nearly legged it. But the person opening the door was a young woman, and usually women don't give me much trouble. This one had red rims to her eyes and a really mournful expression on her face. She also had a nasty bruise on her cheekbone that made me think of Little Marvin.

She said, "Where do you think you're going?" She wasn't friendly but she looked as if she had other things on her mind.

"Safe Systems Plc," I said.

"What do you want?" she said. "The office is closed. And haven't you ever heard of a thing called soap and water?"

"I've got something for Safe Systems," I said, and held out the wallet.

"Jesus Christ!" she said and burst into tears.

We stood there like that—me holding the wallet and her staring at it, crying her eyes out.

At last, she said, "I don't want it. Take it away." And she tried to slam the door.

But I stuck my foot in there. "What do I do with it?" I said.

"Lose it," she said, and because I wouldn't let her close the door, she went on, "Look, you silly little cow, don't you come near me with that thing. Drop it in the river—you can give it to Steve for all I care. I'm finished with all that."

She started banging the door on my foot so I hopped back. The door crashed shut and she was gone.

I was so surprised I stood there gawping at the door and I didn't see the big feller coming up behind until he dropped a hand on my shoulder.

"You the one they call Crystal?" he said from a great height.

"Not me," I said. "Never heard of her." I got the wallet back under my top coat without him noticing.

"What you doing at that office then?" he said, not letting go.

"The lady sometimes gives me her spare change," I said, and watched his feet. It's no good watching their eyes. If you want to know what a bloke's going to do, watch his feet. The big man's feet were planted. I did not like him knowing my name.

"What is your name then?" he said.

I nearly said, "Dawn," but I bit it off just in time.

"What?" he said.

"Doreen," I said. "Who's asking?" If he was Steve, I would give him the wallet and run.

"Detective Sergeant Michael Sussex," he said. It was even worse than I thought. Now even the Law knew my name. It made me sweat in spite of the cold.

"I've got a few questions for you," he said, and he tightened his hand on my shoulder.

"I don't know anything," I said. "What about?"

"About where you was last night," he said. "And who you saw."

"I never saw nothing," I said, really nervous.

"Course you didn't," he said. "Come on. I'll buy you breakfast and then we can talk." And he smiled.

Never, never trust the Law when it smiles.

None of this had ever happened to me before. If you must know, I've hardly ever talked to a policeman in my life. I'm much too fast on my feet.

"Where do you live, Crystal?" he said, starting to walk.

"The name's Doreen," I said, and tried to get out from under the big hand.

"Where do you live . . . Doreen?" he said.

The thing you have to know about the Law is that they ask questions and you answer them. You've got to tell them something or they get really upset. It's the same with social workers. If they want an answer, give them an answer, but keep the truth to yourself. I told Detective Sergeant Michael Sussex the address of a hostel in Walworth.

He was walking us in the direction of the Trenches, and I didn't want to go there. So I said, "I've had my breakfast and I ought to go because I've got an appointment with my social worker."

It was a mistake because then he wanted to know who my social worker was and what time I had to be there. Lies breed. It's much better if you don't talk to the Law because then you can keep to the truth.

After a while he said, "Aren't you a bit young to be living on your own . . . Doreen?"

"I'm eighteen," I said. I felt depressed. I hadn't spoken one honest word to the man since he dropped his big hand on my shoulder. Well, you can't, can you? I talked to a social worker once and she tried to put Dawn and me in care. Never again. They would have split us up and then Dawn would never have found herself a man. Say what you like about Dawn's boyfriend, but he did set her up in business, and she does make good money. She feels real. No one can feel real in care.

We were right next to the Trenches by now. For a change it looked completely deserted—no winos, no bonfires, none of us picking through the rubbish dumped there in the night. It's just a big demolition site, really, but since no one is in any hurry to build there, it's become home to all sorts of people.

Detective Sergeant Michael Sussex stopped. He said, "We found a body in there last night."

I said nothing. I couldn't see the bit of wall the dead man had been sitting by, but I knew where it was.

"Yes," he said, as if he was thinking about something else. "Stripped clean, he was. When it comes my turn I'd like to be somewhere no one can get their thieving hands on me."

I was still watching his feet, and now even his boots looked as if they were thinking about something else. So I took off.

I broke clear of his hand. I dodged between two people passing by and hopped over the wire. Then I dropped down into the Trenches.

It was the last place I wanted to be, but it was the only place I could go.

I heard him come down behind me, and as I ran through the rubble I could feel his feet thudding on the ground. He was awfully fast for a big man.

"Stop!" he yelled, and I kept running. This way, that way, over the brickwork, round the rubbish tips, into cellars, up steps. And all the time I could hear his feet and his breath. I couldn't get free of him.

I was getting tired when I saw the drain. I put on one more sprint and dived head first into it. It was the only thing I could think of to do. It was the only place he couldn't come after me.

It was the only place I couldn't get out of.

I know about the drain. I've been in there before to get out of the wind, but it doesn't go anywhere. There is a bend about ten yards from the opening, and after that it's very wet and all stopped up with earth.

Anyway, like it or not, I dived straight in and crawled down. There wasn't much room even for me. I had to get all the way to the bend before I could turn round.

It was totally dark in the drain. There should have been a circle of light at the opening, but Detective Sergeant Michael Sussex had his head and shoulders wedged in it.

He said, "Don't be a fool, Crystal. Come out of there!" His voice boomed.

"Look, I only want a chat," he said. "I'm not going to hurt you."

He wasn't going to hurt me as long as I stayed in the drain and he stayed out of it.

"Come and get me," I said. I would have felt quite cheerful if it hadn't been so dark and wet.

"I don't know what you think you're up to, Crystal," he said. "But you're in a lot of trouble. I can help you."

I nearly laughed. "I don't know any Crystals," I said. "How can you help me?"

"You've got enemies," he said. "The bloke who died had the same enemies. You took something off him and now they're looking for you. They're rough people, Crystal, and you need my help."

"I don't know any dead blokes," I said. "I didn't take anything. What am I supposed to have nicked?"

"You're wasting my time," he said.

"All right," I said. "Then I'll go." There wasn't anywhere to go, but I didn't think he'd know that.

"Wait," he said. "Don't go anywhere till you've heard what I have to say." He fell silent. It was what I always thought. You tell them things. They'd rather eat worms before they tell you something back.

After a bit he said, "You still there?"

"I'm still here," I said. "But not for long. I'm getting wet."

"All right," he said. "You won't understand this but I'll tell you anyway. The dead bloke was a systems analyst."

"What's one of them?" I asked.

"He was a computer expert." Detective Sergeant Michael Sussex sighed. I could hear it from my end of the drain. Sound travels in a drain.

"He wrote programs for computers. He debugged programs. But most of all he wrote safe programs." He sighed again.

"This doesn't mean anything to you," he said. "Why don't you just come out of there like a good girl and give me the number."

"What number?" I said. He was right. I didn't understand. I was very confused. I thought I was in trouble because I'd taken the wallet. I tried to give it back but the woman wouldn't take it. That was confusing. Whoever heard of anyone not taking money when it was offered.

"It doesn't matter what number," he said, sounding angry. "This bloke, this Philip Walker-Jones, he worked for some very funny types. These types don't keep their dealings in books or ledgers anymore. Oh no. They stick them on computer tape, or discs where your average copper won't know how to find them. It's all bleeding high tech now."

He sounded very fed up, and I couldn't tell if it was because I was in a drain out of reach, or because he didn't understand high tech any more than I did.

Just then I heard footsteps, and someone said, "What you doing down there, boss?"

"Taking a bleeding mudbath," Detective Sergeant Michael Sussex said. "What does it look like I'm doing?"

"Did you lose her, then?" the other voice said.

"Course not. This is a new interview technique. Orders from on high: 'Do it in a bleeding land-drain.' " He sounded so down I almost laughed.

"Are you still there?" he said.

"No," I said. "Good-bye." And I scrambled into the bend of the pipe and pulled my knees up to my chest so that I couldn't be seen.

"Shit!" Detective Sergeant Michael Sussex said. "You've scared her off, you bleeding berk."

I could hear him heaving and cursing, and then he said, "You'd better give me a pull out of here, Hibbard."

There was some more heaving and cursing, and then I heard his voice from further off saying, "Where does this bleeding drain come out?"

"Buggered if I know, boss," Hibbard said. "Could be the river for all I know."

"Well, bleeding go and look," Detective Sergeant Michael Sussex said. "And if you find her don't lose her or I'll have you back in uniform quicker than you can say 'crystals balls.' "

"You sure you had the right one?" Hibbard said. He sounded reluctant to go tramping around the Trenches looking for the other end of a drain.

"You saw the description—there can't be two like her."

I didn't like the way he said that, and I didn't like the way he made fun of my name. I was freezing cold and soaked through, but I wasn't going to come out for anyone with that sort of attitude.

So that's where we stayed, him outside in the Trenches and me scrunched up at the end of the drain waiting for him to give up and go away. Sometimes he shone a torch in—to keep himself busy, I suppose. But I stayed stone-still and never made a sound.

Sometimes he paced up and down and muttered foul language to himself. He reminded me of our mum's boyfriend when he thought I'd pinched something off him. We were all at it in those days. He'd pinch things out of our mum's handbag and Dawn and me pinched things off him. We used to hide under the stairs, Dawn and me, while he raged around swearing he'd leather the lights out of us. Sometimes I'd hide from the truant officer too.

I'm used to hiding. All it takes is a bit of patience and a good breakfast in your belly. Don't try it somewhere wet and cold, though—that calls for real talent and I wouldn't recommend it to beginners.

At one stage Hibbard came back. He didn't sound half so cocky now.

"She'll be long gone," he said. "I can't find where this thing comes out."

"It's got to come out somewhere," Detective Sergeant Michael Sussex said. "Use your radio. Get more bodies. Make a bleeding effort."

He stayed where he was, and I stayed where I was.

Another time, Hibbard said, "Why don't we get in the Borough Engineers to dig this whole fucking site up and be done with it?"

And another time Detective Sergeant Michael Sussex said, "Comb the bleeding area. She could've dropped it or stashed it." He was sounding cold and tired too.

"All this for a bleeding number," he said. "And if we don't get it our whole case goes down the bleeding bog. Why couldn't the silly sod pick somewhere else to pop his clogs?"

Hibbard said, "Why are we so sure he had it on him? And why are we so sure she's got it now?"

"We know he had it because he was bringing it to me," Detective Sergeant Michael Sussex said. "And we know she got it because she swiped his wallet. We've got everything else back except that, and unless he had the number tattooed to his bleeding skull under his bleeding hair that's where it is."

"Couldn't he have just had it in his head?" Hibbard said. "Remembered it."

"Twenty-five bleeding digits? Do me a favor. He said it was written down and he said I could have it. You just want to go indoors for your dinner. Well, no one gets any dinner till I get that kid."

So we all sat there without our dinners. Detective Sergeant Michael Sussex made everyone go hungry for nothing. Because I didn't have any number twenty-five digits long.

But it's no use worrying about what you don't have, especially when what really worries you is what you might get. I was worried I might get pneumonia. If you get sick you can't feed yourself. If you can't feed yourself you get weak, and then either the officials grab you and put you in a hospital, or you die. I've seen it happen.

And I'll tell you something else—a very funny thing happened when I got out of the drain. Well, it wasn't a thing, and it didn't really happen. But I thought it did, and it really frightened me.

I became an old woman.

It was when I looked around the bend and couldn't see the circle of light at the end of the drain. I strained my ears and I couldn't hear anything moving out there. And suddenly I thought I'd gone deaf and blind.

I tried to move, but I was so stiff with cold it took me ages to inch my way along to the opening. I didn't care if Detective Sergeant Michael Sussex caught me. In fact I called out to him, and my voice had gone all weak and husky. I wanted him to be there, if you can believe that. I actually wanted him to help me, see, because I thought I'd gone blind, and I was scared.

But he wasn't there, and it was dark and teeming down with rain. And I couldn't straighten up. My back was bent, my knees were bent. There was no strength in my legs. I couldn't have run if they'd set the dogs on me.

I was an old woman out there in the dark—looking at the puddles in the mud, shuffling along, bent over. And I thought about Bloody Mary and the way she is first thing of a morning. There are some of them even older than she is who never have to bend over to look in dustbins because that's the shape they always are.

Of course I come to my senses soon enough. I got my circulation back and I rubbed the stiffness out of my legs. And I knew it was truly dark. I hadn't gone blind. But I did not stop being scared.

Even standing upright I felt helpless. Even with 743 pounds, 89 pence on me. The Law was after me. The bastards who beat up Little Marvin were after me. And I had nowhere to go. I was sick and old, and I needed help. What I needed, I thought, was a mark of my own.

Once having thought that, I became a little more cheerful. Not a lot, mind, because I hadn't had anything to eat since that curry before daybreak, and being hungry brings on the blues like nothing else can. But I pulled myself together and went looking for my mark.

I didn't know her name, but I knew where to find her. It was up the other end of the northern line. I couldn't have walked it that night, not for love nor money. So I caught the tube to Chalk Farm, and I hung around outside one of those bookshops.

I thought I had her once, but she tightened her grip on her shopping and hurried away. It was a mistake I put down to hunger. Usually I don't go wrong on middle-aged women.

But I saw her at last. She was wearing a fawn-colored raincoat and a tartan scarf. She had a green umbrella and she was struggling with her Christmas shopping.

I said, "Carry your bags for you, missus?"

She hesitated. I knew her. She's the one who has her handbag open before you even ask. She doesn't give you any mouth about finding a job or spending money on drink. She just looks sort of sorry and she watches you when you walk away.

She hesitated, but then she gave me a bag to carry. Not the heaviest one either. She's nice. She wants to trust me. At least she doesn't want to distrust me. I knew her. She was my mark.

She said, "Thank you very much. The car is just round the corner."

I followed her, and stood in the rain while she fumbled with her umbrella and car keys. I put her bag in the boot and helped her with the other one.

She looked at me and hesitated again. Not that she'd dream of going off without giving me something. This one just wants to find a polite way of doing it.

She said, "Well, thanks very much," and she started to fumble in her handbag again. I let her get her money out, and then I said, "I don't want your money, missus, thanks all the same for the thought."

She said, "Oh, but you must let me give you something."

I just stood there shaking my head, looking pitiful.

"What is it?" she asked, with that sorry expression on her face.

It was the crucial time. I said. "I've got some money, missus, but I can't spend it." And I held out one of the fifty-pound notes.

She looked at the money and she looked at me.

I said, "I know what you're thinking. That's why I can't spend it. I want to get some decent clothes because I can't get a job looking like this. But every time I try they look at me like I stole the money and they go to call the Law. No one trusts people like me."

She went on looking first at me and then at the money, and said, "I don't mean to sound suspicious, but where *did* you get a fifty-pound note?"

"A nice lady give it to me," I said. "She must've thought it was a fiver. She was a really nice lady because no one's ever given me a fiver before. But when I went in to buy a cup of tea and some chips, the man went to call the Law and I saw she must have made a mistake."

"I see," she said.

"You don't," I said. "Having this money is worse than not having anything."

"I can see that," she said. "How can I help?"

I had her. "Please, missus," I said. "Please help me spend it. All I want's a good coat and some shoes. There's a charity shop just round the corner and I been hanging around for ages but I can't bring myself to go in on my own."

She was good as gold, my lady mark. She bought me a big wool coat for only a couple of quid and she talked to the women in the shop while I looked for jeans and jerseys.

It was all quality stuff and probably it was all donated to the charity by women like her. They don't give any old rubbish to charity. And I'll tell you something else—my lady mark was having the time of her life. It was like a dream come true to her. Someone really and truly wanted her help with something she approved of. She didn't have to worry I was spending her money on drink or drugs because it wasn't her money and I was there under her nose spending it on warm clothes.

Even the women behind the counter had a sort of glow on them when I came out from behind the racks with my arms full. She'd probably told them my story in whispers when my back was turned. And that was why I really had needed her help. Because those nice ladies behind the counter would have chased me out if I'd gone in on my own. They'd have been afraid I'd pinch their charity.

It was still coming down in buckets when we left the shop. This time it was me carrying all the bags.

I was about to go when she said, "Look, don't be insulted, but what you need is a hot bath and somewhere to change." She said it in a rush as if she really was afraid of hurting my feelings.

"I live up the hill," she said. "It won't take any time at all."

"Nah," I said. "I'll get your car seats all dirty."

"It doesn't matter," she said. "Please."

And I thought, why not? She deserved the satisfaction.

She ran me a hot bath and squirted loads of scented oil in. She gave me her shampoo and a whole heap of clean towels. And then my lovely lady mark left me alone in her bathroom.

I swear she had tears in her eyes when I came out in my new clothes.

"Crystal," she said, "you look like a new person." This was just what I wanted to hear.

"You look quite like my own daughter when she was younger," she said. Which was a good thing because the Law and the bastards who beat Marvin up weren't looking for someone who looked like my lady mark's daughter. And no one would bat an eyelash if she had a fifty-pound note. My lady mark's daughter would not turn into an old woman who had to bend over to root around in dustbins.

And nor, I thought, would I, if I could help it.

She cooked me eggs and potatoes for my tea, and when I left she gave me a fiver and her green umbrella.

It was a shame really to have pinched her soap. But you can't break old habits all at once.

She even wanted to give me another ride in her car. But I wouldn't let her. She was a lovely lady, but I didn't think she'd understand about Dawn. Lovely ladies don't.

I could give lessons about what to do when you find your mark, and the last one would be—don't push your luck. Because if you push your luck and let them take over, they start giving you what they think you need instead of what you want. If my lady mark knew too much about Dawn and what was really going on, she'd have got in touch with the Social Services all over again. And far from being a lovely lady she'd have turned into an interfering old cow.

I was doing her a favor, really. I'm sure she'd rather be a lovely lady than an interfering old cow.

No one who saw me knocking at Dawn's door in Paddington would have known I'd spent all day down a drain. Dawn didn't.

" 'Struth, Crystal," she said when she opened up. "You look like one of those girls from that snob school up the hill from ours."

I knew what she meant and I didn't like it much. But I was lucky really. I'd caught her at a slack time when she was just lying around reading her comic and playing records. And now I was all clean and respectable, she didn't mind if I sat on her bed.

"You still need your hair cut," Dawn said.

She got out her scissors and manicure set, and we sat on her bed while she cut my hair and did my nails. Dawn could be a beautician if she wanted. The trouble is she'd never stand for the training and the money wouldn't be enough. She's used to her creature comforts now, is Dawn.

It was a bit like the old days—Dawn and me together listening to records, and her fiddling with my hair. I didn't want to spoil it but I had to ask about the watch.

Because when I was in the lovely lady's bathroom I'd had another search through Philip Walker-Jones's wallet.

Dawn said, "What about the watch?" And she rubbed round my thumb with her little nail file.

"It was real gold," I said, to remind her. "Your Christmas present."

"I can't wear a man's watch," she said. Dawn likes to be very dainty sometimes.

"Where is it?" I said.

"You want it back?" she asked. "Fine Christmas present if you want it back."

I looked at her and she looked at me. Then she said, "Well, Crystal, if you must know, I was going to give it to my boyfriend for Christmas."

"It wasn't for him," I said. "It was for you."

"A man's watch?" she said, and laughed. "I was going to get his name engraved on the back. 'Eternal love, from Dawn.' But there wasn't room. There were all these numbers on the back, and the man at the jewelers said I'd lose too much gold having them rubbed down."

"Hah!" I said. I felt clever. Because all it takes is some good hot food to help you think. And it had come to me in a flash just after I'd put down my last mouthful of egg and potato.

I said, "Bet there were twenty-five of them."

"Loads of numbers," she said. She put the nail file back in her manicure set.

"If you must know, Crystal," she said, "I popped it. And I bought him a real gold cigarette lighter instead."

And she gave me the pawn ticket.

She hadn't got much for a solid gold watch. Dawn isn't practical like I am, so the pawnbroker cheated her. Not that it mattered. It wasn't her watch in the first place, and besides, it would cost me less to get back. If I wanted it back.

Poor Dawn. She needs me to take care of her. She doesn't think she does because she thinks her boyfriend's doing it. She's not like me. She doesn't want to look after herself. That's not her job. And if I told her what I'd been through today to solve my own problems she'd say I was a fool.

But look at it this way—I'd given Detective Sergeant Michael Sussex the slip. I'd dressed up so he wouldn't know me again if I ran slap-bang into him. Nor would Brainy Brian. So he couldn't finger me to the bastards who beat up little Marvin. I'd had a bath and I'd had eggs and potatoes for my tea. I had enough money to sleep in a bed for as many nights as I wanted. And now I had the watch.

Or I could have it any time I wanted. But it was safer where it was.

I still didn't know why the number was so important but I was sure it would be worth something to me sooner or later.

I saw Dawn looking at me.

"Don't get too cocky, Crystal," she said. "You might *look* like a girl from the snob school, but you're still just like me."

That's how much she knew.

The Wasp

PETER LOVESEY

Peter Lovesey is well known to mystery readers the world over as the creator of Victorian age police officers Sergeant Cribb and Constable Thackeray. Other creations include using King Edward VII as a sleuth in another take on the Victorian age. In between these series he has written dozens of short stories, as well as several television plays. He has also won several awards, notably both the Silver and Gold Dagger awards from the Crime Writers Association.

The storm had passed, leaving a keen wind that whipped foam off the waves. Heaps of gleaming seaweed were strewn about the beach. Shells, bits of driftwood, and a few stranded jellyfish lay where the tide had deposited them. Paul Molloy, bucket in hand, was down there as he was every morning, alone and preoccupied.

His wife Gwynneth stood by the wooden steps that led off the beach through a garden of flowering trees to their property.

"Paul! Breakfast time!"

She had to shout it twice more before Paul's damaged brain registered anything. Then he turned and trudged awkwardly toward her.

The stroke last July, a few days before his sixty-first birthday, had turned him into a shambling parody of the fine man he had been. He was left with the physical coordination of a small child, except that he was slower. And dumb.

The loss of speech was the hardest for Gwynneth to bear. She hated being cut off from his thoughts. He was unable even to write, or draw pictures. She had to be content with scraps of communication. Each time he came up from the beach he handed her something he had found, a shell or a pebble. She received such gifts as graciously as she had once accepted roses.

They had said at the hospital that she ought to keep talking to him in an adult way even if he didn't appear to understand. It was a mistake to give up. So she persevered, though inevitably it sounded as if she were addressing a child.

"Darling, what a beautiful shell! Is it for me? Oh, how sweet! I'll take it up to the house and put it on the shelf with all the other treasures you found for me—except that this one must stand in the center." She leaned forward to kiss him and made no contact with his face. He had moved his head to look at a gull.

She helped him up the steps and they started the short, laborious trek to the house. They had brought the land, a few miles north of Bundaberg on the Queensland coast, ten years before Paul retired from his Brisbane-based insurance company. As chairman, he could have carried on for years more, but he had always promised he would stop at sixty—before he got fat and feeble, as he used to say. They had built themselves this handsome retirement home and installed facilities they'd thought they would use: swimming pool, jacuzzi, boat house, and tennis court. Only their guests used them now.

"Come on, love, step out quick," she urged Paul, "there's beautiful bacon waiting for you." And, tirelessly trying for a spark of interest, she added, "Cousin Haydn's still asleep by the look of it. I don't think he'll be joining you for your walks on the beach. Not before breakfast, anyway. Probably not at all. He doesn't care for the sea, does he?"

Gwynneth encouraged people to stay. She missed real conversation. Cousin Haydn was on a visit from Wales. He was a distant cousin she hadn't met before, but she didn't mind. She'd got to know him when she'd started delving into her family history for something to distract her. Years ago, her father had given her an old Bible with a family tree in the front. She'd brought it up to date. Then she had joined a family-history society and learned that a good way of tracking down ancestors was to write to local newspapers in the areas where they had lived. She had managed to get a letter published in a Swansea paper and Haydn had seen it and got in touch. He was an Evans also, and he'd done an immense amount of research. He'd discovered a branch of his family tree that linked up with hers, through Great-Grandfather Hugh Evans of Port Talbot.

Paul shuffled toward the house without even looking up at the drawn curtains.

"Mind you," Gwynneth continued, "I'm not surprised Haydn is used to staying indoors, what with the Welsh weather *I* remember. I expect he reads the Bible a lot, being a man of the cloth." She checked herself for speaking the obvious again and pushed open the kitchen door. "Come on, Paul. Just you and me for breakfast by the look of it."

Cousin Haydn eventually appeared in time for the midmorning coffee. On the first day after he'd arrived, he'd discarded the black suit and dog-collar in favor of a pink T-shirt. Casual clothes made him look several years younger—say, forty-five—but they also revealed what Gwynneth would have called a beer gut had Haydn not been a minister.

"Feel better for your sleep?" she inquired.

"Infinitely better, thank you, Gwynneth." You couldn't mistake him for an Australian when he opened his mouth. "And most agreeably refreshed by a dip in your pool."

"Oh, you had a swim?"

"Hardly a swim. I was speaking of the small circular pool."

She smiled. "The jacuzzi. Did you find the switch?"

"I was unaware that I needed to find it."

"It works the pumps that make the whirlpool effect. If you didn't switch on, you missed something."

"Then I shall certainly repeat the adventure."

"Paul used to like it. I'm afraid of him slipping, so he doesn't get in there now."

"Pity, if he enjoyed it."

"Perhaps I ought to take the risk. The specialist said he may begin to bring other muscles into use that aren't affected by the stroke—isn't that so, my darling?"

Paul gave no sign of comprehension.

"Does he understand much?" Haydn asked.

"I convince myself he does, even if he's unable to show it. If you don't mind, I don't really care to talk about him in this way, as if he's not one of us."

Cousin Haydn gave an understanding nod. "Let's talk about something less depressing, then. I have good news for you. Gwynneth."

She responded with a murmur that didn't convey much enthusiasm. Sermons in church were one thing, her kitchen was another place altogether.

It emerged that Haydn's good news wasn't of an evangelical character. "One of the reasons for coming here—apart from following up our fascinating correspondence—is to tell you about a mutual ancestor, Sir Tudor Evans."

"*Sir* Tudor? We had a title in the family?"

"Back in the seventeenth century, yes."

"I don't recall seeing him on my family tree."

Haydn gave the slight smile of one who has a superior grasp of genealogy. "Yours started in the seventeen eighties, if I recall."

"Oh, yes."

"To say that it started then is, of course, misleading. Your eighteenth-century forebears had parents, as did mine—and they in turn had parents. And so it goes back—first to Sir Tudor, and ultimately to Adam."

"Never mind Adam. Tell me about Sir Tudor." Gwynneth swung around to Paul, who was sucking the end of his thumb. "Bet you didn't know I came from titled stock, darling."

Haydn said, "A direct line. Planter Evans, they called him. He owned half of Barbados once, according to my research. Made himself a fortune in sugar cane."

"Really? A fortune. What happened to it?"

"Most of it went down with the *Gloriana* in 1683. One of the great tragedies of the sea. He'd sold the plantations to come back to the land of his fathers. He was almost home when a great storm blew up in the Bristol Channel and the ship was lost with all hands. Sir Tudor and his wife Eleanor were among those on board."

"How very sad!"

"God rest their souls, yes."

Gwynneth put her hand to her face. "I'm trying to remember. Last year was such a nightmare for us. A lot of things passed right over my head. The *Gloriana*. Isn't that the ship they found—those treasure hunters? I read about this somewhere."

"It was in all the papers," Haydn confirmed. "I have some of the cuttings with me, in my briefcase."

"I do remember. The divers were bringing up masses of stuff—coins by the bucketful, and silverware and the most exquisite jewelry. Oh, how exciting—can we make a claim?"

Cousin Haydn shook his head. "Out of the question, my dear. One would need to hire lawyers. Besides, it may be too late."

"Why?"

"As I understand it, when treasure is recovered from a wreck around the British coasts, it has to be handed over to the local receiver of wrecks or the Customs. The lawful owner then has a year and a day to make a claim. After that, the pieces are sold and the proceeds go to the salvager."

"A year and a day," said Gwynneth. "Oh, Haydn, this is too tantalizing. When did these treasure hunters start bringing up the stuff?"

"Last March."

"Eleven months! Then there's still time to make a claim. We must do it."

Haydn sighed heavily. "These things can be extremely costly."

"But we'd get it all back if we could prove our right to the treasure."

He put out his hand in a dissenting gesture. "*Your* right, my dear, not mine. Your connection is undeniable, mine is very tenuous. No, I have no personal interest here. Besides, a man of my calling cannot serve God and mammon."

"Do you really believe I have a claim?"

"The treasure hunters would dispute it, I'm sure."

"We're talking about millions of pounds, aren't we? Why should I sit back and let them take it all? I need to get hold of some lawyers—and fast."

Haydn coughed. "They charge astronomical fees."

"I know," said Gwynneth. "We can afford it—can't we, Paul?"

Paul made a blowing sound with his lips that probably had no bearing on the matter.

Gwynneth assumed so. "What is it they want—a down payment?"

"A retainer, I think is the expression."

"I can write a check tomorrow if you want. I look after all our personal finances now. There's more than enough in the deposit account. The thing is, how do I find a reliable lawyer?"

Haydn cupped his chin in his hands and looked thoughtful. "I wouldn't go to an Australian firm. Better find someone on the spot. Jones, Heap, and Jones of Cardiff are the best in Wales. I'm sure they could take on something like this."

"But is there time? We're almost into March now."

"It is rather urgent," Haydn agreed. "Look, I don't mind cutting my holiday short by a few days. If I got back to Wales at the weekend I could see them on Monday."

"I couldn't ask you to do that," said Gwynneth in a tone that betrayed the opposite.

"No trouble," said Haydn breezily.

"You're an angel. Would they accept a check in Australian pounds?"

"That might be difficult, but it's easily got around. Traveler's checks are the thing. I use them all the time. In fact, if you're serious about this—"

"Oh, yes."

"You could buy sterling traveler's checks in my name and I could pay the retainer for you."

"Would you really do that for me?"

"Anything to be of service."

She shivered with pleasure. "And now, if you've got them nearby, I'd love to have ten minutes with those press cuttings."

He left them with her, and she read them through several times during the afternoon when she was alone in her room and Paul had gone for one of his walks along the beach. Three pages cut from a color supplement had stunning pictures of the finds. She so adored the ruby necklace and the gold bracelets that she thought she would refuse to sell them. Cousin Haydn had also given her a much more detailed family tree than she had seen before. It proved beyond doubt that she was the only direct descendant of Sir Tudor Evans.

Was it all too good to be true?

One or two doubts crept into her mind later that afternoon. Presumably the treasure hunters had invested heavily in ships, divers, and equipment. They must have been confident that anything they brought up would belong to them. Maybe her claim wasn't valid under the law. She wondered also whether Cousin Haydn's research was entirely accurate. She didn't question his good faith—how could one in the circumstances?—but she knew from her own humble diggings in family history that it was all too easy to confuse one Evans with another.

On the other hand, she told herself, that's what I'm hiring the lawyers to find out. It's their business to establish whether my claim is lawful.

There was an unsettling incident toward evening. She walked down to the beach to collect Paul. The stretch where he liked to wander was never particularly crowded, even at weekends, and she soon spotted him kneeling on the sand. This time he didn't need calling. He got up, collected his bucket, and tottered toward her. Automatically she held out her hand for the gift he had chosen for her. He peered into the bucket and picked something out and placed it on her open palm.

A dead wasp.

She almost snatched her hand away and let the thing drop. She was glad she didn't, because it was obvious that he'd saved it for her and she would have hated to hurt his feelings.

She said, "Oh, a little wasp. Thank you, darling. So thoughtful. We'll take it home and put it with all my pretty pebbles and shells, shall we?"

She took a paper tissue from her pocket and folded the tiny corpse carefully between the layers.

In the house she unwrapped it and made a space on the shelf among the shells and stones. "There." She turned and smiled at Paul.

He put his thumb on the wasp and squashed it.

"Darling!"

The small act of violence shocked Gwynneth. She found herself quite stupidly reacting as if something precious had been destroyed. "You shouldn't have done that, Paul. You gave it to me. I treasure whatever you give me. You know that."

He shuffled out of the room.

That evening over dinner she told Cousin Haydn about the incident, once again breaking her own rule and discussing Paul while he was sitting with them. "I keep wondering if he meant anything by it," she said. "It's so unlike him."

"If you want my opinion," said Haydn, "he showed some intelligence. You don't want a wasp in the house, dead or alive. As a matter of fact, I've got quite a phobia about them. It's one of the reasons I avoid the beach. You can't sit for long on any beach without being troubled by them."

"Perhaps you were stung once."

"No, I've managed to avoid them, but one of my uncles was killed by one."

"Killed by a wasp?"

"He was only forty-four at the time. It happened on the front at Aberystwyth. He was stung here, on the right temple. His face went bright red and he fell down on the shingle. My aunt ran for a doctor, but all he could do was confirm that Uncle was dead."

Clearly the tragedy had made a profound impression on Haydn. His account of the incident, spoken in simple language instead of his usual florid style, carried conviction.

"Dreadful. It must have been a rare case."

"Not so uncommon as you'd think. I tell you, Gwynneth, the wasp is one of God's creatures I studiously avoid at all times." He turned to Paul and for the first time addressed him directly, trying to end on a less grave note. "So I say more power to your thumbs, boyo."

Paul looked at him blankly.

Toward the end of the meal Haydn announced he would be leaving in the morning. "I telephoned the airport. I am advised I can get something called a standby. They say it's better before the weekend, so I'm leaving tomorrow."

"Tomorrow?" said Gwynneth, her voice pitched high in alarm. "But you can't. We haven't bought those traveler's checks."

"That's all right, my dear. There's a place to purchase them at the airport. All you need to do is write me a check. In fact, you could write it now in case we forget in the morning."

"How much?"

"I don't know. I'm not too conversant with the scale of fees lawyers charge these days. Are you sure you want to get involved in expense?"

"Absolutely. If I have no right to make a claim they'll let me know, won't they?"

"I'll let you know myself, my dear. How much can you spare without running up an overdraft? It's probably better for me to take more rather than less."

She wrote him a check for ten thousand Australian dollars.

"Then if you will excuse me, I'll go and pack my things and have a quiet hour before bedtime."

"Would you like an early breakfast tomorrow?"

Haydn smiled. "Early by my standards, yes. Say about eight? That gives me ample time to do something I promised myself—try the jacuzzi with the switch on. Goodnight and God bless you, my dear. And *you*, Paul, old fellow."

Gwynneth slept fitfully. At one stage in the night she noticed that Paul had his eyes open. She found his hand and gripped it tightly and talked to him as if he understood.

"I keep wondering if I've done the right thing, giving Haydn that check. It's not as if I don't trust him—I mean, you've got to trust a man of God, haven't you? I just wonder if you would have done what I did, my darling—giving him the check, I mean—and somehow I don't think so. In fact, I ask myself if you were trying to tell me something when you gave me the wasp. It was such an unusual thing for you to do. Then squashing it like that."

She must have drifted off soon after, because when she next opened her eyes the grey light of dawn was picking out the edges of the curtains. She sighed and turned toward Paul, but his side of the bed was empty. He must have gone down to the beach already.

She showered and dressed soon after, wanting to make an early start on cooking the breakfast. She would get everything ready first, she decided, and then fetch Paul from the beach before she started the cooking.

However, this was a morning of surprises.

For some unfathomable reason Paul had already come up from the beach without being called. He was seated in his usual place in the kitchen.

"Paul! You gave me quite a shock," Gwynneth told him. "What is it? Are you extra hungry this morning or something? I'll get this started presently. Would you like some bread while you're waiting? I'd better give Cousin Haydn a call first and make sure he's awake."

It crossed her mind as she went to tap on Haydn's door that Paul hadn't brought her anything from the beach. She wondered if she'd hurt his feelings by talking about the wasp as she had.

She didn't like knocking on Haydn's door in case she was interrupting his morning prayers, but it had to be done this morning in case he overslept.

He answered her call. "Thank you. Is there time for me to sample the jacuzzi?"

"Of course. Shall we say twenty minutes?"

"That should be ample."

She returned to the kitchen and made a sandwich for Paul. The bucket he always took to the beach was beside him. Without being too obvious about it, Gwynneth glanced inside to see if the customary gift of a shell or a pebble was there. It was silly, but she was feeling quite neglected.

Empty.

She said nothing about it, simply busied herself setting the table for breakfast. Presently she started heating the frying pan.

Fifteen minutes later when everything was cooked and waiting in the oven, Haydn had not appeared. "He's really enjoying that jacuzzi," she told Paul. "We'd better start, I think."

They finished.

"I'd better go and see," she said.

When she went to the door, the leg of Paul's chair was jammed against it, preventing her from opening it. "Do you mind, darling? I can't get out."

He made no move.

"Maybe you're right," Gwynneth said, always willing to assume that Paul's behavior was deliberate and intelligent. "I shouldn't fuss. It won't spoil for being left a few minutes more."

She allowed another quarter of an hour to pass. "Do you think something's happened to him? I'd better go and see, really I had. Come on, dear. Let me through."

As she took Paul by the arm and helped him to his feet, he reached out and drew her toward him, pressing his face against hers. She was surprised and delighted. He hadn't embraced her once since the stroke. She turned her face and kissed him before going to find Cousin Haydn.

Haydn was lying face down on the tile surround of the jacuzzi, which was churning noisily. He was wearing black swimming-trunks. He didn't move when she spoke his name.

"I think he may be dead," Gwynneth told the girl who took the emergency call.

The girl told her to try the kiss of life, an ambulance was on its way.

Gwynneth was still on her knees trying to breathe life into Cousin Haydn when the police arrived. They had come straight round the back of the house. "Let's have a look, lady," the sergeant said. Then, after a moment: "He's gone—no question. Who is he—your husband?"

She explained about Cousin Haydn.

"This is where you found him?"

"Well, yes. Was it an electric shock, do you think?"

"You tell me, lady. Was the jacuzzi on when you found him?"

"Yes." Gwynneth suddenly realized it was no longer running. Paul must have switched it off while she was phoning for help. She didn't want Paul brought into this. "I don't know. I may be mistaken about that."

"There could be a fault," the sergeant speculated. "We'll get it checked. Is your husband about?"

"He was." She called Paul's name. "He must have gone down to the beach. That's where he goes." She told them about the stroke.

More policemen arrived, some in plainclothes. One introduced himself as Detective Inspector Perry. He talked to Gwynneth several times in the next two hours. He went into Cousin Haydn's room and opened the suitcase he had packed for the flight home. He turned to Gwynneth and smiled.

"You say you knew this man as Haydn Evans, your cousin from Wales?"

"That's who he was."

"A distant cousin?"

Gwynneth didn't care for his grin. "I can show you the family tree if you like."

"No need for that, Mrs. Molloy. His luggage is stuffed with family trees, all as bogus as his Welsh accent. He wasn't a minister of any church or chapel. His name was Brown. Michael Herbert Brown. An English con man we've been after for months. He was getting too well known to Scotland Yard, so he came out to Queensland this summer. He's been stinging people for thousands with the treasure-hunting story. Here's your check. Lucky escape, I'd say."

They finally took the body away in an ambulance.

Detective Inspector Perry phoned late in the afternoon. "I just thought I'd let you know that your jacuzzi is safe to use, Mrs. Molloy. There's no electrical fault. I have the pathologist's report and I can tell you that Brown was not electrocuted."

"What killed him, then?"

He laughed. "Something rather appropriate. It was a sting."

Gwynneth frowned and put her hand to her throat. "A sting from a wasp?"

"In a manner of speaking." There was amusement in his voice. "Not the wasp you had in mind."

"I don't understand."

"No mystery in it, Mrs. Molloy. A sea-wasp got him. You know what a sea-wasp is?"

She knew. Everyone on the coast knew. "A jellyfish. An extremely poisonous jellyfish."

"Right, a killer."

"But the man didn't swim in the sea. He kept off the beach."

"That explains it, then."

"How?"

"He wouldn't have known about the sea-wasps. That storm washed quite a number onto the beaches. It looks as if Brown decided to take one look at the sea before he left this morning. He'd put on his swimming gear—and he must have waded in. Didn't need to go far. There were sea-wasps stranded in the shallows. You and I know how deadly they are, but I reckon an Englishman wouldn't. He got bitten, staggered back to the house, and collapsed beside the jacuzzi."

"I see." She knew it was nonsense.

"Try and remember, Mrs. Molloy. Did you see him walk down to the beach?"

"I was cooking breakfast."

"Pity. Where was your husband?"

"Paul?" She glanced over at Paul, now sitting in his usual armchair with his arms around his bucket. "He was with me in the kitchen." She was about to add that Paul had come up from the beach, but the inspector was already onto other possibilities.

"Maybe someone else saw Brown on the beach. I believe it's pretty deserted at that time."

"Yes."

"Be useful to have a witness for the inquest. All right, I heard what you said about him normally keeping off the beach, but it's a fact that he died from a sea-wasp sting. That's been established."

"I'm not questioning it."

"I ask you, Mrs. Molloy, how else could it have happened? There's only one other possibility I can think of. But how could a jellyfish get into a jacuzzi, for Christ's sake?"

Looking for Thelma

GILLIAN SLOVO

Born in South Africa, Gillian Slovo has lived in England since she was twelve. A journalist and television producer, she has written several excellent mystery novels featuring London-based Kate Baeier, including *Morbid Symptoms* and *Death by Analysis.*

I was in the middle of doing my accounts when the doorbell rang. Or, to be more accurate, my accounts were in the middle of doing me. The center column was being cooperative: it was the ones either side of it that were making trouble.

The bell sounded again. I ignored it: I didn't feel like visitors, and besides, I'd just made a momentous decision. I'd decided to compromise—a few pence to the left subtracted from the right would achieve the proper balance. It wasn't entirely on the level, but if the customs and excise noticed, all they would learn was what they must already know—namely, that I couldn't add to save my life.

"The door was open," a timid voice said.

Frowning at the distraction, I looked toward the door. My eyes came to rest not on a face but on a wide patent-leather belt. I shifted my gaze upward.

The man in front of me was huge—nearer to seven than six feet—with a body to match. He was made to be noticed, and he flaunted the fact. He had shaved his head clean, and his bald pate shone a deep black against the rest of his clothes. It was quite an outfit—his three-piece suit was tailored to fit his broad frame and sewed from all colors of the rainbow, a broad silver tie nestled under the garish waistcoat, and a pair of shining black shoes that seemed to go on forever had silver buckles the size of my hands. I gulped.

"The door was open," he said again.

The voice was not only small but melodic with it. On the principle that there was no point in antagonizing giants, even ones with ingratiating voices, I threw a smile his way. My neck hurt with the effort of twisting so I stood in an attempt to equalize the distance. He strode toward me.

The man was big, real big, and close up he towered above me. There was no point in competing. I sat.

"Can I help you?" I asked. *Good*, I thought, *my voice sounds normal*.

He smiled, and the long gray-brown scar that ran the full length of his left cheek smiled with him. He lowered himself onto the chair in front of me and planted two huge fists on my desk. I backed away and hit the wall with my head. I rubbed it surreptitiously.

"I hope you can help," he said.

I turned the rub into an encouraging nod and waited. I was ready for anything.

"I want you to find somebody for me," he said. "Name of Thelma."

Something clicked in my head, so tangibly that I bet I lost a hundred thousand brain cells making the connection. *Got it in one*, I thought. Smiling cynically, I leaned my chair against the wall and stretched my legs out so that my feet landed on the desk, right in the middle of my accounts book. My only regret was that I didn't have a cigarette to hang out of the side of my mouth and complete the impression.

"And what's your name?" I asked. "Moose, by any chance?"

He looked puzzled. "Moose?" he thought about it a bit. "No, Martin. Martin Malloy."

I smiled again, and this time the cynicism was not an act. "That figures," I said.

He leaned across and shifted my feet to the right, uncovering the columns of numbers. His thick index finger pointed at the center row.

"But this doesn't," he said. "You've inverted one of those numbers, there in the middle. Easily done."

I returned my legs to the ground and pulled the book nearer to me, meaning to close it. But I couldn't help looking at where his finger had once been, and I couldn't help seeing that he was right. I frowned.

He grinned almost by way of apology. "I'm good at figures," he explained. "Always have been. And I learned to read upside down when I was inside."

"You've been in prison, then," I stated.

He nodded.

"And this Thelma put you there."

His brow creased, and I remembered his size and the scar that creased in its redness on his cheek. He was no longer doing an impression of the genial giant: I had angered him. I pulled at the telephone wire, edging the instrument closer to me.

"Thelma didn't put me there," he said. "In fact, if anybody got me out, it was Thelma." He glared at me. "I don't like people who say bad things about Thelma," he concluded.

With a supreme effort of will I fixed his eyes with mine. I kept looking at him while I nudged the receiver off the phone and let it drop on my lap. I rested my hand on the headless phone, thanking the heavens that I now had digital dialing. His frown deepened.

"Tell me more," I said in a voice that was more fear than fake. I hit the first nine on the phone while I tried to work out whether I could manage to make a successful break for the door.

In one effortless motion he reached across the desk and pulled the receiver from my lap. He put it down on the desk. He stretched across again.

He put a finger on one of the buttons and pressed it down.

"That makes two nines," he said. "You've only got to dial one more and you're connected. Go ahead, I won't stop you."

The brain cells were going fast by now. It was a dare, I thought; he'd get me before my first cry for help. He was toying with me, and probably enjoying it. And yet what option did I have? I was isolated and alone, up in my grimy office in the center of London. A cry for help wafting to the street would be cause for a quickening of pace rather than investigation. I had no choice: without the phone, I had no line to the world.

I lifted my hand slowly as the seconds expanded. I could try it, I thought, and maybe I'd succeed. My hand began to shake.

"I'm really a gentle guy," he said slowly, watching that hand. "My size militates against me, but I wouldn't harm a fly. Certainly not a woman, that's for sure."

"And what's that?" I asked, using the poised finger to point at his scar. "Shaving accident?"

He shrugged, and I saw how the rocks in his shoulders bulged. "Prison's a rough place," he said. "It makes you or it breaks you."

"And it made you?"

"Thelma made me," he said. "That's why I want to find her."

We were both back in fiction land. I replaced the receiver on the phone and breathed out. I no longer felt scared, only foolish—a foolishness tinged with anger. He was a pro, I thought, a real good actor, and I might as well face the fact that he had me. He and whoever had sent him—and I had a good idea as to who that was. Well, all I had to do was get rid of him, finish my accounts, close the office for perhaps the last time, and then be free to wreak my own kind of revenge.

But I'd do it subtly, I thought. I reached into the top drawer of my desk and pulled out a pad. As a heading I chose the name M. MALLOY. I underlined it: it looked better that way. On the next line I inscribed the name THELMA in block capitals.

"Parsons," he said. "Thelma Parsons."

"A dancer?" I asked without looking up.

"A social worker," he said. He blinked. "But she did like to dance. She showed me pictures of herself when she was a kid. All dressed up in a white tutu, she was."

Social worker, I wrote, *failed ballet dancer*.

"Thelma never failed at anything," he said loudly. It was the first time he had raised his voice.

I smiled placatingly. It took two to tango, I thought, and I was finally in step. I wasn't going to break my rhythm for any fake display of righteous anger by a giant gullible enough to involve himself in one of Sam's pranks.

"Why don't you tell me the whole story?" I suggested.

He leaned back in the chair. It creaked. He frowned and began to toy with the gold watch fob that was attached to his waistcoat. "Thelma liked to visit me in prison," he began. "She turned me on to books."

I glanced up and my eyes strayed to my accounts.

He laughed, or at least I think that was what described the creaking that issued from his big mouth. "Not those kind," he said, "I always had a knack with them. That's what got me into trouble in the first place. No, Thelma revealed the world of literature to me."

Social worker reforms con by opening his eyes to the joys of the nineteenth century, I wrote.

"Modern literature," he said loudly.

I gulped. I kept forgetting that he could read upside down.

"It changed my whole world view," he continued. "Opened new horizons. I want to be able to thank her, not in the claustrophobia of prison, but in the real world. In the free world."

Free world, I thought, *more like anticommunist modern literature, then*.

"So go round to her office and thank her," I said.

He shook his head unhappily. "She's left her job," he said. "She was never happy with it, it cramped her style, she said, and now she's had the courage to leave. They won't tell me where she went—they don't do that on principle in case some ex-con has a grudge against them."

"And you want me to find her?" I stated.

"That's it," he said, delighted that the slow pupil had finally caught on.

"And then you will thank her."

He nodded. He reached a fist into a pocket of his garish plaid suit. *Here comes the punch line,* I thought.

He placed a piece of paper in front of me, right side up. On it was written the name Thelma Parsons along with an address in Islington.

"That's where Thelma used to work?" I asked.

For reply he reached once more into his pocket. *Ahaa*, I thought, *here it comes*.

I was wrong again. In front of me, dead in front, he placed a wad of new bank notes. I stared at him, and he smiled. I picked up the notes and felt their crispness.

"Two hundred and fifty pounds," he said. "Retainer."

"Is that what they said it would cost?" I asked

"They?" He frowned. I resolved in future not to aggravate the scar. "It's a guess," he continued. "Your retainer plus something toward expenses. Give me a record when you finish, and I'll settle up with you. I'm good at figures, you know."

I didn't say anything, and he had finished as well. I watched as he stood up and began to stride to the door.

"I suppose that you'll be in touch with me rather than leaving me your address," I said.

He turned. "That's right," he said. "Circumstances have conspired to make me a bit of an itinerant at the moment." He waved a hand in my direction before turning away again. "I'll be in touch," he said.

"One more thing," I called just as he had bent his head down far enough to fit. "Ever read any Chandler?"

"No, I haven't," he replied without bothering to look back. "And my reading days are over. I only want to thank Thelma and then I can get on with my life."

They were conveniently seated around the kitchen table when I arrived, all three of them, the ones I had decided were guilty. Sam was doing what he liked best—explaining in layperson's terms a particularly neat solution to the latest space-time continuum problem—while

Anna and Daniel were doing what they did best—pretending to understand.

Into this cozy scene I strolled. I took a swig from the half bottle of Bells I'd picked up on the way.

"Bad day?" Sam asked.

I shoved the bottle into my jacket pocket. It bulged in the linen, but you can't have everything. At least I was suitably crumpled, I thought. I shook my head.

"Great day," I said. "I was having problems balancing the books, but Moose solved that for me."

They looked at one another, and the first hint of a doubt insinuated itself into my mind. They were giving a good impression of confusion, I thought, but then I discarded the thought. Anna and Daniel must surely have picked up some tips from the actors they directed, and as for Sam, well, he'd learned impassivity from years of teaching aspirant Nobel winners.

I changed tack. I reached into my bag, pulled out the wad of money, and threw it at them. It landed just where I had wanted it to, plum in Sam's lap. Both Anna and Daniel stretched across the table to get a better look.

"Nice crisp notes," Daniel commented. "Did this Moose rob a bank?"

"Maybe Sam did," I said. "Let's ask him."

Sam looked at the notes in that abstracted way he had. "Moose," he said speculatively. "*The Big Sleep?*"

"*Farewell, My Lovely*," Daniel said impatiently. "I thought mathematicians were literate these days."

Sam opened his mouth to defend himself. I decided that it was time to stop playing.

"I know you think I should give up the business," I said. "As a matter of fact, I was coming to the same conclusion myself. But sending a nine-foot Moose to my office is not what I call a subtle hint. Nor is it funny."

This time there was no mistaking the confusion in their eyes. I knew them well, these three, and they knew me. They wouldn't, I thought, continue the game this far. Would they?

"Except he said his name was Martin," I told them in a voice that was no longer so certain. "Martin Malloy. Looking for Thelma."

They glanced briefly at one another, but they didn't speak. I saw Anna's eyes come to rest on my jacket pocket. The concern in her eyes spoke of her innocence, spoke of all their innocence. I gulped, took the whiskey out, walked to them, and deposited it on the table. I pulled myself a chair and sat heavily on it.

"I better start again," I said.

I told them all about it, each piece of stinted dialogue, and by the time I had finished I was sure they weren't involved. Which left me with a problem. A big one.

"So who sent him?" I asked.

They had no answer to that, and neither did I. Like most individuals I knew people who didn't like me, and I knew people I didn't like, but they could hardly be called enemies. Not the kind who would go to such elaborate lengths to hoax me—never mind produce 250 crisp new ones to aid them.

"Any dissatisfied clients?" Daniel asked.

No dissatisfied clients—no clients at all, come to think of it.

"So what are you going to do?" Anna's voice broke into my reverie.

I drew myself up straight as if I had already made the decision that was only then forming in my brain.

"Investigate," I answered. "Find Thelma. What else can I do?"

"What if the money's stolen?"

I shrugged. "I guess I'll cross that bridge when I come to it," I said. I picked up the bottle of Bells and dropped it lightly into the dustbin. "Let's celebrate with a real whiskey," I said, "now that I'm no longer filing for a divorce from the lot of you."

I was nicely oiled by the time I arrived at Tony's Golders Green office.

Street Times was peopled by hacks like Tony who'd wakened up one day to the realization that their ulcers were never going to get any smaller. A few of them got together and decided that if they were going to start developing bosses' diseases, they might as well be their own bosses. They'd started a London-based magazine that—now in its middle age—no longer tried to compete for the youth market. In a way, I suppose, they were one of the few remaining relics of the sixties although they had long since grown away from nostalgia or angst and had settled, instead, for what they could do in a world grown increasingly hostile.

Their new offices were, however, not exactly friendly. Workaday would be a better description, sited between a Dorothy Perkins and a grimy solicitor, with a smell courtesy of Grodzinski, the baker, giving the only hint of atmosphere. I made a mental note to pick up a sliced rye and some cheese Danish as I located Tony in his glass cubicle. His shirt sleeves, I observed, were held up by rubber bands.

"Still preserving the image," I commented.

Tony glanced up from his computer and shot what, for him, approximated a smile.

"Bloody kid bit the buttons off," he said.

"And how is she?"

This time the smile was definite. "Great," he gushed. Catching himself, he ran a hand through his mousey brown hair. "For a monster. Want a coffee?"

"If it comes with a Danish," I said.

Tony frowned. "They make them by machine now," he said, "in some warehouse out in Bromley. The smell's bottled to give us the impression that the good old days are still with us."

"I'll pass then," I said. I perched myself on the edge of his desk and peered around in an attempt to read his screen. "Impressive symbols," I said. "*Street Times* going postmodernist?"

Tony moved the screen away. "Accounts," he said curtly. He didn't need to say more; I knew all about accounts. Which brought me to my business.

"Name of Martin Malloy mean anything to you?" I asked.

Tony yawned. "I'm losing my knack," he said. "You're no longer even bothering with the foreplay." He yawned again. "You used to at least pretend to be giving me something in exchange for my gems of information," he explained, "but since we've been exiled to the Green, I suppose you think I come cheap."

I shrugged. "Nothing much to offer," I said. "Business is slow."

"Slow to get off the ground, or slow to die?"

"The latter."

"Well, in that case," Tony said. He hit a cue on his keyboard and the machine began to whir. "Bloody noisy, this new technology," he said. "Now let's see if the data base moved with us." He typed fast with two fingers. "Malloy," he said out loud. "Martin, Mr."

I waited while he squinted his eyes at the screen, and then, a few seconds later, he hit a key and the bytes of information stopped rolling. "Thought I remembered him," Tony said. "An interesting case, Martin Malloy."

So he actually existed, I thought—interesting indeed.

"Martin, aka 'Mouse,' Malloy," Tony offered.

"Mouse?"

"A reference to his size. Never met him, but apparently he's on the big side."

"You could say that."

"And Mouse as well on account of the fact that he never talked to the cops." Tony's eyes scanned rapidly down the screen. "Malloy's a genius with numbers," he said. "When his face first hit the front pages, the gutter press got excited and tried to pin an idiot-savant label on him. He wouldn't play ball, so they dumped him."

"What was their interest in the first place?" I asked.

"Malloy was associated with some East End hoods," Tony answered, "part of a crack gang—you know the scene—New York comes to London. The word was that the police picked the Mouse up in an attempt to get him to finger the big men. He didn't, and someone started to kick up a stink about habeas corpus. The cops eventually got themselves out of trouble by persuading the inland revenue to charge him with tax evasion."

"Tax evasion."

Tony grinned. "Modern, innit? The case against him was weak, but all the jury saw was a giant, and a black giant to boot, who refused to talk. They threw the book at him. Sad, really, although by the sounds of his physique, he'd have no trouble in jail."

I thought about the scar and wondered. "Any woman involved?" I asked.

Tony hit another key. "Not that I can see." He rolled the screen on again and then, finding nothing, wiped it clear. "Want me to check this out further?"

"If you have the time."

Tony yawned again. "Sure," he said. "I'll be in touch if . . ." He didn't finish the sentence: he started up on his computer again. That was it, no good-bye, he had done with me. It wasn't personal—Tony never was one for social niceties, and I knew he'd contact me if he found anything of interest. And besides, who was I to stand between a man and his collective's accounts? I left him to them.

Or tried to. I'd forgotten how much Tony liked to hold his conversations in transit. "Kate," he called when I was almost at the door.

I turned.

"Maybe you should let the business die," he said.

I shrugged and left.

I spent the evening on my own—alone, that is, so long as you don't count my alto. I counted it, I'd just had the whole thing resprung, and I spent a few hours rediscovering both its range and my limitations.

I usually played to get away from work, but this time I failed. An image of a man they called the Mouse kept weaving its way through the blues I played. I saw him as he stood there in my office, his bright clothes, contrasting with those sad eyes, a man with no home trapped for tax evasion. I was beginning to feel sorry for him—sorry that I had treated his visit as a hoax, sorry that I hadn't asked him more. That, I thought, was why I liked the job—and why I would miss it so much when I was forced to close. It wasn't often that you get the opportunity to meet giants who want to thank their social worker for introducing them to literature. Thelma must be quite a woman, I thought—certainly more trusting than I. I should have been more friendly; I should have tried harder.

I shook my head, moved the beat up tempo to fit with my version of South African township jazz, and put a brake on my regrets. Thelma, if she existed, was the social worker, not me. I would try and find her, that's all I could do. I had enough troubles of my own, I had the business to worry about.

Without noticing I slipped back into the blues.

It was hot when I got up, the kind of heat that visits London once every thirteen years. I opened the wardrobe in the hall, the one where I stored the clothes I never got a chance to wear, and stared at the uninspiring choices. In the end I decided to go for broke, fitted myself out in a tight black cotton skirt and flimsy pink T-shirt, threw a pair of thonged sandals on my feet, and took a jacket for protection from the vagaries of the English climate.

The flimsy pink number was already showing signs of wilting when I arrived at the address Martin Malloy had given me. What's more, it clashed with my destination.

The building was plum in the middle of the Arsenal, a cheerful item if ever I saw one. It was round and squat, and red and yellow—a low thing in the middle of a long row of detached gray brick. A kind of eighties version of a sixties domed tent, it was part of the council's attempt to decentralize its services in order to benefit the community.

The community, consisting mainly of women and children, who were crowded into a big room with narrow slanted windows, did not look impressed. I can't say I blamed them: the place was hot and, although cheerful, downright uncomfortable. When I asked for the duty social worker, I was told to take a seat. I gingerly lowered myself into a red plastic item that, bolted to the floor, resembled a bucket with large holes.

"Gets to your bum after an hour or two," said the woman to my left.

"Our Johnny got stuck in one once," said the woman to my right. "Had to get the fire brigade to cut him out. They blamed me, of course." She reached over and slapped her Johnny, who seemed to be making a second bid for fire brigade fame.

"Miss Baeier," a voice called.

I was shown into a small cubicle of a room, airless and lit by fluorescent, in which stood two chairs, a table, and a woman in her early thirties. She smiled at me from her seat and gestured to the second one. When I sat, I could hardly see her for the mound of papers piled in front of her.

She shifted to the right, pulled a manila file from the pile, and opened it. It was, I saw, lined with blank paper. She frowned, turned to her side, dug into a bag that could have doubled as a haversack and that hung on the back of her chair, and pulled out a biro. I saw that it was doing extra work as an advert for sausages. She used the pen to transfer my name from the slip I had filled in onto the first sheet of paper.

"What can I do for you?" she asked.

"I'm trying to find someone," I said.

The woman glanced up sharply, saw that I wasn't joking, and shut the file with a bang. "Ms. Baeier," she said clearly, "we are not all-powerful. We have strict guidelines to which we always adhere. I can tell you, without needing to check, that we draw the line at tracing missing persons. You might care to try the police—we never have much luck with them, but don't let that stop you." The lines in her face belied the aggression in her voice: she looked too tired to have only just started work.

I smiled at her. "Bad morning?"

She half returned my smile. "The worst," she said. "Except for yesterday and tomorrow."

"I won't waste your time then," I said. "I'm looking for a Thelma Parsons."

A look of alarm crossed the woman's face, a flash of response quickly concealed as she ducked behind the pile of papers. When she reemerged, she had gone bland again: I wondered whether I'd been imagining the sheer panic that had cut through her fatigue. She raised an eyebrow.

"Thelma was a social worker," I continued, "based here once. Hated the job as much as you all do and managed to escape. She's an old friend of mine. I was hoping you could help me find her."

It was weak and I knew it. Marlowe would have done better. But then I wasn't Marlowe, was I? I was just a private detective in a land that didn't like detectives, and a woman, not a man.

But then, I thought brightly, as her face seemed to soften at the mention of my friendship with Thelma, neither was this woman a reluctant witness with something to hide—just an overworked social worker fighting the disillusionment that seemed to come with the job these days. Maybe it would work.

It didn't. "We never release addresses of former employees," she said. "Nor, for that matter, of current employees." She was good at her job, but not good enough. Her eyes were narrowed, beaming hostility, contradicting her seeming unconcern.

I opened my mouth to try again, but she shook her head in the general direction of the door, dismissing me with a determined finality. She discarded the manila file and began her way through the one underneath. I got the message: I left.

My way out was blocked by a woman who thrust a small child toward me.

"Here, do me a favor and watch him for a second," she said. "Got to change the baby, and those chairs are useless." She was a pro: she sped down the corridor with yelling infant in arms. I looked down at the abandoned child.

He was a cute enough item if you managed to ignore the effluent issuing from his nose. I couldn't ignore it, so I took a tissue from my bag and moved it downward. He was out of range before the tissue had even a chance of reaching his face.

I recognized him. "Johnny?" I asked.

He wiped his nose with the back of his hand and nodded sullenly. I smiled. A gift from heaven, I thought, snot and all.

"How'd you like to earn fifty pence?" I asked.

Visibly he sized me up. "A pound," he said.

"Seventy pence?"

"A quid or nuffing," he said firmly. He folded his small arms together and stood there, facing me, his feet planted stubbornly on the ground.

I knew when I was beaten. I knelt down beside him and explained what I wanted. He nodded. When I had finished, he held out his hand, palm up. Into it I placed a pound coin that rapidly disappeared into his pocket. Then he nodded again.

As agreed, I walked away from him until I had rounded the corner. Then I waited.

Nothing happened. I waited some more—still nothing. *I've been had*, I thought. *Maybe Tony's right, I'm no detective*. Then suddenly, from around the corner, issued a scream, a bloodcurdling scream, the likes of which I had never before had the privilege of hearing. Once it came, paused, and then once again.

It worked like a dream. I heard a door open and a woman, my woman, call out, "What the hell's going on?"

She got another scream for a reply and some words this time. "My browver," Johnny screamed. "My browver, he's stuck."

"Oh save me," the woman muttered.

Johnny screamed again.

"All right, all right," she said. "I'll get him out. Just do me a favor and stop screaming, will you?"

They rounded the corner at a brisk pace, Johnny leading, the woman following. As they passed me, Johnny let out another yell and the woman quickened her pace, giving him a push as she did so.

I walked fast in the opposite direction, running when I had rounded the corner. I opened the door of her office and stumbled over to her chair. I grabbed her bag and began to rifle through it, one ear on the commotion outside.

It was a bottomless chasm I faced and a messy one at that. I pulled things out at random. The screaming had stopped and I heard the sound of a slap. I had little time left.

The bag was incredible. I dug deep, throwing out old Kleenex, keys, a plethora of credit cards (*social workers must be better paid these days*, I thought), and the occasional half-eaten nut. None of the contents fitted my preconception of what should be there. I dug again.

I was on the verge of giving up when I found what I'd been looking for—an address book, small and black. Except I was probably too late. I heard footsteps outside.

I opened the book to the *P* section. No Parsons there. The footsteps were coming closer.

I turned to the *T* section. And there it was, the name Thelma, no surname, just Thelma. Except it did me no good because underneath the name was a blank piece of paper, stuck on, tight. I know it was tight because I tried to get it off. No luck: I heard a rustling outside the door. So I did what I had to. I pulled the page out, shoved the book along with the rest of the garbage back into the bag, threw the bag over the chair, and ran for the door.

I collided with her there.

"Forgot my pen," I said. "One day I'll forget my head."

The anger in her face faded. "Tell me about it," she muttered before closing the door on me.

In a workers' café across the road I sat over a cup of milky hot water masquerading as tea and stared at the stolen page. There was no way I could remove the covering blankness. I'd tried again and all I'd managed to do was to tear a corner off it.

I turned the paper over. I could see the writing there, faint and inviting, but still indecipherable. I held the page up to the light and it became clearer but still incomprehensible. *Well, it would be*, I thought. *It's backward*.

I left my tea to its own devices and went to the toilet. I held the back of the page up to the scratched mirror above the basin—again the writing appeared, but still illegibly. I got a pen out of my bag and, holding the paper up to the exposed bulb, I slowly started to trace the lines that I could see.

It took a long time, but I managed it in the end. And when I'd finished, I could see, in writing that was not mine, an address, clearly written.

My tea was still waiting for me. I put some coins beside it and left them all to their own devices.

Thelma lived in a small terraced house almost opposite the football ground. Hers was in the middle of a row of look-alikes, all built from dingy gray brick, with lace curtains covering small square windows, low front gardens whose walls could never hold back the tide of litter from the fans, and dark-red-stained front steps that would once, in another age, have been daily scrubbed.

I stood on the steps and rang her bell. I got no response, no sound at all. I rang again but again without luck. I turned to go and it was then that, out of the corner my eye, I saw a portion of the dingy lace twitch. I waited but still nothing happened. I got the message. I turned away and walked back to my car, climbed in, revved it ostentatiously, and drove off. I drove around the block and then returned to her street, parking a few doors down, away from the lace curtain. I switched off the engine and waited.

It was two hours before anything happened. I concentrated mostly on my business or lack of it. I sat and I boiled and I wondered what I was doing, trapped in my own car on a sunny day, watching the minutes tick by and the money diminish, waiting for a frictional Thelma to make a move so I could report back to the fantastic Mouse. Tony was right, I thought, and Sam as well—it was time to move on, time to reenter the real world.

My hand was on my car keys, ready to switch on and leave, when I heard the footsteps. I ducked down, landing heavily on the floor. I strained my neck as I peered through the side mirror. It was her, all right, the woman from Thelma's old office, walking briskly down the pavement. She crossed in front of my car, so close that I could almost smell the anxiety emanating from her, and walked purposively up to Thelma's door.

It was opened almost immediately and kept open. I saw a hint of blue, but otherwise my social worker concealed her protagonist from me. For protagonists they obviously were: I didn't need to hear their conversation to guess that it was ugly—I could see it in the gestures of the social worker, in the hard set of her back, in the way she reached into her bag and flung something toward the door, in the way she walked away, and in the bang that sounded as the door closed.

I crouched down as she passed by me, but I needn't have bothered. She walked fast and angrily, lost in a world of her own making, muttering to herself. At one point she stopped and hit herself—quite literally hit herself on the head with the flat of her hand. I heard the sound of the blow from twenty yards away.

She started up again, and only when she had turned the corner did I get out of my car. I ignored the front of the house and instead walked round the block, counting houses until I reached Thelma's back gate. I pressed against it and it yielded slightly. One long push was enough to break the lock.

I made my way down the narrow path, past the overflowing dustbin and the small outhouse that must once have been the house's only toilet until I reached the kitchen door. I put my hand on the doorknob, and it opened as if it had been waiting for me. I stepped in.

I found myself in a kitchen that stank of neglect. Dishes were piled on both sides of the sink, unwashed and uncleared. On the floor stood two saucers, one with the dregs of old milk, the other piled high with cat food. Plants wilted on the windowsill, geraniums that instead of enjoying the sun were being finished off by it.

And yet it was not a kitchen that I would ever have described as poor. It was packed with consumer durables, with microwaves, coffee percolators, automatic juicers, stainless steel knives, still wrapped and shinning, and a variety of food processors of the latest design. An ideal home gone mad, I thought, as I walked through the room and into the hall.

I was faced with the choice of two doors that opened onto the narrow corridor, and I chose the one at the front, the one from which the lace curtain movement had originated. I found myself in a small room, dirty but tastefully furnished. There was one person in it, a woman in her middle thirties, clad in jeans and a low-slung silk blouse, her thin blond hair hanging weakly down the sides of her long face. She was standing by a small antique maple desk, staring at something on it.

She turned and saw me as soon as I entered, but otherwise she didn't move. Her face did, but not her body. On that pale face, a gamut of emotions crossed—displays of shock, of fear, and finally of a kind of resignation.

"What are you doing here?" she asked dully.

"The door was open," I said. "The back door."

"Have you got a warrant?" she asked.

I shook my head. "I'm not the police," I said. I watched as the resignation turned to slow anger.

"Well, in that case," she said, "I'll call them." She reached across the desk for the phone and picked up the receiver. But the movement seemed to have exhausted her. She stood still, holding it and staring at me. "What do you want?" she asked. The anger was replaced with despair.

I walked over and looked behind her. On the desk, I saw, were pieces of paper, scrawled with writing. There was some tracing paper there too, askew on one piece of the writing, but when she saw my eyes light on it she brushed against it, catapulting it to the floor. She stared at me defiantly.

"My name's Kate Baeier," I said. "I'm a private detective. A man called Martin Malloy hired me to find you."

"Martin?" Her voice rose and she repeated it. "Martin?"

"You used to visit him in prison," I said.

Her face cleared as she remembered and then it disintegrated again, not in fear, this time, but rather in hilarity. The laughter came slowly at first, from deep inside her, surfacing as a giggle but soon transformed into near hysteria. I stood and waited as she laughed in my face, laughed and laughed until the tears streamed down her cheeks.

Gradually the laugh subsided. She sniffed and wiped her eyes with the back of one hand. She looked at me and giggled again, controlling herself only by looking away.

"A private detective," she muttered. "You're not for real."

I shrugged. "Martin wants to see you," I said.

"Well, he can't." Her words had a final ring to them.

"He just wants to thank you," I explained.

The look she threw me was one of pure contempt, not for me, I thought, but for Martin.

"Gimme a break," she said.

"To thank you for opening up the world of fiction to him."

She looked as if she was going to laugh again, and I didn't really blame her. Put like that, it sounded ridiculous. If I hadn't met Martin Malloy, I too would have laughed.

And Thelma had met Martin. She didn't laugh. She smiled but not in mirth.

"He taught me something too," she said in a voice that was pure malice. "The dumb bastard."

I didn't know until then how much I had cared, how much I wanted to deliver to Martin Malloy what he had requested. I acted without thinking. First, I saw the tracing paper on the floor with new eyes, with eyes that were looking at a mirror, then I took in the writing on the desk, and then I acted. I quickly moved behind her and wrenched open a drawer. She was too surprised to prevent me, and we both watched as it tumbled to the floor, spilling its contents. She flung herself on them, but too late to stop me from confirming what I had already guessed.

"Fraud," I said. "That's what it is."

From the floor she looked up at me, surrounded by small pieces of plastic, her eyes flashing anger. I remembered the social worker's bag, and the visit that she had just paid, and I remembered the goods in the kitchen. It made sense.

"Credit card fraud," I said, thinking out loud. "The tracing paper is how you copy the signatures."

She was down but not out, no longer vulnerable, in a way. She glared up at me. "So what are you going to do about it?" she shot.

I didn't answer and she didn't need me to.

"Nothing," she said. "You're the do-gooder type, aren't you? I should know, I've tried that game. It gets you nowhere."

"Except the occasional thanks," I commented.

"Don't give me that," she said. "Thanks never buttered any bread.

I've met enough Martin Malloys in my time, I don't need to meet any more. A casualty of the system, that's all he is, a well-meaning idiot without a chance. He even gave me tips on how to forge signatures, until he realized that my interest was more than academic. Then he had the cheek to lecture me, as if I was the one who had been jailed. Well, I've served my own kind of time, I'm free now. I don't owe anybody anything; I don't owe Martin Malloy the time of day. I can tell you . . ."

I knew she was right; she could have told me. She looked set to go on for a good few hours. I didn't need to listen. I walked out of the room, through the hall, opened the front door, and stepped into the bright sunshine. I left the door open, hoping that some of the air would flow in. I wasn't optimistic.

Martin Malloy turned up two days later. I was in my office waiting for him. I had nothing else to do but wait, and I couldn't shake off the feeling of uselessness that had settled on me ever since I'd met Thelma.

I'd left the door open and he didn't bother to ring the bell this time. He just arrived in my office, a huge man with a surprisingly light tread.

"Did you find her?" he asked.

I nodded.

When he smiled, his face opened up like an exotic flower that the scar did nothing to spoil. "When can we meet?" he asked.

I stood up. "She doesn't want to see you," I said.

I don't know what I expected—fury, sorrow, violence even, but all I got was a vague look of disappointment. He nodded and made as if he were about to go. But then he changed his mind.

"Is Thelma all right?" he asked.

Wrong-footed, I didn't know how to answer. I looked into those warm brown eyes and I shivered. I remembered the sight of that smile, and I knew that I didn't want to disappoint it.

"She's fine," I lied. "Just busy."

I should have known better: Malloy was no fool.

"Don't try and kid me," he said, and his voice was as hard as his body. "Don't treat me like a child."

I sat down. "I'm sorry," I said. "I shouldn't have pretended. Thelma is far from fine. She's involved in some kind of credit card fiddle." I paused. "And I'm not sure she's doing too well." I finished quickly, feeling somehow that I had betrayed someone. I looked away, out the window and at the faultless blue sky.

"Anything I could do to help?" he asked. "She helped me, you know." His voice was sad.

I shook my head and looked at him again. "I'm not sure—" I started.

But he was lost in his own thoughts, and he spoke them out loud. "I knew it was something stupid," he said. "I tried to tell her that people like us just don't win. I thought if I was no longer behind bars, she would listen to me."

I remembered what Thelma had said about him, and I couldn't help myself. "She's a bitch," I snapped. "Beyond saving."

"Don't say that," he said. "She's just confused. Nobody's beyond saving."

I nodded in recognition of sentiment rather than in agreement with the meaning. I reached into my desk and pulled out his money, the money that I had not yet touched.

"It didn't take me long," I said. "You're due some back."

He looked at me and smiled, but his smile was no longer open. "Keep it," he said airily. "There's plenty more where that came from. Payment for keeping my trap shut. Guilt money for doing hard time." His face softened. "I knew Thelma was desperate," he said. "That's why I wanted to thank her. I thought if somebody, anybody, told her how much she'd done for them, it might give her hope. I guess I was too late."

I didn't say anything. What was there to say?

He hadn't finished.

"Did you get somebody to look for me?" he asked.

I nodded.

"My landlord chucked me out," he said. "You should have known nobody wants to house a convict. Especially one who looks like me. Why did you do it?"

I felt I owed him the truth and so I gave it to him. "Because I wasn't sure you really existed," I said.

He nodded, to himself rather than me. "I feel sorry for your type, you know," he said, again almost as if to himself. "I came to literature late, but there's one thing I can do that you can't. I can distinguish between fact and fiction."

I shrugged and I looked at him, at this huge man, dressed this time in gold threads that shimmered when he moved. I smiled. "It's not always easy," I said.

He saw my look and he returned my smile. He strode over to me, enfolded one of my hands in his big paws, and clasped it. "Nice to have met you, Kate Baeier," he said. He let go of my hand. "Can I give you one last piece of advice?"

"How can I refuse?"

"Open the windows," he said. "Let the sun shine in. Breathe the air."

"Thanks," I said.

He shrugged and looked at me. "A balance sheet isn't everything," he said. "I should know, I'm good at numbers. Business will pick up. You're good at your job—you found Thelma, didn't you?"

He left the room as quietly as he had arrived. I climbed on my chair so I could watch him in the street, but somehow I missed his exit.

I was in the right position, so I took his advice.

I opened the windows.

It was difficult, but I managed.

A *Study in White*

NICHOLAS BLAKE

Nicholas Blake was born Cecil Day Lewis in Ballintogher, Ireland, on April 27, 1904. He was educated in England and graduated from Oxford, where with W. H. Auden and Stephen Spender he launched the "new" poetry of the 1930s. He taught school until 1935, when he retired to writing. In 1968 he was named Poet Laureate. Seventeen of the twenty crime novels he wrote as Nicholas Blake were about his amateur detective, Nigel Strangeways. He reviewed the detective story for *The Spectator* for many years and described it as "the folk myth of the 20th century." He died in 1972.

"Seasonable weather for the time of year," remarked the Expansive Man in a voice succulent as the breast of a roast goose.

The Deep Chap, sitting next to him in the railway compartment, glanced out at the snow, swarming and swirling past the window-pane. He replied:

"You really like it? Oh, well, it's an ill blizzard that blows nobody no good. Depends what you mean by seasonable, though. Statistics for the last fifty years would show—"

"Name of Joad, sir?" asked the Expansive Man, treating the compartment to a wholesale wink.

"No, Stansfield, Henry Stansfield." The Deep Chap, a ruddy-faced man who sat with hands firmly planted on the knees of his brown tweed suit, might have been a prosperous farmer but for the long, steady, meditative scrutiny which he now bent upon each of his fellow-travelers in turn.

What he saw was not particularly rewarding. On the opposite seat, from left to right, were a Forward Piece, who had taken the Expansive Man's wink wholly to herself and contrived to wriggle her tight skirt farther up from her knee; a desiccated, sandy, lawyerish little man who fumed and fussed like an angry kettle, consulting every five minutes his gold watch, then shaking out his *Times* with the crackle of a legal parchment; and a Flash Card, dressed up to the nines of spivdom, with the bold yet uneasy stare of the young delinquent.

"Mine's Percy Dukes," said the Expansive Man. "P.D. to my friends. General Dealer. At your service. Well, we'll be across the border in an hour and a half, and then hey for the bluebells of bonny Scotland!"

"Bluebells in January? You're hopeful," remarked the Forward Piece.

"Are you Scots, master?" asked the Comfortable Body sitting on Stansfield's left.

"English outside"—Percy Dukes patted the front of his gray suit, slid a flask from its hip pocket, and took a swig—"and Scotch within." His loud laugh, or the blizzard, shook the railway carriage. The Forward Piece giggled.

"You'll need that if we run into a drift and get stuck for the night," said Henry Stansfield.

"Name of Jonah, sir?" The compartment reverberated again.

"I do not apprehend such an eventuality," said the Fusspot. "The stationmaster at Lancaster assured me that the train would get through. We are scandalously late already, though." Once again the gold watch was consulted.

"It's a curious thing," remarked the Deep Chap meditatively, "the way we imagine we can make Time amble withal or gallop withal, just by keeping an eye on the hands of a watch. You travel frequently by this train, Mr.—?"

"Kilmington. Arthur J. Kilmington. No, I've only used it once before." The Fusspot spoke in a dry Edinburgh accent.

"Ah, yes, that would have been on the seventeenth of last month. I remember seeing you on it."

"No, sir, you are mistaken. It was the twentieth." Mr. Kilmington's thin mouth snapped tight again, like a rubber band round a sheaf of legal documents.

"The twentieth? Indeed? That was the day of the train robbery. A big haul they got, it seems. Off this very train. It was carrying some of the extra Christmas mail. Bags just disappeared, somewhere between Lancaster and Carlisle."

"Och, deary me," sighed the Comfortable Body. "I don't know what we're coming to, really, nowadays."

"We're coming to the scene of the crime, ma'am," said the expansive Mr. Dukes. The train, almost dead-beat, was panting up the last pitch towards Shap Summit.

"I didn't see anything in the papers about where the robbery took place," Henry Stansfield murmured. Dukes fastened a somewhat bleary eye upon him.

"You read all the newspapers?"

"Yes."

The atmosphere in the compartment had grown suddenly tense.

Only the Flash Card, idly examining his fingernails, seemed unaffected by it.

"Which paper did you see it in?" pursued Stansfield.

"I didn't." Dukes tapped Stansfield on the knee. "But I can use my loaf. Stands to reason. You want to tip a mail-bag out of a train—get me? Train must be moving slowly, or the bag'll burst when it hits the ground. Only one place between Lancaster and Carlisle where you'd *know* the train would be crawling. Shap Bank. And it goes slowest on the last bit of the bank, just about where we are now. Follow?"

Henry Stansfield nodded.

"O.K. But you'd be balmy to tip it off just anywhere on this God-forsaken moorland," went on Mr. Dukes. "Now, if you'd traveled this line as much as I have, you'd have noticed it goes over a bridge about a mile short of the summit. Under the bridge runs a road: a nice, lonely road, see? The only road hereabouts that touches the railway. You tip out the bag there. Your chums collect it, run down the embankment, dump it in the car they've got waiting by the bridge, and Bob's your uncle!"

"You oughta been a detective, mister," exclaimed the Forward Piece languishingly.

Mr. Dukes inserted his thumbs in his armpits, looking gratified. "Maybe I am," he said with a wheezy laugh. "And maybe I'm just little old P.D., who knows how to use his loaf."

"Och, well now, the things people will do," said the Comfortable Body. "There's a terrible lot of dishonesty today."

The Flash Card glanced up contemptuously from his fingernails. Mr. Kilmington was heard to mutter that the system of surveillance on railways was disgraceful, and the guard of the train should have been severely censured.

"The guard can't be everywhere," said Stansfield. "Presumably he has to patrol the train from time to time, and—"

"Let him do so, then, and not lock himself up in his van and go to sleep," interrupted Mr. Kilmington, somewhat unreasonably.

"Are you speaking from personal experience, sir?" asked Stansfield.

The Flash Card lifted up his voice and said, in a Charing Cross Road American accent, "Hey, fellas! If the gang was gonna tip out the mail-bags by the bridge, like this guy says—what I mean is, how could they rely on the guard being out of his van just at that point?" He hitched up the trousers of his loud check suit.

"You've got something there," said Percy Dukes. "What I reckon is, there must have been two accomplices on the train—one to get the guard out of his van on some pretext, and the other to chuck off the bags." He turned to Mr. Kilmington, "You were saying something about the guard locking himself up in his van. Now if I was of a suspicious turn of mind, if I was little old Sherlock H. in person"—he bestowed another prodigious wink upon Kilmington's fellow-travelers—"I'd begin to wonder about you, sir. You were traveling on this train when the robbery took place. You went to the guard's van. You *say* you found him asleep. You didn't by any chance call the guard out, so as to—?"

"Your suggestion is outrageous! I advise you to be very careful, sir, very careful indeed," enunciated Mr. Kilmington, his precise voice crackling with indignation, "or you may find you have said something actionable. I would have you know that, when I—"

But what he would have them know was to remain undivulged. The train, which for some little time had been running cautiously down from Shap Summit, suddenly began to chatter and shudder, like a fever patient in high delirium, as the vacuum brakes were applied: then, with the dull impact of a fist driving into a feather pillow, the engine buried itself in a drift which had gathered just beyond the bend of a deep cutting.

It was just five minutes past seven.

"What's this?" asked the Forward Piece, rather shrilly, as a hysterical outburst of huffing and puffing came from the engine.

"Run into a drift, I reckon."

"He's trying to back us out. No good. The wheels are slipping every time. What a lark!" Percy Dukes had his head out of the window on the lee side of the train. "Coom to Coomberland for your winter sports!"

"Guard! Guard, I say!" called Mr. Kilmington. But the blue-clad figure, after one glance into the compartment, hurried on up the corridor. "Really! I *shall* report that man."

Henry Stansfield, going out into the corridor, opened a window. Though the coach was theoretically sheltered by the cutting of this windward side, the blizzard stunned his face like a knuckleduster of ice. He joined the herd of passengers who had climbed down and were stumbling towards the engine. As they reached it, the guard emerged from the cab: no cause for alarm, he said; if they couldn't get through, there'd be a relief engine sent down to take the train back to Penrith; he was just off to set fog-signals on the line behind them.

The driver renewed his attempts to back the train out. But what with its weight, the up-gradient in its rear, the icy rails, and the clinging grip of the drift on the engine, he could not budge her.

"We'll have to dig out the bogeys, mate," he said to his fireman. "Fetch them shovels from the forward van. It'll keep the perishers from freezing, anyhow." He jerked his finger at the knot of passengers who, lit up by the glare of the furnace, were capering and beating their arms like savages amid the swirling snow-wreaths.

Percy Dukes, who had now joined them, quickly established himself as the life and soul of the party, referring to the grimy-faced fireman as "Snowball," adjuring his companions to "Dig for Victory," affecting to spy the approach of a herd of St. Bernards, each with a key of brandy slung round its neck. But after ten minutes of hard digging, when the leading wheels of the bogey were cleared, it could be seen that they had been derailed by their impact with the drift.

"That's torn it, Charlie. You'll have to walk back to the box and get 'em to telephone through for help," said the driver.

"*If* the wires aren't down already," replied the fireman lugubriously. "It's above a mile to that box, and uphill. Who d'you think I am, Captain Scott?"

"You'll have the wind behind you, mate, anyhow. So long."

A buzz of dismay had risen from the passengers at this. One or two, who began to get querulous, were silenced by the driver's offering to take them anywhere they liked if they would just lift his engine back onto the metals first. When the rest had dispersed to their carriage, Henry Stansfield asked the driver's permission to go up into the cab for a few minutes and dry his coat.

"You're welcome." The driver snorted: "Would you believe it? 'Must get to Glasgow tonight.' Damn ridiculous! Now Bert—that's my guard—it's different for him: he's entitled to fret a bit. Missus been very poorly. Thought she was going to peg out before Christmas; but he got the best surgeon in Glasgow to operate on her, and she's mending now, he says. He reckons to look in every night at the nursing home, when he goes off work."

Stansfield chatted with the man for five minutes. Then the guard returned, blowing upon his hands—a smallish, leathery-faced chap, with a noticeably anxious look in his eye.

"We'll not get through tonight, Bert. Charlie told you?"

"Aye. I doubt some the passengers are going to create a rumpus," said the guard dolefully.

Henry Stansfield went back to his compartment. It was stuffy, but with a sinster hint of chilliness, too: he wondered how long the steam heating would last: depended upon the amount of water in the engine boiler, he supposed. Among the wide variety of fates he had imagined for himself, freezing to death in an English train was not included.

Arthur J. Kilmington fidgeted more than ever. When the guard came along the corridor, he asked him where the nearest village was, saying he must get a telephone call through to Edinburgh—most urgent appointment—must let his client know, if he was going to miss it. The guard said there was a village two miles to the northeast; you could see the lights from the top of the cutting; but he warned Mr. Kilmington against trying to get there in the teeth of this blizzard—better wait for the relief engine, which should reach them before nine P.M.

Silence fell upon the compartment for a while; the incredulous silence of civilized people who find themselves in the predicament of castaways. Then the expansive Mr. Dukes proposed that, since they were to be stuck here for an hour or two, they should get acquainted. The Comfortable Body now introduced herself as Mrs. Grant, the Forward Piece as Inez Blake; the Flash Card, with the over-negligent air of one handing a dud half-crown over a counter, gave his name as Macdonald—I. Macdonald.

The talk reverted to the train robbery and the criminals who had pepetrated it.

"They must be awfu' clever," remarked Mrs. Grant, in her sing-song Lowland accent.

"No criminals are clever, ma'am," said Stansfield quietly. His ruminative eye passed, without haste, from Macdonald to Dukes. "Neither the small fry nor the big operators. They're pretty well subhuman, the whole lot of 'em. A dash of cunning, a thick streak of cowardice, and the rest is made up of stupidity and boastfulness. They're too stupid for anything but crime, and so riddled with inferiority that they always give themselves away, sooner or later, by boasting about their crimes. They like to think of themselves as the wide boys, but they're as narrow as starved eels—why, they haven't even the wits to alter their professional methods: that's how the police pick 'em up."

"I entirely agree, sir," Mr. Kilmington snapped. "In my profession I see a good deal of the criminal classes. And I flatter myself none of them has ever got the better of me. They're transparent, sir, transparent."

"No doubt you gentlemen are right," said Percy Dukes comfortably. "But the police haven't picked up the chaps who did this train robbery yet."

"They will. And the Countess of Axminister's emerald bracelet. Bet the gang didn't reckon to find that in the mailbag. Worth all of twenty-five thousand pounds."

Percy Dukes' mouth fell open. The Flash Card whistled. Overcome, either by the stuffiness of the carriage or the thought of twenty-five thousand pounds worth of emeralds, Inez Blake gave a little moan and fainted all over Mr. Kilmington's lap.

"Really! Upon my soul! My dear young lady!" exclaimed that worthy. There was a flutter of solicitude, shared by all except the cold-eyed young Macdonald who, after stooping over her a moment, his back to the others, said. "Here you—stop pawing the young lady and let her stretch out on the seat. Yes, I'm talking to you, Kilmington."

"How dare you! This is an outrage!" The little man stood up so abruptly that the girl was almost rolled onto the floor. "I was merely trying to—"

"I know your sort. Nasty old men. Now, keep your hands off her. I'm telling you."

In the shocked silence that ensued, Kilmington gobbled speechlessly at Macdonald for a moment; then, seeing razors in the youth's cold-steel eye, snatched his black hat and briefcase from the rack and bolted out of the compartment. Henry Stansfield made as if to stop him, then changed his mind. Mrs. Grant followed the little man out, returning presently, her handkerchief soaked in water, to dab Miss Blake's forehead. The time was just 8:30.

When things were restored to normal, Mr. Dukes turned to Stansfield. "You were saying this necklace of—who was it?—the Countess of Axminister, it's worth twenty-five thousand pounds? Fancy sending a thing of that value through the post! Are you sure of it?"

"The value? Oh, yes." Henry Stansfield spoke out of the corner of his mouth, in the manner of a stupid man imparting a confidence. "Don't let this go any further. But I've a friend who works in the Cosmopolitan—the company where it's insured. That's another thing that didn't get into the papers. Silly woman. She wanted it for some big family do in Scotland at Christmas, forgot to bring it with her, and wrote home for it to be posted to her in a registered packet."

"Twenty-five thousand pounds," said Percy Dukes thoughtfully. "Well, stone me down!"

"Yes. Some people don't know when they're lucky, do they?"

Dukes' fat face wobbled on his shoulders like a globe of lard.

Young Macdonald polished his nails. Inez Blake read her magazine. After a while Percy Dukes remarked that the blizzard was slackening; he'd take an airing and see if there was any sign of the relief engine yet. He left the compartment.

At the window the snowflakes danced in their tens now, not their thousands. The time was 8:55. Shortly afterwards Inez Blake went out; and ten minutes later Mrs. Grant remarked to Stansfield that it had stopped snowing altogether. Neither Inez nor Dukes had returned when, at 9:30, Henry Stansfield decided to ask what had happened about the relief. The guard was not in his van, which adjoined Stansfield's coach, towards the rear of the train. So he turned back, walked up the corridor to the front coach, clambered out, and hailed the engine cab.

"She must have been held up," said the guard, leaning out. "Charlie here got through from the box, and they promised her by nine o'clock. But it'll no' be long now, sir."

"Have you seen anything of a Mr. Kilmington—small, sandy chap—black hat and overcoat, blue suit—was in my compartment? I've walked right up the train and he doesn't seem to be on it."

The guard pondered a moment. "Och aye, yon wee fellow? Him that asked me about telephoning from the village. Aye, he's awa' then."

"He did set off to walk there, you mean?"

"Nae doot he did, if he's no' on the train. He spoke to me again—juist on nine, it'd be—and said he was awa' if the relief didna turn up in five minutes."

"You've not seen him since?"

"No, sir. I've been talking to my mates here this half-hour, ever syne the wee fellow spoke to me."

Henry Stansfield walked thoughtfully back down the permanent way. When he passed out of the glare shed by the carriage lights on the snow, he switched on his electric torch. Just beyond the last coach the eastern wall of the cutting sloped sharply with the track. Although the snow had stopped altogether, an icy wind from the northeast still blew, raking and numbing his face. Twenty yards farther on his torch lit up a track, already half filled in with snow, made by several pairs of feet, pointing away over the moor, towards the northeast. Several passengers, it seemed, had set off for the village, whose lights twinkled like frost in the far distance. Stansfield was about to follow this track when he heard footsteps scrunching the snow farther up the line. He switched off the torch; at once it was as if a sack had been thrown over his head, so close and blinding was the darkness. The steps came nearer. Stansfield switched on his torch, at the last minute, pinpointing the squat figure of Percy Dukes. The man gave a muffled oath.

"What the devil! Here, what's the idea, keeping me waiting half an hour in that blasted—?"

"Have you seen Kilmington?"

"Oh, it's you. No, how the hell should I have seen him? Isn't he on the train? I've just been walking up the line, to look for the relief. No sign yet. Damn parky, it is—I'm moving on."

Presently Stansfield moved on, too, but along the track towards the village. The circle of his torchlight wavered and bounced on the deep snow. The wind, right in his teeth, was killing. No wonder, he thought, as after a few hundred yards he approached the end of the trail, those passengers turned back. Then he realized they had not all turned back. What he had supposed to be a hummock of snow bearing a crude resemblance to a recumbent human figure, he now saw to be a human figure covered with snow. He scraped some of the snow off it, turned it gently over on its back.

Arthur J. Kilmington would fuss no more in this world. His briefcase was buried beneath him; his black hat was lying where it had fallen, lightly covered with snow, near the head. There seemed, to Stansfield's cursory examination, no mark of violence on him. But the eyeballs started, the face was suffused with a pinkish-blue color. So men look who have been strangled, thought Stansfield, or asphyxiated. Quickly he knelt down again, shining his torch in the dead face. A qualm of horror shook him. Mr. Kilmington's nostrils were caked thick with snow, which had frozen solid in them, and snow had been rammed tight into his mouth also.

And here he would have stayed, reflected Stansfield, in this desolate spot, for days or weeks, perhaps, if the snow lay or deepened. And when the thaw at last came (as it did that year, in fact, only after two months), the snow would thaw out from his mouth and nostrils, too, and there would thaw out from his mouth and nostrils, too, and there would be no vestige of murder left—only the corpse of an impatient little lawyer who had tried to walk to the village in a blizzard and died for his pains. It might even be that no one would ask how such a precise, pernickety little chap had ventured the two-mile walk in these shoes and without a torch to light his way through the pitchy blackness; for Stansfield, going through the man's pockets, had found the following articles—and nothing more: pocketbook, fountain pen, handkerchief, cigarette case, gold lighter, two letters, and some loose change.

Stansfield started to return for help. But only twenty yards back he noticed another trail of footprints, leading off the main track to the left. This trail seemed a fresher one—the snow lay less thickly in the indentations—and to have been made by one pair of feet only. He followed it up, walking beside it. Whoever made this track had walked in a slight right-handed curve back to the railway line, joining it about one hundred and fifty yards up the line from where the main trail came out. At this point there was a platelayers' shack. Finding the door unlocked, Stansfield entered. There was nothing inside but a coke brazier, stone cold, and a smell of cigar smoke. . . .

Half an hour later, Stansfield returned to his compartment. In the meanwhile, he had helped the train crew to carry back the body of Kilmington, which was now locked in the guard's van. He had also made an interesting discovery as to Kilmington's movements. It was to be presumed that, after the altercation with Macdonald, and the brief conversation already reported by the guard, the lawyer must have gone to sit in another compartment. The last coach, to the rear of the guard's van, was a first-class one, almost empty. But in one of its compartments Stansfield found a passenger asleep. He woke him up, gave a description of Kilmington, and asked if he had seen him earlier.

The passenger grumpily informed Stansfield that a smallish man, in a dark overcoat, with the trousers of a blue suit showing beneath it, had come to the door and had a word with him. No, the passenger had not noticed his face particularly, because he'd been very drowsy himself, and besides, the chap had politely taken off his black Homburg hat to address him, and the hat screened as much of the head as was not cut off from his view by the top of the door. No, the chap had not come into his compartment: he had just stood outside, inquired the time (the passenger had looked at his watch and told him it was 8:50); then the chap had said that, if the relief didn't turn up by nine, he intended to walk to the nearest village.

Stansfield had then walked along to the engine cab. The guard, whom he found there, told him that he'd gone up the track about 8:45 to meet the fireman on his way back from the signal-box. He had gone as far as the place where he'd put down his fog-signals earlier; here, just before nine, he and the fireman met, as the latter corroborated. Returning to the train, the guard had climbed into the last coach, noticed Kilmington sitting alone in a first-class compartment (it was then that the lawyer announced to the guard his intention of walking if the relief engine had not arrived within five minutes). The guard then got out of the train again, and proceeded down the track to talk to his mates in the engine cab.

This evidence would seem to point incontrovertibly at Kilmington's having been murdered shortly after nine P.M., Stansfield reflected as he went back to his own compartment. His fellow-passengers were all present now.

"Well, did you find him?" asked Percy Dukes.

"Kilmington? Oh, yes, I found him. In the snow over there. He was dead."

Inez Blake gave a little, affected scream. The permanent sneer was wiped, as if by magic, off young Macdonald's face, which turned a sickly white. Mr. Dukes sucked in his fat lips.

"The puir wee man," said Mrs. Grant. "He tried to walk it then? Died of exposure, was it?"

"No," announced Stansfield flatly, "he was murdered."

This time, Inez Blake screamed in earnest; and, like an echo, a hooting shriek came from far up the line: the relief engine was approaching at last.

"The police will be awaiting us back at Penrith, so we'd beter all have our stories ready." Stansfield turned to Percy Dukes. "You, for instance, sir. Where were you between eight-fifty-five when you left the carriage, and nine-thirty-five when I met you returning? Are you sure you didn't see Kilmington?"

Dukes, expansive no longer, his piggy eyes sunk deep in the fat of his face, asked Stansfield who the hell he thought he was.

"I am an inquiry agent, employed by the Cosmopolitan Insurance Company. Before that, I was a Detective Inspector in the C.I.D. Here is my card."

Dukes barely glanced at it. "That's all right, old man. Only wanted to make sure. Can't trust anyone nowadays." His voice had taken on the ingratiating, oleaginous heartiness of the small business man trying to clinch a deal with a bigger one. "Just went for a stroll, y'know—stretch the old legs. Didn't see a soul."

"Who were you expecting to see? Didn't you wait for someone in the platelayers' shack along there, and smoke a cigar while you were waiting? Who did you mistake me for when you said, 'What's the idea, keeping me waiting half an hour?' "

"Here, draw it mild, old man." Percy Dukes sounded injured. "I certainly looked in at the huts: smoked a cigar for a bit. Then I toddled back to the train, and met up with your good self on the way. I didn't make no appointment to meet—"

"Oo! Well I *must* say," interrupted Miss Blake virtuously. She could hardly wait to tell Stansfield that, on leaving the compartment shortly after Dukes, she'd overheard voices on the track below the lavatory window. "I recognized this gentleman's voice," she went on, tossing her head at Dukes. "He said something like: 'You're going to help us again, chum, so you'd better get used to the idea. You're in it up to the neck—can't back out now.' And another voice, sort of mumbling, might have been Mr. Kilmington's—I dunno—sounded Scotch anyway—said, 'All right. Meet you in five minutes: platelayers' hut a few hundred yards up the line. Talk it over.' "

"And what did you do then, young lady?" asked Stansfield.

"I happened to meet a gentleman friend, farther up the train, and sat with him for a bit."

"Is that so?" remarked Macdonald menacingly. "Why, you four-flushing little—!"

"Shut up!" commanded Stansfield.

"Honest I did," the girl said, ignoring Macdonald. "I'll introduce you to him, if you like. He'll tell you I was with him for, oh, half an hour or more."

"And what about Mr. Macdonald?"

"I'm not talking," said the youth sullenly.

"Mr. Macdonald isn't talking. Mrs. Grant?"

"I've been in this compartment ever since, sir."

"Ever since—?"

"Since I went out to damp my hankie for this young lady, when she'd fainted. Mr. Kilmington was just before me, you'll mind. I saw him go through into the guard's van."

"Did you hear him say anything about walking to the village?"

"No, sir. He just hurried into the van, and then there was some havers about its no' being lockit this time, and how he was going to report the guard for it."

"I see. And you've been sitting here with Mr. Macdonald all the time?"

"Yes, sir. Except for ten minutes or so he was out of the compartment, just after you'd left."

"What did you go out for?" Stansfield asked the young man.

"Just taking the air, brother."

"You weren't taking Mr. Kilmington's gold watch, as well as the air, by any chance?" Stansfield's keen eyes were fastened like a hook into Macdonald's, whose insolent expression visibly crumbled beneath them.

"I don't know what you mean," he tried to bluster. "You can't do this to me."

"I mean that a man has been murdered, and when the police search you, they will find his gold watch in your possession. Won't look too healthy for you, my young friend."

"Naow! Give us a chance! It was only a joke, see?" The wretched Macdonald was whining now, in his native cockney. "He got me riled—the stuck-up way he said nobody'd ever got the better of him. So I thought I'd just show him—I'd have given it back, straight I would, only I couldn't find him afterwards. It was just a joke, I tell you. Anyway, it was Inez who lifted the ticker."

"You dirty little rotter!" screeched the girl.

"Shut up, both of you. You can explain your joke to the Penrith police. Let's hope they don't die of laughing."

At this moment the train gave a lurch, and started back up the gradient. It halted at the signal-box, for Stansfield to telephone to Penrith, then clattered south again.

On Penrith platform Stansfield was met by an inspector and a sergeant of the County Constabulary, with the police surgeon. Then, after a brief pause in the guard's van, where the police surgeon drew aside the guard's black off-duty overcoat that had been laid over the body, and began his preliminary examination, they marched along to Stansfield's compartment. The guard who, at his request, had locked this as the train was drawing up at the platform and was keeping an eye on its occupants, now unlocked it. The inspector entered.

His first action was to search Macdonald. Finding the watch concealed on his person, he then charged Macdonald and Inez Blake with theft. The inspector next proceeded to make an arrest on the charge of wilful murder. . . .

Whom did the Inspector arrest for the murder of Arthur J. Kilmington?

You have been given no less than eight clues by the author: these eight clues should tell you, by logical deduction, not only the identity of the murderer but also the motive of the crime and the method by which it was committed.

We urge you accept the author's challenge before going further, and when you have interpreted the eight clues, compare your solution with Mr. Blake's, which now follows.

The inspector arrested the guard for the wilful murder of Arthur J. Kilmington.

Kilmington's pocket had been picked by Inez Blake, when she pretended to faint at 8:25, and his gold watch was at once passed by her to her accomplice, Macdonald. Now Kilmington was constantly consulting his watch. It is inconceivable, if he was not killed till after 9 P.M., that he should not have missed the watch and made a scene. This point was clinched by the first-class passenger who had said that a man, answering to the description of Kilmington, had asked him the time at 8:50: if it had really been Kilmington, he would certainly, before inquiring the time of anyone else, have first tried to consult his own watch, found it gone, and reported the theft. The fact that Kilmington neither reported the loss to the guard, nor returned to his original compartment to look for the watch, proves he must have been murdered *before he became aware of the loss*—i.e., shortly after he left the compartment at 8:27. But the guard claimed to have spoken to Kilmington at 9 P.M. Therefore the guard was lying. And why should he lie, except to create an alibi for himself? This is Clue Number One.

The guard claimed to have talked with Kilmington at 9 P.M. Now, at 8:55 the blizzard had diminished to a light snowfall, which soon afterwards ceased. When Stansfield discovered the body, it was buried under snow. Therefore Kilmington must have been murdered *while the blizzard was still raging*—i.e., some time before 9 P.M. Therefore the guard was lying when he said Kilmington was alive at 9 P.M. This is Clue Number Two.

Henry Stansfield, who was investigating on behalf of the Cosmopolitan Insurance Company the loss of the Countess of Axminster's emeralds, reconstructed the crime as follows:

Motive: The guard's wife had been gravely ill before Christmas: then, just about the time of the train robbery, he had got her the best surgeon in Glasgow and put her in a nursing home (evidence of engine-driver: Clue Number Three). A guard's pay does not usually run to such expensive treatment: it seemed likely, therefore, that the man, driven desperate by his wife's need, had agreed to take part in the robbery in return for a substantial bribe. What part did he play? During the investigation the guard had stated that he had left his van for five minutes, while the train was climbing the last section of Shap Bank, and on his return found the mail-bags missing. But Kilmington, who was traveling on this train, had found the guard's van locked at this point, and now (evidence of Mrs. Grant: Clue Number Four) declared his intention of reporting the guard. The latter knew that

Kilmington's report would contradict his own evidence and thus convict him of complicity in the crime, since he had locked the van for a few minutes to throw out the mail-bags himself, and pretended to Kilmington that he had been asleep (evidence of Kilmington himself) when the latter knocked at the door. So Kilmington had to be silenced.

Stansfield already had Percy Dukes under suspicion as the organizer of the robbery. During the journey Dukes gave himself away three times. First, although it had not been mentioned in the papers, he betrayed knowledge of the point on the line where the bags had been thrown out. Second, though the loss of the emeralds had been also kept out of the Press, Dukes knew it was an emerald *necklace* which had been stolen: Stansfield had laid a trap for him by calling it a bracelet, but later in conversation Dukes referred to the "necklace." Third, his great discomposure at the (false) statement by Stansfield that the emeralds were worth £25,000 was the reaction of a criminal who believes he has been badly gypped by the fence to whom he has sold them. Dukes was now planning a second train robbery, and meant to compel the guard to act as accomplice again. Inez Blake's evidence (Clue Number Five) of hearing him say, "You're going to help us again, chum," etc., clearly pointed to the guard's complicity in the previous robbery: it was almost certainly the guard to whom she had heard Dukes say this, for only a railway servant would have known about the existence of a platelayer's hut up the line, and made an appointment to meet Dukes there; moreover, if Dukes had talked about his plans for the next robbery, on the train itself, to anyone *but* a railway servant suspicion would have been incurred should they have been seen talking together.

Method: At 8:27 Kilmington goes into the guard's van. He threatens to report the guard, though he is quite unaware of the dire consequences this would entail for the latter. The guard, probably on the pretext of showing him the route to the village, gets Kilmington out of the train, walks him away from the lighted area, stuns him (the bruise was a light one and did not reveal itself in Stansfield's brief examination of the body), carries him to the spot where Stansfield found the body, packs mouth and nostrils tight with snow. Then, instead of leaving well alone, the guard decides to create an alibi for himself. He takes his victim's hat, returns to train, puts on his own dark, off-duty overcoat, finds a solitary passenger asleep, masquerades as Kilmington inquiring the time, and strengthens the impression by saying he'd walk to the village if the relief engine did not turn up in five minutes, then returns to the body and throws the hat beside it (Stansfield found the hat only lightly covered with snow, as compared with the body: Clue Number Six). Moreover, the passenger noticed that the inquirer was wearing blue trousers (Clue Number Seven). The guard's regulation suit was blue; but Duke's suit was gray, and Macdonald's a loud check—therefore, the masquerader could not have been either of them.

The time is now 8:55. The guard decides to reinforce his alibi by going to intercept the returning fireman. He takes a short cut from the body to the platelayers' hut. The track he now makes, compared with the beaten trail towards the village, is much more lightly filled in with snow when Stansfield finds it (Clue Number Eight): therefore, it must have been made some time after the murder, and could not incriminate Percy Dukes. The guard meets the fireman just after 8:55. They walk back to the train. The guard is taken aside by Dukes, who has gone out for his "airing," and the conversation overheard by Inez Blake takes place. The guard tells Dukes he will meet him presently in the platelayers' hut: this is aimed to incriminate Dukes, should the murder by any chance be discovered, for Dukes would find it difficult to explain why he should have sat alone in a cold hut for half an hour just around the time when Kilmington was presumably murdered only one hundred and fifty yards away. The guard now goes along to the engine and stays there chatting with the crew for some forty minutes. His alibi is thus established for the period from 8:55 to 9:40 P.M. His plan might well have succeeded, but for three unlucky factors he could not possibly have taken into account—Stansfield's presence on the train, the blizzard stopping soon after 9 P.M., and the theft of Arthur J. Kilmington's watch.

The Clue of the Red Wig

JOHN DICKSON CARR

They usually put the paper to press at two a.m. MacGrath, the news editor, who was not feeling well after the Christmas celebrations, went home early to his own bed and left things at the office to young Patterson. MacGrath was sleeping a shivering sleep when the telephone at his bedside rang.

MacGrath made unearthly noises, like a ghost roused before midnight. But he answered the phone.

"Hazel Loring?" he repeated. "What about her?"

"She's dead," answered Patterson. "Murdered, it's pretty certain. Do you know Victoria Square?"

"No."

"It's a quiet little residential square in Bayswater. Hazel Loring lived there. In the middle of the square there's a garden reserved for the use of residents. About eleven o'clock a policeman on his rounds found Hazel Loring dead in the garden with practically no clothes on—"

"What?" shouted MacGrath; and the sleep was struck from his eyes.

"Well, only a brassiere and a pair of step-ins. She was sitting on a bench, dead as Cleopatra, with the rest of her clothes folded up on the bench beside her."

"In *this* weather?"

"Yes. The policeman saw her go into the garden an hour before. Cause of death was a fractured skull, from several blows with a walking stick whose handle was loaded with lead. Signs of a struggle behind the bench."

"Right!" said MacGrath. "Splash it on the front page. Every

woman in the land will want to know what happened to Hazel Loring!"

Everybody knew the name of Hazel Loring, the face of Hazel Loring, the opinions of Hazel Loring. "Smile and Grow Fit" was the title of her weekly column in the *Daily Banner*, a deadly rival of MacGrath's own *Daily Record*. "Smile and Grow Fit" was also the title of the booklets, sold by the thousand, in which she explained to housewives how they might keep slim without anguish. She was no grim taskmistress of health. She did not sternly order them to eat a dry biscuit, and like it.

"I've devised these exercises on the advice of a doctor," she wrote. "Just three minutes each morning; and don't bother any more about it. If you like chocolates, in heaven's name eat chocolates. Only mind you do my exercises: and then eat what you like."

Her chatty, intimate manner warmed their hearts. She became more than an adviser on health. She counselled them about love and hats and husbands. Everybody had seen pictures of the strong, square, pleasant face, showing fine teeth in a smile, and with a dimple at each corner of the mouth. She was slim, with a good figure, and intensely active. She was well dressed, but not offensively so. Her brown hair was bobbed, her brown eyes grave. Her age might have been thirty-five. Thousands felt that they knew her personally, and wrote to tell her so.

Yet somebody killed her, half-dressed, in a public garden on a bitter December night.

If truth must be told, even in MacGrath, hard-boiled as he was, the first reaction was a twinge of pity. His wife was even more emphatic.

"Poor woman!" said Mrs. MacGrath from the opposite bed. "Poor woman!"

"Ho? Is that how it strikes you?" asked MacGrath, his news-sense instantly on the alert.

"Of course it is. Of all the brutal, senseless—!"

"Then that's how we'll play the story. I think I'm getting an inspiration. But Hazel Loring. Oh Lord!"

The next day he carried his inspiration to Houston, the managing editor.

The offices of the *Daily Record* occupy a huge modernistic building, a sort of chromium-plated goldfish bowl. Fleet Street was buzzing with gossip. The murder of Hazel Loring, though they could not yet call it a murder, was considered so important that they held a conference in the managing editor's office. Here, in a cubist-designed room with bright curtains, the stately Houston sat behind a desk topped with black glass, and drew down the corners of his mouth.

"Impossible," Houston said. "We can't do it. Dignity."

"All right. *Be* dignified," said MacGrath. "But don't pass up a thing like this. Now see here, J. H. This is a woman's crime; it oozes feminine interest. It's good for a daily story. Our-Correspondent-Watches-Police; Developments-Day-By-Day. So, with half the women in England crying for news of their favorite, what do we do? Why, we put a woman to cover it."

Houston passed a hand over his thin, high forehead.

"A woman doing police reporting?"

"Why not? She can be dignified, can't she? Womanly and kind, with a touch of sadness? Man, they'll eat it up!"

Houston hunched up his shoulders. "She'd have to be tough," he pointed out. "Covering a war is one thing; covering a murder is another. I don't know who I could assign to it."

"What about that French girl? Jacqueline Dubois. Only been with us a week. Came over when things there went to blazes. But I'll tell you something, J. H. She had the reputation of being the smartest news-hawk in Paris; Richart of *L'Oeil* recommended her in superlatives, and I think he's right."

"She speaks English?"

"She's half English. Her mother was a Cockney. She speaks English all right."

"And she will be—er—dignified?"

"Absolutely. I guarantee it, J. H."

"Get her," said Houston.

Nevertheless, he was uneasy until he actually set eyes on Jacqueline Dubois. Then he drew a breath of relief, and almost beamed.

MacGrath, on the other hand, was jarred. In recommending this girl MacGrath had been acting on a hunch; he knew little about her beyond Richart's word. And, at his first sight of Jacqueline, he had a panicky feeling that Richart must have been indulging in a deplorable Gallic sense of humour.

Jacqueline entered the office so timidly that Houston rose to draw out a chair for her. She was a golden blonde, small and plump, with one of those fair skins which flush easily, and those dark blue eyes which are either wide open or modestly lowered. Her mouth expressed confusion, but anxiety to please. Her fur coat was good but unobtrusive; from her plain grey dress to her tan stockings and shoes she was trim and yet retiring. She kept her big eyes fixed on Houston except when he looked directly at her. In a soft, sweet voice she hesitantly asked what was wanted.

While MacGrath stood in despair, Houston told her.

"And that's the idea, Miss Dubois. Your purpose is to—"

"To pester the police," groaned MacGrath.

"To print," said Houston sternly, "all desirable news which will be of interest to our public. Would you like the assignment?"

Jacqueline raised her limpid blue eyes.

"Would I like it?" she breathed. "Hot ziggety damn!"

Houston sat back with a start. She was covered in confusion, modesty struggling with gratitude.

"I thank you on my knees," she went on, clasping her hands together. "Miss Loring. The poor lady who has so unfortunately kicked the ghost. I had wished to cover that story, yes; but, blimey, I never thought I should get it. Oh, you are a dear. Would you like me to kiss you?"

"Good heavens, no!" said Houston.

But Jacqueline was not listening. She was utterly absorbed. The toe of her shoe tapped the carpet. Her eyes were turned inwards, a pucker of concentration between the brows; and, as she reflected, she nodded to herself.

"I am handicap," she confessed. "I am new to England and I do not know the ropes yet. If I get you a scoop, I must get it funny-ways. Who is the head of your whole police department?"

"The Assistant Commissioner for the Criminal Investigation Department," said MacGrath.

"Good!" said Jacqueline briskly. "I make love to him."

Houston gave her a long, slow look.

"No, no, no!" he said.

"Yes, yes, yes!" said Jacqueline, continuing to nod briskly.

"But you can't do that, Miss Dubois!"

"I do not understand," complained Jacqueline, breaking off to look at him with shy astonishment. "You do not wish me to do it? Why?"

"To explain that fully, Miss Dubois, might take a long time. I can sum up by saying that it would hardly be in accord with the policy of this newspaper. Besides, there are—er—practical considerations. In the first place, you'd never get near him. In the second place, even if you did you wouldn't get any story."

A twinkle appeared in Jacqueline's limpid eyes.

"Ha, ha, ha," she said. "That is what they tell me when I make eyes at Mornay, the *juge d'instruction*. He has whiskers this long"—her gesture indicated a beard of improbable dimensions—"but I get from him the official photographs of De La Rive shooting at all the gendarmes in the rue Jean Goujoun, and I scoop the town! Still, if you do not wish it?"

"Definitely not."

Jacqueline sighed. "Orright," she conceded. "Then I must find out the name of the policeman in charge of the case, and make love to *him*. Also, please, I should like a newspaper photographer to go with me all the time."

"A photographer? Why?"

"First because it is practical. I have got some fine pictures when I work for *L'Oeil*. Once I get a picture of the Comtesse de la Tour St. Sulpice, which is a kleptomaniac, pinching a necklace out of Paulier's in the rue de la Paix."

"Is that so?"

"Oo la la, what a sensation!" She gurgled delightedly. "Then too it is useful if you can get a picture of a police officer doing something he should not. You tell him you will publish the picture unless he gives you a story."

Houston had been listening under a kind of hypnosis. Jacqueline seemed to be surrounded by a rose-leaf cloud of innocence, like a figure on a valentine. He could not have been more startled if the Mona Lisa had suddenly leaned out of her frame and put out her tongue at him. He found his voice.

"We begin with vamping and pass on to blackmail," he said. "MacGrath, I can't do it. Young woman, you're fired! You'd ruin this paper in a week."

"If she's fired," roared MacGrath, "I resign. Splendor of saints, here's a newspaperman at last!"

"Do you want the Home Office to put us out of business?"

"We've got subeditors to read her copy, haven't we? I tell you, J. H., if—"

"Then there is another thing," pursued Jacqueline timidly. "One of your photographers is called Henry Ashwin. He is a good fellow, though I think he drink too much visky-soda. He is the photographer I want, please."

"Ashwin? Why Ashwin?"

"I find out he is making the goo-goo eyes at Hazel Loring's maidservant. Yes! That is something the others pass up, eh? So I give him visky-soda and I talk to him. Already I get much information, you see."

"Before you were assigned to the story?"

Jacqueline raised her eyebrows.

"But yes, yes, yes! Of course. Listen! This Miss Loring, her age is thirty-five. In private life she is very bad-tempered. Henry Ashwin thinks she is what you call a phony, somehow, but he is not sure about what. Also she is good-goody, what you call a prude. Is she married? No! But she has a fiancé, a lawyer which is called Edward Hoyt; and he hang about her for five years and still it is no soap. Why does she not marry him, eh?"

"Well?"

"I find out," answered Jacqueline simply. "Now I tell you something the police have not told you."

"Go on," muttered Houston, still hypnotized.

"This is what her maid say to Henry Ashwin, and Henry Ashwin say to me. When Miss Loring is found sitting on the bench in that garden, wearing only the brassiere and the step-ins and her shoes, the other clothes are folded up on the bench beside her."

MacGrath was instantly alert. "We know that. It's in all the papers."

"Yes! *But*," said Jacqueline, "there are other things too. Folded up in the clothes (so) there is a red wig and a pair of dark spectacles."

Houston and MacGrath stared at each other, wondering whether this might be some obscure French metaphor. But Jacqueline left them in no doubt.

"A red wig," she insisted, tapping her golden hair. "And the smoky spectacles you look through." She cupped her hands over her eyes in mimicry. "Why should Miss Loring have them, eh? Blimey, but that is not all! It is certain she undressed herself, and was not undressed by anybody. Her maid tells Henry Ashwin that Miss Loring has a special way of folding stockings, like . . . ah, zut! . . . would you like me to take off mine and show you?"

"No, no!"

"Orright. I only ask. But it is special. Also the way of folding the dress. So she take her own dress off, and she have a wig and spectacles. Please, will you let me find out why?" Her big blue eyes turned reproachfully on Houston. "You say you will fire me, and that is not nice. I know I am a goofy little beasel; that is what they all say in Paris; but if you will please be a nice man and give me a chance I will get you that story, cross my heart. Yes?"

Houston had the darkest misgivings. But he was a journalist.

"Hop to it," he said.

Inspector Adam Bell, Criminal Investigation Department, stood in the prim little front parlor of number 22 Victoria Square. He looked alternately out of the window, towards the garden in the center, and then back to the white-faced man opposite him.

Sedate and dun-colored was Victoria Square, Bayswater, in the bleak winter afternoon. The house fronts were sealed up. In the garden, surrounded by teeth of spiked iron railings, the branches of trees showed black and knotted against a muddy twilight; its gravel paths wound between iron benches and skeleton bushes, on grass hard with frost.

Inspector Bell, in the white, antiseptic front parlor of the dead woman's house, faced Hazel Loring's fiancé. Inspector Bell was a young and very serious-minded product of Hendon, but his sympathetic manner had already done much.

"And you can't tell me anything more, Mr. Hoyt?"

"Nothing!" said Edward Hoyt, and fingered his black tie. "I wanted to take her to a concert last night, but she refused, and I went alone. I—er—don't read the sensational press. So I knew nothing about this business until Hazel's secretary, Miss Alice Farmer, telephoned me this morning."

Inspector Bell shared Hoyt's views about the sensational press: the house was triple-guarded against reporters, though a hundred eyes came to stop and stare in the square.

Edward Hoyt suddenly sat down beside the small fire in the white grate. He was a long, lean, pleasant-faced man of just past forty, with big knuckly hands and a patient manner. He had certainly, Bell reflected, been a patient suitor. His eyes in the firelight were faintly bloodshot, and he turned them often towards a sofa on which lay a neat wig, a pair of dark spectacles, and a heavy blackthorn walking stick.

"It's fantastic and degrading," he went on, "and I still don't believe it. Can't *you* tell me anything, Inspector? Anything at all?"

Bell was noncommittal.

"You've heard the evidence, sir. Miss Farmer, her secretary, testifies that at a few minutes before ten last night Miss Loring left the house, refusing to say where she was going." He paused. "It wasn't the first time Miss Loring had gone out like that: always about ten o'clock, and usually staying out two or three hours."

Hoyt did not comment.

"From here," said Bell, "she must have gone straight across to the garden—"

"But why, in heaven's name," Hoyt burst out, "the *garden?*"

Bell ignored this. "A policeman on his rounds heard someone fumbling at the gate of the garden. He flashed his light, and saw Miss Loring opening the gate with a key. He questioned her, but she explained that she lived in the square and had a right to use the garden, even on a blacked-out December night.

"The constable let her go. But he was worried. About an hour later, his beat brought him round to the garden again. The gate was still open: he heard it creak. He went in, and found Miss Loring sitting on a bench . . . there . . . at the first turn of the gravel path, about fifteen feet from the gate."

Bell paused.

He visualized the scene, sharp in its loneliness. The gate squeaking in a raw wind; the brief, probing light on icy flesh and white silk underclothing; the head hanging down over the back of the bench; and the high-heeled shoes with button-fastening undone.

"The rest of her clothing—fur coat, dress, suspender-belt, and stockings—lay beside her: folded in such a way that her maid, Henrietta Simms, swears she took off the clothes herself. Her handbag was untouched. The key to the garden gate, with a large cardboard label attached, lay on the path."

Each time Bell made a statement, Edward Hoyt nodded at the fire.

Bell went over to the sofa and picked up the walking stick. It was top-heavy, because its nickel-plated head contained half a pound of lead.

"She'd been killed," Bell went on, "behind that bench. The ground was hard, but there were prints of those high heels of hers all over the place. There'd been a struggle: she wasn't any weakling."

"No," agreed Hoyt.

"Her skull was fractured over the left temple with this stick." Bell weighed it in his hand. "No doubt about this as the weapon. Microscopic traces of blood, and a hair, on the handle: though the wound hardly bled at all outwardly. Our laboratory identifies—"

He broke off apologetically.

"I beg your pardon, sir. I'm not trying to give you the third degree with this. I only brought it along to see whether anybody could identify it."

Hoyt spoke with old-fashioned courtesy.

"And I beg *your* pardon, Inspector. It is a pleasure to deal with a gentleman." He got to his feet, and drew the back of his hand across his mouth. "I'm glad there was no blood," he added. "I'm glad she wasn't—knocked about."

"Yes."

"But is that reasonable, Inspector? A fatal injury, with so little blood?"

"Oh yes. It's the rupture of brain-tissues that counts. A friend of mine got concussion from being struck by the door of a railway carriage and never knew there was anything wrong with him until he collapsed." Bell's tone changed; he spoke sharply. "Now, sir, I've spoken my piece. Have you anything to tell me?"

"Nothing. Except—"

"Well?"

Hoyt hesitated. "I'd been a bit worried about her. She hasn't been looking at all well lately. I'm afraid she had a tendency to overeat." There was the ghost of a smile on his face, contradicted by the bloodshot eyes. "But she said, 'So long as I do my exercises every morning, as thousands of my followers are doing'—she was very proud of her position, Inspector—"

This was hardly what Bell wanted.

"I mean, do you know any reason why anybody should have wanted to kill her?"

"None. I swear!"

"Or why she should have undressed herself in order to get killed?"

Hoyt's mouth tightened. But he was prevented from answering by the entrance of a soft, quiet, but quick-moving woman in horn-rimmed spectacles. Miss Alice Farmer, the perfect secretary, resembled the old-time notion of a schoolmistress. Her face, though not unattractive, was suggestive of a buttered bun; her brown hair was dressed untidily; she wore paper cuffs and flat-heeled shoes.

Miss Farmer had many times shown her devotion to Hazel Loring during six years' service. Now her eyelids looked pink and sanded, and occasionally she reached under the spectacles to dab at them with the tip of a handkerchief.

"Ghouls!" she said, gripping the handkerchief hard. "Ghouls! Inspector, I—I know poor Hazel's body has been taken away. But didn't you give orders that *none* of those horrible reporters was to be admitted to the square over there?"

"Yes, of course. Why?"

"Well," said Miss Farmer, putting out her chin bravely, "they're there now. You can see them from my window upstairs. Two of them. One is a man taking pictures; and the other, if you please, is a *woman*. How any *decent* woman could lower herself to write for the—" She stopped, and her face grew scarlet. "I mean *report*, of course; not write *nice* things; that's altogether different. Oh, dear. You do see what I mean, don't you?"

Inspector Bell saw only that his orders had been disobeyed. He stiffened.

"You're sure they're reporters?"

"Just *look* for yourself!"

Bell's pleasant face grew sinister. He drew a deep breath. He picked up his overcoat and his bowler hat from a chair.

"Excuse me just one moment," he said formally. "I'll attend to them."

By the time he left the house, Bell was running. The garden gate, on the west side of the square, was almost opposite Hazel Loring's house. The iron bench—once green, but now of a rust color—itself faced due west, where the gravel path curved in front of it.

Round it prowled a small golden-haired figure in a fur coat, and a large untidy figure with a mackintosh and a camera. Inspector Bell "Oi'd" at them; then he squared himself in front of them and began to talk.

Henry Ashwin, the photographer, took it stolidly. All he did was to pull his hat farther on a pair of large projecting ears, and shrug his shoulders in an apologetic way. But Jacqueline, between indignation and utter astonishment, was struck dumb. She sincerely felt that she was helping in the investigation, and she could not understand what this man was going on about.

"You must not be such a grimy camel!" she cried, reasoning with him kindly. "You do not understand at all. I am Dubois of the *Record*. This is Mr. Ashwin of the *Record*."

"I know Mr. Ashwin," said Bell grimly. "Now, for the last time, madam: will you get out of here, or must you be taken out by main force?"

"But you do not mean that!"

Bell stared at her.

"What makes you think so?"

"And you should not talk so to the Press. It is not nice and you get yourself into trouble. Henry, I do not like this man. Kick him out of here and then we get on with our work."

"Ashwin," said Bell, "is this girl completely off her head?"

Ashwin intervened in a protesting rumble. "Sorry, Inspector; I'll fix it. Look here, Jackie, things aren't the same here as they are in France. That's what I've been trying to tell you. In England, reporters aren't allowed to—"

"You will not do it?"

"I can't, Jackie!"

"Now I am mad," said Jackie, folding her arms with an air of cold grandeur. "Blimey, now I am good and mad; and just for that I do not tell you anything about the clue I have discovered."

"Clue?" said Bell sharply.

"Ha, *now* you are interested, eh?" cried Jacqueline, wagging her head. Her tone changed: it became timid and pleading. "Please, I like to be nice, and I like you to be nice too. I could help you if you would let me. I think I know what happen here last night. As soon as I hear about Miss Loring's shoes being unbuttoned, and hear about the wig and spectacles—"

Bell whirled round on her.

"How do you know her shoes were unbuttoned? And about any wig and spectacles? That wasn't given out to the Press!"

Twilight was deepening over the spiky trees of the garden. Not a gleam showed in Victoria Square except the hooded sidelights of a taxi, which circled the square with its engine clanking noisily. Jacqueline opened her handbag, and drew out a large oblong of glazed paper.

It was a photograph of Hazel Loring's body, taken from in front and some dozen feet away. The shadows were behind it, so that every detail showed with crude realism: the upright posture but limp arms, the head thrown back, the slim muscular legs and shoes whose open fastenings were visible at a glance.

"Where," Bell shouted, "did you get this?"

"*I* got it, Inspector," Ashwin admitted. "I climbed over the fence this morning, before they'd moved anything. If I'd used a flashbulb your men would have spotted me straightaway; but there was a good strong sun up to ten o'clock, so I just took a snap and hared off."

Ashwin's little eyes blinked out of the shadow of his shabby hat. It had grown so dark in the garden that little more could be seen of him except the shift and shine of his eyes, and the fact that he needed a shave. If ordinarily he might have been something of a swaggerer, he was subdued now. He also had found Jacqueline a handful.

"I wasn't even going to use the picture, I swear!" he went on, and stated his real grievance. "This girl pinched it from me, when I wasn't even going to show—"

"Shoes!" insisted Jacqueline.

Bell swung round again. "What about the shoes?"

"They is clues," said Jacqueline simply. "You must not ask me how I get my information. The wig and the spectacles I learn about from Miss Loring's maid, in a way. But I do not mind telling you what will solve your case for you, strike me pink."

Bell hesitated.

"If this is some sort of game," he snapped, "there's going to be a lot of trouble in store for certain people I could mention. Now, I warn you! But if you've got anything to tell me, let's hear it."

Jacqueline was complacent.

"You do not see that the shoes show what has happen here?"

"Frankly, I don't."

"Ah! That is why you need a woman to detect for you when a woman is murdered. Now I show you. You see in the picture that the shoes have very high heels. Yes?"

"Yes."

"And they fasten only with one strap and one button across the . . . the . . . ah, zut!"

"Instep?"

"I am spikking the English very well, thank you," said Jacqueline, drawing herself up coldly. "I do not need your help to be pure. And I have already think to say instep. But you still do not tumble? No?" She sidled closer. Coaxing and honey-sweet, her voice caressed him out of the twilight. "If I tell you, then you do something for me? You will be a nice man and let me print what I like?"

"I most certainly will not."

"Orright. Then I will not tell you."

Adam Bell's wrath boiled clear to the top. Never in his career had he met anyone quite like this. It is true that his career had not been a long one; but then Jacqueline's could not have been so very long either. Now he meant to have no more nonsense. He would put her in her place, and with no uncertain adjectives.

He had opened his mouth to do this, when there was a flicker of a shrouded light across the square. The door of number 22 opened and closed.

Bell had a sharp premonition of disaster as soon as he heard the flat-heeled footsteps rapping and ringing on frosty pavements. A squat little figure, coatless and with wisps of hair flying, hurried across the street into the garden.

When the figure came closer, Bell saw that tears were trickling down Miss Alice Farmer's face.

"It's all your fault," she said accusingly to Bell. "Oh dear, if only you hadn't left! If only you'd stayed with him!"

"Easy now. What is it? Steady, Miss Farmer!"

"Your sergeant's phoned for the ambulance; and he says they may pull him through, but oh dear, if they don't I don't know what I shall do. Oh dear, it's even more dreadful than—"

Then she pulled herself together.

"I'm sorry. It's poor Mr. Hoyt. He's taken poison. You'd better come over to the house at once."

Adam Bell was not able to interview Hoyt until the following day. That morning's edition of the *Daily Record* was in Bell's pocket: he wondered what the Assistant Commissioner would have to say about Jacqueline Dubois's story.

A nurse conducted him to a small private room, where Edward Hoyt lay propped up among the pillows of a white iron bed. Alice Farmer sat in a squeaky rocking chair by the window, looking out at the snowflakes that had begun to thicken over Kensington Gardens.

"Rather a foolish thing to do, wasn't it, sir?" Bell asked quietly.

"I recognize that, Inspector."

"Why did you do it?"

"Can't you guess?"

Hoyt even managed a sour smile. His hands, snake-veined, lay listless on the coverlet; his gaze wandered over the ceiling without curiosity. Yesterday he had seemed in his middle forties: now he looked ten years older.

"The curious thing is," he went on, frowning, "that I had no intention of doing it. That's a fact, Inspector. I hadn't realized—by George, I hadn't!—how terrible and irresistible a mere *impulse* can be."

He paused, as tough to get his breath.

"I went upstairs," he said, "to have a look at Hazel's room. That's all. It honestly is all. I glanced into the bathroom. I saw the medicine cabinet open, and a bottle of morphine tablets inside. Before I had any notion of what I meant, I had filled a glass of water, and swallowed seven or eight of the tablets as fast as I could get them down. At that time, I admit, I didn't want to live any longer."

"No, sir?"

"No. But I have changed my mind now. I am sorry: it was, as you say, a very foolish thing to do."

Always the gentleman, thought Inspector Bell.

From the direction of the window came a sharp, almost malignant squeak from the rocking chair. Alice Farmer glanced over her shoulder, and back again quickly. The snow shed shifting lights into the warm, close room.

"Of course I realize," Bell said awkwardly, "that as Miss Loring's fiancé—"

"It is not quite accurate to call me her fiancé," returned Hoyt, with detached calmness.

His tone made Inspector Bell sit up sharply.

"Meaning, sir?"

"Hazel never intended to get married, to me or anybody else."

"How do you know that?"

"She told me so. But I kept on patiently waiting. I have always had a fancy for the senseless role of the *preux chevalier*. God knows I'm cured of that now." Hoyt closed his eyes, and opened them again. "You see that I am being frank."

"You mean she didn't love you?"

Hoyt smiled faintly. "I doubt if Hazel was ever in love with anybody. No: I wasn't referring to that."

"Well?"

"I think she was married already. One moment!" The weak voice sharpened and grew firm. "I have absolutely no evidence for saying that. It's a guess. An impression. A—well, Inspector, I haven't known Hazel Loring for five years without learning something about her beyond those famous eyebrows and dimples. I knew her moods. And her heart. And her mind: which was, after all, a second-rate mind. Lord forgive me, what am I saying?"

He broke off, looking still more ill. There was another squeak from the rocking chair as Alice Farmer got up to pour him a glass of water from the bedside table.

Hoyt thanked her with a grateful nod; and she hardly glanced at him. But to Inspector Bell, watching every turn of lip or hand, that glance meant much. Bell thought to himself, with a rush of realization: if Hazel Loring wasn't in love with Edward Hoyt, I know who else is.

Miss Farmer fluttered back to her chair.

"I tell you that," pursued Hoyt, setting down the glass, "because I want to see this mess cleared up. If Hazel *had* a husband tucked away somewhere in secret, she could hardly divorce him. She had set herself up in too pious a position before the world."

Drawing up the collar of his overcoat, Bell went out of the nursing-home into the falling snow. Jacqueline Dubois, wearing a fur coat and a hat with an outrageous veil, was waiting for him at the foot of the steps.

Inspector Bell took one look at her, and then began to run.

His excuse for this was a bus, which would set him down beside a hotel in a side street only a few yards away from Victoria Square. The bus was already some distance away, and lumbering fast. Bell sprinted hard after it, sprang aboard, and climbed up to a deserted top deck. He had no sooner settled back than Jacqueline, flushed and panting, was beside him.

The girl was almost in tears.

"You are not genteel!" she wailed. "I have twist my ankle. Would you like it that I should hurt myself bad?"

"Candidly," said Bell, "yes."

"You do not like me at *all?*"

"No. Remember, I've read your story in the *Record* this morning."

"You do not like it? But, *chéri*, I wrote it to please you!"

"In the course of that story," said Bell, "you four times described me as 'handsome.' How I'm going to dare show my face back at Scotland Yard again I don't know. What is more important, you headlined—"

"You are not angry?"

"Oh, no. Not at all."

"Besides, I have a clue."

Despite everything, Bell suddenly found himself chuckling. Rules were rules; but still, he reflected, he had been behaving like a good deal of a stuffed shirt. This girl need give him no trouble. And in her way Jacqueline was rather attractive.

"Not again?" he said.

"No, no, no! It is the same clue. You will not let me explain. You will not let me explain how I know that Miss Loring was not killed in the garden at all, but that the assassin kill her somewhere else and carry her to the garden afterwards."

The bus lurched round a snow-rutted curve.

Bell, taking two tickets from the conductor, almost dropped both of them.

"Is this," he demanded, "another stunt?"

"It is the truth! I know it by the shoes. The shoes have very high heels, and their straps are not buttoned."

"Well?"

"She could not have walked in them. Yes, I tell you so! She could not have walked a step in them. It is impossible. Either the shoes fall off, or *she* fall off.

"Listen! You say to yourself, 'Miss Loring has entered the garden; she had started to undress herself.' So? Then why does she take off her stockings and put her shoes back on? You say, 'While she is like this, the assassin catch her; there is a struggle; she is hit; the assassin pick her up and put her on the bench.' I say, no, no, no! She could not have walked in those shoes. It is jolly sure she could not have *fight* in them. They would just fall off, and then there would be marks on her feet. And there were no marks, eh?"

"Go on," said Bell, after a pause.

"It jumps to the eyes that the assassin has put the shoes on Miss Loring after she is dead."

"But—"

"Now I tell you something else. What is it that puzzle you so much, *chéri?* What is the big headache? It is the reason why Miss Loring should have undress herself in the open with the weather freezing zero. Yes? But she did not.

"She had gone first to the garden. Then she has left the garden, and gone somewhere else which is indoors; and there she has undressed herself. There the assassin catch her and kill her. Then he take her back to the garden in the blackout, to make you think she was killed there. He is just starting to dress her fully when he is interrupted, and has to run. Yes?"

Their bus had gone clanking up Gloucester Terrace, and was turning into Hargreaves Street, which led to Victoria Square. Already Bell could see the square ahead. Bell smote his hand against the top of the seat in front of them.

"By all the—" he burst out, and stopped. "I wonder if it could be?"

"I do not wonder," said Jacqueline. "I am sure it is true. For any woman to take off her clothes outdoors in such weather is not practical; and even if I am a goofy little beasel I see that straightaway, gorblimey!"

"Just a minute. What about the heel marks of the struggle in the earth behind the bench?"

"They is phony," returned Jacqueline calmly. "I do not think there be any marks with the ground so hard. The assassin has made them too."

Stopping with a jolt, the bus threw them against the bench ahead. They climbed down to the pavement beside the quiet hotel only a few steps from Victoria Square. Though Jacqueline was dancing round him, Bell would not be hurried either mentally or physically.

"It's nonsense," he decided.

"You are a nasty man and I do not like you. Why is it nonsense?"

"Well, where did the woman go? You say Miss Loring went somewhere and 'undressed.' Where? Apparently she didn't go back home. Where could any woman go at that hour of the night in order to undr—?"

He checked himself, and raised his eyes. A raw wind shouted down Hargreaves Street, whipping the snow to powder. The grimy red-brick building in front of them had two entrances. Across the top of one was blazoned in gilt letters the name of the hotel. On the glass doors of the other were smaller letters in white enamel, but they were letters which made Bell jump. They said:

LADIES' AND GENTLEMEN'S
TURKISH BATHS.
OPEN DAY AND NIGHT.

The woman behind the counter was scandalized. When she first caught a glimpse of them, coming down in the automatic lift into the warm, dim basement-foyer, she threw up the flap of the counter and ran out.

"You, sir!" she cried. "You can't come in here!"

"I am a police officer—," Bell began.

The woman hesitated only a second. "Sorry, sir, but you still aren't allowed here. This is Wednesday. It's Ladies' Day. Didn't you see the notice upstairs?"

"*I* can come in?" cooed Jacqueline.

"Yes, madam, of course."

" 'Ow much?" asked Jacqueline, opening her handbag.

Taking hold of Jacqueline's arm in a grip that made her squeal, Bell drove the other woman before him until she retreated behind the counter. First he showed his warrant card. Then he drew out a large close up photograph of Hazel Loring's face.

"Did you ever see this lady before?"

"I—I don't know. There are so many people here. What do you want?"

On the counter lay a tray of pens and pencils. With a coloured pencil Bell drew on the photograph a crude representation of an auburn wig. To this he added a pair of dark spectacles.

"Did you ever see *this* lady before?"

"I did and all!" admitted the woman. "Of course I did. She was always coming here at night. If you'd just tell me what you—"

"Was she here on Monday night?"

The attendant, who seemed less frightened than anxious that Bell should not get beyond the doors at the left, admitted this too.

"Yes, she was. She came in about a quarter past ten, a little later than usual. I noticed because she looked awfully groggy; sick like; and her hands were shaky and she didn't leave any valuables here at the desk."

"What time did she leave?"

"I don't know. I—I don't remember." A puzzled look, a kind of spasm, flickered across the attendant's face. "Here's Mrs. Bradford," she added. "She'll give you what-for if you don't get out of here!"

It was very warm and faintly damp in the tiled basement. A dim humming noise throbbed beyond it. Soft lights shone on the counter, on the wall of steel boxes behind it; and, towards the left, on leather-covered swing doors studded with brass nailheads.

One of these doors was pushed open. A stocky, medium-sized woman, with dark hair drawn behind her ears and eyebrows that met over the top of her nose, first jerked back as though for flight, and then stood solidly. Her face was impassive and rather sinister. She wore a white duck coat and skirt; her bare feet were thrust into beach sandals.

"Mrs. Bradford—," the attendant began.

Mrs. Bradford gave the newcomers a long, slow look. Emotion, harsh and pressed to bursting, filled that foyer as thickly as the damp. Voices, faint laughter, made a ghostly background beyond.

"You'd better come in here," she told them. Opening a door which led into a small office, she nodded at them to precede her. When they were inside, she closed and locked the door. Then she flopped down in an office-chair and presently began to cry.

"I knew I couldn't get away with it," she said.

* * *

"So that's it," Bell muttered ten minutes later. "Hoyt told me that Miss Loring was fond of overeating."

Mrs. Bradford uttered a contemptuous snort. She was sitting forward, her elbows carelessly on her knees; she seemed to feel better now that she had been given a cigarette.

"Overeating!" she growled. "She'd have been as big as a barrage-balloon if she hadn't nearly killed herself with more Turkish baths than any human being ought to take. Yes, and keeping a medicine cabinet full of slimming drugs that were downright dangerous. I warned her. But, oh, no! She wouldn't listen. She was making too much money out of this slimming campaign of hers."

"You knew her?"

"I've known Hazel Loring for twenty years. We were kids together in the north. She was always the lady. Not like me. And she was clever: I give her that."

Bell was putting many facts together now.

"Then the simple-exercises-and-keep-fit campaign—?"

"It was all," said Mrs. Bradford, wagging her head and blowing out smoke contemptuously, "a fake. Mind, her exercises maybe did do some people good. There's some women could hypnotize themselves into believing anything. And, if they thought it kept 'em slim . . . why, perhaps it did. But not little Hazel. That's why she had to sneak over here in a damn silly disguise, like a film star or something. She was desperately frightened somebody'd spot her."

"And yet," said Bell, "somebody murdered her. It was you, I suppose?"

The cigarette dropped out of Mrs. Bradford's hand.

"Murdered!" she whispered; and missed the cigarette altogether when she tried to stamp it out with her foot. Then her voice rose to a screech. "Man, what's the matter with you? Are you clean daft? Murdered?"

"Sh-h!"

"Murdered?" said Mrs. Bradford. "She fell down and died in the steamroom. I had to get her out of here on the q.t., or the scandal would have ruined us."

"She died from concussion of the brain."

Mrs. Bradford's eyes seemed to turn inwards.

"Ah? So that was it! I noticed she'd got a kind of red mark on her temple, half under the wig. I supposed she had hit her head on the edge of the marble bench when she collapsed—"

"No," said Bell. "She was beaten to death with a lead-loaded walking stick. The laboratory can prove that."

Distant fans whirred and hummed: the air was astir. Mrs. Bradford slid up from her chair, with a lithe motion for a woman so stocky, and began to back away.

"Don't you try to bluff a woman that's always been honest," she said, in a thin unnatural voice. "It was an accident, I tell you! Either heart failure, or hitting her head when she fell. It's happened before, when people can't stand the heat. And now you come and tell me—"

"Just a moment," said Bell quietly.

The tone of his voice made Mrs. Bradford pause, her hand half-lifted as though to take an oath.

"Now tell me," Bell continued, "did you see Miss Loring arrive here on Monday night?"

"Yes."

"How did she look? Ill, for instance?"

"Very ill. Lucy at the desk can tell you that. All shaky and funny. That's why I kept an eye on her."

"What happened then? No, I'm not accusing you of lying! Just tell me what happened."

Mrs. Bradford stared at him.

"Well . . . she went to one of the booths, and took off her clothes, and wrapped herself up in that cotton robe they wear, and went on to the hot rooms. I'm manager here: I don't act as masseuse usually, but I did it for her so that nobody shouldn't discover about the wig. I was nervous because she looked so ill. Afterwards I went up to the steam room, and there she was lying on the floor. Alone. Dead. I thought: Holy mother, I knew something would happen, and now—!"

"Go on."

"Well, what could I do? I couldn't carry her down to where her clothes were, because there were ten or a dozen other women here and they'd know what had happened."

"Go on."

"I had to get rid of her. I *had* to! I ran down and rolled her clothes and handbag up into a bundle and ran back up to the steam room. But I couldn't dress her there, because somebody might have walked in any minute. Don't you see?"

"Go on."

Mrs. Bradford moistened her lips. "Upstairs there's a door that leads out into an alley by the hotel. I slung her over my shoulder, and carried her out into the blackout wrapped in that cotton robe.

"I knew where to put her, too. Beside her handbag there'd been a big key, with a cardboard label saying it was the key to the garden in Victoria Square. I got her into the garden and sat her down on the first bench I came to. Then I started to dress her properly so nobody shouldn't know she'd ever been at the baths. I'd just got the underclothes on, and slipped the shoes on her feet so they'd be handy, when I heard a noise. I slipped back a little; and it's a good thing I did, for there was a great big blazing light—"

"Did I not say it?" murmured Jacqueline softly. "Did I not say the policeman has come in and interrupted her?"

"So I hopped it," concluded Mrs. Bradford, wiping her eyes. "I still had the cotton robe in my hand; but I forgot the wig and spectacles." Her face grew harsh and ugly. "That's what I did. I admit it. But that's all I did. She wasn't murdered in these baths!"

"As a matter of fact," replied Bell calmly, "I don't think she was. For all practical purposes, I think she was dead before she got here."

It was not easy to frighten Jacqueline Dubois. Only her imagination could do this. Her imagination conjured up wild visions of a dead woman in a red wig, the face already bloodless, walking into the foyer and confronting the attendant with blind black spectacles. It unnerved her. Even the humming of the fans unnerved her.

She cried out at Bell, but he silenced her.

"Queer thing," Bell mused. "I was telling Mr. Hoyt yesterday about a friend of mine. He was struck by the door of a railway carriage. He got up, brushed himself, assured everybody he wasn't hurt, went home, and collapsed an hour later with concussion of the brain. Such cases are common enough. You'll find plenty of them in Taylor's *Medical Jurisprudence*. That's what happened to Hazel Loring, in my opinion."

"You mean . . ."

"Mind!" Bell held hard to his caution. "Mind, I don't promise anything. Whether they'll want to hold you as accessory after the fact, Mrs. Bradford, I can't say. But, just between ourselves, I don't think you've got a lot to worry about.

"As I read it, Hazel Loring met the murderer in the garden at ten o'clock. There was a fight. The murderer struck her down and left her for dead. She got to her feet, thought she was all right, and came over here to the baths. In the steam room she collapsed and died. And you, finding the key to the garden, carried her body straight back to the real scene of the crime."

Bell drew a deep breath and his forehead wrinkled in thought.

"Talk about the wheel revolving!" he added. "All we want now is the murderer."

Edward Hoyt, released from the nursing home on Friday morning, took a taxi to Victoria Square under a bright, watery sun which was turning the snow to slush.

The exposure of Hazel Loring's racket, appearing in Thursday's *Daily Record*, was both a revelation and a revolution. It was a real scoop for the paper.

MacGrath, the news editor, danced the saraband. Henry Ashwin, the photographer, swallowed three quick whiskies and went out to find Jacqueline. Sir Claude Champion, owner of the *Daily Banner*, swallowed aspirins and vowed vengeance. All over the country it made wives pause in the very act of the patent exercises. Yet nobody was satisfied. Through the excitement ran a bitter flavor: however much of a fake the dead woman might have been, still she was dead by a brutal attack and her murderer still walked and talked in the town.

Edward Hoyt's face seemed to express this as he went up the steps of number 22. The door was opened for him by Alice Farmer, whose face brightened with joy. And this performance was watched with interest by Jacqueline Dubois and Henry Ashwin, the photographer, lurking behind the railings in the garden opposite.

"The point is," insisted Ashwin, giving her a sideways glance, "what is Bell doing? He now seems to think you're a kind of mascot—"

Jacqueline was not without modest pride.

"He think I am pretty good," she admitted. "I just try to give him ideas, that is all. But between you and me and the pikestaff, I do not know *what* he is doing. He is very mysterious."

"Beaten, eh? Shame on you!"

Jacqueline's color went up like a flag.

"I am not beaten either! But maybe perhaps I am wrong about him. First I think he is only a stupid Englishman, all dumb and polite, and now I think his mind may work funnier than I expect. He keep talking about lights."

"Lights?"

"Big lights. Oi! Look!"

She pointed. There was another visitor for number 22. Mrs. Eunice Bradford, almost unrecognizable in an oversmart outfit and a saucer hat, strode briskly along the street. The morning sun streamed full on the doorway; they saw Mrs. Bradford punching the doorbell with assurance. She was admitted by Miss Farmer.

"Got 'em taped," said the voice of Inspector Bell.

Jacqueline felt a shock. Bell, followed by Sergeant Rankin and a uniformed constable, was coming across the slush-marshy garden with the sun behind him.

"Don't sneak up like that, Inspector!" protested Ashwin. He nodded towards the house across the way. "So it's a gathering of the suspects, eh?"

"It is."

"And you're going to nab somebody over there?"

"I am."

Jacqueline began to shiver, though the air held an almost spring-like thaw. Bell's expression was guileless.

"You can come along, if you like," he said to Jacqueline. "In fact, I might say you've got to come along. A good deal of my evidence depends on you, though you may not know it. I'll give you some poetic justice too. You've spent half your time in this business worming things out of people or pinching things from people. I've taken the liberty of pinching something from you."

"You go away!" said Jacqueline. "Please, what is this? I do not understand."

Bell opened the briefcase he was carrying. "You remember," he said, "how you solved your part of the problem by deducing something from the unbuttoned shoes in a photograph taken the morning after the murder?"

"Yes."

Bell drew a large glazed oblong of paper from the briefcase. It was the picture they had all seen: Hazel Loring's body on the bench, every detail sharp-etched with the shadows behind.

"Is this the same photograph?"

"Ah, zut! Of course it is."

Bell glanced inquiringly at Ashwin.

"You confirm that? This is the same photograph you took at about ten o'clock on Tuesday morning?"

Ashwin, with a face of hideous perplexity, merely nodded. Sergeant Rankin suddenly guffawed: a sharp sound which he covered up with a cough.

"Then it's very curious," said Bell. He held up the photograph. "It's the most curious thing we've come across yet. Look at it. Every shadow in this picture, as we see, falls straight behind bench and body.

Yet the bench, as we've known from the start, faces due west and has its back to the east.

"Look at the bench now. See how the shadows fall in front of it along the path. In other words, this photograph couldn't possibly have been taken in the morning. It couldn't have been taken at any time during the day, because the sun was gone in the afternoon. That bright light and those dead-black shadows could have been made in only one way. The photograph must have been taken, after dark, by the glare of a flashbulb: which was the 'great big blazing light' Mrs. Bradford saw when she—"

Jacqueline screamed.

One face in the group altered and squeezed up as though it were crumpling like a wet paper mask. A pair of hands flung forward to grab the photograph from Bell and rend it in pieces; but Sergeant Rankin's arm was round the man's throat and the two of them went over backwards in a crashing cartwheel on the path.

Bell's voice remained level.

"Henry Ashwin, I arrest you for the murder of your wife, Hazel Loring. I have to warn you that anything you say will be taken down in writing and may be used as evidence against you at your trial."

To Jacqueline, that night, Bell was a little more communicative.

"There's nothing much to tell," he said off handedly. "Once I got Hoyt's tip, and we put the organization to work, it didn't take long to discover that one Hazel Ann Loring and one Henry Fielding Ashwin had been married at the Hampstead Registry Office in 1933." He grinned. "That's where the official police will always score over you amateurs."

Jacqueline was agog.

"He try the blackmail on her. Yes?"

"Yes, in a small way. A nasty bit of work is Ashwin. In the first place, he was a no-good who would take some explaining; in the second place, she couldn't afford to have the gaff blown about her racket. That was why Ashwin was pretending to make what you call goo-goo eyes at Hazel Loring's maid: he had to have some excuse for hanging round the house so constantly.

"But Hazel was getting fed up with it. She issued an ultimatum, and arranged to meet him in the garden. There was a wild, blind row: both of them, we know, had ugly tempers. Ashwin laid her out, and then ran. It wasn't a planned crime: he just ran.

"After he'd had a couple of drinks, he began to get scared. He'd left that stick behind. He didn't *think* they could trace it to him; but suppose they did? So he went back to the square—and must have thought he was losing his mind. For he saw Eunice Bradford bringing the body back.

"In any case, he thought it was a gift from heaven. If he could frame any evidence against her, Mrs. Bradford would swing for the crime as sure as eggs. He set his flashbulb and fired blindly for a picture. But in the dark his aim was bad; Mrs. Bradford had jumped back; and he didn't get her in the picture at all. He saw that when he developed the picture. Of course he'd never have shown that photograph to anyone. He'd have torn up the pictures and destroyed the negative. Only—"

Jacqueline nodded radiantly.

"I pinch it from him," she declared, with pride. "And then he have to stew up some explanation for it."

"Yes. Of course, I saw that the dim, paper-covered torch of the policeman who discovered the body could never have produced that 'great big blazing light' described by Mrs. Bradford. Then, once you looked closely at the photograph and noticed the fall of the shadows, that tore it. I gathered the obvious suspects in one house to throw Ashwin off his guard; and got him to confirm his previous story before police witnesses. That's all."

He chuckled.

"There's one good result from it, anyway," he added. "Edward Hoyt and Alice Farmer should be extremely comfortable with each other."

But Jacqueline was not listening. Her eyes were shining and absorbed. She put her hand with innocent fervor on his arm.

"If I had not pinch the picture," she said, "and if I had not deduce those things, maybe you would not have solved the case. Eh?"

"Maybe not."

"You do not think I am such a goofy little beasel. No?"

"No."

"In fact, day by day in every way I am becoming indispensable to you. Yes?"

The hair froze on Bell's head. "Hold on! Take it easy! I didn't say that!"

"But *I* say it," declared Jacqueline, with fiery earnestness. "I think we go well together, yes? I pinch things for you; and if you like you can be my Conscience and go gobble-gobble at me, but you do not be too mad when I help you. Then each day I get an exclusive inter—inter—"

"Interview," suggested Bell.

"Okay, if you say so, though my knowledge of English is formidable and you do not have to tell me. If I like you very much and am a good girl, will you let me help with the detecting when I ask to?"

Bell looked down at the flushed, lovely face.

"I will," he said, "*ou je serai l'oncle d'un singe!* My knowledge of French is formidable too."

Woodrow Wilson's Necktie

PATRICIA HIGHSMITH

Patricia Highsmith (1921–1995) was known for turning the conventional mystery story upside down in her novels and short fiction. Either by showing the world through the eyes of a criminal or starting with a (relatively) innocent man or woman and showing their gradual descent into crime, as in *Strangers on a Train,* or madness, examined in the novel *Edith's Diary,* she redefined the suspense story, combining subtle social or political commentary with the study of crime in her elegantly plotted stories. Her work attracted interest from Hollywood, most notable *Strangers on a Train* which was adapted and filmed by Alfred Hitchcock. The movie has been hailed as a masterpiece of taut, white-knuckled suspense. The Ripley novels have also garnered interest, with a version of *The Talented Mr. Ripley* released in the year 1999.

The façade of MADAME THIBUALT'S WAXWORK HORRORS glittered and throbbed with red and yellow lights, even in the daytime. Knobs of golden balls—the yellow lights—pulsated amid the red lights, attracting the eye and holding it.

Clive Wilkes loved the place, the inside and the outside equally. Since he was a delivery boy for a grocery store, it was easy for him to say that a certain delivery had taken him longer than had been expected—he'd had to wait for Mrs. So-and-so to get home because the doorman had told him she was due back any minute, or he'd had to go five blocks to find some change because Mrs. Smith had had only a twenty-dollar bill. At these spare moments—and Clive managed one or two a week—he visited MADAME THIBAULT'S WAXWORK HORRORS.

Inside the establishment you went through a dark passage—to be put in the mood—and then you were confronted by a bloody murder scene on the left: a girl with long blond hair was sticking a knife into the neck of an old man who sat at a kitchen table eating his dinner. His dinner consisted of two wax frankfurters and wax sauerkraut. Then came the Lindbergh kidnapping scene, with Hauptmann climbing down a ladder outside a nursery window; you could see the top of the ladder outside the window, and the top half of Hauptmann's figure, clutching the little boy. Also there was Marat in his bath with Charlotte nearby. And Christie with his stocking, throttling a woman.

Clive loved every tableau, and they never became stale. But he didn't look at them with the solemn, vaguely startled expression of the other people who looked at them. Clive was inclined to smile, even to laugh. They were amusing. So why not laugh?

Farther on in the museum were the torture chambers—one old, one modern, purporting to show Twentieth Century torture methods in Nazi Germany and in French Algeria. Madame Thibault—who Clive strongly suspected did not exist—kept up to date. There were the Kennedy assassination and the Tate massacre, of course, and some murder that had happened only a month ago somewhere.

Clive's first definite ambition in regard to MADAME THIBAULT'S WAXWORK HORRORS museum was to spend a night there. This he did one night, providently taking along a cheese sandwich in his pocket. It was fairly easy to accomplish. Clive knew that three people worked in the museum proper—down in the bowels, as he thought of it, though the museum was on street level—while a fourth, a plumpish middle-aged man in a nautical cap, sold tickets at a booth in front. The three who worked in the bowels were two men and a woman; the woman, also plump and with curly brown hair and glasses and about 40, took the tickets at the end of the dark corridor, where the museum proper began.

One of the inside men lectured constantly, though not more than half the people ever bothered to listen. "Here we see the fanatical expression of the true murderer, captured by the supreme wax artistry of Madame Thibault"—and so on. The other inside man had black hair and black-rimmed glasses like the woman, and he just drifted around, shooing away kids who wanted to climb into the tableaux, maybe watching for pickpockets, or maybe protecting women from unpleasant assaults in the semidarkness. Clive didn't know.

He only knew it was quite easy to slip into one of the dark corners or into a nook next to one of the Iron Molls—maybe even into one of the Iron Molls; but slender as he was, the spikes might poke into him, Clive thought, so he ruled out this idea. He had observed that people were gently urged out around 9:15 P.M., as the museum closed at 9:30 P.M. And lingering as late as possible one evening, Clive had learned that there was a sort of cloakroom for the staff behind a door in one back corner, from which direction he had also heard the sound of a toilet flushing.

So one night in November, Clive concealed himself in the shadows, which were abundant, and listened to the three people as they got ready to leave. The woman—whose name turned out to be Mildred—was lingering to take the money box from Fred, the ticket seller, and to count it and deposit it somewhere in the cloakroom. Clive was not interested in the money. He was interested only in spending a night in the place and being able to boast he had.

"Night, Mildred—see you tomorrow," called one of the men.

"Anything else to do? I'm leaving now," said Mildred. "Boy, am I tired! But I'm still going to watch Dragon Man tonight."

"Dragon Man," the other man repeated, uninterested.

Evidently the ticket seller, Fred, left from the front of the building after handing in the money box, and in fact Clive recalled seeing him close up the front once, cutting the lights from inside the entrance door, then locking the door and barring it on the outside.

Clive stood in a nook by an Iron Moll. When he heard the back door shut and the key turn in the lock, he waited for a moment in delicious silence, aloneness, and suspense, and then ventured out. He went first, on tiptoe, to the room where they kept their coats, because he had never seen it. He had brought matches—also cigarettes, though smoking was not allowed, according to several signs—and with the aid of a match he found the light switch. The room contained an old desk, four metal lockers, a tin wastebasket, an umbrella stand, and some books in a bookcase against a grimy wall that had once been white. Clive slid open a drawer and found the well-worn wooden box which he had once seen the ticket seller carrying in through the front door. The box was locked. He could walk out with the box, Clive thought, but he didn't care to, and he considered this rather decent of himself. He gave the box a wipe with the side of his hand, not forgetting the bottom where his fingertips had touched. That was funny, he thought, wiping something he wasn't going to steal.

Clive set about enjoying the night. He found the lights and put them on so that the booths with the gory tableaux were all illuminated. He was hungry, took one bite of his sandwich, then put it back in the paper napkin in his pocket. He sauntered slowly past the John F. Kennedy assassination—Mrs. Kennedy and the doctors bending anxiously over the white table on which JFK lay. This time, Hauptmann's descent of the ladder made Clive giggle. Charles Lindbergh, Jr.'s face looked so untroubled that one would think he might be sitting on the floor of his nursery, playing with blocks.

Clive swung a leg over a metal bar and climbed into the Judd-Snyder tableau. It gave him a thrill to be standing right *with* them, inches from the throttling-from-behind which the lover of the woman was administering to the husband. Clive put a hand out and touched the red-paint blood that was seeming to come from the man's throat where the cord pressed deep. Clive also touched the cool cheekbones of the victim. The popping eyes were of glass, vaguely disgusting, and Clive did not touch those.

Two hours later he was singing church hymns, *Nearer My God to*

Thee and *Jesus Wants Me for a Sunbeam*. Clive didn't know all the words. And he smoked.

By two in the morning he was bored and tried to get out by both the front door and the back, but couldn't—both were barred on the outside. He had thought of having a hamburger at an all-night diner between here and home. However, his enforced incarceration didn't bother him, so he finished the now-dry cheese sandwich and slept for a bit on three straight chairs which he arranged in a row. It was so uncomfortable that he knew he'd wake up in a while, which he did—at 5 A.M. He washed his face, then went for another look at the wax exhibits. This time he took a souvenir—Woodrow Wilson's necktie.

As the hour of 9:00 approached—MADAME THIBAULT'S WAXWORK HORRORS opened at 9:30 A.M.—Clive hid himself in an excellent spot, behind one of the tableaux whose backdrop was a black-and-gold Chinese screen. In front of the screen was a bed and in the bed lay a wax man with a handlebar mustache, who was supposed to have been poisoned by his wife.

The public began to trickle in shortly after 9:30 A.M., and the taller, more solemn man began to mumble his boring lecture. Clive had to wait till a few minutes past ten before he felt safe enough to mingle with the crowd and make his exit, with Woodrow Wilson's necktie rolled up in his pocket. He was a bit tired, but happy—though on second thought, who would he tell about it? Joey Vrasky, that dumb cluck who worked behind the counter at Simmons' Grocery? Hah! Why bother? Joey didn't deserve a good story. Clive was half an hour late for work.

"I'm sorry, Mr. Simmons, I overslept," Clive said hastily, but he thought quite politely, as he came into the store. There was a delivery job awaiting him. Clive took his bicycle and put the carton on a platform in front of the handlebars.

Clive lived with his mother, a thin highly strung woman who was a saleswoman in a shop that sold stockings, girdles, and underwear. Her husband had left her when Clive was nine. She had no other children. Clive had quit high school a year before graduation, to his mother's regret, and for a year he had done nothing but lie around the house or stand on street corners with his pals. But Clive had never been very chummy with any of them, for which his mother was thankful, as she considered them a worthless lot. Clive had had the delivery job at Simmons' for nearly a year now, and his mother felt that he was settling down.

When Clive came home that evening at 6:30 P.M. he had a story ready for his mother. Last night he had run into his old friend Richie, who was in the Army and home on leave, and they had sat up at Richie's house talking so late that Richie's parents had invited him to stay over, and Clive had slept on the couch. His mother accepted this explanation. She made a supper of baked beans, bacon, and eggs.

There was really no one to whom Clive felt like telling his exploit of the night. He couldn't have borne someone looking at him and saying, "Yeah? So what?" because what he had done had taken a bit of planning, even a little daring. He put Woodrow Wilson's tie among his others that hung over a string on the inside of his closet door. It was a gray silk tie, conservative and expensive-looking. Several times that day Clive imagined one of the two men in the museum, or maybe the woman named Mildred, glancing at Woodrow Wilson and exclaiming, "Hey! What happened to Woodrow Wilson's tie, I wonder?"

Each time Clive thought of this he had to duck his head to hide a smile.

After twenty-four hours, however, the exploit had begun to lose its charm and excitement. Clive's excitement only rose again—and it could rise two or three times a day—whenever he cycled past the twinkling façade of MADAME THIBAULT'S WAXWORK HORRORS. His heart would give a leap, his blood would run a little faster, and he would think of all the motionless murders going on in there, and all the stupid faces of Mr. and Mrs. Johnny Q. Public gaping at them. But Clive didn't even buy another ticket—price 65 cents—to go in and look at Woodrow Wilson and see that his tie was missing and his collar button showing—his work.

Clive did get another idea one afternoon, a hilarious idea that would make the public sit up and take notice. Clive's ribs trembled with suppressed laughter as he pedaled toward Simmons', having just delivered a bag of groceries.

When should he do it? Tonight? No, best to take a day or so to plan it. It would take brains. And silence. And sure movements—all the things Clive admired.

He spent two days thinking about it. He went to his local snack bar and drank beer and played the pinball machines with his pals. The pinball machines had pulsating lights too—*More Than One Can Play* and *It's More Fun To Compete*—but Clive thought only of MADAME THIBAULT'S as he stared at the rolling, bouncing balls that mounted a score he cared nothing about. It was the same when he looked at the rainbow-colored jukebox whose blues, reds, and yellows undulated, and when he went over to drop a coin in it. He was thinking of what he was going to do in MADAME THIBAULT'S WAXWORK HORRORS.

On the second night, after a supper with his mother, Clive went to MADAME THIBAULT'S and bought a ticket. The old guy who sold tickets barely looked at people, he was so busy making change and tearing off the stubs, which was just as well. Clive went in at 9:00 P.M.

He looked at the tableaux, though they were not so fascinating to him tonight as they had been before. Woodrow Wilson's tie was still missing, as if no one had noticed it, and Clive chuckled over this. He remembered that the solemn-faced pickpocket-watcher—the drifting snoop—had been the last to leave the night Clive had stayed, so Clive assumed he had the keys, and therefore he ought to be the last to be killed.

The woman was the first. Clive hid himself beside one of the Iron Molls again, while the crowd ambled out, and when Mildred walked by him, in her hat and coat, to leave by the back door, having just said something to one of the men in the exhibition hall, Clive stepped out and wrapped an arm around her throat from behind.

She made only a small *ur-rk* sound.

Clive squeezed her throat with his hands, stopping her voice. At last she slumped, and Clive dragged her into a dark, recessed corner to the left of the cloakroom. He knocked an empty cardboard box of some kind over, but it didn't make enough noise to attract the attention of the two men.

"Mildred's gone?" one of the men asked.

"I think she's in the office."

"No, she's not." The owner of this voice had already gone into the corridor where Clive crouched over Mildred and had looked into the empty cloakroom where the light was still on. "She's left. Well, I'm calling it a day too."

Clive stepped out then and encircled this man's neck in the same manner. The job was more difficult, because the man struggled, but Clive's arm was thin and strong; he acted with swiftness and knocked the man's head against the wooden floor.

"What's going on?" The thump had brought the second man.

This time Clive tried a punch to the man's jaw, but missed and hit his neck. However, this so stunned the man—the little solemn fellow, the snoop—that a quick second blow was easy, and then Clive was able to take him by the shirtfront and bash his head against the plaster wall which was harder than the wooden floor. Then Clive made sure that all three were dead. The two men's heads were bloody. The woman was bleeding slightly from her mouth. Clive reached for the keys in the second man's pockets. They were in his left trousers pocket and with them was a penknife. Clive also took the knife.

Then the taller man moved slightly. Alarmed, Clive opened the pearl-handled penknife and plunged it into the man's throat three times.

Close call, Clive thought, as he checked again to make sure they were all dead. They most certainly were, and that was most certainly real blood, not the red paint of MADAME THIBAULT'S WAXWORK HORRORS. Clive switched on the lights for the tableaux and went into the exhibition hall for the interesting task of choosing exactly the right places for the three corpses.

The woman belonged in Marat's bath—not much doubt about that. Clive debated removing her clothing, but decided against it, simply because she would look much funnier sitting in a bath wearing a fur-trimmed coat and hat. The figure of Marat sent him off into laughter. He'd expected sticks for legs, and nothing between the legs, because you couldn't see any more of Marat than from the middle of his torso up; but Marat had no legs at all and his wax body ended just below the waist in a fat stump which was planted on a wooden platform so that it would not topple. This crazy waxwork Clive carried into the cloakroom and placed squarely in the middle of the desk. He then carried the woman—who weighed a good deal—onto the Marat scene and put her in the bath. Her hat fell off, and he pushed it on again, a bit over one eye. Her bloody mouth hung open.

Good lord, it *was* funny!

Now for the men. Obviously, the one whose throat he had knifed would look good in the place of the old man who was eating wax franks and sauerkraut, because the girl behind him was supposed to be stabbing him in the throat. This took Clive some fifteen minutes. Since the figure of the old man was in a seated position, Clive put him on the toilet off the cloakroom. It was terribly amusing to see the old man seated on the toilet, throat apparently bleeding, a knife in one hand and a fork in the other. Clive lurched against the door jamb, laughing loudly, not even caring if someone heard him, because it was so comical it was even worth getting caught for.

Next, the little snoop. Clive looked around him and his eye fell on the Woodrow Wilson scene which had depicted the signing of the armistice in 1918. A wax figure sat at a huge desk signing something, and that was the logical place for a man whose head was almost split open. With some difficulty Clive got the pen out of the wax man's fingers, laid it to one side on the desk, and carried the figure—it didn't weigh much—into the cloakroom, where Clive seated him at the desk, rigid arms in an attitude of writing. Clive stuck a ballpoint pen into his right hand. Now for the last heave. Clive saw that his jacket was now quite spotted with blood and he would have to get rid of it, but so far there was no blood on his trousers.

Clive dragged the second man to the Woodrow Wilson tableau, lifted him up, and rolled him toward the desk. He got him onto the chair, but the head toppled forward onto the green-blottered desk, onto the blank wax pages, and the pen barely stood upright in the limp hand.

But it was done. Clive stood back and smiled. Then he listened. He sat down on a straight chair and rested for a few minutes, because his heart was beating fast and he suddenly realized that every muscle in his body was tired. Ah, well, he now had the keys. He could lock up, go home, and have a good night's rest, because he wanted to be ready to enjoy tomorrow.

Clive took a sweater from one of the male figures in a log-cabin tableau of some kind. He had to pull the sweater down over the feet of the waxwork to get it off, because the arms would not bend; it stretched the neck of the sweater, but he couldn't help that. Now the wax figure had a sort of bib for a shirtfront, and naked arms and chest.

Clive wadded up his jacket and went everywhere with it, erasing fingerprints from whatever he thought he had touched. He turned the lights off, made his way carefully to the back door, locked and barred it behind him, and would have left the keys in a mailbox if there had been one; but there wasn't, so he dropped the keys on the rear doorstep. In a wire rubbish basket he found some newspapers; he wrapped up his jacket in them and walked on with it until he found another wire rubbish basket, where he forced the bundle down among candy wrappers, beer cans, and other trash.

"A new sweater?" his mother asked that night.

"Richie gave it to me—for luck."

Clive slept like the dead, too tired even to laugh again at the memory of the old man sitting on the toilet.

The next morning Clive was standing across the street when the ticket seller arrived just before 9:30 A.M. By 9:35 A.M. only four people had gone in; but Clive could not wait any longer, so he crossed the street and bought a ticket. Now the ticket seller was doubling as ticket taker, and telling people, "Just go on in. Everybody's late this morning."

The ticket man stepped inside the door to put on some lights, then walked all the way into the place to put on the display lights for the tableaux, which worked from switches in the hall that led to the cloakroom. And the funny thing, to Clive who was walking behind him, was that the ticket man didn't notice anything odd, didn't even notice Mildred in her hat and coat sitting in Marat's bathtub.

The other customers so far were a man and a woman, a boy of fourteen or so in sneakers, alone apparently, and a single man. They looked expressionlessly at Mildred in the tub as if they thought it quite "normal," which would have sent Clive into paroxysms of mirth, except that his heart was thumping madly and he could hardly breathe for the suspense. Also, the man with his face in franks and sauerkraut brought no surprise either. Clive was a bit disappointed.

Two more people came in, a man and a woman.

Then at last, in front of the Woodrow Wilson tableau, there was a reaction. One of the women, clinging to her husband's arm, asked, "Was someone shot when the armistice was signed?"

"I don't know. I don't *think* so," the man replied vaguely.

Clive's laughter pressed like an explosion in his chest; he spun on his heel to control himself, and he had the feeling he knew *all* about history, and that no one else did. By now, of course, the real blood had turned to a rust color. The green blotter was now splotched, and blood had dripped down the side of the desk.

A woman on the other side of the room, where Mildred was, let out a scream.

A man laughed, but only briefly.

Suddenly everything happened. A woman shrieked, and at the same time a man yelled, "My God, it's *real!*"

Clive saw a man climbing up to investigate the corpse with his face in the frankfurters.

"The blood's *real!* It's a *dead* man!"

Another man—one of the public—slumped to the floor. He had fainted.

The ticket seller came bustling in. "What's the trouble here?"

"Coupla corpses—*real* ones!"

Now the ticket seller looked at Marat's bathtub and fairly jumped into the air with surprise. "Holy Christmas! *Holy* cripes!—it's *Mildred!*"

"And this one!"

"And the one here!"

"My God, got to—got to call the police!" said the ticket seller.

One man and woman left hurriedly. But the rest lingered, shocked, fascinated.

The ticket seller had run into the cloakroom, where the telephone was, and Clive heard him yell something. He'd seen the man at the desk, of course, the wax man, and the half body of Marat on the desk.

Clive thought it was time to drift out, so he did, sidling his way through a group of people peering in the front door, perhaps intending to come in because there was no ticket seller.

That was good, Clive thought. That was all right. Not bad. Not bad at all.

He had not intended to go to work that day, but suddenly he thought it wiser to check in and ask for the day off. Mr. Simmons was of course as sour as ever when Clive said he was not feeling well, but as Clive held his stomach and appeared weak, there was little old Simmons could do. Clive left the grocery. He had brought with him all his ready cash, about $23.

Clive wanted to take a long bus ride somewhere. He realized that suspicion might fall on him, if the ticket seller remembered his coming to MADAME THIBAULT's often, or especially if he remembered Clive being there last night; but this really had little to do with his desire to take a bus ride. His longing for a bus ride was simply, somehow, irresistible. He bought a ticket westward for $8 and change, one way. This brought him, by about 7:00 P.M., to a good-sized town in Indiana, whose name Clive paid no attention to.

The bus spilled a few passengers, Clive included, at a terminal, where there was a cafeteria and a bar. By now Clive was curious about the newspapers, so he went to the newsstand near the street door of the cafeteria. And there were the headlines:

Triple Murder in Waxworks

Mass Murder in Museum

Mystery Killer Strikes: Three Dead in Waxworks

Clive liked the last one best. He bought the three newspapers, and stood at the bar with a beer.

"This morning at 9:30 A.M., ticket man Fred J. Carmody and several of the public who had come to see Madame Thibault's Waxwork Horrors, a noted attraction of this city, were confronted by three genuine corpses among the displays. They were the bodies of Mrs. Mildred Veery, 41; George P. Hartley, 43; and Richard K. McFadden, 37, all employed at the waxworks museum. The two men were killed by concussion and stabbing, and the woman by strangulation. Police are searching for clues on the premises. The murders are believed to have taken place shortly before 10:00 P.M. last evening, when the three employees were about to leave the museum. The murderer or murderers may have been among the last patrons of the museum before closing time at 9:30 P.M. It is thought that he or they may have concealed themselves somewhere in the museum until the rest of the patrons had left. . . ."

Clive was pleased. He smiled as he sipped his beer. He hunched over the papers, as if he did not wish the rest of the world to share his pleasure, but this was not true. After a few minutes Clive stood up and looked to the right and left to see if anyone else among the men and women at the bar was also reading the story. Two men were reading newspapers, but Clive could not tell if they were reading about him, because their newspapers were folded.

Clive lit a cigarette and went through all three newspapers to see if any clue to him was mentioned. He found nothing. One paper said specifically that Fred J. Carmody had not noticed any person or persons entering the museum last evening who looked suspicious.

". . . Because of the bizarre arrangement of the victims and of the displaced wax figures in the exhibition, in whose places the victims were put, police are looking for a psychopathic killer. Residents of the area have been warned by radio and television to take special precautions on the streets and to keep their houses locked."

Clive chuckled over that one. Psychopathic killer! He was sorry about the lack of detail, the lack of humor in the three reporters' stories. They might have said something about the old guy sitting on the toilet. Or the fellow signing the armistice with the back of his head bashed in. Those were strokes of genius. Why didn't they appreciate them?

When he had finished his beer, Clive walked out onto the sidewalk. It was now dark and the streetlights were on. He enjoyed looking around in the new town, looking into shop windows. But he was aiming for a hamburger place, and he went into the first one he came to. It was a diner made up to look like a crack railway car.

Clive ordered a hamburger and a cup of coffee. Next to him were two Western-looking men in cowboy boots and rather soiled broad-brimmed hats. Was one a sheriff, Clive wondered? But they were talking, in a drawl, about acreage somewhere. Land. They were hunched over hamburgers and coffee, one so close that his elbow kept touching Clive's. Clive was reading his newspapers all over again and he had propped one against the napkin container in front of him.

One of the men asked for a napkin and disturbed Clive, but Clive smiled and said in a friendly way, "Did you read about the murders in the waxworks?"

The man looked blank for a moment, then said, "Yep, saw the headlines."

"Someone killed the three people who worked in the place. Look." There was a photograph in one of the papers, but Clive didn't much like it because it showed the corpses lined up on the floor. He would have preferred Mildred in the bathtub.

"Yeah," said the Westerner, edging away from Clive as if he didn't like him.

"The bodies were put into a few of the exhibits. Like the wax figures. They say that, but they don't show a picture of it," said Clive.

"Yeah," said the Westerner, and went on eating.

Clive felt let down and somehow insulted. His face grew a little warm as he stared back at his newspapers. In fact, anger was growing quickly inside him, making his heart go faster, as it always did when he passed MADAME THIBAULT'S WAXWORK HORRORS, though now the sensation was not at all pleasant.

Clive put on a smile, however, and turned to the man on his left again. "I mention it, because I did it. That's my work there." He gestured toward the picture of the corpses.

"Listen, boy," said the Westerner casually, "you just keep to yourself tonight. Okay? We ain't botherin' you, so don't you go botherin' us." He laughed a little, glancing at his companion.

His friend was staring at Clive, but looked away at once when Clive stared back.

This was a double rebuff, and quite enough for Clive. He got out his money and paid for his unfinished food with a dollar bill. He left the change and walked to the sliding-door exit.

"But y'know, maybe that guy ain't kiddin'," Clive heard one of the men say.

Clive turned and said, "I *ain't* kiddin'!" Then he went out into the night.

Clive slept at a Y.M.C.A. The next day he half-expected he would be picked up by a passing cop on the beat, but he wasn't. He got a lift to another town, nearer his hometown. The day's newspapers brought no mention of his name, and no mention of clues. In another café that evening, almost the identical conversation took place between Clive and a couple of fellows his own age. They didn't believe him. It was stupid of them, Clive thought, and he wondered if they were pretending? Or lying?

Clive hitched his way home and headed for the police station. He was curious as to what *they* would say. He imagined what his mother would say after he confessed. Probably the same thing she had said to her friends sometimes, or that she'd said to a policeman when he was sixteen and had stolen a car.

"Clive hasn't been the same since his father went away. I know he needs a man around the house, a man to look up to, imitate, you know. That's what people tell me. Since he was fourteen Clive's been asking me questions like, 'Who am I, anyway?' and 'Am I a person, mom?' " Clive could see and hear her in the police station.

"I have an important confession to make," Clive said to a deskman in the front.

The man's attitude was rude and suspicious, Clive thought, but he was told to walk to an office, where he spoke with a police officer who had gray hair, and a fat face. Clive told his story.

"Where do you go to school, Clive?"

"I don't. I'm eighteen." Clive told him about his job at Simmons' Grocery.

"Clive, you've got troubles, but they're not the ones you're talking about," said the officer.

Clive had to wait in a room, and nearly an hour later a psychiatrist was brought in. Then his mother. Clive became more and more impatient. They didn't believe him. They were saying his was a typical case of false confession in order to draw attention to himself. His mother's repeated statements about his asking questions like "Am I a person?" and "Who am I?" only seemed to corroborate the opinions of the psychiatrist and the police.

Clive was to report somewhere twice a week for psychiatric therapy.

He fumed. He refused to go back to Simmons' Grocery, but found another delivery job, because he liked having a little money in his pocket, and he was fast on his bicycle and honest with the change.

"You haven't *found* the murderer, have you?" Clive said to the police psychiatrist. "You're all the biggest bunch of jackasses I've ever seen in my life!"

The psychiatrist said soothingly, "You'll never get anywhere talking to people like that, boy."

Clive said, "Some perfectly ordinary strangers in Indiana said, 'Maybe that guy ain't kidding.' They had more sense than *you!*"

The psychiatrist smiled.

Clive smoldered. One thing might have helped to prove his

story—Woodrow Wilson's necktie, which still hung in his closet. But these dumb clucks damned well didn't deserve to see that tie. Even as he ate his suppers with his mother, went to the movies, and delivered groceries, he was planning. He'd do something more important next time—like starting a fire in the depths of a big building or planting a bomb somewhere or taking a machine gun up to some penthouse and letting 'em have it down on the street. Kill a hundred people at least, or a thousand. They'd have to come up in the building to get him. *Then* they'd know. *Then* they'd treat him like somebody who really existed, like somebody who deserved an exhibit of himself in MADAME THIBAULT'S HORRORS.

Nothing to Lose

FRANCES FYFIELD

Frances Fyfield is the best-selling author of seven crime novels. *A Question of Guilt, Trial by Fire, Deep Sleep, Shadow Play,* and *A Clear Conscience* feature Crown Prosecutor Helen West and the detective Geoffrey Bailey. As Frances Hegarty, she has also written two psychological thrillers, and a new novel, *Let's Dance,* was published in the UK by Viking in October 1995. Frances Fyfield is a practicing solicitor in London, currently working with the Crown Prosecution Service in a specialized capacity.

"You like my country?"

"Oh yes. I like. I like very much."

She liked the way he regarded her with a smile so full of sweetness it was better than a pineapple, fresh plucked and sold for cents, sliced for her as if she were royalty at a banquet. She liked the way no one on this West African beach looked askance at her figure, but smiled into her eyes. She liked: she liked so very much that she had almost lost her command of English. Much, very. Words of more than two syllables had slipped to the edge.

Wherever Audrey looked, she was blinded by what she saw. The sand was canary yellow, the sky was blue; the colors of cotton iridescent. All skin was as brown and various as the polished wood of her own antique furniture. Walnut, mahogany, oak, stained pine, nothing quite black. There was no such thing as really black wood. Black was not a color, it was an illusion.

"It's good? Is it good?"

"What?" For a moment, she was confused. What was good?

"The pineapple?"

"Oh, very."

"See you later."

"Not much later?"

"Of course." She watched his progress away from her and knew she would wait. For him to come back and look at her with the great kind eyes of a man who could not harm a fly.

Abdoulie had been squatting beside her heavy wooden sunbed, his pose laconic and restive, full of the spring of a tiger. He could look at ease with his elbows on his knees, his buttocks almost touching the sand, his long arms hanging loose until he spoke, and then his arms and fingers became the whirling tools of gestures. His was hesitant English, better by far than her own command of any foreign language, but still the level of fluency which would scarcely gain him admission to many an old-fashioned English secondary school. Mrs. Audrey Barett was aware of that. At home, she commuted from her village to teach difficult children in a school where half the problem was language. Punjabi versus English, own goal. In rapid reverse of her own childish belief that anyone who spoke a foreign language must be sublimely clever in order to get their tongues round all those sounds, she had advanced beyond the stage of imagining that either soul or intelligence could be gauged by what words came out of the mouth. Goodness had nothing to do with linguistics. She was also beyond imagining that her own admirable culture (and she did admire it, without apology) was better equipped than any other to rule the world. Audrey was an intelligent, middle-aged lady who read the quality newspapers and the better kind of novel which made one think. She was liberal and conservative in the same breath, her life without blame, and yet she still felt a sense of failure. No one had ever shouted admiration at Audrey Barett.

She chewed her nails, something she had always done. These days, she exerted control over her shyness.

"How many childrens, many, many, I think, Mrs. B., I think?" the hotel manager had asked, questioning her respectability and looking for a common denominator. People would always talk about their children, and in his family, any woman over fifty was obliged to be a grandmother by now.

"Thousands," she had said, grandly, startling him a little until she explained. She failed to add, two, of my own. Anxious girls, long gone, phoning every week from London, which is very different from the North of England, you know. Long gone, along with their father. Such is history. She could not quite imagine how she had come by them, except for the fact that hormones do not dictate the best choice of partner. Her own husband had been a little vicious; something she liked to forget and translated into a fondness for men who would never consider violence, but splendid results sometimes arrive as the result of bad mistakes, her best friend Molly was fond of saying, and the mistakes can last for years, as hers had done.

"Abdoulie is a good boy," the manager said meaningfully. "He will look after you." Then he bent toward her, speaking confidentially. "He has had a sad life, that boy."

* * *

The description of "boy" was inaccurate, Audrey thought when she saw him. Abdoulie was not a boy; he was a man of almost forty and he needed looking after. There were fabulous young men on this Gambian beach; Audrey watched them, early on the first morning, with the same disinterested fascination she might have given to a series of moving pictures. They worked their lithe bodies with exercise, hoping for a big break into the football team; fitness could catapult a boy into employment, even stardom. Abdoulie was not one of these. He was immensely tall, with dark coffee skin, a broad torso, and a slight squint in one eye. His wife and child had long since died in a fire, he said, and he was not eligible enough or prosperous enough to begin again. He did what he could, he said. He might have been, in his own estimation, too old for hope and he was not a glamorous young lion. Audrey would not have looked at him twice if he had been a youth. As he was, in the high street of the prosperous village where Audrey lived, under her gray skies and mirrored in the green eyes of the inhabitants, he would surely look like a god.

In all her careful and independent life, Audrey had avoided the trauma of rash deeds just as she normally avoided sunshine. Nor had she ever gone out looking for a man. Europe had been the setting for travels where she made friends with other woman travelers. Africa was a brutal assault on the senses similar to a series of blows from a spiked mallet. The poverty moved her to despair; the corruption angered her beyond belief, the smells made her delirious, the colors invaded her eyes, and the sun made her beautiful.

That was June: this was November. Abdoulie lay on her spare bed in the tiny spare bedroom of her small cottage and he had shrunk to fit. He had never been more prosperous, and he looked like a dying man. The squint in his eye and the crookedness of his teeth were more noticeable than they ever had been against the golden sand or the green vegetation which had crept down to the shore. He was as pale as he could be against her own white pillow. She perspired inside her blouse; the sweat on his skin shone like water.

She loved him to death and she wanted, more than anything else in the world, to kill him.

They had been married ten weeks.

They did not seem to notice a woman's age, these Africans with the endless smiles for the tourists. Abdoulie had trembled when she touched him; he seemed drawn to her by invisible strings. He did not look at girls; he looked at her as if she were beauty incarnate. They had managed a whole repertoire of jokes with the aid of a small store of words and the universal language of gesture. The understanding between them seemed infinite. Undeniably genuine, provided it had seen its limitation, which was the scenery in which it grew. Neither of them saw this flowering love as being bounded by the beach. It was too fine a plant to depend on habitat. The hotel manager smiled benignly and touched his nose.

"Love is in the air, I think, Mrs. Barett. Or is it spring?"

After all, she reasoned then, while wondering gleefully about how Molly would react, what did she have to lose? It did not seem to her any great act of courage to fall in love and propose marriage; in fact it would have taken far more courage to walk away and know that she would spend the rest of her life wondering how it might have been. Sitting in her cottage with the roses round the door after the next round of educational cuts she had come away to escape, prematurely retired, financially okay and emotionally barren. No pupils, no one to look after, no sense of purpose. The opposite beckoned when Abdoulie told her he loved her and that love always found a way. Audrey Barett would educate this funny, sorrowful man who did not know the meaning of malice; she lulled herself to sleep with visions of benign influence while the air-conditioned hotel room chilled her overheated body to ice; she dreamed of her own triumph.

Now she was not only contemplating murder most foul; she was set on it. The light from the lamp outside cast strange shadows on the ceiling as the branches of the tree waved at her in breezy mockery. Fool, fool, fool; sighing and scolding at her, telling there is no fool like a liberated one. Audrey had aged a decade in as many weeks. They had never quite known one another in the biblical sense, as her daughter primly defined it. That had been one of those stored-up treats, which remained stored until after the use-by date until forgotten and no longer relevant. The knowledge gave her an inkling of what it had been like to be proud. There was something about herself she had not relinquished, even if the failure to do so had been because he had not wanted it; both of them had been paralyzed. There was still a little piece of England, perfectly preserved.

"I'm going to get married, Molly."

"You never!"

"Well, he's a widower and I met him on holiday and we get along just fine, why not?" There had not been a single tremor of doubt as long as she had been acting alone, organizing things, booking his flight as soon as she got home, paying for it without a murmur, looking into the whole vexed business of entry, being appalled and outraged, all that. Easier by far than telling Molly or her daughters, which certainly took the air out of her lungs.

"He's black, of course," she added as a throwaway line, not courageous enough to add that black was an illusion of a color and it was finding him asleep outside her bedroom door which had been the final decision time. Abdoulie slept like an angel, but the whole cut of his body adjusted to a concrete floor. A man accustomed to such, without the option of a bed, was a man who deserved better. You could not do damage to a man who had nothing. You could only transform him.

Silence on the end of a phone line was unnerving.

"Congratulate me, darling?"

More silence.

"Say something then."

"I can't. You must be mad."

There was nothing like resistance to get her going and make her prove she was right. Audrey had always moved sideways in the face of conflict, found another way. She did not fight, she merged into shadows until the fuss was over and then came out triumphantly and went on as before. Besides, it was not so much her daughters and Molly she wanted to impress; it was neighbors who had seen her as dull, sensible, sexless Mrs. Barett, manless and dutiful this twenty years in an area where to be without a mate was to be without sin or life. Boring and sad, in other words. Audrey did not want that kind of respect, and there she would be, in the eyes of the newsagents, the butcher and the baker, in the eyes of her contemporaries at school, taking life in both hands and embarking on adventure. With a man so much taller, so much kinder, than any of theirs.

How was she going to kill him? It was three in the morning and the cold was complete. Poor little Abbie had pneumonia. All she had to do was open the window and strip the bed. He was used to sleeping on mud floors, let him try this.

Audrey tucked the duvet round his chin and sat back. There was never a violent burglar high on drugs and homicidally inclined when you wanted one. She would have paid such a beast to make a decent job of it, although she would have preferred to donate her life savings to an undertaker who would make it look as if her brand-new husband had died a natural and dignified death.

It was a long vigil, midnight to dawn, leaving far too much room for thought. There were many options, apart from the brutal remedy of ice. She could give him extra antibiotics, not known to kill a man, but never mind. Extra sleeping tablets. A parcel of antidepressants saved from a long and distant time, in the fridge. She could give him a cocktail of pills, she could poison him with the alcohol he loathed and say he had done it to himself. He was weak: he was sick to death. The doctor had given her an armory.

Abdoulie opened his eyes. He had the nerve to smile.

"Banjie," he murmured. "Banjie."

The name of a girl, the name of a town. Never her name.

Audrey was a neat-figured, neat-faced person with a good crop of outstanding gray-black hair, better-looking than many, but not so vain as to contemplate a wedding with white gown and all the jazz. Besides, they would need the money for other things. Someone would give him a job, surely, on the basis of his gentle temperament alone. Audrey had worked it all out on a piece of graph paper. It would take him a year, she reckoned; a year or less to learn the system. In the meantime, there was enough to buy him the clothes he patently adored, or there might have been if the man had the faintest idea of the value of money. He did not. He could not understand that if she was willing to buy him a suit worth eighty pounds, she would balk at the one priced at three hundred which he preferred. He did not understand why she lived in a cottage with low ceilings when there were other houses on the market. He did not (and she laughed herself sick at this one) understand the difference between rich and poor. If you had any money at all, you could buy the world. All this from a man who could sleep on concrete. Whose shoe size defeated condescending persons in shops and whose feet ached from the cold.

Abdoulie looked like a puzzled giant at their nuptials. These took place two weeks after his arrival. She had asked him if he was sure.

"Of course. Of course. I am very sure." He had fingered the cloth of his imperfect suit, doubtfully, smiled his crooked smile. Moved from the embrace of her arms, where her head nestled against his chest.

"Then," he said, "we make love."

Oh yes, he had caused a stir. But the modesty of the wedding, the Anglo-Saxon reserve of it, was simply another of her mistakes. He wanted her to look like something from television, the way she had never looked. He spoke his lines with the aplomb of Sir Laurence Olivier and he looked like Othello, but he might as well have killed her then, the way she would kill him now.

This kind of wedding meant nothing to him. He had no particular belief, he had said. Only the beliefs which were buried in his bones, made him mutter alien prayers and meant that this was no wedding at all. The same beliefs which made him a kind of thief.

Audrey was the sum of all her parts. She had wanted a man, this man, so gentle, malleable and different from the last, to complete the circle of her existence and surround that hole in the middle, making the vacuum a captive space which no longer bothered her. There's always that space, her friend Molly had said: we are none of us born to know contentment at all times. Look at what you have achieved, Audrey, dear; take pride in that. A lovely home with roses round the door, the liking and respect of your peers, freedom, the ability to live with grace.

"Grace is a virtue; virtue is a grace,
Grace is a naughty girl who will not wash her face. . . ."

Audrey chanted the words under her breath and wiped Abdoulie's face, roughly. She could put the pillow over his head, press down and wait: she doubted he would even fight because he had never had any fight in him.

It would be a lovely funeral, better than a wedding.

She sat and considered how his premature death would give back to her what she had lost. She could see herself following the coffin to the crematorium, dignified in grief, wearing her black suit, holding her head high, admired by those who would give her the accolades of their pity, talking about her admiringly behind her back. Oh, she's so brave. Brave to marry again in the first place, and them so happy, and him dying so soon. Extraordinarily sad. Tragic. She would be restored to her place in the pecking order, with the added cachet of widowhood and eccentricity. After all, no one had heard them quarrel. She and Abdoulie had never quarreled. They had merely been silent, with him frozen into ghostly quietness by his own despair. He could not admit mistakes; nor tell her in words the devastating homesickness which began to eat him like a cancer as soon as he finally got it into his mind that this was where, and how, he was supposed to live.

The despair had followed fast on the heels of novelty.

"What's so wrong with it, Abbie? Why do you negate me by hating everything about this place? Why have you fouled up everything important to me?"

She spoke softly, the venom in her mind turning to plaintive speculation. He hated the cold, he hated the low beams of her cottage, he shied like a frightened animal in the supermarket, he did not like the food, and he treated her cat like something with the evil eye. The doctor said he could be allergic to the cat; the pneumonia was compounded by fits of wheezing. What a joke that would be if it was the cat killed him. She could bring it into the room, wake him up and watch him expire out of terror. Pathetic, a big man like that. And what was more to the point, it was his frigid, frightened, monumental, animal loathing which made her follow and detest all the same things which so affected him. She looked at her possessions and her status and wondered what they meant, mistrusting everything she had done and all she owned. All turned to dust as she gazed at it. He was like someone who had seized an exquisite piece of crochet and systematically reduced it to threads. He, who was without violence, had smashed everything to pieces.

On the nights on which murders take place, or so she had read, the wind howled outside; thunder and lightning heralded the worst crime known to man, but at the time, murder seemed the most natural thing in the world and the night had grown calm and clear. She looked out of the window at the village street, a tidy piece of England, far from the sea.

"Banjie," he muttered, turning so that his face pointed to the white ceiling. "Banjie." Then he opened his eyes, looked straight into her own as she moved closer to him. In his dream he screamed. Once, loudly. A single expulsion of desperate sound, before his eyes closed again.

Poor man, who would not hurt a fly.

You are not really a tolerant person, Molly had said. None of us, apart from those peculiarly gifted to the point of being a little mad, are so tolerant that we can be comprehensive about what we are able to accept about another. You liked his country; you didn't love it or understand it, which isn't your fault. Why should he suddenly love yours?

Because he loved me.

That, said Molly, is nowhere near enough. You can't put cactus in a pond and expect it to grow. You can't expect a husky dog to love the desert, even if it is a champion breed. Molly was expert on gardening and dogs.

He is so gentle, Audrey said; I cannot bear it.

There was sobbing from the bed. Audrey sat on the edge. She touched his face. His hand held her palm against his hot skin. She cradled his head and gave him water. She knew she had the power of life and death. He knew it, too and did not seem to mind.

"You had nothing," she whispered to him. "Nothing." That was where he had lied. He had had plenty. The only thing not included had been money.

The dawn was beginning when she went downstairs to let the cat back indoors. Autumn had been fine. The sky was streaked with red, delicately pretty. No comparison to the awesome splendor of the West African sunset, where Audrey had fallen in love. Where a man could bury his heart in the sand and let the clouds take his head. Murder belonged with the dark. Audrey became efficient with the daylight. She waited, impatiently, for the hour when other people would be in their offices, ready to receive calls and respond to her authoritative voice. In the meantime, she busied herself, frowned over her bank balance, shrugged and planned the week. She pushed down the bitterness inside her with the same determination she used to knead bread. She suppressed all the feelings of insult and outrage and put them to one side together with all those comfortingly violent sensations which had been her companions for the night. She was not, after all, that kind of woman.

Yes, she was. She was no better than she ought to be and worse than he was, suffering in silence, turning his face to the wall while she planned necessary termination. He had not pleaded; he had not even considered violence. He was what she first discovered, a good man, in his way. He had never wished her harm, would never do as she had done, contemplate hurting her. Audrey was not ashamed about any of her decisions.

It was ten o'clock when she went upstairs. His eyes were closed, his sleep profound and peaceful, as if he had known what she was doing. She flung back the curtains and let in the sun. Pale, watery, English sun.

"You're going home," she said firmly. "In a day or two. When you feel a bit better, eh?"

It was the look of intense relief that he could not begin to hide as his eyes flew open and his face came alive, which made her want to weep. Such an innocent, totally unaware of what she had been thinking. Of course he would rather have nothing.

After he had gone, both of them laughing and crying at the airport and making meaningless promises, she came home and cleaned the house. Stripped his bed and wondered if she would ever use it again. Prepared a barrage of explanations to save what dignity she could. Vowed she would never say a bad word about him. Audrey felt bereft and utterly relieved about her soldierly behavior. He had never seen into her soul, never guessed she could be so foul.

Turning the mattress in order to resettle it upside down against the divan base, she found the knife at the level of the pillow. It was an unfamiliar, lethal-looking thing, sharper than the ones the tourists bought for fun.

Ready for her.

On balance, Molly said, she should be grateful. The discovery redressed the delicate balance of one, last night.

Poison Peach

GILLIAN LINSCOTT

Gillian Linscott has written five novels set in Edwardian England and featuring radical suffragette Nell Bray. A former Parliamentary reporter for the BBC, she has also written a historical mystery set in Alaska as well as a contemporary mystery series featuring expoliceman turned physical trainer Birdie Linnett. Her short fiction appears in such anthologies as *Murder, They Wrote.*

If there's one thing I love about summer, it's going to visit one of the many orchards near Cabot Cove. There's nothing like being able to enjoy the fruits of your labors after a pleasant day of picking. Of course, for some people, even the sweetest fruit can leave a bad taste in their mouth. In this story, the Valance family discovers this in a most unusual way.

". . . care must be taken not to bruise any part of the shoot; the wounds made by the knife heal quickly, but a bruise often proves incurable."

—*The Gardener's Monthly Volume:*
"The Peach." George W.
Johnson and R. Errington.
October 1847.

January was the time for pruning. In the peach house the journeyman gardeners untied the branches from their wires on the whitewashed wall and spread them out as delicately as spiders spinning webs. The fruit house foreman stepped among them with his bone-handled knife, trimming off the dead wood that had carried last year's fruit, choosing the shoots for this year's. Behind him an apprentice moved like an altar boy with a small basket, picking up every piece of branch as it fell. Few words were said, or needed to be said. In the eighty years since the peach houses had been built by the grandfather of the present owner, this same ritual had gone on, winter after winter. Victoria ruled an empire and died, apprentices took root and grew into head gardeners, the nineteenth century turned the corner into the twentieth, and always just after the turn of the year, with the solstice past but the days not yet perceptibly lengthening, the trees were pruned in the peach house at Briarley.

From the door between the peach house and the grape house, Henry Valance watched as his father and his grandfather had watched before him, all of them decent, careful men, accepting their role of guarding, cautiously improving, passing on to sons. What was different this January was that Henry's wife, Edwina, stood beside him, staring out through the sloping glass at the brassicas and bare soil of the kitchen garden. In the five years they'd been married, Edwina hadn't taken a great interest in the garden, being more concerned with the house and the duties of a hostess—although not yet of a mother. She didn't seem very interested now, but in the last few months had accepted her husband's timid suggestions on how to spend her time as if they were commands, following him dutifully but without the animation that had once sparked in her every word or movement. Her hair under the turban hat was still as glossy as the shoulder of a chestnut horse, her tall figure graceful in the long astrakhan coat she wore because it was cold, even inside the glass houses. But her hands, smoothly gloved in silver-gray kid, were clasped tightly together and her face was as blank as the winter sky.

Her husband moved closer to her so that the men working on the peaches couldn't hear them.

"I've had a letter from Stephen."

Over the past few months they'd fallen into the habit of talking about the things that mattered in almost public places, with the servants not far away. It limited the scope for damage. She moved her head a little, still looking out at the vegetable garden, as if the stiff rows of brussels sprouts might creep away if not watched.

"It seems he's written a book."

"What kind of book?"

"A novel."

"Why would he do that?"

Her voice had always been low. Now it was scarcely alive.

"He says he needs to make a career for himself." She said nothing. He glanced at her face, then away at the peach pruning. "I've written offering to pay him. I've told him I'll double whatever he's expecting to make from it, if he'll agree not to publish."

"He won't accept."

She said it with flat certainly. They stood for a while, then he gave her his arm and they walked away through the glass galleries of the grape house and the empty melon house scrubbed clean for winter, their feet echoing on the iron gratings. In the peach house, the foreman watched as two journeymen used strips of cloth to tie to the wall, fanshaped, the tree he'd pruned back. He signaled them to stop, stepped forward with his pruning knife, hesitated over a fruiting spur, and then, without cutting, nodded to them to carry on. The shape was right after all and the shoot should live to carry its peach. Behind the fruit houses men were cleaning and riddling the great boiler that fed hot water into the pipes under the floor gratings. Soon, when the pruning was finished and the stopcock turned to start the artificial indoor spring, the sap would begin to rise up the narrow trunks, along the spread branches, and into that spur, along with the rest. For a day or two longer the peach trees could rest.

By April the peach house was warm and full of pink blossoms, although the air outside hadn't lost the edge of winter. Amongst the petals, the gardeners fought their campaign against small pests that might threaten the setting of the fruit. An apprentice with a brass syringe walked the aisles between the trees, spraying the leaves with tobacco water to control the aphids. A journeyman with a paintbrush worked a mixture of sulfur and soft soap into every joint and crevice to kill off the eggs of red spiders and kept an eye on the apprentice at the same time.

"Careful with that bloody thing. You nearly knocked that spur clean off."

In fact, the apprentice's momentary carelessness had scarcely dislodge a petal and the journeyman's attention was not wholly on the killing of spider eggs and aphids. Things were happening that even the apprentices knew about and the waves that had started in the family rooms of the house had spread out through the upper staff down to the kitchens, out through the scullery door to the gardeners who carried up baskets of vegetables every day. A collection had been organized among the journeyman gardeners and a discreet order placed at the bookshop in the nearest town. The groom was to collect the result of it when he went down to the station, along with the other copies ordered by the upstairs staff, the kitchen staff, and the stables. The butler, who had connections in London, was believed to have got his hands on a copy already but wasn't showing anybody. At lunchtime the journeyman gardeners gathered in their bothy behind the wall at the back of the fruit houses, made themselves as comfortable as possible on sacks and buckets, and elected a reader. His attempts to make an orderly start at the beginning of chapter one were immediately voted down.

"That's not what all the trouble's about. Start at the business between him and her and we'll go back to the beginning later."

"If we want to."

Laughter, but muted. They were allowed half an hour in the bothy for their bread and cheese, but what they were doing was no part of their duties and could lead to trouble, and even dismissal for impudence, if discovered. The door had been firmly shut in the noses of the apprentices but was no protection against foreman or head gardener. The reader asked, plaintively, how he was supposed to know where the business was.

"They don't put it in the margins like they do with the Bible."

"I heard it was chapter ten."

The reader rustled pages, scanned silently, then whistled between his teeth.

Several voices told him to get on with it and not keep it to himself.

"It's where she calls him in to give him a piece of her mind because he's been getting too friendly with one of the maids."

"Is that how they put it—too friendly?"

"Oh, get on with it."

Now it had come to it, they were all a little embarrassed. The man trusted with the book read it in a fast mutter so that they had to crane forward to hear him. The lady calls the gentleman into her boudoir. She is stern. She does not usually listen to servants' gossip, but he must realize that the young housemaids are in her care and as employer she has a moral duty to them and to their parents. If the gentleman can assure her that these rumors are baseless then she will take severe action against the people spreading them. A sound outside. The men froze, but it was only two apprentices trying to listen and they were seen off, nursing cuffed ears.

"Go on."

The gentleman cannot give her that assurance. He compliments her instead on her good taste in employing such very attractive housemaids. She is unbelieving at first, then furious. He remains calm, then asks her if she is not, perhaps, jealous. She loses control and actually tries to hit him. He grabs her by the wrist and she falls back across the sofa, her furious black eyes gazing up at him. He stands looking down at her, smiling a little inward smile.

"Well, what happens after that?"

"Nothing. It's the end of the chapter."

He turned the book toward them to show the blank half page.

"Well, go on to the next one them."

He turned the page.

"It doesn't go on. Not with that, anyway. It goes back to the husband at his club."

"Well, what does he—"

The bothy door opened suddenly. In the doorway was the square, bowler-hatted figure of the head gardener himself, who could dismiss all of them with a snap of his fingers, quick as pulling an earwig in half.

"What do you men think you're doing? You've been nearly an hour in here."

Then he saw the book and snatched it out of the reader's hand.

"I'm ashamed of you all. You should know where this filth belongs."

With the journeymen trailing shamefaced after him and the apprentices peering from behind the pot shed, he marched across the yard to the barrel that held liquid fertilizer, pats of cow dung seething in rainwater. He nodded to one of the men to remove the lid, tossed the book into it, and waited while it globbed into the viscous depths. Another nod, and the lid went back.

"If I catch anybody in my gardens dirtying his hands with that again, if I catch anybody even mentioning it or looking as if he's thinking about it, he'll be applying for a new post without a character. Now get back to your work, all of you."

Dispiritedly they went, two of them toward the fruit houses.

"Tell you what, though, he got one thing wrong."

"What's that?"

"Her eyes aren't black—they're brown."

They laughed at that but sobered up when they found Hobbes, the fruit foreman, waiting for them and couldn't meet his eyes.

". . . neither peaches nor nectarines acquire perfection, either in richness or in flavour, unless they be exposed to the full influence of the sun during their last swelling."

—*An Encyclopedia of Gardening.*
J. C. Loudon. 1835.

By late June the peaches were close to perfection. Cosseted and watched over from the time the first green knobs formed behind the blossom, scrutinized and selected until there was just one fruit to every spur, all they waited for now was their final ripening. In case the midsummer sun should be too strong and scorch them through the glass, early every morning Hobbes would stand among the orderly rows of leaves, looking up, then say a few words, quietly as in church, to his assistant. The assistant would operate a wheel to open rows of ventilating panes, inch by inch, until they were at the exact angle to give a gentle circulation of air, and the process would be repeated every few hours as the sun climbed. Once the ventilators were open the peach house was tidied as carefully as a drawing room, every fragment of loam swept off the path, every tree checked for the slightest sign of insect damage, because by this time the season was at its height and the peaches were out in society. Briarley was famous for its fruit houses and a stroll between breakfast and lunch past the swelling grapes, under green and golden melons hanging among their heavy leaves, was almost a social duty for guests. In fact, there'd not been many guests at Briarley that season, but the fruit houses were always kept ready for them, as they always had been. Today Henry Valance came on his morning visit alone. Alone, that is, apart from the train that followed him at a respectful distance, first the head gardener, then Hobbes the foreman, then the two journeymen with particular responsibility for fruit.

Occasionally he'd pause, palpate and sniff a melon, finger a grape. When this happened the head gardener would catch up with him and a few serious words would be exchanged. The procession made its slow way to the peach house and stopped between the rows of trees.

"Nearly ripe then, are they?"

A nod from the head gardener signaled to Hobbes to come closer. It was a sign of the respect he had for Hobbes as a master in his own field that he allowed the foreman to answer the employer's question directly. Hobbes stood there in his dark suit and hat among in the green-dappled shade, gardening apron discarded for this formal visit, watch chain gleaming.

"The Hale's Early should be ripe by next Monday, sir, and the Early Beatrice not long after. Then the Rivers and the Mignonnes are coming on very nicely."

"Excellent. We'll look forward to that."

Henry's father and grandfather had stood in the same place and used much the same words. The difference was in the flatness of his voice that said everything he might have looked forward to was already in the past. Then, with an effort:

"You'll make sure we have plenty ripe for the second weekend in July, won't you? We have a lot of people coming, house quite full."

The two journeymen exchanged glances. It would be the first house party since it happened. The staff had been speculating that there wouldn't be any this year.

"We'll make sure, sir."

His question had not been necessary. It was the work of them all to see that there were ripe peaches all through the summer, whether there were guests to eat them or not. Still, there was no resentment that he'd asked it. He was, on the whole, liked by the gardening staff—and pitied.

> *"Nets . . . are perfectly useless in keeping off wasps and other insects, as they will alight on the outside and, folding their wings, pass through those of the smallest meshes."*
>
> *—An Encylopaedia of Gardening.*

There was the sound of footsteps coming through the glass galleries from the direction of the house, too light and quick for a gardener's, too confident for a maid's. Hurrying steps. The man went tense.

"Henry."

His wife's voice, with scarcely controlled panic in it. He met her in the doorway.

"A letter for you. It's just arrived."

She held it out to him. At first he'd looked simply puzzled. Dozens of letters arrived every day, and it was no part of Edwina's duties to chase him round the estate with them. Then he saw the handwriting. Took it from her and read.

"He's heard about the house party. He's inviting himself."

"No!"

The gardeners were in an impossible position. To eavesdrop on employers' private conversation was unthinkable. On the other hand, it was equally unthinkable to melt away through the door into the kitchen garden, since they'd been given no sign to go. They made a great business of scrutinizing the peach leaves, which they already knew were perfect.

"Write to him. Tell him he can't come."

"I can't do that. He is my brother, after all."

"He can't come if you don't let him."

"He'd come in any case, and what could I do then? Call the police to bring a van and drag him away? Tell the men to throw him in the lake, with the house full of visitors? It would mean that people would go on talking about it for years."

"That's what he wants."

"Yes, and the only way we can prevent him from getting it is facing it out, letting him come here."

"No."

But it was a different word now, numb and dispirited. He put out a hand to her but she moved away and her slow steps back toward the house seemed to go on for a long time.

The head gardener said kindly: "The figs are doing very nicely, sir. Would you care to look at them?"

"Figs. Yes, certainly, figs."

As they were moving off, the head gardener stopped suddenly.

"Excuse me, sir, but look at that."

He pointed at one of the peaches. An intake of breath from the gardeners.

"A wasp. Early for them, isn't it?"

The insect was sitting, wings folded, on the down of a peach. Hobbes stepped forward, mortified.

"I'm sorry, sir."

One of the journeymen ventured, unasked: "The lad was saying he'd seen a nest of them at the back of the pot shed."

The head gardener glared at him.

"Well, why didn't you do something about it? See to it, will you, Hobbes." His instruction to the foreman was less brusque than it might have been, considering the shame of the wasp's invasion. Hobbes nodded and the party moved on.

> *"A gentle squeeze at the point where the stalk joins the fruit will soon determine whether it be ripe enough."*
>
> —*The Gardener's Monthly Volume*: "The Peach."

July, and the scent of ripe peaches hung on the air like a benignant gas. Every morning the foreman would pick the ripest and lay them gently onto a padded tray held by the apprentice, ready for the house party at lunch. All but a few. It was a custom at Briarley that some of the best fruit should be left on the trees for the look of it when the visitors walked round, glowing through green like the eyes of a sleepy animal. But the party hadn't reached the peach house yet, lingering on the way to admire the ripe purple clusters on the grapevine. Murmurs of admiration and white-gloved hands reaching out, almost touching but stopping just before making contact, unwilling to smudge a bloom on the fruit like the first morning in Eden. But one pair of hands, male and gloveless, kept moving, breached the invisible barrier, picked a grape. A little shiver, half shocked, half pleased, ran through the party. Relishing the attention, the picker put the grape in his mouth.

His lips were full, for a man's, and as he munched he let the underside of his lower lip show, slick and smooth.

"Is it good?"

The woman guest who asked the question had dark piled hair and wide eyes. She smelt of carnations and her dressmaker had been perhaps a shade too attentive in cutting her dress so exactly to the curve of her full breasts. Instead of answering in words, the man picked another grape and held it half an inch from her lips. Her eyes flickered sideways to where her host and hostess were standing, then she opened her lips in a little round pout just wide enough to let the grape in, dipped her head, and took it from his fingers like a bird.

"Yes, very good."

A silence, then from the side of the group, their host's voice: "Shall we go and look at the peaches?" But he couldn't stop himself adding: "If you've had enough, Stephen."

"Oh, enough for now, don't you think?"

The party moved on in silence.

> *"It is common practice to lay littery material beneath the trees to save from bruising the fruit which falls, and sometimes those which fall are extremely luscious."*
>
> —*The Gardener's Monthly Volume*: "The Peach."

On Sunday morning the day started later. Only a few guests came to the fruit houses between breakfast and lunch. Host and hostess went to church as usual. A few of the house party went with them, but it was a hot day and most preferred to stroll by the lake or in the lime avenue. After lunch, with the weekend drawing to its close, the strolls became lazier and polite slow-motion competition developed for places on rustic benches under the trees. Afterward, nobody knew who had proposed another tour of the fruit houses. It might have been a suggestion from the host—certainly not one from Edwina, because she had a headache and had retired to the drawing room after lunch, with an old friend in attendance. The suggestion might have come from Stephen, as he'd been the focus of the younger set in the party for most of the weekend. A stranger might have taken him for the host instead of his brother, although his behavior toward Henry and Edwina had been entirely correct throughout. He'd let it be known that he enjoyed being back at the old place so much that he thought he might stay for the week. Whoever suggested it, the proposal collected a little following and about a dozen people joined the tour, including the woman who smelt of carnations. Some of the older guests felt that for a woman whose husband was working abroad she'd been a little too eager for Stephen's company over the weekend. Late at night, among some of the men lingering in the billiard room after too much port, there'd been jokes about Stephen doing research for his next novel, only not in Henry's hearing. Only one more night to go and she'd be leaving on Monday morning. The men in the billiard room had even been placing bets.

Sun, food, and wine swept away the touch of solemnity that usually went with the fruit house tour. Stephen was triumphant, unstoppable. He ranged along the fruit-smelling avenues like a big child, greedy to see, touch, taste. The younger element in the party had caught his mood. The woman who'd eaten the grape had competition now as they all fingered, dared, ate. A melon was parted from its stem and thrown from hand to hand until golden flesh and pips splattered on the red-tiled floor. Henry watched, impassive. Farther back, not part of the party, the head gardener watched, equally impassive. He stayed ten yards behind them as they laughed and pattered through the grape house, leaving the bunches blemished with bare stems and torn tongues of purple skin.

When they got to the green-dappled shade of the peach house Hobbes was at work there, and it looked for a moment as if he were going to commit the sackable sin of rudeness to his employer's guests in defense of his cherished peaches. He actually stood for a moment in the path of the party until the head gardener caught his eye and he stood reluctantly aside. This little stutter of opposition seemed to increase Stephen's pleasure. He challenged one of the women to eat a peach without picking it. She moved her lips toward a red and golden fruit that trembled on its stem with ripeness. Hobbes started toward her, perhaps intending to hand it to her with proper respect for lady and peach. The head gardener looked alarmed at the impending breach of etiquette and might have stopped him, but at the last minute the woman drew her face away from the peach, giggling.

"You can't. It would fall. Nobody could."

"Yes you can. All you need is a soft mouth. Look."

In silence, with them all watching him, Stephen advanced on the largest peach in sight. It hung conveniently on a level with his chin, standing out from the leaves on its spur. He bent a little at the knees and turned his head back so that the fruit was almost resting on his mouth. His teeth closed on it. Juice ran down his chin, dribbled onto the lapel of his white jacket. A little gasp from one of the women, hushed at once. The peach shifted a little, rotating on its stem, but still didn't fall. His neck muscles tensed and he took another, larger bite. Then there was a little cracking sound and he was falling, falling backward with the peach clenched in his jaws. This time the gasps weren't hushed but turned to screams. Because of the way he'd been standing, the back of his head hit the iron grating with a crash that sent every leaf in the place quivering. Then voices.

"Choking. For heaven's sake, get it out of his mouth."

"Air. Get some air in here."

"Get the ladies out."

"Isn't there a doctor?"

Henry was at the front of the group, along with the head gardener and the foreman. They turned Stephen over, wrenched the peach from his teeth. From the look of his contorted face it seemed likely that he'd choked on the fruit before his head hit the grating, but since he couldn't be dead twice over that didn't seem to matter. Henry got to his feet coughing, staggered backward against the wall, then was violently sick.

"Get him outside. Get him into the air."

"Everybody outside."

"A piece of cloth fastened to a stick, soaked in a saturated solution of cyanide of potassium, is immediate death to all wasps within or returning to the nest."

—*"The Fruit Grower's Guide.*
John Wright. 1892.

It took some time for the doctor to reach Briarley and while they waited for him doubts were already setting in, mainly because of the smell. Several of the men besides Henry were coughing as they came out of the peach house, and a woman collapsed and had to be revived. When Henry and most of the party were on their way back to the house, the head gardener, Hobbes, and a few of the male guests covered the body with clean sacks. Then they shut the door firmly and waited on the other side of it in the grape house, the guests smoking, the two gardeners standing a little apart from them. When the doctor arrived at last they followed him in but stood at a safe distance, although most of the smell had worn off by then. He peeled back the sack from the face.

"What did you say happened?"

"He was eating a peach and he choked."

He examined the body briefly, then told them they should cover it up again but not do anything else until the police arrived. He was a comparatively new doctor in the village, Scottish and conscientious. The old doctor might have managed things more tactfully.

The verdict was never in doubt: Stephen Valance had deserved what he got. If you seduce your brother's maidservant, then his wife, and—for a profit—tell the world about it, you can't complain if your peach turns out to contain cyanide. Even those who had quite liked Stephen and watched his career with interest felt a kind of satisfaction that there was a limit after all, although there had been some sporting interest in seeing how far and fast a man could go before he hit it. Stephen had chosen to ride his course that way and by the natural law of things he was heading for a fall. No more needed to be done and very little said, except in private when the servants were out of the room.

That, at any rate, was the immediate verdict of society. The verdict of the country's system of justice was another matter and at first seemed likely to throw up more difficulties. That Stephen had died by cyanide poisoning and that the carrier of the poison had been the peach was never seriously in doubt. The hopeful theory of suicide in a moment of well-earned remorse was abandoned instantly by anybody who had the slightest acquaintance with Stephen or his reputation. Which left . . .

"Well, I suppose if it comes right down to it, it has to be murder."

The discussion was going on very late at night in the billiard room. Not that anybody had actually tried to play billiards, which would have been totally inappropriate on a Sunday, with the hostess prostrate upstairs, the host at her bedside, and the host's younger brother in the mortuary. The men who had influence had naturally congregated there—not the giddier sort who had followed Stephen but the more sober ones who had known Henry's father, who sat as magistrates and chose men to stand for Parliament.

"You can't blame him. I'd have done the same thing myself."

"Not very nice, poison."

"Quick, though. Practically painless, I'd have thought. Anyway, what can you do? I mean, you can't challenge a man to a duel in this day and age."

"I suppose the next thing's the inquest. They can bring in murder by person or persons unknown. . . ."

"Or they can even name the person they think did it, if they think there's enough evidence."

Silence, while they considered it.

"Of course, there's always accidental death."

"There was a glass vial of cyanide in that peach. How does that get in there accidentally?"

"They use cyanide to kill wasp nests in glass houses. At any rate, my gardener does, and I don't suppose Henry's are any different. You get a lot of wasps after peaches."

More silence, finally broken by the oldest man amongst them.

"I think I'd better have a word with his head gardener in the morning."

"Only professional men can use it safely."
—The Fruit Grower's Guide

Hobbes stood in a shaft of sunlight in the coroner's court, dark-suited in his Sunday best, new bowler hat on the table in front of him, and gave his evidence. By that point the court had already heard from the brother of the deceased, from two doctors, from a police officer, and from the head gardener, who clearly remembered telling the fruit foreman to do something about the wasps in the peach house. The coroner had been respectful to the brother's grief, businesslike with the doctors and the head gardener. To the fruit foreman his tone was colder, and Hobbes answered respectfully. He had been in Mr. Valance's employment for twenty years. Yes, he had used potassium cyanide on a wasp's nest; they kept a drum of it for the purpose in the pot shed. No, he did not know how it had come to contaminate a peach. Yes, he had been warned to be careful with it and knew that it was poisonous. If any of it had somehow come onto the fruit, from his gardening gloves or some tool, then that was very great carelessness. Could he think of any other way that the cyanide might have come onto the peach? No sir, he could think of no other way. There was a rustling and sighing in the court, like heavy leaves in a breeze. The coroner paused to let the answer sink in, then turned to another aspect of the matter. The doctor who had certified death and the police officer had noticed small fragments of glass in the peach.

"It was put on the floor, sir, by one of the gentlemen, when they took it out of his mouth."

"You're suggesting that was when the glass became attached to it?"

"Yes, sir."

"Are you accustomed to leaving glass fragments lying on the floor of your employer's fruit houses?"

"Not accustomed, no sir."

"And yet glass fragments were there?"

"Yes sir."

"Should we assume that this was another example of carelessness?"

It took Hobbes some time to realize that an answer was required. When he did he said "Yes sir" again in the same respectful voice. At last he was permitted to stand down. The head gardener—who would hardly allow a petal to settle on the floor of the glass houses for more than a second or two—looked straight ahead throughout the foreman's evidence, face expressionless. In his summing-up the coroner had some hard things to say about carelessness by men who should know better. Hobbes took them all, head bent over the bowler hat that rested on his knees. The verdict was accidental death.

Outside the court, one of Henry Valance's friends went up to Hobbes as he stood on his own among departing cars and carriages.

"Well, Hobbes, always best to own up to things."

"Yes sir."

"I gather Mr. Valance is letting you keep your position."

"Yes sir."

"A very generous man, Mr. Valance. I'm sure you're grateful."

"Yes sir."

And although he'd been one of the chief movers in arranging things so satisfactorily, the friend really did feel that Henry was acting generously. The coroner's rebuke had wrapped itself around Hobbes and his deplorable carelessness with cyanide was now a fact of history, officially recorded.

"Anyway, I don't suppose it will happen again."

"No sir."

Both men took their hats off as the Valances' motor car drove slowly past, with Edwina sitting very upright beside her husband, pale under her heavy veil.

By October the peach season was almost over. A few Prince of Wales and Lady Palmerstons still gleamed among the leaves but there hadn't been much call for peaches from the household, or many tours of the glass houses. Henry made his dutiful rounds from time to time and exchanged a few words with Hobbes about indifferent things, but that was all. One morning when there was already a frosty feel to the air outside the head gardener came in while Hobbes was retieing labels on wires. There was nobody else within hearing.

"All well, Hobbes?"

"Yes."

The head gardener looked out through the panes to where the men were digging over a potato plot.

"Some people are saying you got left with the dirty end of the stick. Still, you said your piece very well and you didn't lose by it."

No response. The head gardener's attention seemed to be all on the men outside, then he said: "Funny, the things you find when you dig."

The wire under Hobbes's hand suddenly tightened and began vibrating. He kept his head down.

"What are you thinking of?"

"End of July, I was in the herb garden and I noticed this little freshly dug patch right at the back of the angelica. Now I hadn't told anyone to dig there. I went and got a spade from the shed and turned it over to have a look. What do you suppose I found there?"

Hobbes's grip on the wire was now so tight that the tree branch it supported was quivering too.

"Peaches, that's what I found. I backed off quickly, I can tell you. There's a paving slab over them now, in case of any more accidents."

The tree branch was near to breaking when Hobbes released his grip of the wire and straightened up. The head gardener took his arm, not roughly.

"Of course, you couldn't be sure he'd take that one peach so you'd have to do a few of them. And you were going to stop the lady when she looked like biting into one of them instead."

Hobbes nodded. "How did you know?"

"That it was you? Well, Mr. Valance might have done the one of them, but to do more than one like that you needed to be neat-fingered and you needed to have time. Nobody has more time in the peach house than you do, and nobody's got neater fingers. I've watched you grafting fruit trees."

Hobbes took the compliment with another nod.

"And another thing I know—I know why you did it, and I don't blame you."

The foreman looked at the head gardener's face, then the words surged out of him.

"They were all talking about what he'd done to her, to Mrs. Valance, as if my girl didn't matter. All this about the book, everybody reading about what he'd done to the housemaid, to my girl, and the lady calling him in to talk about it and then he . . . When I knew he had the face to come back here, laughing at us, I started thinking—supposing I did so and so. And, well, I did it."

The head gardener's hand stayed on his arm. Anybody looking into the peach house from outside would have seen nothing but two men enjoying the autumn sunshine on their employer's time.

"How is your girl?"

"Gone to her aunt in Wales. They've put it about that the father's a sailor lost at sea. She won't be coming back here."

Silence. They were two men used to patience, but Hobbes gave way first.

"Let's be going and get it over with."

"It *is* over. You've been careless. The coroner said so."

"But—"

"Be quiet. I'm thinking."

"I thought you'd already done the thinking."

"That space over there. Do you think another couple of Rivers or maybe Lord Napiers instead?"

Hobbes stared first at the blank white wall, then at him.

"You're asking me that—now?"

"Why not? None too soon for you to start planning for next year, is it?"

"For next year . . ."

It took him some time to understand. When he did he said thank you and turned back to the fruit trees. A spur, fruitless now, snagged at his cuff, but he freed it with a hand still shaking a little and went on with his work.

The Four Suspects

AGATHA CHRISTIE

Agatha Christie (1890–1976) rightfully earned the title "the grand dame of mystery," with her detectives Hercule Poirot and Miss Jane Marple crisscrossing the English countryside to solve numerous crimes. Born on the south coast of Devon, she had aspirations of becoming a pianist but could not overcome her extreme shyness. After serving as a volunteer nurse in the Royal Air Corps, she later accompanied her second husband, Max Mallowan, on several archaological digs, functioning as the photographer for the expeditions. All of these life experiences served her well in writing her 66 novels and 144 short stories.

The conversation hovered round undiscovered and unpunished crimes. Everyone in turn vouchsafed an opinion: Colonel Bantry, his plump amiable wife, Jane Helier, Dr. Lloyd, and even old Miss Marple. The one person who did not speak was the one best fitted in most people's opinion to do so. Sir Henry Clithering, ex-Commissioner of Scotland Yard, sat silent, twisting his moustache—or rather stroking it—and half smiling, as though at some inward thought that amused him.

"Sir Henry," said Mrs. Bantry at last, "if you don't say something, I shall scream. Are there a lot of crimes that go unpunished, or are there not?"

"You're thinking of newspaper headlines, Mrs. Bantry. SCOTLAND YARD AT FAULT AGAIN. And a list of unsolved mysteries to follow."

"Which really, I suppose, form a very small percentage of the whole?" said Dr. Lloyd.

"Yes, that is so. The hundreds of crimes that are solved and the perpetrators punished are seldom heralded and sung. But that isn't quite the point at issue, is it? When you talk of undiscovered crimes and unsolved crimes, you are talking of two different things. In the first category come all the crimes that Scotland Yard never hears about, the crimes that no one even knows have been committed."

"But I suppose there aren't very many of those?" said Mrs. Bantry.

"Aren't there?"

"Sir Henry! You don't mean there are?"

"I should think," said Miss Marple thoughtfully, "that there must be a very large number."

The charming old lady, with her old-world, unruffled air, made her statement in a tone of the utmost placidity.

"My dear Miss Marple," said Colonel Bantry.

"Of course," said Miss Marple, "a lot of people are stupid. And stupid people get found out, whatever they do. But there are quite a number of people who aren't stupid, and one shudders to think of what they might accomplish unless they had very strongly rooted principles."

"Yes," said Sir Henry, "there are a lot of people who aren't stupid. How often does some crime come to light simply by reason of a bit of unmitigated bungling, and each time one asks oneself the question: If this hadn't been bungled, would anyone ever have known?"

"But that's very serious, Clithering," said Colonel Bantry. "Very serious, indeed."

"Is it?"

"What do you mean, is it? Of course it's serious."

"You say crime goes unpunished, but does it? Unpunished by the law perhaps, but cause and effect works outside the law. To say that every crime brings its own punishment is by way of being a platitude, and yet in my opinion nothing can be truer."

"Perhaps, perhaps," said Colonel Bantry. "But that doesn't alter the seriousness—the—er—seriousness—" He paused, rather at a loss.

Sir Henry Clithering smiled.

"Ninety-nine people out of a hundred are doubtless of your way of thinking," he said. "But you know, it isn't really guilt that is important—it's innocence. That's the thing that nobody will realize."

"I don't understand," said Jane Helier.

"I do," said Miss Marple. "When Mrs. Trent found half a crown missing from her bag, the person it affected most was the daily woman, Mrs. Arthur. Of course the Trents thought it was her, but being kindly people and knowing she had a large family and a husband who drinks, well—they naturally didn't want to go to extremes. But they felt differently toward her, and they didn't leave her in charge of the house when they went away, which made a great difference to her; and other people began to get a feeling about her too. And then it suddenly came out that it was the governess. Mrs. Trent saw her through a door reflected in a mirror. The purest chance—though I prefer to call it Providence. And that, I think, is what Sir Henry means. Most people would be only interested in who took the money, and it turned out to be the most unlikely person—just like in detective stories! But the real person it was life and death to was poor Mrs.

Arthur, who had done nothing. That's what you mean, isn't it, Sir Henry?"

"Yes, Miss Marple, you've hit off my meaning exactly. Your charwoman person was lucky in the instance you relate. Her innocence was shown. But some people may go through a lifetime crushed by the weight of a suspicion that is really unjustified."

"Are you thinking of some particular instance, Sir Henry?" asked Mrs. Bantry shrewdly.

"As a matter of fact, Mrs. Bantry, I am. A very curious case. A case where we believe murder to have been committed, but with no possible chance of ever proving it."

"Poison, I suppose," breathed Jane. "Something untraceable."

Dr. Lloyd moved restlessly and Sir Henry shook his head.

"No, dear lady. Not the secret arrow poison of the South American Indians! I wish it were something of that kind. We have to deal with something much more prosaic—so prosaic, in fact, that there is no hope of bringing the deed home to its perpetrator. An old gentleman who fell downstairs and broke his neck; one of those regrettable accidents which happen every day."

"But what happened really?"

"Who can say?" Sir Henry shrugged his shoulders. "A push from behind? A piece of cotton or string tied across the top of the stairs and carefully removed afterward? That we shall never know."

"But you do think that it—well, wasn't an accident? Now why?" asked the doctor.

"That's rather a long story, but—well, yes, we're pretty sure. As I said, there's no chance of being able to bring the deed home to anyone—the evidence would be too flimsy. But there's the other aspect of the case—the one I was speaking about. You see, there were four people who might have done the trick. One's guilty, but the other three are innocent. And unless the truth is found out, those three are going to remain under the terrible shadow of doubt."

"I think," said Mrs. Bantry, "that you'd better tell us your long story."

"I needn't make it so very long after all," said Sir Henry. "I can at any rate condense the beginning. That deals with a German secret society—the *Schwartze Hand*—something after the lines of the Camorra or what is most people's idea of the Camorra. A scheme of blackmail and terrorization. The thing started quite suddenly after the war and spread to an amazing extent. Numberless people were victimized by it. The authorities were not successful in coping with it, for its secrets were jealously guarded, and it was almost impossible to find anyone who could be induced to betray them.

"Nothing much was ever known about it in England, but in Germany it was having a most paralyzing effect. It was finally broken up and dispersed through the efforts of one man, a Dr. Rosen, who had at one time been very prominent in Secret Service work. He became a member, penetrated its inmost circle, and was, as I say, instrumental in bringing about its downfall.

"But he was, in consequence, a marked man, and it was deemed wise that he should leave Germany—at any rate for a time. He came to England, and we had letters about him from the police in Berlin. He came and had a personal interview with me. His point of view was both dispassionate and resigned. He had no doubts of what the future held for him.

" 'They will get me, Sir Henry,' he said. 'Not a doubt of it.' He was a big man with a fine head and a very deep voice, with only a slight guttural intonation to tell of his nationality. 'That is a foregone conclusion. It does not matter, I am prepared. I faced the risk when I undertook this business. I have done what I set out to do. The organization can never be gotten together again. But there are many members of it at liberty, and they will take the only revenge they can—my life. It is simply a question of time, but I am anxious that that time should be as long as possible. You see, I am collecting and editing some very interesting material—the result of my life's work. I should like, if possible to be able to complete my task.'

"He spoke very simply, with a certain grandeur which I could not but admire. I told him we would take all precautions, but he waved my words aside.

" 'Some day, sooner or later, they will get me,' he repeated. 'When that day comes, to not distress yourself. You will, I have no doubt, have done all that is possible.'

"He then proceeded to outline his plans which were simple enough. He proposed to take a small cottage in the country where he could live quietly and go on with his work. In the end he selected a village in Somerset—King's Gnaton, which was seven miles from a railway station and singularly untouched by civilization. He bought a very charming cottage, had various improvements and alterations made, and settled down there most contentedly. His household consisted of his niece, Greta; a secretary; an old German servant who had served him faithfully for nearly forty years; and an outside handy man and gardener who was a native of King's Gnaton."

"The four suspects," said Dr. Lloyd softly.

"Exactly. The four suspects. There is not much more to tell. Life went on peacefully at King's Gnaton for five months and then the blow fell. Dr. Rosen fell down the stairs one morning and was found dead about half an hour later. At the time the accident must have taken place, Gertrud was in her kitchen with the door closed and heard nothing—so she says.

Fäulein Greta was in the garden, planting some bulbs—again, so she says. The gardener, Dobbs, was in the small potting shed having his elevenses—so he says; and the secretary was out for a walk, and once more there is only his own word for it. No one had an alibi—no one can corroborate anyone else's story. But one thing is certain. No one from outside could have done it, for a stranger in the little village of King's Gnaton would be noticed without fail. Both the back and the front doors were locked, each member of the household having his own key. So you see it narrows down to those four. And yet each one seems to be above suspicion. Greta, his own brother's child. Gertrud, with forty years of faithful service. Dobbs, who has never been out of King's Gnaton. And Charles Templeton, the secretary—"

"Yes," said Colonel Bantry, "what about him? He seems the suspicious person to my mind. What do you know about him?"

"It is what I knew about him that put him completely out of court—at any rate, at the time," said Sir Henry gravely. "You see, Charles Templeton was one of my own men."

"Oh!" said Colonel Bantry, considerably taken aback.

"Yes. I wanted to have someone on the spot, and at the same time I didn't want to cause talk in the village. Rosen really needed a secretary. I put Templeton on the job. He's a gentleman, he speaks German fluently, and he's altogether a very able fellow."

"But, then, which do you suspect?" asked Mrs. Bantry in a bewildered tone. "They all seem so—well, impossible."

"Yes, so it appears. But you can look at the thing from another angle. Fräulein Greta was his niece and a very lovely girl, but the war has shown us time and again that brother can turn against sister, or father against son, and so on, and the loveliest and gentlest of young girls did some of the most amazing things. The same thing applies to Gertrud, and who knows what other forces might be at work in her case? A quarrel, perhaps, with her master, a growing resentment all the more lasting because of the long faithful years behind her. Elderly women of that class can be amazingly bitter sometimes. And Dobbs? Was he right outside it because he had no connection with the family?

Money will do much. In some way Dobbs might have been approached and bought.

"For one thing seems certain: Some message or some order must have come from outside. Otherwise, why five months' immunity? No, the agents of the society must have been at work. Not yet sure of Rosen's perfidy, they delayed till the betrayal had been traced to him beyond any possible doubt. And then, all doubts set aside, they must have sent their message to the spy within the gates—the message that said. 'Kill.' "

"How nasty!" said Jane Helier, and shuddered.

"But how did the message come? That was the point I tried to elucidate—the one hope of solving my problem. One of those four people must have been approached or communicated with in some way. There would be no delay—I knew that; as soon as the command came, it would be carried out. That was a peculiarity of the *Schwartze Hand*.

"I went into the question, went into it in a way that will probably strike you as being ridiculously meticulous. Who had come to the cottage that morning? I eliminated nobody. Here is the list."

He took an envelope from his pocket and selected a paper from its contents.

"The butcher, bringing some neck of mutton. Investigated and found correct.

"The grocer's assistant, bringing a packet of corn flour, two pounds of sugar, a pound of butter, and a pound of coffee. Also investigated and found correct.

"The postman, bringing two circulars for Fräulein Rosen, a local letter for Gertrud, three letters for Dr. Rosen, one with a foreign stamp, and two letters for Mr. Templeton, one also with a foreign stamp."

Sir Henry paused and then took a sheaf of documents from the envelope.

"It may interest you to see these for yourself. They were handed me by the various people concerned or collected from the wastepaper basket. I need hardly say they've been tested by experts for invisible ink, et cetera. No excitement of that kind is possible."

Everyone crowded round to look. The catalogues were respectively from a nurseryman and from a prominent London fur establishment. The two bills addressed to Dr. Rosen were a local one for seeds for the garden and one from a London stationery firm. The letter addressed to him ran as follows:

My Dear Rosen—Just back from Dr. Helmuth Spath's. I saw Edgar Jackson the other day. He and Amos Perry have just come back from Tsingtau. In all Honesty I can't say I envy them the trip. Let me have news of you soon. As I said before: Beware of a certain person. You know who I mean, though you don't agree.

—Yours,
Georgina.

"Mr. Templeton's mail consisted of this bill which, as you see, is an account rendered from his tailor, and a letter from a friend in Germany," went on Sir Henry. "The latter, unfortunately, he tore up while out on his walk. Finally we have the letter received by Gertrud."

Dear Mrs. Swartz,—We're hoping as how you be able to come the social on friday evening. The vicar says has he hopes you will—one and all being welcome. The resipy for the ham was very good, and I thanks you for it. Hoping as this finds you well and that we shall see you friday i remain

Yours faithfully,
Emma Greene.

Dr. Lloyd smiled a little over this and so did Mrs. Bantry.

"I think the last letter can be put out of court," said Dr. Lloyd.

"I thought the same," said Sir Henry, "but I took the precaution of verifying that there was a Mrs. Greene and a church social. One can't be too careful, you know."

"That's what our friend Miss Marple always says," said Dr. Lloyd, smiling. "You're lost in a daydream, Miss Marple. What are you thinking out?"

Miss Marple gave a start.

"So stupid of me," she said. "I was just wondering why the word Honesty in Dr. Rosen's letter was spelled with a capital H."

Mrs. Bantry picked it up.

"So it is," she said. "Oh!"

"Yes, dear," said Miss Marple. "I thought you'd notice!"

"There's a definite warning in that letter," said Colonel Bantry. "That's the first thing caught my attention. I notice more than you'd think. Yes, a definite warning—against whom?"

"There's rather a curious point about that letter," said Sir Henry. "According to Templeton, Dr. Rosen opened the letter at breakfast and tossed it across to him, saying he didn't know who the fellow was from Adam."

"But it wasn't a fellow," said Jane Helier. "It was signed 'Georgina.' "

"It's difficult to say which it is," said Dr. Lloyd. "It might be Georgey, but it certainly looks more like Georgina. Only it strikes me that the writing is a man's."

"You know, that's interesting," said Colonel Bantry. "His tossing it across the table like that and pretending he knew nothing about it. Wanted to watch somebody's face. Whose face—the girl's? Or the man's?"

"Or even the cook's?" suggested Mrs. Bantry. "She might have been in the room bringing in the breakfast. But what I don't see is . . . it's most peculiar—"

She frowned over the letter. Miss Marple drew closer to her. Miss Marple's finger went out and touched the sheet of paper. They murmured together.

"But why did the secretary tear up the other letter?" asked Jane Helier suddenly. "It seems—oh, I don't know—it seems queer. Why should he have letters from Germany? Although, of course, if he's above suspicion, as you say—"

"But Sir Henry didn't say that," said Miss Marple quickly, looking up from her murmured conference with Mrs. Bantry. "He said four suspects. So that shows that he includes Mr. Templeton. I'm right, am I not, Sir Henry?"

"Yes, Miss Marple. I have learned one thing through bitter experience. Never say to yourself that anyone is above suspicion. I gave you reasons just now why three of these people might after all be guilty, unlikely as it seemed. I did not at that time apply the same process to Charles Templeton. But I came to it at last through pursuing the rule I have just mentioned. And I was forced to recognize this: That every army and every navy and every police force has a certain number of traitors within its ranks, much as we hate to admit the idea. And I examined dispassionately the case against Charles Templeton.

"I asked myself very much the same questions as Miss Helier has just asked. Why should he, alone of all the house, not be able to produce the letter he had received—a letter, moreover, with a German stamp on it. Why should he have letters from Germany?

"The last question was an innocent one, and I actually put it to him. His reply came simply enough. His mother's sister was married to a German. The letter had been from a German girl cousin. So I learned something I did not know before—that Charles Templeton had relations with people in Germany. And that put him definitely on the list of suspects—very much so. He is my own man—a lad I have always liked and trusted; but in common justice and fairness I must admit that he heads that list.

"But there it is—I do not know! I do not know. . . . And in all probability I never shall know. It is not a question of punishing a murderer. It is a question that to me seems a hundred times more important. It is the blighting, perhaps, of an honorable man's whole career . . . because of suspicion—a suspicion that I dare not disregard."

Miss Marple coughed and said gently:

"Then Sir Henry, if I understand you rightly, it is this young Mr. Templeton only who is so much on your mind?"

"Yes, in a sense. It should, in theory, be the same for all four, but that is not actually the case. Dobbs, for instance—suspicion may attach to him in my mind, but it will not actually affect his career. Nobody in the village has ever had any idea that old Dr. Rosen's death was anything but an accident. Gertrud is slightly more affected. It must make, for instance, a difference in Fräulein Rosen's attitude toward her. But that, possibly, is not of great importance to her.

"As for Greta Rosen—well, here we come to the crux of the matter. Greta is a very pretty girl and Charles Templeton is a good-looking young man, and for five months they were thrown together with no outer distractions. The inevitable happened. They fell in love with each other—even if they did not come to the point of admitting the fact in words.

"And then the catastrophe happens. It is three months ago now, and a day or two after I returned, Greta Rosen came to see me. She had sold the cottage and was returning to Germany, having finally settled up her uncle's affairs. She came to me personally, although she knew I had retired, because it was really about a personal matter she wanted to see me. She beat about the bush a little, but at last it all came out. What did I think? That letter with the German stamp—she had worried about it and worried about it—the one Charles had torn up. Was it all right? Surely it must be all right. Of course she believed his story, but—oh, if she only knew! If she knew—for certain.

"You see? The same feeling: the wish to trust—but the horrible lurking suspicion, thrust resolutely to the back of the mind, but persisting nevertheless. I spoke to her with absolute frankness and asked her to do the same. I asked her whether she had been on the point of caring for Charles and he for her.

" 'I think so,' she said. 'Oh yes, I know it was so. We were so happy. Every day passed so contentedly. We knew—we both knew. There was no hurry—there was all the time in the world. Some day he would tell me he loved me, and I should tell him that I, too—Ah! But you can guess! And now it is all changed. A black cloud has come between us—we are constrained, when we meet we do not know what to say. It is, perhaps, the same with him as with me. . . . We are each saying to ourselves, "If I were sure!" That is why, Sir Henry, I beg of you to say to me, "You may be sure, whoever killed your uncle, it was not Charles Templeton!" Say it to me! Oh, say it to me! I beg—I beg!'

"I couldn't say it to her. They'll drift farther and farther apart, those two—with suspicion like a ghost between them—a ghost that can't be laid."

He leaned back in his chair; his face looked tired and grey. He shook his head once or twice despondently.

"And there's nothing more can be done, unless—" He sat up straight again and a tiny whimsical smile crossed his face. —"unless Miss Marple can help us. Can't you, Miss Marple? I've a feeling that letter might be in your line, you know. The one about the church social. Doesn't it remind you of something or someone that makes everything perfectly plain? Can't you do something to help two helpless young people who want to be happy?"

Behind the whimsicality there was something earnest in his appeal. He had come to think very highly of the mental powers of this frail, old-fashioned maiden lady. He looked across at her with something very like hope in his eyes.

Miss Marple coughed and smoothed her lace.

"It does remind me a little of Annie Poultny," she admitted. "Of course the letter is perfectly plain—both to Mrs. Bantry and myself. I don't mean the church-social letter, but the other one. You living so much in London and not being a gardener, Sir Henry, would not have been likely to notice."

"Eh?" said Sir Henry. "Notice what?"

Mrs. Bantry reached out a hand and selected a catalogue. She opened it and read aloud with gusto:

" 'Dr. Helmuth Spath. Pure lilac, a wonderfully fine flower, carried on exceptionally long and stiff stem. Splendid for cutting and garden decoration. A novelty of striking beauty.

" 'Edgar Jackson. Beautifully shaped chrysanthemum-like flower of a distinct brick-red color.

" 'Amos Perry. Brilliant red, highly decorative.

" 'Tsingtau. Brilliant orange-red, showy garden plant and lasting cut flower.

" 'Honesty—' "

"With a capital H, you remember," murmured Miss Marple.

" 'Honesty. Rose and white shades, enormous perfect-shaped flower.' "

Mrs. Bantry flung down the catalogue and said with immense explosive force:

"Dahlias!"

"And their initial letters spell 'Death,' " explained Miss Marple.

"But the letter came to Dr. Rosen himself," objected Sir Henry.

"That was the clever part of it," said Miss Marple. "That and the warning in it. What would he do, getting a letter from someone he didn't know, full of names he didn't know. Why, of course, toss it over to his secretary."

"Then, after all—"

"Oh no!" said Miss Marple. "Not the secretary. Why, that's what makes it so perfectly clear that it wasn't him. He'd never have let that letter be found if so. And equally he'd never have destroyed a letter to himself with a German stamp on it. Really, his innocence is—if you'll allow me to use the word—just shining."

"Then who—"

"Well, it seems almost certain—as certain as anything can be in this world. There was another person at the breakfast table, and she would—quite naturally under the circumstances—put out her hand for the letter and read it. And that would be that. You remember that she got a gardening catalogue by the same post—"

"Greta Rosen," said Sir Henry slowly. "Then her visit to me—"

"Gentlemen never see through these things," said Miss Marple. "And I'm afraid they often think we old women are—well, cats, to see things the way we do. But there it is. One does know a great deal about one's own sex, unfortunately. I've no doubt there was a barrier between them. The young man felt a sudden inexplicable repulsion. He suspected, purely through instinct, and couldn't hide the suspicion. And I really think that the girl's visit to you was just pure spite. She was safe enough really, but she just went out of her way to fix your suspicions definitely on poor Mr. Templeton. You weren't nearly so sure about him until after her visit."

"I'm sure it was nothing that she said—" began Sir Henry.

"Gentlemen," said Miss Marple calmly, "never see through these things."

"And that girl—" He stopped. "She commits a cold-blooded murder and gets off scot-free!"

"Oh no, Sir Henry," said Miss Marple. "Not scot-free. Neither you nor I believe that. Remember what you said not long ago. No. Greta Rosen will not escape punishment. To begin with, she must be in with a very queer set of people—blackmailers and terrorists—associates who will do her no good and will probably bring her to a miserable end. As you say, one mustn't waste thoughts on the guilty—it's the innocent who matter. Mr. Templeton, who I daresay will marry that German cousin, his tearing up her letter looks—well, it looks suspicious—using the word in quite a different sense from the one we've been using all the evening. A little as though he were afraid of the other girl noticing or asking to see it? Yes, I think there must have been some little romance there. And then there's Dobbs—though, as you say, I daresay it won't much matter to him. His elevenses are probably all he thinks about. And then there's that poor old Gertrud—the one who reminded me of Annie Poultny. Poor Annie Poultny. Fifty years' faithful service and suspected of making away with Miss Lamb's will, though nothing could be proved. Almost broke the poor creature's faithful heart. And then after she was dead it came to light in the secret drawer of the tea caddy where old Miss Lamb had put it herself for safety. But too late then for poor Annie.

"That's what worries me so about that poor old German woman. When one is old, one becomes embittered very easily. I felt much more sorry for her than for Mr. Templeton, who is young and good-looking and evidently a favorite with the ladies. You will write to her, won't you, Sir Henry, and just tell her that her innocence is established beyond doubt? Her dear old master dead, and she no doubt brooding and feeling herself suspected of . . . Oh! It won't bear thinking about!"

"I will write, Miss Marple," said Sir Henry. He looked at her curiously. "You know, I shall never quite understand you. Your outlook is always a different one from what I expect."

"My outlook, I'm afraid, is a very petty one," said Miss Marple humbly. "I hardly ever go out of St. Mary Mead."

"And yet you have solved what may be called an international mystery," said Sir Henry. "For you have solved it. I am convinced of that."

Miss Marple blushed, then bridled a little.

"I was, I think, well educated for the standard of my day. My sister and I had a German governess—a Fräulein. A very sentimental creature. She taught us the language of flowers—a forgotten study nowadays, but most charming. A yellow tulip, for instance, means 'Hopeless Love,' while a China aster means 'I Die of Jealousy at Your Feet.' That letter was signed Georgina, which I seem to remember as dahlia in German, and that of course made the whole thing perfectly clear. I wish I could remember the meaning of dahlia, but alas, that eludes me. My memory is not what it was."

"At any rate, it didn't mean 'Death.' "

"No, indeed. Horrible, is it not? There are very sad things in the world."

"There are," said Mrs. Bantry with a sigh. "It's lucky one has flowers and one's friends."

"She puts us last, you observe," said Dr. Lloyd.

"A man used to send me purple orchids every night to the theater," said Jane dreamily.

" 'I Await Your Favors'—that's what that means," said Miss Marple brightly.

Sir Henry gave a peculiar sort of cough and turned his head away.

Miss Marple gave a sudden exclamation.

"I've remembered. Dahlias mean 'Treachery and Misrepresentation.' "

"Wonderful," said Sir Henry. "Absolutely wonderful."

And he sighed.

The Two Bottles of Relish

LORD DUNSANY

Edward John Moreton Drax Plunkett, eighteenth Baron Dunsany, managed to cram his writing career into a life of genteel pursuits, including traveling, hunting, and cricket. Fantasy and mystery are often combined in his plays and short stories.

Perhaps his best-known tale is the classic "The Two Bottles of Relish" (1934), which appeared in the anthology *Powers of Darkness: A Collection of Uneasy Tales.*

Smithers is my name. I'm what you might call a small man and in a small way of business. I travel for Num-numo, a relish for meats and savories—the world-famous relish, I ought to say. It's really quite good, no deleterious acids in it, and does not affect the heart; so it is quite easy to push. I wouldn't have got the job if it weren't. But I hope some day to get something that's harder to push, as of course the harder they are to push, the better the pay. At present I can just make my way, with nothing at all over; but then I live in a very expensive flat. It happened like this, and that brings me to my story. And it isn't the story you'd expect from a small man like me, yet there's nobody else to tell it. Those that know anything of it besides me are all for hushing it up. Well, I was looking for a room to live in in London when first I got my job. It had to be in London, to be central; and I went to a block of buildings, very gloomy, they looked, and saw the man that ran them and asked him for what I wanted. Flats, they called them; just a bedroom and a sort of a cupboard. Well, as he was showing a man round at the time who was a gent, in fact more than that, so he didn't take much notice of me—the man that ran all those flats didn't, I mean. So I just ran behind for a bit, seeing all sorts of rooms and waiting till I could be shown my class of thing. We came to a very nice flat, a sitting room, bedroom, and bathroom, and a sort of little place that they called a hall. And that's how I came to know Linley. He was the bloke that was being shown round.

"Bit expensive," he said.

And the man that ran the flats turned away to the window and picked his teeth. It's funny how much you can show by a simple thing like that. What he meant to say was that he'd hundreds of flats like that, and thousands of people looking for them, and he didn't care who had them or whether they all went on looking. There was no mistaking him, somehow. And yet he never said a word, only looked away out of the window and picked his teeth. And I ventured to speak to Mr. Linley then; and I said, "How about it, sir, if I paid half, and shared it? I wouldn't be in the way, and I'm out all day, and whatever you said would go, and really I wouldn't be no more in your way than a cat."

You may be surprised at my doing it; and you'll be much more surprised at him accepting it—at least, you would if you knew me, just a small man in a small way of business. And yet I could see at once that he was taking to me more than he was taking to the man at the window.

"But there's only one bedroom," he said.

"I could make up my bed easy in that little room there," I said.

"The hall," said the man, looking round from the window without taking his toothpick out.

"And I'd have the bed out of the way and hid in the cupboard by any hour you like," I said.

He looked thoughtful, and the other man looked out over London; and in the end, do you know, he accepted.

"Friend of yours?" said the flat man.

"Yes," answered Mr. Linley.

It was really very nice of him.

I'll tell you why I did it. Able to afford it? Of course not. But I heard him tell the flat man that he had just come down from Oxford and wanted to live for a few months in London. It turned out he wanted just to be comfortable and do nothing for a bit while he looked things over and chose a job, or probably just as long as he could afford it. Well, I said to myself, what's the Oxford manner worth in business, especially a business like mine? Why, simply everything you've got. If I picked up only a quarter of it from this Mr. Linley I'd be able to double my sales, and that would soon mean I'd be given something a lot harder to push, with perhaps treble the pay. Worth it every time. And you can make a quarter of an education go twice as far again, if you're careful with it. I mean you don't have to quote the whole of the *Inferno* to show that you've read Milton; half a line may do it.

Well, about the story I have to tell. And you mightn't think that a little man like me could make you shudder. Well, I soon forgot about the Oxford manner when we settled down in our flat. I forgot it in the sheer wonder of the man himself. He had a mind like an acrobat's body, like a bird's body. It didn't want education. You didn't notice whether he was educated or not. Ideas were always leaping up in him, things you'd never have thought of. And not only that, but if any ideas were about, he'd sort of catch them. Time and again I've found him knowing just what I was going to say. Not thought reading, but what they call intuition. I used to try to learn a bit about chess, just to take my thoughts off Num-numo in the evening, when I'd done with it. But problems I never could do. Yet he'd come along and glance at my problem and say, "You probably move that piece first," and I'd say, "But where?" and he'd say. "Oh, one of those three squares." And I'd say, "But it will be taken on all of them." And the piece a queen all the time, mind you. And he'd say, "Yes, it's doing no good there: you're probably meant to lose it."

And, do you know, he'd be right.

You see, he'd been following out what the other man had been thinking. That's what he'd been doing.

Well, one day there was that ghastly murder at Unge. I don't know if you remember it. But Steeger had gone down to live with a girl in a bungalow on the North Downs, and that was the first we had heard of him.

The girl had £200, and he got every penny of it, and she utterly disappeared. And Scotland Yard couldn't find her.

Well, I'd happened to read that Steeger had bought two bottles of Num-numo; for the Otherthorpe police had found out everything about him, except what he did with the girl; and that of course attracted my attention, or I should have never thought again about the case or said a word of it to Linley. Num-numo was always on my mind, as I always spent every day pushing it, and that kept me from forgetting the other thing. And so one day I said to Linley, "I wonder with all that knack you have for seeing through a chess problem, and thinking of one thing and another, that you don't have a go at that Otherthorpe mystery. It's a problem as much as chess," I said.

"There's not the mystery in ten murders that there is in one game of chess," he answered.

"It's beaten Scotland Yard," I said.

"Has it?" he asked.

"Knocked them endwise," I said.

"It shouldn't have done that," he said. And almost immediately after he said, "What are the facts?"

We were both sitting at supper, and I told him the facts, as I had them straight from the papers. She was a pretty blonde, she was small, she was called Nancy Elth, she had £200, they lived at the bungalow for five days. After that he stayed there for another fortnight, but nobody ever saw her alive again. Steeger said she had gone to South America, but later said he had never said South America, but South Africa. None of her money remained in the bank where she had kept it, and Steeger was shown to have come by at least £150 just at that time. Then Steeger turned out to be a vegetarian, getting all his food from the greengrocer, and that made the constable in the village of Unge suspicious of him, for a vegetarian was something new to the constable. He watched Steeger after that, and it's well he did, for there was nothing that Scotland Yard asked him that he couldn't tell them about him, except of course the one thing. And he told the police at Otherthorpe five or six miles away, and they came and took a hand at it too. They were able to say for one thing that he never went outside the bungalow and its tidy garden ever since she disappeared. You see, the more they watched him the more suspicious they got, as you naturally do if you're watching a man; so that very soon they were watching every move he made, but if it hadn't been for his being a vegetarian they'd never have started to suspect him, and there wouldn't have been enough evidence even for Linley. Not that they found out anything much against him, except that £150 dropping in from nowhere, and it was Scotland Yard that found that, not the police of Otherthorpe. No, what the constable of Unge found out was about the larch trees, and that beat Scotland Yard utterly, and beat Linley up to the very last, and of course it beat me. There were ten larch trees in the bit of a garden, and he'd made some sort of an arrangement with the landlord, Steeger had, before he took the bungalow, by which he could do what he liked with the larch trees. And then from about the time that little Nancy Elth must have died he cut every one of them down. Three times a day he went at it for nearly a week, and when they were all down he cut them all up into logs no more than two foot long and laid them all in neat heaps. You never saw such work. And what for? To give an excuse for the ax was one theory. But the excuse was bigger than the ax; it took him a fortnight, hard work every day. And he could have killed a little thing like Nancy Elth without an ax, and cut her up too. Another theory was that he wanted firewood, to make away with the body. But he never used it. He left it all standing there in those neat stacks. It fairly beat everybody.

Well, those are the facts I told Linley. Oh yes, and he bought a big butcher's knife. Funny thing, they all do. And yet it isn't so funny after all; if you've got to cut a woman up, you've got to cut her up; and you can't do that without a knife. Then, there were some negative facts. He hadn't burned her. Only had a fire in the small stove now and then, and only used it for cooking. They got on to that pretty smartly, the Unge constable did, and the men that were lending him a hand from Otherthorpe. There were some little woody places lying round, shaws, they call them in that part of the country, the country people do, and they could climb a tree handy and unobserved and get a sniff at the smoke in almost any direction it might be blowing. They did that now and then, and there was no smell of flesh burning, just ordinary cooking. Pretty smart of the Otherthorpe police that was, though of course it didn't help to hang Steeger. Then later on the Scotland Yard men went down and got another fact—negative, but narrowing things down all the while. And that was that the chalk under the bungalow and under the little garden had none of it been disturbed. And he'd never been outside it since Nancy disappeared. Oh yes, and he had a big file besides the knife. But there was no sign of any ground bones found on the file, or any blood on the knife. He'd washed them, of course. I told all that to Linley.

Now I ought to warn you before I go any further. I am a small man myself, and you probably don't expect anything horrible from me. But I ought to warn you this man was a murderer, or at any rate somebody was; the woman had been made away with, a nice pretty little girl too, and the man that had done that wasn't necessarily going to stop at things you might think he'd stop at. With the mind to do a thing like that, and with the long thin shadow of the rope to drive him further, you can't say what he'll stop at. Murder tales seem nice things sometimes for a lady to sit and read all by herself by the fire. But murder isn't a nice thing, and when a murderer's desperate and trying to hide his tracks he isn't even as nice as he was before. I'll ask you to bear that in mind. Well, I've warned you.

So I says to Linley, "And what do you make of it?"

"Drains?" said Linley.

"No," I says, "you're wrong there. Scotland Yard has been into that. And the Otherthorpe people before them. They've had a look in the drains, such as they are, a little thing running into a cesspool beyond the garden; and nothing has gone down it—nothing that oughtn't to have, I mean."

He made one or two other suggestions, but Scotland Yard had been before him in every case. That's really the crab of my story, if you'll excuse the expression. You want a man who sets out to be a detective to take his magnifying glass and go down to the spot; to go to the spot before everything; and then to measure the footmarks and pick up the clues and find the knife that the police have overlooked. But Linley never even went near the place, and he hadn't got a magnifying glass, not as I ever saw, and Scotland Yard were before him every time.

In fact they had more clues than anybody could make head or tail of. Every kind of clue to show that he'd murdered the poor little girl; every kind of clue to show that he hadn't disposed of the body; and yet the body wasn't there. It wasn't in South America either, and not much more likely in South Africa. And all the time, mind you, that enormous bunch of chopped larchwood, a clue that was staring everyone in the face and leading nowhere. No, we didn't seem to want any more clues, and Linley never went near the place. The trouble was to deal with the clues we'd got. I was completely mystified; so was Scotland Yard; and Linley seemed to be getting no forwarder; and all the while the mystery was hanging on me. I mean if it were not for the trifle I'd chanced to remember, and if it were not for one chance word I said to Linley, that mystery would have gone the way of all the other mysteries that men have made nothing of, a darkness, a little patch of night in history.

Well, the fact was Linley didn't take much interest in it at first, but I was so absolutely sure that he could do it that I kept him to the idea. "You can do chess problems," I said.

"That's ten times harder," he said, sticking to his point.

"Then why don't you do this?" I said.

"Then go and take a look at the board for me," said Linley.

That was his way of talking. We'd been a fortnight together, and I knew it by now. He meant to go down to the bungalow at Unge. I know you'll say why didn't he go himself; but the plain truth of it is that if he'd been tearing about the countryside he'd never have been thinking, whereas sitting there in his chair by the fire in our flat there was no limit to the ground he could cover, if you follow my meaning. So down I went by train next day, and got out at Unge station. And there were the North Downs rising up before me, somehow like music.

"It's up there, isn't it?" I said to the porter.

"That's right," he said. "Up there by the lane; and mind to turn to your right when you get to the old yew tree, a very big tree, you can't mistake it, and then . . ." and he told me the way so that I couldn't go wrong. I found them all like that, very nice and helpful. You see, it was Unge's day at last. Everyone had heard of Unge now; you could have got a letter there any time just then without putting the county or post town; and this was what Unge had to show. I daresay if you tried to find Unge now . . . well, anyway, they were making hay while the sun shone.

Well, there the hill was, going up into sunlight, going up like a song. You don't want to hear about the spring, and all the may rioting, and the color that came down over everything later on in the day, and all those birds; but I thought, "What a nice place to bring a girl to." And then when I thought that he'd killed her there, well, I'm only a small man, as I said, but when I thought of her on that hill with all the birds singing, I said to myself, "Wouldn't it be odd if it turned out to be me after all that got that man killed, if he did murder her." So I soon found my way up to the bungalow and began prying about, looking over the hedge into the garden. And I didn't find much, and I found nothing at all that the police hadn't found already, but there were those heaps of larch logs staring me in the face and looking very queer.

I did a lot of thinking, leaning against the hedge, breathing the smell of the may, and looking over the top of it at the larch logs, and the neat little bungalow the other side of the garden. Lots of theories I thought of, till I came to the best thought of all; and that was that if I left the thinking to Linley, with his Oxford-and-Cambridge education, and only brought him the facts, as he had told me, I should be doing more good in my way than if I tried to do any big thinking. I forgot to tell you that I had gone to Scotland Yard in the morning. Well, there wasn't really much to tell. What they asked me was what I wanted. And, not having an answer exactly ready, I didn't find out very much from them. But it was quite different at Unge; everyone was most obliging; it was their day there, as I said. The constable let me go indoors, so long as I didn't touch anything, and he gave me a look at the garden from the inside. And I saw the stumps of the ten larch trees, and I noticed one thing that Linley said was very observant of me, not that it turned out to be any use, but anyway I was doing my best: I noticed that the stumps had been all chopped anyhow. And from that I thought that the man that did it didn't know much about chopping. The constable said that was a deduction. So then I said that the ax was blunt when he used it; and that certainly made the constable think, though he didn't actually say I was right this time. Did I tell you that Steeger never went outdoors, except to the little garden to chop wood, ever since Nancy disappeared? I think I did. Well, it was perfectly true. They'd watched him night and day, one or another of them, and the Unge constable told me that himself. That limited things a good deal. The only thing I didn't like about it was that I felt Linley ought to have found all that out instead of ordinary policemen, and I felt that he could have too. There'd have been romance in a story like that. And they'd never have done it if the news hadn't gone round that the man was a vegetarian and only dealt at the greengrocer's. Likely as not even that was only started out of pique by the butcher. It's queer what little things may trip a man up. Best to keep straight is my motto. But perhaps I'm straying a bit away from my story. I should like to do that forever—forget that it ever was; but I can't.

Well, I picked up all sorts of information; clues, I suppose I should call it in a story like this, though they none of them seemed to lead anywhere. For instance, I found out everything he ever bought at the village, I could even tell you the kind of salt he bought, quite plain with no phosphates in it, that they sometimes put in to make it tidy. And then he got ice from the fishmonger's, and plenty of vegetables, as I said, from the greengrocer, Mergin & Sons. And I had a bit of a talk over it all with the constable. Slugger, he said his name was. I wondered why he hadn't come in and searched the place as soon as the girl was missing. "Well, you can't do that," he said. "And besides, we didn't suspect at once, not about the girl, that is. We only suspected there was something wrong about him on account of him being a vegetarian. He stayed a good fortnight after the last that was seen of her. And then we slipped in like a knife. But, you see, no one had been inquiring about her, there was no warrant out."

"And what did you find?" I asked Slugger, "when you went in?"

"Just a big file," he said, "and the knife and the ax that he must have got to chop her up with."

"But he got the ax to chop trees with," I said.

"Well, yes," he said, but rather grudgingly.

"And what did he chop them for?" I asked.

"Well, of course, my superiors has theories about that," he said, "that they mightn't tell to everybody."

You see, it was those logs that were beating them.

"But did he cut her up at all?" I asked.

"Well, he said that she was going to South America," he answered. Which was really very fair-minded of him.

I don't remember now much else that he told me. Steeger left the plates and dishes all washed up and very neat, he said.

Well, I brought all this back to Linley, going up by the train that started just about sunset. I'd like to tell you about the late spring evening, so calm over that grim bungalow, closing in with a glory all round it as though it were blessing it; but you'll want to hear of the murder. Well, I told Linley everything, though much of it didn't seem to me to be worth the telling. The trouble was that the moment I began to leave anything out, he'd know it, and make me drag it in. "You can't tell what may be vital," he'd say. "A tin tack swept away by a housemaid might hang a man."

All very well, but be consistent, even if you are educated at Eton and Harrow, and whenever I mentioned Num-numo, which after all was the beginning of the whole story, because he wouldn't have heard of it if it hadn't been for me, and my noticing that Steeger had bought two bottles of it, why then he said that things like that were trivial and we should keep to the main issues. I naturally talked a bit about Num-numo, because only that day I had pushed close on fifty bottles of it in Unge. A murder certainly stimulates people's minds, and Steeger's two bottles gave me an opportunity that only a fool could have failed to make something of. But of course all that was nothing at all to Linley.

You can't see a man's thoughts, and you can't look into his mind, so that all the most exciting things in the world can never be told of. But what I think happened all that evening with Linley, while I talked to him before supper, and all through supper, and sitting smoking afterward in front of our fire, was that his thoughts were stuck at a barrier there was no getting over. And the barrier wasn't the difficulty of finding ways and means by which Steeger might have made away with the body, but the impossibility of finding why he chopped those masses of wood every day for a fortnight, and paid, as I'd just found out, £25 to his landlord to be allowed to do it. That's what was beating Linley. As for the ways by which Steeger might have hidden the body, it seemed to me that every way was blocked by the police. If you said he buried it, they said the chalk was undisturbed, if you said he carried it away, they said he never left the place; if you said he burned it, they said no smell of burning was ever noticed when the smoke blew low, and when it didn't they climbed trees after it. I'd taken to Linley wonderfully, and I didn't have to be educated to see there was something big in a mind like his, and I thought that he could have done it. When I saw the police getting in before him like that, and no way that I could see of getting past them, I felt real sorry.

Did anyone come to the house, he asked me once or twice. Did anyone take anything away from it? But we couldn't account for it that way. Then perhaps I made some suggestion that was no good, or perhaps I started talking of Num-numo again, and he interrupted me rather sharply.

"But what would you do, Smithers?" he said. "What would you do yourself?"

"If I'd murdered poor Nancy Elth?" I asked.

"Yes," he said.

"I can't ever imagine doing such a thing," I told him.

He sighed at that, as though it were something against me.

"I suppose I should never be a detective," I said. And he just shook his head.

Then he looked broodingly into the fire for what seemed an hour. And then he shook his head again. We both went to bed after that.

I shall remember the next day all my life. I was till evening, as usual, pushing Num-numo. And we sat down to supper about nine. You couldn't get things cooked at those flats, so of course we had it cold. And Linley began with a salad. I can see it now, every bit of it. Well, I was still a bit full of what I'd done in Unge, pushing Num-numo. Only a fool, I know, would have been unable to push it there; but still, I *had* pushed it; and about fifty bottles, forty-eight to be exact, are something in a small village, whatever the circumstances. So I was talking about it a bit; and then all of a sudden I realized that Num-numo was nothing to Linley, and I pulled myself up with a jerk. It was really very kind of him; do you know what he did? He must have known at once why I stopped talking, and he just stretched out a hand and said, "Would you give me a little of your Num-numo for my salad?"

I was so touched I nearly gave it him. But of course you don't take Num-numo with salad. Only for meats and savories. That's on the bottle.

So I just said to him, "Only for meats and savories." Though I don't know what savories are. Never had any.

I never saw a man's face go like that before.

He seemed still for a whole minute. And nothing speaking about him but that expression. Like a man that's seen a ghost, one is tempted to write. But it wasn't really at all. I'll tell you what he looked like. Like a man that's seen something that no one has ever looked at before, something he thought couldn't be.

And then he said in a voice that was all quite changed, more low and gentle and quiet, it seemed, "No good for vegetables, eh?"

"Not a bit," I said.

And at that he gave a kind of sob in his throat. I hadn't thought he could feel things like that. Of course I didn't know what it was all about; but, whatever it was, I thought all that sort of thing would have been knocked out of him at Eton and Harrow, an educated man like that. There were no tears in his eyes, but he was feeling something horribly.

And then he began to speak with big spaces between his words, saying, "A man might make a mistake, perhaps, and use Num-numo with vegetables."

"Not twice," I said. What else could I say?

And he repeated that after me as though I had told of the end of the world, and adding an awful emphasis to my words, till they seemed all clammy with some frightful significance, and shaking his head as he said it.

Then he was quite silent.

"What is it?" I asked.

"Smithers," he said.

"Yes," I said.

"Smithers," said he.

And I said, "Well?"

"Look here, Smithers," he said, "you must phone down to the grocer at Unge and find out from him this."

"Yes?" I said.

"Whether Steeger bought those two bottles, as I expect he did, on the same day, and not a few days apart. He couldn't have done that."

I waited to see if any more was coming, and then I ran out and did what I was told. It took me some time, being after nine o'clock, and only then with the help of the police. About six days apart, they said; and so I came back and told Linley. He looked up at me so hopefully when I came in, but I saw that it was the wrong answer by his eyes.

You can't take things to heart like that without being ill, and when he didn't speak I said, "What you want is a good brandy, and go to bed early."

And he said, "No. I must see someone from Scotland Yard. Phone round to them. Say here at once."

But I said, "I can't get an inspector from Scotland Yard to call on us at this hour."

His eyes were all lit up. He was all there, all right.

"Then tell them," he said, "they'll never find Nancy Elth. Tell one of them to come here, and I'll tell him why." And he added, I think only for me, "They must watch Steeger, till one day they get him over something else."

And, do you know, he came. Inspector Ulton; he came himself.

While we were waiting I tried to talk to Linley. Partly curiosity, I admit. But I didn't want to leave him to those thoughts of his, brooding away by the fire. I tried to ask him what it was all about. But he wouldn't tell me. "Murder is horrible" is all he would say. "And as a man covers his tracks up it only gets worse."

He wouldn't tell me. "There are tales," he said, "that one never wants to hear."

That's true enough. I wish I'd never heard this one. I never did, actually. But I guessed it from Linley's last words to Inspector Ulton, the only ones that I overheard. And perhaps this is the point at which to stop reading my story, so that you don't guess it too; even if you think you want murder stories. For don't you rather want a murder story with a bit of a romantic twist, and not a story about real foul murder? Well, just as you like.

In came Inspector Ulton, and Linley shook hands in silence, and pointed the way to his bedroom; and they went in there and talked in low voices, and I never heard a word.

A fairly hearty-looking man was the inspector when they went into that room.

They walked through our sitting room in silence when they came out, and together they went into the hall, and there I heard the only words they said to each other. It was the inspector that first broke that silence.

"But why," he said, "did he cut down the trees?"

"Solely," said Linley, "in order to get an appetite."

The Two Ladies of Rose Cottage

PETER ROBINSON

A Yorkshire native who now resides in Toronto, Peter Robinson constructs a touching mystery in this story that encompasses an entire lifetime. Robinson is the author of the Inspector Banks series *(Gallows View, A Dedicated Man, A Necessary End, The Hanging Valley, Past Reason Hated, Wednesday's Child, Final Account,* and *Innocent Grave). Past Reason Hated* won the Crime Writers of Canada Award for best novel in 1992, and one of Robinson's short stories, "Innocence" won the CWC Award for best short story in 1991.

In our village, they were always known as the "Two Ladies of Rose Cottage": Miss Eunice, with the white hair, and Miss Teresa with the gray. Nobody really knew where they came from, or exactly how old they were, but the consensus held that they had met in India, America, or South Africa, and decided to return to the homeland to live out their days together. And, in 1939, they were generally believed to be in or approaching their nineties.

Imagine our surprise, then, one fine day in September, when the police car pulled up outside Rose Cottage, and when, in a matter of hours, rumors began to spread throughout the village: rumors of human bones dug up in a distant garden; rumors of mutilation and dismemberment; rumors of murder.

Lyndgarth is the name of our village. It is situated in one of the most remote Yorkshire dales, about twenty miles from Eastvale, the nearest large town. The village is no more than a group of limestone houses with slate roofs, clustered around a bumpy, slanted green that always reminded me of a handkerchief flapping in the breeze. We have the usual amenities—grocer's shop, butcher's, news-agent's, post office, school, two churches, three public houses—and proximity to some of the most beautiful countryside in the world.

I was fifteen in 1939, and Miss Eunice and Miss Teresa had been living in the village for twenty years, yet still they remained strangers to us. It is often said that you have to "winter out" at least two years before being accepted into village life, and in the case of a remote place like Lyndgarth, in those days, it was more like ten.

As far as the locals were concerned then, the two ladies had served their apprenticeship and were more than fit to be accepted as fully paid-up members of the community, yet there was about them a certain detached quality that kept them ever at arm's length.

They did all their shopping in the village and were always polite to people they met in the street; they regularly attended church services at St. Oswald's and helped with charity events; and they never set foot in any of the public houses. But still there was that sense of distance, of not quite being—or not *wanting* to be—a part of things.

The summer of 1939 had been unusually beautiful despite the political tensions. Or am I indulging in nostalgia for childhood? Our dale can be one of the most grim and desolate landscapes on the face of the earth, even in August, but I remember the summers of my youth as days of dazzling sunshine and blue skies. In 1939, every day was a new symphony of color—golden buttercups, pink clover, mauve crane's-bill—ever-changing and recombining in fresh palettes. While the tense negotiations went on in Europe, while Ribbentrop and Molotov signed the Nazi-Soviet pact, and while there was talk of conscription and rationing at home, very little changed in Lyndgarth.

Summer in the dale was always a season for odd jobs—peat-cutting, wall-mending, sheep-clipping—and for entertainments, such as the dialect plays, the circus, fairs, and brass bands. Even after war was declared on the third of September, we still found ourselves rather guiltily having fun, scratching our heads, shifting from foot to foot, and wondering when something really warlike was going to happen.

Of course, we had our gas masks in their cardboard boxes, which we had to carry everywhere; streetlighting was banned, and motor cars were not allowed to use their headlights. This latter rule was the cause of numerous accidents in the dale, usually involving wandering sheep on the unfenced roads.

Some evacuees also arrived from the cities. Uncouth urchins for the most part, often verminous and ill-equipped for country life, they seemed like an alien race to us. Most of them didn't seem to have any warm clothing or Wellington boots, as if they had never seen mud in the city. Looking back, I realize they were far from home, separated from their parents, and they must have been scared to death. I am ashamed to admit, though, that at the time I didn't go out of my way to give them a warm welcome.

This is partly because I was always lost in my own world. I was a bookish child, and had recently discovered the stories of Thomas Hardy, who seemed to understand and sympathize with a lonely village lad and his dreams of becoming a writer. I also remember how much he thrilled and scared me with some of the stories. After "The Withered Arm," I wouldn't let anyone touch me for a week, and I didn't dare go to sleep after "Barbara of the House of Grebe" for fear that there was a horribly disfigured statue in the wardrobe, that the door would slowly creak open and . . .

I think I was reading *Far from the Madding Crowd* that hot July day, and, as was my wont, I read as I walked across the village green, not looking where I was going. It was Miss Teresa I bumped into, and I remember thinking that she seemed remarkably resilient for such an old lady.

"Do mind where you're going, young man!" she admonished me, though when she heard my effusive apologies, she softened her tone somewhat. She asked me what I was reading, and when I showed her the book, she closed her eyes for a moment, and a strange expression crossed her wrinkled features.

"Ah, Mr. Hardy," she said after a short silence. "I knew him once, you know, in his youth. I grew up in Dorset."

I could hardly hold back my enthusiasm. Someone who actually *knew* Hardy! I told her that he was my favorite writer of all time, even better than Shakespeare, and that when I grew up I wanted to be a writer, just like him.

Miss Teresa smiled indulgently. "Do calm down," she said, then she paused. "I suppose," she continued, with a glance toward Miss Eunice, "that if you are really interested in Mr. Hardy, perhaps you might like to come to tea someday?"

When I assured her I would be delighted, we made an arrangement that I was to call at Rose Cottage the following Tuesday at four o'clock, after securing my mother's permission, of course.

That Tuesday visit was the first of many. Inside, Rose Cottage belied its name. It seemed dark and gloomy, unlike ours, which was always full of sunlight and bright flowers. The furnishings were antique, even a little shabby. I recollect no family photographs of the kind that embellished most mantelpieces, but there was a huge gilt-framed painting of a young girl working alone in a field hanging on one wall. If the place sometimes smelled a little musty and neglected, the aroma of Miss Teresa's fresh-baked scones more often than not made up for it.

"Mr. Hardy was full of contradictions," Miss Teresa told me on one occasion. "He was a dreamer, of course, and never happier than when wandering the countryside, alone with his thoughts. But he was also a fine musician. He played the fiddle on many social occasions, such as dances and weddings, and he was often far more gregarious and cheerful than many of his critics would have imagined. He was also a scholar, head forever buried in a book, always studying Latin or Greek. I was no dullard, either, you know, and I like to think I held my own in our conversations, though I had little Latin and less Greek." She chuckled, then turned serious again. "Anyway, one never felt one really *knew* him. One was always looking at a mask. Do you understand me, young man?"

I nodded. "I think so, Miss Teresa."

"Yes, well," she said, staring into space as she sometimes did while speaking of Hardy. "At least that was *my* impression. Though he was a good ten years older than me, I like to believe I got glimpses of the man behind the mask. But because the other villagers thought him a bit odd, and because he was difficult to know, he also attracted a lot of idle gossip. I remember there was talk about him and that Sparks girl from Puddletown. What was her first name, Eunice?"

"Tryphena."

"That's right." She curled her lip and seemed to spit out the name. "Tryphena Sparks. A singularly dull girl, I always thought. We were about the same age, you know, she and I. Anyway, there was talk of a child. Utter rubbish, of course." She gazed out of the window at the green, where a group of children were playing a makeshift game of cricket. Her eyes seemed to film over. "Many's the time I used to walk through the woodland past the house, and I would see him sitting there at his upstairs window seat, writing or gazing out on the garden. Sometimes he would wave and come down to talk." Suddenly she stopped, then her eyes glittered, and she went on. "He used to go and watch hangings in Dorchester. Did you know that?"

I had to confess that I didn't, my acquaintance with Hardy being recent and restricted only to his published works of fiction, but it never occurred to me to doubt Miss Teresa's word.

"Of course, executions were public back then." Again she paused, and I thought I saw, or rather *sensed* a little shiver run through her. Then she said that was enough for today, that it was time for scones and tea.

I think she enjoyed shocking me like that at the end of her little narratives, as if we needed to be brought back to reality with a jolt. I remember on another occasion she looked me in the eye and said, "Of course, the doctor tossed him aside as dead at birth, you know. If it hadn't been for the nurse, he would never have survived. That must do something to a man, don't you think?"

We talked of many other aspects of Hardy and his work, and, for the most part, Miss Eunice remained silent, nodding from time to time. Occasionally, when Miss Teresa's memory seemed to fail her on some point, such as a name or what novel Hardy might have been writing in a certain year, she would supply the information.

I remember one visit particularly vividly. Miss Teresa stood up rather more quickly than I thought her able to, and left the room for a few moments. I sat politely, sipping my tea, aware of Miss Eunice's silence and the ticking of the grandfather clock out in the hall. When Miss Teresa returned, she was carrying an old book, or rather two books, which she handed to me.

It was a two-volume edition of *Far from the Madding Crowd*, and, though I didn't know it at the time, it was the first edition, from 1874, and was probably worth a small fortune. But what fascinated me even more than Helen Paterson's illustrations was the brief inscription on the flyleaf: *To Tess, With Affection, Tom.*

I knew that Tess was a diminutive of Teresa, because I had an Aunt Teresa in Harrogate, and it never occurred to me to question that the "Tess" in the inscription was the person sitting opposite me, or that the "Tom" was any other than Thomas Hardy himself.

"He called you Tess," I remember saying. "Perhaps he had you in mind when he wrote *Tess of the d'Urbervilles?*"

Miss Teresa's face drained of color so quickly I feared for her life, and it seemed that a palpable chill entered the room. "Don't be absurd, boy," she whispered. "Tess Durbeyfield was hanged for murder."

We had been officially at war for about a week, I think, when the police called. There were three men, one in uniform and two in plainclothes. They spent almost two hours in Rose Cottage, then came out alone, got in their car, and drove away. We never saw them again.

The day after the visit, though, I happened to overhear our local constable talking with the vicar in St. Oswald's churchyard. By a great stroke of fortune, several yews stood between us and I was able to remain unseen while I took in every word.

"Murdered, that's what they say," said P. C. Walker. "Bashed his 'ead in with a poker, then chopped 'im up in little pieces and buried 'em in t' garden. Near Dorchester, it were. Village called 'igher Bockhampton. People who lived there were digging an air-raid shelter when they found t' bones. 'Eck of a shock for t' bairns."

Could they possibly mean Miss Teresa? That sweet old lady who made such delightful scones and had known the young Thomas Hardy? Could she really have bashed someone on the head, chopped him up into little pieces, and buried them in the garden? I shivered at the thought, despite the heat.

But nothing more was heard of the murder charge. The police never returned, people found new things to talk about, and after a couple of weeks Miss Eunice and Miss Teresa reappeared in village life much as they had been before. The only difference was that my mother would no longer allow me to visit Rose Cottage. I put up token resistance, but by then my mind was full of Spitfires, secret codes, and aircraft carriers anyway.

Events seemed to move quickly in the days after the police visit, though I cannot be certain of the actual time period involved. Four things, however, conspired to put the murder out of my mind for some time: Miss Teresa died, I think in the November of that same year; Miss Eunice retreated into an even deeper silence than before; the war escalated; and I was called up to military service.

The next time I gave any thought to the two ladies of Rose Cottage was in Egypt, of all places, in September 1942. I was on night watch with the 8th Army, not far from Alamein. Desert nights have an eerie beauty I have never found anywhere else since. After the heat of the day, the cold surprises one, for a start, as does the sense of endless space, but even more surprising is the desertscape of wrecked tanks, jeeps, and lorries in the cold moonlight, metal wrenched and twisted into impossible patterns like some petrified forest or exposed coral reef.

To spoil our sleep and shatter our nerves, Rommel's Afrika Corps had got into the routine of setting up huge amplified speakers and blaring out "Lili Marleen" over and over all night long. It was on a night such as this, while I was trying to stay warm and awake and trying to shut my ears to the music, that I struck up a conversation with a soldier called Sidney Ferris from one of the Dorset regiments.

When Sid told me he had grown up in Piddlehinton, I suddenly thought of the two ladies of Rose Cottage.

"Did you ever hear any stories of a murder around there?" I asked, offering Sid a cigarette. "A place called Higher Bockhampton?"

"Lots of murder stories going around when I was a lad," he said, lighting up, careful to hide the flame with his cupped hand. "Better than the wireless."

"This would be a wife murdering her husband."

He nodded. "Plenty of that and all. And husbands murdering their wives. Makes you wonder whether it's worth getting married, doesn't it? Higher Bockhampton, you say?"

"Yes. Teresa Morgan, I believe the woman's name was."

He frowned. "Name don't ring no bell," he said, "but I do recall a tale about some woman who was supposed to have killed her husband, cut him up in pieces, and buried them in the garden. A couple of young lads found some bones when they was digging an air-raid shelter a couple of years back. Animal bones, if you ask me."

"But did the villagers believe the tale?"

He shrugged. "Don't know about anyone else, but I can't say as I did. So many stories like that going around, they can't all be true, or damn near all of us would be murderers or corpses. Stands to reason, doesn't it?" And he took a long drag on his cigarette, holding it in his cupped hand, like most soldiers, so the enemy wouldn't see the pinpoint of light.

"Did anyone say what became of the woman?" I asked.

"She went away some years later. There was talk of someone else seen running away from the farmhouse, too, the night they said the murder must have taken place."

"Could it have been him? The husband?"

Sid shook his head. "Too slight a figure. Her husband was a big man, apparently. Anyway, that led to more talk of an illicit lover. There's always a lover, isn't there? Have you noticed? You know what kind of minds these country gossips have."

"Did anyone say who the other person might have been?"

"Nobody knew. Just rumors of a vague shape seen running away. These are old wives' tales we're talking about."

"But perhaps there's some tru—"

But at that point I was relieved of my watch, and the next weeks turned out to be so chaotic that I never even saw Sid again. I heard later that he was killed at the battle of Alamein just over a month after our conversation.

I didn't come across the mystery of Rose Cottage again until the early 1950s. At that time, I was living in Eastvale, in a small flat overlooking the cobbled market square. The town was much smaller and quieter than it is today, though little about the square has changed, from the ancient market cross, the Queen's Arms on the corner, the Norman church, and the Tudor-fronted police station.

I had recently published my first novel and was still basking in that exquisite sensation that comes only once in a writer's career: the day he holds the first bound and printed copy of his very first work. Of course, there was no money in writing, so I worked part-time in a bookshop on North Market Street, and on one of my mornings off, a market day, as I remember, I was absorbed in polishing the third chapter of what was to be my second novel when I heard a faint tap at my door. This was enough to startle me, as I rarely had any visitors.

Puzzled and curious, I left my typewriter and went to open the door. There stood a wizened old lady, hunch-shouldered, white-haired, carrying a stick with a brass lion's head handle and a small package wrapped in brown paper, tied with string.

She must have noticed my confused expression, because, with a faint smile, she said, "Don't you recognize me, Mr. Riley? Dear, dear, have I aged that much?"

Then I knew her, knew the voice.

"Miss Eunice!" I cried, throwing my door open. "Please forgive me. I was lost in my own world. Do come in. And you must call me Christopher."

Once we were settled, with a pot of tea mashing beside us—though, alas, none of Miss Teresa's scones—I noticed the dark circles under Miss Eunice's eyes, the yellow around the pupils, the parchmentlike quality of her skin, and I knew she was seriously ill.

"How did you find me?" I asked.

"It didn't take a Sherlock Holmes. Everyone knows where the famous writer lives in a small town like Eastvale."

"Hardly famous," I demurred. "But thank you anyway. I never knew you took the trouble to follow my fortunes."

"Teresa would have wished it. She was very fond of you, you know. Apart from ourselves and the police, you were the only person in Lyndgarth who ever entered Rose Cottage. Did you know that? You might remember that we kept ourselves very much to ourselves."

"Yes, I remember that," I told her.

"I came to give you this."

She handed me the package and I untied it carefully. Inside was the Smith, Elder & Co. first edition of *Far from the Madding Crowd,* complete with Hardy's inscription to "Tess."

"But you shouldn't," I said. "This must be very valuable. It's a fir—"

She waved aside my objections. "Please take it. It is what Teresa would have wished. And I wish it, too. Now listen," she went on. "That isn't the only reason I came. I have something very important to tell you, to do with why the police came to visit all those years ago. The thought of going to my grave without telling someone troubles me deeply."

"But why me? And why now?"

"I told you. Teresa was especially fond of you. And you're a writer," she added mysteriously. "You'll understand. Should you wish to make use of the story, please do so. Neither Teresa nor I have any living relatives to offend. All I ask is that you wait a suitable number of years after my death before publishing any account. And that death is expected to occur at some point over the next few months. Does that answer your second question?"

I nodded. "Yes. I'm sorry."

"You needn't be. As you may well be aware, I have long since exceeded my three score and ten, though I can hardly say the extra years have been a blessing. But that is God's will. Do you agree to my terms?"

"Of course. I take it this is about the alleged murder?"

Miss Eunice raised her eyebrows. "So you've heard the rumors?" she said. "Well, there was a murder all right. Teresa Morgan murdered her husband, Jacob, and buried his body in the garden." She held out her tea cup and I poured. I noticed her hand was shaking slightly. Mine was, too. The shouts of the market vendors came in through my open windows.

"When did she do this?" was all I could manage.

Miss Eunice closed her eyes and pursed her cracked lips. "I don't remember the exact year," she said. "But it really doesn't matter. You could look it up, if you wanted. It was the year the Queen was proclaimed Empress of India."

I happened to know that was in 1877. I have always had a good memory for historical dates. If my calculations were correct. Miss Teresa would have been about twenty-seven at the time. "Will you tell me what happened?" I asked.

"That's why I'm here," Miss Eunice said rather sharply. "Teresa's husband was a brute, a bully, and a drunkard. She wouldn't have married him, had *she* had any choice in the matter. But her parents approved the match. He had his own small farm, you see, and they were only tenants. Teresa was a very intelligent girl, but that counted for nothing in those days. In fact, it was a positive disadvantage. As was her willfulness. Anyway, he used to beat her to within an inch of her life—where the bruises wouldn't show, of course. One day she'd had enough of it, so she killed him."

"What did she do?"

"She hit him with the poker from the fireplace and, after darkness had fallen, she buried him deep in the garden. She was afraid that if the matter went to court the authorities wouldn't believe her, and she would be hanged. She had no evidence, you see. And Jacob was a popular man among the other fellows of the village, as is so often the case with drunken brutes. And Teresa was terrified of being publicly hanged."

"But did no one suspect her?"

Miss Eunice shook her head. "Jacob was constantly talking about leaving his wife and heading for the New World. He used to berate her for not bearing him any children—specifically sons—and threatened that one day she would wake up and he would be gone. Gone to another country to find a woman who could give him the children he wanted. He repeated these threats in the ale-house so often that no one in the entire county of Dorset could fail to know about them."

"So when he disappeared, everyone assumed he had followed through on his threats to leave her?"

"Exactly. Oh, there were rumors that his wife had murdered him, of course. There always are when such mysteries occur."

Yes, I thought, remembering my conversation with Sid Ferris one cold desert night ten years ago: rumors and fancies, the stuff of fiction. And something about a third person seen fleeing from the scene. Well, that could wait.

"Teresa stayed on at the farm for another ten years," Miss Eunice went on. "Then she sold up and went to America. It was a brave move, but Teresa no more lacked for courage than she did for beauty. She was in her late thirties then, and even after a hard life, she could still turn heads. In New York, she landed on her feet and eventually married a financier. Sam Cotter. A good man. She also took a companion."

"You?" I asked.

Miss Eunice nodded. "Yes. Some years later, Sam died of a stroke. We stayed on in New York for a while, but we grew increasingly homesick. We came back finally in 1919, just after the Great War. For obvious reasons, Teresa didn't want to live anywhere near Dorset, so we settled in Yorkshire."

"A remarkable tale," I said.

"But that's not all," Miss Eunice went on, pausing only to sip some tea. "There was a child."

"I thought you said—"

She took one hand off her stick and held it up, palm out. "Christopher, please let me tell the story in my own way. Then it will be yours to do with as you wish. You have no idea how difficult this is for me." She paused and stared down at the brass lion's head for so long I feared she had fallen asleep, or died. Outside in the market square a butcher was loudly trying to sell a leg of lamb. Just as I was about to go over to Miss Eunice, she stirred. "There was a child," she repeated. "When Teresa was fifteen, she gave birth to a child. It was a difficult birth. She was never able to bear any other children."

"What happened to this child?"

"Teresa had a sister called Alice, living in Dorchester. Alice was five years older and already married with two children. Just before the pregnancy started to show, both Teresa and Alice went to stay with relatives in Cornwall for a few months, after it had been falsely announced that Alice was with child again. You would be surprised how often such things happened. When they came back, Alice had a fine baby girl."

"Who was the father?"

"Teresa would never say. The one thing she did make clear was that no one had forced unwanted attentions on her, that the child was the result of a love match, an infatuation. It certainly wasn't Jacob Morgan."

"Did she ever see the child again?"

"Oh, certainly. What could be more natural than visiting one's sister and seeing one's niece grow up? When the girl was a little older, she began to pay visits to the farm, too."

Miss Eunice stopped here and frowned so hard I thought her brow would crack like dry paper. "That was when the problems began," she said quietly.

"What problems?"

Miss Eunice put her stick aside and held out her tea cup. I refilled it. Her hands steady now, she held the cup against her scrawny chest as if its heat were the only thing keeping her alive. "This is the most difficult part," she said in a faint voice. "The part I didn't know whether I could ever tell anyone."

"If you don't wish—"

She waved my objection aside. "It's all right, Christopher. I didn't know how much I could tell you before I came here, but I know now.

I've come this far. I can't go back now. Just give me a few moments to collect myself."

Outside, the market was in full swing, and during the ensuing silence I could hear the clamor of voices selling and buying, arguing over prices.

"Did I ever tell you that Teresa was an extremely beautiful young girl?" Miss Eunice asked after a while.

"I believe you mentioned it, yes."

She nodded. "Well, she was. And so was her daughter. When she began coming by herself to the house, she was about twelve or thirteen years of age. Jacob didn't fail to notice her, how well she was 'filling out' as he used to say. One day, Teresa had gone into the village for firewood and the child arrived in her absence. Jacob, just home from the ale-house, was there alone to greet her. Need I say more, Mr. Riley?"

I shook my head. "I don't mean to excuse him in any way, but I'm assuming he didn't know the girl was his step-daughter?"

"That is correct. He never knew. Nor did *she* know Teresa was her mother. Not until much later."

"What happened next?"

"Teresa came in before her husband could have his way with the struggling, half-naked child. Everything else was as I said. She picked up the poker and hit him on the head. Not once, but six times. Then they cleaned up and waited until after dark and buried him deep in the garden. She sent her daughter back to her sister's and carried on as if her husband had simply left her, just as he had threatened to do."

So the daughter was the mysterious third person seen leaving the farm in Sid Ferris's account. "What became of the poor child?" I asked.

Miss Eunice paused again and seemed to struggle for breath. She turned terribly pale. I got up and moved toward her, but she stretched out her hand. "No, no. I'm all right, Christopher. Please sit."

A motor car honked outside and one of the street vendors yelled a curse.

Miss Eunice patted her chest. "That's better. I'm fine now, really I am. Just a minor spasm. But I do feel ashamed. I'm afraid I haven't been entirely truthful with you. It's so difficult. You see, I was, I *am* that child."

For a moment my mouth just seemed to flap open and shut and I couldn't speak. Finally, I managed to stammer, "You? *You* are Miss Teresa's daughter? But you can't be. That's not possible."

"I didn't mean to shock you," she went on softly, "but, really, you only have yourself to blame. When people see two old ladies together, all they see is two old ladies. When you first began calling on us at Rose Cottage fifteen years ago, Teresa was ninety and I was seventy-six. I doubt a fifteen-year-old boy could tell the difference. Nor could most people. And Teresa was always remarkably robust and well-preserved."

When I had regained my composure, I asked her to continue.

"There is very little left to say. I helped my mother kill Jacob Morgan and bury him. And we didn't cut him up into little pieces. That part is pure fiction invented by scurrilous gossip-mongers. My foster-parents died within a short time of one another, around the turn of the century, and Teresa wired me the money to come and live with her in New York. I had never married, so I had no ties to break. I think that experience with Jacob Morgan, brief and inconclusive as it was, must have given me a lifelong aversion to marital relations. Anyway, it was in New York where Teresa told me she was really my mother. She couldn't tell Sam, of course, so I remained there as her companion, and we always lived more as friends than as mother and daughter." She smiled. "When we came back to England, we chose to live as two spinsters, the kind of relationship nobody really questions in a village because it would be in bad taste to do so."

"How did the police find you after so long?"

"We never hid our identities. Nor did we hide our whereabouts. We bought Rose Cottage through a local solicitor before we returned from America, so it was listed as our address on all the official papers we filled in." She shrugged. "The police soon recognized that Teresa was far too frail to question, let alone put on trial, so they let the matter drop. And to be quite honest, they didn't really have enough evidence, you know. You didn't know it--and Teresa would never have told you—but she already knew she was dying before the police came. Just as I know I am dying now."

"And did she really die without telling you who your father was?"

Miss Eunice nodded. "I wasn't lying about that. But I always had my suspicions." Her eyes sparkled for a moment, the way a fizzy drink does when you pour it. "You know, Teresa was always unreasonably jealous of that Tryphena Sparks, and Mr. hardy did have an eye for the young girls."

Forty years have passed since Miss Eunice's death, and I have lived in many towns and villages in many countries of the world.

Though I have often thought of the tale she told me, I have never been moved to commit it to paper until today.

Two weeks ago, I moved back to Lyndgarth, and as I was unpacking, I came across that first edition of *Far from the Madding Crowd.* 1874: the year Hardy married Emma Gifford. As I puzzled again over the inscription, words suddenly began to form themselves effortlessly in front of my eyes, and all I had to do was copy them down.

Now that I have finished, I suddenly feel very tired. It is a hot day, and the heat haze has muted the greens, grays, and browns of the steep hillsides. Looking out of my window, I can see the tourists lounging on the village green. The young men are stripped to the waist, some bearing tattoos of butterflies and angels across their shoulder blades; the girls sit with them, in shorts and T-shirts, laughing, eating sandwiches, drinking from pop or beer bottles.

One young girl notices me watching and waves cheekily, probably thinking I'm an old pervert, and as I wave back I think of another writer—a far, far greater writer than I could ever be—sitting at his window seat, writing. He looks out of the window and sees the beautiful young girl passing through the woods at the bottom of the garden. He waves. She waves back. And she lingers, picking wild flowers, as he puts aside his novel and walks out into the warm summer air to meet her.

Eyes for Offa Rex

JONATHAN GASH

Lovejoy, the randy antique dealer you love to hate, and his penchant for getting mixed up in all sorts of wild misadventures, has earned for himself and his creator, Jonathan Gash, a large and loyal following among mystery readers. Antiques play a major role in such Lovejoy novels as *The Judas Pair, The Vatican Rip, Firefly Gadroon,* and *Pearlhanger.* One also plays a large role in "Eyes for Offa Rex"—an antique coin, to be exact—although Lovejoy is absent from this tense tale of murder and numismatics.

Councillor Ash waited in the silent darkness, watching the road. A clear night with stars tingling overhead, the sort which made you remember. He pondered seriously for a moment, worried by the possibility of an untidy detail, before memory flooded in to clear his irritation away. That phrase . . . Tennyson, wasn't it? *Shivered to the tingling stars*. You had to learn by heart once. Too bloody idle to learn anything at all these days, he thought in some annoyance. Look at the way kids come slouching in for jobs, thinking everybody owed them a living. And the state of some of them.

The lonely spot was ideal. Bright moon, blind bend, frosted white skeletal trees, and a road covered with black ice. A night worth waiting half a year for, since that summer evening when Gordon had refused to sell the Offa Rex—and thereby had condemned himself to death.

Ash congratulated himself for choosing well. Short of unforeseen calamities—like that drunken sot parking to neck with his tart last Friday night and spoiling the plan—he would kill tonight. He found himself sweating heavily despite the subzero temperature. Concentration did that, made a man sweat. Concentration and sex.

His watch said tennish. Gordon would be saying his farewells in the Goat and Compass before driving this way. Luckily Gordon was no mechanic, never had been since he was a kid. Too reflective, too indrawn. Ash desperately wanted a smoke. Gordon of course never smoked. How the hell a cold fish like him ever won Janey . . . In other circumstances Ash would have made a contest of it. As it was, there were bigger things at stake than a girl, though once Gordon was dead . . . Even if Janey did have a good job in the local hospital laboratory, well, widows were known to be receptive to consolation from somebody attentive in just the right way. He found himself grinning without humor and switched his face off. Discipline.

The poem came back for a fleeting second. It was where that knight was carrying the dying Arthur through those icy caves, his clashing harness echoes among the stalactites. An eerie funeral scene. Appropriate to remember that, in a way.

The exciting part would come in a month's time, when Janey disposed of Gordon's estate and sold the Offa Rex. Ash realized his hands were trembling. Concentration to lift a man's temperature, he thought wryly, and lust to quiver him like a pointer.

Ice was beautiful. No real snow to speak of for several days, then persistent fog all yesterday, a faint suggestion of a thaw early this morning and a snap frost at dusk. Black ice warnings were out on the motorways with the radio ominous with warnings all day. Ash knew this stretch of country road like his own hand, but then so did Gordon. They had cycled along it often enough. No lights of course in these ancient curling East Anglian village roads. Near the river black ice tended to form faster, almost heaven-sent.

Before settling in to wait Ash had examined the surface beyond the medieval humpback bridge. Lovely. Worse than a skating rink. Tires needed chains for grip on a night like this. Gordon's never had even a trace of tread on them. Ash knew because he had looked. Served the fool right. The iron-hard frozen roadside would hold no imprints, so Ash had selected a slight recess to the right of the road. Gordon would come over the bridge onto the black ice which covered the road for almost a hundred yards—only to find a strange car cutting across suddenly from his right, where there should only be trees . . . Gordon's sudden instinctive braking on black ice would cause his death. Not really murder. You couldn't call it that. It would be a sort of suicide, or an accident. The narrow road dog-legged left where the oxbow river curved again, and the parapet was too low, always had been. Ash himself had complained in council meetings about the possibility of cars crashing through at that point into the slow, deep river so far below. . . .

Black ice was essential. The more usual pale stuff was always easier. And it shone white in moonlight, giving ample warning to change gear before taking the bridge. That was the bewitchingly sinister beauty of black ice. Roads always looked innocent and bone-dry, innocently black as the tar beneath but more slippery than any mirror. Ash found himself grinning despite his nervousness. If only he'd allowed himself the radio, perhaps a nip in a flask to keep the cold out or a cigarette. But no. Discipline always paid well.

A beam lit the sky, waved once, and was gone. A car was coming. "Good old Gordon," Ash growled.

He fired the engine, a first time start. Keep a cool head. The Jaguar would be reported missing fairly soon. Surprising how easy it had been. Ash's own car was waiting in the same pub yard. Pinching the Jag to do the job was probably overcautious but had actually proved very little risk. Unpleasantly simple, in fact. And it was vital for Gordon not to recognize Ash's select green Humber, should things go wrong.

The headlights swathed the sky again. The oncoming car was at the Dragonswell turnoff. Sure enough, the lights flickered on to the side road. It had to be him. Ash gunned the engine into a deep sustained roar. Three hundred yards. Ash clenched his hands a few times to loosen them, the way the army made you prepare for action. Then into first gear with the throttle slightly dipped and the clutch slammed flat. At the last minute he decided the powerful engine could cope and shifted into second, a simple modification to his plan proving complete adaptability and control, something he would be able to look back on with justifiable pride.

The oncoming car lurched, its lights jerking skywards once, then dipping to silhouette the humped bridge's ancient stones.

Now.

Ash rolled the Jaguar onto the road. A horn sounded, despair already in the note. A faint squeal, then Ash was trundling among the trees on the opposite side of the road, quickly turning with some difficulty and having to reverse to make the road again. Pinching a car with chained tires really had been a brainwave, he complimented himself. He managed the turn without difficulty. Six seconds and he was off in the direction from which Gordon had been driving.

Ash put the headlights on after two hundred yards. One glance in his mirror showed only darkness over the river valley. No lights shone there at all. Poor Gordon. He reached now for a cigarette. Soon the Offa Rex would be his.

Hardwick, the golf club secretary, approved of the doctor and the policeman even if they hadn't played a round in years. He expressed it best to Mrs. Aspern when going over her catering accounts. "Without the quack and the local C.I.D. a golf club's missing something—tone, perhaps."

Mrs. Aspern would have none of it. "A lady doctor lays herself open to scandal," she shot back, "coming in bold as brass—"

Hardwick sighed. "Times have changed, Mrs. Aspern." They had the same argument every Saturday. "And lunch in a crowded clubroom's hardly the height of depravity." It was hopeless. Mrs. Aspern had a trick of exclaiming, lips tight shut, which discredited any innocent explanation.

Across the restaurant Dr. Baxter was trying to reason with Inspector Young. "You're reading too much into it, George," she was saying, about his disappointingly simple road crash case. "The dead man's wife has every right to feel aggrieved with the police."

"Why?" George Young found to his surprise he was losing the argument. "The bloody woman drove me mad."

"Well, was she irrational?"

"No. Calm but uptight, if you know what I mean. My point is, there's no such thing as murder without trace, Clare."

"But any theory's possible, George—"

"That's her very argument!" George realized he had raised his voice and caused some heads to turn. He smiled to show all was well. Clare grinned and passed the salt to give him time. "But surely you can see how illogical the statement is?" He salted his veal unnecessarily. "A so-called 'murder' without evidence of murder *is* an accident. By definition."

Clare was becoming interested. "There's another way of putting that, George."

"Go on, then."

"The way the woman did. Her husband might have been killed deliberately. Your people failed to elicit any evidence for what she *knows* to be true."

George growled, "We've combed the riverbank, the bridge, the roadside—"

"Here." Clare was looking thoughtful. "Is it that case in today's local rag? Black ice, the car?"

"That's it, Summerston."

"I read it," Clare said. "Doesn't ice leave marks?"

"Not after it melts, love," the inspector said dryly. "Mrs. Summerston believes another car lay in wait, pulled out, causing her husband to lose control."

"It's quite possible."

"Not to a local man," said the inspector doggedly. "He knew the road in all weathers."

"I've driven over the bridge several times," Clare cut in. "With ice around you put both feet on the floor so the car slows without braking."

"So he'd had a few drinks and forgot."

"Or was made to brake suddenly, instinctively." Clare put her knife and fork down. "Another car hidden in the dip by the old bridge . . . You'd slam the brake down by reflex action."

"Only if there *was* another car, Clare. You're as daft as his wife." George waited in silence for a moment.

The doctor tilted her head inquiringly. "Come on, out with it. There's something you haven't admitted."

George shrugged uncomfortably. "She says she knows whose car it was."

Clare gasped audibly. "And you've done nothing?"

"Of course we did." George refilled their glasses. Clare had chosen the wine this Saturday, a German *spätlese*, somewhat too sweet but ripe enough. "We checked every damned thing. The suspect's own car was parked until well after closing time at a tavern several miles away."

"Vouched for?" Clare must have touched a nerve. George's reply sounded bitter.

"You think I'd forget to check on that, too?"

"Sorry," Clare said meekly. "But only most of the evening, not all?"

"He hinted that he has this girl . . ." George admitted sheepishly as Clare smiled with understanding. "But Janey Summerston claims that's all a front. She said it's the sort of thing the other chap would do."

"Was he rich?"

"The deceased? Far from it. And there seems no funny business, nothing we hang action on. The only rum point is they were friends, grew up together."

"How terrible!" Clare sipped at her chilled glass. "Bitter friends lifelong?"

George was beginning to feel uncomfortable for some reason. "Look, Clare. Can I make my original point?"

"What was it, George dear?" Clare fluttered her eyes disarmingly to make him laugh.

"Be serious. It's that some people are incapable of accepting the truth, even if it's there before their very eyes. They'll lie, make accusations, go demented—even pillory a best friend to disprove reality."

"Well, distressed people do behave irrationally."

"More than that." George now felt he was winning. "There's guilt. *Her* guilt. A twenty-six-year-old husband who prefers to spend his evening drinking with the lads in a pub rather than go home . . . *She's* guilty, see? Needs a scapegoat. So she picks on the only person she can think of, a bloke whose name was probably often heard around the house. Comes along to the cop shop and accuses him."

"Did she have a motive as rational as the rest of her story?"

"As *ir*rational, Clare," George reproved, catching her smile.

Mrs. Aspern also caught the smile and the inspector's sudden seriousness as he decided to tell Clare Janey Summerston's account of Ash's motive in killing Gordon. Her lips thinned. She closed the office hatch thinking of Mr. Hardwick's gullibility and that all men are fools. Like children.

Inspector Young would have enjoyed meeting Janey Summerston on practically any other occasion than just before her deceased husband was subjected to inquest. She was pleasantly slender, neat without seeming obsessional, and even wore colorful clothes. Her sweater set matched the pleated skirt and the shoes showed sense instead of flamboyance. The only indications of grief were the dark rings beneath her eyes. Other than that she seemed composed but full of conviction.

"I know what you're thinking, Inspector," she had said. "That I'm deranged, and that in another week or two I'll come to my senses. That is not the case. I'm in earnest."

George Young kept his calm. That was a familiar reaction and you had to make allowances. He said mildly, "Mrs. Summerston, we need something more than supposition."

"It is not supposition," Janey Summerston said evenly. "I'm sure it's truc."

"But Councillor Ash is a well-respected man—"

"So was Dr. Crippen."

"—and was known to be a friend of . . . of your husband."

"They grew up together, went to the same school." Janey Summerston nodded as if acknowledging something to herself. "Their paths diverged."

"They didn't see each other much?" The inspector found himself drawn in despite exasperation at the uselessness of it all.

"No, not for the past few years. Except at occasional meetings."

"A club?"

"No. The coin-collectors' circle."

"So they were no longer well acquainted," Young said firmly. "So neither evidence nor motive."

"There *is* motive," Janey said. "Gordon's collection."

Inspector Young heard Sergeant Brent cough twice, his signal for some additional information on the subject. He clicked his pencil to show the hint was taken.

"Is Gordon's collection valuable, Mrs. Summerston?"

"Not really."

"Does any agreement exist that will allow Councillor Ash, or any other named person, to take possession of the collection in the event of your husband's death?"

"No."

"Is there anything in that collection which they own jointly?"

"No."

The interview had ended only after an hour's arguing. Janey Summerston insisted that Ash had somehow engineered her husband's accident. As George told Clare Baxter when describing Janey, there was simply no reason to believe a single word the grieving woman uttered.

". . . though everything's possible, Doctor," he concluded with mock formality, making Clare pull a face at him. She had won a telling point the previous week using the selfsame words.

"I still have a funny feeling she may have something, George."

"Look," he threatened. "If you're going to claim woman's intuition . . ."

"I shan't." Clare laughed. "We've both agreed there's no such thing."

Mrs. Aspern watched them rise and go through into the club lounge.

Clare drove to the surgery straight from the golf club though she was off duty call until midnight. Anderson, only one year her partner in the practice, looked up with surprise from the notes he was completing.

"Hello, Clare," he said, taking in her appearance. "I thought it was boutique and a hairdo on Saturdays."

Clare quickly crossed the surgery to shut the door which communicated with Nurse Hargreaves's domain. The younger doctor's casually modern manner still rankled with her, though they had had this out several times and he remained as amused as ever at her propriety.

"Gordon Summerston's one of ours, isn't he, Derek?" she asked, moving behind him to the record files.

"From Dragonswell? Yes; did an insurance medical on him last month. Fit as a flea."

"Dead," Clare said. "Accident."

Anderson stopped writing and grimaced around at her. "Hell fire. Third this month. It's a bloody epidemic." He saw Clare hesitate before speaking. "What's up?"

She flipped through the envelopes and found Gordon Summerston's. "I don't know. Something really rather odd. Nothing important in his records, though."

"Road accidents aren't mysterious, Clare. They're just an utterly stupid waste of people."

"I suppose you're right, Derek." She dropped the envelope on Anderson's desk and opened the side door to let herself out. "Have fun."

"You know," her younger colleague said, eyeing her legs and grinning, "for a geriatric girl you're not at all bad. If you play your cards right you could have me."

"Get on with you."

Nurse Hargreaves overheard as the door closed and lifted her head, interested, wondering about Dr. Baxter and Derek Anderson. You could never tell with some women, she told herself, especially ones like Clare Baxter. Except sometimes.

Inspector Young sat at his desk leafing through sales catalogs. Sergeant Brent had gotten them for him from Constable MacAndrews, the station's one avid collector. It had been interesting just to see MacAndrews, normally rather taciturn, come alive when asked about his hobby. Rather than look down on his inspector's transparent ignorance about numismatics, the lad obviously had been delighted to explain the inner politics of local collecting circles. Collectors of hammered coinage evidently were the aristocracy among numismatologists, it seemed. Summerston and Ash were even more specialized than this, having focused in a modest sort of way on royal coinage of the pre-Conquest period. And MacAndrews had even been moved to wax lyrical when enlarging on the greatest yet the most obscure of the ancient kings. George Young had never heard of him, but to hear the young constable talk there should have been no such era as the Dark Ages. That whole period was apparently illuminated by the blinding brilliance of the mighty but mysterious Offa Rex.

Afterwards Young had thanked MacAndrews and sent him back to his point duty. He flipped the catalogs over curiously, looking at the photograph of the old coins. "Bloody lunatics," he muttered. "An old penny's an old penny, no matter how rare." He stared at the pictures so long he began to imagine things. "Bloody lunatics," he said again, and shoved them aside. He would have to see Ash. He'd put it off long enough.

Ash watched the inspector's car leave, and turned back toward the house conscious now of the immensity of his success. He'd done it, achieved the impossible. Murder that even the law agreed was an accident.

Janey was too impoverished to keep Gordon's collection. The Offa would be sold with the rest of it at auction, seeing she knew nothing about numismatics herself. And guess who would be at the auction? He chuckled. Probably within the month the Offa silver would be his, in his hand. Unique and glowing, with its frontal portrait and those pellet eyes staring from the surface. Clever of her to spot the way he had killed Gordon, though. The interesting thought came that only a woman who knew a man really well could have sensed the truth as Janey had done. But *how* well did she know him? Maybe she, too, had felt that flicker of desire. Maybe she sometimes found herself thinking of the aggressive Councillor Ash instead of her drippy husband. He found it an erotic idea. Janey *and* the Offa Rex? Maybe.

Funny to think that soon he would be able to look into the eyes of Offa, the greatest hero king between Alexander and the Conqueror. Unless, he thought wryly, this bloody welfare state increases the widow subsidy. He chuckled inwardly at the idea. Maybe he should propose that to the council. He was still smiling an hour later over a brandy.

Early the following day Janey Summerston faced Mr. Watkins in his office. The shoddiness of the place contrasted sharply with the sleek auction premises next door, but this was as the elderly auctioneer liked it. What is traditional is best, was his favorite saying. The old man was less embarrassed by Janey's tragedy than her obvious courage.

"Are you sure you wouldn't rather take Gordon's things somewhere else, Janey?"

"No, Mr. Watkins."

"I mean, because I am an old friend of your father's I can't guarantee a higher percentage. There are rules about auctions. You know that?"

"I understand."

"Very well. Think about it a few days and—"

"No." Her surprising firmness took him aback. "Before the end of the month, please."

Janey Summerston herself had met widows sentimentally clinging to outmoted belongings, unsuitable houses, and even whole lifestyles in obedience to some inner compulsion they assumed was loyalty. To her they always seemed pathetic. It was something she would not do. She explained this attitude while her father's erstwhile bowling companion listened gravely.

"And are you going to include that Offa piece Gordon bought here some years ago?"

"That, too."

"It may cause quite a stir among local collectors."

"So I believe."

"You have quite decided not to sell it privately?" Mr. Watkins fiddled with his spectacles to give her an opportunity of replying before launching his rather Edwardian sales talk. "I am certain that an auction is the proper place, and will produce at least the yield which any private sale would."

"Thank you, Mr. Watkins." Janey Summerston rose to go, pausing a moment to add, "I am sure you will achieve the best result, only . . ."

"Yes?"

"Can . . . can I lay down conditions?"

"Why, yes, within limits. A reserve price, that sort of thing?"

"Nothing like that. But . . . I would like the best piece from Gordon's collection to be quite safe."

"I assure you, Janey, that—"

"Please." She drew a breath and confronted him with that almost belligerent decisiveness. "I want one piece to stay enclosed in a separate container until the buyer takes possession."

"We must allow proper inspection, Janey."

Janey was shaking her head. "That will be all right. Two sides of its case will be glass. Free inspection will be quite in order, but it must not be removed at any time."

"Very well." Mr. Watkins made a note. "Er, which piece is it, my dear?"

Something flashed in Janey's eyes as she spoke. Even before the words fell the old man knew the answer.

"The Offa Rex," she said.

A few moments later he watched the door close behind Janey. He felt uneasy, conscious that something was wrong. Not a mere clerical error which could be traced and accounted for, but a gross violation in his way of life. Something irrevocable.

In the town library Gillanders was being distrait. "Nobody borrowed that book in a twelvemonth," he was complaining to his deputy in the library office. "Then we have four simultaneous demands for the wretched thing. It's just too much. Has there been some exhibition we haven't heard about?"

"We must ask for an extra copy, sir." Miss Mortimer loved any excuse to increase the library's stock.

"We certainly must not," Gillanders snapped at her. She didn't have to face the town's sour finance committee. "We'll no sooner get ourselves fitted out with extra copies of J. J. North and of Dolley and nobody will want them. It happened before. Remember that stupid flute-maker's biography? A sheer waste of money, Anglo-Saxon coins, indeed."

Miss Mortimer knuckled under. "Yes, Mr. Gillanders." She knew a tantrum when she saw one.

The auction sale went off with surprising simplicity. MacAndrews was excited at the idea of being seconded from traffic duty to attend in plainclothes. Inspector Young thought it dull as ditchwater. The previous week he had spent some time with Mr. Watkins, who had gone over the auction procedure for his benefit. A careful record would be kept of all buyers. Surely nothing could go wrong.

The Offa looked so ordinary to George Young. It was in a gray metal box, heavy as lead, with glass top and bottom. Even the glass was heavy, so thick and dark he only saw through to the piece with difficulty.

"Lovely, isn't it?" some enthusiast said as the auctioneer droned away on the rostrum.

"Er, aye," the inspector said doubtfully. A strip light showed the contents of the box. One coin, goldish in appearance, somehow set suspended in a sheet of gray metal. That must be the Offa Rex, though MacAndrews had said it was silver, not gold. The metal container was like a small safe. "Can we open it and look, please?" he asked an attendant.

"No, sir. Instructions," the man said.

So Janey Summerston's demands were being met. Young glanced round the throng and saw Charles Ash seated in the third row. Item two hundred and nine. At the rate the auctioneer was going it would be well into the afternoon before the Offa coin was sold. As he turned to go he noticed the metal sides of the container were engraved. He bent and read, "The Property of Gordon Summerston, deceased twelfth of December." The same legend was inscribed on all four of the metal sides and, he observed with puzzlement, even on the glass surfaces. Odd. The engraving looked new. Maybe the case had been made specifically for this auction?

At the door he bumped into Janey Summerston. He said hello, but she avoided his gaze and determinedly swept past. Come to see how high a price her husband's precious Offa fetched, no doubt. As he stepped outside onto the pavement he gave a barely imperceptible nod in MacAndrews's direction, but the bloody man was listening rapturously to the bids. He told himself it was stupid to worry. The annoying part was this irritating feeling of having arrived at a football match where nobody would tell you the score.

Ash drove home faster than usual and was in his study almost before the engine had silenced. He lifted the heavy box out onto a piece of felt as soon as he could tear off his coat. He opened the windows, though he knew his wife would play hell about drafts. Cigar smoke was death to a coin's patina. That and the acids which oak gave off into the atmosphere, hence the preponderance of mahogany and teak in his study.

Lamp, magnifying glass, a glass of brandy and he practically fell on the heavy box. He had waited years.

"Not yet," he shouted when his wife called for him to come down for supper.

It had been a cinch. Old Watkins had looked disappointed at the low price. Maybe he'd expected a Christie's level. The thought made Ash laugh aloud. If Janey hadn't been so foolish as to try the cheap trick of washing a gilt paint over the Offa Rex the price might have soared. As it was, her pathetically obvious device of gilding had brought the price down to within easy reach of his pocket. At least two London dealers had shone their beam quartzes at the Offa through the thick glass and then drifted across to the pub in disgust and not returned. Gordon should have taught her better, Ash thought contentedly. No numismatist wants a precious surface tinkered with. Still, it would only take a few minutes and the right chemical solvents to get that muck off—and then he could gaze serenely at the tiny eyes on the coin portrait of the great Offa Rex. Eye to eye. It would need care, though, and the daylight of morning which was so essential for proper numismatic work.

He looked for a moment at Gordon's engraved name on the case. Quite well made and solid lead, but Ash wasn't having somebody else's name labeling *his* prize item at any price. No, sir. The box had to go. His own cabinet would display the Offa to the fullest possible advantage. And a small side lamp, perhaps opposite his desk . . .

It took a moment's work with a screwdriver to unscrew the interlocked edges of the box's sides. Ash smiled triumphantly as he finally lifted out the middle section holding the Offa piece and placed it gently down on the felt.

He brushed the surface using a small painter's brush. Typical of women, always wanting to gild the gingerbread. If she'd left it untouched it possibly would have gone for a fortune. He turned the Offa over and bent closer, enthralled. He stared at the portrait so long his eyes began to prickle.

He looked up eventually after what seemed only mere minutes and was surprised to notice it had started snowing outside. Strange, he thought, there had been no such forecast. Then he blinked to clear his eyes and saw the late afternoon skies were only dulled and gray. Not snowing after all. He smiled. It must be the strain of peering at his new acquisition for too long, that and the excitement. After all, you could count the owners of an Offa Rex on one hand these days.

Upstairs that night the organism was sleeping beside its mate. Its component cells were synchronized, bathed in homeostatically controlled fluids. Its organs were subtordinated to autonomic feedbacks beyond the main organism's conscious awareness as its vagal impulses rhythmically modulated the respiration. Yet it slept disturbed. Epithelial cells were starting to replicate out of time along the margins of the organism's eyelids. The exquisitely beautiful polarized membranes hugging each nucleus were now punctured and leaking, the semipermeability which protected and sustained the delicate internal genome's milieu already starting to bleed translucent fluids inwards to stifle the shimmering opalescent chains of cistrons. Deeper still in the organism's eye the vital ganglion cells were dying. The retinal structure appeared intact, but the ganglion cells themselves had been deformed some hours. Tomorrow the retinal rods would still be aligned, but the cones would begin to show the gross deformities revealing their spreading metabolic doom.

Councillor Ash groaned in his sleep, once.

Downstairs in the darkness of the study the Offa Rex was concealed under a layer of green felt, a covering which failed to impede the steady emission radiating from the coin's surface. The lifeless silver molding the face of the great king beat with silent vigor. The open pellet eyes, pressed directly against the felt covering, stared blindly upwards as if to follow the unseen rays streaming out through the cloth and piercing the very substance of the elegant cabinet's solid wood beating outwards and filling the air of the silent room.

Three days later a freezing fog came over the sea marshes. The dark hawthorns and the thin sloe hedges showed no whitening frost. Instead the chill remained hanging in the air, coating paths and trees and surfaces with an ominously transparent coating of ice. On the main coast roads the streams of night traffic dwindled to a trickle, and finally ended. By the sixth day every one of the low Hundreds was overlaid with black ice and the small fishing fleets were back, closely staithed in the silent estuaries. The town quietened. The villages recovered their lost medieval pace. Wise travelers chained their tires and hoped for snow or thaw. Wiser people stayed at home.

On that sixth day Janey Summerston phoned Charles Ash. "Charles? Janey Summerston."

Ash tried to perk up on hearing her voice, though he'd been terrible just lately. The wife was in bed though it was only nine. No reason to stay up on such a lousy night, and she had telly up there. She had been useless lately anyway; always was, when he felt unwell.

"That you, Janey? How good to hear you." He modulated his voice, politically trained to instant solicitude. It had gone hoarse at the weekend, probably part of this illness. Maybe a bug going round. "I haven't really had a chance to express my sincere condolences about poor Gordon."

She cut in quite briskly. "Never mind that, Charles. How are you?"

"Quite well," he said, puzzled.

"Are you sure?" Janey's voice paused, then went on, "No sickness, Charles? No loss of appetite? Eyes as good as ever?" He could almost hear her smile. She surely hadn't rung just to ask after his well-being . . . had she?

"Your voice is hoarser than it was at the auction, Charles."

Ash felt the blood drain from his face, the vessels prickling and tightening. "How did you know I've been off color?" He doubled at a sudden gripe.

She went on, her voice cooing, "Tired these days, Charles? Listless?"

"What's the meaning of this, Janey?" He needed to suck moisture into his tongue to get the words out.

"How—?"

"Listen carefully, Charles. You'd better sit down while I explain, seeing you are so ill. It might prove a shock." She surely had no way of knowing anything about his illness, not having seen him since the auction. "For the past six days, Charles," she coursed on, "your eyesight has deteriorated quite drastically. You can no longer see to read. There are sores round your eyelids and mouth."

It was true. He had seen Smithson at the clinic only the previous day. The best eye man in the country, Smithson had made a number of tests. He had obviously been puzzled.

"You are too tired to bother with anything." Janey might have been reading from a list. "Ulcers on your face, Charles. You've developed a cough. I'll bet your wife has said how pale you've gone. Soon you will vomit after every meal."

Ash, thinking fast, said nothing.

"I do hope you are paying attention, Charles, because this is really rather important. Your blood cells have begun to decrease, Charles. Your count will fall and fall—"

He began shaking. His arm quivered uncontrollably. He held the receiver away to silence the woman's brisk professional voice. Twice he brought a handkerchief to his mouth to stifle a sudden retching. The bitch had done something, got at him somehow.

"How do you know this? What have you done to me?" He knew she would still be there, listening and waiting.

"A little preliminary explanation, Charles," Janey reprimanded. "You ought to know that there are some sixteen thousand effective and available poisons—"

"*Poison?*" And he knew. "In the gilding on the—"

The crisp detached voice called him back. "Please don't interrupt. I was about to say that if you call the police I shall deny any allegations you make. And calling a doctor will not help you. I've been careful enough to select a combination of poisons that produce a very complex symptomatology, as you now know." So she knew he had been to the clinic. Of course, she worked at the hospital. "By the time they work out the antidotes it will be impossibly late."

"Janey," Ash said brokenly. "I swear to God I had nothing to do with Gordon's accident. Please. That inspector came by and told me what you said—"

"There's not really time for blustering, Charles," Janey cooed. "You've begun to *die*, Charles. Don't you understand?"

She was insane. There could be no other explanation. "I'll give you anything, Janey. Honest to God. If it's money—"

"To tell you the antidote?" Janey's laughing tapped against his eardrum. "I've got it here, waiting."

"Waiting?"

"Don't be so mistrustful, Charles. I know your motive in getting rid of Gordon. It was me, wasn't it, dear?"

Her? Ash was sweating heavily. He rubbed his free hand along his thigh in an attempt to dry the palm. Of course he fancied her, always had, but *kill* for the lunatic? Yet he had to agree with whatever the mad bitch said. Once he'd got the antidote he'd streak over to Dr. Baxter and get her to inject it . . .

"You guessed," he managed to get out, somewhat too carefully.

"And now I'm making sure, Charles. Of you."

Ash hesitated. "What do you want me to do?" Instinctively he was more guarded on the instant. Begging had been new to him, but bargaining was something he understood. The main thing was to get that antidote.

"Charles? Come here. Now."

"In this fog? There's fog, black ice." She made no answer, the bitch, knowing he had to obey. "I'll come, Janey. I can hire a car."

"No. You come alone, Charles."

She was asking the impossible. "But my eyes. For Christ's sake. And it's atrocious on the roads."

"Very well," she said sweetly. "Let's leave it a few days, shall we?"

"No! No! I'll . . . I'll come, of course." He cleared his throat. "Darling."

"I'll be waiting," she replied. "Darling."

Click. Brrr. Ash replaced his receiver, still shaky but conscious there was a way out. The bitch. Figuring him out like that. And putting the poison in the gilt, washing it over the Offa Rex, guessing he would be unable to resist examining it. Some stuff that needed only a trace to produce its effects. No wonder the eye consultant had been puzzled. He must get over there. Fast. And everything would be all fine again soon. She *had* felt the pull between them both. He rose to get his car keys and his coat, almost grinning with relief though he felt rotten. That old fatal Ash charm. Women like a man who's aggressive, bit of a showoff. If she would go to these lengths to get him, maybe more than a little care was called for. She would need careful handling, careful yet firm. The old sex game, at which he'd always been a permanent winner.

His car started first time. Beautiful smooth movement. He moved at a crawl out onto the drive, never hearing his wife's voice calling. The ice-filled fog was everywhere. Its density froze the car lights a few feet ahead. He had to sit perched forward on the edge of the seat to peer with his fading eyes. The bloody specialist had wanted to admit him to the hospital immediately, as if anyone with a councillor's responsibilities can drop everything just like that. Ash suddenly remembered his eyedrops, but they'd be useless now after what Janey had told him. He decided to press on with his ulcerated and bloodshot eyes straining into the fog. It had to be the antidote.

Luckily there were few cars out, and he managed a steady crawl. But by the time he reached the Dragonswell turnoff he was driving about five miles an hour, with the side windows wound down so as to see the blur of the grass verge. The largest of the ulcers along his upper lids were bleeding now from the cold. Every few yards he was having to stop to dab inexpertly at the blood and pus. He had used three handkerchiefs. Twice he stopped and tried squeezing his eyes shut tight for a moment, hoping the vision would improve. It was definitely fading. His inner rage surfaced momentarily and even overcame his fear, making him groan aloud. As soon as he'd got that antidote he'd see she suffered for giving him this fright, by God he would. Play her along, then put the boot in. That's all some women could understand, the sadistic cow. If she'd wanted him, for Christ's sake, why hadn't she just phoned and said so when Gordon was out? She had more than sex coming to her. He'd see to that. By God . . .

He approached the humpbacked bridge gingerly. The thought had crossed his mind that this was all a ruse, a come-on, to get him out here in these appalling conditions. But if so, she was foiled. He was hardly going fast enough to skid downhill, let alone on a comparatively level road. And his tires would stay chained until April. Still, it was with relief he saw his head beams regain the road, dipping from the hump to follow the few feet of the hedgerow remaining visible.

The next danger would be the end of this straight bit where the road dog-legged from the river parapet. It would be more dangerous than usual because the bloody council roadmen had stayed at home on account of the weather. And there was no parapet. Gordon had demolished it. Thankfully, Ash saw four orange road-lights blipping ahead indicating where the road bent. At least the road-safety man had earned his pence. Ash leaned farther from his car and, craning to see, accelerated slightly but thankfully toward the orange lights.

On the far side of the river Janey watched his shrouded lights approach. In silhouette she could just make out the gap in the parapet. Beside her on the bank the four lights blinked their warning, popping faintly with every flash. They even looked quite pretty spaced out like that. She stood quite proudly among them, in line on the wrong side of the river.

Ash only realized when his car tilted, hesitated, then slid elegantly forward into the river ice with a loud crack. Its onward motion caused it to slip quite a distance from the bank and away from the hole it had made on entry. His head, projecting from the side window, was jerked forward with a snap and flipped against the door margin. The last thing he knew was the gruesome, sordid nature of the act of dying. Janey was unable to see most of the events. And, regretfully, she could not stay to listen to the bubbling and sucking beneath the ice where the car lights were fading deep in the water. She had a job to do. She took four cloth covers from a shoulderbag and hooded each warning light into darkness. Being on trestles, they weighed heavily, so she could only carry two at a time. And she had to go all the way round, along this bank to the humpback bridge, and then walk all the way along the road to replace the warning lights by the gap in the parapet.

Thirty minutes later Janey somewhat breathlessly unhooded the last of the trestled lights spaced out along the road, in place again to warn drivers about the parapet. Just as they should be, she thought, pleased. Of course, it would have been easier to carry them across on the ice, but she'd decided against that. She hadn't wanted to risk an accident.

Inspector Young knew the county pathologist vaguely from his attendances at coroners' courts. Henderson was one of those slender, rather creaky, bespectacled men who must have looked elderly even as a gangly lad. His twinkly yet detached manner always impressed and conveyed confidence. Only once had the inspector seen him flustered, and that had been over a minute typographical error most men would hardly have noticed. He seated himself in the chair Dr. Henderson indicated, trying to avoid looking at the specimens on the low bookcase behind the pathologist.

"Ash, I presume?" Henderson's reedy voice matched his frame.

Young nodded, wondering if his own personality was as entire as Henderson's appeared to be. "Question of foul play," he said.

"You surprise me." Henderson turned the pages of the file. "Typical road-accident injuries. Death due to multiple injuries. Even if he had survived the trauma he would probably have drowned. Shock, that temperature, bewildered under the ice, concussed. As it was, his broken neck did the job a fraction speedier, that's all."

"I viewed the deceased," the inspector said. "What was all that round his eyes?"

"Odd ulceration. He'd been to the opthalmology clinic recently. Our surgeon was unsure. Extensive ulceration, possibly chemical or toxic. And his vision."

"Could he not see properly?"

"No. The eye surgeon found massive retinal scarring, atrophy—"

"He was going blind." It was intended as a question but emerged as a flat statement.

"Yes. Dr. Smithson wanted to admit him."

"Why?"

"Well." Henderson paused to consider the confidentiality issue before conceding. "I spoke to Smithson after the post mortem. He, too, had seen nothing like it, except once. And that was a case of irradiation burns from dangerous emitters. Some military job."

The inspector thought hard. Lead boxes are used for carrying radioactive stuff. That heavy lead box, its dark glass top—dark because lead-containing glass is basically darker than the modern colorless kind?

A faint nausea came which he recognized as fear. He, like others, had bent to squint at the Offa Rex for a moment. Maybe some irradiation had got at him, too.

"Are you all right, Inspector?" the pathologist was asking.

"Just suppose, Doctor," he said slowly, "I wanted to display something, a coin, say, covered in an irradiation chemical, yet wanted to avoid injuring people. How could I do it?"

"Depends. A lead box, with a thick window of lead glass," Henderson said. "And stopping people getting near. The inverse square law operates." He drummed his fingers on the notes. "Of course, for this degree of eye damage you'd need to be pretty close."

"What quantity would be needed? The amount you could get on to, say, a penny?"

"Easily."

Inspector Young drew breath. "Can you examine a house for traces of a radioactive chemical?"

Henderson smiled thinly. "Again, just supposing, Inspector?"

The C.I.D. man thought over the somber joke for a moment. "No," he said. "Real."

"What's it all about, or am I not to ask?"

The C.I.D. man did not reply immediately. There was a faint risk that Janey Summerston was friendly with one of Henderson's own people, maybe from some shared training course at a technical college. A small chance, but why take it? "A private worry," he said at last. "Nothing much."

"Loose ends?"

They agreed that Dr. Henderson would arrange for the dead man's car to be monitored for radiation with a minimum of fuss. Samples would be taken from the house drains, the contents of Ash's study and the garden examined for the presence of radioactive isotopes and reports sent direct.

"We want this done absolutely confidentially, please," Inspector Young said.

"If you wish," Dr. Henderson assured him, eyeing him quizzically.

"Are the tests for radiation really, er, good, efficient?"

Dr. Henderson smiled thinly. "If there's a trace we'll find it." On the way out of the building he stopped at the porter's desk to ask if he knew a technician called Janey Summerston.

"Not here, guv," the gray-haired man said. "Probably over at the hospital. They have hundreds. Overpaid and underworked."

Inspector Young left, satisfied there was now no chance that Janey might hear of Henderson's forthcoming investigations for radioactivity at Ash's home. No harm making sure. For the first time he felt one move ahead of Janey.

They met at the golf club the following Saturday under Mrs. Aspern's disapproving gaze. Neither Clare nor George made any pretense that they were lunching to chat over the weather.

"I've put two and two together, George," Clare announced as soon as they had ordered.

"And made five?"

"Stop it." She watched the wine being poured, knowing the instant he spoke that he was more than a little depressed. "We may be only a rural village practice, but we do get the newspapers. And there's gossip."

"Shall I start?"

Clare was in no doubt. "No. Me. See how close I get to the truth." She fortified herself with a sip of wine and waved absently to friends who tried to beckon her over. "Mrs. Summerston somehow persuaded Ash to drive to Dragonswell that evening. Maybe she phoned him. Despite the terrible deterioration in his sight he drove that way and suffered the same consequences Gordon Summerston had. Right?"

"In a way, Clare."

She looked at him blankly. "Well? What do you think?"

"All right so far. Go on."

"That's as far as I've got," she said, pleased.

George recounted the tale of the Offa Rex piece and the auction.

"It only occurred to me too late," he admitted. "I think Janey put some chemical on the Offa Rex, some gold-colored corrosive which would blind anyone coming too close. It certainly was in a hell of a box."

"Which nobody was allowed to open except the purchaser?"

"Correct."

"There's a way of finding out, George," Clare observed. "You'll have to get your forensic experts to search the box and Janey's home for whatever chemical—" She halted as George shook his head. "What's wrong with that?"

"It won't work, Clare. In fact it didn't."

"You must ask Henderson, the county pathologist. He's a good man."

"We did. The traces have all gone. Janey knew that Ash would buy the Offa Rex. No traces at the Ash house, in the car, Ash's office, his study. Everything negative, clean as a whistle. The Offa piece as well. Every bloody place and thing we could think of."

Clare was intrigued. "If you suspected all this, George, you should have at least *some* evidence to catch her."

"The pathologist was very helpful," George continued miserably. "We talked it over. He got the very best technologist to do all those things. In absolute confidence. Sampled everything."

"And he found not even a trace—?"

"*She* found sod all," George was unable to resist the vulgarity. "Nothing."

"Radiation." Light dawned and Clare grasped George's arm vehemently. "It really must have been radiation, George! That's it! She put—"

"Shhh. Keep your voice down."

Clare sank her voice to an excited whisper. "Janey put some radioactive isotope, perhaps cobalt, into a gilt wash. Safely shielded, so only Ash himself got the full effects on opening the case." She shuddered. "How really horrid. It's well, almost snakelike. If we're right."

"Oh, we're right. She'd learned enough about coin collectors to know that a gilt wash would bring the price down to something Ash could afford, and that only the actual purchaser would have the right to handle it afterwards." And stare affectionately, he thought with his spine tingling, into those sinister little pellet eyes of Offa Rex, eyes which would beam an unseen but lethal irradiation into the retinas of the observer. As inevitable as night following day. He shivered at the unpleasant analogy.

"I don't understand. You can easily detect radioactive isotopes, George," Clare breathed. "The hospital has a good radioactive isotope laboratory, best in the eastern counties. Why not use it?"

"I know." George watched her carefully. "It's the one Henderson calls in when he needs help of this kind. He hasn't a radiation lab of his own. The only point I forgot to check."

"Then let's phone the radiation lab now," Clare suggested, still eager.

"No. Because Janey Summerston would answer." George did not look at her as he said this. "That's why, love." He felt her aghast silence for a moment before continuing. "She's the head technician in the radio-isotope section at the hospital. Naturally, Henderson got them to do the job—in strictest confidence, of course. I was being so bloody cautious I didn't even tell Henderson all my suspicions, in case Janey somehow got word."

"And *she* was the technician sent out to examine—?"

"I believed I'd thought of everything."

"Giving her the opportunity to clean up every single trace of radiation," Clare cried softly.

"Bloody marvelous," George said bitterly, "letting ourselves fall for it. Practically arranging for a murderer to examine in private every possible clue."

"Crime?" Clare asked. "Are we sure it was a crime?"

"Well, wasn't it?" George asked, honestly seeking an opinion now.

"Maybe not," Clare offered. "After all, we're only guessing." They both recognized her kindness, but George persisted.

"But maybe? You still admit it might be?"

Clare hesitated. "I don't know. There's no way of knowing anymore, is there?"

George bit back his irritation. Sometimes Clare made him furious. She seemed to have an innate skill at escaping the point.

"A crime's a crime, Clare. Ash may subconsciously have guessed how Janey was blinding him. He wasn't humbly accepting his punishment. A man doesn't do that. He was driving to Janey to ask her to undo the damage she'd inflicted on him. Maybe he had bribery in mind, perhaps even a confession."

"Did you call on Janey Summerston?" Clare could not avoid asking.

"Of course we did. She claimed ignorance of the whole thing."

They sat in silence for a minute.

"*Would* she have helped him, Clare?" George asked eventually.

Clare shrugged. "Who knows? A woman can be very touched when faced with the harm she's done."

"Or she can put the boot in," George countered. "Worse than any man."

"Women don't do that sort of thing," Clare said primly. "Anyhow, George," she finished, "maybe he just lost the road in the fog."

"Maybe," George said.

"Like Summerston."

The remark came almost under her breath.

As the soup arrived George looked carefully at her expression, wondering if a woman really could be so vengeful as he guessed Janey Summerston had been. Clare was half smiling, the way she sometimes did when making a joke, but in the moderate light of the club restaurant he couldn't quite tell.

One Morning They'll Hang Him

MARGERY ALLINGHAM

Margery Allingham was born in London in 1904, the eldest child of H. J. Allingham, whose serials appeared in the popular weeklies of the day. In 1927 she married Philip Youngman Carter, an artist, and the following year she wrote *The Crime at Black Dudley*, her first novel featuring the mild, bespectacled Albert Campion. Her novels before 1934 were mostly pure entertainment; those written later place her in the forefront of the generation of detection writers who attempted to fuse the police novel and the novel of character and psychology.

It was typical of Detective Inspector Kenny, at that time D.D.I. of the L. Division, that, having forced himself to ask a favor, he should set about with the worst grace possible. When at last he took the plunge, he heaved his two hundred pounds off Mr. Campion's fireside couch and set down his empty glass with a clatter.

"I don't know if I needed that at three in the afternoon," he said ungratefully, his small blue eyes baleful, "but I've been up since two this morning dealing with women, tears, minor miracles, and this perishing rain." He rubbed his broad face, and presented it scarlet and exasperated at Mr. Campion's back. "If there's one thing that makes me savage it's futility!" he added.

Mr. Albert Campion, who had been staring idly out of the window watching the rain on the roofs, did not glance round. He was still the lean, somewhat ineffectual-looking man to whom the Special Branch had turned so often in the last twenty years. His very fair hair had bleached into whiteness and a few lines had appeared round the pale eyes which were still, as always, covered by large horn-rimmed spectacles, but otherwise he looked much as Kenny first remembered him—"Friendly and a little simple—the old snake!"

"So there's futility in Barraclough Road too, is there?" Campion's light voice sounded polite rather than curious.

Kenny drew a sharp breath of annoyance.

"The Commissioner has 'phoned you? He suggested I should look you up. It's not a great matter—just one of those stupid little snags which has some perfectly obvious explanation. Once it's settled the whole case is open-and-shut. As it is, we can't keep the man at the station indefinitely."

Mr. Campion picked up the early edition of the evening paper from his desk.

"This is all I know," he said, holding it out. "Mr. Oates didn't 'phone. There you are, in the Stop Press. *Rich Widow shot in Barraclough Road West. Nephew at police station helping investigation*. What's the difficulty? His help is not altogether wholehearted, perhaps?"

To his surprise an expression remarkably like regret flickered round Kenny's narrow lips.

"Ruddy young fool," he said, and sat down abruptly. "I tell you, Mr. Campion, this thing is in the bag. It's just one of those ordinary, rather depressing little stories which most murder cases are. There's practically no mystery, no chase—nothing but a wretched little tragedy. As soon as you've spotted what I've missed, I shall charge this chap and he'll go before the magistrates and be committed for trial. His counsel will plead insanity and the jury won't have it. The Judge will sentence him, he'll appeal, their Lordships will dismiss it. The Home Secretary will sign the warrant and one morning they'll take him out and they'll hang him." He sighed. "All for nothing," he said. "All for nothing at all. It'll probably be raining just like it is now," he added inconsequentially.

Mr. Campion's eyes grew puzzled. He knew Kenny for a conscientious officer and, some said, a hard man. This philosophic strain was unlike him.

"Taken a fancy to him?" he inquired.

"Who? Me? I certainly haven't." The Inspector was grim. "I've got no sympathy for youngsters who shoot up their relatives however selfish the old besoms may be. No, he's killed her and he must take what's coming to him, but it's hard on—well, on some people. Me, for one." He took out a large old-fashioned notebook and folded it carefully in half. "I stick to one of these," he remarked virtuously. "None of your backs of envelopes for me. My record is kept as neatly as when I was first on the beat, and it can be handed across the court whenever a know-all counsel asks to see it." He paused. "I sound like an advertisement, don't I? Well, Mr. Campion, since I'm here, just give your mind to this, if you will. I don't suppose it'll present any difficulty to you."

"One never knows," murmured Mr. Campion idiotically. "Start with the victim."

Kenny returned to his notebook.

"Mrs. Mary Alice Cibber, aged about seventy or maybe a bit less. She had heart trouble which made her look frail and, of course, I didn't see her until she was dead. She had a nice house in Barraclough Road, a good deal too big for her, left her by her husband who died ten years ago. Since then she's been alone except for a maid who cleared off in the war and now for another old party who calls herself a companion. *She* looks older still, poor old girl, but you can see she's been kept well under—" he put his thumb down expressively—"by Mrs. C. who appears to have been a dictator in her small way. She was the sort of woman who lived for two chairs and a salad bowl."

"I beg your pardon?"

"Antiques." He was mildly contemptuous. "The house is crammed with them, all three floors and the attic, everything kept as if it was brand-new. The old companion says she loved it more than anything on earth. Of course she hadn't much else *to* love, not a relation in the world except the nephew—"

"Whose future you see so clearly?"

"The man who shot her," the Inspector agreed. "He's a big, nervy lad, name of Woodruff, the son of the old lady's brother. His mother, father, and two young sisters all got theirs in the blitz on Portsmouth. Whole family wiped out."

"I see." Campion began to catch some of Kenny's depression. "Where was he when that happened?"

"In the Western Desert." The D.D.I.'s protuberant eyes were dark with irritation. "I told you this was just an ordinary miserable slice of life. It goes on the same way. This boy, Richard Woodruff—he's only twenty-eight now—did very well in the war. He was in the landings in Sicily and went through the fighting in Italy where he got the M.C. and was promoted major. Then he copped in for the break-through in France and just before the finish he became a casualty. A bridge blew up with him on it—or something of the sort, my informant didn't know exactly—and he seems to have become what the boys call 'bomb happy.' It used to be 'shell shock' in my day. As far as I can gather, he always had been quick-tempered, but this sent him over the edge. He sounds to me as if he wasn't safe for a while. That may help him in his defense, of course."

"Yes." Campion sounded depressed. "Where's he been since then?"

"On a farm mostly. He was training to be an architect before the war but the motherly old Army knew what was best for him and when he came out of the hospital they bunged him down to Dorset. He's just got away. Some wartime buddy got him a job in an architect's office under the old pals' act and he was all set to take it up." He paused and his narrow mouth, which was not entirely insensitive, twisted bitterly. "Ought to have started Monday," he said.

"Oh dear," murmured Mr. Campion inadequately. "Why did he shoot his aunt? Pure bad temper?"

Kenny shook his head.

"He had a reason. I mean one can see why he was angry. He hadn't anywhere to live, you see. As you know London is crowded, and rents are fantastic. He and his wife were paying through the nose for a cupboard of a bed-sitting room off the Edgware Road."

"His wife?" The lean man in the horn-rims was interested. "Where did she come from? You're keeping her very quiet."

To Campion's surprise the Inspector did not speak at once. Instead he grunted and there was regret, and surprise at it, in his little smile. "I believe I would if I could," he said sincerely. "He found her on the farm. They've been married six weeks. I don't know if you've ever seen love, Mr. Campion? It's very rare—the kind I mean." He put out his hands deprecatingly. "It seems to crop up—when it does—among the most unexpected people, and when you do see it, well, it's very impressive." He succeeded in looking thoroughly ashamed of himself. "I shouldn't call myself a sentimental man," he said.

"No." Campion was reassuring. "You got his war history from her, I suppose?"

"I had to, but we're confirming it. He's shut up as a watch—or a hand grenade. 'Yes' and 'No' and 'I did not shoot her'—that's about all his contribution amounted to, and he's had a few hours of expert treatment. The girl is quite different. She's down there too. Won't leave. We put her in the waiting room finally. She's not difficult—just sits there."

"Does she know anything about it?"

"No." Kenny was quite definite. "She's nothing to look at," he went on presently, as if he felt the point should be made. "She's just an ordinary nice little country girl, a bit too thin and a bit too brown, natural hair and inexpert make-up, and yet with this—this blazing, radiant steadfastness about her!" He checked himself. "Well, she's fond of him," he amended.

"Believes he's God," Campion suggested.

Kenny shook his head. "She doesn't care if he isn't," he said sadly. "Well, Mr. Campion, some weeks ago these two approached Mrs. Cibber about letting them have a room or two at the top of her house. That must have been the girl's idea; she's just the type to have old-fashioned notions about blood being thicker than water. She made the boy write. The old lady ignored the question but asked them both to an evening meal last night. That invitation was sent a fortnight ago, so you can see there was no eager bless-you-my-children about it."

"Only that she had to have notice if she was giving a party. The old companion explained that to me. There was the silver to get out and clean, and the best china to be washed, and so on. Oh, there was nothing simple and homely about the household!" He sounded personally affronted. "When they got there, of course there was a blazing row."

"Hard words or flying crockery?"

Kenny hesitated. "In a way, both," he said slowly. "It seems to have been a funny sort of flare-up. I had two accounts of it—one from the girl and one from the companion. I think they are both trying to be truthful but they both seem to have been completely foxed by it. They both agree that Mrs. Cibber began it. She waited until there were three oranges and a hundredweight of priceless early Worcester dessert service on the table, and then let fly. Her theme seems to have been the impudence of Youth in casting its eyes on its inheritance before Age was in its grave, and so on and so on. She then made it quite clear that they hadn't a solitary hope of getting what they wanted, and conveyed that she did not care if they slept in the street so long as her precious furniture was safely housed. There's no doubt about it that she was very aggravating and unfair."

"Unfair?"

"Ungenerous. After all she knew the man quite well. He used to go and stay with her by himself when he was a little boy." Kenny returned to his notes. "Woodruff then lost his temper in his own way which, if the exhibition he gave in the early hours of this morning is typical, is impressive. He goes white instead of red, says practically nothing, but looks as if he's about to 'incandesce'—if I make myself plain."

"Entirely." Mr. Campion was deeply interested. This new and human Kenny was an experience. "I take it he then fished out a gun and shot her?"

"Lord, no! If he had, he'd have a chance at least of Broadmoor. No. He just got up and asked her if she had any of his things, because if so he'd take them and not inconvenience her with them any longer. It appears that when he was in hospital some of his gear had been sent to her, as his next of kin. She said yes, she had, and it was waiting for him in the boot cupboard. The old companion, Miss Smith, was sent trotting out to fetch it and came staggering in with an old officers' hold-all, bursted at the sides and filthy. Mrs. Cibber told her nephew to open it and see if she'd robbed him, and he did as he was told. Of course, one of the first things he saw among the ragged bush shirts and old photographs was a revolver and a clip of ammunition." He paused and shook his head. "Don't ask me how it got there. You know what hospitals were like in the war. Mrs. Cibber went on taunting the man in her own peculiar way, and he stood there examining the gun and presently loading it, almost absently. You can see the scene?"

Campion could. The pleasant, perhaps slightly overcrowded room was vivid in his mind, and he saw the gentle light on the china and the proud, bitter face of the woman.

"After that," said Kenny, "the tale gets more peculiar, although both accounts agree. It was Mrs. C. who laughed and said, 'I suppose you think I ought to be shot?' Woodruff did not answer but he dropped the gun in his side pocket. Then he packed up the hold-all and said 'Goodbye.' " He hesitated. "Both statements say that he then said something about *the sun having gone down*. I don't know what that meant, or if both women mistook him. Anyway, there's nothing to it. He has no explanation to offer. Says he doesn't remember saying it. However, after that he suddenly picked up one of his aunt's beloved china fruit-bowls and simply dropped it on the floor. It fell on a rug, as it happened, and did not break, but old Mrs. Cibber nearly passed out, and the girl hurried him off home."

"With the gun?"

"With the gun." Kenny shrugged his heavy shoulders. "As soon as the girl heard that Mrs. Cibber had been shot, she jumped up with a tale that he had *not* taken it. She said she'd sneaked it out of his pocket and put it on the window sill. The lamest story you ever heard! She's game and she's ready to say absolutely anything, but she won't save him, poor kid. He was seen in the district at midnight."

Mr. Campion put a hand through his sleek hair. "Ah. That rather tears it."

"Oh, it does. There's no question that he did it. It hardly arises. What happened was this. The young folk got back to their bed-sitting room about ten to nine. Neither of them will admit it, but it's obvious that Woodruff was in one of those boiling but sulky rages which made him unfit for human society. The girl left him alone—I should say she has a gift for handling him—and she says she went to bed while he sat up writing letters. Quite late, she can't or won't say when, he went out to the post. He won't say anything. We may or may not break him down, he's a queer chap. However, we have a witness who saw him somewhere about midnight at the Kilburn end of Barraclough Road.

Woodruff stopped him and asked if the last eastbound 'bus had gone. Neither of them had a watch, but the witness is prepared to swear it was just after midnight—which is important because the shot was fired at two minutes before twelve. We've gotten that time fixed."

Mr. Campion, who had been making notes, looked up in mild astonishment.

"You got that witness very promptly," he remarked. "Why did he come forward?"

"He was a plainclothesman off duty," said Kenny calmly. "One of the local men who had been out to a reunion dinner. He wasn't tight but he had decided to walk home before his wife saw him. I don't know why he hadn't a watch"—Kenny frowned at this defect—"anyway, he hadn't, or it wasn't going. But he was alert enough to notice Woodruff. He's a distinctive chap, you know. Very tall and dark, and his manner was so nervy and excitable that the dick thought it worth reporting."

Campion's teeth appeared in a brief smile.

"In fact, he recognized him at once as a man who looked as though he'd done a murder?"

"No." The Inspector remained unruffled. "No, he said he looked like a chap who had just got something off his mind and was pleased with himself."

"I see. And meanwhile the shot was fired at two minutes to twelve."

"That's certain." Kenny brightened and became businesslike. "The man next door heard it and looked at his watch. We've got his statement and the old lady's companion. Everyone else in the street is being questioned, but nothing has come in yet. It was a cold wet night and most people had their windows shut; besides, the room where the murder took place was heavily curtained. So far, these two are the only people who seem to have heard anything at all. The man next door woke up and nudged his wife who had slept through it. But then he may have dozed again, for the next thing he remembers is hearing screams for help. By the time he got to the window, the companion was out in the street in her dressing gown, wedged in between the lamp post and the mail box, screeching her little gray head off. The rain was coming down in sheets."

"When exactly was this?"

"Almost immediately after the shot, according to the companion. She had been in bed for some hours and had slept. Her room is on the second floor, at the back. Mrs. Cibber had not come up with her but had settled down at her bureau in the drawing-room, as she often did in the evening. Mrs. C. was still very upset by the scene at the meal, and did not want to talk. Miss Smith says she woke up and thought she heard the front door open. She won't swear to this, and at any rate she thought nothing of it, for Mrs. Cibber often slipped out to the mail box with letters before coming to bed. Exactly how long it was after she woke that she heard the shot she does not know, but it brought her scrambling out of bed. She agrees she might have been a minute or two finding her slippers and a wrapper, but she certainly came down right away. She says she found the street door open, letting in the rain, and the drawing-room door, which is next to it, wide open as well, and the lights in there full on." He referred to his notes and began to read aloud. " 'I smelled burning'—she means cordite—'and I glanced across the room to see poor Mrs. Cibber on the floor with a dreadful hole in her forehead. I was too frightened to go near her, so I ran out of the house shouting "Murder! Thieves!" ' "

"That's nice and old-fashioned. Did she see anybody?"

"She says not, and I believe her. She was directly under the only lamp post for fifty yards and it was certainly raining hard."

Mr. Campion appeared satisfied but unhappy. When he spoke his voice was very gentle.

"Do I understand that your case is that Woodruff came back, tapped on the front door, and was admitted by his aunt; after some conversation, which must have taken place in lowered tones since the companion upstairs did not hear it, he shot her and ran away, leaving all the doors open?"

"Substantially, yes. Although he may have shot her as soon as he saw her."

"In that case she'd have been found dead in the hall."

Kenny blinked. "Yes, I suppose she would. Still, they couldn't have talked much."

"Why?"

The Inspector made a gesture of distaste. "This is the bit which gets under my skin," he said. "They could hardly have spoken long—*because she'd forgiven him*. She had written to her solicitor—the finished letter was on her writing pad ready for the post. She'd written to say she was thinking of making the upper part of her house into a home for her nephew, and asked if there was a clause in her lease to prevent it. She also said she wanted the work done quickly, as she had taken a fancy to her new niece and hoped in time there might be children. It's pathetic, isn't it?" His eyes were wretched. "That's what I meant by futility. She'd forgiven him, see? She wasn't a mean old harridan, she was just quick-tempered. I told you this isn't a mystery tale, this is ordinary sordid life."

Mr. Campion looked away.

"Tragic," he said. "Yes. A horrid thing. What do you want me to do?"

Kenny sighed. "Find the gun," he murmured.

The lean man whistled.

"You'll certainly need that if you're to be sure of a conviction. How did you lose it?"

"He ditched it somewhere. He didn't get rid of it in Barraclough Road because the houses come right down to the street, and our chaps were searching for it within half an hour. At the end of the road he caught the last 'bus, which ought to come along at midnight but was a bit late last night, I'm morally certain. These drivers make up time on the straight stretch by the park; it's more than their jobs are worth, so you never get them to admit it. Anyhow, he didn't leave the gun on the 'bus, and it's not in the house where his room is. It's not in the old lady's house at 81 Barraclough Road because I've been over that house myself." He peered at the taller man hopefully. "Where would you hide a gun in this city at night, if you were all that way from the river? It's not so easy, is it? If it had been anywhere obvious it would have turned up by now."

"He may have given it to someone."

"And risked blackmail?" Kenny laughed. "He's not as dumb as that. You'll have to see him. He says he never had it—but that's only natural. Yet where did he put it, Mr. Campion? It's only a little point but, as you say, it's got to be solved."

Campion grimaced.

"Anywhere, Kenny. Absolutely anywhere. In a drain—"

"They're narrow gratings in Barraclough Road."

"In a sandbin or a static water tank—"

"There aren't any in that district."

"He threw it down in the street and someone, who felt he'd rather like to have a gun, picked it up. Your area isn't peopled solely with the lawabiding, you know."

Kenny became more serious. "That's the real likelihood," he admitted gloomily. "But all the same, I don't believe he's the type to throw away a gun casually. He's too intelligent, too cautious. Do you know how this war has made some men cautious even when they're being the most reckless? He's one of those. He's hidden it. Where? Mr. Oates said you'd know if anyone did."

Campion ignored this blatant flattery. He stood staring absently out of the window for so long that the Inspector was tempted to nudge him, and when at last he spoke, his question did not sound promising.

"How often did he stay with his aunt when he was a child?"

"Quite a bit, I think, but there's no kid's hiding-place there that only he cold have known, if that's what you're after." Kenny could hardly conceal his disappointment. "It's not that kind of house. Besides, he hadn't the time. He got back about twenty past twelve; a woman in the house confirms it—she met him on the stairs. He was certainly spark-out when we got there at a quarter after four this morning. They were both sleeping like kids when I first saw them. She had one skinny little brown arm round his neck. He just woke up in a rage, and she was more astounded then frightened, I swear—"

Mr. Campion had ceased to listen.

"Without the gun the only real evidence you've got is the plainclothesman's story of meeting him," he said. "And even you admit that gallant officer was walking for his health after a party. Imagine a good defense lawyer enlarging on that point."

"I have," the Inspector agreed, dryly. "That's why I'm here. You must find the gun for us, sir. Can I fetch you a raincoat? Or," he added, a faintly smug expression flickering over his broad face, "will you just sit in your armchair and do it there?"

To his annoyance his elegant host appeared to consider the question.

"No, perhaps I'd better come with you," he said at last. "We'll go to Barraclough Road first, if you don't mind. And if I might make a suggestion, I should send Woodruff and his wife back to their lodgings—suitably escorted, of course. If the young man was going to crack, I think he would have done so by now, and the gun, wherever it is, can hardly be at the police station."

Kenny considered. "He may give himself away and lead us to it," he agreed, although without enthusiasm. "I'll telephone. Then we'll go anywhere you say, but as I told you I've been over the Barraclough Road house myself and if there's anything there it's high time I retired."

Mr. Campion merely looked foolish, and the Inspector sighed and let him have his way.

He came back from the telephone smiling wryly.

"That's settled," he announced. "He's been behaving like a good soldier interrogated by the enemy, silly young fool—after all, we're only trying to hang him! The girl has been asking for him to be fed, and reporters are crawling up the walls. Our boys won't be sorry to get rid of 'em for a bit. They'll be looked after. We shan't lose 'em. Now, if you've set your heart on the scene of the crime, Mr. Campion, we'll go."

In the taxi he advanced a little idea.

"I was thinking of that remark he is alleged to have made," he said, not without shame. "You don't think that it could have been 'Your sun has gone down,' and that we could construe it as a threat within the meaning of the act?"

Campion regarded him owlishly.

"We could, but I don't think we will. That's the most enlightening part of the whole story, don't you think?"

If Inspector Kenny agreed he did not say so, and they drove to the top of Barraclough Road in silence. There Campion insisted on stopping at the first house next to the main thoroughfare. The building had traded on its proximity to the shopping centre and had been converted into a dispensing chemist's. Campion was inside for several minutes, leaving Kenny in the cab. When he came out he offered no explanation other than to observe fatuously that they had a "nice time," and settled back without troubling to look out at the early Victorian stucco three-story houses which lined the broad road.

A man on duty outside, and a handful of idlers gaping apathetically at the drawn blinds, distinguished 81 Barraclough Road. Kenny rang the bell and the door was opened after a pause by a flurried old lady with a duster in her hand.

"Oh, it's you, Inspector," she said hastily. "I'm afraid you've found me in a muddle. I've been trying to tidy up a little. *She* couldn't have borne the place left dirty after everyone had been trampling over it. Yet I don't mean to say that you weren't all very careful."

She led them into a spotless dining room which glowed with old mahogany and limpid silver, and the wan afternoon light showed them her reddened eyes and worn navy-blue housedress. She was a timid-looking person, not quite so old as Kenny had suggested, with very neat gray hair and a skin which had never known cosmetics. Her expression was closed and secret with long submission, and her shoulder blades stuck out a little under the cloth of her dress. Her hands still trembled slightly from the shock of the evening before.

Kenny introduced Campion. "We shan't be long, Miss Smith," he said cheerfully. "Just going to have another little look around."

Campion smiled at her reassuringly. "It's difficult to get help these days?" he suggested pleasantly.

"Oh, it is," she said earnestly. "And Mrs. Cibber wouldn't trust just anyone with her treasures. They are so very good." Her eyes filled with tears. "She was so fond of them."

"I daresay she was. That's a beautiful piece, for instance." Campion glanced with expert interest at the serpentine sideboard with its genuine handles and toilet cupboard.

"Beautiful," echoed Miss Smith dutifully. "And the chairs, you see?"

"I do." He eyed the Trafalgar set with the cherry-leather seats. "Is this where the quarrel took place?"

She nodded and trembled afresh. "Yes. I—I shall never forget it, never."

"Was Mrs. Cibber often bad-tempered?"

The woman hesitated, and her firm small mouth moved without words.

"Was she?"

She shot a swift unhappy glance at him.

"She was quick," she said. "Yes, I think I ought to say she was quick. Now, would you like to see the rest of the house or—?"

Campion glanced at his watch and compared it with the Tompion bracket clock on the mantelshelf.

"I think we've just time," he said, idiotically. "Upstairs first, Inspector."

The next thirty-five minutes reduced Kenny to a state of jitters rare in him. After watching Campion with breathless interest for the first five, it slowly dawned on him that the expert had forgotten the crime in his delight at discovering a treasure trove. Even Miss Smith, who betrayed a certain proprietorial pride, flagged before Campion's insatiable interest. Once or twice she hinted that perhaps they ought to go down, but he would not hear of it. By the time they had exhausted the third floor and were on the steps to the attic, she became almost firm. There was really nothing there but some early Georgian children's toys, she said.

"But I must just see the toys. I've got a 'thing' on toys, Kenny." Campion sounded ecstatic. "Just a minute—"

A vigorous tattoo on the front door interrupted him and Miss Smith, whose nerves were suffering, emitted a little squeak.

"Oh, dear. Somebody at the door. I must go down."

"No, no." Campion was uncharacteristically effusive. "I'll see who it is and come back. I shan't be a moment."

He flung himself downstairs with boyish enthusiasm. Miss Smith behind him, and Kenny, seeing escape at last, following quickly.

They reached the hall just in time to see him closing the door. "Only the post," he said, holding out a package. "Your library book, Miss Smith."

"Oh, yes," she came forward, hand outstretched. "I was expecting that."

"I rather thought you were." His voice was very soft and suddenly menacing. He held the cardboard book box high over his head with one hand, and with the other released the flap which closed it. The soft gleam of metal appeared in the light from the transom, and a service revolver crashed heavily to the parquet floor.

For a long minute there was utter silence.

Miss Smith appeared frozen in mid air, her hands clawing at the box.

Then, most dreadfully, she began to scream . . .

A little over an hour later Kenny sat on a Trafalgar chair in a room which still seemed to quiver and shudder with terrible sound. He was pale and tired-looking. His shirt was torn and there were three livid nail scratches down his face.

"God," he said, breathing hard. "God, can you beat that?"

Mr. Campion sat on the priceless table and scratched his ear.

"It was a bit more than I bargained for," he murmured. "It didn't occur to me that she'd become violent. I'm afraid they may be having trouble in the van. Sorry. I ought to have thought of it."

The C.I.D. man grunted. "Seems to me you thought of plenty," he muttered. "It came as a shock to me—I don't mind admitting it since I can't very well help it. When did it come to you? Did you have it from the start?"

"Oh, Lord, no." Campion sounded apologetic. "It was that remark of Woodruff's you quoted about the sun going down. That's what set me on the train of thought. Weren't you ever warned as a kid, Kenny, and by an aunt perhaps, never to let the sun go down on your wrath?"

"I've heard it, of course. What do you mean? It was a sort of saying between them?"

"I wondered if it was. They knew each other well when he was a child, and they were both quick-tempered people. It seemed to me that he was reminding her that the sun *had* gone down, and he showed her he could have smashed her precious bowl if he liked. It would have broken, you know, if he hadn't taken care it shouldn't. I wondered if, like many quick-tempered people, they got sorry just as quickly. Didn't you think it odd, Kenny, that directly after the row they should *both* have settled down to write letters?"

The detective stared at him.

"She wrote to her solicitor," he began slowly. "And he—? Good Lord! You think he wrote to her to say he was sorry?"

"Almost certainly, but we shall never find his letter. That's in the kitchen stove by now. He came back to deliver it, pushed it through the door, and hurried off looking, just as your plainclothesman said, as if he'd got something off his chest. Then he could sleep. The sun had not gone down on his wrath." He slid off the table and stood up. "The vital point is, of course, that *Mrs. Cibber knew he would.* She sat up waiting for it."

Kenny sucked in his breath.

"And Miss Smith knew?"

"Of course, she knew. Mrs. Cibber hadn't the kind of temperament one can keep a secret. Miss Smith knew from the moment that Mrs. Cibber received the initial letter that the nephew would get his way in the end—*unless she could stop it somehow!* She was the one with the bee in her bonnet about the furniture. I realized that as soon as you said the whole house was kept like a bandbox. No woman with a weak heart can keep a three-story house like a palace, or compel another to do it—unless the other wants to. Miss Smith was the one with the mania. Who was to get the house if the nephew died in the war? Mrs. Cibber must have made some provision."

Kenny rubbed his head with both hands. "I knew!" he exploded. "The lawyer's clerk told me this morning when I rang up to find out if Woodruff was the heir. I was so keen to confirm that point that I discounted the rest. If he died the campanion was to have it for her lifetime."

Campion looked relieved.

"I thought so. There you are, you see. She had to get rid of them both—Woodruff and his new wife. With a young and vigorous woman in the house there was a danger of the companion becoming—well, redundant. Don't you think?"

Kenny was fingering his notebook.

"You think she'd planned it for a fortnight?"

"She'd thought of it for a fortnight. She didn't see how to do it until the row occurred last night. When she found the gun on the window sill, where young Mrs. Woodruff left it, and Mrs. Cibber told her that the boy would come back, the plan was obvious." He shivered. "Do you realize that she must have been waiting, probably on the stairs, with the gun in one hand and the book box addressed to herself in the other, listening for Woodruff's letter to slide under the door? As soon as she heard it, she had to fly down and get it and open the door. Then she had to walk into the drawing-room, shoot the old lady as she turned to see who it was, and put the gun in the book box. The instant she was certain Mrs. Cibber was dead, she then had to run out screaming to her place between the lamp post and the mail box and—*post the package!*"

Kenny put down his pencil and looked up.

"Now there," he said with a honest admiration, "there I hand it to you. How in the world did you get on to that?"

"You suggested it."

"*I* did?" Kenny was pleased in spite of himself. "When?"

"When you kept asking me where one could hide a gun in a London street with no wide gratings and no sandbins. There was only the mail box. I guessed she'd posted it to herself—no one else would have been safe. Even the dead letter office eventually gives up its dead. That's why I was so keen to get her to the top of the house—as far away from the front door as possible." He sighed. "The book box was misguided genius. The gun was an old Luger, did you notice? Loot. That's why he never had to turn it in. It just fitted in the box. She must have had a thrill when she discovered that."

Kenny shook his head wonderingly. "Well, blow me down!" he said inelegantly. "Funny that *I* put you onto it!"

Mr. Campion was in bed that night when the telephone rang. It was Kenny again.

"I say, Mr. Campion?"

"Yes?"

"Sorry to bother you at this time of night but there's something worrying me. You don't mind, do you?"

"Think nothing of it."

"Well. Everything is all right. Smith has been certified by three medicos. The little girl is very happy comforting her boy, who seems to be upset about his aunt's death. The Commissioner is very pleased. But I can't get off to sleep. Mr. Campion, *how did you know what time the afternoon post is delivered in Barraclough Road?*"

The lean man stifled a yawn.

"Because I went into the chemist's shop on the corner and asked," he said. "Elementary, my dear Kenny."

Home Is The Hunter

CATHERINE AIRD

"Ever had anything to do with an Extradition Order, Sloan?" asked Police Superintendent Leeyes.

"No, sir," said Detective Inspector Sloan warily.

"Now's your chance then," said Leeyes.

"Sir?"

"It's never too late to learn," said Leeyes. "All the good books say so."

"Yes, sir," said Sloan, since this was very true.

The superintendent consulted a piece of paper on his desk. "It's from France."

"A friendly power."

The superintendent, suspecting irony, ignored this. "A Madam Vercollas of 17 Rue de la Pierre Blanche, St Amand d'Huiss . . . Huisse . . ." Leeyes gave up the unequal struggle to pronounce Huisselot. "Anyway she's here in Berebury now, which is all that matters to us."

"Keeps it simple," agreed Sloan.

"Nothing like your own patch." The superintendent's xenophobia was well known to embrace the next county to Calleshire as well as the next country to England. He had always been one to equate stranger with enemy.

"And the French would like her back would they, sir?" asked Sloan, getting out his notebook.

"They would," growled Leeyes. He pushed the Extradition Order from the Home Office across the desk. "She's wanted on a charge of murdering her husband, Louis Vercollas, at a place called Corbeaux last September."

"*His* convenience," added Anne Pickford tartly.

"What happened next?" asked Crosby, who was still a bachelor.

"The hotel proprietor sent for the doctor. I explained about Louis's illness and showed him all the medicines he had been having for it. He said that since we were strangers in Corbeaux he would telephone our doctor in Huisselot."

"Then what?"

"At first everything was all right—well, straightforward anyway. I saw the undertaker and so forth and went to have a look at the cemetery—the French make rather a thing of their cemeteries."

Sloan nodded. Even he had heard of *pompe funèbre.*

"It was outside the town and I couldn't find Louis's map in the car, but I got there in the end." She looked at the two policemen. "There was no point in my taking him back to Huisselot. It hadn't been his home town or anything, and when I came to think of it I didn't even know where his parents and sister were buried. It had never cropped up, and in any case he was a very secretive man."

"Quite so," said Sloan.

"All I knew was their names—Henri Georges and Clothilde Marie. The sister was Clémence . . ." Her voice trailed away as if she had just remembered something.

"What is it?" asked Sloan sharply.

"Nothing." She shook her head. "I arranged the funeral and ordered some of those marble *éternelles* that aren't allowed in England, and then . . ."

"Then?" prompted Sloan.

"Then the doctor said that there would have to be a post mortem after all. All of his sleeping draught had gone, you see."

"That's when they found out about the narcotic poisoning?" said Sloan soberly.

She nodded.

"Didn't the fools think about suicide?" said Crosby, forgetting all about the professional *Entente Cordiale* that was supposed to exist between national police forces.

"There was no note," said Laura Vercollas with the air of one repeating a well-rehearsed list. "There had been no threats to end his life at any time. He wasn't in pain, and generally speaking physically ill people don't do it. To say nothing," she added painfully, "of its being a funny time and place to choose—the first night in a strange hotel in a strange town."

"Looks black, doesn't it," agreed Crosby ingenuously.

"Louis wasn't exactly poor either." Laura Vercollas apparently couldn't resist piling Pelion upon Ossa. "That interested the French police a lot."

"I'll bet," said the constable warmly.

"That's all very well," said Laura Vercollas with spirit, "but I didn't put that sleeping draught into the wine or the soup, no matter what anyone says."

Had Crosby been French he might have said "*Bravo*" to that. Instead he looked distinctly mournful. "They've got everything on a plate, though, haven't they?"

"A strange hotel in a strange town," said Sloan slowly, "and yet your husband found it easily enough."

"He had a map."

"No," said Sloan quietly. "You couldn't find the map, could you?"

She stared at him.

"And the only mistake he made in getting to the hotel was directing you up a one-way street."

"Ye . . . es," she said uncertainly.

"Streets that have been two-way can be made one-way."

"What do you mean?"

"When you mentioned your husband's parents' names just now," said Sloan swiftly, "you were going to say something else."

"It was nothing, Inspector. Only a coincidence."

"Coincidence and circumstantial evidence sometimes go hand in hand," said Sloan sternly, hoping that he might be forgiven by an unknown number of defence counsels for picking one of their best lines.

"It was when I was in the cemetery," said Laura Vercollas. "I wandered about a bit, as one does, and I just happened to notice a tombstone to another husband and wife called Henri Georges and Clothilde Marie, that's all. Not the same surname. It was just a coincidence."

"And Clémence?" asked Sloan softly.

She shook her head. "There was a Clémence but in another part of the ceme . . ." She stopped and stared at him.

"Madame Vercollas," he said, "think carefully. You arrived in Corbeaux after dark."

"Yes."

"You yourself went into the hotel and arranged the room. Not your husband."

"Yes."

"You had your meal not in the dining room but in your bedroom."

"Yes."

"Who answered the door to the waiter who brought it up?"

"I did."

"Did he see your husband?"

"No. He was in the bathroom when he came."

"So no one in Corbeaux actually saw your husband?"

"No one."

"Did that not strike you as very strange?"

"I hadn't thought about it."

Sloan watched her face intently. "Had your husband ever mentioned Corbeaux in the past?"

"He never mentioned the past at all, Inspector," responded Laura Vercollas.

"The Occupation?"

"He wouldn't talk about the war at all except to say that he wanted to forget it."

"So he might," said Sloan vigorously. "And he succeeded, didn't he? Except perhaps," he added meaningfully, "when he was asleep."

"Those names, you mean?"

"Hercule, Jean-Paul, François," said Sloan.

"And the doctor," put in Crosby.

"Madam," said Sloan, "you told us the address of the hotel, didn't you?"

"Yes, I did," she replied quickly. "It was Le Coq d'Or, Place Dr Jacques Colliard . . . Place Dr Jacques Colliard." She stiffened. "Inspector, there was a plaque in the square. I noticed it particularly."

"Yes?" said Sloan into the sudden silence that had fallen in the neat sitting room in suburban Berebury.

Madame Vercollas's voice had sunk to a whisper. "It said 'Place Dr Jacques Colliard, Martyr de la Résistance'."

"The doctor," said Crosby almost under his breath.

"If what I am suggesting is so," said Sloan carefully, "there will be other memorials too. Such men are not forgotten in France."

She moistened her lips. "You mean Louis arranged to go back to Corbeaux to die? But why didn't he just . . ."

Sloan put the thought delicately: "Perhaps he wouldn't have been welcome."

She looked up.

"Perhaps," he went on, "if they had known in Corbeaux who he was they wouldn't have had him in their churchyard . . ."

"Are you saying, Inspector, he might have betrayed those men?"

"They were hard times in France," said Sloan obliquely. "No one knows what sort of unimaginable pressure . . ."

"The names he couldn't stop dreaming about."

"The Gestapo," said Sloan evenly, "might have gone on a 'shopping expedition', so to speak, that he would have found it hard to resist. Who are we to judge, Madam? We are too young to know."

"It would explain how he knew the way in the dark," she said.

"And why he would never come to England," said Anne Pickford intelligently, the teapot still in her hand.

Crosby looked puzzled.

"Vercollas wouldn't have been his real name and he couldn't have got a passport," she said.

Laura Vercollas was sitting very still. "Inspector, if those names that Louis couldn't stop remembering in his sleep are on the Corbeaux war memorial, the French police will have to think again, won't they?"

"They will." Sloan relaxed. "There's something you mustn't say to them, though, Madam."

"What's that?"

"Honi soit qui mal y pense."

Family Business

MICHAEL Z LEWIN

Michael Z. Lewin has written more than a dozen comedic mystery novels featuring either private detective Albert Samson or police lieutenant Leroy Powder. He has gained an international reputation, garnering several awards, including the Falcon, a Japanese award for best foreign mystery, and the German Marlowe award. A former science teacher and basketball columnist, he has also written several plays for both stage and radio. He lives with his family in Somerset, England.

1

At 09.38 hours Gina heard footsteps on the stairs. She sat up from the typewriter and ran a hand through her hair. When the door opened she was ready with businesslike attention.

In the old days the door had the words 'Please knock before entering' lettered at the bottom of the glass, but when Gina took over as receptionist/secretary she pointed out that nobody could come up the stairs without being heard and suggested that the door could do without being knocked on. The Old Man, of course, hadn't changed the door, but one of the first things Angelo had done was get the sign painter in to alter the lettering to 'No need to knock before entering'. It was longer and that disturbed the symmetry and the Old Man didn't like it and Gina's idea had been to paint out all the stuff about knocking, but Angelo had gone one better and that was Angelo for you.

When the door opened a woman looked hesitantly into the room.

'Hello,' Gina said. 'Come in.'

The woman was about forty with greying brown hair. Despite the invitation she was still uncertain. 'Is this the detective agency?' she asked.

'That's right,' Gina replied. 'Can we help you?'

The woman looked as if she was reminding herself of a decision already made. She stepped in and closed the door carefully. Then she turned to face Gina. 'Is the detective in?'

'We have a number of operatives,' Gina said, 'but they are all out working at the moment.'

'Oh,' the woman said.

'Mr Angelo Lunghi is the head of the agency. I can ring him on his car 'phone if it is an emergency.'

'I know all about car 'phones,' the woman said. But it didn't sound like an emergency.

Gina said, 'Perhaps the best thing is if you sit down and tell me generally what the problem is.'

'You?' the woman said. Her face said, 'You? The receptionist?'

'That's right. What you say to me is entirely confidential, I promise you. And although Mr Lunghi supervises all our cases personally, I can certainly assess whether we are likely to be able to help you.'

'I see,' the woman said.

'As well as being receptionist and secretary here,' Gina said, 'I am also Mrs Lunghi.'

2

Dinner was served at 19.10, the Lunghis' traditional Thursday evening meal, a hot curry made by Rosetta, Angelo's sister, whose domestic duties doubled with a part-time role as agency accountant. Thursday was a full family evening, which meant that the Old Man and Momma came down from their flat and that the two children, David and Marie, were expected to organise their school and social lives in such a way as to be there. Only Sal—Salvatore, Angelo's older brother, the painter—was not regularly there on Thursdays, Sunday afternoons and Tuesdays. But sometimes he came and sometimes he brought one of his models, as he called them. It was not an issue.

Gina's parents lived in another city these days.

Tonight Angelo rubbed his hands together as he sat down. 'Good good good,' he said.

'Hey, and what's wrong with spaghetti?' the Old Man asked. But it was in a friendly way and he said that sort of thing often. Spaghetti, or some other pasta, was on Sunday.

'Sorry I didn't get back to the office,' Angelo said.

'We coped,' Gina said.

'You know that guy Hardwick?'

They all knew that guy Hardwick, as various bits of investigation for Hardwick's solicitors had formed the major part of the agency's work for more than four weeks.

'Suddenly friend Hardwick decides that he *does* remember where he was on the night of April eighteenth.'

A groan went up from around the table.

'If he's going to be stupid enough to plead amnesia,' the Old Man said, 'then he ought to be smart enough to remember that he has amnesia.'

Everybody laughed.

'So what came into the office today?' Angelo asked.

'We were quite busy.'

'Good good good,' Angelo said and rubbed his hands.

David mimicked his father a moment after. 'Gooda gooda gooda.'

'Smart alec,' Angelo said, and swatted David on the top of the head. 'Tufty smart alec.'

David reconstructed his hair. It was all good-humoured.

'The main thing was a woman whose son has too much money.'

'We should all have such a problem,' Momma said.

'But as far as the woman can tell, the son doesn't work for it. He doesn't have a regular job and won't explain where it comes from.'

Everyone was listening now. Most agency work was for solicitors or involved missing relatives or related to faithless spouses, though the Old Man had once had a murder and would only too happily tell the whole thing yet again. But a son with too much money was unusual. They began to vie gently for the chance to ask Gina questions.

Several began to speak. Angelo held up his hand and established chairmanship. 'Marie.'

'How old is the son?' Marie, fourteen, asked.

'Too old for you, my girl.'

Marie blushed, but smiled. She enjoyed her position as the family heartbreaker.

'The boy is twenty-two,' Gina said.

'And still lives at home?' Angelo asked.

'You still live at home,' the Old Man said.

'Our situation is not an ordinary one,' Momma said.

'That's right,' David said. They all looked at him. 'Our house is bigger than most people's.' They laughed. A pretender for 'family wit'.

'Twenty-two years of age.' The Old Man looked thoughtful. 'So what does he do that his mother doesn't know what he does?'

Gina said, 'Well, he's been on the social for fifteen months, though he stays up late and sleeps in the day a lot and he goes out evenings and nights. His last job was interior-decorating.' Gina's face suggested that there was some unusual bit of information about the boy that was awaiting the right question.

'He's got boyfriends?' Momma asked.

'No.'

'He's a bloody artist?' This was the Old Man.

Gina shook her head.

'He's enrolled in the Open University and that's why he stays up at night, 'cause they don't have a video,' Rosetta, the accountant, offered.

'That's pretty tricky thinking,' David said.

Rosetta smiled.

Angelo considered, staring at his wife. 'So what's it going to be?' he asked himself aloud. 'So what's it going to be?'

'Give up?' Gina asked.

'Never,' the Old Man said.

Gina said, 'This unemployed layabout kid has a one-year-old car and a car telephone. And when he goes out at night and his mother asks him what he's been doing, all he will say is, "Driving." '

'Well well well,' Angelo said. He looked around the table. Everyone else was looking at him. It was a matter of who had driving licenses. And who could be asked to stay up all night following the son.

'We could ask Salvatore,' Momma said. She didn't like the Old Man to be out at night. There'd been enough of that, one way or another, when he was younger.

Gina said, 'Yes. He'd be interested in the work.'

'Work?' the Old Man said. 'He wants work, he can come here to work, he wants work. Right, Angelo?'

'Sally knows he's always got a place here if he wants it, Poppa,' Angelo said. 'But he'll never do it.'

'Never is a long time,' the Old Man said. 'But while I'm alive I think I agree with you.'

'That'll be forever,' Marie said, and the Old Man—who doted on his only granddaughter—beamed and said, 'There. Now there's a child.'

'I'm glad you like my handiwork, Poppa,' Gina said.

The Old Man looked at Gina for a moment and then burst into loud laughter. He also liked his daughter-in-law.

'So how's it left with this woman?' Angelo asked.

'It's left I got the car and its registration number and the address, the car 'phone number, the names, all that.'

'You mean we're on tonight?'

'I already rang Salvatore. He'd happy to do the night, or split shifts if you prefer. I didn't know exactly what you had to do tomorrow about the Hardwick.'

'Right,' Angelo said. 'Or we could use Max, or Johnny.'

'Outside ops are expensive,' Rosetta said.

'Salvatore ain't cheap,' Angelo said.

'At least he's in the family,' Momma said.

'*I*'m in the family,' the Old Man said. 'What's this you treat me like I couldn't follow a giraffe in a herd of mice? Am I not here or something? I got bad breath?'

'I haven't forgotten you, Poppa,' Angelo said.

'You're on shoplifting at Quicks again tomorrow,' Gina said.

'Cheaper to get a store detective replacement for me daytime than hire an outside op short notice tonight.'

'We're not going to hire anybody tonight except Sal,' Angelo said. 'I don't know what all this is about. We can cover it. We can cover most things.'

'Dad?' David asked.

'Uh huh?'

'Can I come out with you tonight?'

'I don't know I'm going out.'

'Can I go out with Uncle Sal, then?'

'Not on a school night,' Gina said.

David said, 'I could try to spin you a story about not having school, the teachers having one of those funny days they have or something, but it *is* a school day tomorrow.'

'Is that supposed to be news?' Angelo asked.

'But it's not an important day. No tests and I've got no homework. It's a good day for me to be out the night before.'

'Nice try,' Angelo said.

'Aw Dad!'

'If we're still on it tomorrow night, maybe then. A Friday or a Saturday night.'

'Or both?'

'We'll see. We'll see.' Angelo turned back to Gina. 'What's the financial?'

'The mother has some money an aunt left her. She intended to fix the house up, but she's too worried about this kid. She's sure he's up to no good.'

'What's the name?'

'The boy is John Anson Hatwell.'

'Form?'

'I rang Charlie. It's mixed. He had some DC when he was sixteen, for some muggings and he admitted two burglaries to be taken into account. He's been arrested twice again, for burglaries, but charges were dropped.'

'It sounds like a bit of a problem,' Angelo said.

'I asked her what she expected if we found out he was engaged in criminal activities. Of course, she wants a chance to "handle" it herself. I told her that really depended on what we found out, if we found out anything.'

'Sal will find out tonight whether the kid is going to be easy to tail or whether we'll need a team.'

'So you want Sally on all night? No shifts?'

'Not unless he needs it. If he does then maybe Poppa will cover it.' Angelo looked at his father. The Old Man looked at his wife. His wife looked at Gina. 'I'll talk to Sally,' Gina said, 'but we left it that he would do the night unless he heard different.'

'So,' Angelo said, 'you said it was busy. What else came in?'

'Well,' Gina said, 'there was this woman who found a comb in the back seat of her husband's car. She wanted *him* followed.'

'Suddenly it's follow follow follow,' Angelo said.

'But she didn't realise how expensive it was or how long it might take.'

'To follow a comb?' David asked.

'She went home to think about just how bad she wants to find out who belongs to the comb.'

'You should get a grant from the marriage guidance people,' Angelo said, 'the good advice you give out for free.'

'Free free free,' David said.

3

At 10.55 the next morning Salvatore dropped in to report to Gina on his night's activities.

'The Big Man going to need me again tonight?'

'I don't know yet, Sal,' Gina said.

'It's just I got a model booked. I can unbook her if it's important.'

'I'll call him on the car 'phone.'

'Or leave a message in his Filofax?'

'Don't be naughty, Salvatore.'

Gina tried to ring Angelo, but he wasn't in his car. 'Sorry,' she said. 'I'll try him later.'

'I thought it through,' Sal said, 'and this one, it isn't that important I know ahead. Just let me know around dinner-time, eh?'

'You want to come over for dinner tonight?'

'No thanks, kid.' In a playful way he said, 'You ever done any modelling?'

'Only in my spare time.' An obvious joke since everyone acknowledged that Gina never had spare time.

'Get hard up, give me a ring.'

'You want the money for last night now?'

'Yeah, I'll take it now, now you mention it.' He laughed. They both knew who was hard up for what.

Dinner was early on a Friday night to make it easier for David and Marie, who liked to go out. Rosetta went out Fridays too, with her fiancé of the last four years who was agonising over the morality of divorce, if not necessarily over other moralities. Gina always cooked on Fridays, unless it was busy, in which case they went out for a pub meal.

Angelo was already in when Gina came home from the office. He had scrubbed some potatoes.

'So what did Sally have to say?' Angelo asked.

Normally they would have waited to talk about it till mealtime, but with the possibility that David would be riding if Angelo went out, they needed to plan ahead.

'Sally said that John Anson Hatwell didn't have a clue he was being followed and that he should be easy for one car.'

'That's something.'

'What did he do?'

'Sal got there about twenty hundred. Twenty-one thirty-five Hatwell left his home address alone. He drove into the city and went to a backstreet café called Henry's. Do you know it?'

'That's on Morris Street, isn't it?'

'That's it. Do you know what it is?'

'Give me a clue.'

'Stays open all night.'

'Cabbies?'

Gina smiled.

Angelo considered the information. 'How long was Hatwell there?'

'Only about half an hour. Then drove around till two a.m.'

'Just drove around?'

'That's what Sally says. He took down the street names for a while, but the kid didn't stop anywhere. He just drove till two-o-eight. He might have been making calls from his car phone but Sally didn't think so.'

'If he did, who to?'

Gina shrugged.

'And what happened then?'

'He picked up a prostitute at two-o-eight.'

'I see.'

'Dropped her off again at two thirty-two.'

'He may have too much money but he doesn't like to waste it on frills, eh?'

'And then he went home,' Gina said.

'Hmmmm.'

'His mother says often he stays out till five or six, so this probably wasn't typical. I don't know what he does during the days. It was the evenings and nights that really worried her and I told her that's what we would concentrate on.'

'I think we stick at that for the time being. What she's worried about is how he makes his money, not how he spends it.'

Gina nodded.

'I'll take him tonight. Maybe Sally again tomorrow.'

'And David?'

They looked at each other. Angelo said, 'I more or less promised him.'

'Yes,' Gina said. 'All right.'

4

Angelo and David arrived at Hatwell's house at 18.30. Their car was well-stocked for a long night. Thermos flasks, cassette tapes, food, blankets. Specimen jars in case of emergency. David had been out before and knew the drill.

'Which car is it, Dad?'

'The Opel across the street. Under the light.'

'I see.'

'How're your eyes these days, son? Can you read the number plate?'

David read the number plate. Then he said, 'Grandad told Mum that he wanted to come along tonight.'

'She didn't say anything to me.'

'I think Gran talked him out of it.'

'More likely there's a private-eye film on TV. He loves to pick holes in the stories.'

'Coincidences like that don't happen in real life,' David said, mimicking his grandfather.

Angelo smiled. 'That's it.'

'Did you ever think of being something other than a private detective, Dad?'

'I didn't get much choice once Uncle Sal went to art college.'

'Do you mind?'

'I don't think about it.'

'What else would you have wanted to do?'

Angelo considered. 'I don't know.'

'A painter like Uncle Sal?'

'You got to be able to draw,' he said.

'Uncle Sal's stuff doesn't look like you have to draw so well.'

'You've got to be able to draw to make it look like you can't,' Angelo said.

'Oh,' David said. Then, 'What time do you think this Hatwell bloke is going to come out of his house?'

'Not for a while yet,' Angelo said. 'He didn't go out till twenty-one thirty last night.'

But Angelo was wrong, because three minutes later, 19.22 John Anson Hatwell left his mother's house and got into his car.

'Write it down,' Angelo said to David as he started his car.

David took up the clipboard and wrote a note of the time that they had begun the active phase of their surveillance.

5

Hatwell's night began much as the previous night had begun. He drove to Henry's Café, parked and went in.

The windows of the café were large and clear enough that Hatwell could be seen going to the counter, placing an order and then moving to a table where another man already sat. Hatwell had entered the café at 19.49.

The man behind the counter carried a tray to Hatwell at 19.53. The man sitting with Hatwell rose and left the café at 19.59. This man got into one of the taxis up the street.

'Binoculars,' Angelo said with some urgency, but David already had the large-lens binoculars out of the case and resting on the dashboard for support.

When the man pulled his taxi into the road, David read out the vehicle's registration number and the name of the taxi company. Angelo recorded these on the clipboard sheet.

The binoculars intensified light from dim images. It was as if one's eyes were suddenly five times as big: more light from the object was caught.

At 20.06 Angelo took some money from his coin purse. 'What say you go in and ask for a couple of doughnuts?'

'Really?'

'See whether Hatwell is talking to anybody else, but if he gets up to leave, just walk back to the car.'

'Okay, Dad.'

'And don't tell your mother.'

David winked and put out his hand for the money.

By 20.13 he was back in the car. 'Hatwell isn't talking to anybody else. What he's got left is some chips on a small plate and he took a drink from whatever he had a cup of.'

Angelo began to speak but David interrupted him. 'There was a mirror behind the counter,' he said. 'I watched him in that.'

'Good boy,' he said. Then, 'Hang on. I think we're rolling.'

Hatwell had risen from his table and was walking towards the café door.

'Got a time for me, Dad?' David asked.

6

Hatwell drove to a petrol station. Angelo pulled into a street on the opposite side of the road, turned around and waited, ready to go in whichever direction Hatwell chose after his stop.

Hatwell filled his Opel with petrol. David practised with the binoculars and saw that the car had taken 41.42 litres.

'Litres?' Angelo asked. 'How much is that in real?'

'A bit more than nine gallons,' David said.

'Oh,' Angelo said, not having expected an answer. He wrote it down.

Hatwell left the petrol station and drove around for about half an hour. Then, at 21.02, he pulled to the side of the road and stopped suddenly. Angelo had to drive past him. David turned to see what was happening in the Opel.

'It looks like he's talking on the 'phone, Dad,' David said.

Angelo again used a sidestreet and turned around quickly. They could just make out Hatwell's car.

After another minute on the 'phone, Hatwell put it away and

made a squealing U-turn. Angelo pulled out to follow him and already it was obvious that the car was being driven in a much more positive manner than before.

This went on for thirteen minutes as they followed the Opel across town. Then suddenly Hatwell slowed down. Taking a chance, Angelo—who felt he was lucky still to be with the car—slowed down, too, rather than overtake it as he had done the time before.

Hatwell did not *seem* to notice them.

'If he'd been looking for us,' Angelo said to his quiet son, 'he'd have spotted us a dozen times.'

Hatwell appeared instead to be intent on finding a house number. After a few moments of slow cruising, he parked. Angelo pulled past him and parked on the other side of the street.

'Stay here and stay low,' he said to David.

Angelo got out of his car. As he pretended to lock the vehicle door he saw which way Hatwell had turned. Angelo turned in the other direction and walked till he found a telephone pole. In a sideways movement he dropped into its shadow and turned back to watch Hatwell.

Hatwell had not moved far. For several seconds he studied the front of a semi-detached house. Then he began to walk. Angelo followed unseen.

Hatwell walked around the block. When he got to the front of the semi again, he walked up the path and then through the gate between the house and its garage.

Angelo slipped back into his car where David waited eagerly.

'What's up, Dad?'

'I think he's committing a burglary,' Angelo said. 'If I had to guess, that would be it.' He started his car.

'Where are we going?'

'I want to get in a better position in case he leaves fast.'

Angelo turned around in the street and reparked several yards behind Hatwell's Opel.

They waited for nearly an hour, but eventually Hatwell reappeared. He carried two suitcases and was not in any apparent hurry.

'A cool son of a bitch,' Angelo said tensely.

David was pleased that his father used such language with him. Gina would have disapproved.

Hatwell did not have to unlock his boot. A push of a button and the lid flew up. In a moment the cases were in and the lid back down.

Hatwell got into his car then, and, still without seeming to rush, he drove away.

'What do we do now, Dad?'

'Follow follow follow,' Angelo said. He pulled out to do just that but he was in deep thought.

7

Angelo and David came home when Hatwell finally returned to his mother's house, parked and went in. David, who knew he had been along for something unusual, *said* he was too excited to sleep. But when Angelo sent him upstairs he went with a yawn, not a murmur. He was too tired to be too excited to sleep.

Angelo left a note on the kitchen table for Gina to wake him at 08.00 and to get the Old Man down. On another day Rosetta would have been summoned, but normally she stayed out on a Friday night and did not return on Saturday until noon.

At 08.22, when everyone was together and Angelo had had a cup of coffee he said, 'It's tough to know exactly what to do.'

He explained what they had done and seen. That Hatwell had pulled up to use his car 'phone a second time and had driven to look for and find a second address after that. But something had perhaps looked wrong to him. He had not stayed long and had not gone on to the property at the second address.

'And then,' Angelo said, 'cool as can be, he drives back to Henry's and has some more food. This is at three-twelve in the morning. He's got two suitcases of stolen goods in the boot of his car and he still hasn't locked it because when he finally went back to his mother's house, he locked it before he went inside. We have to decide what to do.'

'What does the client want you to do?' the Old Man asked.

Gina said, 'She said she wanted to know if there was anything criminal before we told the police.'

'How much money have you had?' the Old Man asked.

'Fee for three nights, but no expenses.'

'She seem flush?'

'She didn't hesitate writing the cheque,' Gina said.

'Our responsibility is to her,' the Old Man said.

'I am tempted to follow Hatwell this morning,' Angelo said. 'To find out what he does with it all. He must be going to take it to a fence today.'

'Who's paying you to do that?' the Old Man asked. 'Suddenly you're an independent working on commission from the police?'

'I know I know I know, Pop,' Angelo said. 'All I said was that I am tempted. How often do we get something like this?'

'Not often, but so what?'

'Who paid you to solve the murder of Norman Stiles?'

'At least I was being paid to check a suspect's alibi. So I stumbled on to a different way to alibi him. At least I was being paid.'

'You never got paid.'

'So at least I was owed,' the Old Man said with dignity.

'I know I know I know,' Angelo said. 'But I am still tempted.'

'I think we should contact Mrs Hatwell,' Gina said. 'She is the client.'

The Old Man looked at Gina fondly.

'I was also tempted to try to look in the boot while Hatwell was in Henry's.'

'Not with David there!'

'But Hatwell parked right in front of the café second time.'

They sat quietly for a moment. 'We have an obligation to the client,' Angelo said. 'And an obligation to the police. But if it came to it I think I could deal with the police.'

At the time they didn't ask him what he meant by that.

Instead, Gina said, 'How tired are you?'

'I'm all right.'

'This is what we do,' Gina said. 'We drive two cars to the Hatwells'. I go up to the door to see if I can talk to Mrs Hatwell myself. You wait outside and you follow the son if he goes anywhere. Poppa mans the office.'

'Who's paying, he goes anywhere?' the Old Man demanded again.

'Maybe if we recover what's in the suitcases the owners will pay us,' Gina said.

8

Gina and Angelo arrived at 09.49. Before Gina went in, Angelo slipped into her passenger seat. 'I'm not that happy about you going in cold,' Angelo said.

'I'll be all right.'

He raised his eyebrows. 'Tell her you're there only as a courtesy. We have to tell the police. We have no choice.'

She nodded and got out.

And it was true enough. Police everywhere are territorial. It is not enough that justice be done in the end. If it's their justice, they are loathe for anybody else to administer it. The bulk of a detective-agency's business does not require direct involvement in, or knowledge of, illegality; but to be in the bad books of the local police can obstruct detective work a hundred times in a year. It is not something to risk casually.

But Angelo was still tempted to let Hatwell have a little rope and to see where he would take the suitcases.

In the end, however, stronger forces determined his actions.

Gina went to the door of the house at 09.54. She was admitted to the house at 09.55 by Mrs Hatwell.

By 10.15 Angelo was tired of waiting. He sorely wished he had put a wire on her. Or at least a call device, a button to be pushed in case of emergency. They had relied too much on the assumption that the young Hatwell's routine of sleeping late would be followed. Angelo felt he had been careless from fatigue. He felt that he had put Gina at risk. He began to think that he should go to the house himself.

Having begun to think that, he began to decide to do it.

He got out of his car. He walked towards the house. He stood by the Opel. Gina did not emerge.

Angelo looked at the house. Then he began to walk up the path.

Suddenly the front door burst open. John Anson Hatwell ran out.

Angelo froze. He was in no-man's-land. He couldn't get back to his own car to follow without it being obvious. And Gina still did not appear.

So Angelo tackled Hatwell himself as the young man ran by.

The act was a surprise to both of them. But with Hatwell on the ground, Angelo knew enough to be able to keep him there.

Hatwell swore and spluttered and made enquiries as to what Angelo thought he was doing.

Angelo informed him that he was making a citizen's arrest, something he was perfectly entitled to do as long as he was willing to take the consequences of false citizen's arrest.

Angelo fretted, however, because all he could do was sit there holding Hatwell immobile when what he wanted to do was go into the house to make sure Gina was all right.

Why had Hatwell come out running? What had he done? What

had happened to the two women inside. Angelo at first *asked* for answers from Hatwell. Then he screamed at his prisoner.

9

Rosetta served Sunday dinner at 14.00 sharp. It was an even-numbered Sunday in the month so her 'fiancé', Walter, was in attendance. Salvatore was there, too, having brought a model named Carol.

'This is my father,' Sal said, introducing her to the Old Man. 'And my mother. And this is Carol. She models for me.'

'Hello,' Momma said tersely. Carol didn't *look* like a potential wife.

'Welcome and make yourself at home,' the Old Man said. He shook Carol's hand warmly.

'My niece and nephew, Marie and David.'

'Hello.'

'Hello.'

'Hello.'

'Gina you met at the door. That's Rosetta behind the salad bowl and Walter next to her. And the man with the black eye is my brother Angelo. He's about to tell us how he got it.'

Carol exchanged greetings with the rest of the family and everyone sat down.

In fact the one thing that Angelo didn't remember was when he had been hit in the eye. 'I was just worried that the creep had done something to my Gina.'

Gina said, 'The boy's mother was crying. I was trying to console her. She was a client after all.'

'But I didn't know.'

'No.'

'So there I was sitting on this kid,' Angelo began, 'having made a citizen's arrest.'

'Tricky,' the Old Man said. 'Very tricky.'

'I thought I had him bang to rights,' Angelo said. 'I thought he had two suitcases of stolen goods locked in the boot of his car. I had seen him put them there. I had seen him lock it. I thought—'

'But it was four hours later.'

'I know I know I know. Nobody was more surprised than me when the police opened the boot and it was flaming empty.'

'That was a very tense moment,' Gina agreed.

'I was thinking I'm going to go down for GBH,' Angelo said. 'A friend Charlie may be over there, but he's not going to be able to get me off GBH.'

Angelo paused to look around the room.

'So come on,' Salvatore said. 'Get on with it. How come you're here and smiling instead of being held on remand in a tin hut somewhere out in the country?'

Gina said, 'My Angelo did say before we went out that he thought he could deal with the police.'

Angelo said, 'I was bothered by this Hatwell's car telephone.'

'He didn't use it the night I was out,' Sal said.

'But with David and me . . .' Angelo turned to David who beamed at the guests. 'With David and me he used it twice. Each time he then goes to a house somewhere. First time it's suitcases. Second time nothing. But it bothered me. And then I'm thinking, each night he's down at this taxi drivers' café. First night he eats alone. Second night he eats with a cabby. You see, the problem about these 'phone calls is who is it he's talking to?'

'So my boy puts two and two together,' the Old Man said to Carol proudly.

'And he got twenty-two,' David said.

'And this time I am lucky,' Angelo said.

'Who was it then?' Carol asked.

'What I decided was that Hatwell was working with a taxi driver. The driver picked up fares from a house. He noticed whether they locked up when they left, whether it looked like it was empty. Then after he took them to their destination, he telephoned Hatwell. Gave him the address. Hatwell went to the address, confirmed to his own satisfaction that the house was empty. And burgled it if he thought it was right.'

'Gosh,' Carol said.

'Some nights the driver got no appropriate fares or maybe he was just off work—that's what I think happened your night, Sal.'

Salvatore nodded.

'But Friday night they had a big hit. The police figured there was nearly two grand's worth in the suitcases, when they recovered them from the cabby. Who drove home at the end of his shift via Hatwell's house. Duplicate key to Hatwell's boot. Takes the cases at six in the morning. Who sees?'

'They were still in his taxi when the police got there,' Gina said.

'And how did you know who the taxi driver was?' Carol asked.

'Ah, that was down to David,' Angelo said. 'He was the one who spotted the man's registration number when he went on shift. A word with his despatcher and he was despatched.'

'All in a night's work, ma'am,' David said.

Carol smiled.

'The police say they think it will resolve about forty outstanding burglaries,' Gina said.

'Well done, brother,' Salvatore said with genuine pride.

'Thanks.'

'Are people ready to eat?' Rosetta asked.

'So what's today?' the Old Man asked.

'Linguini, with my special sauce,' Rosetta said.

'That's Italian for "little tongues",' the Old Man said.

'Oh,' Carol said.

'So,' the Old Man said to Rosetta, 'what's wrong with some curry?'

There was a quiet groan from several places around the table.

'A family joke,' Salvatore explained.

'You know, Carol,' the Old Man said, 'one time, one time only, I was involved in an actual *murder* case.'

'Gosh!' Carol said.

'The man's name was Norman Stiles and he was a small-time bookmaker.'

A second, louder, groan was heard. But not by the Old Man.

Justice in My Own Hands

ELIZABETH FERRARS

Elizabeth Ferrars (1907–1995) is the pseudonym of Morna Brown, the prolific author of more than 70 novels published over more than four decades. She was married to a Robert Brown, a distinguished professor of botany, and spent much of her time at scientific meetings, the results of which appear in several of her novels. One of her series detectives, Andrew Basnett, is even a retired botany professor, and appears to be based on an amalgam of characteristics of her and her husband. Her other series, which she was working on when she died, featured Virginia and Felix Freer, a separated-but-not-divorced husband and wife amateur sleuthing team. A founding member of the Crime Writers' Association, the leading mystery writers organization in Great Britain.

I have never committed a murder.

I once took justice into my own hands and if this had happened fifty years ago it might have led to something which perhaps could be described as murder, since capital punishment then was still normal. And to send a person to the gallows, even if this was deserved according to the law, might have been regarded in its way as homicidal. But a sentence for what is called life, but which is a mere ten years or so, with time off for good behavior, is altogether a different thing. Only too different, I realise, as the years pass. . . .

It is about eight years ago now that my Grandaunt Emma telephoned me one morning and begged me pressingly to come and see her.

'Dorothy, dear, I know you're very busy, but couldn't you spare a couple of days to come down here at the weekend?' she said. 'You know I've not been well, don't you, and there's something I want to talk to you about before . . . Well, as soon as possible.'

Her old voice creaked and was a little shaky. She was eighty-six, and a few months before—as I had heard from my sister Marion, who lived with her—had suffered a slight stroke. Considering her age, the old woman had made a very good recovery. She had apparently become a little more absent-minded than before, but had not been paralysed in any way and could still enjoy reading and watching television, and could even walk around the house a little without assistance.

She had had to give up cooking, which irked her because it had been one of the main interests in her life. At one time she had even written articles about it for one of the women's magazines. And she had stubbornly gone on with it until her stroke, since when, unfortunately for Marion—who could produce a very presentable shepherd's pie and even grill a chop with some success—Aunt Emma had become more critical than ever and not as grateful as she might have been for all that Marion did for her.

If the telephone call that morning had been a cry for help from Marion, badly wanting a few days off to meet some friends, go to a theatre and do some shopping in London, it would have puzzled me less than our aunt's anxious invitation.

For anxious it certainly was. It sounded almost frightened. The stroke, I thought, must have affected her more than Marion had told me, more perhaps than Marion, spending as much time as she did with the old woman and being too used to her to notice a gradual change, had even realised. Aunt Emma had always been an intrepid character, always busy with half-a-dozen worthy causes, and had once stood for Parliament as an independent candidate. She had lost her deposit but had always referred to the experience as if it gave her some kind of special importance. Apart from that, she was rich, generous and affectionate.

'Yes, of course I could come if you really want me,' I said, 'though it isn't just the easiest thing at the moment.'

'Please, Dorothy, please!' she implored. 'This weekend. Can't you do it?'

I could if it was really that urgent, though I usually worked over the weekend. At that time I was employed by a literary agent and often took manuscripts home with me on Fridays to read in the quiet of my small flat in Hampstead. In the office there were always interruptions, telephone calls, committee meetings, visiting authors, discussions with publishers. And recently I had been letting the manuscripts pile up. . . . But if it was really that important to Aunt Emma, the manuscripts would just have to wait.

'Very well,' I said. 'On Saturday morning, will that be all right?'

'Yes, yes, if you can't come sooner. Couldn't you come on Friday evening?'

'I suppose I could.'

'Then, do! Come in time for dinner. After all, it's only an hour from London and you can take a taxi from the station.'

'Can't Charles or Marion meet me with the car? I think there's a train at six which gets to Oxford just after seven.'

'Perhaps they could. Yes. No. I don't know. I'll speak to them about it.' The anxiety in her voice was almost strident.

'You mean you haven't said anything yet about this visit of mine to Marion?' I said.

'How could I, till I knew you'd come?'

That made sense, but I had a sudden uncomfortable feeling that with her new absent-mindedness Aunt Emma might forget to mention my visit to my sister, which might be inconvenient, if not actually upsetting for her. So I suggested that, if Marion was in at that moment, perhaps I might have a few words with her—but Aunt Emma replied in an odd, hurried way that she was not in and, anyway, there were always lots of taxis at the station. So I accepted it and left it at that. I could telephone Marion later, I thought.

I called her that evening, but it turned out to have been unnecessary. Aunt Emma *had* told her of my plans. I was not sure, though, that Marion sounded too pleased.

'But what's she so worried about?' I asked. 'Because she is worried, isn't she?'

'I think it's just that she's got it into her head that she's bound to have another stroke soon,' Marion answered, 'and she wants to be sure of seeing you once more before it happens. You were always her favorite, you know.'

I did know it. Marion, living with her in Oxford, had always done far more for Aunt Emma than I had, yet we both knew that I occupied a place in her affections that Marion could never come close to.

'Well, I'll see you on Friday,' I said, 'and don't bother about meeting me. I'll take a taxi.'

'Oh, I'll meet you,' she said, 'or else Charles will.'

In the event it was Charles who came to the station.

I had never been able to make up my mind about Charles. There had been a time when I had thought that he was in love with me, but it was Marion whom he had married. However, this had not done much more than damage my *amour propre*, leaving my heart intact. He was an oddly nondescript kind of man, fairly tall, fairly thin, rather stooping, with grey eyes, and a long, pale face topped by shaggy fair hair which always looked as if he had forgotten to have it cut rather than deliberately let it grow long. He was a university lecturer in Social History and according to some people was brilliant, as would be generally recognised, they said, when he finished his book.

Unfortunately, the book showed no signs of ever nearing an end, and that, to someone in my profession, only too used to people who at some future date were going to produce a work of genius, was no recommendation. All the same, I had always found him a curiously exciting man, though I could not have said why. Perhaps it was his air of wary detachment, his cautious avoidance of becoming more than superficially involved with anyone. It was a kind of challenge.

'It's good of you to come,' he said, as we drove away from the station. 'The poor old thing seems to want you badly. She's made up her mind she hasn't long to live and God knows I hate to say it, but I suppose she's right. When it happens it's going to be what people call a merciful release. Don't you find that a disgusting phrase?'

'I hadn't realised, from what Marion told me, that she was as ill as that,' I said.

'I'm not sure that she is. But she thinks she is, which is what counts. I believe every night, when she goes to sleep, she says to herself that she probably won't wake up in the morning. "If I should die before I wake, I beg the Lord my soul to take. . . ." I believe death is on her mind all the time, frightening her out of her wits.'

But he was wrong. It was not death that was frightening Aunt Emma. It was something which I personally found more horrible. She was afraid of going mad.

I discovered this during the first talk I had alone with her in her bedroom after the dinner that she and Charles and Marion and I had together in the stately but somehow unwelcoming dining room. Charles and I had arrived at the house in North Oxford, in Elwell Street, which is a turning off the Banbury Road, at about a quarter past seven and we had found Aunt Emma sitting by the fire in the drawing room, dressed in a pretty flowered blouse and a long black skirt, from under the hem of which woolly bedroom slippers protruded. The slippers and the stick which was propped against her chair were the only indications that she was not as well as she had been when I saw her last. She had always been proud of her feet and ankles and would never have appeared in public in anything but the most elegant of shoes, probably Italian and very expensive.

The blouse looked new, however, as if she had been shopping not long before, and her white hair was clearly cut, while her small, wrinkled face, with its pointed features and dazzlingly blue eyes, showed no signs of recent illness.

Marion joined us briefly, but said that she was busy in the kitchen and soon left us. We had drinks and chatted about my journey, about the recent cold spell, about the shocking cost of nearly everything and the state of the country, and pretended that there was nothing amiss.

Marion and I were rather alike to look at, though I was slightly the taller and two years the older. Actually, I am the same age as Charles, who at that time was forty. She and I were both brown-haired and brown-eyed, with oval faces which no one could call distinguished, long, thin necks, and narrow, sloping shoulders. We were slim and I suppose might have made something of this, but neither of us had much dress sense; however, I had learnt to manage a little better than Marion, having found that there was some virtue in it if you worked in a London office, whereas in North Oxford it seemed not to be very important. I had also learnt to cook somewhat better than she did. What she gave us that evening was soup out of a tin, Irish stew, trifle made with custard powder, and instant coffee.

As soon as the meal was over Aunt Emma said that she was sorry but she was very tired and was going straight to bed, and hoped that perhaps I would come upstairs presently and talk to her for a little. I helped Marion clear the table and stack the dishwasher, waited for about half an hour, then went up to Aunt Emma's bedroom.

She looked very small and shrunken in the big bed, propped up against several pillows. She wore a pale blue quilted bedjacket and had a book open on her knee, but I noticed that she had not put on her spectacles, so she could not have been reading. They were on the table on the far side of the bed under a lamp which was the only light in the room. As I sat down beside her she closed the book and put it on the table, then reached out and took my hand. Her small, thin fingers dug almost painfully into my wrist.

'Dorothy, do you understand why I wanted to see you?' she asked with a disturbing note of excitement in her usually calm though creaky voice. 'My dear, I think I'm going out of my mind.'

I gave a laugh, which I dare say sounded rather patronising, patted her hand and said, 'Aunt Emma, you're probably the sanest person I know.'

Then I realised that she was serious and wished I had chosen a different tone.

'It's just from time to time,' she went on as if I had not spoken. 'I don't think the others have noticed it yet. I have these blackouts. Suddenly I can't remember anything. I find myself in the middle of a room and I can't remember how I got there or where I was going. And I begin a sentence and get lost halfway through it and I begin to wonder if it sounds as nonsensical to other people as it does to me. And sometimes it's worse than that. I *see* things. . . . Only yesterday I saw poor Bertram standing at the end of the bed, pointing at me and laughing at me. As if he would ever do such a thing! But I knew it was an illusion, I knew it as well as I know you're really sitting here beside me, but I couldn't make him go away.' Her voice rose slightly. 'Dorothy, I'm so frightened they'll find out and then I'll be helpless!'

Bertram was her long-dead husband. It was from him that she had inherited her wealth. He had died of viral pneumonia about thirty years ago.

'Does it matter if they do find out?' I asked. 'They'll take care of you. You aren't frightened they'll try to put you into a mental home or something like that, are you? People can't do that sort of thing nowadays. It's extremely difficult to have a person put into one of those places, if they don't want to go, even when they're truly crazy. And you know no one could say that about you. Anyway, Marion and Charles have always been very good to you, haven't they?'

'But there's the money, you see.'

I did not see at once, though I recognised that most things in the end come down to money.

She withdrew her hand from mine and crossed it with the other on the hump her knees made in the bed.

'What I want, Dorothy, is to give you power of attorney over my affairs,' she said. 'Will you see to that for me?'

I was very puzzled.

'Of course,' I said, 'but wouldn't it be better to give it to Charles and Marion?'

'I don't think you understand,' she said. 'You can't give power of attorney to anyone unless it's evident that you're in your right mind and you know what you're doing. And I'm afraid if I wait, perhaps—perhaps—well, I told you, I get frightened sometimes that I'm not quite sane any more and that perhaps I'm going to get worse. You know, I really wish that stroke had finished me off. It would have made everything so much simpler. But if I don't give power of attorney soon to someone there may be a terrible muddle to clear up when I get really peculiar, and then, even if Charles and Marion don't put me into a mental home, they'll be able to do what they like with me. They'll put me into a home of some sort and everyone will say how wonderfully good they've always been to me. But they won't be able to afford a really nice home where I'd be comfortable and well looked after unless they've got control of my money, and so I want to be sure that the person who's got it is someone I trust. So I want to be sure it's you.'

I took a moment to answer. Then I said, 'Why don't you trust Charles and Marion?'

'Well, Marion doesn't like me, you know,' she replied. 'She never has. She only came here because it was a way of giving Charles the sort of good home he likes that doesn't cost him anything. But she's very bored and she'd love to be back in her old job.'

Marion had been a librarian in St Botolph's College for several years before she married Charles and in those days had had a nice little cottage of her own in Cumnor.

Aunt Emma continued: 'She thinks she could get the job back if she hadn't got me to look after, so she's going to pop me into a home the first moment she can. But even if they have control of my money and could arrange to move me into somewhere nice, it would actually be into the cheapest thing they could find, and the last years of my life, or months, or weeks, whatever it turns out to be, would be pretty wretched.'

I think I was frowning.

'Then just what is it you want me to do?' I asked.

'First of all, fix up the power of attorney,' she said. 'You'll have to get in touch with Mr Baybridge. He's my solicitor. Of course, he won't be in his office on a Saturday morning, but if you ring his home this evening and tell him it's urgent, I'm sure he'll come to see me tomorrow. Then as soon as that's been sorted out and you're in charge, I want you to tell Charles and Marion that they aren't needed here any more because you're going to get in a woman from an agency to look after me. I've the address of a good agency who'll send someone who'll do the shopping and the cooking and everything. It's very expensive but, after all, I can afford it—particularly as it may not be for long—and meanwhile I'll feel . . .' She paused, then continued softly: 'I'll feel *safe*.'

That was the first time I started to wonder if she *was* in her right mind and fit to give me power of attorney. Whereas it should have been the time when I began to take her seriously. . . .

'Very well,' I said, 'if you're sure it's what you want. It'll be a little hard on Charles and Marion, suddenly being turned out, but I suppose they'll be able to find lodgings till they can buy a place of their own. And the first step you want me to take is to ring up Mr Baybridge this evening and ask him to call on you here to fix up this power of attorney thing.'

She nodded. 'And please don't tell Charles and Marion about any of this. I know you think I'm being ungrateful, but really . . . really, Dorothy . . .'

She did not finish the sentence and it was only later that I guessed what she had nearly said.

The telephone was on a table in the hall at the bottom of the stairs. I found Mr Baybridge's number in a notebook beside the telephone, rang him up and arranged with him that he should call on my aunt next morning at eleven o'clock. I did not say anything about why she wanted to see him, but only that she would be very grateful if he would come. But the door of the drawing room where Marion and Charles were sitting was open and as I joined them Charles said, 'So she's going to change her will.'

'Change her will?' I said. 'She hasn't said anything about that to me.'

'Isn't that why she wants Baybridge to come round?'

'Not that I know of.'

Aunt Emma's will, to the best of my knowledge, left everything she had divided equally between Marion and me. It seemed to me very unlikely that she should think of changing it.

'Of course, if she did we could contest it,' Charles went on. 'I think Dr Summers would be willing to say that the balance of her mind wasn't all that it should be at the time she did it. Then we might add—' He paused and gave me one of the odd brilliant smiles that could transform his rather nondescript face into one which, at least to me, had always been surprisingly exciting. 'We could talk about undue influence, couldn't we? I mean, in view of the time you've spent with her this evening.'

'She never mentioned her will all the time I was with her and neither did I,' I answered truthfully.

'Anyway, there's nothing wrong with the balance of her mind,' Marion said. 'She's old, that's all, and it happens she doesn't like you and me, Charles. I don't know why, but it's her right, isn't it? I hope no one thinks my mind is unhinged simply because I dislike some of the people I do.'

I said something I was later to regret.

'*I* don't think her mind is unhinged, but she's afraid it's going to be.'

Charles gave me a sombre look. 'Is that really true? It hadn't occurred to me.'

I remembered that Aunt Emma had said that she did not think that Charles and Marion had noticed her blackouts and other peculiarities.

Trying to make amends to her, I said, 'Oh, I don't know. I expect it's just the after-effects of her stroke. She's more helpless than she's ever been in her life and she can't come to terms with it.'

'All the same, you think she's afraid—' He checked himself, and exchanged a long look with Marion which made me wonder if, in spite of his having said otherwise, the two of them might not already have discussed it.

Feeling guilty, as if I had somehow let Aunt Emma down, I said good night to them and went to bed.

Next morning I was awakened by Marion who came into my room with a pot of tea on a tray. As she put it down on the table by my bed, I said, 'This is very nice of you. You shouldn't have bothered.'

'It's no bother. I always do it for Aunt Emma,' she replied. 'Come down when you feel like it. You'll probably find me in the kitchen.'

'I think I'd like a bath,' I said. 'Does anyone else want the bathroom?'

'No, go ahead when you like.' She turned to the door.

Sitting up, reaching for the tray and balancing it on my knees, I said, 'Marion, last night before I went to sleep I started thinking about the things we'd been talking about. Honestly, Aunt Emma never said anything to me about changing her will. I'd a feeling you and Charles didn't believe me when I told you that.'

She gave a shrug of her shoulders. I was sure I saw disbelief in her eyes. But she said, 'It wouldn't break my heart if she did change it. What I want is to get back to my job. I don't think I'm cut out to be a nurse, any more than you are. But you've been lucky, no one's ever suggested you ought to give up that job of yours to do the sort of things I've had to do recently. You've always got away with everything you wanted.'

Except, I thought, marrying Charles, which was something that at one time I had wanted very badly.

'But you're fond of Aunt Emma, aren't you?' I said. 'She's always been very good to us both.'

'Oh yes, of course,' she answered indifferently. 'But I'm no more domesticated than you are, you know. I can't cook and I'm not nearly as good as you are at entertaining people, which is something Charles would like me to do, and doing the shopping and being shut up half the time in this great house bores me beyond words. However, I'm sorry, I didn't mean to start grumbling so early in the morning. It's usually something that works up gradually through the day, if I've got a sympathetic listener. I'll give you a dose of it later!'

She went out and I heard her go downstairs.

I drank my tea, then got out of bed, put on my dressing-gown, collected my sponge and toothbrush and went to the bathroom.

I ran a deep bath, washed lazily and lay comfortably back in the warm water, thinking how strange it was to discover that Marion's life, which I had always to some extent envied, should apparently to her be a kind of trap. I did not believe that Aunt Emma's money was unimportant to her and Charles. If it were, why had they not moved out long ago and left Aunt Emma to find herself a good housekeeper? The truth was, I thought, that Marion was one of those people who want to have everything without giving up anything to achieve it. She wanted marriage, and her job, and more money than she could earn at it, and a luxurious home to live in. . . .

It was at that point that I heard the shout, or the scream, or whatever the dreadful noise was, and Marion's voice crying out distinctly, 'Don't! Don't!'

Then I heard a shot.

I jumped out of the bath, grabbed my dressing-gown and still struggling into it ran out on to the landing. A draught from an open window sent a chill over my wet body. The door of Aunt Emma's bedroom was open. I entered.

What I saw gave me the worst shock of my life. Aunt Emma was lying in her bed with half of her head blown away. Her pillows were a mass of blood. One of her eyes seemed to have come adrift and was hanging half out of its socket. There was a strange smell in the room which I did not recognise, because I had never before been on the spot when a gun had just gone off. A revolver, or an automatic pistol, or whatever it was, was lying on the floor just beside the bed and one of her hands hung down over the edge of the bed, almost touching the gun. Marion was in the middle of the room, shrieking.

Perhaps the right thing to have done would have been to slap her face. One reads that that is the thing to do with a case of hysterics. But I was very near shrieking myself so, without even knowing what I was doing, I wasted a moment fumbling with the zip of my dressing-gown—though even when I had dragged it shut, I found myself shivering inside it. However, when I was no longer half-naked I felt more able to cope with things and I took hold of Marion by the shoulders and shook her. Actually by then she had stopped shrieking and was simply standing there, shaking.

'What happened?' I yelled at her. 'For God's sake, what happened?'

'I couldn't stop her,' she answered frantically. 'I shouted at her not to do it, but I was too late. I shouted "Don't!" but she went ahead and pulled the trigger. I saw her do it, Dorothy, I *saw* her. I came in, bringing her the tea, and there she was, holding the gun to her head. And it was as if she didn't know I was there. She didn't even look at me. She just pulled the trigger . . . Oh . . . Oh . . . !'

I thought the shrieking was going to start again, but she only took a few steps away from the bed, dropped into a chair and hid her face in her hands.

I saw the tea-tray where she had put it down on the table next to the bed.

'Where did the gun come from?' I asked. 'Do you know?'

'I think it must be one Uncle Bertram brought back from the war,' Marion answered. 'I've heard her speak of it, though I don't know where she kept it.'

'But why—why should she do it? When we talked yesterday evening, she—well—she had other plans.'

Marion dropped her hands. 'Wasn't she afraid of going mad? That's what you said yourself. And isn't that a good reason for killing oneself?'

At that moment Charles came into the room.

When he saw Aunt Emma and the blood and the gun and the dreadful displaced eye, he exclaimed something that sounded like, 'Oh, my Christ!' but it was in a hoarse, muffled tone and might have been anything. His face had gone a strange grey-white. Turning to Marion, he asked her almost exactly the same questions as I had just asked her and she gave him the same answer, though her voice was steadier now. But she kept her eyes shut, as if she could not bear to look at the thing on the bed.

'You really saw her do it?' he asked. 'You'll swear to that?'

'Of course I will—but why should I have to?' she asked.

'Because there'll be an inquest and you'll have to do it then,' he answered. 'I'm going to 'phone Summers now, and then—there's no point in putting it off—I'll phone the police.'

Dr Summers had been Aunt Emma's doctor for about the last ten years. She had regarded him with some distrust as a not very responsible young man, though he was well into his fifties and had several grown-up children. She used to talk wistfully of a Dr Charters, who had been nearly as old as she was. But young and irresponsible or not, Dr Summers would not have much difficulty in diagnosing the cause of her death.

Marion stood up. She looked at me.

'Why don't you go and get dressed?' she said, and it was astonishing how calm she sounded. 'We're going to have plenty of company presently and it may not be convenient to do it then.'

It seemed good sense so I went to my bedroom.

I heard Charles go downstairs and the tinkle of the telephone bell as he started dialling, first, I supposed, the doctor, and then the police. Presently, as I was combing my hair in front of the mirror, I smelt coffee and realised that Marion must have gone downstairs too, and I felt very glad that she had thought of it. Coffee was just what I wanted then. Yet I did not go down immediately.

Something was nagging at my mind, something about that room where Aunt Emma lay dead, something that was trying to surface in my thoughts, something that did not make sense.

I found the door of her bedroom closed and I opened it softly, as if I were afraid of disturbing her, or perhaps someone else who might be in there. But of course there was no one and everything was just as it had been when I had been in the room before. But was it really just the same? Why did I feel that something had altered?

I am not sure how long I stood there, gazing at the desolate room that already had the smell of blood in it, before I realised what had changed. It was the tea-tray. When I had first burst into the room to find Marion in the middle of it, screaming, the tea-tray had been on the table beside the bed. But now the tray was no longer there. Apparently Marion had taken it down to the kitchen to wash the tea-pot. It seemed an odd thing to have done at a time like this, but then it is just at such times that people do do very odd things, dictated simply by habit. Probably Marion had not even been aware of what she was doing.

Then I saw that she had not taken the tray downstairs. It was on a chest of drawers, just inside the door.

So far as I could tell, nothing else in the room had been moved. The gun still lay on the carpet beside the bed. Aunt Emma's dead hand dangled above it. But the tray, with a small silver tea-pot on it, a milk-jug, a cup and saucer and a plate with two biscuits on it, had mysteriously been moved from the bedside table to the chest of drawers by the door.

I solved the mystery of why it had happened quite soon, though it seemed to me a long time that I stood there, thinking about it. But when I went downstairs the coffee was only just ready, so I could not have stayed in Aunt Emma's room for more than a few minutes. We drank the coffee in the kitchen, waiting for the doctor's ring at the doorbell. It came after about a quarter of an hour and when he had taken one look at Aunt Emma's body, the only thing he said was, 'You've phoned the police, of course.'

'Of course,' Charles answered.

We all went downstairs again and Marion gave Dr Summers some coffee.

Sipping it, he said thoughtfully, 'I suppose we ought to have expected something like this. She seemed to get over that stroke very well, but I've realised she was depressed, not at all the high-spirited person she used to be. But I'm surprised that she shot herself. I'd have expected an overdose of the pills I've been giving her. They're fairly harmless, but if you took enough of them they might do the job. Did you know she'd a gun?'

'Yes, I was telling my sister about it,' Marion said. 'I think it was a souvenir my granduncle brought back from the war. I've heard my aunt speak of it. But I didn't know where she kept it or that she'd any ammunition for it. The reason she did it—well, something my sister told us yesterday evening makes us fairly sure she'd a belief she might be going insane. And perhaps she was, though my husband and I hadn't noticed anything particularly strange about her. Some depression, yes, but she always seemed to be completely on the spot when one talked to her.'

'The insane, though that isn't the fashionable word for them nowadays, can be remarkably cunning at concealing their peculiarities from the people round them,' the doctor responded. 'But I don't expect there'll be any difficulties at the inquest. If you know she'd that fear in her mind, it gave her a good reason for doing what she did.'

The police arrived only a few minutes later.

A shortish, stolid-looking man in plain clothes, who introduced himself as Detective Inspector Foskin, was in charge, and a uniformed sergeant and a constable were with him. Charles and Dr Summers took the three men up to Aunt Emma's room while Marion and I waited in the drawing room below, listening for sounds from upstairs. But after the first tramping about there was a remarkable silence.

Then one of the men came down and used the telephone in the hall. I thought he would be ringing for an ambulance, but it seemed to be a call to the police station, asking for a photographer to be sent as well as someone connected with fingerprints. I heard Marion let out a long breath. She was standing rigidly in front of the fireplace, where the ashes from yesterday's fire were still in a heap. A woman who cleaned the house and cleared the grate and laid a new fire came in on most mornings, but not on a Saturday.

The sergeant who had been telephoning entered the drawing room and said that Inspector Foskin would be glad if Marion and I would join him upstairs and tell him exactly what had happened that morning.

We went up, the sergeant following us, and into the bedroom.

I heard Marion give a little gasp of shock. It did not surprise me. The tea-tray, which had been on the chest of drawers by the door when she had left the room, was now back on the bedside table where it had been when I had first entered the room that morning.

Inspector Foskin seemed very interested in it.

'I understand from your husband,' he said to Marion, 'that it was you who discovered the body this morning. Would you mind telling me exactly what happened?'

She stood there, staring at the tea-tray. Then she turned and gave me a long look. Then she turned back to the inspector.

'I came in, as I usually do, about a quarter to eight,' she said. 'I brought my aunt her tea, as I did every morning, and I saw her with the gun at her head. I think I shouted, "Don't!" or something like that, and I ran across the room to her, but before I got to her bedside she'd pulled the trigger. And I believe I started screaming. I'm not really sure what I did. The next thing I remember clearly is my sister shaking me and asking what had happened.'

'But the tray you were carrying,' the detective said in his stolid way. 'What did you do with it?'

'The tray?' she repeated stupidly, as if she did not know what he was talking about, although her attention had been on it ever since she and I had come into the room. 'I don't know. I suppose I put it down somewhere.'

'Here on this table,' he said, pointing. 'Although you saw your aunt with a gun at her head, you carried the tray across the room and round the foot of the bed and you put it down here and only then started screaming. I find that very hard to envisage. If you'd simply dropped the whole works on the floor, or put it down on the nearest thing you could—that chest of drawers by the door, for instance—I could understand it and I should probably believe your story. As it is, I'm inclined to believe it may have been you who pulled the trigger *after* you'd put the tray down on this table.'

Marion's eyes met mine again. I suppose she was thinking of the time, while she had been making coffee, that I had had to myself, getting dressed and then no doubt returning to this room and putting the tray back where I had seen it when I first came into the room.

Believing that she had rectified her error of leaving it on the bedside table before she killed Aunt Emma, she had been feeling reasonably safe. And so she might still have been if she had kept her head, if she had not turned on me and tried to scratch my eyes out with her nails! The evidence against her was actually very scanty.

But she was not really the type to attempt murder, any more than I am myself. I went so far as to deny that I had touched the tray and as I had been very careful to leave no fingerprints on it I was believed. In the end, after another attack of shrieking, she broke down completely and confessed that she had killed Aunt Emma. To the end she believed that Aunt Emma had been about to change her will, cutting her and Charles out of it.

She was sentenced to life.

But of course a life sentence does not literally mean for life and the years have been passing. Charles and I have been living together for a long time now, but I am not quite sure what will happen when Marion is released from prison. I think he is happy with me. I gave up my job long ago and we live in the old house in Elwell Street. We have plenty of money and entertain a good deal, which he enjoys. But the scandal of the murder did him a fair amount of damage and he never obtained the professorship that he would have liked.

I still do not know for certain if he was involved in the shooting of my aunt, or if the whole guilt was Marion's, and I do not like to dig too deep. She never said anything to incriminate him, but perhaps, as his wife, she would not have been able to do so. However, he has always claimed that he really did not know what she intended to do that morning when she went downstairs to make the tea. All the same, sometimes I see him looking at me in a way that makes me wonder about the future. . . .

Means of Evil

RUTH RENDELL

The most recent of our Britannic investigators, Inspector Reginald Wexford, initially appeared in 1964 in *From Doon with Death.* This was Ruth Rendell's first published novel, although she had written several others. "I wrote many novels before my first was accepted," she has said. "The first novel I did submit to a publisher was a sort of drawing room comedy. . . . This was kept for a long time and then returned . . . and they asked if I had done anything else. I had written a detective story just for my own entertainment. . . ." And that was how Inspector Wexford came into the world. He soon became one of the most popular of current British detectives. Not quite the traditional police inspector, Wexford grows and changes from novel to novel. In her subsequent novels about him, Ruth Rendell has chosen to deal "with the psychological, emotional aspects of human nature rather than the puzzle, forensics. . . ." In our story you'll find Wexford and his associate, Burden, dealing with both the psychological and the forensic.

"Blewits," said Inspector Burden, "parasols, horns of plenty, morels and boletus. Mean anything to you?"

Chief Inspector Wexford shrugged. "Sounds like one of those magazine quizzes. What have these in common? I'll make a guess and say they're crustacea. Or sea anemones. How about that?"

"They are edible fungi," said Burden.

"Are they now? And what have edible fungi to do with Mrs. Hannah Kingman throwing herself off, or being pushed off, a balcony?"

The two men were sitting in Wexford's office at the police station, Kingsmarkham, in the County of Sussex. The month was November, but Wexford had only just returned from his holiday. And while he had been away, enjoying in Cornwall an end of October that had been more summery than the summer, Hannah Kingman had committed suicide. Or so Burden had thought at first. Now he was in a dilemma, and as soon as Wexford had walked in that Monday morning, Burden had begun to tell the whole story to his chief.

Wexford, getting on for sixty, was a tall, ungainly, rather ugly man who had once been fat to the point of obesity but had slimmed to gauntness for reasons of health. Nearly twenty years his junior, Burden had the slenderness of a man who has always been thin. His face was ascetic, handsome in a frosty way. The older man, who had a good wife who looked after him devotedly, nevertheless always looked as if his clothes came off the peg from the War on Want Shop, while the younger, a widower, was sartorially immaculate. A tramp and a Beau Brummell, they seemed to be, but the dandy relied on the tramp, trusted him, understood his powers and his perception. In secret he almost worshipped him.

Without his chief he had felt a little at sea in this case. Everything had pointed at first to Hannah Kingman's having killed herself. She had been a manic-depressive, with a strong sense of her own inadequacy; apparently her marriage, though not of long duration, had been unhappy, and her previous marriage had failed. Even in the absence of a suicide note or suicide threats, Burden would have taken her death for self-destruction—if her brother hadn't come along and told him about the edible fungi. And Wexford hadn't been there to do what he always could do, sort out sheep from goats and wheat from chaff.

"The thing is," Burden said across the desk, "we're not looking for proof of murder so much as proof of *attempted* murder. Axel Kingman could have pushed his wife off that balcony—he has no alibi for the time in question—but I had no reason to think he had done so until I was told of an attempt to murder her some two weeks before."

"Which attempt has something to do with edible fungi?"

Burden nodded. "Say with administering to her some noxious substance in a stew made from edible fungi. Though if he did it, God knows how he did it, because three other people, including himself, ate the stew without ill effects. I think I'd better tell you about it from the beginning."

"I think you had," said Wexford.

"The facts," Burden began, very like a Prosecuting Counsel, "are as follows. Axel Kingman is thirty-five years old and he keeps a health-food shop here in the High Street called Harvest Home. Know it?" When Wexford signified by a nod that he did, Burden went on, "He used to be a teacher in Myringham, and for about seven years before he came here he'd been living with a woman named Corinne Last. He left her, gave up his job, put all the capital he had into this shop, and married a Mrs. Hannah Nicholson."

"He's some sort of food freak, I take it," said Wexford.

Burden wrinkled his nose. "Lot of affected nonsense," he said. "Have you ever noticed what thin pale weeds these health-food people are? While the folks who live on roast beef and suet and whisky and plum cake are full of beans and rarin' to go."

"Is Kingman a thin pale weed?"

"A feeble—what's the word?—aesthete, if you ask me. Anyway, he and Hannah opened this shop and took a flat in the high-rise tower our planning geniuses have been pleased to raise over the top of it. The fifth floor. Corinne Last, according to her and according to Kingman, accepted the situation after a while and they all remained friends."

"Tell me about them," Wexford said. "Leave the facts for a bit and tell me about them."

Burden never found this easy. He was inclined to describe people as "just ordinary" or "just like anyone else," a negative attitude which exasperated Wexford. So he made an effort. "Kingman looks the sort who wouldn't hurt a fly. The fact is, I'd apply the word gentle to him if I wasn't coming round to thinking he's a cold-blooded wife-killer. He's a total abstainer with a bee in his bonnet about drink. His father went bankrupt and finally died of alcoholism, and our Kingman is an anti-booze fanatic.

"The dead woman was twenty-nine. Her first husband left her after six months of marriage and went off with some girl friend of hers. Hannah went back to live with her parents and had a part-time job helping with the meals at the school where Kingman was a teacher. That was where they met."

"And the other woman?" said Wexford.

Burden's face took on a repressive expression. Sex outside marriage, however sanctioned by custom and general approval, was always distasteful to him. That, in the course of his work, he almost daily came across illicit sex had done nothing to mitigate his disapproval. As Wexford sometimes derisively put it, you would think that in Burden's eyes all the suffering in the world, and certainly all the crime, somehow derived from men and women going to bed together outside the bonds of wedlock. "God knows why he didn't marry her," Burden now said. "Personally I think things were a lot better in the days when education authorities put their foot down about immorality among teachers."

"Let's not have your views on that now, Mike," said Wexford. "Presumably Hannah Kingman didn't die because her husband didn't come to her a pure virgin."

Burden flushed slightly. "I'll tell you about this Corinne Last. She's very good-looking, if you like the dark sort of intense type. Her father left her some money and the house where she and Kingman lived, and she still lives in it. She's one of those women who seem to be good at everything they put their hands to. She paints and sells her paintings. She makes her own clothes, she's more or less the star in the local dramatic society, she's a violinist and plays in some string trio. Also she writes for health magazines and she's the author of a cookery book."

"It would look then," Wexford put in, "as if Kingman split up with her because all this was more than he could take. And hence he took up with the dull little school-meals lady. No competition from her, I fancy."

"I daresay you're right. As a matter of fact, that theory has already been put to me."

"By whom?" said Wexford. "Just where did you get all this information, Mike?"

"From an angry young man, the fourth member of the quartet, who happens to be Hannah's brother. His name is John Hood and I think he's got a lot more to tell. But it's time I left off describing the people and got on with the story.

"No one saw Hannah fall from the balcony. It happened last Thursday afternoon at about four. According to her husband, he was in a sort of office behind the shop doing what he always did on early-closing day—stock-taking and sticking labels on various bottles and packets.

"She fell onto a hard-top parking area at the back of the flats, and her body was found by a neighbor a couple of hours later between two parked cars. We were sent for, and Kingman seemed to be distraught. I asked him if he had had any idea that his wife might have wished to take her own life and he said she had never threatened to do so but had lately been very depressed and there had been quarrels, principally about money. Her doctor had put her on tranquilizers—of which, by the way, Kingman disapproved—and the doctor himself, old Dr. Castle, told me Mrs. Kingman had been to him for depression and because she felt her life wasn't worth living and she was a drag on her husband. He wasn't surprised that she had killed herself and neither, by that time, was I. We were all set for an inquest verdict of suicide while the balance of the mind was disturbed when John Hood walked in here and told me Kingman had attempted to murder his wife on a previous occasion."

"He told you just like that?"

"Pretty well. It's plain he doesn't like Kingman, and no doubt he was fond of his sister. He also seems to like and admire Corinne Last. He told me that on a Saturday night at the end of October the four of them had a meal together in the Kingmans' flat. It was a lot of vegetarian stuff cooked by Kingman—he always did the cooking—and one of the dishes was made out of what I'm old-fashioned enough, or narrow-minded enough, to call toadstools. They all ate it and they were all OK but for Hannah, who got up from the table, vomited for hours, and apparently was quite seriously ill."

Wexford's eyebrows went up. "Elucidate, please," he said.

Burden sat back, put his elbows on the arms of the chair, and pressed the tips of his fingers together. "A few days before this meal was eaten, Kingman and Hood met at the squash club of which they are both members. Kingman told Hood that Corinne Last had promised to get him some edible fungi called shaggy caps from her own garden, the garden of the house which they had at one time shared. A crop of these things show themselves every autumn under a tree in this garden. I've seen them myself, but we'll come to that in a minute.

"Kingman's got a thing about using weeds and whatnot for cooking, makes salads out of dandelion and sorrel, and he swears by this fungi rubbish, says they've got far more flavour than mushrooms. Give me something that comes in a plastic bag from the supermarket every time, but no doubt it takes all sorts to make a world. By the way, this cookbook of Corinne Last's is called *Cooking for Nothing*, and all the recipes are for making dishes out of stuff you pull up by the wayside or pluck from the hedgerow."

"These warty blobs or spotted puffets or whatever, had he cooked them before?"

"Shaggy caps," said Burden, grinning, "or *coprinus comatus*. Oh, yes, every year, and every year he and Corinne had eaten the resulting stew. He told Hood he was going to cook them again this time, and Hood says he seemed very grateful to Corinne for being so—well, magnanimous."

"Yes, I can see it would have been a wrench for her. Like hearing 'our tune' in the company of your ex-lover and your supplanter." Wexford put on a vibrant growl. " 'Can you bear the sight of me eating our toadstools with another?' "

"As a matter of fact," said Burden seriously, "it could have been just like that. Anyway, the upshot of it was that Hood was invited round for the following Saturday to taste these delicacies and was told that Corinne would be there. Perhaps it was that fact which made him accept. Well, the day came. Hood looked in on his sister at lunchtime. She showed him the pot containing the stew which Kingman had already made and she said *she had tasted it* and it was delicious. She also showed Hood half a dozen specimens of shaggy caps which she said Kingman hadn't needed and which they would fry for their breakfast. This is what she showed him."

Burden opened a drawer in the desk and produced one of those plastic bags which he had said so inspired him with confidence. But the contents of this one hadn't come from a supermarket. He removed the wire fastener and tipped out four whitish scaly objects. They were egg-shaped, or rather elongated ovals, each with a short fleshy stalk.

"I picked them myself this morning," he said, "from Corinne Last's garden. When they get bigger, the egg-shaped bit opens like an umbrella, or a pagoda really, and there are sort of black gills underneath. You're supposed to eat them when they're in the stage these are."

"I suppose you've got a book on fungi?" said Wexford.

"Here." This also was produced from the drawer. *British Fungi, Edible and Poisonous*. "And here we are—shaggy caps."

Burden had opened it at the *Edible* section and at a line and wash drawing of the species he held in his hand. He passed it to the chief inspector.

"*Coprinus Comatus*," Wexford read aloud, *"a common species, attaining when full-grown a height of nine inches. The fungus is frequently to be found, during late summer and autumn, growing in fields, hedgerows and often in gardens. It should be eaten before the cap opens and disgorges its inky fluid, but is at all times quite harmless."* He put the book down but didn't close it. "Go on, please, Mike," he said.

"Hood called for Corinne and they arrived together. They got there just after eight. At about eight-fifteen they all sat down to table and began the meal with avocado *vinaigrette*. The next course was to be the stew, followed by nut cutlets with a salad and then an apple-cake. Very obviously, there was no wine or liquor of any sort on account of Kingman's prejudice. They drank grape juice from the shop.

"The kitchen opens directly out of the living-dining room. Kingman brought in the stew in a large tureen and served it himself at the table, beginning, of course, with Corinne. Each one of those shaggy caps had been sliced in half lengthwise and the pieces were floating in a thickish gravy to which carrots, onions and other vegetables had been added. Now, ever since he had been invited to this meal, Hood had been feeling uneasy about eating fungi, but Corinne had reassured him, and once he began to eat it and saw the others were eating it quite happily, he stopped worrying for the time being. In fact, he had a second helping.

"Kingman took the plates out and the tureen and immediately *rinsed them under the tap*. Both Hood and Corinne Last have told me this, though Kingman says it was something he always did, being fastidious about things of that sort."

"Surely his ex-girl friend could confirm or deny that," Wexford put in, "since they lived together for so long."

"We must ask her. All traces of the stew were rinsed away. Kingman then brought in the nut concoction and the salad, but before he could begin to serve them Hannah jumped up, covered her mouth with her napkin, and rushed to the bathroom.

"After a while Corinne went to her. Hood could hear a violent vomiting from the bathroom. He remained in the living room while Kingman and Corinne were both in the bathroom with Hannah. No one ate any more. Kingman eventually came back, said that Hannah must have picked up some 'bug' and that he had put her to bed. Hood went into the bedroom where Hannah was lying on the bed with Corinne beside her. Hannah's face was greenish and covered with sweat and she was evidently in great pain because while he was there she doubled up and groaned. She had to go to the bathroom again and that time Kingman had to carry her back.

"Hood suggested Dr. Castle should be sent for, but this was strenuously opposed by Kingman who dislikes doctors and is one of those people who go in for herbal remedies—raspberry leaf tablets and camomile tea and that sort of thing. Also he told Hood rather absurdly that Hannah had had quite enough to do with doctors and that if this wasn't some gastric germ it was the result of her taking 'dangerous' tranquilizers.

"Hood thought Hannah was seriously ill and the argument got heated, with Hood trying to make Kingman either call a doctor or take her to a hospital. Kingman wouldn't and Corinne took his part. Hood is one of those angry but weak people who are all bluster, and although he might have called a doctor himself, he didn't. The effect on him of Corinne again, I suppose. What he did was tell Kingman he was a fool to mess about cooking things everyone knew weren't safe, to which Kingman replied that if the shaggy caps were dangerous, how was it they weren't all ill? Eventually, at about midnight, Hannah stopped retching, seemed to have no more pain, and fell asleep. Hood drove Corinne home, returned to the Kingmans' and remained there for the rest of the night, sleeping on their sofa.

"In the morning Hannah seemed perfectly well, though weak, which rather upset Kingman's theory about the gastric bug. Relations between the brothers-in-law were strained. Kingman said he hadn't liked Hood's suggestions and that when he wanted to see his sister he, Kingman, would rather he came there when he was out or in the shop. Hood went off home, and since that day he hasn't seen Kingman.

"The day after his sister's death he stormed in here, told me what I've told you, and accused Kingman of trying to poison Hannah. He was wild and nearly hysterical, but I felt I couldn't dismiss this allegation as—well, the ravings of a bereaved person. There were too many peculiar circumstances, the unhappiness of the marriage, the fact of Kingman rinsing those plates, his refusal to call a doctor. Was I right?"

Burden stopped and sat waiting for approval. It came in the form of a not very enthusiastic nod.

After a moment Wexford spoke. "Could Kingman have pushed her off that balcony, Mike?"

"She was a small fragile woman. It was physically possible. The back of the flats isn't overlooked. There's nothing behind but the parking area and then open fields. Kingman could have gone up by the stairs instead of using the lift and come down by the stairs. Two of the flats on the lower floors are empty. Below the Kingmans lives a bedridden woman whose husband was at work. Below that the tenant, a young married woman, was in but she saw and heard nothing. The invalid says she thinks she heard a scream during the afternoon but she did nothing about it, and if she did hear it, so what? It seems to me that a suicide, in those circumstances, is as likely to cry out as a murder victim."

"OK," said Wexford. "Now to return to the curious business of this meal. The idea would presumably be that Kingman intended to kill her that night but that his plan misfired because whatever he gave her wasn't toxic enough. She was very ill but she didn't die. He chose those means and that company so that he would have witnesses to his innocence. They all ate the stew out of the same tureen, but only Hannah was affected by it. How then are you suggesting he gave her whatever poison he did give her?"

"I'm not," said Burden frankly, "but others are making suggestions. Hood's a bit of a fool, and first of all he would only keep on about all fungi being dangerous and the whole dish being poisonous. When I pointed out that this was obviously not so, he said Kingman must have slipped something into Hannah's plate, or else it was the salt."

"What salt?"

"He remembered that no one but Hannah took salt with the stew. But that's absurd because Kingman couldn't have known that would happen. And, incidentally, to another point we may as well clear up now—the avocados were quite innocuous. Kingman halved them *at the table* and the *vinaigrette* sauce was served in a jug. The bread was not in the form of rolls but a home-made wholemeal loaf. If there was anything there which shouldn't have been it was in the stew all right.

"Corinne Last refuses to consider the possibility that Kingman might be guilty. But when I pressed her she said she was not actually sitting at the table while the stew was served. She had got up and gone into the hall to fetch her handbag. So she didn't see Kingman serve Hannah." Burden reached across and picked up the book Wexford had left open at the description and drawing of the shaggy caps. He flicked over to the *Poisonous* section and pushed the book back to Wexford. "Have a look at some of these."

"Ah, yes," said Wexford. "Our old friend, the fly agaric. A nice-looking little red job with white spots, much favoured by illustrators of children's books. They usually stick a frog on top of it and a gnome underneath. I see that when ingested it causes nausea, vomiting, tetanic convulsions, coma and death. Lots of these agarics, aren't there? Purple, crested, warty, verdigris—all more or less lethal. Aha! The death cap, *amanita phalloides*. How very unpleasant. The most dangerous fungus known, it says here. Very small quantities will cause intense suffering and often death. So where does all that get us?"

"The death cap, according to Corinne Last, is quite common round here. What she doesn't say, but what I infer, is that Kingman could have got hold of it easily. Now suppose he cooked just one specimen separately and dropped it into the stew just before he brought it in from the kitchen? When he comes to serve Hannah he spoons up for her this specimen, or the pieces of it, in the same way as someone might select a special piece of chicken for someone out of a casserole. The gravy was thick, it wasn't like thin soup."

Wexford looked dubious. "Well, we won't dismiss it as a theory. If he had contaminated the rest of the stew and others had been ill, that would have made it look even more like an accident, which was presumably what he wanted. But there's one drawback to that, Mike. If he meant Hannah to die, and was unscrupulous enough not to mind about Corinne and Hood being made ill, why did he rinse the plates? To *prove* that it was an accident, he would have wanted above all to keep some of that stew for analysis when the time came, for analysis would have shown the presence of poisonous as well as non-poisonous fungi, and it would have seemed that he had merely been careless.

"But let's go and talk to these people, shall we?"

The shop called Harvest Home was closed. Wexford and Burden went down an alley at the side of the block, passed the glass-doored main entrance, and went to the back to a door that was labelled *Stairs and Emergency Exit*. They entered a small tiled vestibule and began to mount a steepish flight of stairs.

On each floor was a front door and a door to the lift. There was no one about. If there had been and they had had no wish to be seen, it would only have been necessary to wait behind the bend in the stairs until whoever it was had got into the lift. The bell by the front door on the fifth floor was marked *A. and H. Kingman*. Wexford rang it.

The man who admitted them was smallish and mild-looking and he looked sad. He showed Wexford the balcony from which his wife had fallen. It was one of two in the flat, the other being larger and extending outside the living-room windows. This one was outside a glazed kitchen door, a place for hanging washing or for gardening of the window-box variety. Herbs grew in pots, and in a long trough there still remained frost-bitten tomato vines. The wall surrounding the balcony was about three feet high, the drop sheer to the hard-top below.

"Were you surprised that your wife committed suicide, Mr. Kingman?" said Wexford.

Kingman didn't answer directly. "My wife set a very low valuation on herself. When we got married I thought she was like me, a simple sort of person who doesn't ask much from life but has quite a capacity for contentment. It wasn't like that. She expected more support and more comfort and encouragement than I could give. That was especially so for the first three months of our marriage. Then she seemed to turn against me. She was very moody, always up and down. My business isn't doing very well and she was spending more money than we could afford. I don't know where all the money was going and we quarrelled about it. Then she'd become depressed and say she was no use to me, she'd be better dead."

He had given, Wexford thought, rather a long explanation for which he hadn't been asked. But it could be that these thoughts, defensive yet self-reproachful, were at the moment uppermost in his mind. "Mr. Kingman," he said, "we have reason to believe, as you know, that foul play may have been involved here. I should like to ask you a few questions about a meal you cooked on October 29th, after which your wife was ill."

"I can guess who's been telling you about that."

Wexford took no notice. "When did Miss Last bring you these—er, shaggy caps?"

"On the evening of the 28th. I made the stew from them in the morning, according to Miss Last's own recipe."

"Was there any other type of fungus in the flat at the time?"

"Mushrooms, probably."

"Did you at any time add any noxious object or substance to that stew, Mr. Kingman?"

Kingman said quietly, wearily, "Of course not. My brother-in-law has a lot of ignorant prejudices. He refuses to understand that that stew, which I have made dozens of times before in exactly the same way, was as wholesome as, say, a chicken casserole. More wholesome, in my view."

"Very well. Nevertheless, your wife was very ill. Why didn't you call a doctor?"

"Because my wife was not 'very' ill. She had pains and diarrhoea, that's all. Perhaps you aren't aware of what the symptoms of fungus poisoning are. The victim doesn't just have pain and sickness. His vision is impaired, he very likely blacks out or has convulsions of the kind associated with tetanus. There was nothing like that with Hannah."

"It was unfortunate that you rinsed those plates. Had you not done so and called a doctor, the remains of that stew would almost certainly have been sent for analysis, and if it was harmless as you say, all this investigation could have been avoided."

"It was harmless," Kingman said stonily.

Out in the car Wexford said, "I'm inclined to believe him, Mike. And unless Hood or Corinne Last has something really positive to tell us, I'd let it rest. Shall we go and see her next?"

The cottage Corinne had shared with Axel Kingman was on a lonely stretch of road outside the village of Myfleet. It was a stone cottage with a slate roof, surrounded by a well-tended pretty garden. A green Ford Escort stood on the drive in front of a weatherboard garage. Under a big old apple tree, from which the yellow leaves were falling, the shaggy caps, immediately recognisable, grew in three thick clumps.

She was a tall woman, the owner of this house, with a beautiful, square-jawed, high-cheekboned face and a mass of dark hair. Wexford was at once reminded of the Klimt painting of a languorous red-lipped woman, gold-neckleted, half covered in gold draperies, though Corinne Last wore a sweater and a denim smock. Her voice was low and measured. He had the impression she could never be flustered or caught off her guard.

"You're the author of a cookery book, I believe?" he said.

She made no answer but handed him a paperback which she took down from a bookshelf. *Cooking for Nothing. Dishes from Hedgerow and Pasture* by Corinne Last. He looked through the index and found the recipe he wanted. Opposite it was a coloured photograph of six people eating what looked like brown soup. The recipe included carrots, onions, herbs, cream, and a number of other harmless ingredients. The last lines read: *Stewed shaggy caps are best served piping hot with wholewheat bread. For drinkables, see page 171.* He glanced at page 171, then handed the book to Burden.

"This was the dish Mr. Kingman made that night?"

"Yes." She had a way of leaning back when she spoke and of half lowering her heavy glossy eyelids. It was serpentine and a little repellent. "I picked the shaggy caps myself out of this garden. I don't understand how they could have made Hannah ill, but they must have done because she was fine when we first arrived. She hadn't got any sort of gastric infection, that's nonsense."

Burden put the book aside. "But you were all served stew out of the same tureen."

"I didn't see Axel actually serve Hannah. I was out of the room." The eyelids flickered and almost closed.

"Was it usual for Mr. Kingman to rinse plates as soon as they were removed?"

"Don't ask me." She moved her shoulders. "I don't know. I do know that Hannah was very ill just after eating that stew. Axel doesn't like doctors, of course, and perhaps it would have—well, embarrassed him to call Dr. Castle in the circumstances. Hannah had black spots in front of her eyes, she was getting double vision. I was extremely concerned for her."

"But you didn't take it on yourself to get a doctor, Miss Last? Or even support Mr. Hood in his allegations?"

"Whatever John Hood said, I knew it couldn't be the shaggy caps." There was a note of scorn when she spoke Hood's name. "And I was rather frightened. I couldn't help thinking it would be terrible if Axel got into some sort of trouble, if there was an inquiry or something."

"There's an inquiry now, Miss Last."

"Well, it's different now, isn't it? Hannah's dead. I mean, it's not just suspicion or conjecture any more."

She saw them out and closed the front door before they had reached the garden gate. Farther along the roadside and under the hedges more shaggy caps could be seen as well as other kinds of fungi Wexford couldn't identify—little mushroom-like things with pinkish gills, a cluster of small yellow umbrellas, and on the trunk of an oak tree, bulbous smoke-coloured swellings that Burden said were oyster mushrooms.

"That woman," said Wexford, "is a mistress of the artless insinuation. She damned Kingman with almost every word, but she never came out with anything like an accusation." He shook his head. "I suppose Kingman's brother-in-law will be at work?"

"Presumably," said Burden, but John Hood was not at work. He was waiting for them at the police station, fuming at the delay, and threatening "if something wasn't done at once" to take his grievances to the Chief Constable, even to the Home Office.

"Something is being done," said Wexford quietly. "I'm glad you've come here, Mr. Hood. But try to keep calm, will you, please?"

It was apparent to Wexford from the first that John Hood was in a different category of intelligence from that of Kingman and Corinne Last. He was a thick-set man of perhaps no more than twenty-seven or twenty-eight, with bewildered, resentful blue eyes in a puffy flushed face. A man, Wexford thought, who would fling out rash accusations he couldn't substantiate, who would be driven to bombast and bluster in the company of the ex-teacher and that clever subtle woman.

He began to talk now, not wildly, but still without restraint, repeating what he had said to Burden, reiterating, without putting forward any real evidence, that his brother-in-law had meant to kill his sister that night. It was only by luck that she had survived. Kingman was a ruthless man who would have stopped at nothing to be rid of her. He, Hood, would never forgive himself that he hadn't made a stand and called the doctor.

"Yes, yes, Mr. Hood, but what exactly were your sister's symptoms?"

"Vomiting and stomach pains, violent pains," said Hood.

"She complained of nothing else?"

"Wasn't that enough? That's what you get when someone feeds you poisonous rubbish."

Wexford merely raised his eyebrows. Abruptly, he left the events of that evening and said, "What had gone wrong with your sister's marriage?"

Before Hood replied, Wexford could sense he was keeping something back. A wariness came into his eyes and then was gone. "Axel wasn't the right person for her," he began. "She had problems, she needed understanding, she wasn't . . ." His voice trailed away.

"Wasn't what, Mr. Hood? What problems?"

"It's got nothing to do with all this," Hood muttered.

"I'll be the judge of that. You made this accusation, you started this business off. It's not for you now to keep anything back." On a sudden inspiration, Wexford said, "Had these problems anything to do with the money she was spending?"

Hood was silent and sullen. Wexford thought rapidly over the things he had been told—Axel Kingman's fanaticism on one particular subject, Hannah's desperate need of an unspecified kind of support during the early days of her marriage. Later on, her alternating moods, and then the money, the weekly sums of money spent and unaccounted for.

He looked up and said baldly, "Was your sister an alcoholic, Mr. Hood?"

Hood hadn't liked this directness. He flushed and looked affronted. He skirted round a frank answer. Well, yes, she drank. She was at pains to conceal her drinking. It had been going on more or less consistently since her first marriage broke up.

"In fact, she was an alcoholic," said Wexford.

"I suppose so."

"Your brother-in-law didn't know?"

"Good God, no. Axel would have killed her!" He realised what he had said. "Maybe that's why. Maybe he found out."

"I don't think so, Mr. Hood. Now I imagine that in the first few months of her marriage she made an effort to give up drinking. She needed a good deal of support during this time but she couldn't, or wouldn't, tell Mr. Kingman why she needed it. Her efforts failed, and slowly, because she couldn't manage without it, she began drinking again."

"She wasn't as bad as she used to be," Hood said with pathetic eagerness. "And only in the evenings. She told me she never had a drink before six, and after that she'd have a few more, gulping them down on the quiet so Axel wouldn't know."

Burden said suddenly, "Had your sister been drinking that evening?"

"I expect so. She wouldn't have been able to face company, not even just Corinne and me, without a drink."

"Did anyone besides yourself know that your sister drank?"

"My mother did. My mother and I had a sort of pact to keep it dark from everyone so that Axel wouldn't find out." He hesitated and then said rather defiantly, "I did tell Corinne. She's a wonderful person, she's very clever. I was worried about it and I didn't know what to do. She promised she wouldn't tell Axel."

"I see." Wexford had his own reasons for thinking she hadn't done so. Deep in thought, he got up and walked to the other end of the room where he stood gazing out of the window. Burden's continuing questions, Hood's answers, reached him only as a confused murmur of voices. Then he heard Burden say more loudly, "That's all for now, Mr. Hood, unless the chief inspector has anything more to ask you."

"No, no," said Wexford abstractedly, and when Hood had somewhat truculently departed, "Time for lunch. It's past two. Personally, I shall avoid any dish containing fungi, even *psalliota compestris*."

After Burden had looked that one up and identified it as the common mushroom, they lunched and then made a round of such wineshops in Kingsmarkham as were open at that hour. At the Wine Basket they drew a blank, but the assistant in the Vineyard told them that a woman answering Hannah Kingman's description had been a regular customer, and that on the previous Wednesday, the day before her death, she had called in and bought a bottle of Courvoisier Cognac.

"There was no liquor of any kind in Kingman's flat," said Burden. "Might have been an empty bottle in the rubbish, I suppose." He made a rueful face. "We didn't look, didn't think we had any reason to. But she couldn't have drunk a whole bottle on the Wednesday, could she?"

"Why are you so interested in this drinking business, Mike? You don't seriously see it as a motive for murder, do you? That Kingman killed her because he'd found out, or been told, that she was a secret drinker?"

"It was a means, not a motive," said Burden. "I know how it was done. I know how Kingman tried to kill her that first time." He grinned. "Makes a change for me to find the answer before you, doesn't it? I'm going to follow in your footsteps and make a mystery of it for the time being, if you don't mind. With your permission we'll go back to the station, pick up those shaggy caps and conduct a little experiment."

Michael Burden lived in a neat bungalow in Tabard Road. He had lived there with his wife until her untimely death and continued to live there with his sixteen-year-old daughter, his son being away at university. But that evening Pat Burden was out with her boy friend, and there was a note left for her father on the refrigerator. *Dad, I ate the cold beef from yesterday. Can you open a tin for yourself? Back by 10.30. Love, P.*

Burden read this note several times, his expression of consternation deepening with each perusal. And Wexford could precisely have defined the separate causes which brought that look of weariness into Burden's eyes, that frown, that drooping of the mouth. Because she was motherless his daughter had to eat not only cold but leftover food, she who should be carefree was obliged to worry about her father, loneliness drove her out of her home until the appallingly late hour of half-past ten. It was all nonsense, of course, the Burden children were happy and recovered from their loss, but how to make Burden see it that way? Widowhood was something he dragged about with him like a physical infirmity. He looked up from the note, screwed it up and eyed his surroundings vaguely and with a kind of despair. Wexford knew that look of desolation. He saw it on Burden's face each time he accompanied him home.

It evoked exasperation as well as pity. He wanted to tell Burden—once or twice he had done so—to stop treating John and Pat like retarded paranoiacs, but instead he said lightly, "I read somewhere the other day that it wouldn't do us a scrap of harm if we never ate another hot meal as long as we lived. In fact, the colder and rawer the better."

"You sound like the Axel Kingman brigade," said Burden, rallying and laughing which was what Wexford had meant him to do. "Anyway, I'm glad she didn't cook anything. I shouldn't have been able to eat it and I'd hate her to take it as criticism."

Wexford decided to ignore that one. "While you're deciding just how much I'm to be told about this experiment of yours, d'you mind if I phone my wife?"

"Be my guest."

It was nearly six. Wexford came back to find Burden peeling carrots and onions. The four specimens of *coprinus comatus*, beginning to look a little wizened, lay on a chopping board. On the stove a saucepanful of bone stock was heating up.

"What the hell are you doing?"

"Making shaggy cap stew. My theory is that the stew is harmless when eaten by non-drinkers, and toxic, or toxic to some extent, when taken by those with alcohol in the stomach. How about that? In a minute, when this lot's cooking, I'm going to take a moderate quantity of alcohol, then I'm going to eat the stew. Now say I'm a damned fool if you like."

Wexford shrugged. He grinned. "I'm overcome by so much courage and selfless devotion to the duty you owe the taxpayers. But wait a minute. Are you sure only Hannah had been drinking that night? We know Kingman hadn't. What about the other two?"

"I asked Hood that when you were off in your daydream. He called for Corinne Last at six, at her request. They picked some apples for his mother, then she made him coffee. He did suggest they call in at a pub for a drink on their way to the Kingmans', but apparently she took so long getting ready that they didn't have time."

"OK. Go ahead then. But wouldn't it be easier to call in an expert? There must be such people. Very likely someone holds a chair of fungology or whatever it's called at the University of the South."

"Very likely. We can do that after I've tried it. I want to know for sure *now*. Are you willing to?"

"Certainly not. I'm not your guest to that extent. Since I've told my wife I won't be home for dinner, I'll take it as a kindness if you'll make me some innocent scrambled eggs."

He followed Burden into the living room where the inspector opened a door in the sideboard. "What'll you drink?"

"White wine, if you've got any, or vermouth if you haven't. You know how abstemious I have to be."

Burden poured vermouth and soda. "Ice?"

"No, thanks. What are you going to have? Brandy? That was Hannah Kingman's favourite tipple apparently."

"Haven't got any," said Burden. "It'll have to be whisky. I think we can reckon she had two double brandies before that meal, don't you? I'm not so brave I want to be as ill as she was." He caught Wexford's eye. "You don't think some people could be more sensitive to it than others, do you?"

"Bound to be," said Wexford breezily. "Cheers!"

Burden sipped his heavily watered whisky, then tossed it down. "I'll just have a look at my stew. You sit down. Put the television on."

Wexford obeyed him. The big coloured picture was of a wood in autumn, pale blue sky, golden beech leaves. Then the camera closed in on a cluster of red-and-white-spotted fly agaric. Chuckling, Wexford turned it off as Burden put his head round the door.

"I think it's more or less ready."

"Better have another whisky."

"I suppose I had." Burden came in and re-filled his glass. "That ought to do it."

"What about my eggs?"

"Oh, God, I forgot. I'm not much of a cook, you know. Don't know how women manage to get a whole lot of different things brewing and make them synchronise."

"It is a mystery, isn't it? I'll get myself some bread and cheese, if I may."

The brownish mixture was in a soup bowl. In the gravy floated four shaggy caps, cut lengthwise. Burden finished his whisky at a gulp.

"What was it the Christians in the arena used to say to the Roman Emperor before they went to the lions?"

"Morituri, te salutamus," said Wexford. " 'We who are about to die salute thee.' "

"Well . . ." Burden made an effort with the Latin he had culled from his son's homework. *"Moriturus, te saluto*. Would that be right?"

"I daresay. You won't die, though."

Burden made no answer. He picked up his spoon and began to eat. "Can I have some more soda?" said Wexford.

There are perhaps few stabs harder to bear than derision directed at one's heroism. Burden gave him a sour look. "Help yourself. I'm busy."

Wexford did so. "What's it like?" he said.

"All right. It's quite nice, like mushrooms."

Doggedly he ate. He didn't once gag on it. He finished the lot and wiped the bowl round with a piece of bread. Then he sat up, holding himself rather tensely.

"May as well have your telly on now," said Wexford. "Pass the time." He switched it on again. No fly agaric this time, but a dog fox moving across a meadow with Vivaldi playing. "How d'you feel?"

"Fine," said Burden gloomily.

"Cheer up. It may not last."

But it did. After fifteen minutes had passed, Burden still felt perfectly well. He looked bewildered. "I was so damned positive. I *knew* I was going to be retching and vomiting by now. I didn't put the car away because I was certain you'd have to run me down to the hospital."

Wexford only raised his eyebrows.

"You were pretty casual about it, I must say. Didn't say a word to stop me, did you? Didn't it occur to you it might have been a bit awkward for you if anything had happened to me?"

"I knew it wouldn't. I said to get a fungologist." And then Wexford, faced by Burden's aggrieved stare, burst out laughing. "Dear old Mike, you'll have to forgive me. But you know me, d'you honestly think I'd have let you risk your life eating that stuff? I knew you were safe."

"May one ask how?"

"One may. And you'd have known too if you'd bothered to take a proper look at that book of Corinne Last's. Under the recipe for shaggy cap stew it said, 'For drinkables, see page 171.' Well, I looked at page 171, and there Miss Last gave a recipe for cowslip wine and another for sloe gin, both highly intoxicating drinks. Would she have recommended a wine and a spirit to drink with those fungi if there'd been the slightest risk? Not if she wanted to sell her book she wouldn't. Not unless she was risking hundreds of furious letters and expensive lawsuits."

Burden had flushed a little. Then he too began to laugh.

After a little while they had coffee.

"A little logical thinking would be in order, I fancy," said Wexford. "You said this morning that we were not so much seeking to prove murder as attempted murder. Axel Kingman could have pushed her off that balcony, but no one saw her fall and no one heard him or anybody else go up to that flat during the afternoon. If, however, an attempt to murder her was made two weeks before, the presumption that she was eventually murdered is enormously strengthened."

Burden said impatiently, "We've been through all that. We know that."

"Wait a minute. The attempt failed. Now just how seriously ill was she? According to Kingman and Hood, she had severe stomach pains and she vomited. By midnight she was peacefully sleeping and by the following day she was all right."

"I don't see where all this is getting us."

"To a point which is very important and which may be the crux of the whole case. You say that Axel Kingman attempted to murder her. In order to do so he must have made very elaborate plans—the arranging of the meal, the inviting of the two witnesses, the ensuring that his wife tasted the stew earlier in the same day, and the preparation for some very nifty sleight of hand at the time the meal was served. Isn't it odd that the actual method used should so signally have failed? That Hannah's *life* never seemed to have been in danger? And what if the method had succeeded? At post-mortem some noxious agent would have been found in her body or the effects of such. How could he have hoped to get away with that since, as we know, neither of his witnesses actually watched him serve Hannah and one of them was even out of the room?

"So what I am postulating is that no one attempted to murder her, but someone *attempted* to make her ill so that, taken in conjunction with the sinister reputation of nonmushroom fungi and Hood's admitted suspicion of them, taken in conjunction with the known unhappiness of the marriage, *it would look as if there had been a murder attempt*."

Burden stared at him. "Kingman would never have done that. He would either have wanted his attempt to succeed or not to have looked like an attempt at all."

"Exactly. And where does that get us?"

Instead of answering him, Burden said on a note of triumph, his humiliation still rankling, "You're wrong about one thing. She *was* seriously ill, she didn't just have nausea and vomiting. Kingman and Hood may not have mentioned it, but Corinne Last said she had double vision and black spots before her eyes and . . ." His voice faltered. "My God, you mean . . . ?"

Wexford nodded. "Corinne Last only of the three says she had those symptoms. Only Corinne Last is in a position to say, because she lived with him, if Kingman was in the habit of rinsing plates as soon as he removed them from the table. What does she say? That she doesn't know. Isn't that rather odd? Isn't it rather odd too that she chose that precise moment to leave the table and go out into the hall for her handbag?

"She knew that Hannah drank because Hood had told her so. On the evening that meal was eaten you say Hood called for her at her own request. Why? She has her own car, and I don't for a moment believe that a woman like her would feel anything much but contempt for Hood."

"She told him there was something wrong with the car."

"She asked him to come at six, although they were not due at the Kingmans' till eight. She gave him *coffee*. A funny thing to drink at that hour, wasn't it, and before a meal? So what happens when he suggests calling in at a pub on the way? She doesn't say no or say it isn't a good idea to drink and drive. She takes so long getting ready that they don't have time.

"She didn't want Hood to drink any alcohol, Mike, and she was determined to prevent it. She, of course, would take no alcohol and she knew Kingman never drank. But she also knew Hannah's habit of having her first drink of the day at about six.

"Now look at her motive, far stronger than Kingman's. She strikes me as a violent, passionate and determined woman. Hannah had taken Kingman away from her. Kingman had rejected her. Why not revenge herself on both of them by killing Hannah and seeing to it that Kingman was convicted of the crime? If she simply killed Hannah, she had no way of ensuring that Kingman would come under suspicion. But if she made it look as if he had previously attempted her life, the case against him would become very strong indeed.

"Where was she last Thursday afternoon? She could just as easily have gone up those stairs as Kingman could. Hannah would have admitted her to the flat. If she, known to be interested in gardening, had suggested that Hannah take her on to that balcony and show her the pot herbs, Hannah would willingly have done so. And then we have the mystery of the missing brandy bottle with some of its contents surely remaining. If Kingman had killed her, he would have left that there as it would greatly have strengthened the case for suicide. Imagine how he might have used it. 'Heavy drinking made my wife ill that night. She knew I had lost respect for her because of her drinking. She killed herself because her mind was unbalanced by drink.'

"Corinne Last took that bottle away because she didn't want it known that Hannah drank, and she was banking on Hood's keeping it dark from us just as he had kept it from so many people in the past. And she didn't want it known because the fake murder attempt that *she* staged depended on her victim having alcohol present in her body."

Burden sighed, poured the last dregs of coffee into Wexford's cup. "But we tried that out," he said. "Or I tried it out, and it doesn't work. You knew it wouldn't work from her book. True, she brought the shaggy caps from her own garden, but she couldn't have mixed up poisonous fungi with them because Axel Kingman would have realised at once. Or if he hadn't, they'd all have been ill, alcohol or no alcohol. She was never alone with Hannah before the meal, and while the stew was served she was out of the room."

"I know. But we'll see her in the morning and ask her a few more questions." Wexford hesitated, then quoted softly, " 'Out of good still to find some means of evil.' "

"What?"

"That's what she did, isn't it? It was good for everyone but Hannah, you look as if it's done you a power of good, but it was evil for

Hannah. I'm off now, Mike, it's been a long day. Don't forget to put your car away. You won't be making any emergency trips to hospital tonight."

They were unable to puncture her self-possession. The languorous Klimt face was carefully painted this morning, and she was dressed as befitted the violinist or the actress or the author. She had been forewarned of their coming and the gardener image had been laid aside. Her long smooth hands looked as if they had never touched the earth or pulled up a weed.

Where had she been on the afternoon of Hannah Kingman's death? Her thick shapely eyebrows went up. At home, indoors, painting. Alone?

"Painters don't work with an audience," she said rather insolently, and she leaned back, dropping her eyelids in that way of hers. She lit a cigarette and flicked her fingers at Burden for an ashtray as if he were a waiter.

Wexford said, "On Saturday, October 29th, Miss Last, I believe you had something wrong with your car?"

She nodded lazily.

In asking what was wrong with it, he thought he might catch her. He didn't.

"The glass in the offside front headlight was broken while the car was parked," she said, and although he thought how easily she could have broken that glass herself, he could hardly say so. In the same smooth voice she added, "Would you like to see the bill I had from the garage for repairing it?"

"That won't be necessary." She wouldn't have offered to show it to him if she hadn't possessed it. "You asked Mr. Hood to call for you here at six, I understand."

"Yes. He's not my idea of the best company in the world, but I'd promised him some apples for his mother and we had to pick them before it got dark."

"You gave him coffee but had no alcohol. You had no drinks on the way to Mr. and Mrs. Kingman's flat. Weren't you a little disconcerted at the idea of going out to dinner at a place where there wouldn't even be a glass of wine?"

"I was used to Mr. Kingman's ways." But not so used, thought Wexford, that you can tell me whether it was normal or abnormal for him to have rinsed those plates. Her mouth curled, betraying her a little. "It didn't bother me, I'm not a slave to liquor."

"I should like to return to these shaggy caps. You picked them from here on October 28th and took them to Mr. Kingman that evening. I think you said that?"

"I did. I picked them from this garden."

She enunciated the words precisely, her eyes wide open and gazing sincerely at him. The words, or perhaps her unusual straightforwardness, stirred in him the glimmer of an idea. But if she had said nothing more, that idea might have died as quickly as it had been born.

"If you want to have them analysed or examined or whatever, you're getting a bit late. Their season's practically over." She looked at Burden and gave him a gracious smile. "But you took the last of them yesterday, didn't you? So that's all right."

Wexford, of course, said nothing about Burden's experiment. "We'll have a look in your garden, if you don't mind."

She didn't seem to mind, but she had been wrong. Most of the fungi had grown into black-gilled pagodas in the twenty-four hours that had elapsed. Two new ones, however, had thrust their white oval caps up through the wet grass. Wexford picked them, and still she didn't seem to mind. Why, then, had she appeared to want their season to be over? He thanked her and she went back into the cottage. The door closed. Wexford and Burden walked out into the road.

The fungus season was far from over. From the abundant array by the roadside it looked as if the season would last weeks longer. Shaggy caps were everywhere, some of them smaller and greyer than the clump that grew out of Corinne Last's well-fed lawn. There were green and purple agarics, horn-shaped toadstools, and tiny mushrooms growing in fairy rings.

"She doesn't exactly mind our having them analysed," Wexford said thoughtfully, "but it seems she'd prefer the analysis to be done on the ones you picked yesterday than on those I picked today. Can that be so or am I just imagining it?"

"If you're imagining it, I'm imagining it too. But it's no good, that line of reasoning. We know they're not potentiated—or whatever the word is—by alcohol."

"I shall pick some more all the same," said Wexford. "Haven't got a paper bag, have you?"

"I've got a clean handkerchief. Will that do?"

"Have to," said Wexford, who never had a clean one. He picked a dozen more young shaggy caps, big and small, white and grey, immature and fully grown. They got back into the car and Wexford told the driver to stop at the public library. He went in and emerged a few minutes later with three books under his arm.

"When we get back," he said to Burden, "I want you to get on to the university and see what they can offer us in the way of an expert in fungilogy."

He closeted himself in his office with the three books and a pot of coffee. When it was nearly lunchtime, Burden knocked on the door.

"Come in," said Wexford. "How did you get on?"

"It's not fungologist or fungilogist," said Burden with triumphant severity. "It's *mycologist* and they don't have one. But there's a man on the faculty who's a toxicologist and who's just published one of those popular science books. This one's about poisoning by wild plants and fungi."

Wexford grinned. "What's it called? *Killing for Nothing?* He sounds as if he'd do fine."

"I said we'd see him at six. Let's hope something will come of it."

"No doubt it will." Wexford slammed shut the thickest of his books. "We need confirmation," he said, "but I've found the answer."

"For God's sake! Why didn't you say?"

"You didn't ask. Sit down." Wexford motioned him to the chair on the other side of the desk. "I said you'd done your homework, Mike, and so you had, only your textbook wasn't quite comprehensive enough. It's got a section on edible fungi and a section on poisonous fungi—*but nothing in between*. What I mean by that is, there's nothing in your book about fungi which aren't wholesome yet don't cause death or intense suffering. There's nothing about the kind that can make people ill in certain circumstances."

"But we know they ate shaggy caps," Burden protested.

"And if by 'circumstances' you mean the intake of alcohol, we know shaggy caps aren't effected by alcohol."

"Mike," said Wexford quietly, "*do* we know they ate shaggy caps?" He spread out on the desk the haul he had made from the roadside and from Corinne Last's garden. "Look closely at these, will you?"

Quite bewildered now, Burden looked at and fingered the dozen or so specimens of fungi. "What am I to look *for?*"

"Differences," said Wexford laconically.

"Some of them are smaller than the others, and the smaller ones are greyish. Is that what you mean? But, look here, think of the differences between mushrooms. You get big flat ones and small button ones and . . ."

"Nevertheless, in this case it is that small difference that makes all the difference." Wexford sorted the fungi into two groups. "All the small greyer ones," he said, "came from the roadside. Some of the larger whiter ones came from Corinne Last's garden and some from the roadside."

He picked up between forefinger and thumb a specimen of the former. "This isn't a shaggy cap, it's an ink cap. Now listen." The thick book fell open where he had placed a marker. Slowly and clearly he read: "*The ink cap*, coprinus atramentarius, *is not to be confused with the shaggy cap*, coprinus comatus. *It is smaller and greyer in colour, but otherwise the resemblance between them is strong. While* coprinus atramentarius *is usually harmless when cooked, it contains, however, a chemical similar to the active principle in* Antabuse, *a drug used in the treatment of alcoholics, and if eaten in conjunction with alcohol will cause nausea and vomiting.*"

"We'll never prove it."

"I don't know about that," said Wexford. "We can begin by concentrating on the one lie we know Corinne Last told when she said she picked the fungi she gave Axel Kingman *from her own garden*."

Octopussy

IAN FLEMING

Ian Fleming (1908–1964) is known the world over as the creator of the British superspy James Bond. Although the novels were critically panned for their depictions of sex and violence, they gained a huge popular following, were endorsed by President John F. Kennedy, and single-handedly revived literary interest in the spy novel. Fleming's career before turning to writing is as varied as the adventures of his fictional hero, including working as the Moscow news correspondent for Reuters, and later, *The Times,* as well as various stints as a merchant banker, stockbroker, and publisher. He served in the Royal Naval Volunteer Reserve as the personal assistant to the Director of Naval Intelligence. Many of his novels were translated into successful movies, with James Bond portrayed by a variety of actors, the most recent being Pierce Brosnan in the film *The World Is Not Enough,* released in 1999.

"You know what?" said Major Dexter Smythe to the octopus. "You're going to have a real treat today if I can manage it."

He had spoken aloud, and his breath had steamed up the glass of his Pirelli mask. He put his feet down to the sand beside the coral boulder and stood up. The water reached to his armpits. He took off the mask and spat into it, rubbed the spit round the glass, rinsed it clean, and pulled the rubber band of the mask back over his head. He bent down again.

The eye in the mottled brown sack was still watching him carefully from the hole in the coral, but now the tip of a single small tentacle wavered hesitatingly an inch or two out of the shadows and quested vaguely with its pink suckers uppermost. Dexter Smythe smiled with satisfaction. Given time—perhaps one more month on top of the two during which he had been chumming the octopus—and he would have tamed the darling. But he wasn't going to have that month. Should he take a chance today and reach down and offer his hand, instead of the expected lump of raw meat on the end of his spear, to the tentacle. Shake it by the hand, so to speak? No, Pussy, he thought. I can't quite trust you yet. Almost certainly other tentacles would whip out of the hole and up his arm. He only needed to be dragged down less than two feet for the cork valve on his mask to automatically close, and he would be suffocated inside it or, if he tore it off, drowned. He might get in a quick lucky jab with his spear, but it would take more than that to kill Pussy. No. Perhaps later in the day. It would be rather like playing Russian roulette, and at about the same five-to-one odds. It might be a quick, a whimsical, way out of his troubles! But not now. It would leave the interesting question unsolved. And he had promised that nice Professor Bengry at the Institute. . . . Dexter Smythe swam leisurely off toward the reef, his eyes questing for one shape only, the squat, sinister wedge of a scorpionfish, or, as Bengry would put it, *Scorpaena plumieri*.

Major Dexter Smythe, O.B.E., Royal Marines (Retd.), was the remains of a once brave and resourceful officer and a handsome man who had had the sexual run of his teeth all his life, particularly among the Wrens and Wracs and ATS who manned the communications and secretariat of the very special task force to which he had been attached at the end of his service career. Now he was fifty-four and slightly bald, and his belly sagged in his Jantzen trunks. And he had had two coronary thromboses, the second (the "second warning" as his doctor, Jimmy Greaves, who had been at one of their high poker games at Prince's Club when Dexter Smythe had first come to Jamaica, had half jocularly put it) only a month before. But, in his well-chosen clothes, with his varicose veins out of sight, and with his stomach flattened by a discreet support belt behind an immaculate cummerbund, he was still a fine figure of a man at a cocktail party or dinner on the North Shore. And it was a mystery to his friends and neighbors why, in defiance of the two ounces of whiskey and the ten cigarettes a day to which his doctor had rationed him, he persisted in smoking like a chimney and going to bed drunk, if amiably drunk, every night.

The truth of the matter was that Dexter Smythe had arrived at the frontier of the death wish. The origins of this state of mind were many and not all that complex. He was irretrievably tied to Jamaica, and tropical sloth had gradually riddled him so that, while outwardly he appeared a piece of fairly solid hardwood, inside the varnished surface, the termites of sloth, self-indulgence, guilt over an ancient sin, and general disgust with himself had eroded his once hard core into dust. Since the death of Mary two years before, he had loved no one. (He wasn't even sure that he had really loved her, but he knew that, every hour of the day, he missed her love of him and her gay, untidy, chiding, and often irritating presence.) And though he ate their canapés and drank their martinis, he had nothing but contempt for the international riffraff with whom he consorted on the North Shore. He could perhaps have made friends with the more solid elements—the gentleman-farmers inland, the plantation owners on the coast, the professional men, the politicians—but that would mean regaining some serious purpose in life which his sloth, his spiritual accidie, prevented, and cutting down on the bottle, which he was definitely unwilling to do. So Major Smythe was bored, bored to death, and, but for one factor in his life, he would long ago have swallowed the bottle of barbiturates he had easily acquired from a local doctor. The lifeline that kept him clinging to the edge of the cliff was a tenuous one. Heavy drinkers veer toward an exaggeration of their basic temperaments, the classic four—sanguine, phlegmatic, choleric, and melancholic. The sanguine drunk goes gay to the point of hysteria and idiocy; the phlegmatic sinks into a morass of sullen gloom; the choleric is the fighting drunk of the cartoonists who spends much of his life in prison for smashing people and things; and the melancholic succumbs to self-pity, mawkishness, and tears. Major Smythe was a melancholic who had slid into a drooling fantasy woven around the birds and insects and fish that inhabited the five acres of Wavelets (the name he had given his small villa was symptomatic), its beach, and the coral reef beyond. The fish were his particular favorites. He referred to them as "people," and since reef fish stick to their territories as closely as do most small birds, he knew them all, after two years, intimately, "loved" them, and believed that they loved him in return.

They certainly knew him, as the denizens of zoos know their keepers, because he was a daily and a regular provider, scraping off algae and stirring up the sand and rocks for the bottom-feeders, breaking up sea eggs and sea urchins for the small carnivores, and bringing out scraps of offal for the larger ones. And now, as he swam slowly and heavily up and down the reef and through the channels that led out to deep water, his "people" swarmed around him fearlessly and expectantly, darting at the tip of the three-pronged spear they knew only as a prodigal spoon, flirting right up to the glass of the Pirelli, and even, in the case of the fearless, pugnacious demoiselles, nipping softly at his feet and legs.

Part of Major Smythe's mind took in all these brilliantly colored little "people" and he greeted them in unspoken words. ("Morning, Beau Gregory" to the dark blue demoiselle sprinkled with bright blue spots—the jewelfish that exactly resembles the starlit fashioning of a bottle of Guerlain's Dans La Nuit; "Sorry. Not today, sweetheart" to a fluttering butterflyfish with false black eyes on its tail; and "You're too fat anyway, Blue Boy," to an indigo parrotfish that must have weighed a good ten pounds.) But today he had a job to do and his eyes were searching for only one of his "people"—his only enemy on the reef, the only one he killed on sight, a scorpionfish.

The scorpionfish inhabits most of the southern waters of the world, and the rascasse that is the foundation of bouillabaisse belongs to the family. The West Indian variety runs up to only about twelve inches long and perhaps a pound in weight. It is by far the ugliest fish in the sea, as if nature were giving warning. It is a mottled brownish gray with a heavy wedge-shaped shaggy head. It has fleshy pendulous "eyebrows" that droop over angry red eyes and a coloration and broken silhouette that are perfect camouflage on the reef. Though a small fish, its heavily toothed mouth is so wide that it can swallow whole most of the smaller reef fishes, but its supreme weapon lies in its erectile dorsal fins, the first few of which, acting on contact like hypodermic needles, are fed by poison glands containing enough dotoxin to kill a man if they merely graze him in a vulnerable spot—in an artery, for instance, or over the heart or in the groin. It constitutes the only real danger to the reef swimmer, far more dangerous than the barracuda or the shark, because, supreme in its confidence in its camouflage and armory, it flees before nothing except the very close approach of a foot or actual contact. Then it flits only a few yards, on wide and bizarrely striped pectorals, and settles again watchfully either on the sand, where it looks like a lump of overgrown coral, or among the rocks and seaweed where it virtually disappears. And Major Smythe was determined to find one and spear it and give it to his octopus to see if it would take it or spurn it—to see if one of the ocean's great predators would recognize the deadliness of another, know of its poison. Would the octopus consume the belly and leave the spines? Would it eat the lot? And if so, would it suffer from the poison? These were the questions Bengry at the Institute wanted answered, and today, since it was going to be the beginning of the end of Major Smythe's life at Wavelets—and though it might mean the end of his darling Octopussy—Major Smythe had decided to find out the answers and leave one tiny memorial to his now futile life in some dusty corner of the Institute's marine biological files.

For, in only the last couple of hours, Major Dexter Smythe's already dismal life had changed very much for the worse. So much for the worse that he would be lucky if, in a few weeks' time—time for an exchange of cables via Government House and the Colonial Office to the Secret Service and thence to Scotland Yard and the Public Prosecutor, and for Major Smythe's transportation to London with a police escort—he got away with a sentence of imprisonment for life.

And all this because of a man called Bond, Commander James Bond, who had turned up at ten-thirty that morning in a taxi from Kingston.

* * *

The day had started normally. Major Smythe had awakened from his Seconal sleep, swallowed a couple of Panadols (his heart condition forbade him aspirin), showered, skimped his breakfast under the umbrella-shaped sea almonds, and spent an hour feeding the remains of his breakfast to the birds. He then took his prescribed doses of anticoagulant and blood-pressure pills and killed time with the *Daily Gleaner* until it was time for his elevenses, which, for some months now, he had advanced to ten-thirty. He had just poured himself the first of two stiff brandy and ginger ales (The Drunkard's Drink) when he heard the car coming up the drive.

Luna, his colored housekeeper, came out into the garden and announced "Gemmun to see you, Major."

"What's his name?"

"Him doan say, Major. Him say to tell you him come from Govment House."

Major Smythe was wearing nothing but a pair of old khaki shorts and sandals. He said, "All right, Luna. Put him in the living room and say I won't be a moment." And he went round the back way into his bedroom and put on a white bush shirt and trousers and brushed his hair. Government House! Now what the hell?

As soon as he had walked through into the living room and seen the tall man in the dark tropical suit standing at the picture window looking out to sea, Major Smythe had somehow sensed bad news. And, when the man had turned slowly toward him and looked at him with watchful, serious gray-blue eyes, he had known that this was officialdom, and when his cheery smile was not returned, inimical officialdom. And a chill had run down Major Smythe's spine. "They" had somehow found out.

"Well, well. I'm Smythe. I gather you're from Government House. How's Sir Kenneth?"

There was somehow no question of shaking hands. The man said, "I haven't met him. I only arrived a couple of days ago. I've been out round the island most of the time. My name's Bond, James Bond. I'm from the Ministry of Defense."

Major Smythe remembered the hoary euphemism for the Secret Service. He said bonhomously, "Oh. The old firm?"

The question had been ignored. "Is there somewhere we can talk?"

"Rather. Anywhere you like. Here or in the garden? What about a drink?" Major Smythe clinked the ice in the glass he still held in his hand. "Rum and ginger's the local poison. I prefer the ginger by itself." The lie came out with the automatic smoothness of the alcoholic.

"No thanks. And here would be fine." The man leaned negligently against the wide mahogany windowsill.

Major Smythe sat down and threw a jaunty leg over the low arm of one of the comfortable planters' chairs he had had copied from an original by the local cabinetmaker. He pulled out the drink coaster from the other arm, took a deep pull at his glass, and slid it, with a consciously steady hand, down into the hole in the wood. "Well," he said cheerily, looking the other man straight in the eyes, "what can I do for you? Somebody been up to some dirty work on the North Shore and you need a spare hand? Be glad to get into harness again. It's been a long time since those days, but I can still remember some of the old routines."

"Do you mind if I smoke?" The man had already got his cigarette case in his hand. It was a flat gun-metal one that would hold around twenty-five. Somehow this small sign of a shared weakness comforted Major Smythe.

"Of course, my dear fellow." He made a move to get up, his lighter ready.

"It's all right, thanks." James Bond had already lit his cigarette. "No, it's nothing local. I want to . . . I've been sent out to . . . ask you to recall your work for the Service at the end of the war." James Bond paused and looked down at Major Smythe carefully. "Particularly the time when you were working with the Miscellaneous Objectives Bureau."

Major Smythe laughed sharply. He had known it. He had known it for absolutely sure. But when it came out of this man's mouth, the laugh had been forced out of Major Smythe like the scream of a hit man. "Oh Lord, yes. Good old MOB. That was a lark all right." He laughed again. He felt the anginal pain, brought on by the pressure of what he knew was coming, build up across his chest. He dipped his hand into his trouser pocket, tilted the little bottle into the palm of his hand, and slipped the white TNT pill under his tongue. He was amused to see the tension coil up in the other man, the way the eyes narrowed watchfully. *It's all right, my dear fellow. This isn't a death pill.* He said, "You troubled with acidosis? No? It slays me when I go on a bender. Last night. Party at Jamaica Inn. One really ought to stop thinking one's always twenty-five. Anyway, let's get back to MOB Force. Not many of us left, I suppose." He felt the pain across his chest withdraw into its lair. "Something to do with the Official History?"

James Bond looked down at the tip of his cigarette. "Not exactly."

"I expect you know I wrote most of the chapter on the Force for the War Book. It's fifteen years since then. Doubt if I'd have much to add today."

"Nothing more about that operation in the Tirol— place called Oberaurach, about a mile east of Kitzbühel?"

One of the names he had been living with for fifteen years forced another harsh laugh out of Major Smythe. "That was a piece of cake! You've never seen such a shambles. All those Gestapo toughs with their doxies. All of 'em hog-drunk. They'd kept their files all ticketty-boo. Handed them over without a murmur. Hoped that'd earn 'em easy treatment I suppose. We gave the stuff a first going-over and shipped all the bods off to the Munich camp. Last I heard of them. Most of them hanged for war crimes I expect. We handed the bumf over to HQ at Salzburg. Then we went on up the Mittersill valley after another hideout." Major Smythe took a good pull at his drink and lit a cigarette. He looked up. "That's the long and the short of it."

"You were Number Two at the time, I think. The CO was an American, a Colonel King from Patton's army."

"That's right. Nice fellow. Wore a mustache, which isn't like an American. Knew his way among the local wines. Quite a civilized chap."

"In his report about the operation he wrote that he handed you all the documents for a preliminary run-through as you were the German expert with the unit. Then you gave them all back to him with your comments?" James Bond paused. "Every single one of them?"

Major Smythe ignored the innuendo. "That's right. Mostly lists of names. Counterintelligence dope. The CI people in Salzburg were very pleased with the stuff. Gave them plenty of new leads. I expect the originals are lying about somewhere. They'll have been used for the Nuremberg Trials. Yes, by Jove!"—Major Smythe was reminiscent, pally—"those were some of the jolliest months of my life, haring around the country with MOB Force. Wine, women, and song! And you can say that again!"

Here, Major Smythe was saying the whole truth. He had had a dangerous and uncomfortable war until 1945. When the commandos were formed in 1941, he had volunteered and been seconded from the Royal Marines to Combined Operations Headquarters under Mountbatten. There his excellent German (his mother had come from

Heidelberg) had earned him the unenviable job of being advanced interrogator on commando operations across the Channel. He had been lucky to get away from two years of this work unscathed and with the O.B.E. (Military), which was sparingly awarded in the last war. And then, in preparation for the defeat of Germany, the Miscellaneous Objectives Bureau had been formed jointly by the Secret Service and Combined Operations, and Major Smythe had been given the temporary rank of lieutenant colonel and told to form a unit whose job would be the cleaning up of Gestapo and Abwehr hideouts when the collapse of Germany came about. The OSS got to hear of the scheme and insisted on getting into the act to cope with the American wing on the front, and the result was the creation of not one but six units that went into operation in Germany and Austria on the day of surrender. They were units of twenty men, each with a light armored car, six jeeps, a wireless truck, and three lorries, and they were controlled by a joint Anglo-American headquarters in SHAEF, which also fed them with targets from the Army Intelligence units and from the SIS and OSS. Major Smythe had been Number Two of "A" Force, which had been allotted the Tirol—an area full of good hiding places with easy access to Italy and perhaps out of Europe—that was known to have been chosen as funkhole Number One by the people MOB Force was after. And, as Major Smythe had just told Bond, they had had themselves a ball. All without firing a shot—except, that is, two fired by Major Smythe.

James Bond said casually, "Does the name of Hannes Oberhauser ring a bell?"

Major Smythe frowned, trying to remember. "Can't say it does." It was eighty degrees in the shade, but he shivered.

"Let me refresh your memory. On the same day as those documents were given to you to look over, you made inquiries at the Tiefenbrünner Hotel, where you were billeted, for the best mountain guide in Kitzbühel. You were referred to Oberhauser. The next day you asked your CO for a day's leave, which was granted. Early next morning you went to Oberhauser's chalet, put him under close arrest, and drove him away in your jeep. Does that ring a bell?"

That phrase about "refreshing your memory." How often had Major Smythe himself used it when he was trying to trap a German liar? *Take your time! You've been ready for something like this for years*. Major Smythe shook his head doubtfully. "Can't say it does."

"A man with graying hair and a gammy leg. Spoke some English, he'd been a ski teacher before the war."

Major Smythe looked candidly into the cold, clear blue eyes. "Sorry. Can't help you."

James Bond took a small blue leather notebook out of his inside pocket and turned the leaves. He stopped turning them. He looked up. "At that time, as side arms, you were carrying a regulation Webley-Scott forty-five with the serial number eight-nine-six-seven-three-sixty-two."

"It was certainly a Webley. Damned clumsy weapon. Hope they've got something more like the Luger or the heavy Beretta these days. But I can't say I ever took a note of the number."

"The number's right enough," said James Bond. "I've got the date of its issue to you by HQ and the date when you turned it in. You signed the book both times."

Major Smythe shrugged. "Well then, it must have been my gun. But"—he put rather angry impatience into his voice—"what, if I may ask, is all this in aid of?"

James Bond looked at him almost with curiosity. He said, and now his voice was not unkind, "You know what it's all about, Smythe." He paused and seemed to reflect. "Tell you what. I'll go out into the garden for ten minutes or so. Give you time to think things over. Give me a hail." He added seriously, "It'll make things so much easier for you if you come out with the story in your own words."

Bond walked to the door into the garden. He turned around. "I'm afraid it's only a question of dotting the i's and crossing the *t*'s. You see I had a talk with the Foo brothers in Kingston yesterday." He stepped out onto the lawn.

Something in Major Smythe was relieved. Now at least the battle of wits, the trying to invent alibis, the evasions, were over. If this man Bond had got to the Foos, to either of them, they would have spilled the beans. The last thing they wanted was to get in bad with the government, and anyway there was only about six inches of the stuff left.

Major Smythe got briskly to his feet and went to the loaded side-board and poured himself out another brandy and ginger ale, almost fifty-fifty. He might as well live it up while there was still time! The future wouldn't hold many more of these for him. He went back to his chair and lit his twentieth cigarette of the day. He looked at his watch. It said eleven-thirty. If he could be rid of the chap in an hour, he'd have plenty of time with his "people." He sat and drank and mar-shaled his thoughts. He could make the story long or short, put in the weather and the way the flowers and pines had smelled on the mountain, or he could cut it short. He would cut it short.

Up in that big double bedroom in the Tiefenbrünner, with the wads of buff and gray paper spread out on the spare bed, he hadn't been looking for anything special, just taking samples here and there and concentrating on the ones marked in red, KOMMANDOSACHE—HÖCHST VERTRAULICH. There weren't many of these, and they were mostly confidential reports on German top brass, intercepts of broken allied ciphers, and information about the whereabouts of secret dumps. Since these were the main targets of "A" Force, Major Smythe had scanned them with particular excitement—food, explosives, guns, espionage records, files of Gestapo personnel. A tremendous haul! And then, at the bottom of the packet, there had been the single envelope sealed with red wax and the notation ONLY TO BE OPENED IN FINAL EMERGENCY. The envelope contained one single sheet of paper. It was unsigned, and the few words were written in red ink. The heading said VALUTA, and beneath it was written: WILDE KAISER. FRANZISKANER HALT 100 M. OSTLICH STEINHUGEL. WAFFENKISTEZWEI BAR 24 KT. Under that was a list of measurements in centimeters. Major Smythe held his hands apart as if telling a story about a fish he had caught. The bars would be about as wide as his shoulders and about two by four inches. And one single English sovereign of only eighteen carats was selling nowadays for two to three pounds! This was a bloody fortune! Forty, fifty thousand pounds worth! Maybe even a hundred! He didn't stop to think, but, quite coolly and speedily, in case anyone should come in, he put a match to the paper and the envelope, ground the ashes to powder, and swilled them down the lavatory. Then he took out his large-scale Austrian ordnance map of the area and in a moment had his finger on the Franziskaner Halt. It was marked as an uninhabited mountaineers' refuge on a saddle just below the highest of the easterly peaks of the Kaiser mountains, that awe-inspiring range of giant stone teeth that gave Kitzbühel its threatening northern horizon. And the cairn of stones would be about there—his fingernail pointed—and the whole bloody lot was only ten miles and perhaps a five hours' climb away!

The beginning had been as this fellow Bond had described. He had gone to Oberhauser's chalet at four in the morning, had arrested him, and had told his weeping, protesting family that Smythe was taking him to an interrogation camp in Munich. If the guide's record was clean he would be back home within a week. If the family kicked up a fuss it would only make trouble for Oberhauser. Smythe had refused to give his name and had had the forethought to shroud the numbers on his jeep. In twenty-four hours, "A" Force would be on its way, and by the time military government got to Kitzbühel, the incident would already be buried under the morass of the Occupation tangle.

Oberhauser had been a nice enough chap once he had recovered from his fright, and when Smythe talked knowingly about skiing and climbing, both of which he had done before the war, the pair, as Smythe intended, became quite pally. Their route lay along the bottom of the Kaiser range to Kufstein, and Smythe drove slowly, making admiring comments on the peaks that were now flushed with the pink of dawn. Finally, below the peak of gold, as he called it to himself, he slowed to a halt and pulled off the road into a grassy glade. He turned in his seat and said with an assumption of candor, "Oberhauser, you are a man after my own heart. We share many interests together, and from your talk, and from the man I think you to be, I am sure you did not cooperate with the Nazis. Now I will tell you what I will do. We will spend the day climbing on the Kaiser, and I will then drive you back to Kitzbühel and report to my commanding officer that you have been cleared at Munich." He grinned cheerfully. "Now. How about that?"

The man had been near to tears of gratitude. But could he have some kind of paper to show that he was a good citizen? Certainly. Major Smythe's signature would be quite enough. The pact was made, the jeep was driven up a track and well hidden from the road, and they were off at a steady pace, climbing up through the pine-scented foothills.

Smythe was well dressed for the climb. He had nothing on except his bush shirt, shorts, and a pair of the excellent rubber-soled boots issued to American parachutists. His only burden was the Webley-Scott, and, tactfully, for Oberhauser was after all one of the enemy, Oberhauser didn't suggest that he leave it behind some conspicuous rock. Oberhauser was in his best suit and boots, but that didn't seem to bother him, and he assured Major Smythe that ropes and pitons would not be needed for their climb and that there was a hut directly up above them where they could rest. It was called the Franziskaner Halt.

"Is it indeed?" said Major Smythe.

"Yes, and below it there is a small glacier. Very pretty, but we will climb round it. There are many crevasses."

"Is that so?" said Major Smythe thoughtfully. He examined the back of Oberhauser's head, now beaded with sweat. After all, he was only a bloody kraut, or at any rate of that ilk. What would one more or less matter? It was all going to be as easy as falling off a log. The only thing that worried Major Smythe was getting the bloody stuff down the mountain. He decided that he would somehow sling the bars across his back. After all, he could slide it most of the way in its ammunition box or whatnot.

It was a long, dreary hack up the mountain, and when they were above the treeline, the sun came up and it was very hot. And now it was all rock and scree, and their long zigzags sent boulders and rubble rumbling and crashing down the slope that got steeper as they approached the final crag, gray and menacing, that lanced away into the blue above them. They were both naked to the waist and sweating, so that the sweat ran down their legs into their boots, but despite Oberhauser's limp, they kept up a good pace, and when they stopped for a drink and a swabdown at a hurtling mountain stream, Oberhauser congratulated Major Smythe on his fitness. Major Smythe, his mind full of dreams, said curtly and untruthfully that all English soldiers were fit, and they went on.

The rock face wasn't difficult. Major Smythe had known that it wouldn't be or the climbers' hut couldn't have been built on the shoulder. Toeholds had been cut in the face, and there were occasional iron pegs hammered into crevices. But he couldn't have found the more difficult traverses by himself, and he congratulated himself on deciding to bring a guide.

Once, Oberhauser's hand, testing for a grip, dislodged a great slab of rock, loosened by five years of snow and frost, and sent it crashing down the mountain. Major Smythe suddenly thought about noise. "Many people around here?" he asked as they watched the boulder hurtle down into the treeline.

"Not a soul until you get near Kufstein," said Oberhauser. He gestured along the arid range of high peaks. "No grazing. Little water. Only the climbers come here. And since the beginning of the war. . . ." He left the phrase unfinished.

They skirted the blue-fanged glacier below the final climb to the shoulder. Major Symthe's careful eyes took in the width and depth of the crevasses. Yes, they would fit! Directly above them, perhaps a hundred feet up under the lee of the shoulder, were the weather-beaten boards of the hut. Major Smythe measured the angle of the slope. Yes, it was almost a straight dive down. Now or later? He guessed later. The line of the last traverse wasn't very clear.

They were up at the hut in five hours flat. Major Smythe said he wanted to relieve himself and wandered casually along the shoulder to the east, paying no heed to the beautiful panoramas of Austria and Bavaria that stretched away on either side of him perhaps fifty miles into the heat haze. He counted his paces carefully. At exactly one hundred and twenty there was the cairn of stones, a loving memorial perhaps to some long dead climber. Major Smythe, knowing differently, longed to tear it apart there and then. Instead he took out his Webley-Scott, squinted down the barrel, and twirled the cylinder. Then he walked back.

It was cold up there at ten thousand feet or more, and Oberhauser had got into the hut and was busy preparing a fire. Major Smythe controlled his horror at the sight. "Oberhauser," he said cheerfully, "come out and show me some of the sights. Wonderful view up here."

"Certainly, Major." Oberhauser followed Major Smythe out of the hut. Outside, he fished in his hip pocket and produced something wrapped in paper. He undid the paper to reveal a hard wrinkled sausage. He offered it to the major. "It is only what we call a *Soldat*," he said shyly. "Smoked meat. Very tough but good." He smiled. "It is like what they eat in Wild West films. What is the name?"

"Pemmican," said the major. Then—and later this had slightly disgusted him with himself—he said, "Leave it in the hut. We will share it later. Come over here. Can we see Innsbruck? Show me the view on this side."

Oberhauser bobbed into the hut and out again. The major fell in just behind him as he talked, pointing out this or that distant church spire or mountain peak.

They came to the point above the glacier. Major Smythe drew his revolver, and at a range of two feet, fired two bullets into the base of Hannes Oberhauser's skull. No muffing! Dead-on!

The impact of the bullets knocked the guide clean off his feet and over the edge. Major Smythe craned over. The body hit twice only, and then crashed onto the glacier. But not onto its fissured origin. Halfway down and on a patch of old snow! "Hell!" said Major Smythe.

The deep boom of the two shots, which had been batting to and fro among the mountains, died away. Major Smythe took one last look at the black splash on the white snow and hurried off along the shoulder. First things first!

He started on the top of the cairn, working as if the devil were after him, throwing the rough, heavy stones indiscriminately down the mountain to right or left. His hands began to bleed, but he hardly noticed. Now there were only two feet or so left, and nothing! Bloody nothing! He bent to the last pile, scrabbling feverishly. And then! Yes! The edge of a metal box. A few more rocks away, and there was the whole of it! A good old gray Wehrmacht ammunition box with the trace of some lettering still on it. Major Smythe gave a groan of joy. He sat down on a hard piece of rock, and his mind went orbiting through Bentleys, Monte Carlo, pent-house flats, Cartier's, champagne, caviar, and, incongruously (but because he loved golf), a new set of Henry Cotton irons.

Drunk with his dreams, Major Smythe sat there looking at the gray box for a full quarter of an hour. Then he looked at his watch and got briskly to his feet. Time to get rid of the evidence. The box had a handle at each end. Major Smythe had expected it to be heavy. He had mentally compared its probable weight with the heaviest thing he had ever carried—a forty-pound salmon he had caught in Scotland just before the war—but the box was certainly double that weight, and he was only just able to lift it out of its last bed of rocks onto the thin alpine grass. Then he slung his handkerchief through one of the handles and dragged it clumsily along the shoulder to the hut. Then he sat down on the stone doorstep, and, his eyes never leaving the box, he tore at Oberhauser's smoked sausage with his strong teeth and thought about getting his fifty thousand pounds—for that was the figure he put it at—down the mountain and into a new hiding place.

Oberhauser's sausage was a real mountaineer's meal—tough, well-fatted, and strongly garlicked. Bits of it stuck uncomfortably between Major Smythe's teeth. He dug them out with a sliver of matchstick and spat them on the ground. Then his Intelligence-wise mind came into operation, and he meticulously searched among the stones and grass, picked up the scraps, and swallowed them. From now on he was a criminal—as much a criminal as if he had robbed a bank and shot the guard. He was a cop turned robber. He must remember that! It would be death if he didn't—death instead of Cartier's. All he had to do was to take infinite pains. He would take those pains, and by God they would be rich and happy. After taking ridiculously minute trouble to eradicate any sign of entry into the hut, he dragged the ammunition box to the edge of the last rock face and, aiming it away from the glacier, tipped it, with a prayer, into space.

The gray box, turning slowly in the air, hit the first steep slope below the rock face, bounded another hundred feet, and landed with an iron clang in some loose screen and stopped. Major Smythe couldn't see if it had burst open. He didn't mind one way or the other. He had tried to open it without success. Let the mountain do it for him!

With a last look around, he went over the edge. He took great care at each piton, tested each handhold and foothold before he put his weight on it. Coming down, he was a much more valuable life than he had been climbing up. He made for the glacier and trudged across the melting snow to the black patch on the icefield. There was nothing to be done about footprints. It would take only a few days for them to be melted down by the sun. He got to the body. He had seen many corpses during the war, and the blood and broken limbs meant nothing to him. He dragged the remains of Oberhauser to the nearest deep crevasse and toppled it in. Then he went carefully around the lip of the crevasse and kicked the snow overhang down on top of the body. Then, satisfied with his work, he retraced his steps, placing his feet exactly in his old footprints, and made his way on down the slope to the ammunition box.

Yes, the mountain had burst open the lid for him. Almost casually he tore away the cartridge-paper wrappings. The two great hunks of metal glittered up at him under the sun. There were the same markings on each—the swastika in a circle below an eagle, and the date 1943—the mint marks of the Reichsbank. Major Smythe gave a nod of approval. He replaced the paper and hammered the crooked lid half-shut with a rock. Then he tied the lanyard of his Webley around one of the handles and moved on down the mountain, dragging his clumsy burden behind him.

It was now one o'clock, and the sun beat fiercely down on his naked chest, frying him in his own sweat. His reddened shoulders began to burn. So did his face. To hell with them! He stopped at the stream from the glacier, dipped his handkerchief in the water, and tied it across his forehead. Then he drank deeply and went on, occasionally cursing the ammunition box as it caught up with him and banged at his heels. But these discomforts, the sunburn and the bruises, were nothing compared with what he would have to face when he got down to the valley and the going leveled out. For the time being he had gravity on his side. There would come at least a mile when he would have to carry the blasted stuff. Major Smythe winced at the thought of the havoc the eighty pounds or so would wreak on his burned back. "Oh well," he said to himself almost lightheadedly, *"il faut souffrir pour être millionaire!"*

When he got to the bottom and the time had come, he sat and rested on a mossy bank under the firs. Then he spread out his bush shirt and heaved the two bars out of the box and onto its center and tied the tails of the shirt as firmly as he could to where the sleeves sprang from the shoulders. After digging a shallow hole in the bank and burying the empty box, he knotted the two cuffs of the sleeves firmly together, knelt down, and slipped his head through the rough sling, got his hands on either side of the knot to protect his neck, and staggered to his feet, crouching far forward so as not to be pulled over on his back. Then, crushed under half his own weight, his back on fire under the contact with his burden, and his breath rasping through his constricted lungs, coolie-like, he shuffled slowly off down the little path through the trees.

To this day he didn't know how he had made it to the jeep. Again and again the knots gave under the strain and the bars crashed down on the calves of his legs, and each time he had sat with his head in his hands and then started all over again. But finally, by concentrating on counting his steps and stopping for a rest at every hundredth, he got to the blessed little jeep and collapsed beside it. And then there had been the business of burying his hoard in the wood, amongst a jumble of big rocks that he would be sure to find again, of cleaning himself up as best he could, and of getting back to his billet by a circuitous route that avoided the Oberhauser chalet. And then it was all done, and he had got drunk by himself off a bottle of cheap schnapps and eaten and gone to bed and fallen into a stupefied sleep. The next day, MOB "A" Force had moved off up the Mittersill valley on a fresh trail, and six months later Major Smythe was back in London and his war was over.

But not his problems. Gold is difficult stuff to smuggle, certainly in the quantity available to Major Smythe, and it was now essential to get his two bars across the Channel and into a new hiding place. So he put off his demobilization and clung to the red tabs of his temporary rank, and particularly to his Military Intelligence passes, and soon got himself sent back to Germany as a British representative at the Combined Interrogation Center in Munich. There he did a scratch job for six months, during which, on a weekend's leave, he collected his gold and stowed it in a battered suitcase in his quarters. Then he resigned his post and flew back to England, carrying the two bars in a bulky briefcase. The hundred yards across the tarmac at each end of the flight, and the handling of his case as if it contained only papers, required two benzedrine tablets and a will of iron, but at last he had his fortune safe in the basement of an aunt's flat in Kensington and could get on with the next phase of his plans at leisure.

He resigned from the Royal Marines and got himself demobilized and married one of the many girls he had slept with at MOB Force Headquarters, a charming blond Wren from a solid middle-class family named Mary Parnell. He got passages for them both in one of the early banana boats sailing from Avonmouth to Kingston, Jamaica, which they both agreed would be a paradise of sunshine, good food, cheap drink, and a glorious haven from the gloom and restrictions and Labour Government of postwar England. Before they sailed, Major Smythe showed Mary the gold bars from which he had chiseled away the mint marks of the Reichsbank.

"I've been clever, darling," he said. "I just don't trust the pound these days, so I've sold out all my securities and swapped the lot for gold. Must be about fifty thousand pounds' worth there. That should give us twenty-five years of the good life, just cutting off a slice now and then and selling it."

Mary Parnell was not to know that such a transaction was impossible under the currency laws. She knelt down and ran her hands lovingly over the gleaming bars. Then she got up and threw her arms around Major Smythe's neck and kissed him. "You're a wonderful, wonderful man," she said, almost in tears. "Frightfully clever and handsome and brave, and now I find out that you're rich as well. I'm the luckiest girl in the world."

"Well, anyway we're rich," said Major Smythe. "But promise me you won't breathe a word, or we'll have all the burglars in Jamaica around our ears. Promise?"

"Cross my heart."

Prince's Club, in the foothills above Kingston, was indeed a paradise. Pleasant enough members, wonderful servants, unlimited food, cheap drink—and all in the wonderful setting of the tropics, which neither of them had known before. They were a popular couple, and Major Smythe's war record earned them the entrée to Government House society, after which their life was one endless round of parties, with tennis for Mary and golf (with the Henry Cotton irons!) for Major Smythe. In the evenings there was bridge for her and the high poker game for him. Yes, it was paradise all right,while in their homeland people munched their Spam, fiddled in the black market, cursed the government, and suffered the worst winter's weather for thirty years.

The Smythes met all their initial expenditures from their combined cash reserves, swollen by wartime gratuities, and it took Major Smythe a full year of careful sniffing around before he decided to do business with the Messrs. Foo, import and export merchants. The brothers Foo, highly respected and very rich, were the acknowledged governing junta of the flourishing Chinese community in Jamaica. Some of their trading was suspected to be devious—in the Chinese tradition—but all Major Smythe's casually meticulous inquiries confirmed that they were utterly trustworthy. The Bretton Woods Convention, fixing a controlled world price for gold, had been signed, and it had already become common knowledge that Tangier and Macao were two free ports that, for different reasons, had escaped the Bretton Woods net; there a price of at least one hundred dollars per ounce of gold, ninety-nine fine, could be obtained, compared with the fixed world price of thirty-five dollars per ounce. And, conveniently, the Foos had just begun to trade again with a resurgent Hong Kong, already the port of entry for gold smuggling into the neighboring Macao. The whole setup was, in Major Smythe's language, "ticketty-boo." He had a most pleasant meeting with the Foo brothers. No questions were asked until it came to examining the bars. At this point the absence of mint marks resulted in a polite inquiry as to the original provenance of the gold.

"You see, Major," said the older and blander of the brothers behind the big bare mahogany desk, "in the bullion market the mint marks of all respectable national banks and responsible dealers are accepted without question. Such marks guarantee the fineness of the gold. But of course there are other banks and dealers whose methods of refining"—his benign smile widened a fraction—"are perhaps not quite, shall we say, so accurate."

"You mean the old gold brick swindle?" asked Major Smythe with a twinge of anxiety. "Hunk of lead covered with gold plating?"

Both brothers tee-heed reassuringly. "No, no, Major. That of course is out of the question. But"—the smiles held constant—"if you cannot recall the provenance of these fine bars, perhaps you would have no objections if we were to undertake an assay. There are methods of determining the exact fineness of such bars. My brother and I are competent in these methods. If you would care to leave these with us and perhaps come back after lunch . . . ?"

There had been no alternative. Major Smythe had to trust the

Foos utterly now. They could cook up any figure, and he would just have to accept it. He went over to the Myrtle Bank and had one or two stiff drinks and a sandwich that stuck in his throat. Then he went back to the cool office of the Foos.

The setting was the same—the two smiling brothers, the two bars of gold, the briefcase—but now there was a piece of paper and a gold Parker pen in front of the older brother.

"We have solved the problem of your fine bars, Major———"

Fine! Thank God, thought Major Smythe.

"———And I am sure you will be interested to know their probable history."

"Yes indeed," said Major Smythe, with a brave show of enthusiasm.

"They are German bars, Major. Probably from the wartime Reichsbank. This we have deduced from the fact that they contain ten percent of lead. Under the Hitler regime, it was the foolish habit of the Reichsbank to adulterate their gold in this manner. This fact rapidly became known to dealers, and the price of German bars, in Switzerland for instance, where many of them found their way, was adjusted downward accordingly. So the only result of the German foolishness was that the national bank of Germany lost a reputation for honest dealing it had earned over the centuries." The Oriental's smile didn't vary. "Very bad business, Major. Very stupid."

Major Smythe marveled at the omniscience of these two men so far from the great commercial channels of the world, but he also cursed it. *Now what?* He said, "That's very interesting, Mr. Foo. But it is not very good news for me. Are these bars not 'Good delivery,' or whatever you call it in the bullion world?"

The older Foo made a slight throwaway gesture with his right hand. "It is of no importance, Major. Or rather, it is of very small importance. We will sell your gold at its true mint value, let us say, eighty-nine fine. It may be re-fined by the ultimate purchaser, or it may not. That is not our business. We shall have sold a true bill of goods."

"But at a lower price."

"That is so, Major. But I think I have some good news for you. Have you any estimate as to the worth of these two bars?"

"I thought around fifty thousand pounds."

The older Foo gave a dry chuckle. "I think—if we sell wisely and slowly—you should receive one hundred thousand pounds, Major, subject that is, to our commission, which will include shipping and incidental charges."

"How much would that be?"

"We were thinking about a figure of ten percent, Major. If that is satisfactory to you."

Major Smythe had an idea that bullion brokers received a fraction of one percent. But what the hell? He had already as good as made forty thousand pounds since lunch. He said "Done" and got up and reached his hand across the desk.

From then on, every quarter, he would visit the office of the Foos carrying an empty suitcase. On the broad desk there would be one thousand new Jamaican pounds in neat bundles and the two gold bars, which diminished inch by inch, together with a typed slip showing the amount sold and the price obtained in Macao. It was all very simple and friendly and highly businesslike, and Major Smythe didn't think that he was being submitted to any form of squeeze other than the duly recorded ten percent. In any case, he didn't particularly care. Four thousand net a year was good enough for him, and his only worry was that the income tax people would get after him and ask him what he was living on. He mentioned this possibility to the Foos. But they said he was not to worry, and for the next four quarters, there was only nine hundred pounds instead of a thousand on the table and no comment was made by either side. Squeeze had been administered in the right quarter.

And so the lazy, sunshiny days passed by for fifteen happy years. The Smythes both put on weight, and Major Smythe had the first of his two coronaries and was told by his doctor to cut down on his alcohol and cigarettes, to take life more easily, to avoid fats and fried food. Mary Smythe tried to be firm with him, but when he took to secret drinking and to a life of petty lies and evasions, she tried to backpedal on her attempts to control his self-indulgence. But she was too late. She had already become the symbol of the caretaker to Major Smythe, and he took to avoiding her. She berated him with not loving her anymore. And when the continual bickering became too much for her simple nature, she became a sleeping pill addict. And one night, after one flaming drunken row, she took an overdose—"just to show him." It was too much of an overdose and it killed her. The suicide was hushed up, but the cloud did Major Smythe no good socially, and he retreated to the North Shore, which, although only some thirty miles across the island from the capital, is, even in the small society of Jamaica, a different world. And there he had settled in Wavelets and, after his second coronary, was in the process of drinking himself to death when this man named Bond arrived on the scene with an alternative death warrant in his pocket.

Major Smythe looked at his watch. It was a few minutes after twelve o'clock. He got up and poured himself another stiff brandy and ginger ale and went out onto the lawn. James Bond was sitting under the sea almonds gazing out to sea. He didn't look up when Major Smythe pulled up another aluminum garden chair and put his drink on the grass beside him.

When Major Smythe had finished telling his story, Bond said unemotionally, "Yes, that's more or less the way I figure it."

"Want me to write it all out and sign it?"

"You can if you like. But not for me. That'll be for the court-martial. Your old corps will be handling all that. I've got nothing to do with the legal aspects. I shall put in a report to my own Service of what you've told me, and they'll pass it on to the Royal Marines. Then I suppose it'll go to the Public Prosecutor via Scotland Yard."

"Could I ask a question?"

"Of course."

"How did they find out?"

"It was a small glacier. Oberhauser's body came out at the bottom of it earlier this year. When the spring snows melted. Some climbers found it. All his papers and everything were intact. His family identified him. Then it was just a question of working back. The bullets clinched it."

"But how did you get mixed up in the whole thing?"

"MOB Force was a responsibility of my, er, Service. The papers found their way to us. I happened to see the file. I had some spare time on my hands. I asked to be given the job of chasing up the man who did it."

"Why?"

James Bond looked Major Smythe squarely in the eyes. "It just happened that Oberhauser was a friend of mine. He taught me to ski before the war, when I was in my teens. He was a wonderful man. He was something of a father to me at a time when I happened to need one."

"Oh, I see." Major Smythe looked away. "I'm sorry."

James Bond got to his feet. "Well, I'll be getting back to Kingston." He held up a hand. "No, don't bother. I'll find my way to the car." He looked down at the older man. He said abruptly, almost harshly—perhaps, Major Smythe thought, to hide his embarrassment—"It'll be about a week before they send someone out to bring you home." Then he walked off across the lawn and through the house, and Major Smythe heard the iron whirr of the self-starter and the clatter of the gravel on the unkempt drive.

Major Smythe, questing for his prey along the reef, wondered what exactly those last words of the Bond man had meant. Inside the Pirelli his lips drew mirthlessly back from the stained teeth. It was obvious, really. It was just a version of the corny old act of leaving the guilty officer alone with his revolver. If the Bond man had wanted to, he could have telephoned Government House and had an officer of the Jamaica Regiment sent over to take Major Smythe into custody. Decent of him, in a way. Or was it? A suicide would be tidier, save a lot of paperwork and taxpayers' money.

Should he oblige the Bond man and be tidy? Join Mary in whatever place suicides go to? Or go through with it—the indignity, the dreary formalities, the headlines, the boredom and drabness of a life sentence that would inevitably end with his third coronary? Or should he defend himself—plead wartime, a struggle with Oberhauser, prisoner trying to escape, Oberhauser knowing of the gold cache, the natural temptation of Smythe to make away with the bullion, he, a poor officer of the commandos confronted with sudden wealth?

Should he dramatically throw himself on the mercy of the court? Suddenly Major Smythe saw himself in the dock—a splendid, upright figure, in the fine bemedaled blue and scarlet of the ceremonial uniform that was the traditional rig for court-martial. (Had the moths got into the japanned box in the spare room at Wavelets? Had the damp? Luna would have to look to it.) A day in the sunshine, if the weather held. A good brushing. With the help of his corset, he could surely still get his forty-inch waist into the thirty-four-inch trousers Gieves had made for him twenty, thirty, years ago. And, down on the floor of the court, at Chatham probably, the Prisoners' Friend, some staunch fellow, at least of colonel's rank in deference to his own seniority, would be pleading his cause. And there was always the possibility of appeal to a higher court. Why, the whole affair might become a cause célèbre . . . he would sell his story to the papers, write a book. . . .

Major Smythe felt the excitement mounting in him. Careful, old boy! Careful! Remember what the good old snip-cock had said! He put his feet to the ground and had a rest amidst the dancing waves of the northeast trades that kept the North Shore so delightfully cool until the torrid months—August, September, October—of the hurricane season. He would soon be having his two pink gins, skimpy lunch, and happily sodden siesta, after which he would have to give all this more careful thought. And then there were cocktails with the Arundels and dinner at the Shaw Park Beach Club with the Marchesis. Then some high bridge and home to his seconal sleep. Cheered by the prospect of the familiar routine, the black shadow of Bond retreated into the background. Now then, scorp, where are you? Octopussy's waiting for her lunch! Major Smythe put his head down, and his mind freshly focused and his eyes questing, continued his leisurely swim along the shallow valley between the coral clumps that led out toward the white-fringed reef.

Almost at once he saw the two spiny antennae of a lobster, or rather of its cousin, the West Indian langouste, weaving inquisitively toward him, toward the turbulence he was creating, from a deep fissure under a coral boulder. From the thickness of the antennae, it would be a big one, three or four pounds! Normally, Major Smythe would have put his feet down and delicately stirred up the sand in front of the lair to bring the lobster farther out, for they are an inquisitive family. Then he would have speared it through the head and taken it back for lunch. But today there was only one prey in his mind, one shape to concentrate on—the shaggy, irregular silhouette of a scorpionfish. And, ten minutes later, he saw a clump of seaweedy rock on the white sand that wasn't just a clump of seaweedy rock. He put his feet softly down and watched the poison spines erect themselves along the back of the thing. It was a good-sized one, perhaps three-quarters of a pound. He got his three-pronged spear ready and inched forward. Now the red angry eyes of the fish were wide open and watching him. He would have to make a single quick lunge from as nearly the vertical as possible; otherwise, he knew from experience, the barbed prongs, needle-sharp though they were, would almost certainly bounce off the horny head of the beast. He swung his feet up off the ground and paddled forward very slowly, using his free hand as a fin. Now! He lunged forward and downward. But the scorpionfish had felt the tiny approaching shockwave of the spear. There was flurry of sand, and it had shot up in a vertical takeoff and whirred, in almost birdlike flight, under Major Smythe's belly.

Major Smythe cursed and twisted around in the water. Yes, it had done what the scorpionfish so often does—gone for refuge to the nearest algae-covered rock, and there, confident in its superb camouflage, gone to ground on the seaweed. Major Smythe had only to swim a few feet, lunge down again, this time more accurately, and he had it, flapping and squirming on the end of his spear.

The excitement and the small exertion had caused Major Smythe to pant, and he felt the old pain across his chest lurking, ready to come at him. He put his feet down, and after driving his spear all the way through the fish, held it, still flapping desperately, out of the water. Then he slowly made his way back across the lagoon on foot and walked up the sand of his beach to the wooden bench under the sea-grape. Then he dropped the spear with its jerking quarry on the sand beside him and sat down to rest.

It was perhaps five minutes later that Major Smythe felt a curious numbness more or less in the region of his solar plexus. He looked casually down, and his whole body stiffened with horror and disbelief. A patch of his skin, about the size of a cricket ball, had turned white under his tan, and, in the center of the patch, there were three punctures, one below the other, topped by little beads of blood. Automatically, Major Smythe wiped away the blood. The holes were only the size of pinpricks. Major Smythe remembered the rising flight of the scorpionfish, and he said aloud, with awe in his voice, but without animosity, "You got me, you bastard! By God, you got me!"

He sat very still, looking down at his body and remembering what it said about scorpionfish stings in the book he had borrowed from the Institute and had never returned—*Dangerous Marine Animals*, an American publication. He delicately touched and then prodded the white area around the punctures. Yes, the skin had gone totally numb, and now a pulse of pain began to throb beneath it. Very soon this would become a shooting pain. Then the pain would begin to lance all over his body and become so intense that he would throw himself on the sand, screaming and thrashing about, to rid himself of it. He would vomit and foam at the mouth, and then delirium and convulsions would take over until he lost consciousness. Then, inevitably in his case, there would ensue cardiac failure and death. According to the book the whole cycle would be complete in about a quarter of an hour—that was all he had left—fifteen minutes of hideous agony! There were curses, of course—procaine, antibiotics, and antihistamines—if his weak heart would stand them. But they had to be near at hand. Even if he could climb the steps up to the house, and supposing Dr. Cahusac had these modern drugs, the doctor couldn't possibly get to Wavelets in under an hour.

The first jet of pain seared into Major Smythe's body and bent him over double. Then came another and another, radiating through his stomach and limbs. Now there was a dry, metallic taste in his mouth, and his lips were prickling. He gave a groan and toppled off the seat onto the beach. A flapping on the sand beside his head reminded him of the scorpionfish. There came a lull in the spasms of pain. Instead, his whole body felt as though it were on fire, but, beneath the agony, his brain cleared. But of course! The experiment! Somehow, somehow he must get out to Octopussy and give her her lunch!

"Oh Pussy, my Pussy, this is the last meal you'll get."

Major Smythe mouthed the refrain to himself as he crouched on all fours, found his mask, and struggled to force it over his face. Then he got hold of his spear, tipped with the still flapping fish, and clutching his stomach with his free hand, crawled and slithered down the sand and into the water.

It was fifty yards of shallow water to the lair of the octopus in the coral cranny, and Major Smythe, screaming all the while into his mask, crawling mostly on his knees, somehow made it. As he came to the last approach and the water became deeper, he had to get to his feet, and the pain made him jiggle to and fro, as if he were a puppet manipulated by strings. Then he was there, and with a supreme effort of will, he held himself steady as he dipped his head down to let some water into his mask and clear the mist of his screams from the glass. Then, blood pouring from his bitten lower lip, he bent carefully down to look into Octopussy's house. Yes! The brown mass was still there. It was stirring excitedly. Why? Major Smythe saw the dark strings of his blood curling lazily down through the water. Of course! The darling was tasting his blood. A shaft of pain hit Major Smythe and sent him reeling. He heard himself babbling deliriously into his mask. *Pull yourself together, Dexter, old boy! You've got to give Pussy her lunch!* He steadied himself, and holding the spear well down the shaft, lowered the fish down toward the writhing hole.

Would Pussy take the bait? The poisonous bait that was killing Major Smythe but to which an octopus might be immune? If only Bengry could be here to watch! Three tentacles, weaving excitedly, came out of the hole and wavered around the scorpionfish. Now there was a gray mist in front of Major Smythe's eyes. He recognized it as the edge of unconsciousness and feebly shook his head to clear it. And then the tentacles leaped! But not at the fish! At Major Smythe's hand and arm. Major Smythe's torn mouth stretched in a grimace of pleasure. Now he and Pussy had shaken hands! How exciting! How truly wonderful!

But then the octopus, quietly, relentlessly pulled downward, and terrible realization came to Major Smythe. He summoned his dregs of strength and plunged his spear down. The only effect was to push the scorpionfish into the mass of the octopus and offer more arm to the octopus. The tentacles snaked upward and pulled more relentlessly. Too late, Major Smythe scrabbled away his mask. One bottled scream burst out across the empty bay, then his head went under and down, and there was an explosion of bubbles to the surface. Then Major Smythe's legs came up and the small waves washed his body to and fro while the octopus explored his right hand with its buccal orifice and took a first tentative bite at a finger with its beaklike jaws.

The body was found by two young Jamaicans spinning for needlefish from a canoe. They speared the octopus with Major Smythe's spear, killed it in the traditional fashion by turning it inside out and biting its head off, and brought the three corpses home. They turned Major Smythe's body over to the police, and had the scorpionfish and the seacat for supper.

The local correspondent for the *Daily Gleaner* reported that Major Smythe had been killed by an octopus, but the paper translated this into "found drowned" so as not to frighten away the tourists.

Later, in London, James Bond, privately assuming "suicide," wrote the same verdict of "found drowned," together with the date, on the last page and closed the bulky file.

It is only from the notes of Dr. Cahusac, who performed the autopsy, that it has been possible to construct some kind of a postscript to the bizarre and pathetic end of a once valuable officer of the Secret Service.

Heroes

ANNE PERRY

Anne Perry is the writer of two series of mystery novels, both set in Victorian England and characterized by strong female characters and a keen attention to detail. The first, more long-running series is about police inspector, Thomas Pitt, and his wife, Charlotte, who both solve crimes in the late 19th century and made their first appearance in *The Cater Street Hangman.* The second series, began in 1990 with *The Face of a Stranger* and features an amnesiac police detective who must rediscover himself as he works to solve mysteries. Both series examine not only the Victorian Age's hypocrisy and social injustice but also comment on the role of women during that age.

Nights were always the worst, and in winter they lasted from dusk at about four o'clock until dawn again toward eight the following morning. Sometimes star shells lit the sky, showing the black zigzags of the trenches stretching as far as the eye could see to left and right. Apparently now they went right across France and Belgium all the way from the Alps to the Channel. But Joseph was only concerned with this short stretch of the Ypres Salient.

In the gloom near him someone coughed, a deep, hacking sound coming from down in the chest. They were in the support line, farthest from the front, the most complex of the three rows of trenches. Here were the kitchens, the latrines and the stores and mortar positions. Fifteen-foot shafts led to caves about five paces wide and high enough for most men to stand upright. Joseph made his way in the half dark now, the slippery wood under his boots and his hands feeling the mud walls, held up by timber and wire. There was an awful lot of water. One of the sumps must be blocked.

There was a glow of light ahead and a moment later he was in the comparative warmth of the dugout. There were two candles burning and the brazier gave off heat and a sharp smell of soot. The air was blue with tobacco smoke, and a pile of boots and greatcoats steamed a little. Two officers sat on canvas chairs talking together. One of them recited a joke—gallows humor, and they both laughed. A gramophone sat silent on a camp table, and a small pile of records of the latest music-hall songs was carefully protected in a tin box.

"Hello, Chaplain," one of them said cheerfully. "How's God these days?"

"Gone home on sick leave," the other answered quickly, before

Joseph could reply. There was disgust in his voice, but no intended irreverence. Death was too close here for men to mock faith.

"Have a seat," the first offered, waving toward a third chair. "Morris got it today. Killed outright. That bloody sniper again."

"He's somewhere out there, just about opposite us," the second said grimly. "One of those blighters the other day claimed he'd got forty-three for sure."

"I can believe it," Joseph answered, accepting the seat. He knew better than most what the casualties were. It was his job to comfort the terrified, the dying, to carry stretchers, often to write letters to the bereaved. Sometimes he thought it was harder than actually fighting, but he refused to stay back in the comparative safety of the field hospitals and depots. This was where he was most needed.

"Thought about setting up a trench raid," the major said slowly, weighing his words and looking at Joseph. "Good for morale. Make it seem as if we were actually doing something. But our chances of getting the blighter are pretty small. Only lose a lot of men for nothing. Feel even worse afterward."

The captain did not add anything. They all knew morale was sinking. Losses were high, the news bad. Word of terrible slaughter seeped through from the Somme and Verdun and all along the line right to the sea. Physical hardship took its toll, the dirt, the cold, and the alternation between boredom and terror. The winter of 1916 lay ahead.

"Cigarette?" The major held out his pack to Joseph.

"No thanks," Joseph declined with a smile. "Got any tea going?"

They poured him a mugful, strong and bitter, but hot. He drank it, and half an hour later made his way forward to the open air again and the travel trench. A star shell exploded high and bright. Automatically he ducked, keeping his head below the rim. They were about four feet deep, and in order not to provide a target, a man had to move in a half crouch. There was a rattle of machine-gun fire out ahead and, closer to, a thud as a rat was dislodged and fell into the mud beside the duckboards.

Other men were moving about close to him. The normal order of things was reversed here. Nothing much happened during the day. Trench repair work was done, munitions shifted, weapons cleaned, a little rest taken. Most of the activity was at night, most of the death.

" 'Lo, Chaplain," a voice whispered in the dark. "Say a prayer we get that bloody sniper, will you?"

"Maybe God's a Jerry?" someone suggested in the dark.

"Don't be stupid!" a third retorted derisively. "Everyone knows God's an Englishman! Didn't they teach you nothing at school?"

There was a burst of laughter. Joseph joined in. He promised to offer up the appropriate prayers and moved on forward. He had known many of the men all his life. They came from the same Northumbrian town as he did, or the surrounding villages. They had gone to school together, nicked apples from the same trees, fished in the same rivers, and walked the same lanes.

It was a little after six when he reached the firing trench beyond whose sandbag parapet lay no-man's-land with its four or five hundred yards of mud, barbed wire, and shell holes. Half a dozen burnt tree stumps looked in the sudden flares like men. Those gray wraiths could be fog, or gas.

Funny that in summer this blood-and horror-soaked soil could still bloom with honeysuckle, forget-me-nots, and wild larkspur, and most of all with poppies. You would think nothing would ever grow there again.

More star shells went up, lighting the ground, the jagged scars of the trenches black, the men on the fire steps with rifles on their shoulders illuminated for a few, blinding moments. Sniper shots rang out.

Joseph stood still. He knew the terror of the night watch out beyond the parapet, crawling around in the mud. Some of them would be at the head of saps out from the trench, most would be in shell holes, surrounded by heavy barricades of wire. Their purpose was to check enemy patrols for unusual movement, any signs of increased activity, as if there might be an attack planned.

More star shells lit the sky. It was beginning to rain. A crackle of machine-gun fire, and heavier artillery somewhere over to the left. Then the sharp whine of sniper fire, again and again.

Joseph shuddered. He thought of the men out there, beyond his vision, and prayed for strength to endure with them in their pain, not to try to deaden himself to it.

There were shouts somewhere ahead, heavy shells now, shrapnel bursting. There was a flurry of movement, flares, and a man came sliding over the parapet, shouting for help.

Joseph plunged forward, slithering in the mud, grabbing for the wooden props to hold himself up. Another flare of light. He saw quite clearly Captain Holt lurching toward him, another man over his shoulder, deadweight.

"He's hurt!" Holt gasped. "Pretty badly. One of the night patrol. Panicked. Just about got us all killed." He eased the man down into

Joseph's arms and let his rifle slide forward, bayonet covered in an old sock to hide its gleam. His face was grotesque in the lantern light, smeared with mud and a wide streak of blood over the burnt cork that blackened it, as all night patrol had.

Others were coming to help. There was still a terrible noise of fire going on and the occasional flare.

The man in Joseph's arms did not stir. His body was limp and it was difficult to support him. Joseph felt the wetness and the smell of blood. Wordlessly others materialized out of the gloom and took the weight.

"Is he alive?" Holt said urgently. "There was a hell of a lot of shot up there." His voice was shaking, almost on the edge of control.

"Don't know," Joseph answered. "We'll get him back to the bunker and see. You've done all you can." He knew how desperate men felt when they risked their lives to save another man and did not succeed. A kind of despair set in, a sense of very personal failure, almost a guilt for having survived themselves. "Are you hurt?"

"Not much," Holt answered. "Couple of grazes."

"Better have them dressed, before they get poisoned," Joseph advised, his feet slipping on the wet boards and banging his shoulder against a jutting post. The whole trench wall was crooked, giving way under the weight of mud. The founds had eroded.

The man helping him swore.

Awkwardly carrying the wounded man, they staggered back through the travel line to the support trench and into the light and shelter of a bunker.

Holt looked dreadful. Beneath the cork and blood his face was ashen. He was soaked with rain and mud and there were dark patches of blood across his back and shoulders.

Someone gave him a cigarette. Back here it was safe to strike a match. He drew in smoke deeply. "Thanks," he murmured, still staring at the wounded man.

Joseph looked down at him now, and it was only too plain where the blood had come from. It was young Ashton. He knew him quite well. He had been at school with his older brother.

The soldier who had helped carry him in let out a cry of dismay, strangled in his throat. It was Mordaff, Ashton's closest friend, and he could see what Joseph now could also. Ashton was dead, his chest torn open, the blood no longer pumping, and a bullet hole through his head.

"I'm sorry," Holt said quietly. "I did what I could. I can't have got to him in time. He panicked."

Mordaff jerked his head up. "He never would!" The cry was desperate, a shout of denial against a shame too great to be borne. "Not Will!"

Holt stiffened. "I'm sorry," he said hoarsely. "It happens."

"Not with Will Ashton, it don't!" Mordaff retorted, his eyes blazing, pupils circled with white in the candlelight, his face gray. He had been in the front line two weeks now, a long stretch without a break from the ceaseless tension, filth, cold, and intermittent silence and noise. He was nineteen.

"You'd better go and get that arm dressed, and your side," Joseph said to Holt. He made his voice firm, as to a child.

Holt glanced again at the body of Ashton, then up at Joseph.

"Don't stand there bleeding," Joseph ordered. "You did all you could. There's nothing else. I'll look after Mordaff."

"I tried!" Holt repeated. "There's nothing but mud and darkness and wire, and bullets coming in all directions." There was a sharp thread of terror under his shell-thin veneer of control. He had seen too many men die. "It's enough to make anyone lose his nerve. You want to be a hero—you mean to be—and then it overwhelms you—"

"Not Will!" Mordaff said again, his voice choking off in a sob.

Holt looked at Joseph again, then staggered out.

Joseph turned to Mordaff. He had done this before, too many times, tried to comfort men who had just seen childhood friends blown to pieces, or killed by a sniper's bullet, looking as if they should still be alive, perfect except for the small, blue hole through the brain. There was little to say. Most men found talk of God meaningless at that moment. They were shocked, fighting against belief and yet seeing all the terrible waste and loss in front of them. Usually it was best just to stay with them, let them speak about the past, what the friend had been like, times they had shared, just as if he were only wounded and would be back, at the end of the war, in some world one could only imagine, in England, perhaps on a summer day with sunlight on the grass, birds singing, a quiet riverbank somewhere, the sound of laughter, and women's voices.

Mordaff refused to be comforted. He accepted Ashton's death; the physical reality of that was too clear to deny, and he had seen too many other men he knew killed in the year and a half he had been in Belgium. But he could not, would not accept that Ashton had panicked. He knew what panic out there cost, how many other lives it jeopardized. It was the ultimate failure.

"How am I going to tell his mam?" he begged Joseph. "It'll be all I can do to tell her he'd dead! His pa'll never get over it. That proud of him, they were. He's the only boy. Three sisters he had, Mary, Lizzie, and Alice. Thought he was the greatest lad in the world. I can't tell 'em he panicked! He couldn't have, Chaplain! He just wouldn't!"

Joseph did not know what to say. How could people at home in England even begin to imagine what it was like in the mud and noise out here? But he knew how deep shame burned. A lifetime could be consumed by it.

"Maybe he just lost sense of direction," he said gently. "He wouldn't be the first." War changed men. People did panic. Mordaff knew that, and half his horror was because it could be true. But Joseph did not say so. "I'll write to his family," he went on. "There's a lot of good to say about him. I could send pages. I'll not need to tell them much about tonight."

"Will you?" Mordaff was eager. "Thanks . . . thanks, Chaplain. Can I stay with him . . . until they come for him?"

"Yes, of course," Joseph agreed. "I'm going forward anyway. Get yourself a hot cup of tea. See you in an hour or so."

He left Mordaff squatting on the earth floor beside Ashton's body and fumbled his way back over the slimy duckboards toward the travel line, then forward again to the front and the crack of gunfire and the occasional high flare of a star shell.

He did not see Mordaff again, but he thought nothing of it. He could have passed twenty men he knew and not recognized them, muffled in greatcoats, heads bent as they moved, rattling along the duckboards, or standing on the fire steps, rifles to shoulder, trying to see in the gloom for something to aim at.

Now and again he heard a cough, or the scamper of rats' feet and the splash of rain and mud. He spent a little time with two men swapping jokes, joining in their laughter. It was black humor, self-mocking, but he did not miss the courage in it, or the fellowship, the need to release emotion in some sane and human way.

About midnight the rain stopped.

A little after five the night patrol came scrambling through the wire, whispered passwords to the sentries, then came tumbling over the parapet of sandbags down into the trench, shivering with cold and relief. One of them had caught a shot in the arm.

Joseph went back with them to the support line. In one of the dugouts a gramophone was playing a music-hall song. A couple of men sang along with it; one of them had a beautiful voice, a soft, lyric tenor. It was a silly song, trivial, but it sounded almost like a hymn out here, a praise of life.

A couple of hours and the day would begin: endless, methodical duties of housekeeping, mindless routine, but it was better than doing nothing.

There was still a sporadic crackle of machine-gun fire and the whine of sniper bullets.

An hour till dawn.

Joseph was sitting on an upturned ration case when Sergeant Renshaw came into the bunker, pulling the gas curtain aside to peer in.

"Chaplain?"

Joseph looked up. He could see bad news in the man's face.

"I'm afraid Mordaff got it tonight," he said, coming in and letting the curtain fall again. "Sorry. Don't really know what happened. Ashton's death seems to have. . . . well, he lost his nerve. More or less went over the top all by himself. Suppose he was determined to go and give Fritz a bloody nose, on Ashton's account. Stupid bastard! Sorry, Chaplain."

He did not need to explain himself, or to apologize. Joseph knew exactly the fury and the grief he felt at such a futile waste. To this was added a sense of guilt that he had not stopped it. He should have realized Mordaff was so close to breaking. He should have seen it. That was his job.

He stood up slowly. "Thanks for telling me, Sergeant. Where is he?"

"He's gone, Chaplain." Renshaw remained near the doorway. "You can't help 'im now."

"I know that. I just want to . . . I don't know . . . apologize to him. I let him down. I didn't understand he was . . . so . . ."

"You can't be everybody's keeper," Renshaw said gently. "Too many of us. It's not been a bad night otherwise. Got a trench raid coming off soon. Just wish we could get that damn sniper across the way there." He scraped a match and lit his cigarette. "But morale's good. That was a brave thing Captain Holt did out there. He wanted the chance to do something to hearten the men. He saw it and took it. Pity about Ashton, but that doesn't alter Holt's courage. Could see him, you know, by the star shells. Right out there beyond the last wire, bent double, carrying Ashton on his back. Poor devil went crazy. Running around like a fool. Have got the whole patrol killed if Holt hadn't gone after him. Hell of a job getting him back. Fell a couple of times. Reckon that's worth a mention in dispatches, at least. Heartens the men, knowing our officers have got that kind of spirit."

"Yes . . . I'm sure," Joseph agreed. He could only think of Ashton's white face, and Mordaff's desperate denial, and how Ashton's mother would feel, and the rest of his family. "I think I'll go and see Mordaff just the same."

"Right you are," Renshaw conceded reluctantly, standing aside for Joseph to pass.

• • •

Mordaff lay in the support trench just outside the bunker two hundred yards to the west. He looked even younger than he had in life, as if he were asleep. His face was oddly calm, even though it was smeared with mud. Someone had tried to clean most of it off in a kind of dignity, so that at least he was recognizable. There was a large wound in the left side of his forehead. It was bigger than most sniper wounds. He must have been a lot closer.

Joseph stood in the first paling of the darkness and looked at him by candlelight from the open bunker curtain. He had been so alive only a few hours ago, so full of anger and loyalty and dismay. What had made him throw his life away in a useless gesture? Joseph racked his mind for some sign that should have warned him Mordaff was so close to breaking, but he could not see it even now.

There was a cough a few feet away, and the tramp of boots on duckboards. The men were stood down, just one sentry per platoon left. They had returned for breakfast. If he thought about it he could smell cooking.

Now would be the time to ask around and find out what had happened to Mordaff.

He made his way to the field kitchen. It was packed with men, some standing to be close to the stoves and catch a bit of their warmth, others choosing to sit, albeit farther away. They had survived the night. They were laughing and telling stories, most of them unfit for delicate ears, but Joseph was too used to it to take any offense. Now and then someone new would apologize for such language in front of a chaplain, but most knew he understood too well.

"Yeah," one answered his question through a mouthful of bread and jam. "He came and asked me if I saw what happened to Ashton. Very cut up, he was."

"And what did you tell him?" Joseph asked.

The man swallowed. "Told him Ashton seemed fine to me when he went over. Just like anyone else, nervous . . . but, then, only a fool isn't scared to go over the top!"

Joseph thanked him and moved on. He needed to know who else was on the patrol.

"Captain Holt," the next man told him, a ring of pride in his voice. Word had got around about Holt's courage. Everyone stood a little taller because of it, felt a little braver, more confident. "We'll pay Fritz back for that," he added. "Next raid—you'll see."

There was a chorus of agreement.

"Who else?" Joseph pressed.

"Seagrove, Noakes, Willis," a thin man replied, standing up. "Want some breakfast, Chaplain? Anything you like, on the house—as long as it's bread and jam and half a cup of tea. But you're not particular, are you? Not one of those fussy eaters who'll only take kippers and toast?"

"What I wouldn't give for a fresh Craster kipper," another sighed, a faraway look in his eyes. "I can smell them in my dreams."

Someone told him good-naturedly to shut up.

"Went over the top beside me," Willis said when Joseph found him quarter of an hour later. "All blacked up like the rest of us. Seemed okay to me then. Lost him in no-man's-land. Had a hell of a job with the wire. As bloody usual, it wasn't where we'd been told. Got through all right, then Fritz opened up on us. Star shells all over the sky." He sniffed and then coughed violently. When he had control of himself again, he continued. "Then I saw someone outlined against the flares, arms high, like a wild man, running around. He was going toward the German lines, shouting something. Couldn't hear what in the noise."

Joseph did not interrupt. It was now broad daylight and beginning to drizzle again. Around them men were starting the duties of the day: digging, filling sandbags, carrying ammunition, strengthening the wire, resetting duckboards. Men took an hour's work, an hour's sentry duty, and an hour's rest.

Near them somebody was expending his entire vocabulary of curses against lice. Two more were planning elaborate schemes to hold the water at bay.

"Of course that lit us up like a target, didn't it!" Willis went on. "Sniper fire and machine guns all over the place. Even a couple of shells. How none of us got hit I'll never know. Perhaps the row woke God up, and He came back on duty!" He laughed hollowly. "Sorry,

Chaplain. Didn't mean it. I'm just so damn sorry poor Ashton got it. Holt just came out of nowhere and ran after him. Obsessed with being a hero, or he'd not even have tried. I can see him in my mind's eye floundering through the mud. If Ashton hadn't got caught in the wire he'd never have got him."

"Caught in the wire?" Joseph asked, memory pricking at him.

"Yeah. Ashton must have run right into the wire, because he stopped sudden—teetering, like—and fell over. A hell of a barrage came over just after that. We all threw ourselves down."

"What happened then?" Joseph said urgently, a slow, sick thought taking shape in his mind.

"When it died down I looked up again, and there was Holt staggering back with poor Ashton across his shoulders. Hell of a job he had carrying him, even though he's bigger than Ashton—well, taller, anyway. Up to his knees in mud, he was, shot and shell all over, sky lit up like a Christmas tree. Of course we gave him what covering fire we could. Maybe it helped." He coughed again. "Reckon he'll be mentioned in dispatches, Chaplain? He deserves it." There was admiration in his voice, a lift of hope.

Joseph forced himself to answer. "I should think so." The words were stiff.

"Well, if he isn't, the men'll want to know why!" Willis said fiercely. "Bloody hero, he is."

Joseph thanked him and went to find Seagrove and Noakes. They told him pretty much the same story.

"You going to have him recommended?" Noakes asked. "He earned it this time. Mordaff came and we said just the same to him. Reckon he wanted the Captain given a medal. He made us say it over and over again, exactly what happened."

"That's right." Seagrove nodded, leaning on a sandbag.

"You told him the same?" Joseph asked. "About the wire, and Ashton getting caught in it?"

"Yes, of course. If he hadn't got caught by the legs he'd have gone straight on and landed up in Fritz's lap, poor devil."

"Thank you."

"Welcome, Chaplain. You going to write up Captain Holt?"

Joseph did not answer, but turned away, sick at heart.

He did not need to look again, but he trudged all the way back to the field hospital anyway. It would be his job to say the services for both Ashton and Mordaff. The graves would be already dug.

He looked at Ashton's body again, looked carefully at his trousers. They were stained with mud, but there were no tears in them, no marks of wire. The fabric was perfect.

He straightened up.

"I'm sorry," he said quietly to the dead man. "Rest in peace." And he turned and walked away.

He went back to where he had left Mordaff's body, but it had been removed. Half an hour more took him to where it also was laid out. He touched the cold hand and looked at the brow. He would ask. He would be sure. But in his mind he already was. He needed time to know what he must do about it. The men would be going over the top on another trench raid soon. Today morale was high. They had a hero in their number, a man who would risk his own life to bring back a soldier who had lost his nerve and panicked. Led by someone like that, they were equal to Fritz any day. Was one pistol bullet, one family's shame, worth all that?'

What were they fighting for anyway? The issues were so very big, and at the same time so very small and immediate.

• • •

He found Captain Holt alone just after dusk, standing on the duckboards below the parapet, near one of the firing steps.

"Oh, it's you, Chaplain. Ready for another night?"

"It'll come, whether I am or not," Joseph replied.

Holt gave a short bark of laughter. "That doesn't sound like you. Tired of the firing line, are you? You've been up here a couple of weeks; you should be in turn for a step back any day. Me too, thank God."

Joseph faced forward, peering through the gloom toward no-man's-land and the German lines beyond. He was shaking. He must control himself. This must be done in the silence, before the shooting started up again. Then he might not get away with it.

"Pity about that sniper over there," he remarked. "He's taken out a lot of our men."

"Damnable," Holt agreed. "Can't get a line on him, though. Keeps his own head well down."

"Oh, yes." Joseph nodded. "We'd never get him from here. It needs a man to go over in the dark and find him."

"Not a good idea, Chaplain. He'd not come back. Not advocating suicide, are you?"

Joseph chose his words very carefully and kept his voice as unemotional as he could.

"I wouldn't have put it like that," he answered. "But he has cost us a lot of men. Mordaff today, you know?"

"Yes . . . I heard. Pity."

"Except that wasn't the sniper, of course. But the men think it was, so it comes to the same thing, as far as morale is concerned."

"Don't know what you mean, Chaplain." There was a slight hesitation in Holt's voice in the darkness.

"Wasn't a rifle wound, it was a pistol," Joseph replied. "You can tell the difference, if you're actually looking for it."

"Then he was a fool to be that close to German lines," Holt said, facing forward over the parapet and the mud. "Lost his nerve, I'm afraid."

"Like Ashton," Joseph said. "Can understand that, up there in no-man's-land, mud everywhere, wire catching hold of you, tearing at you, stopping you from moving. Terrible thing to be caught in the wire with the star shells lighting up the night. Makes you a sitting target. Takes an exceptional man not to panic, in those circumstances . . . a hero."

Holt did not answer.

There was silence ahead of them, only the dull thump of feet and a squelch of duckboards in mud behind, and the trickle of water along the bottom of the trench.

"I expect you know what it feels like," Joseph went on. "I notice you have some pretty bad tears in your trousers, even one in your blouse. Haven't had time to mend them yet."

"I daresay I got caught in a bit of wire out there last night," Holt said stiffly. He shifted his weight from one foot to the other.

"I'm sure you did," Joseph agreed with him. "Ashton didn't. His clothes were muddy, but no wire tears."

There were several minutes of silence. A group of men passed by behind them, muttering words of greeting. When they were gone the darkness closed in again. Someone threw up a star shell and there was a crackle of machine-gun fire.

"I wouldn't repeat that, if I were you, Chaplain," Holt said at last. "You might make people think unpleasant things, doubts. And right at the moment morale is high. We need that. We've had a hard time recently. We're going over the top in a trench raid soon. Morale is important . . . trust. I'm sure you know that, maybe even better than I do. That's your job, isn't it? Morale, spiritual welfare of the men?"

"Yes . . . spiritual welfare is a good way of putting it. Remember what it is we are fighting for, and that it is worth all that it costs . . . even this." Joseph gestured in the dark to all that surrounded them.

More star shells went up, illuminating the night for a few garish moments, then a greater darkness closed in.

"We need our heroes," Holt said very clearly. "You should know that. Any man who would tear them down would be very unpopular, even if he said he was doing it in the name of truth, or justice, or whatever it was he believed in. He would do a lot of harm, Chaplain. I expect you can see that. . . ."

"Oh, yes," Joseph agreed. "To have their hero shown to be a coward who laid the blame for his panic on another man, and let him be buried in shame, and then committed murder to hide that, would devastate men who are already wretched and exhausted by war."

"You are perfectly right." Holt sounded as if he were smiling. "A very wise man, Chaplain. Good of the regiment first. The right sort of loyalty."

"I could prove it," Joseph said very carefully.

"But you won't. Think what it would do to the men."

Joseph turned a little to face the parapet. He stood up onto the fire step and looked forward over the dark expanse of mud and wire.

"We should take that sniper out. That would be a very heroic thing to do. Good thing to try, even if you didn't succeed. You'd deserve a mention in dispatches for that, possibly a medal."

"It would be posthumous!" Holt said bitterly.

"Possibly. But you might succeed and come back. It would be so daring, Fritz would never expect it," Joseph pointed out.

"Then you do it, Chaplain!" Holt said sarcastically.

"It wouldn't help you, Captain. Even if I die, I have written a full account of what I have learned today, to be opened should anything happen to me. On the other hand, if you were to mount such a raid, whether you returned or not, I should destroy it."

There was silence again, except for the distant crack of sniper fire a thousand yards away and the drip of mud.

"Do you understand me, Captain Holt?"

Holt turned slowly. A star shell lit his face for an instant. His voice was hoarse.

"You're sending me to my death!"

"I'm letting you be the hero you're pretending to be and Ashton really was," Joseph answered. "The hero the men need. Thousands of us have died out here, no one knows how many more there will be.

Others will be maimed or blinded. It isn't whether you die or not, it's how well."

A shell exploded a dozen yards from them. Both men ducked, crouching automatically.

Silence again.

Slowly Joseph unbent.

Holt lifted his head. "You're a hard man, Chaplain. I misjudged you."

"Spiritual care, Captain," Joseph said quietly. "You wanted the men to think you a hero, to admire you. Now you're going to justify that and become one."

Holt stood still, looking toward him in the gloom, then slowly he turned and began to walk away, his feet sliding on the wet duckboards. Then he climbed up the next fire step and up over the parapet.

Joseph stood still and prayed.